Praise for the Pushcart Prize...

" In its 38th edition, the Pushcart Prize anthology features a diverse selection of fiction, poetry and non-fiction from hundreds of small presses. Exceptional fiction includes "A Full-Service Shelter," Amy Hempel's tale of tireless animal shelter volunteers taking on the Sisyphean task of saving animals slated for execution, as well as Lorrie Moore's "Wings," in which a washed-up musician finds an unlikely companion in her elderly neighbor. While some experimental fiction selections lack depth, the collection is more than redeemed by its striking non-fiction and essays, such as Andre Dubus III's "Writing & Publishing a Memoir," which is about reconciling his past with the version of it he presents in his coming-of-age memoir Townie; "The Healing Powers of the Western Oystercatcher," in which Howard Norman recovers from the shock of a brutal murder-suicide that occurred in his home; and Bill Cotter's account of being tasked with curating a collection of "the most important works of literature of all time," in "The Gentle Man's Library, a Nowaday Redux." The collection's poetry, selected by guest editors Patricia Smith and Arthur Sze, captures a variety of styles and subjects with standouts from Louise Glück, Jeffrey Harrison, David Hernandez and Eduardo C. Corral. With large publishing houses facing an uncertain future, the Pushcart Prize is more valuable than ever in highlighting the unique voices thriving in America's small presses."

PUBLISHERS WEEKLY (*starred review*)

" A cosmos of candor, humor, conviction and lyricism...generous, glimmering, and hopeful."

BOOKLIST

" Of all the anthologies, Pushcart's is the most rewarding."

CHICAGO TRIBUNE

" These authors are the guardians of our language."

LIBRARY JOURNAL

" A treasure trove."

LOS ANGELES TIMES

" Like discovering yet one more galaxy."

WORLD LITERATURE TODAY

" Big, colorful, cheerful, gratifying..."

NEW YORK TIMES BOOK REVIEW

2014

PUSHCART
PRIZE XXXVIII
BEST OF THE
SMALL PRESSES

EDITED BY BILL HENDERSON
WITH THE PUSHCART PRIZE EDITORS

Note: nominations for this series are invited from any small, independent, literary book press or magazine in the world, print or online. Up to six nominations—tear sheets or copies, selected from work published, or about to be published, in the calendar year—are accepted by our December 1 deadline each year. Write to Pushcart Fellowships, P.O. Box 380, Wainscott, N.Y. 11975 for more information or consult our websites www.pushcartprize.com. or pushcart press.org.

Acknowledgments
Selections for The Pushcart Prize are reprinted with the permission of authors and presses cited. Copyright reverts to authors and presses immediately after publication.

Distributed by W. W. Norton & Co.
500 Fifth Ave., New York, N.Y. 10110

Library of Congress Card Number: 76-58675
ISBN (hardcover): 978-1-888889-70-3
ISBN (paperback): 978-1-888889-71-0
ISSN: 0149-7863

For
Harvey Shapiro (1924–2013)
Poet, editor, friend

INTRODUCTION

Forty years ago Pushcart Press got its start.

Our first publication was *The Publish It Yourself Handbook*, a homely tome (as in homemade), set with an electric typewriter and press type. Our office was a studio apartment in that literary capital of the world – Yonkers, NY.

The Handbook was our shout of defiance at a commercial publishing world that had rejected my first great American novel – ten years in the writing. I was joined in my shouting by 26 other writers who had rejected the commercial rejecters with success. Among them Anaïs Nin, Leonard and Virginia Woolf, and Stewart Brand.

We were angry not only at commercial publishers, like Doubleday, where I was then an about-to-be-fired junior editor, but vanity outfits, particularly the lead huckster, Vantage Press. Martin Baron, an ex-editor at Vantage, contributed a chapter warning writers to avoid these sharks at all cost. (Ironically, just this year Vantage collapsed into bankruptcy).

Pushcart's 1973 Yonkers publication was also a history of do-it-yourselfers, Whitman, Twain, Poe, Sandburg and Joyce, among others. All of them had done without the money folks. They paid no one to "publish" their works. Whitman sold *Leaves of Grass* from his wheelbarrow (and also wrote his best reviews himself). Anaïs Nin set her own type letter by letter for *Winter of Artifice* and *Under a Glass Bell*. Our contributors included a winner of the National Book Award, a playwright, editors of magazines and journals and a cookbook author.

Pushcart's *Handbook*, produced with the last of our minimal savings, sold 75,000 copies over the years and earned the funds that enabled us to publish the first Pushcart Prize in 1976.

I bring up all this because 40 years may have given this writer a bit of insight on what's become of our literary culture over the decades.

Judging from the nominations that arrive every fall at Pushcart there has been a terrific increase in both quantity and quality. We started with 450 pages in PPI and now even 650 pages won't hold the astonishing work of today's writers. (Please consider seriously the Special Mention section at the end of this volume. All of these authors are must-reads. It is sheer agony to pick who is reprinted and who is mentioned.)

On the other hand, as I have stated before, I am concerned about the effect of the internet on young writers. It's far too easy to burp out a blog and consider yourself an accomplished author. And the vanity sharks are swimming in a new guise. What's a vanity shark? Any outfit that demands you give them money to "publish" your book, poem, story, etc. At one count 250,000 vanity books were published last year. Almost all of it rubbish.

And while we are at it let's consider literary prizes – 6000 of them according to a recent New York *Times* accounting. It's now very probable that you will win a prize of some sort. Many of these prizes are of significance, most not so. Some wag even started a web site dedicated to telling writers how to write in order to win themselves a prize. Imagine!

Let me state flat out, for me writing is a form of worship. Not the kind of worship you do in church perhaps, maybe it's even dark, bleak or anti-religious. Literature should be akin to prayer. To write in order to win a prize, including a Pushcart, is my idea of blasphemy.

If you want to win a prize make up your own prize. Print a certificate off your computer, inscribe your name upon it. Frame it and hang the thing on your wall. Impress your friends. Seduce whomsoever. There you've won a prize. Now get serious about writing. Consult your heart, mind and soul. The rest is too often mere fluff.

We face in this marvelous computer age another problem far beyond mere prize deluge. Clutter. As I mentioned in last year's introduction, this is the age of clutter censorship. Thousands of TV channels, more than 600 million internet sites, and 8 million bloggers. What reader can sort through this cacophony?

Well, as I said, there's an upside – decades of small press effort, have produced a literature that continues, against all clutter and commercial competition, to be glorious. Some of that literature is in this PP issue. Lots more can be discovered with a subscription to some of the little magazines listed herein and a visit to your local bookstore. These stores happily seem to be holding their own against the onslaught of Amazon, e-books, and faltering and failed chains like Borders.

What's interesting about this Pushcart Prize endeavor is that we are perhaps one of the last remaining collectives from the 60's and 70's – over 200 Contributing Editors send in nominations every fall plus 700 or more presses – print and online. What's more astonishing, actual editors read the nominations. Real people. I was amazed recently to learn that computers have been employed to read student essays for universities. Soon I'm sure computers will grade short stories and poems. That certainly will make our job at Pushcart a lot simpler. E-mail your efforts to us, a computer will have a look, and in the end publish the winners too. And while we're at it, why not have a machine write your stuff – and print out a prize certificate. Life will be so much easier for all of us.

But for now Pushcart is staffed by real people who can really read. Our guest poetry editors this year are Patricia Smith of New Jersey and Arthur Sze of New Mexico. Every year I ask the guest poetry editors to comment on the impossible job of considering thousands of poems. Here's what they say.

Arthur Sze is the author of eight books of poetry including *The Redshifting Web: Poems 1970-1998*. A ninth collection, *Compass Rose*, is forthcoming from Copper Canyon Press. He is also a translator and editor and has published *The Silk Dragon: Translations From the Chinese* and edited *Chinese Writers On Writing*. He is the recipient of various awards including the 2013 Jackson Poetry Prize, a Guggenheim Fellowship, a Lannan Literary Award, an American Book Award and two Pushcart Prizes. He comments:

> "In December and then in March a large box of poetry came by UPS to my door. I'm guessing there were over 2000 poems to consider. In reading and re-reading the poems I was struck by the sheer diversity and energy of contemporary American poetry. No particular style was dominant; rather, there were singular voices with remarkable visions and the poems ranged from short lyrics that valued compression to expansive sequences that unfolded over time . . . I would like to point readers to the wonderful poems that received Special Mentions and were not possible to include and also to translations from such languages as Chinese and Russian."

Patricia Smith is the author of six books of poetry including *Blood Dazzler*, a finalist for the National Book Award, and her latest *Shoulda Been Jimi Savannah*. She was a 2012 Fellow at both the MacDowell Colony and Yaddo, a two-time Pushcart Prize winner and a four-time individual champion of The National Poetry Slam, the most successful poet in the competition's history. She writes:

"Is poetry dead? Did someone actually ask that question--out loud? Did thousands of writers, readers and instigators rush to their battle stations to debate the merit of the aforementioned theory? Honestly? Because after immersing myself in roughly 41,611 poems (well, the boxes WERE big), I can unequivocally assure you that not only is contemporary poetry infused with a relentless, bellowing pulse, it's moving in directions that will knock the naysayers back on their prim little keisters. Judging the Pushcart was taxing and intoxicating, exasperating and illuminating, an arduous honor that forever changed the way I feel about the possibilities of the canon. On a personal note, I discovered dozens of new literary journals, and have now crafted a harrowing submission schedule. But the experience yielded a much larger lesson. For months, I was surrounded by the voices of those impassioned and driven by the power of the word, and that sweet collective noise proved one thing once and for all--poetry, ladies and gentlemen, won't be dying anytime soon. If ever."

My profound thanks to Arthur and Patricia, and also to our guest prose editors. You will find them listed on the masthead.

PP38 includes 68 brilliant selections from 53 stalwart presses (17 of them new to the series, a record).

Blessings on you honored reader. We keep the faith for you. Please keep the faith for us.

Bill Henderson

THE PEOPLE WHO
HELPED

FOUNDING EDITORS—Anaïs Nin (1903-1977), Buckminster Fuller (1895-1983), Charles Newman (1938-2006), Daniel Halpern, Gordon Lish, Harry Smith (1936–2013), Hugh Fox (1932-2011), Ishmael Reed, Joyce Carol Oates, Len Fulton, Leonard Randolph, Leslie Fiedler (1917-2003), Nona Balakian (1918-1991), Paul Bowles (1910-1999), Paul Engle (1908-1991), Ralph Ellison (1914-1994), Reynolds Price (1933-2011), Rhoda Schwartz, Richard Morris, Ted Wilentz (1915-2001), Tom Montag, William Phillips (1907-2002). Poetry editor: H. L. Van Brunt

CONTRIBUTING EDITORS FOR THIS EDITION—Dan Albergotti, Dick Allen, John Allman, Antler, Philip Appleman, Tony Ardizzone, M. C. Armstrong, Renee Ashley, David Baker, Kim Barnes, Ellen Bass, Rick Bass, Claire Bateman Charles Baxter, Bruce Beasley, Marvin Bell, Molly Bendall, Bruce Bennett, Linda Bierds, Diann Blakely, Marianne Boruch, Michael Bowden, Geoffrey Brock, Fleda Brown, Rosellen Brown, Michael Dennis Browne, Christopher Buckley, E. S. Bumas, Richard Burgin, Sarah Busse, Richard Cecil, Suzanne Cleary, Michael Collier, Billy Collins, Jeremy Collins, Martha Collins, Lydia Conklin, Stephen Corey, Lisa Couturier, Michael Czyzniejewski, Phil Dacey, Claire Davis, Ted Deppe, Jaquira Diaz, Stuart Dischell, Anthony Docrr, Jack Driscoll, John Drury, Karl Elder, Angie Estes, Gary Fincke, Ben Fountain, Alice Friman, Joanna Fuhrman, John Fulton, Richard Garcia, Christine Gelineau, Gary Gildner, Elton Glaser, Sarah Green, Linda Gregerson, Susan Hahn, Mark Halliday, James Harms, Jeffrey Harrison, Matt Hart, Tim Hedges, Robin Hemley, Daniel L. Henry, William Heyen, Bob Hicok, Kathleen Hill, Jane Hirshfield, Jen Hirt, Ted Hoagland, Andrea Hollander, Caitlin Horrocks, Helen Houghton, Christopher Howell, Andrew Hudgins, Maria Hummel, Karla Huston, Colette Inez, Mark Irwin, David Jauss, Bret Anthony Johnston,

Nalini Jones, Laura Kasischke, George Keithley, Brigit Pegeen Kelly, Thomas E. Kennedy, Junse Kim, Kristin King, David Kirby, John Kistner, Judith Kitchen, Ted Kooser, Richard Kostelanetz, Maxine Kumin, Wally Lamb, Fred Leebron, Don Lee, Sandra Leong, Dana Levin, Philip Levine, Daniel S. Libman, Rachel Loden, Jennifer Lunden, Margaret Luongo, William Lychack, Paul Maliszewski, Kathryn Maris, Matt Mason, Dan Masterson, Alice Mattison, Gail Mazur, Robert McBrearty, Nancy McCabe, Rebecca McClanahan, Davis McCombs, Jill McDonough, Erin McGraw, Nancy Mitchell, Jim Moore, Joan Murray, Kirk Nesset, Michael Newirth, Aimee Nezhukumatathil, Celeste Ng, Risteard O'Keitinn, Joyce Carol Oates, Dzvinia Orlowsky, Peter Orner, Alicia Ostriker, Alan Michael Parker, Edith Pearlman, Benjamin Percy, Jen Percy, Donald Platt, Joe Ashby Porter, Elizabeth Powell, Kevin Prufer, Lia Purpura, James Reiss, Donald Revell, Nancy Richard, David Rigsbee, Atsuro Riley, Laura Rodley, Jessica Roeder, Jay Rogoff, Gibbons Ruark, Maxine Scates, Alice Schell, Brandon R. Schrand, Grace Schulman, Philip Schultz, Lloyd Schwartz, Salvatore Scibona, Maureen Seaton, Diane Seuss, Ravi Shankar, Anis Shivani, Jeanne Shoemaker, Gary Short, Arthur Smith, Anna Solomon, David St. John, Maura Stanton, Maureen Stanton, Paul Stapleton, Pamela Stewart, Patricia Strachan, Terese Svoboda, Chad Sweeney, Jennifer K. Sweeney, Joan Swift, Mary Szybist, Ron Tanner, Katherine Taylor, Elaine Terranova, Susan Terris, Robert Thomas, Jean Thompson, Pauls Toutonghi, William Trowbridge, Lee Upton, Laura van den Berg, G. C. Waldrep, Anthony Wallace, B. J. Ward, Don Waters, Michael Waters, Marc Watkins, William Wenthe, Philip White, Naomi J. Williams, Eleanor Wilner, S.L. Wisenberg, Mark Wisniewski, David Wojahn, Carolyne Wright, Robert Wrigley, Christina Zawadiwsky, Paul Zimmer

PAST POETRY EDITORS—H.L. Van Brunt, Naomi Lazard, Lynne Spaulding, Herb Leibowitz, Jon Galassi, Grace Schulman, Carolyn Forché, Gerald Stern, Stanley Plumly, William Stafford, Philip Levine, David Wojahn, Jorie Graham, Robert Hass, Philip Booth, Jay Meek, Sandra McPherson, Laura Jensen, William Heyen, Elizabeth Spires, Marvin Bell, Carolyn Kizer, Christopher Buckley, Chase Twichell, Richard Jackson, Susan Mitchell, Lynn Emanuel, David St. John, Carol Muske, Dennis Schmitz, William Matthews, Patricia Strachan, Heather McHugh, Molly Bendall, Marilyn Chin, Kimiko Hahn, Michael Dennis Browne, Billy Collins, Joan Murray, Sherod Santos, Judith Kitchen, Pattiann Rogers, Carl Phillips, Martha Collins,

CONTENTS

HUMAN SNOWBALL

by DAVY ROTHBART

from THE PARIS REVIEW

On February 14, 2000, I took the Greyhound bus from Detroit to Buffalo to visit a girl named Lauren Hill. Not Lauryn Hill, the singer who did that song "Killing Me Softly," but another Lauren Hill, who'd gone to my high school, and now, almost ten years later, was about to become my girlfriend, I hoped. I'd seen her at a party when she was home in Michigan over the holidays, and we'd spent the night talking and dancing. Around four in the morning, when the party closed down, we'd kissed for about twelve minutes out on the street, as thick, heavy snowflakes swept around us, melting on our eyebrows and eyelashes. She'd left town the next morning, and in the six weeks since, we'd traded a few soulful letters and had two very brief, awkward phone conversations. As Valentine's Day came near, I didn't know if I should send her flowers, call her, not call her, or what. I thought it might be romantic to just show up at her door and surprise her.

I switched buses in Cleveland and took a seat next to an ancient-looking black guy who was in a deep sleep. Twenty minutes from Buffalo, when darkness fell, he woke up, offered me a sip of Jim Beam from his coat pocket, and we started talking. His name was Vernon. He told me that when midnight rolled around, it was going to be his hundred-and-tenth birthday.

"A *hundred and ten?*" I squealed, unabashedly skeptical.

Happy to prove it, he showed me a public-housing ID card from Little Rock, Arkansas, that listed his birth date as 2/15/90.

"Who was president when—"

"Benjamin Harrison," he said quickly, cutting me off before I was

19

even done with my question, as though he'd heard it many times before. I had no clue if this was true, but he winked and popped a set of false teeth from his mouth, and in the short moment they glistened in his hand, it seemed suddenly believable that he was a hundred and ten, and not just, like, eighty-nine. His bottom gums, jutting tall, were shaped like the Prudential rock and were the color of raw fish, pink and red with dark gray speckles. The skin on his face was pulled taut around his cheekbones and eye sockets, as leathery and soft-looking as some antique baseball mitt in its display case at Cooperstown.

I found myself telling Vernon all about Lauren Hill and explained how nervous I was to see her—surely he'd have some experience he could draw on to help me out. I told him I thought I was taking a pretty risky gamble by popping up in Buffalo unannounced. Things were either going to be really fucking awesome or really fucking weird, and I figured I'd probably know which within the first couple of minutes I saw her. Vernon, it turned out, was in a vaguely similar situation. After a century plus of astonishingly robust health, he'd been ailing the past eighteen months, and before he kicked off he wanted to make amends with his great-granddaughter, whom he was the closest to out of all of his relatives. But, he admitted, he'd let her down so many times—with the drinking, the drugs, and even stealing her money and kitchen appliances—that she might not be willing to let him past the front door. Twice he used my cell phone to try calling her, but nobody answered. So much for sage advice.

We both got quiet and brooded to ourselves as the bus rolled off the freeway ramp and wound its way through empty downtown streets lined with soot-sprayed mounds of snow and ice. Buffalo in winter is a bleak Hoth-like wasteland, and the only sign of life I saw was a pair of drunks who'd faced off in front of an adult bookstore and begun to fight, staggering like zombies. One of them had a pink stuffed animal and was clubbing the other in the face with it. A steady snow began to fall, and I felt a wave of desperate sorrow crash over me. Whatever blind optimism I'd had about the night and how Lauren Hill might receive me had been lost somewhere along the way (maybe at the rest stop in Erie, Pennsylvania, in the bathroom stall with shit smeared on the walls). The trip, I realized now, was a mistake, but at the same time I knew that the only thing to do was to go ahead with my fucked-up plan anyway and go surprise Lauren, because once you're sitting there and you've got a needle in your hands, what else is there to do but poke your finger and see the blood?

At the greyhound station, a sort-of friend of mine named Chris Hendershot was there to pick me up in a shiny black Ford Explorer with only four hundred miles on the odometer but its front end and passenger side bashed to shit. "You get in a rollover?" I asked him, after hopping in up front.

"Naw, I just boosted this bitch yesterday in Rochester, it was already like this. Who's your friend?"

"This is Vernon. He's gonna ride with us, if that's cool. In a few hours it's gonna be his hundred-and-tenth birthday."

"No shit?" Chris glanced in the rearview and nodded to Vernon, in the backseat. "Fuck if I make it to twenty-five," he said, gunning it out of the lot.

Chris was the kind of guy who always made these sorts of claims, hoping, perhaps, to sound tougher, but really he was a sweetheart with a swashbuckler's twinkle who was rarely in serious danger and probably had decades of fun times ahead of him, if he could stay out of prison. He had pale white skin, a rash of acne on his neck, and his own initials carved into his buzz-cut hair in several places. He looked Canadian and sounded Canadian and was indeed Canadian—he'd grown up on the meanest street of Hamilton, Ontario, and, as he'd told me more than a few times, he and his older brother had stolen seventy-six cars before getting finally caught when Chris was nineteen. Chris did the time— three years—while his brother skated. Then Chris moved in with an uncle in Cincinnati and got a job as an airline reservationist, which was how I'd met him a couple of years before. He had a gregarious nature, and after we'd found ourselves in deep conversation while I was buying tickets over the phone, he'd come to Chicago a few weekends in a row and stayed on my couch while pursuing his dream of becoming a stand-up comic. The problem was that he was absolutely sorry as a stand-up comic, just woefully bad. I saw him perform once, at the ImprovOlympic at Clark and Addison, and it was one of the hardest, saddest things I've ever had to watch—someone's dream unraveling and being chopped dead with each blast of silence that followed his punch lines. But where I would've been destroyed by this, Chris was over it by the next morning, and freshly chipper. He told me the lesson he'd learned was that he needed to focus on his strengths, and he knew himself to be an ace car thief. Before long, he'd moved to Buffalo and was working at his older brother's "mechanic" shop. When I called and told him I was coming to town and explained why, he told me he actually knew Lauren Hill, because for a while he'd been a regular at Freighter's, the bar where she worked, though he doubted she knew him by name, and anyway, he said, he wasn't allowed in there anymore because he'd left twice without paying when he'd realized at the end of the night that he'd left his cash at home. "I'll tell you one thing," he said. "That girl's beautiful. Every guy who wanders into that damn bar, they leave in love with her."

Vernon had asked if he could roll with us for a bit while he kept trying to reach his great-granddaughter. If nothing else, he suggested, we could drop him off later at the YMCA and he'd track her down the next morning. He sat quietly in the backseat, looking out the window while we cruised toward the east side of town, running every sixth light, Chris catching me up on some of his recent escapades, half-shouting to make himself heard over the blare of a modern-rock station out of Niagara Falls, Ontario, that slipped in and out of range. "Hey, check this out," he said. He reached beneath the driver's seat and passed me a fat roll of New York Lottery scratch tickets. "You can win like ten grand!" he cried. "Scratch some off if you want."

"Where'd you get these, man?"

"Get this—they were in the car when I got it! Just sitting in the back-seat! I already scratched off some winners, like forty bucks' worth." He passed me a tin Buffalo Sabres lighter from his coat pocket, its sharp bottom edge gummed with shavings from the tickets he'd scratched. "Go on," he said, "make us some money."

I tore off a long band of tickets and handed them back to Vernon, along with a quarter from the center console, and Chris cranked up the volume until the windows shook and piloted us through his frozen, desolate town toward Lauren Hill's apartment, singing along to the radio, while me and Vernon scratched away: "*You make me come./You make me complete./You make me completely miserable.*" I looked up and saw him grinning at me and nodding his head, as if to ask, Doesn't this song fucking rock? I grinned and nodded back, because yes, in a crazy way it kind of did. A barely perceptible but definitely perceptible drip of hopefulness had started to seep back into the night.

No one was home at Lauren's place; in fact, the lights were out in all six apartments in her building even though it was only seven-thirty.

Chris cracked his window and flicked a pile of my losing scratch tickets through like cigarette butts. "She's probably at the bar," he said. "She works every night, and she's there hanging out even when she ain't working. We'll go find her." He whipped the Explorer around the corner and we fishtailed a bit in the gathering snow.

A mile down, five tiny side streets spilled together at a jagged-shaped intersection, and from its farthest corners, two squat and battered bars glared across at each other like warring crabs, panels of wood nailed over the windows and painted to match the outside walls and one neon beer sign hanging over each door—Yuengling and Budweiser—as though they were the names of the bars.

Chris pulled over and pointed to the bar with the Yuengling sign. "That's Freighter's," he said. "See if she's in there. And if she is, see if you can call off the dogs so I can get in there, too."

I jumped out and took a few steps, then had a thought and went back to the truck and asked Vernon if he wanted to come in with me. I was nervous to see Lauren and afraid she would find something creepy and stalker-like about me taking a Greyhound bus a few hundred miles to make an uninvited appearance on Valentine's Day. If I rolled in there with Vernon, it seemed to me, any initial awkwardness might be diffused.

Vernon was a little unsteady on his feet, either from the whiskey or the quilt of fresh snow lining the street paired with his ludicrously advanced age, so I held him by the arm as we crossed the intersection. A plume of merriment rose in my chest that was six parts the gentle glow of heading into any bar on a cold, snowy night, and four parts the wonderful, unpredictable madness of having a hundred-and-ten-year-old man I'd just met on the Greyhound bus as my wingman. I heaved open the heavy door to Freighter's, letting out a blast of noise and hot, smoky air, and once Vernon shuffled past, I followed him in.

Inside, it was so dark and hot and loud it took me a few seconds to get my bearings. People shouted over the thump of a jukebox and the rattle of empty bottles being tossed into a metal drum. Directly overhead, two hockey games roared from a pair of giant TVs. It smelled like someone had puked on a campfire. All of which is to say, just the way I liked it and just like the 8 Ball Saloon back in Michigan where Lauren had worked before moving to Buffalo for school.

A hulking, tattooed guy on a stool was asking me and Vernon for our IDs. I flashed him mine, while Vernon pulled out the same fraying ID card he'd showed me earlier. The doorman plucked it from his hand, inspected it, and passed it back, shaking his head. "Nope," he shouted

23

over the din. "I need a driver's license or state ID." At first I laughed, thinking he was just fucking with us, but then I saw he was serious.

I leaned to his ear and protested, "But he's a hundred and ten years old! Look at the guy!"

The doorman shook his head and pointed at the exit. It was useless to try to reason with him over the din, and I figured once I found Lauren, she'd help me get Vernon and Chris in.

"Wait in the truck," I shouted in Vernon's ear. "I'll come get you guys in a few minutes."

He nodded and slipped out into the cold. I took a few steps further in. The place was packed, mostly older, rugged-looking dudes—factory workers, construction workers, bikers, and their equally rugged-looking girlfriends—with a sprinkling of younger indie kids and punk rockers mixed in. All of a sudden I caught sight of Lauren Hill behind the bar and my heart twisted like a wet rag—she had her back turned to me and was getting her shoulders thoroughly massaged by a tall, skinny, dark-haired guy in a sleeveless shirt, dozens of tattoos slathered on his arms. My first thought was to immediately leave, but I also knew that would be silly—this was surely just some guy who worked with her, not a true threat. The guy finished his little rubdown and they both turned back to the bar. Lauren's beauty made my stomach lurch. She had long, straight hair, dyed black; big, expressive eyes; and her usual enormous, bright smile. I made my way over, feeling stupid for having spent the last eight hours on buses without the foresight to dream up a single witty or romantic thing to say when I greeted her.

I edged between a few guys at the bar and pulled a ten-dollar bill from my back pocket. When Lauren came close, I called out, "Can I get a Bell's Amber?"—a local Michigan brew that wasn't served in Buffalo—my spontaneous, wilted stab at a joke. Even Chris Hendershot could've conjured up something funnier.

She looked at me and the smile drained off her face. "Davy? Oh my God, what the hell are you doing here?" There was no way to hug across the bar; instead, Lauren offered what seemed to me a slightly awkward and tepid two-handed high five.

I slapped her hands and said, "I came here to surprise you," feeling suddenly lost in space.

"Oh, that's so awesome," she said, sounding possibly genuine. "But what are you doing in Buffalo?"

"No, I came to Buffalo because I wanted to see you." I shrugged and heard the next words tumble out of my mouth, even as I instantly regretted them. "Happy Valentine's Day!"

Just then, a bar-back rushing past with a tub full of empty glasses crashed into her, knocking her a couple of feet to the side. Now she was within shouting range of a few guys further along the bar, and they started barking out their drink orders. She leaned back toward me and hollered, "I'm sorry, Monday nights are always like this, and we're short a guy. Can you come back later? It'll be less insane."

"Sure, no problem," I said, putting both hands up idiotically for another slap of hands, but she'd already turned and was cranking the caps off a row of Yuenglings. I slowly lowered my hands, waited another fifteen seconds or so until she happened to glance my way, and gave her a little wave. She flashed a polite smile in return, and I whirled and slunk out the door, utterly defeated, making a promise to myself not to come back later in the night unless she called my phone in the next few hours and begged me to. It was just past eight o'clock. I'd give her till midnight.

"Should we come inside?" Chris asked as I climbed in the backseat; Vernon had made it back to the car and was up riding shotgun.

"It's kind of busy in there. Let's get some grub and come back later."

"Well, how'd it go?" asked Vernon, once we were moving again.

"Not too bad. I don't know. Not too good, either." I told them what had gone down. They both tried to reassure me that Lauren was probably really excited I was in town, but that it's always hard when someone pops in to see you and you're busy at work. I granted them that, but it still seemed like she could've maybe flipped me the keys to her apartment, in case I wanted to take a nap or chill out and watch a movie until she got home. Or really had done anything to give me the sense that she was happy I'd rolled in.

"Don't worry, man," Vernon said. "Trust me, it'll be cool." This from the guy who was now using Chris's cell phone—and had been the whole time I was in the bar—to try to reach his great-granddaughter, to no avail. He was hoping we could stop by her house, which was on the west side of town, about a twenty-minute drive.

"I'm down," I said. "Chris?"

"Rock 'n' roll." He pumped up the Green Day song on the radio, zoomed through side streets to the on-ramp for an expressway, and looped the Explorer back toward the lights of downtown, slapping the steering wheel along to the music. Vernon tore off a few scratch tickets for himself, passed me the rest of the roll, and we both went to work.

Each losing ticket I scratched out socked me a little blow to the heart. Why didn't scratch cards just have a single box that told you if you'd won or not? Why the slow build, all the teasing hoopla of tic-tac-toe game boards and wheels of fortune? You kept thinking you were getting close and then, once again: loser. All of the unanswered questions made my head hurt: Had I blown things by coming to Buffalo and putting unfair pressure on Lauren Hill? Should I simply have come on any day other than Valentine's Day? Had she meant all the things she'd said in her letters? Some of it? None of it? And what would be the best way to salvage the night when I went back to the bar? (Because, face it, I was headed back there later whether she called me or not.) A small heap of losing tickets gathered at my feet.

"Holy shit!" cried Vernon from up front. "I think we got a winner!"

"How much?" said Chris, suddenly alert, punching the radio off.

"Wait a second. Did I win? Yeah, I did. Ten bucks!"

"Not bad." Chris nodded enthusiastically. "That's yours to keep," he told Vernon. "You guys just keep on scratching."

"You bet your goddamn ass," said Vernon, still believing a bigger payday was near.

His minor stroke of glory made me glad, but to me, winning ten bucks instead of ten grand was like getting a drunken kiss on the corner of the mouth from a stranger at the bar that you'll never see again. What I really wanted was to spend the night in Lauren Hill's arms, kissing her and holding her tight; to wake up with her at dawn, make love once or twice, and walk hand in hand through the woodsy park I'd glimpsed by her apartment, which by morning, I imagined—if it kept snowing the way it was now—would be transformed into a place of quiet and exquisite majesty. That was my wish. Anything less I'd just as soon chuck out the window.

From the outside, Vernon's great-granddaughter's house looked like a haunted mansion out of *Scooby-Doo*. It sat on a wide section of an abandoned half-acre lot overgrown with weeds, brambles, and the remaining debris from houses that had been leveled on either side. Across the street, TVs flickered dimly from the windows of a low-rise housing project, and at the end of the block a closed-down liquor store with both doors missing gaped like a sea cave, open to the elements. As we pulled up in front, Vernon looked back at me and said, "Hey, would you come inside with me?" It was my turn to be wingman.

I followed him up the front walk and up three stairs to the porch, and he lifted the enormous, rusted horseshoe knocker on the front door and let it land with a heavy thud. We waited. I watched snowflakes touch down on the Explorer's windshield and instantly melt. The knocker squeaked as he lifted it again, but then, from somewhere deep in the house, came a woman's voice, "I hear you, I'm coming."

Her footsteps padded near and Vernon edged back until he was practically hiding behind me. "Who's there?" the woman called.

I looked over to Vernon, waiting for him to respond. He had the look of a dog who'd strewn trash through the kitchen. "It's your grand-daddy," he said at last, weakly.

"Who?"

"Vernon Wallace." He kicked the porch concrete. "Your great-granddaddy."

The door opened a couple of inches and a woman's face appeared, eyebrows raised, hair wrapped in a towel above her head. She was in maybe her early fifties. Through a pair of oversize glasses, she took a long look at Vernon, sighed, shook her head, and said, "Granddaddy, what're you doing up here in the wintertime?" As he cleared his throat and began to respond, she said, "Hold on, let me get my coat." The door closed, and for a half-minute Vernon painted hieroglyphics with the toe of his old shoe in a pyramid of drifting snow, looking suddenly frail and ancient. Exhaust panted from the Explorer's tailpipe out on the street, and I could make out the hard-rock bass line rattling its windows but didn't recognize the song.

After a moment, the door opened again and the woman stepped out and joined us on the front porch, hair still tucked up in a towel. Over a matching pink sweat suit she wore a puffy, oversize, black winter coat, and her feet, sockless, were stuffed into a pair of unlaced low-top Nikes. She gave Vernon a big, friendly hug, and said, "I love you, Grand-daddy, it's good to see you," and then turned to me and said, "Hi there, I'm Darla Kenney," and once I'd introduced myself she said, "Well, it's good to meet you, I appreciate you bringing Vernon by." She turned back to face him and crossed her arms. "What you been drinking to-night, Granddaddy?"

He flinched slightly but didn't respond.

"Listen," she said, "I love you, but I ain't got no money. You know my whole situation. You're gonna have to stay with your friend here, 'cause I can't just invite you in."

Vernon nodded deeply, unable to meet her gaze. "I was just hoping we could spend time together."

"We can!" she said. "But not tonight. I got all kinds of shit to deal with tonight. I can't even get the damn car started. You got to learn to call people ahead of time so they know you coming." She softened. "How long you gonna stay in town for?"

Vernon shrugged. "A week or two?"

"Okay, then. Look, you give me a call tomorrow, or the next day, and we'll go for a drive, we'll play cards at Calvin's. He know you're in town?"

Vernon shook his head.

Darla looked past us, to the Explorer out on the street, its motor revving, Chris Hendershot behind the wheel, slapping his hands on the dash and crooning to himself. "That your friend?" she asked me.

"Yeah. That's Chris."

Darla tugged her coat closed and fought with the zipper. "Hey, listen," she said. "I got cables. Think I can get a jump?"

Ten minutes later, Chris was shouting instructions to me, banging under the hood of Darla Kenney's '84 Lincoln Continental with a wrench while I pounded the gas and jammed the ignition. Is there any sound more full of frustration and futility than a car that won't start when you turn the key? Click-click-click-click-click. All I could think of was Lauren Hill's dismayed expression in the bar when she'd first seen me.

"Okay, cut it!" Chris shouted. I felt his weight on the engine block as he bobbed deep within. A ping and a clatter. "Now try."

Click-click-click-click.

"Cut it!"

I heard Chris disconnecting the jumper cables, and then he dropped the hood with a magnificent crash. "I'll tell you what's happening, ma'am," he said to Darla, who stood in the street, looking on, still in her unlaced sneakers and coat with a towel on her head. "Your battery cable's a little frizzy, down by the starter relay. We get this in the shop, it's nothing—ten minutes, you're on your way. Tonight, though, no tools? Ain't gonna be easy." He passed her the jumper cables and put a consoling hand on her shoulder. "I'm really sorry. Usually I can get anything moving." I was touched by his level of kindness—if this was how sweetly he treated a woman he'd just met, it was hard to imagine there was anything he wouldn't do for his friends.

I climbed from the car and joined Chris and Darla. Vernon was sitting in the Explorer, keeping warm up front, scratching off lotto tickets.

"Well, it was nice of you to try," said Darla. She looked back and forth between us. "How do you guys know my granddaddy, anyhow?"

I wasn't sure how to answer. "Well, we met on a Greyhound bus once; we were seatmates." The word "once" tossed in there made it seem like this was years ago.

But Darla saw through it. "Oh, okay, when was that?"

"Well. Tonight."

She weighed this for a second. "Is he staying with you guys?"

"I don't know," I said. "I think he was saying something about the Y." The way my awesome surprise had gone over with Lauren Hill, I'd probably end up in the next bunk.

"I stay with my brother," Chris piped up. "But we got a cot at the garage, right around the corner. It's heated. I mean, that's where we work. Shit, he can stay in my room and I'll stay on the cot."

"We're not gonna leave him on the street," I said. I meant to be reassuring, but realized a second later that my words could be taken as an accusation.

Darla toyed with the clamps of the jumper cables in her hands; the metal jaws, squeaking open and shut, looked like angry, puppet-size gators shit-talking back and forth. As little as she seemed to want to deal with Vernon, she also seemed aware that he was her responsibility as much as anyone else's, and she wasn't ready to ditch him with two white kids he'd met an hour before. "Here's the thing," she said. "He can't stay at my house, and I got no money to give him right now. But I've got a tenant that owes me four hundred fifty dollars—I was gonna stop there tonight anyhow. We get some of that money together, I'll give my granddaddy half and put him up a week at the Front Park Inn."

Me and Chris nodded. "That'll work," I said. Fuck the Y—maybe at the Front Park Inn there'd be an extra bed for me.

Darla went to the Lincoln, heaved open the back door, and tossed the jumper cables on the floor behind the driver's seat. She turned back toward us. "Can I get a ride over to this house with you guys? It's really close, like ten, fifteen blocks from here. Larchmont, just the other side of Lake Avenue."

"Ain't no thing," said Chris.

I asked Darla if she wanted to get dressed first, at least pull on some socks, but she was already climbing into the backseat of Chris's Explorer and sliding over to make room for me. "We're just going and coming right back," she said. "Come on, hop in."

The snow kept falling. On the way to her tenant's house, Darla filled me in on a few things while Chris blasted music up front. It both irritated and charmed me that he kept the radio going max force no matter who was in the car with him. Even when he'd stayed with me in Chicago all those weekends, every time we were in my truck he'd reach over and crank the volume. Vernon rode shotgun, dozing, the dwindling spool of lotto tickets in his lap.

Darla had four children, she told me. She'd had the same job—quality control at a metal-stamping plant—for almost thirty years, and as she was careful with her money, she'd been able to buy homes for each of her children in nearby West Buffalo neighborhoods. "Nothing fancy," she said, "but a roof over their heads." One daughter had split up with her husband two years before and moved to Tampa, Florida. Darla rented out one half of their house to a friend from work, and the ex had stayed on in the other half, though Darla had begun to charge him three hundred bucks a month in rent, which was more than fair, she said, and less than what she could get from somebody else. But her daughter's ex, whose name was Anthony, and who was, overall, a decent, hardworking man, had fallen behind—he still owed her for January, and now half of February. It was time for her to pay a visit, Darla said.

She coached Chris through a few turns. We crossed a big four-lane road and the neighborhood deteriorated, making Darla's street look regal by comparison. Every third house was shuttered or burned-out. On a side street I glimpsed four guys loading furniture out of a squat apartment building into a U-Haul trailer. "Okay," said Darla, "take this right and it's the first one on the right."

We pulled up in front of a tiny, ramshackle house with cardboard taped over a missing window and its gutters hanging off, dangling to the ground. Still, the dusting of snow softened its features, and there were hopeful signs of upkeep—Christmas lights draped over a hedge by the side door and a pair of well-stocked bird feeders, swinging from low branches in the front yard, which had attracted a gang of sickly but grateful-looking squirrels.

"I'll be back in a couple minutes," said Darla, stepping gingerly down to the snow-filled street. She closed her door, picked her way across the lawn to the side of the house, knocked a few times, and disappeared inside.

Chris's cell phone rang and he answered it and had a quick, angry spat with his older brother. He'd explained to me that he'd been in hot water with his brother all month. His brother had a rule that anytime Chris boosted a car he was supposed to get it immediately to their shop to be dismantled (or at least stripped of its VIN) and resold. Chris admitted that he had a habit of keeping stolen cars for a while and driving around in them to impress girls. A couple of weeks before, another guy who worked with them had landed a cherry-red PT Cruiser in Pittsburgh, and Chris had whipped it around Buffalo over Super Bowl weekend while his brother was out of town. His brother found out, of course, and had been hounding him about it ever since. Now he seemed to be giving Chris grief for driving the Explorer; I could hear his brother on the other end of the phone, shouting at him to bring it back to base. "Fuck that motherfucker!" Chris shouted, hanging up and slamming his phone on the dash. "Who the fuck does he think he is?" To me, there was something ecstatically rich and appealing in someone who acted so gangsta but sounded so Canadian; at the same time, I could see in the rearview mirror that Chris's eyes had gone teary, and I felt a guilty and despairing tug of responsibility for dragging him around town and sticking him deeper into his brother's doghouse.

The shouting roused Vernon from his mini-nap, and without missing a beat he resumed work scratching off the squares of each lotto ticket. A heaviness had settled over him. He inspected a ticket after scratching it off, sighed greatly, and let it slip from his fingers.

In the front yard of the house next door, a band of ragtag little kids wrestled in the snow and hurled snowballs at parked cars and each other, shouting, "I'ma blast you, nigga!" The oldest of them, a boy around ten, was trying to rally the rest of them through the early stages of building a snowman. I powered my window down a few inches so I could hear his pitch. "Start with a giant snowball," he said breathlessly, as he worked on packing one together, then placed it on the ground. "Then we keep rolling this thing, and rolling it, and rolling it, until it's as big as a house, and then we'll have the biggest snowman in all of Buffalo!" The other kids dove in to help him, and they slid around the yard, accumulating more snow, then breaking off chunks accidentally as they pushed in opposite directions. Everyone shouted instructions at everyone else: "Roll it that way!" "Get those Doritos off it!" "You're fucking it up!"

31

Lauren Hill had been about the same age—nine or ten—when her dad was killed by a drunk driver. She'd told me the story in the most recent letter she'd sent me; her mom had appeared at the park where Lauren was playing with her friends and pulled her away and told her the news. Even though that had happened in summertime, I couldn't help but picture a fifth-grade Lauren Hill building a snowman with her neighborhood pals, her mom galloping up, crazed and wild-eyed, and dragging her away to a sucky, dadless future in a grim apartment complex near the Detroit airport, populated by creepy neighbors and a steady stream of her mom's low-life live-in boyfriends. When you first got involved with any girl who'd been punctured by that kind of sadness, I'd learned, you had to be extra cautious about flooding them with goodness and light. A gentle and steady kindness appealed to them, but too much love straight out of the gate was uncomfortable, even painful, and impossible to handle. I felt like an idiot for coming to Buffalo and freaking Lauren out.

"Hey, Vernon," I said, leaning between the front seats. "Did you ever get married?"

"Yes I did. Wanda May. Fifty years we were married." He paused, passing a scratch-off to Chris. "I think this one wins a free ticket." Then, to me, with a sudden touch of melancholy, "She died in 1964."

"Damn. That's way before I was born."

Vernon slipped his whiskey bottle out, touched it to his lips, and gave me a look. "You want some advice?" he said.

"Definitely."

"You should marry this girl you came to see. Marry her right away. Tomorrow, if you want. You don't know how much time you get with someone, so you might as well start right away."

"The problem is, it's not up to me. She gets a say."

"It's more up to you than you think."

I let that sink in, watching the kids in the neighbor's yard. Their snowman's round trunk had quickly swelled from the size of a soccer ball to the size of a dorm fridge. It took all of them, pushing and shouldering it together, to keep it rolling across the lawn. Finally they ran out of juice and came to a stop, slumping against their massive boulder of snow, tall as the oldest boy. There seemed to be two opinions about what to do next. The boy in charge wanted to go down the street and recruit his older cousin and some of his cousin's friends to keep pushing. But one tiny girl pointed out that the snowman had already gotten too big for them to add a middle and a top. Also, she suspected that if the boy's cousin and his friends glimpsed the half-built snowman, all they'd want to do is destroy it. "We made it, we should get to knock it down," she said.

Vernon passed his bottle to Chris, who took a long gulp and passed it back to me. I drained the last of the whiskey down and watched as the kids gave their big, round heap of snow a pair of stick arms, then collaborated on the face—two deep holes for eyes, a Dorito for a nose, and, strangely, no mouth.

By now, Chris and Vernon were watching them, too. "You want some more advice?" Vernon asked.

"Yes, I do."

"Okay. Don't outlive your wife."

The oldest kid pulled off his red knit cap and plopped it on top of the snowman's head, and at last the whole crew of munchkins stood back to silently admire their handiwork. It was surely the saddest, fattest, strangest, and most beautiful snowman I'd ever seen.

After a few long moments, there was the sound of voices, as Vernon's great-granddaughter Darla banged her way through the side door of the house she owned. The towel on her head had been replaced by a black baseball cap, and she was trailed by two others in heavy coats with their hoods pulled up. Her appearance seemed to somehow release the kids in the neighbors' yard from their spell. The oldest boy let out a mighty cry and charged the snowman—he plowed into its shoulder, driving loose its left arm and a wedge of its face, before crashing to the ground. The other kids followed, flailing with arms and feet, and even using the snowman's own arms to beat its torso quickly to powdery rubble.

Darla and her two companions crossed the yard toward us.

Vernon turned to me and Chris. "That's how long I was married, feels like," he said, eyes blazing. "As long as that snowman was alive."

We took on two new passengers—Anthony, the ex-husband of Darla's daughter who owed Darla all the back rent, and his shy, pregnant girlfriend, Kandy. They squeezed in back with me and Darla, and we circled around the block and headed back the way we'd come. Our next destination was a Chinese restaurant where Anthony worked as a dishwasher, on the east end of town, not far from Lauren Hill's bar. Anthony told us that his car was dead, too; apparently, one of the few operational vehicles in all of Buffalo was Chris's Explorer, which he'd driven off the lot of a body shop in Rochester the night before.

Anthony and Darla continued a conversation they must have started in the house. Anthony—dark skinned, small and compact, with a thin mustache, roughly forty years old—spoke softly, but had a thoughtful, commanding presence. He was explaining why he hadn't quit his job, even though he hadn't been paid in a month. "Here's the thing about Mr. Liu," he said. "Last winter, business got so slow, sometimes there was no customers in there, he could've sent me home. But he knows I got bills, and I'm scheduled to work, so he gave me the hours and found shit for me to do. You know, shovel the parking lot, clean out the walk-in cooler. Sometimes he paid me just to sit on a stool in back and watch basketball. Now his wallet thin for a minute, how'm I just gonna walk out on him?"

"What if he goes out of business?" Darla asked. "He gonna pay you those paychecks?"

"That's what *I'm* saying," said Kandy. She sat on the far side of the backseat, deeply ensconced in the hood of her jacket; it was hard for me to get a good look at her, but she seemed no older than me or Chris, and was maybe seven months pregnant.

"We talked about that," said Anthony. "First of all, we ain't goin' out of business. It's slow every winter, Mr. Liu just had some extra costs this winter. Second of all, he do go out of business? Mr. Liu told me he's gonna sell the building and all the equipment an' shit, and he'll have plenty enough to pay me what he owe."

The general plan, it seemed, was for Anthony to ask his boss for at least a portion of his paycheck so he could turn the money over to Darla, who might then have enough to support Vernon during his visit and buy him a ticket home to Little Rock. My own plan was to get some shrimp lo mein and ask Chris for a ride back to Freighter's. I wondered if bringing Lauren a carton of Chinese food would be a sweet gesture or just seem demented.

Chris had been quiet since the phone call with his brother, but now he dropped the music a few notches, glanced back at Kandy, and said, "You having a girl or a boy?"

"A boy," she peeped.

"What you gonna name it?"

"Floyd."

"That was her granddaddy's name," Anthony offered.

Chris nodded. "I like that name. Question is, he gonna take after his mom or his dad?"

"Not his dad, I hope," Anthony said cryptically.

"Well, I'll tell you what," said Vernon. "I'm sick of these scratch tickets." Over the seat, he handed back what remained of the roll. "Here ya go. I'm too old for this shit." His night, like mine, was not going the way he'd hoped. He reached for the radio, turned the volume back up, and sank into his seat, eyes out the window.

This was a song I knew: "What It's Like" by Everlast. Chris slid us back onto the Kensington Expressway, and the swirling snow gusted this way and that, rocking the SUV like a baby plane in turbulence. I closed my eyes and let myself sway.

Then you really might know what it's like.
Yeah, then you really might know what it's like . . . to have to lose.

Mr. Liu's chinese restaurant anchored a shambling commercial strip between a Popeyes and a defunct video store. It was called the Golden Panda, though just the right letters had burned out on the neon sign in its front window to leave THE GOLDEN AN. "Look!" I cried, rallying from the darkness, "it's the Golden AN!" Everyone stared at me flatly. "You know, from *Sesame Street*?"

"Wait a second," said Chris. "I know this fucking place. My brother loves this place. He always gets takeout here. It's so fucking *nasty* but he loves it." He looked at Anthony in the rearview mirror. "I mean, no offense."

Vernon and Kandy hung back in the Explorer while me, Chris, and Darla followed Anthony inside. The place had an odd, foul, but unidentifiable smell. It had just closed for the night, and a pretty Chinese girl in her late teens was blowing out red candles on each table that I supposed had been set out for Valentine's Day, and loading an enormous tray with dirty dishes. "Hey, Anthony," she said, tired but friendly. "If you came for dinner, you better let my mom know, she's shutting down the kitchen right now." She flipped a switch for the overhead fluorescents, and as they flickered on, the restaurant's interior grew more drab and dingy.

Anthony asked the girl if her dad was still around, and the girl told him he was. "Hey, Mary, these are my friends," he said, and told us he'd be back in a minute.

"Hi, Anthony's friends," she said. "You can have a seat if you want."

"Oh," said Anthony. "Did you hear back yet?"

"Not yet," said the girl. "The admissions office, they were supposed to call or e-mail everybody last week, but they never called me. So that's not a good sign. That reminds me, I need to check my e-mail."

"Well, look, if it don't work out, you just keep on trying." Anthony pushed his way through a blue silk curtain at the back of the dining area and disappeared down a hallway.

The three of us found a table that the girl had already cleared and sat down. Darla lowered her voice and said, "That's a fine young man right there. You know, that baby, Floyd, that's not even his baby. But he's gonna raise it and take care of that baby like it is." She shook her head. "I still call him my son. And that baby will be my grandson." Then, in a near whisper, "I hate putting the squeeze on him, but that ain't right he ain't getting paid." She eyed Mary, the owner's daughter, and said, under her breath, "This ain't the plantation. This is Buffalo!"

"I'm sure the guy'll give him some cash," I said.

As if on cue, a sudden, jarring eruption of shouting rose from deep in back. It was Anthony's voice, but the only word I could make out was "motherfucker." Soon a second voice joined the fray—Mr. Liu, no doubt, shouting back. And then a woman's voice jumped in, yelling in Chinese, followed by the sound of pots and pans clattering to the floor. Mary set down her tray and rushed through the blue curtains, and Darla said, "Oh no," and leapt up and dashed after her.

Chris gave me a dismal look and sank his head to the table. "Today's retarded," he said, sounding truly pained, his voice cracking a bit. "You know what sucks?"

"Yeah," I said, as the shouting in back increased. "That old man out there, Vernon, he thinks I should marry Lauren Hill tomorrow, but I don't think she wants anything to do with me, and you know, she's probably fucking this dude at her work."

"Yeah, that does suck," said Chris. "And I'll tell you what else sucks. I am really, really, incredibly fucking hungry."

"Maybe it'll all boil over back there and mellow out," I suggested, and again, Anthony's timing was splendid—he came ripping through the curtain just then, shouting and cursing, Darla at his heels, tugging at his sleeve and begging him to chill out.

"Get your fucking hands off me!" he said. "Fuck that motherfucker. I'll kill that slant-eyed faggot." He stopped in his tracks, turned, and screamed full force, "Fuck you, Mr. Liu! Suck my fucking dick, you little bitch!" From in back somewhere, Mr. Liu was shouting in return. Anthony kicked over a chair, and said, "Come get some of this! You want some? Come out here and get some!" Darla grabbed his shoulders and steered him toward the front door. "Fuck this place," Anthony said, deeply aggrieved, shoving her arm away. He fought his way outside.

"Come on," said Darla to me and Chris, holding the door open. "Time to go."

Back in the Explorer, Anthony was still shouting. We sat in the lot, trying to calm him down. Kandy seemed inappropriately entertained, a strange smile on her face as she pleaded with him to explain what had happened.

"That fucker," he said, jaw clenched, breathing hard through flared nostrils. "I told him he better pay me, not the whole month he owes me, just like two weeks, and he's, like"—here Anthony mocked Mr. Liu's Chinese accent—" 'I no have your money. Give me more time.' And I said, 'Fuck that. Pay me.' So then he's, like, 'I can't afford you no more. I hafta let you go.' " Anthony rubbed his face. With great anger, sadness, and shame, he said, "I didn't come all the way down here tonight to get my ass fired." He had tears in his eyes.

I saw that Darla, beside him, had tears in her eyes, too. She put her arm around Anthony and soothed him. "Okay, it'll be all right. It'll all be all right." I caught Chris's gaze in the rearview mirror. Even his eyes were wet. Strangely enough, I realized, mine were, too. I thought of the kids we'd seen building the snowman—how blissfully carefree they'd seemed—and felt a mournful gulf open up inside me. Whatever lumps those kids were taking as they sprouted in their bleak, tundra-like ghetto had nothing on the disappointments and humiliations of adulthood.

Kandy took Anthony's hand and said, "Listen, baby. You need to take a few deep breaths. I got to show you something."

"Five fucking years," said Anthony. "You know how many times I coulda gone somewhere else? My cousin in Syracuse, he's roofing now, twenty bucks an hour. That job coulda been mine." He blasted the back of the front passenger seat with his fist and Vernon bolted upright. "Sorry, Vernon," said Anthony. He looked at the empty front room of the Golden Panda. "Five years. Chinese people don't know shit about loyalty."

"It'll be all right," said Kandy. Her odd smile broadened. "Vernon, come on, will you just tell 'em?"

Vernon turned the radio off and looked around, gathering our attention, wide-eyed and mysterious. Then he melted into a smile, held up a scratched-out lotto ticket, and said, "We just won two thousand dollars."

Darla immediately screamed and slapped her hands to her cheeks in astonishment. Chris's eyes bugged out of his head. Anthony turned to his girlfriend, Kandy: "Say what?"

Kandy laughed. "It's true! I scratched it off!"

Vernon handed the ticket to Chris. "Really, how it is, *you* won two thousand dollars. We were just the first ones to find out."

Everyone grew suddenly quiet, watching Chris as he brought the ticket close to check it out. He nodded slowly, gave a low whistle, and flipped it over to read the fine print on back. "Looks like . . . redeem anywhere," he said softly, to himself. "They just print you a check right there. Damn. Two grand." He twisted around, looked back at all of us, and laughed. "Shit, this ain't a funeral," he said. "If I won, we all won. What the fuck, we're splittin' this fucker!"

Wild, joyous whoops of celebration filled the SUV, and all at the same time Vernon, Darla, Anthony, and Kandy hugged Chris and rubbed his shaved head. Everyone began shaking back and forth and the whole Explorer rocked side to side.

"Chris," I said. "You are a great American."

He was giggling, giddy at this sudden turn of events and all of the combined adulation. "Fuck you, dude. I'm Canadian!" Then he sobered up. "Okay, when I say we're splitting it, what I mean is, I get half, and the rest of you split the other half."

Everyone settled down a little, doing the math in their hands, and then murmured agreeably—this seemed like a more-than-fair arrangement, without asking Chris to be unreasonably generous.

Chris went on, peering back toward the restaurant, where Mr. Liu's daughter, Mary, had emerged to gather the last of the dishes. "Look, Anthony," he said, "I know the last thing you wanna do right now is go back in there. But yo, I got an idea. And I *need* some fried wontons."

A minute later, there were nine people clustered in the cramped, pungent kitchen of the Golden Panda—me, Chris, Old Man Vernon, Darla, Anthony, and Kandy, along with Mr. Liu, his wife, and their daughter, Mary, who sat on a milk crate, pecking away at a laptop. Mr. Liu had small, round glasses and graying hair and wore an apron over a dirty white T-shirt and baggy, brightly patterned swim trunks. He was bent over an industrial-size sink, wiping it out with a blue sponge, still tense, it seemed, from his confrontation with Anthony, who stood behind Vernon, glowering at the floor.

I could guess that Chris was aiming to broker a truce between the two of them, but didn't see the tack he planned on taking even as he dove right in. "Mr. Liu," he said. "I have been a customer of your fine establishment here for a couple of years. My brother, Shawn, he's been coming here for longer than that. I love the food you have here. It's kind of nasty sometimes, but it's good nasty. It's filling. I especially like the pork fried rice. And I like how you give fortune cookies even on to-go orders."

"Thank you," said Mr. Liu, with a heavy accent, standing straight. "I see you in here before. I think I know your brother." His wife, tiny and anxious, wearing a Buffalo Bills hoodie and a hairnet, said a few rapid words in Chinese to Mary, and Mary gave a one-word response without looking up.

"I recently came into some money," Chris went on. "And knowing me, I'll spend it, it'll be gone, and that'll be that." He took a breath. "I've got an idea, though. It'll be a good thing for me, and maybe it'll help you, too. Here's what I'm thinking—I want to come here tomorrow and give you . . . let's say . . . eight hundred bucks, cash money."

Mr. Liu crossed his arms, not quite sure where Chris was going with this.

"I'm thinking I give you eight hundred up front," said Chris, "and me and my brother eat here free for the rest of the year." He explained that they wouldn't take advantage of the arrangement—they'd only come by once or twice a week. Basically, Chris said, he was offering to pay in advance for a year's worth of meals. But he had a few conditions. "I want you to hire Anthony back. He's been loyal to you, you gotta be loyal to him. And you gotta pay him at least half of what you owe him right now in back wages."

Mr. Liu and Anthony glanced up toward each other without actually letting their eyes meet. Mr. Liu said to Chris, "I want Anthony to work. But not enough customers."

"Well, for one thing," Chris said, "you guys need to have delivery. A Chinese place without delivery, that's like a dog with no dick. That's why my brother always sends me down here to pick up. In snowstorms and shit. I hate that shit. You have delivery, you'll double your sales.

Anthony can wash dishes and go on runs, both. You need a delivery car, I can even help you find one, for a good price."

Mr. Liu spoke to his wife in Chinese, translating Chris's appeal. She responded at great length, gesturing at Anthony, Mary, and at Chris. I couldn't help but marvel at Chris's command of the situation. My image of him as a failed comic and petty criminal could barely accommodate the ease and confidence he now seemed to possess. At last Mrs. Liu fell silent, and Mr. Liu turned and said to Anthony, "Okay. You want to work here?"

Without unclenching his jaw, still staring down, burning holes in the tile, Anthony nodded.

"Good," said Chris. "Now hug it out, you two. Seriously. Go on. It's part of the deal."

Shyly, like two bludgeoned boxers embracing at the end of twelve rounds, Anthony and Mr. Liu edged near each other and slumped close in a kind of half hug, patting each other quickly on the back, but not without an evident bit of emotion.

Darla started clapping, and I found myself joining in, unexpectedly stirred; soon Kandy, Vernon, and even Mrs. Liu were clapping, too. Chris was beaming. "That's good," he said. "That's perfect." I had goose bumps. My only sorrow was that Lauren wasn't there to witness the moment.

Chris laughed, growing comfortable in his role as peacemaker. "Now, before we hit the bar to celebrate—and drinks are on me tonight—there's just one more part of the deal."

Mr. Liu eyed him nervously.

"If it's not too inconvenient," Chris said, "I was hoping we could all dig into some grub. Golden Panda leftovers, I don't care. I could eat a horse, this guy's been on a bus the last twenty-four hours"—he pointed at Vernon—"and this girl's eating for two," with a sideways nod toward Kandy. "What do you say?"

"No problem," said Mr. Liu.

All of a sudden, his daughter Mary shrieked and leapt to her feet like she'd been stung on the butt by a bee. She let out some rapid birdsong to her parents in Chinese, and Mr. Liu took the laptop from her hands and inspected the screen while Mrs. Liu threw her arms around Mary and began to sob into her shoulder. Mary looked at Anthony, tearing up herself, and cried, "I got in! I got in! Medaille College e-mailed me! Anthony, I got in!"

A half hour later, well fed, all nine of us were crammed into Chris's Explorer, speeding toward Freighter's. I sat up front in the passenger seat; behind me sat old Vernon Wallace, his great-granddaughter Darla, and Anthony and Kandy. Squashed way in back, and squealing like kindergarteners with every pothole we bounced over, were Mr. Liu and his wife and daughter. Chris was driving, phone clamped between his ear and his shoulder, talking to his older brother. "Shawn, just meet us there. It's good news, I'm saying, though."

I could hear Chris's brother chewing him out on the other end, calling him a moron, a loser, and a punk. All of the merriment and gladness quickly drained from Chris's face. "Yes, Shawn. Okay. Okay, Shawn. Yes, I understand." He closed his phone and tossed it up on the dash, shaking his head and biting at a thumbnail. In the back, full of jolly banter, no one else had caught the exchange.

"Fuck that, dude," I said to Chris. "Shake it off."

"It's not that easy," he said, hurt and sinking. He mashed on the gas pedal and we veered right, back tires sliding out a little, and bolted through a light that had just turned red. A few blocks down, the five-way intersection with Lauren's bar came into sight. I felt supremely nervous, but fortified by the size of my brand-new posse.

Chris clouded over with a look of fierce intensity. He reached for his phone again, dialed his brother, and propped the phone to his ear, battle-ready. Then, without warning, a siren whooped in the night, and a blinding strobe of red and blue lights filled the SUV. "Yo, man," said Anthony, "you just blew right past that stop sign." I twisted around and saw, through the back window, a cop car right on our tail, flashers twirling giddily, high beams punching the air, one-two, one-two.

"No fucking way!" Chris cried, as the phone slipped from his shoulder to the center console and tumbled to the floor at my feet. "What the fuck do we do?" He kept rolling forward, while everyone in back began shouting instructions. I was pretty sure that only Vernon and me knew the truck was stolen. A forlorn tide rose in my chest.

I could hear Shawn's voice on the phone, saying Chris's name. I plucked it up and said, "He's gotta call you back," and folded the phone closed.

"Okay," said Chris frantically. "Here's what we're gonna do. I'm gonna pull over up here, and then all of us, we're just gonna scatter in every direction. Just fuckin' haul ass into the alleyways, all these side streets, into the bushes. They can't get more than one or two of us."

"Are you crazy, boy?" said Darla. "You think my granddaddy's gonna take off running? You think *I* am? I ain't got nothing to hide from. Cops can't fuck with me."

From the way back, Mary said, "You know, there's always policemen at the restaurant. I know a ton of 'em. I got my friend out of a speeding ticket once."

"I'm not worried about a damn ticket," Chris said.

Anthony sat forward and got close to Chris's ear. "Nobody's running," he said. "Chris—listen to me—you got warrants?"

"No."

"Is this shit hot?"

Chris nodded. "Burning."

"Okay. Listen, just pull over and talk to the guy. Just act like it's nothing. Play it cool, like everything's cool. I'm telling you, I've seen dudes talk their way outta way worse."

"I'm not going down tonight," said Chris. He was so deeply spooked, it made me remember the time I'd suggested he incorporate his time in prison into his stand-up routines and he'd told me with a grave, distant stare that there was nothing funny about being in prison.

"That's right," said Anthony. "You're not going down. Now pull over and talk to this man."

Chris pulled to the curb and turned off the radio. He reached slowly for his shoulder belt and clanked it into its buckle.

"The guy's coming!" Mary called from in back.

I watched the cop's cautious approach. He wielded a powerful flashlight and shined it at each of our windows, but they were so fogged up from all the bodies in the car, I doubted he could see much. He took position just behind Chris's window and tapped on the glass with gloved fingers.

Chris lowered the window. "Hello there, sir, good evening," he said, laying on a healthy dose of Canadian politeness.

"License and registration." I couldn't see the cop's face, but he sounded young, which to me seemed like a bad thing. Seasoned cops, I'd found, were more likely to play things fast and loose; rookies went by the book.

"Here's my license," said Chris, passing over his New York State ID. "As far as the registration, I don't have any. I just bought this thing yesterday at an auction in Rochester. I know I shouldn't be driving it around till I get over to the DMV, that's my bad." Fat snowflakes spiraled in through his window and tumbled along the dash.

"You know you ran a light back there?"

"Yes, sir. I believe I ran a stop sign just now, too. I was talking to my brother on the phone and I got distracted. That's my bad. I'm really sorry about that."

Chris was handling things as well as he possibly could, I thought. But once the cop checked the plates, we'd be doomed. If I bailed and ran, it occurred to me, maybe the cop would chase after me and Chris could peel away. My heart jangled, and my fingers crawled to the door handle, ready to make a move.

"You been doing any drinking tonight?" asked the cop.

"Not really, sir," said Chris. He ejected a bark-like laugh. "Planning to, though. We're just going up there to Freighter's." He hitched his thumb toward me. "Even got a designated driver."

The cop bent his head down and poked his flashlight at me. He had dark, close-cropped hair, and was maybe in his mid-thirties. I dropped my hand from the door handle. Then he leaned through Chris's window a shade more and played his light over our bizarre array of passengers—four generations of black folk in the backseat, and a Chinese family in the trunk. His face crinkled up in utter bafflement. Either we were human traffickers with a payload of Asians or a tour bus covering the last leg of the Underground Railroad.

I heard Mr. Liu's daughter call out from the back, "Officer Ralston?"

He ducked his head further into the Explorer. "Who's that?"

"Mary. From the Golden Panda."

"Oh!" said the cop. "Mary! Hey, is that your dad?"

"Yeah. Guess what? I got into Medaille College! We're all going out to celebrate. These are our employees and some of our regulars. You might know some of them."

"But you're not old enough to drink."

"Don't tell the bouncer!" Mary giggled, playfully—even masterfully—redirecting the conversation. "I'm just gonna have a glass of wine."

The cop said, "All right, then," and withdrew his head from inside the truck. He handed Chris back his license. "I'll tell you what," he told Chris. "No more driving with your head up your—you know. Especially when the roads are this bad. You all take care." He doused his flashlight and headed back to his cruiser.

Chris zipped his window up. "Wait for it," he said tersely. "Wait for it."

The cop's flashers went dark, and a moment later his squad car swished past, hung a left at the next side street, and disappeared. Chris turned to look at all of us and broke out into relieved, maniacal laughter. "Holy shit!" he said. "What just happened? This is a magical night!"

Even as everyone began cheering and dancing around in their seats, slapping each other on the back, a cold ball pitted itself in my stomach. It was time to go see Lauren Hill.

"Fuck no, you can't bring all these people in here," the massive bouncer at Freighter's told me, shouting over the music. He eased from his perch and barged forward, using his bulk to crowd us back toward the door. He pointed at Vernon. "That dude didn't have an ID earlier. And this little fucker right here"—he jabbed Chris in the chest—"he's eighty-sixed for life." He took a look at Mary. "She's underage, I'll put money on that. Get these clowns out of my face. Try Cole's, across the street. They'll serve anybody."

I said in his ear, "I'm Lauren Hill's boyfriend. And these are my friends."

"Darrell is Lauren Hill's boyfriend," said the bouncer. "Get your Rainbow Coalition the fuck outta here."

Darrell? Who the *fuck* was Darrell? "Just let me go find Lauren," I pleaded.

"Knock yourself out," said the bouncer. "But these people got to wait outside."

I hustled everyone back through the door, into the freezing night. "Just give me two minutes," I said. "I'll be right back."

I rushed in, my neck hot, blood crashing through my veins. In the three or four hours I'd been away, the Freighter's crowd had gone from tipsy to riotously drunk. Two old bikers had their shirts off and were holding a tough-man contest, affectionately slugging each other in the gut. A pair of young punk rockers dry-humped in a booth. People were screaming along to a song on the jukebox and hooting at hockey highlights on the TVs. At a table in the middle of the room, a man in a winter coat dumped a humongous boot-shaped glass of beer over his own head. I was desperate to be that drunk.

The crowd tossed and turned me like a piece of driftwood, until finally I reached the bar and stood a few feet from Lauren Hill, staring at the back of her neck and her bare shoulders as she mixed a row of drinks at the rear counter. I felt like a vampire, dying to taste her skin.

44

Lauren turned toward me, and the whole scene seemed to grind into slow motion and go mute. I waited for the moment of truth—the expression on her face when she saw that I was back. She set the drinks down in front of the guys next to me, and as she looked up she saw me and smiled—a jolting, radiant, zillion-watt smile. The room's roar slammed back in and the world returned to normal speed. "There you are," she shouted. "What do you want to drink?"

"I made some friends," I shouted back. "Can you help me get 'em in?"

"Just tell Greg I said it was cool."

"I think you better come with me."

She looked around. The other bartender had left and she was now the only person serving drinks, but there seemed to be a momentary lull. "Okay," she said. "Really quick." She ducked under the bar and followed me through the raucous crowd to the front door.

"Come outside for a second," I said. I blasted the door open and we spilled out onto the sidewalk, where a stocky, young white guy in a powder-blue FUBU sweatshirt and Timberland boots was talking to Chris and Mr. Liu while the rest of the crew looked on.

"All the food we want, all year long?" the guy said.

"My guests," said Mr. Liu.

"Rock on!" The guy wrapped his arm over Chris's shoulders, pulled him close, and rubbed his head with his knuckles. "I love you, ya little fuckhead," he said, laughing. "You are just full of surprises." This, I realized, had to be Chris's older brother, Shawn. Chris scrapped his way loose and looked up at me with a magnificent gleam.

"Davy! Let's get our drink on," Chris hollered. "They gonna let us in or what?"

"Yes, sir," I said. "But wait, you guys, everyone come here, I want you meet someone. This is Lauren Hill." The whole group gathered close, joining us in a tight little huddle. "Lauren," I said, "these are my new friends." I went around the circle, introducing her to each of them, and as I introduced them, they each gave her a friendly hello. "This is Mr. and Mrs. Liu, they own the Golden Panda on Fillmore Avenue. And Mary, their daughter, she just found out she got into college tonight! This is Anthony, and this is Kandy—they're having a baby soon." I pointed to Kandy's stomach. "That's little Floyd in there. And this is my Canadian friend Chris I was telling you about, a man of many talents. And, Shawn, right?"

He nodded. "That's right. You're Davy?"

"Yup." I explained to Lauren that Shawn was Chris's older brother.

"And evil boss," said Shawn with a grin.

"But how'd you meet all these people?" Lauren said, a bit dazzled.

"Hold on." I continued around the circle. "This is Darla Kenney. She lives over on the West Side, in Front Park. And here's her grandfather, actually her great-grandfather, Vernon Wallace. Hey, wait a second, what time is it?"

Shawn glanced at his cell phone. "Ten to midnight."

"In ten minutes," I told Lauren, "it's gonna be Vernon's hundred-and-tenth birthday!"

"No way!" she said.

"It's true!" said Darla.

Lauren looked at me with wide, whirling eyes, really taking me in, as beautiful a girl as I'd ever seen in my life. "You were only gone a couple hours," she said. "This is crazy. This is awesome." She shivered.

"Let's go inside and have a drink," I said.

"Let's drink!" Chris echoed.

Lauren reached for the door, glowing. "Okay, all of you come on in, I'll pour a round of birthday shots. Let me tell Greg what's up." Then she paused, giving Chris an odd look. She seemed to recall his status on the Freighter's blacklist. "Except you," she said, pointing at him. "I'm sorry, but . . . you just can't skip out on a tab. Not three or four times. Not here. Not in Buffalo."

"I just, sometimes I leave my wallet at home," Chris sputtered.

"I'm sorry," said Lauren.

"Wait," said Anthony. "What if we pay off everything he owes? Can he be forgiven then?"

Lauren thought about this. "Not forgiven. But if he pays every dollar he owes, plus a twenty-*five* percent tip, then he's allowed back in."

"Done," said Shawn.

"All right, then," Lauren said. She hauled open the door and grasped my hand and led me through. My heart thrummed.

For a moment she leaned close to Greg the bouncer and explained the situation. At last he nodded and Lauren waved everyone past, into the mad melee inside. She squeezed my hand as we swept across the room to the bar and whispered in my ear, so close I could feel her hot breath, "Thank you for being here." The universe had finally, improbably—almost unbelievably—become perfectly aligned.

Our whole crew stood in a crushed knot against the bar. Lauren ducked under and popped up on the far side. "What'll it be?" she shouted, spreading out a constellation of shot glasses.

"It's Vernon's night," said Chris.

Vernon peered around, the tallest of us, soaking it all in like an ancient willow admiring an orchard of saplings. "Knob Creek!" he declared.

Lauren found the bottle and poured nine Knob Creeks, plus a shot of Dr. Pepper for Mrs. Liu, who asked for root beer instead, and, at Kandy's request, a shot of Molson Ice. As Lauren passed them out, I saw Greg, the bouncer, waddling quickly in our direction. I had the gut-shot feeling that everything was about to go from wildly festive to ferociously violent in the next several seconds. But instead, Greg howled, "Let me get in on that!"

Lauren saw the confusion in my face. "Greg loves to be a badass," she said, "but he's just a big softie. He goes to those Renaissance fairs. He swings swords around and wears dresses!"

"They're called kilts!" Greg bellowed, grumpy and happy at the same time. Lauren handed him a shot of whiskey; in his massive paw it looked the size of a thimble.

Lauren slipped under the bar again and pressed herself against me. We all raised our glasses, mashed tightly together, and looked around at one another, everyone's face filled with a golden glow. Darla and Vernon had their arms around each other, as did Anthony and Kandy, and Chris and Shawn Hendershot, and Mr. Liu, Mrs. Liu, and Mary. I put my arm around Lauren's waist and pulled her close.

Later in the night, much later, I ended up telling Lauren that I loved her, and she told me she loved me, too. And the next afternoon, when we woke up, hung over but in fine spirits, we went for the walk I'd fantasized about, through a city transformed by almost two feet of snow. Every tree, every bush, every fire hydrant, and every garbage can was laced with soft, gentle beauty, like we'd crossed through a portal into some distant, magic land. In a few weeks, of course, Lauren Hill was no longer with me, she was with that dude named Darrell, the other bartender at Freighter's, and Mr. Liu's restaurant, I learned, went out of business just a few months after that. Vernon made it to late summer, Darla told me later, then simply lay down on a park bench in Little Rock and died. But don't you see, none of that mattered, none of that mattered, none of that mattered. Because you can take away Lauren Hill, you can take away the love we had for each other, but you can't take away the feeling I had that night at midnight, as I squeezed her hand and looked around at my new, glorious tangle of friends, letting my eyes briefly catch their eyes and linger on each of their faces, the whiskey in each shot glass sparkling like a supernova. If there's ever been a happier moment in my life, I can't remember it.

"To Vernon!" someone cried out.

"To Vernon!" we shouted in chorus.

The Knob Creek went down like a furious, molten potion. I turned and looked at Lauren. She was smiling at me, sweet, soulful, and open.

"Happy Valentine's Day," I said.

"Happy Valentine's Day," she said.

And we kissed.

Nominated by The Paris Review, Katherine Taylor

ENLIGHTENMENT

by NATASHA TRETHEWEY

from THE VIRGINIA QUARTERLY REVIEW

In the portrait of Jefferson that hangs
    at Monticello, he is rendered two-toned:
his forehead white with illumination—

a lit bulb—the rest of his face in shadow,
    darkened as if the artist meant to contrast
his bright knowledge, its dark subtext.

By 1805, when Jefferson sat for the portrait,
    he was already linked to an affair
with his slave. Against a backdrop, blue

and ethereal, a wash of paint that seems
    to hold him in relief, Jefferson gazes out
across the centuries, his lips fixed as if

he's just uttered some final word.
    The first time I saw the painting, I listened
as my father explained the contradictions:

how Jefferson hated slavery, though—*out
    of necessity*, my father said—had to own
slaves; that his moral philosophy meant

he could not have fathered those children:
    would have been impossible, my father said.
For years we debated the distance between

word and deed. I'd follow my father from book
    to book, gathering citations, listen
as he named—like a field guide to Virginia—

each flower and tree and bird as if to prove
    a man's pursuit of knowledge is greater
than his shortcomings, the limits of his vision.

I did not know then the subtext
    of our story, that my father could imagine
Jefferson's words made flesh in my flesh—

the improvement of the blacks in body
    and mind, in the first instance of their mixture
with the whites—or that my father could believe

he'd made me *better*. When I think of this now,
    I see how the past holds us captive,
its beautiful ruin etched on the mind's eye:

my young father, a rough outline of the old man
    he's become, needing to show me
the better measure of his heart, an equation

writ large at Monticello. That was years ago.
    Now, we take in how much has changed:
talk of Sally Hemings, someone asking,

how white was she?—parsing the fractions
    as if to name what made her worthy
of Jefferson's attentions: a near-white,

quadroon mistress, not a plain black slave.
    Imagine stepping back into the past,
our guide tells us then—and I can't resist

whispering to my father: this is where
   we split up. I'll head around to the back.
When he laughs, I know he's grateful

I've made a joke of it, this history
   that links us—white father, black daughter—
even as it renders us other to each other.

Nominated by The Virginia Quarterly Review

CORN MAZE

by PAM HOUSTON

from HUNGER MOUNTAIN

When I was four years old, my father lost his job. We were living in Trenton, New Jersey at the time, where he had lived most of his life. With no college education, he had worked his way up to the position of controller at a Transamerica-owned manufacturing company called Delavalve. The company restructured itself and dismissed him. My parents decided to use his sudden unemployment as an opportunity to take a vacation, to drive whatever Buick convertible we had at the time from New Jersey to California. My parents loved the sun and the beach more than they loved anything except vodka martinis. They promised to take me to Disneyland. We stopped at Las Vegas on the way.

We stayed at the Sands, where my mother had opened, decades before, as a singing, dancing comedian for Frank Sinatra. I got to swim in the kidney shaped pool, and then we ate a giant slab of prime rib each for a dollar. My mother and I went up to the room to bed, and my father stayed downstairs to gamble. I woke up to my mother standing over my bed and sun streaming into the hotel room window. I was four and a half years old. "Pam," she said, "go downstairs and get your father out of the casino."

I found him sitting at an empty blackjack table, looking a hundred and ten. I took his hand and led him through the hazy cigarette air, up the elevator and down the long hall with the zig-zag carpet to our room. He had, of course, lost everything. The money we were meant to live on until he found another job, the money for the trip to California, the money for the hotel bill. Even the car.

My mother's old boss at the Desert Inn loaned us enough to get the car back, to pay the hotel bill, to take me to Disneyland. A few weeks later my father started a new job in Pennsylvania, and we moved there, though when my mother ran away from Spiceland, Indiana at age thirteen to Manhattan, because she had won the bet with her Aunt Ermie, who raised her, that she *could* get straight C's, and as a result had, for the first time in her life, fifty whole dollars, she'd vowed she would never live west of the New Jersey border again.

About five years ago, I was asked to be one of four writers to participate in an evening called "Unveiled" at the Wisconsin Book Festival in Madison. Our assignment was to write something new that had never been tried or tested, and read it aloud to an audience of roughly a thousand. I not only accepted, I took the assignment so literally, I didn't start writing until I was on the plane to Wisconsin. I wrote for the entire plane ride, and all evening in my hotel room. I stayed up all night and wrote, and I wrote all day the day of the reading. When I started to panic that I would not have something ready in time for the reading, I told myself what I tell my students when they get stuck: *write down all of the things out in the world that have arrested your attention lately, that have glimmered at you in some resonant way. Set them next to each other. See what happens.*

By late afternoon I had twelve tiny scenes. I have always, for some reason, thought in twelves. I don't believe this has anything to do with the apostles. One scene was called Georgetown, Great Exuma. Another was called Ozona, Texas. Another was called Juneau, Alaska. Two hours before I was to read, I looked back at my instructions to make sure I had done everything the assignment asked of me. The only caveat, it said, was that the piece had to mention Wisconsin. I knew nothing about Wisconsin, so I left my hotel room and sat on a street corner downtown and waited for something to happen. In less than thirty minutes, something did, and I went back to my room and wrote it down. When I added Madison, Wisconsin to the original twelve, I had to take out Mexican Hat, Utah, but that was okay with me.

"Jesus, Pam," Richard Bausch said, after the reading, "Write a hundred of them, and that's your next book." I thought, "No, not a hundred, but possibly a hundred and forty-four."

When I went on tour with my first book, a collection of short stories called *Cowboys Are My Weakness*, I was asked, more than any other question, *how much of this really happened to you?* "A lot of it," was my honest answer, night after night, but the audience grew dissatisfied with that answer and seemed, more than anything, to want something quantifiable, so I began saying, also honestly, about eighty-two percent.

Eight years later, when I published my first "nonfiction" book, and went on tour with it, I would often be introduced in some version of the following manner: "In the past we have gotten eighty-two percent Pam, and now we are going to get one hundred percent," and I would approach the microphone and feel the need to say, "Well, no, still coming in right about eighty-two."

Between Davis and Dixon, California, in the heart of the Central Valley, just off 1-80, right under the historic sign where the cow jumps over the moon, is the Guinness Book of World Records' Largest Corn Maze. If you get off the highway and drive to it, you find out that technically speaking, it was the Guinness Book of World Records' Largest Corn Maze in 2007, and not in 2010. But, you figure they figure, once a winner, always a winner.

In the corn maze, as in life, there are rules. No running. No smoking. No strollers. No drugs. No inappropriate language. (The corn has ears too!) No tampering with the signs and the maze markers. If you misbehave you will be asked to leave, though in a corn maze, you understand, that is not always so straightforward. Surprisingly, dogs are allowed in the corn maze, and there is nothing in the rules prohibiting handguns. Sex in the corn maze is also apparently okay, as long as you use appropriate language.

The computer-generated grid that the corn maze sits upon runs from A through QQ and one through fifty-two. It contains 2,193 squares. When you enter, they hand you a map. To complete the maze successfully, you will make approximately 189 right turns and 156 left turns, though there are a few places where more than one option will get you out, so your individual numbers may vary.

One ear of corn has approximately 800 kernels in sixteen rows. A pound of corn contains 1,300 kernels. One bushel averages 90,000 kernels. In America we sell more corn than any other crop. The corn in this maze *is* as high as an elephant's eye, if we are talking the world's largest elephant, in heels.

I have a painting in my kitchen by my friend Mark Penner-Howell of a giant ear of corn with the word *Hallelujah* written in red letters run-ning vertically up the ear and lots of little ghostly gas pumps in the background. When my boyfriend Greg eats corn on the cob his lips swell up so much we call him Angelina Jolie.

The reason I have been afraid, until very recently, to make any kind of general, theoretical, or philosophical statements about women, writers, westerners, environmentalists, academics, western women, western women writers, outdoorswomen who grew up in New Jersey and even-tually became academics, women who dreamed of running white water rivers and falling in love with poets and cowboys (though not cowboy poets), women who got on 1-80 West on the other side of the George Washington Bridge one day and just kept driving . . . is that I have never felt comfortable speaking for anyone except myself. Maybe I had been socialized not to make declarative statements. Maybe I thought you had to be fifty before you knew anything about the world. Maybe I was afraid of misrepresenting someone I thought I understood but didn't. Maybe I was afraid of acting hypocritically. Maybe I have always be-lieved it is more honest, more direct, and ultimately more powerful, to tell a story one concrete and particular detail at a time.

So I did. I put my boat into the river, some things happened, and I took it back out on the other side. In time though, I began to suspect that linear narrative was not doing a very good job representing life as I experienced it, but I still tried to stretch the things I originally con-ceived of as Slinkies into straight lines. I don't mean to suggest that I was unique in this. There are so many of us out there, trying to turn Spyrograph flowers into rocket ships. In time I began to gain confi-dence in my Spyrograph flowers and Slinkies. Eventually, I began to speculate about where they came from. Just for starters, I never met any of my grandparents. Also, every single one of my relatives (except a second cousin in Alaska who is oddly afraid of me and his illegitimate son who likes me, but lives in Prague) is dead.

Also, when both of your parents are alcoholics, one thing never leads to another. There is no such thing as how it really happened. When both of your parents are alcoholics, the only way to get to a narrative that is *un*-shattered would be to run the tape backwards, like a car ac-cident in reverse where the windshield that is in a million pieces mag

55

ically mends itself. This is not necessarily the bad news. A mind that moves associatively (as my mind does and probably your mind too) like a firefly in a grassy yard on a late June evening, has more fun (and other things too, of course, like static, like trouble) than a mind that moves logically or even chronologically. Just the other day for instance, someone said the word *tennis*, and I saw in my mind's eye a lady in a pig suit with wings.

Not too long after grad school, I was hired by a magazine to write an article about why women over forty take adventure vacations. I was barely thirty and had no idea why, but I needed the money so I called some power women I knew who had climbed Kilimanjaro or whatever and asked them. They gave flat and predictable answers like, "for the challenge," so I made up some smart, funny women who said surprising and subversive things about why they took adventure vacations, and wrote the article up.

When the fact checker called me, I said, "You're a what?" like an asshole fresh out of graduate school. "You actually believe in things called facts?"

The fact checker, whose name was Bethany, asked for the phone numbers of the six women I wrote about. I gave her the numbers of the three that actually existed.

"What about Katherine and Louise and Samantha?" she said.

"Well, Bethany," I said, "I made them up."

There were five seconds of silence, then she said, "Well, I guess we don't have to call them then, do we?"

In 2010 in Las Vegas, in a gondola, in the canal that runs from Barney's New York to Kenneth Cole (*up*stairs in the mall they call the Palazzo), a very young man is proposing to a very young woman. He is on one knee, and the acne-faced gondolier in his straw hat and red kerchief steadies the wobbling boat. The shoppers pause a minute to look over the railing and watch. The girl is either genuinely surprised or good at pretending. She whispers yes, and then shouts it for the small crowd. The twenty-five of us gathered clap and cheer, and the boy stands up and pumps both fists, the same exact gesture he uses, one imagines, when he hears that his fantasy football quarterback has gone 18 for 24 with four TD's and no interceptions. The gondolier turns the boat

56

around with his single long paddle, and pushes them back toward Bed, Bath and Beyond.

Every day in Vegas is upside down day. Walking along the canal, young men in wife beaters say sentences into their cell phones that, if they were not in Las Vegas, they would never say. "I'll meet you in an hour in St. Mark's Square," or, "I applied for a job with the KGB," or, "Let's meet up in time to see the volcano erupt." People pay money— a lot of it—to see Donny and Marie Osmond. On the poster for the Garth Brooks show in the Wynn Encore theater, there is a picture of Garth in his big black hat and a one word review from the *Los Angeles Times: Genius.*

We are staying at the Golden Nugget, downtown, a hotel where, if you want to, you can go down a water slide, which is really more like a water straw, through a 200,000-gallon shark tank. At the guest relations desk there is a very pretty girl with quarter-inch thick make up and long blonde hair that has been dyed so many times it is leaning toward burnt sienna, and the kind of ultra thick, ultra blunt square false eyelashes that only transvestites wear, and the whole ensemble makes her look like somebody cross-dressed as herself.

Every time we leave the hotel, the junkies are sitting on the steps of the church across the street shooting up under their toenails. The lady in front of the sign that says Hotel-Wedding-Cuban buffet looks right through the driver's side window into my eyes and says, "Put a muffler on it you fucking bitch," right before she sits down in the middle of the street and tries to scratch her own scalp off.

When it was decided (*when* was that again, and by whom?) that we were all supposed to choose between fiction and nonfiction, what was not taken into account was that for some of us truth can never be an absolute, that there can (at best) be only less true and more true and sometimes those two collapse inside each other like a Turducken. Given the failure of memory. Given the failure of language to mean. Given metaphor. Given metonymy. Given the ever-shifting junction of code and context. Given the twenty-five people who saw the same car accident. Given our denial. Given our longings.

Who cares really if she hung herself or slit her wrists when what really matters is that James Frey is secretly afraid that he's the one who killed her. Dear Random House Refund Department: If they were moved, then they got their twenty-four dollars' worth.

Back in the nineties, a magazine sent me to the Ardèche region of France. They wanted me, among other things, to kayak the Ardèche river canyon, one of the five river canyons the French call the Grand Canyon of France. But they sent me in late October, the days were short and getting shorter, all the kayak rental places were boarded up tight for the year, and it was 36 degrees with freezing rain. So I hiked the canyon of the Ardèche, thinking it would be an acceptable substitute.

When I turned in the article the editor said, "We really wanted you to kayak the Ardèche."

"I know," I said, "but it was too cold, all the rental places . . ."

"No," she said, "we really wanted you to kayak the Ardèche. . . ."

"Ah. . . ." I said.

"And while you're at it," she said, "could you make it rain a little less?"

I found her request neither difficult nor surprising. The river had, at that time of year, hardly a riffle on it, and would have been a pretty, if chilly, float. To spice things up, I added a water fight with three Italian kayakers. There was some good-natured flirting across the language barrier. It didn't rain that day at all.

Some years later, the editor of an anthology asked my permission to reprint that essay. He said, "I really liked your story, especially the part about the three Italian kayakers."

"Funny," I said, "I made that part up."

Maybe I should have anticipated the depth of his outrage, but I did not. This was pre-James Frey, of course, and who would have ever anticipated that? The editor called back a few days later and said he had removed the kayak trip from the essay. He had added a scene in which I carry my kayak down to the river's edge, and a fog bank rolls in, and I decide not to go.

"I don't want to be an asshole," I said, which of course wasn't true either. "But if I can't make up three Italian kayakers, I don't think you can make up fog in my essay."

It is hard, all these decades after *The Things They Carried*, to stand here and say the scene with the three Italian kayakers is the truest thing in the entire essay (though, of course it is) even though it never really happened. Nor would I turn an entirely deaf ear to the complaints of those who actually use travel magazines to plan trips. And I'm not even going to mention journalistic coverage of war crimes, genocide, sex offenders, presidents who lie about weapons of mass destruction. . . . Certainly I do believe that sometimes it is necessary for us all to pretend together that language can really mean.

But if you think about it, the fact that I did not *really* have a flirty exchange with three Italian kayakers doesn't make it any less likely that you might. I might even go so far as to argue that you would be more likely to have such an exchange *because* of my (non-existent) kayakers, first because they charmed you into going to the Ardèche to begin with, and second, because if you happened to be floating along on a rainless day in your kayak and a sexy, curly-haired guy glided by and splashed water on you, you would now be much more likely to splash him back.

Due north of Newfoundland, there is a small rocky island in the Labrador Straights called Quirpon (pronounced Kar-poon). The island is roughly ten miles long and three miles across, and on the seaward tip there is a lighthouse and a lighthouse keeper's house—both painted a bright red and white—and no other buildings to speak of. Inside the house, two tough and sweet women named Madonna and Doris fry cod, dry clothes, fix mugs of hot chocolate, and hand out maps to soggy hikers who've come to stay the night.

Marked on the map along with the fox den and the osprey nest is an old townsite called L'Anse au Pigeon, and underneath the name in parentheses it says, "site of mass murder." When I ask Doris about it, she tells me she isn't much of a storyteller, but when I press she takes a deep breath to get into what I recognize as the Newfoundlanders' storytelling mode, a half performance/half trance state that suggests stories are serious matters, whether they are about mass murders or not.

"And now," she says, "I will tell you the story of the mass murders on Quirpon Island." She brings her hands into her lap and folds them as if she's getting ready to pray. "A long long time ago," she says, "not in this time, but in the time before this time, there was a settlement—several fishing families, living together on Quirpon Island. And one day the government saw fit to send them a schoolteacher. Now this schoolteacher mind you, he was a handsome fellow, young and smart, and one of the fishermen's wives fell head over heels in love with him. And the husband was terrible jealous, terrible, terrible, so he decided to trick the schoolteacher into drinking a little bit of the stuff—what is it? I don't know what the stuff is called. . . ."

"Arsenic?"

"No, it's the stuff they use in the lanterns."

"Kerosene?"

"Like kerosene, but different from kerosene."

"White gas?"

"Like white gas, but different from white gas. . . . anyway, he gave it to him a little, a little, a little at a time, and finally the poor handsome schoolteacher died."

Doris nods her head as a kind of punctuation, unfolds her hands and stands. "And that is the story of the mass murder on Quirpon Island."

"But Doris," I say, "why call the death of one schoolteacher a mass murder?"

Doris sighs heavily. She sits back down and brings her hands back into her lap. "A long long time ago," she begins, "not in this time, but in the time before this time, the fisherman who had given the schoolteacher the poison to drink became more and more afraid that the men in the town were getting ready to confront him. There wasn't law back then like we have in these times, so he probably would have gotten away with it, but his guilt made him believe his friends were not his friends. So deep deep into one dark night he soaked one of the fishing boats with the liquid that goes into the lanterns . . ."

"The same liquid," I say, "that he gave the schoolteacher to drink?"

"The very same!"

"The white gas?"

"Like white gas," Doris says, "but different from white gas."

"Didn't they smell it?"

"This is the liquid that has no smell. Anyway, all the men in the town went fishing the next morning and one of 'em struck a match to light his cigarette and the whole lot of them burned up or drowned or died of hypothermia. You can't last long in that iceberg water," she says, nodding her head towards the window. "And that is the story of the mass murder on Quirpon Island."

I was driving over Slumgullion Pass listening to *Ashes of American Flags* at volume 50. There were three feet of new snow on the ground, and I watched a herd of two hundred elk gallop through it. I had spent hours the night before on baby naming websites trying to find something I could search and replace for Pam in my forthcoming novel of

144 chapters. The book is more or less autobiographical. I have, of course, taken massive liberties with the truth.

In past books I have used Millie, Lucy, and Rae. For the sake of sentence rhythm, I was leaning towards something with one syllable, but it would also be convenient to the book if the replacement name meant something as embarrassing as what the name "Pamela" means: which is *all honey*. I had considered Melinda, which on some sites means honey and could be shortened to Mel. I had considered Samantha which means listener, and could be shortened to Sam. But in the car with the elk in the pasture and the snow on the road and Jeff Tweedy in my ears I was all of a sudden very angry at whoever it was who put all that pressure on Oprah Winfrey. This book was in danger of missing the whole point of itself if my name were not Pam in it. If my name were not Pam in it, who was the organizing consciousness behind these 144 tiny miraculous coincident unrelated things?

About ten years ago, I was looking for an epigraph for a book of my travel essays. I arranged a lot of my Asian travel in those days with an excellent San Francisco outfit called Geographic Expeditions, a company famous for their catalogs, which are full of heart-stopping photos and quotes from writers like Goethe, Shakespeare, Chatwin, and Plato. That year's catalog contained a quote from Seamus O'Banion: *Eventually I realized that wanting to go where I hadn't been might be as fruitful as going there, but for the repose of my soul I had to do both.* I found it wise and pleasingly self-effacing, and I shamelessly stole it for my epigraph, without taking time to find the original source.

A season later, I was invited to a cocktail party at the offices of Geographic Expeditions, and since my new book contained essays about trips they had arranged for me, I brought them a copy. "And look," I said, "I thieved my epigraph straight from your catalog," and showed them the O'Banion quote.

When they could contain their laughter long enough to explain it, they said, "There's no such person as Seamus O'Banion. We made him up, one late night several catalogs ago, and now we bring him back whenever we need him to say something profound."

When I told my friend Shannon how rattled I got in Vegas, she twisted up her mouth and said, "Well, it seems to me that Vegas is the distillation of American-style capitalism, where what is desired is a facsimile of old world decadence (Venice) exchangeable only by complete ignorance of its actual cost (the wasteland at its margins). And that the lower-middle class who go there with their obese children are the real fools, because it's their money that keeps everyone else either rich or poor."

For the first time in my life I truly understood the difference between a writer and a cultural critic. A cultural critic goes to Vegas and lets it serve as proof of everything she's been trying to say about the world. A writer goes to Vegas, and it makes her want to kill herself.

It is possible that I will be advised to change the character Pam's name to Melinda. It is also possible, though less so, that I will be advised to change the names I have changed back to the actual names, or that I will be advised, the first time I introduce a character called Rick to say "the man I'll call Rick." It is possible I will be advised to do that with all the characters' names I have changed, which is somewhere in the neighborhood of thirty. In the instances where I have combined two or more real live people into one character, and thrown a little something in there to make them blend—a little storyteller's petit verdot—or even made a character up all together, this method becomes problematic.

The Rick I've put on the page bears only a modest resemblance to the man I love and live with—less and less with every draft. But the point I am trying to make here is that the two wouldn't resemble each other much more than they currently do if I called him by his real name and tried with all my might to make the two characters match. Nor would the Pam on the page resemble me any more or less than she currently does (which is only so much) if I am made to call her Melinda. Except in as much as her name would be Melinda, and my name would still be Pam.

I understand that it is in bad taste to love Venice, the real version. The city exists, now, more or less for the tourists, who number an astounding seven million a year. None of the employees can afford to live there, and the whole city shuts down by ten-thirty each night because the waiters have to run for the last boat/train/bus for the city of Mestre, where there are apartments they can actually afford. Eighty percent of the palazzo windows are dark at night because they are all owned by counts or bankers or corporations, and now, because of the wave action of speedboats, the wood pilings that have stood strong under the town for more than a thousand years are finally rotting, and the whole city is sinking slowly but surely into the Adriatic Sea.

And still, leaving the rent-a-car at the San Marco carpark, and slipping onto a vaporetto at 8:00 pm on a foggy January night, leaving the dock and watching the first palazzos come into view, some of them still adorned with Christmas lights, puttering past a gondola, its gondolier ram-rod straight in his slim black coat, passing under the Bridge of Sighs, with the dark water lapping softly against the bow, it is hard not to feel like you have entered the world's single remaining magical kingdom.

And when you tell the Sicilian owner at Beccafico, "We have only one night here, so just make us whatever you think is best," and he brings a whole fish cooked in wine and capers and olives and so fresh it is like the definition of the words *fresh fish* in your mouth, and afterwards, your sweetheart buys you for your birthday a small piece of venetian glass, various shades of umber, in the shape of a life preserver to wear around your neck, and you drift off to sleep in a room that has had fancy people sleeping in it since at least the 1400s, you think, if the worst thing they ever say about you is that you have an underdeveloped sense of irony that might be quite all right.

Did I mention that when James Frey was an undergraduate, I was his creative writing teacher?

In San Francisco, at Alonzo King's Sheherazade there was one dancer who was head and shoulders above the others. I mean that literally—he was a giant—and figuratively—every time he leapt onto the stage all of our hearts leapt up too.

It was a difficult problem, I imagined, for the choreographer to solve, to have one dancer in a troupe who was so outstanding, so lithe and fluid, so perfectly free inside his own body, that he made all the other dancers, who I am sure were very fine dancers, look clunky, boorish, and uncontrovertibly white (even the black ones). And yet, having seen that dancer perform, wasn't it Alonzo King's duty to let us see him, even if he couldn't be on stage the entire time, even if every time he left the stage, we all died a little bit inside?

I did not actually believe, for example, until I saw the signs with my own eyes, that several places in Vegas offer drive-through windows for weddings.

It has been five years since my trip to Madison, Wisconsin, and I have 144 chapters. 132 of them are titled with a place name, divided into groups of twelve by twelve single stories that take place no place—on an airplane, 39,000 feet above the ground. I had to make a decision as to whether the airplane stories would count as twelve of the 144, or over and above the 144, but that turned out to be easy. If I stuck to 132 non-airplane stories, I needed just twelve airplane stories to serve as both dividers and bookends. If I wrote 144 non-airplane stories, I would have needed thirteen, which would have ruined everything.

In the final stages of editing, I sent an email to my editor saying, "Is it wrong of me to want to call myself Pam in this book? Should I .just change my name to Melinda and be done with it?"

She wrote back saying, "No, I like Pam. I think we want people to think it is both you and not you," and I sat in front of the computer and nearly wept with gratitude.

Six months before my father lost his job and we drove to Las Vegas, he threw me across the room and broke my femur. I think it's possible he meant to kill me, and I spent the rest of my childhood, the rest of his life, really, thinking he probably would. Speaking only for myself, now, I cannot see any way that my subsequent well-being depends on whether or not, or how much, you believe what I am telling you—that is to say—on the difference (if there is any) between eighty-two and one hundred percent true. My well-being (when and if it exists) resides in the gaps language leaves between myself and the corn maze, myself and the Las Vegas junkies, myself and the elk chest-deep in snow. It is there, in that white space of language's limitation that I am allowed to touch everything, and it is in those moments of touching everything, that I am some version of free.

When my agent read the first draft of my forthcoming book, she said in dismay, *you haven't taken us anywhere and yet you have taken us everywhere!* I know what she was asking for was more resolution, which she was right to ask for and which I subsequently provided, but I still don't know how to inflect her sentence in a way in which it doesn't sound like praise.

One thing I am sure of, having spent the last five years inside a shattered narrative, is that time is a worthy opponent. It does not give up quietly. It does not give up kicking and screaming. It does not, in fact, give up at all. Time is like when you break a thermometer and all the mercury runs around the table trying like crazy to reconstitute itself. Or like the way PCB can start out in a glass transformer in Alabama and wind up on the island of Svalbard, inside a polar bear cub's brain. A shattered narrative is still a narrative. We can't escape it; it is what we are.

Nominated by Hunger Mountain, David Jauss, Wally Lamb

MING

by JILL MCDONOUGH

from THE THREEPENNY REVIEW

> *That's why we don't keep things in stairwells.*
> —Mary Warnement, The Boston Athenaeum

When the former curator remembers the Ming,
remembers knocking it over, he remarks, "The thing

took fucking forever to fall." Shaking
his heavy head. Inside, the Ming's still taking

its time. Still falling. Look: he opened the magic door,
invented a way of making more

time. All of us always longing for longer, a few extra hot
days in July, sunshine, more time with the kids. Not

this endless loop, cringing eternity, fucking forever in the poor
guy's vase-sized head. Scott asks if I'd be twenty again. *Not for*

all the money in the world. But then I sort of take
it back, bargain: would I for sure meet Josey? Could I bank

the money I did not give back to the world—just Jeter's share,
net worth of the board of Goldman Sachs—relive those years

and then have the rest of my life with her, her and fewer
jobs? A car, dishwasher, dryer. New roof, newer

shoes, Josey's never-swollen one-shift-a-week knees.
Go back to twenty, to the instant the Ming first leans

into thinner air. This vase makes it through Bruegel,
the new world, microscopes. From bustles to Google

to finally fall. But not finally anything: always it slips
from a half-hearted shelf, fresh from its crated straw, his fingertips

always in reach. You gain a week, say, week of replay, your fault
in the space time continuum, week of stutter and halt

taken back in slivers of seconds, in panicked gasps, sleep rent
again. You gain a week. This is how it's spent.

Nominated by The Threepenny Review,
Sarah Green, Jane Hirshfield,
Maria Hummel, Philip Levine,
Gail Mazur, Jessica Roeder,
Lloyd Schwartz

A FULL-SERVICE SHELTER

fiction by AMY HEMPEL

from TIN HOUSE

> *"They knew me as one who shot reeking crap out of cages with a hose."*
> —Leonard Michaels, "In the Fifties"

They knew me as one who shot reeking crap out of cages with a hose—and liked it. And would rather do that than go to a movie or have dinner with a friend. They knew me as one who came two nights a week, who came at four and stayed till after ten, and knew it was not enough, because there was no such thing as enough at the animal shelter in Spanish Harlem that was run by the city, which kept cutting the funds.

They knew us as the ones who checked the day's euth list for the names of the dogs scheduled to be killed the next morning, who came to take the death-row dogs, who were mostly pit bulls, for a last long walk, brought them good dinners, cleaned out their kennels, and made their beds with beach towels and bath mats and torn sheets and Scooby-Doo fleece blankets still warm from industrial dryers. They knew me as one who made their beds less neatly over the course of a difficult evening, who thought of the artist whose young daughter came to visit his studio, pointed to the painting she liked, and asked, "Why didn't you make them *all* good?"

They knew us as the ones who put pigs' ears on their pillows, like a chocolate in a good hotel. They knew us as vocal vegetarians who brought them cooked meat—roast turkey, rare roast beef, and honey-glazed ham—to top off the canned food we supplied that was still better than what they were fed there. They knew us as the ones who fed them when they were awake, instead of waking them at 2:00 AM for feeding, the way the overnight staff had been ordered by a director who felt they did not have enough to do.

They knew me as one who spoke no Spanish, who could say only "Si, si" when someone said about a dog I was walking, "Que lindo!" And when a thuggish guy approached too fast, then said, "That's a handsome dude," look how we exploded another stereotype in a neighborhood recovering from itself.

They knew us as the ones who had no time for the argument that caring about animals means you don't also care about people; one of us did! Evelyne, a pediatrician who treated abused children.

They knew us as the ones who got tetanus shots and rabies shots—the latter still a series but no longer in the stomach—and who closed the bites and gashes on our arms with Krazy glue—not the medical grade, but the kind you find at hardware stores—instead of going to the ER for stitches, where we would have had to report the dog, who would then be put to death.

They knew us as the ones who argued the names assigned at Intake, saying, "Who will adopt a dog named Nixon?" And when Nixon's name was changed—changed to Dahmer—we ragged on them again, then just let it go when the final name assigned was O.G., Original Gangster. There was always a "Baby" on one of the wards so that staff could write on the kennel card, "No one puts Baby in the corner," and they finally stopped using "Precious" after a senior kennel worker said of a noble, aged Rottie, "I fucking hate this name, but this is a good dog." (Though often they got it right: they named the cowboy-colored pocket pit who thought he was a big stud, Man Man).

They knew me as one who did not bother wearing latex gloves or gauzy scrubs to handle the dogs in sick ward, who wore gloves only when a dog had swallowed his rabies tag, and I had to feel for it in feces. They knew me as one who gave a pit bull a rawhide chew stick swirled in peanut butter, then, after he spit it up and wanted it back, cleaned it off and gave it to him so he could have . . . closure.

They knew us as the ones who put our fingers in mouths to retrieve a watch, a cell phone, a red bicycle reflector that a dog sucked on like a lozenge.

They knew me as one who shot reeking crap out of cages with a hose, who scoured metal walls and perforated metal floors with Trifectant, the syrupy, yellow chemical wash that foamed into the mess, and then towel-dried the kennel and liked the tangible improvement—like mowing a lawn or ironing a shirt—that reduced their anxiety by even that much.

They knew me as one who, early on, went to tell a vet tech the good news that three dogs had been rescued from that morning's list of twelve, to which the tech said, "*That* blows—I already filled twelve syringes."

They knew us as the ones who repeatedly thanked the other vet tech, the one who was reprimanded for refusing to kill Charlie, the pit bull who licked his hand when the tech went to inject him. And Charlie was adopted less than twenty-four hours later by a family who sent us photos of their five-year-old daughter asleep atop Charlie, the whole story like a children's book, or maybe a *German* children's book. And we kept thanking the vet tech, until he was fired for killing two of the wrong dogs, their six-digit ID numbers one digit off. He didn't catch the mistake, but neither had the kennel worker who brought him the wrong dogs, and who still has his job.

They knew us as those who found them magnificent with their wide-spaced eyes and powerfully muscled bodies, their sense of humor and spirit, the way they were "first to the dance and last to leave," even in a House of Horrors, the way stillness would take them over as they pushed their heads into our stomachs while sitting in our laps. They knew us as those whose enthusiasm for them was palpable, Rebecca falling in love with them "at first sight, second sight, third sight," and Yolanda tending to them with broken fingers still in a cast, and Joy and the rest with their surpassing competence and compassion. They knew us as those who would sometimes need to take out a Chihuahua—"like walking an ant," Laurie said—for a break. They knew us as those who didn't mind when they back-washed our coffee, when they licked the paper cup the moment we looked away. They knew us as the ones who worked for free, who felt that an hour stroking a blanket-wrapped dog whose head never left your lap and who was killed the next morning was time well spent.

They knew me as the least knowledgeable one there, whose mistakes were witnessed by those who knew better.

They knew me as one who liked to apply the phrase, "the ideal version of"—as in "Cure Chanel's mange and you'll see the ideal version of herself"—but did not like the term "comfort zone," and thought one should try to move beyond it.

They knew me as one who was unsure of small dogs, having grown up with large breeds and knowing how to read them, but still afraid of the Presa Canarios, the molossers bred in the Canary Islands, with their dark bulk and bloodshot bedroom eyes, since I had lived in San Francisco when a pair of them loose in a tony apartment house had killed a friend of mine who had stopped to get her mail and could not get her door unlocked before the attack began.

They knew me as one who called one of their number a dick when he knocked me over and I slammed into a steel bolt that left me bleeding from just above an eye. They knew me as one who guided them to step over the thick coiled hose in the packed garage that was being used weekly by a member of the board of directors to wash his car the city paid for. He never went inside the building.

They knew us as the ones who attached a life-size plastic horse's head to a tree in the fenced-in junkyard backyard, where the dogs could be taken to run off leash one at a time, and to sniff the horse's head before lifting a leg against it. They knew us as those who circulated photos of two pit littermates dive-bombing each other under the blankets of a bed to get closer to the large-hearted woman who had adopted them both.

They knew us as the ones who took them out, those rated "no concern" and "mild," also "moderate," and even "severe," though never the red-stamped "caution" dogs. Although some of the sweetest dogs were the ones rated "moderate," which was puzzling until we realized that behavior testing was done when a stray was brought in by police or a dog surrendered by his owner, when they were most scared. "Fearful" is the new "moderate." And how do you think a starving dog will score on "resources guarding" when you try to take away a bowl of food! They knew me as one who never handled the "questionable" dogs, because that meant they could turn on you in an instant, you wouldn't know what was coming, and some of us got enough of that outside the shelter.

They knew me as one whom Enrique had it in for, the kennel worker who had asked me to take out a one-hundred-fifty-pound Cane Corso, and when I said, "Isn't he 'severe'?" said, "Naw, he's a good boy," and when I looked up his card he was not only "severe," he was also DOH-HB hold—Department of Health hold for Human Bite. He had bitten his owner.

They knew me as one who forgave Enrique when he slipped on the newly installed floor while subduing a frightened mastiff, fell, and punctured a lung. After voting to spend nearly fifty thousand dollars to replace the facility's floor, the board then had to allocate funds to bring in a crew with sanders to rough up the pricey new floor. The allocated funds were diverted from Supplies, so kennel staff had to ask us, the volunteers, for food when they ran out because feeding the dogs had not factored into the board's decision.

They knew me as one who held the scarred muzzle of a long-nosed mutt in sick ward and sang, "There is a nose in Spanish Harlem" until he slept.

They knew me as one who refused to lock the padlocks on their kennels, the locks a new requirement after someone stole a puppy from Small Dog Adoptions, and which guarantee the dogs will die in the event the place catches fire.

They knew me as one who asked them stupid questions—How did you get so cute?—and answered the questions stupidly, saying on behalf of the giddy dog, "I was born cute and kept getting cuter." They knew me as one who talked baby talk to the babies, and spoke in a normal voice about current events to those who enjoyed this sort of discourse during their one-on-ones. I told an elderly pittie about the World War II hero who died in his nineties this year in a Florida hospital after having been subdued while in emotional distress by the use of a metal cage that was fixed in place over his bed. The Posey Cage had been outlawed in Eastern Europe, yet was still somehow available in Florida. Caged in the space of his bed, "he died like a dog," people said.

They knew us as the ones who wrote Congress in support of laws made necessary by human cruelty and named for canine victims: Oreo's Law, Nitro's Law, the law for the hero dog from Afghanistan, and that's just this year.

They knew me as one who loved in them what I recoiled from in people: the patent need, the clinging, the appetite. They knew me as one who saw their souls in their faces, who had never seen eyes more expressive than theirs in colors of clover honey, root beer, riverbed, and the tricolor "cracked-glass" eyes of a Catahoula, rare to find up north. They knew us as the ones who wrote their biographies to post to rescue groups, campaigning for the rescue of dogs that we likened to Cleopatra, the Lone Ranger, or Charlie Chaplin's little tramp, to John Wayne, Johnny Depp, and, of course, Brad Pitt, asking each other if we'd gone overboard or gone soft, like Lennie in *Of Mice and Men*. They knew us as the ones who tried to gauge what they had been through, as when Laurie said of a dog with shunts draining wounds on his head, "He looks exhausted even when he's asleep."

They knew us as the ones who wrote letters to the mayor pointing out that the Department of Health had vastly underestimated the number of dogs in the city to clear itself of misconduct for failing to license more. The political term for this is "inflating their compliance record." They knew Joy as the stellar investigator who told the rest of us that the governor helped boost the state budget by helping himself to funds that had been set aside to subsidize spay/neuter services throughout the state.

They knew that? They seemed to know that, just as they seemed to appreciate Joy's attempt to make a new worker understand that staff had not "forgotten" to write down the times they had walked certain dogs, that the blank space under dates on the log sheets three days in a row meant that those dogs had not been walked in three days. "When the budget was cut by a million and a half," Joy began. But the new worker did not believe her.

They knew us as the ones who decoded reasons for surrender and knew that "don't have time" for an elderly, ill dog meant the owner had been hit hard by the ruined economy and could not afford veterinary bills. They knew us as the ones who doted on "throwaway moms," lactating dogs left tied to posts in the Bronx after the owners sold their puppies, and the terrified young bait dogs—we would do anything for them—their heads and bodies crossed with scars like unlucky lifelines in a human hand, yet whose tails still wagged when we reached to pet them. They knew me as one who changed her mind about Presa Canarios when I found one wearing an E-collar that kept him from reaching his food. I had to hold his bowl up to his mouth inside the plastic cone for him to eat; I lost my fear of Presas.

They knew me as one who had Bully Project on speed dial, who knew that owning more than five dogs in Connecticut was, legally, hoarding, who regularly "fake-pulled" a much-loved dog when I found that dog on the list, pretending to be a rescue group, so that in the twenty-four hours it took for the shelter manager to learn it was fake, the dog would have that time to be pulled for real.

They knew me as one who got jacked-up on rage and didn't know what to do with it, until a dog dug a ball from a corner of his kennel and brought it to my side, as though to ask, "Have you thought of this?"

They knew me as one who learned a phrase in Spanish: "Lo siento mucho," I am so sorry, and used it often in the lobby when handed over a dog by owners who faced eviction by the New York City Housing Authority if they didn't surrender their pit.

They knew me as one who wrote a plea for a dog named Storm, due to be killed the next morning, and posted the plea and then went home, to learn the next day that there had been two dogs named Storm in the shelter that night, and the one who needed the plea had been killed that morning—I had failed to check the ID number of the dog. So this is not about heroics; it's about an impossible job. I joined them in filth and fear, and then I left them there.

They knew me as one who walked them past the homeless man on East 110th who said, "You want to rescue somebody, rescue *me*."

They knew me as one who saw through the windowed panel in a closed ward door a dog lift first one front paw and then the other, offering a paw to shake though there was no one there, doing a trick he had once been taught and praised for, a dog not yet damaged but desperate.

They knew me as one who decoded the civic boast of a "full-service" shelter, that it means the place kills animals, that the "full-service" offered is death.

They knew me as one who learned that the funds allocated for the dangerous new floor had also been taken from Medical, that the board had determined as "nonessential": the first injection, the sedative before the injection of pentobarbital that kills them, and since it will take up to fifteen seconds for the pentobarb to work, the dogs are then made to walk across the room to join the stack of bodies, only some of which are bagged. This will be the dogs' last image of life on earth. My fantasy has them waking to find themselves paddling with full stomachs in the warm Caribbean, treading the clearest water over rippled white sand until they find themselves refreshed farther out in cooler water, in the *deep blue reef-scarred sea.*

They knew me as one who asked another volunteer if she would mind holding Creamsicle, a young vanilla and orange pup, while I cleaned his soiled kennel and made his bed at the end of a night. I knew that Katerina would leave the shelter in minutes for the hospital nearby where her father was about to die. She rocked the sleepy pup in her arms. She said, "You are working too fast." She kissed the pup. She handed him to me. She said to me, "You should take your time." We were both tired, and took turns holding the pup against our hearts. They saw this; they knew this. The ward went quiet. We took our time.

Nominated by Bret Anthony Johnston, Joyce Carol Oates

DURING A
BREAK FROM FEELING

by MARY RUEFLE

from FORKLIFT, OHIO

Someone will tell you the number of your story
When you are called be ready to act your story
Read the story again to see if you have everything on your list
Act so the other boys and girls will know which story is yours
Do not be disappointed if your story is not as good as the others
Happiness is not always good, it can lead to lacklusterness
Or what is worse, slovenliness
Which can be lovely, to be sure
Do not be afraid no one will hear your story
Wait for another day
The pause may be pregnant
The pause may be pregnant again
During a break from feeling, it may be apparent
None of our words actually become parents
Word is the only word true to itself
It does not refer to something else
Do not argue over your stories
The Argonauts did not argue
The sun does not have diphtheria
Few human experiences are more cordially disliked than pain
Now go tell your story
Giant glory of snow, go tell your story
Little flakes, know when to stop

Nominated by Mark Irwin, Diane Seuss, David Wojahn

THIRST

fiction by TAYMIYA R. ZAMAN

from NARRATIVE

We strode the halls of the overeducated. Ideas were our battlefield. The stakes were highest in our seminar on narrative. A few of us went for the jugular when combating the structuralists, and everyone thought Marxists were passé. Feminists were tedious, unless they engaged Irigaray and Lacan. We loved Foucault but ripped apart his epistemology. We were above personal allegiances. On the first day, the department chair told us to look around the room, because more than half of us would not walk out with a PhD. Some would leave. Others would be screened out of the program at the discretion of our professors. When we saw someone open a slim white envelope and run out of the mail room crying, we were relieved it wasn't us. And we pretended that we had known all along that our newly departing colleague wasn't cut out for a PhD anyway. She barely understood Kristeva's semiotic. She'd be better off in journalism. Sometimes we thought of quitting ourselves, but we couldn't bear the thought of those still standing thinking that they had predicted our departure all along.

Our ambition was a clawing, grasping thing. It got us out of bed and into class and through stacks of books each more incomprehensible than the last. Admitting that a text was difficult was out of the question. Reading fiction was a crime. All our professors had written books that had reconfigured the field and won celebrated awards. Our goal was to master their books, and then, among ourselves, to tear them down, imagining that we would do better than they. We went to conferences. *Yes*, we would say, *he's my adviser*, and bask in the envy of others at less prestigious institutions. Our professors lectured halls of undergraduates, some suitably dazzled and others sleepy. We did the grading. Each time we told an undergraduate that the professor was too busy to see them but they could talk to us instead, our hearts swelled with importance. Someday, we would be that professor. Our teeth would be sharper, our theories more dazzling. The screening process that thinned our numbers weeded out the unfit, kept our program robust, and primed us for success.

We could not understand why Maia Alfieri had been screened out. She might have been the brightest of us all. We had to have an A- average, and she said her grades were fine. One of her research papers was on reserve at the library because the professors jointly teaching the methodology class had deemed it exemplary. Rory Brandt said the paper was reductive and barely took into account the impact of the linguistic turn on gender, but we knew that was only because Rory thought his paper was better. Rumors swirled. Someone said Maia had done well so far only because she was sleeping with the department chair. Someone else said that Maia had skipped a week of classes not to attend a workshop but to have an abortion. Maia called the rumors ludicrous. She said the program screened out a disproportionate number of women and minorities. Someone brought up Priyanka Sharma. Priyanka's adviser, Alison Levin, had written a book on British India. Levin had accused Priyanka of plagiarizing her work. After that, no one had been willing to chair Priyanka's committee, and she had left the program. Priyanka had called Levin racist. At the time, most of us had thought that absurd. Only uneducated hicks were racist. Irfan Alam, the other Indian student in the program, had concurred. He got on fine with Levin.

Although we didn't usually look kindly upon anyone playing the race or gender card, our noses twitched and our ears pricked up at the thought that Maia Alfieri merited further consideration. Maia's case carried the heady risk of profaning the sanctified halls of our graduate program with suggestions of the bodily, unintelligent matters that plagued the masses who read bestsellers and tabloids. We theorized about masculinist modes of signification and sexism, but the actual thought of something akin to a sex scandal had us salivating. More so, if it involved the powerful and happily married chair of our department, Dr. Anthony R. Davis, whose understanding of ancient Greek, Arabic, and Persian ethical treatises was legendary, even outside academia. It helped that Maia was beautiful. We thought ourselves too lofty to be swayed by beauty, and it was not something we came by often. The men in our program were bespectacled, odd but nonetheless brainy, and scarred from being picked on in high school.

The women wore pointy shoes and superfluous scarves, were intelligent but high-strung, and hid behind feminist theory and irony while vying with one another for the men.

Maia was of us but unlike us. Voluptuous and half-Italian, given to red lipstick and leather boots, coy but effortlessly popular, she inspired brainless lust and pangs of envy. She reminded us of things we thought we were too clever to hanker after, such as popularity and charisma. She brought forth echoes of our insecure high school selves, easily stirred to tears or anger when another's ability to glide through life reminded us of our own incompetence. Maia was the girl we knew would always be out of our league, who survived adolescence unscarred by acne or social rejection, who walked through life assured of her value. Rory said he was the only one among us smart enough to see through her charms to what was her barely above mediocre intellect. But we, the anxious and always aspiring, were enraged on Maia's behalf and hoped to gain her friendship by rallying to her defense. Some of us felt secretly vindicated for personal slights from the past we could not entirely name. This we admitted to no one. We sneered at Rory for being small-minded.

We had to do something. Too educated to take to picket lines and slogans, we organized a graduate student committee that would communicate to the faculty our concern about the lack of transparency in screening procedures. Now that we questioned the process, the signs were everywhere. Alison Levin had written an entire chapter on constructs of theft and ownership in British India. Some had criticized her book for subscribing to the very notion of Indians as savages that she hoped to dispel. Wasn't it interesting that she automatically assumed that an Indian student was "stealing" her ideas? Dr. Anthony R. Davis came from a long line of privileged white males with Ivy League PhDs. His work never addressed gender. His wife stayed at home, raised their children, and occasionally came to department events with something or the other she had baked. Unlike us, he probably had no respect for women and failed to take Maia, who wore low-cut blouses and made provocative comments in class, seriously as a scholar. We knew Maia's disregard for feminism was part of an intelligently formulated post-feminist position, but it had clearly landed her in trouble with the male-dominated establishment, which could not see past her appearance the way we could.

Rachel Goldfarb, Maia's closest friend, said that while Maia hadn't told her anything directly, she had asked Rachel to go with her if she ever had to talk to Davis in his office. We noticed that Maia appeared uneasy each time Davis entered a room. If Davis had made a move on Maia, she would hardly have been the only woman in the program who chose to stay silent for fear of ridicule and disbelief. Several of us murmured that we too felt uncomfortable around Davis. As chair, he must have had the final word on Maia. We were outraged. Maia needed us to bring about justice, not just for her, but for the principle of the thing. Irfan, who some suspected was half in love with Maia, pointed out that if this could happen to Maia, it could happen to any of us. We were all vulnerable to a system we trusted blindly, despite having to struggle to prove our worth to professors who pretended their assessments were dispassionate.

Marxism, which we had thought outdated, now made perfect sense. Graduate school was nothing but evidence of false consciousness on our part, a willing suspension of disbelief: we believed we had power but in fact we had none, and the faculty could do with us what they wished. Maia nodded seriously as we expressed our frustration at a meeting in the graduate student lounge. She was angry that she was being painted as sleeping her way to good grades. Logically speaking, she pointed out, if that's what she was doing, she would hardly have been screened out before she could sleep her way to getting a PhD. She had no idea what this was about. She was sick of the rumors. All we wanted, we agreed, was the truth, something to which the faculty supposedly was committed. Maia did not sign the letter from the newly formed Graduate Student Collective demanding a meeting with the faculty, since she was technically no longer a graduate student. But she hoped that a dialogue with the faculty would benefit all of us regardless of her departure. We deserved answers.

That week, we were belligerent. Fangs bared, we snarled at the faculty. Some of us pointedly did not do our readings for class. Or we tore the readings apart more ferociously than usual: What did these scholars know about the realities of the world, the daily injustices that women and people of color had to face, when all they did was theorize about subjectivity as a discursive construct? Sarah Miller called Rory analytically complacent when he agreed with an assigned reading on interdisciplinary methods. Irfan was heard telling Joel Carter that he was going to switch advisers because he was done with Levin. Irfan came to our program from India because he admired Levin's work, but he was disgusted with some of the comments she made about her Indian husband. Joel said that despite his own white privilege, he understood the insidious nature of internalized racism; in fact, that's what his dissertation was partly about. Rachel alluded to sexual harassment and coercion in a class discussion about the pervasiveness of power. The professor snapped at her, confirming for us his complicity in an oppressive system.

The meeting between the faculty and us was held the following week. Since Irfan was the only person of color in our cohort, we chose him as our representative. Sarah suggested that we also choose a woman. She nominated Rachel, and we unanimously agreed. The faculty arranged themselves behind a table. Dr. Anthony R. Davis sat in the middle, with Alison Levin on one side and a junior faculty member, Joshua Green, on the other. Green looked nervous, and Levin's face was pinched. But Davis, gray haired and handsome, still emanated that combination of gravitas and success that drew forth our envy and ire. Joel, his teaching assistant, had been to his house and said it had to be worth nearly a million. We thought of the cramped apartments we shared with people we often didn't like, and we sharpened our claws. Joel and Sarah pointed out that Davis and Levin were tenured; they had deliberately chosen Green because he was untenured and, like us, had no power. *Of course*, we thought. *What else could we expect from these people?*

The meeting began. Maia slipped in sometime after the first few combative words were exchanged. She stood quietly at the back of the crowded room, her long, dark hair loose over her shoulders, her eyes lined with kohl, her lips red, her posture a combination of defiant and demure. We were proud to stand up for her, for ourselves, for principle. Back and forth the accusations flew. Irfan and Rachel highlighted Maia's achievements and brought out the names of other women and minorities who had been screened out or had dropped out. When Irfan said that the department had a problem retaining minorities, we clapped. Levin's face turned red. Each student was assessed on a case-by-case basis, she said, raising her voice. And the need for confidentiality restricted the faculty from bringing to light the weaknesses in anyone's record, including Maia's. Joshua Green said nothing. Rachel called this convenient; hiding behind confidentiality fooled no one. We cheered.

Emboldened, Sarah raised her hand and brought up the question of student vulnerability to a lack of sexual ethics on the part of certain faculty members. Davis told her firmly that insinuations were inappropriate. When he asked her if there was something specific she wanted to discuss, Sarah backed down. We snuck glances at Maia. Her composure did not waver. Rory smirked. Davis reminded us that this was a discussion among adults, premised on collegiality and professionalism. Shamed but still determined, Irfan and Rachel picked up their argument where they had left off. Could the faculty, without violating confidentiality, at least give us some explanation? Levin responded. She said that all students screened out received warnings regarding their grades, or the viability of their proposed dissertation, or their ability to write and conduct independent research. If a student failed to heed such warnings, and a majority of the faculty members at the screening meeting expressed no confidence in his or her ability to complete the degree, the student was screened out. A student could always appeal the decision.

There was a rustle of disquiet among us. None of us knew anything about Maia's dissertation topic or final choice of adviser. We had only her word about her grades, and one exemplary paper. Based on her comments in class, we knew she was capable of excellent work, but so were we all. Maia, still composed, stayed silent. Rachel and Irfan exchanged a look. Rachel weakly said that screening procedures could still use more transparency. Our handbook said we needed to be "in good academic standing" to pass screening, but this language was vague. Davis offered to set up a committee composed of both graduate students and faculty. Together, he promised, we could design a more transparent, concrete, and detailed set of rules. He asked if this was acceptable. Having lost our steam, we mumbled agreement. Some of us began gathering our things, vaguely deflated because there had not been as much blood in the arena as we had imagined and already preoccupied with how much work we had to do for classes that week.

Davis beamed at the room and picked up his jacket. This had been a productive discussion, he said, thanking all of us magnanimously. Levin and Green followed him out of the room. We slunk off toward the library or our apartments. Maia was heard thanking Rachel and Irfan. To those of us who clustered around Maia, hoping to sniff out if she had in fact received warnings, she answered tiredly that of course her work had received criticism, but hadn't everyone's at some point or other? How was she supposed to know when criticism meant that the faculty would decide she needed to leave? She did not see the point of putting herself through an appeals process, but she said she was glad that at least now there would be more transparency for us. Sarah put an arm around Maia. She suggested that maybe now Maia could focus on other things she wanted to do and spend more time with her boyfriend, a lawyer who drove up to see her almost every weekend. As Maia

81

looked into the distance, into a future some of us imagined wistfully as more exciting than ours and others as merely ordinary, we let her go.

Although screening procedures became clearer on paper, half our class, as predicted, did not graduate with a PhD. Rachel Goldfarb dropped out because her husband, who was in high tech, got a job on the West Coast. We liked Rachel, but she had become increasingly preoccupied with her personal life. Neither she nor Maia, now that we thought of it, seemed suited for purely intellectual pursuits. Rory Brandt landed a postdoc followed by a tenure-track job at a research university, and his monograph on Byzantine pederasty came out two years after he had completed his degree. Joel Carter gave it a review that lauded Brandt's efforts toward advancing the field but pointed to several transliteration errors and two areas where his already tenuous argument was further diluted by a lack of conceptual clarity. Married now to Sarah Miller, Joel was a spousal hire at the public university that had hired her on tenure track. Irfan Alam moved back to India after completing his PhD. We had no idea what he was doing. Alison Levin, who had remained his adviser, said she was disappointed that he had chosen to throw away his career by moving to a place where he would be starved for intellectual resources.

Dr. Anthony R. Davis, we learned through the grapevine, divorced his wife and negotiated a move to the only institution in the country more highly ranked than ours. With his new salary, he bought a summer house in Wellfleet. Our jobs paid little. Those of us who were employed had heavy teaching loads in small towns with cold winters. Some of us commuted from one part-time job to another. We lived in small apartments. We were always short on sleep. We ran into one another at conferences and competed over who worked the longest hours and had the worst students. We dreamed of jobs at research universities like the one from which we had graduated, where teaching assistants would grade badly written undergraduate papers while we wrote award-winning books. Anthony Davis's new book was the rage. Widely considered his most brilliant yet, it analyzed romantic love and moral responsibility in poetic traditions in the premodern Mediterranean. Following an untranslated verse in Greek, he dedicated it to his wife, Maia Alfieri, his beautiful muse, his moral compass, and the love of his life.

Nominated by Narrative

BLUES IN FIVE/FOUR THE VIOLENCE IN CHICAGO

by AFAA MICHAEL WEAVER

from IBBETSON STREET

In movies about the end of our civilization
toys fill the broken spaces of cities, flipping over
in streets where children are all hoodlums, big kids
painting themselves in neon colors, while the women
laugh, following the men into a love of madness.

Still shots show emptiness tearing the eyes of the last
of us who grew to be old, the ones the hoodlums
prop up in shadows, throwing garbage at us,
taping open our eyes, forcing us to study the dead
in photos torn from books in burned down libraries.

Chicago used to be Sundays at Gladys' Luncheonette
where church folk came and ate collard greens and chicken
after the sermons that rolled out in black churches, sparkling
tapestries of words from preachers' mouths, prayer books,
tongues from Tell Me, Alabama, and Walk On, Mississippi.

Now light has left us, the sun blocked out by shreds
of what history becomes when apathy shreds it,
becoming a name the bad children give themselves
as they laugh and threaten each other while we starve
for the laughter we were used to before the end came.

Nominated by Ibbetson Street, Martha Collins, Pamela Stewart

WHAT HAPPENS IN HELL

by CHARLES BAXTER

from PLOUGHSHARES

"Sir, I am wondering—have you considered lately what happens in Hell?"

No, I hadn't, but I liked that "lately." We were on our way from the San Francisco Airport to Palo Alto, and the driver for Bay Area Limo, a Pakistani American whose name was Niazi, was glancing repeatedly in the rearview mirror to check me out. After all, there I was, a privileged person—a hegemon of some sort—in the backseat of the Lincoln Town Car, cushioned by the camel-colored leather as I swigged my bottled water. Like other Americans of my class and station, I know the importance of staying hydrated. And there *he* was, up front, behind the wheel on a late sunny Saturday afternoon, speeding down California State Highway 101, missing (he had informed me almost as soon as I got into the car) the prayer service and sermon at his Bay Area mosque. The subject of the sermon would be Islamic inheritance laws—a subject that had led quite naturally to the subject of death and the afterlife.

I don't really enjoy sitting in the backseat of Lincoln Town Cars. I don't like being treated as some sort of important personage. I'm a Midwesterner by location and temperament and don't even cotton to being called "Sir." So I try to be polite ("Just call me Charlie") and take my shoes off, so to speak, in deference to foreign customs, as Mrs. Moore does in *A Passage to India.*

"No," I said, "I haven't. What happens in Hell?" I asked.

"Well," Niazi said, warming up and stroking his beard, "there is no forgiveness over there. There is forgiveness here but not there. The God does not listen to you on the other side."

"He doesn't?"

"No. The God does not care what you say, and He does not forgive you once you are on that side after you die. By then it is over."

"Interesting," I said, nondirectively.

"It is all in the Holy Book," Niazi went on. "And your skin, Sir. Do you know what the God does with your skin?"

"No, I don't," I said. "Tell me." Actually I was most interested in the definite article. Why was the deity referred to as *the* God? Are there still other lesser gods, minor subsidiary deities, set aside somewhere, who must be differentiated from the major god? I drank some more water as I considered this problem.

"It is very interesting, what happens with the skin," Niazi said, as we pulled off the Bayshore Freeway onto University Avenue. "Every day the skin is burned off."

"Yes?"

"Yes. This is known. And then, each day, the God gives you new skin. This new skin is like a sheath."

"Ah." I noticed the repeated use of the word *you*.

"And every day the *new* skin is burned off." He said this sentence with a certain degree of excitement. "It is very painful as you can imagine. And the pain is always *fresh* pain."

Meanwhile, we were proceeding through downtown Palo Alto. On the outskirts of town I had noticed the absence of pickup trucks and rusting American cars; everywhere I looked, I saw Priuses and Saabs and Lexuses and BMWs and Volvos and Mercedes-Benzes and a few Teslas here and there. The mix didn't include convertible Bentleys or Maybachs, the brand names that flash past you on Ocean Boulevard in Santa Monica. Here, ostentation was out; professional-managerial modesty was in. Here the drivers were engaged in Right Thinking and were uncommonly courteous: complete stops at stop signs were the norm, and ditto at the mere sight of a pedestrian at a crosswalk. No one seemed to be in a hurry. There was plenty of time for everything, as if Siddhartha himself were directing traffic.

And the pedestrians! Fit, smiling, upright, well-tended, with not a morbidly obese fellow-citizen in sight, the evening crowd on University Avenue appeared to be living in an earlier America era, one lacking desperation, hysteria, and Fox News. Somehow Palo Alto had remained immune to what one of my students has referred to as "The Great Decline." In this city, the businesses were thriving under blue skies and polished sunshine. I couldn't spot a single boarded-up front window.

Although I saw plenty of panhandlers, no one looked shabby and lower-middle-class. I noted, as an outsider would, the lines outside the luxe restaurants—Bella Luna, Lavanda, and the others—everyone laughing and smiling. The happiness struck me as stagy. What phonies these people were! Having come from Minneapolis, where we have boarded-up businesses in bulk, I felt like—what is the expression?—an ape hanging onto the fence of Heaven watching the gods play.

And it occurred to me at that moment that Niazi felt that way too, apelike, except that I was one of those damn gods, which explained why he had to inform me about Hell.

"You burn forever," Niazi said, drawing me out of my reverie. "And, yes, here we are at your hotel."

"Sir" and "Hell": the two words belong together. After arguing with the hotel desk clerk, who claimed (until I showed him my confirmation number) that I didn't have a reservation and therefore didn't belong there, I went up to my room past a gaggle of beautiful leggy young men and women, track stars, in town for a meet at Stanford University, where I'd been hired to teach as a visiting writer. They were flirting with each other and tenderly comparing relay batons. Off in the bar on the other side of the lobby, drugstore cowboys were whooping it up, throwing back draft beers while the voice of Faith Hill warbled on the jukebox. Nothing is so dispiriting as the sight of strangers getting boisterously happy. It makes you feel like a stepchild, a poor relation. Having checked in, I went upstairs and sat in my room immobilized, unable for a moment even to open my suitcase, puzzled by the persistence of Hell and why I had just been forced to endure a lecture about it.

Rattled, I stared out the window. A soft Bay Area rain was falling, little dribs and drabs dropping harmlessly, impressionistically, out of the sky—Monet rain. A downmarket version of an Audubon bird—how I hate those Audubon birds—was trapped and framed in a picture above the TV.

I am usually an outsider everywhere. I don't mind being one—you're a writer, you choose a certain fate—but the condition is harder to bear in a self-confident city where everyone is playing a role successfully and no one is glancing furtively for the EXIT signs.

In his writings and his clinical practice, the French psychoanalyst Jacques Lacan liked to ask why any particular person would want to believe any given set of ideas. He initially asked the question of behavioral psychologists with their dopey experiments with mice and pigeons, but, inspired by Lacan, you can ask it of anyone. Why do you *desire* to believe the ideas that you hold dear, the cornerstones of your faith? Why do you clutch tightly to the ideas that appear to be particularly repellant and cruel? Why would anyone *want* to suppose that an untold multitude of human souls burn in extreme agony for eternity? Having left a marriage, and now living and working alone, I found myself in that hotel room experiencing the peculiar vacuum of self that arises when you go on working without a clear belief in what (or whom) you're working *for* and are also being exposed randomly to the world's cruelties.

The idea of Hell has a transcendently stupefying ugliness akin to that of torture chambers. This particular ugliness is fueled by the rage and sadism of the believer who enjoys imagining his enemies writhing perpetually down there in the colorful fiery pit. How many of us relish the fairy tale of endless suffering! Nietzsche claimed that all such relishers are in the grip of *ressentiment*, whereby frustration against the rulers, and anger at oneself, are transformed into a morality. Ressentiment is what happens to resentment once it goes Continental and becomes a metaphysical category. After Marx, injustice no longer seemed part of a natural order. And if injustice *isn't* part of a natural order, then ressentiment will naturally arise, the rage of the have-nots against the haves, the losers against the winners. Sometimes the rage is constructive, sometimes not. For Nietzsche, in *On the Genealogy of Morals*, the unequal distribution of power is simply a condition of things-as-they-are:

> It is not surprising that the lambs should bear a grudge against the great birds of prey, but that is no reason for blaming the great birds of prey for taking the little lambs. And when the lambs say among themselves, "These birds of prey are evil, and he who least resembles a bird of prey, who is rather its opposite, a lamb,—should he not be good?"

If you're a loser, you might as well get used to your loserdom and sanctify it. Thus Nietzsche. The eagles will come down sooner or later and grab you and eat you. It's how nature works. But if you, the lamb, claim a superior virtue to the eagle, and you band together with other lambs and consign the eagles to a sadistically picturesque Hell, you will, in another life, find yourself behind the wheel, working for Bay Area

Limo, instructing the hapless pale-skinned passenger from Minnesota about the manner in which some will find themselves scorched forever on the other side, forever and forever, oh, and by the way, here we are at your hotel.

In one of Alice Munro's stories, a character observes that the Irish treat all authority with abject servility followed by savage, sneering mockery. Ressentiment has its comic side, after all.

After washing up, I came back downstairs through the lobby—more beautiful track stars, more flirting, and a little micro-portion of ressentiment on my part against their beauty and youth and sexiness—and ambled to the Poolside Grille, where I ordered the *specialité de la maison*, blackened red snapper (California cuisine: black beans, jasmine rice, salsa fresca, lime sour cream), the snapper itself an endangered species. I hastily gulped down my chardonnay and, like a starving peasant, devoured the fish without tasting it. Gulping and chewing and swallowing, I watched the athletes in their skimpy garb promenading around the hotel, as graceful as swans. Ned Rorem on youth: "We admire them for their beauty, and they want us to admire them for their minds, the little shits." All the while Niazi's voice was in my head: "Every day the God gives you a new skin so that He can burn it away." I paid the bill and returned to my room. Fresh pain! What a phrase. I couldn't read, so I watched TV: *CSI: Crime Scene Investigation*, Captain Jim Brass confessing to human failings, played very well by Paul Guilfoyle. Or did I watch another show, some prepackaged drama interchangeable with that one? I can't remember. I do remember that I drifted off to sleep in my street clothes. There was no one around to tell me not to.

I didn't see Niazi again for another four weeks. On a Wednesday morning in April, he was to meet me in front of my Stanford apartment at 9:30 to take me to the San Francisco Airport so that I could fly back to Minneapolis. I had been commuting almost every week. At 9:25 I stood out in front with my suitcase beside me, waiting for him. I saw his black Lincoln Town Car in the visitors' parking lot. He honked, pulled up, and rushed out to put my suitcase in the trunk.

"Good morning, Sir," he said. "How are you?" His eyes, I noticed, were heavy-lidded and puffy. He looked like a box turtle.

"Fine," I said, settling into the backseat and snapping on the lap-and-shoulder belt. "How about you?" I looked around for a bottle of water. There were two little ones.

"Very tired," he said, checking his watch before flopping in behind the wheel. "I could not sleep last night. I have been in this parking lot since 8:30."

"You should have called me," I said. "We could've left early?"

"No no no," Niazi corrected me. "I have been trying to take the nap."

"Are you still drowsy?" I asked, noting again his nonstandard use of definite articles.

"A little, somewhat," he told me. "But when I am that way, I think of the Holy Book?"

"Ah."

He drove us up to Interstate 280, back in the hills, an alternative route to the airport. Here the rain was falling harder, and I noticed that Niazi didn't bother to turn on the car's windshield wipers. The rain spattered violently against the glass in an almost Midwestern manner. I felt right at home. Stroking his beard, Niazi gazed out at the highway, and after about ten minutes, I saw that, with his eyes half-closed, he was moving his head back and forth, shaking it slowly, as if . . . *was this possible? Was I actually seeing what I was seeing?* He was driving the limo, with me in it, while sleeping.

My brother Tom used to get drowsy behind the wheel and, one winter night in 1961, almost killed himself outside Delano, Minnesota, when he dozed off. Another irony: Delano's major business in those days was the engraving of cemetery monuments, and the town's motto was, "Drive carefully. We can wait." Unable to walk away from his accident, his car in the ditch, my brother had to drag himself on all fours out of the wreck across a snowy field to a farmhouse. As a boy, I was quite accustomed to my brother's sleepiness behind the wheel and would keep him entertained and awake with bright patter, for which I have a gift. So: "Niazi!" I said. "Do you have many jobs today? I'll bet you do!"

"Oh, yes, Sir," he said dispiritedly. "Many. Two this afternoon." Maybe he wasn't asleep after all.

The rain fell harder, unusually hard for Northern California. I looked around at the interior of the Lincoln Town Car, thinking, *We're going to crash. But at least this limo is a very solid car.* With the irony of which life is so fond, I thought of two lines of a creepy song I had heard a few months before, by the group Concrete Blonde. The song was "Tomorrow, Wendy," and two lines serve as the song's refrain:

Hey, hey, goodbye
Tomorrow Wendy's going to die.

And just about then the car began to fishtail. When a car fishtails, you take your foot off the accelerator and tap the brake pedal. Fishtailing occurs often in icy conditions (think: Minnesota winter), less often in rain. But California drivers aren't used to precipitation, so when the car began to lose control, Niazi woke up and slammed on the brakes, throwing the Lincoln into a sideways skid, and when the rear-wheel-drive tires acquired traction again, they pushed us off the freeway, onto the shoulder, and then, very rapidly, down a hill, where the car flipped over sideways and began to roll, turning over and over and over, until it reached the bottom of the hill, right side up. From the moment the car began to lose control until it came to rest, Niazi was screaming. All during the time we turned over down that hill, he continued to scream.

Reader, this essay is about that scream. Please do your best to imagine it.

Men don't scream, as a rule; they bellow or roar with fright or anger, but male screaming is an exceptionally rare phenomenon, and the sound makes your flesh crawl. A woman's scream calls you to protective action. A man's scream provokes horror.

Inside that car, I was holding on to the door's hand rest, clutching it, and I was as quiet as the tomb. I wasn't particularly scared, although things were flying around the car—my cell phone had escaped from my coat pocket and was airborne in front of me, as were various other items from the car, including those free little bottles of water and a clipboard from the front seat—and I heard the sound of crunching or of some huge animal chewing up the car. I thought: *Let this be over soon.* And then it was. They say everything slows down during an accident, but no, not always, and this accident didn't slow down my sense of time until we were at rest and I heard Niazi moaning, and more than anything else I wanted to get out of that car before the gas tank exploded, but my door wouldn't open—the right rear door—but the left rear door did, after I pushed my shoulder against it.

Around and inside the car was a terrible smell of wreckage, oil and burnt rubber, and another smell, which I am tempted to describe as sulfurous.

"Niazi," I said, "are you OK?"

"Oh oh oh oh," he said, "yes, I am OK" (he clearly wasn't), "and you, Mr. Baxter, sir, are you OK?"

"Yes." Where was I? Without a transition, I seemed to be standing in the rain outside the car, and Niazi, making the sounds that precede speech in human history, was trying to get himself off the ground, blood streaming down his face; and his shoes, I noticed, were off, which (I had once heard) is one of the signs of a high-velocity accident. Amid the wreckage, he was barefoot, and blood was dripping onto his feet. I reached out for him.

Suddenly witnesses surrounded us. "You turned over four times!" an Asian American man said, clutching my arm. His face was transfixed by shock. "I saw it. I was behind you. Are you all right? How could you possibly be all right? Surely you are not all right?" He opened his umbrella and lifted it over my head, a perfect gesture of kindness.

"I don't know," I said. I looked down at my Levis. The belt loops had snapped off. How was that possible? I stared in wonderment at the broken belt loops. I looked at the man. "Am I all right?"

He simply stared at me as if I had been resurrected.

The usual confusion followed: EMT guys, California Highway Patrol guys, witness reports. An off-duty cop from San Marino, another witness to the accident, said he couldn't believe I was standing up. He touched my arm with a tender gesture as if I might break. Someone asked me to sign a document, and I did, my hand shaking so violently that my signature looked like that of a third grader. And what was I worried about? My *laptop*. Had it been damaged? Furthermore, I thought, I'm going to be late for my airplane flight! In shock, we lose all sense of proportion. My signature on another official document looked like someone else's, not mine. And now Niazi was standing up, still bloodily barefoot, talking. He appeared to be in stable condition though they were putting a head brace on him and then lowering him onto a wooden stretcher, as if he had been smashed up. The Asian American witness who saw our car turn over four times asked me where I was going, and I said, "To the airport."

"I will take you," he said. "Just put your suitcase in the backseat. We will have to drop off my father-in-law in Millbrae. Do you mind?"

"No," I said. "Thank you."

The driver and his father-in-law spoke Mandarin all the way to Millbrae, the driver politely interpreting for me so that I wouldn't be left out of the conversation. "My father-in-law thinks you must be badly injured," the driver said. "I told him that you said you were fine." Thanks to this gentleman, I arrived at the San Francisco Airport in time for my flight. My ribs hurt, and my back hurt, and I gave off an odd panic-stricken body odor, but all I wanted to do was to get home. At the same time, I was still disoriented. Near the entrance to Terminal One, I noticed, was a sign with a name on it: NOSMO KING. It appeared to me as graffiti on behalf of a deposed potentate. Who was this oddly named Nosmo King? King of what? We were in Northern California! No kings here! Not until I was seated on the airplane did I calm down and realize that I had misread the sign and that, like other public places, the San Francisco Airport did not tolerate lighting up or puffing on cigarettes.

My back still hurts sometimes, especially on long flights. Niazi called me at home a few days later and left a message on my answering machine. His voice was expressive of deep despair combined with physical pain. "Mr. Baxter, sir, I am worried about you. I am . . . I am not all right, but I am lying down, recovering. Would you please call me?"

No. I would not call him, and I did not. I still haven't. I heard from someone else that he had broken his back. Guiltily, shamefully, I left him uncalled, and my inability to dial his number and to ask him how he was recovering surely serves as a sign of a human failing, a personalized grudge that will not be appeased. But all I could think of then and now was: *that expert on Hell almost got me killed.*

The insurance company has promised to send me $500 to compensate me for my pain and suffering.

In another version of the accident, the one I sometimes told myself compulsively, I sit silently while Niazi screams and the car rolls over down the hill. But I didn't just tell myself this story; I told everybody. The accident turned me into a tiresome raconteur. A repetition compulsion had me in its tight narrative grip. I had become like a character in one of my own stories, the sort of madcap who buttonholes an innocent bystander to relieve himself of an obsession. Some stories present themselves as a gift, to be handed on to others as a second gift. But some more dire stories have a certain difficult-to-define taint. They give off an odd smell. They have infected the person who possesses them, and that person peevishly passes on the infection to others. In the story in which I am the victim, I am not an artist, but a garrulous ancient mariner who has come ashore long after his boat has been set adrift and long after his rescue, which does not feel like a rescue but an abandonment.

From the airport I called my wife, from whom I was—and remain—separated, to give her the news. She met me at the airport, and we hugged each other for the first time in months. Near-death trumps marital discord but does not heal it. Then she took me back to my apartment, where she dropped me off.

I sat alone in the apartment for a few days, trying to read, but mostly writing e-mails. At night, I would fall asleep to the remembered sound of Niazi's screams. I announced my accident on Facebook, curious whether any of my FB friends would press the "like" button. A few did. I picked up the phone and started calling people. "Let me tell you what happened to me," I would say. I had become strangely interesting to myself. One friend has called my compulsion to talk about the accident a form of "vocational imperialism," though I think he means *avocational* imperialism. After all, I am a mere tourist in the landscape of Islam. As an unsteady humanist, I don't believe in much, and the virtues that I do believe in—goodness, charity, bravery—abandoned me in the moments after that accident.

All I thought as we tumbled down that hill, as I have said, was the hope that this awfulness would be over soon. We die alone, even if someone else is dying beside us. And—this was my fleeting wish in the backseat of that violently rotating Lincoln Town Car, in the wondrously dark clarity of thought produced by the unexpected, as the plastic bottles of water were flying around my head and my cell phone twirled in the air in front of me—I prayed that the car would land right-side up or, if this was to be the moment of my death, by fire as the gas tank exploded, that it be quick.

Nominated by Marianne Boruch, Nalini Jones, Bill Lychack

AFTER SUICIDE

by MATT RASMUSSEN

from WATER-STONE REVIEW

At the foot of your grave
I planted our black phone

wrapped up in its coiled cord.
I'd hoped its ring would

shudder upward and each blade
of grass become a chime, pealing.

But together we decide
which way the dream goes

like spilled water on a table
we carry across the room.

I wait for the lawn to ring
while the cord sprouts

and a receiver blooms
like a black cucumber.

No one is calling so
I put it to my ear

expecting the steady
dial tone of your voice,

but hear only the dark
breathing of the dirt.

Nominated by Water-Stone Review

TEEN CULTURE

fiction by ELIZABETH ELLEN

from AMERICAN SHORT FICTION

Saul doesn't want to go home and Darius doesn't want to go home and Alondra sure as shit doesn't want to go home so we drive around another half an hour and end up in a back booth at IHOP drinking coffee and eating cheese sticks. Two hours ago we bought three bags of candy at the movies, and Alondra and Ellie and I ate two and Darius and Saul threw the candy from the third bag all over the movie theater floor. Ellie and I don't want to go home, either. Ellie and I are picking at cheese sticks and french fries because we're not really hungry, but we don't want to go home, either.

The waitress brings a bowl of flavored creamers, and Saul tells her she looks like a country music singer, not any country music singer in particular, just a country music singer in general, and the waitress looks pleased with this information. The waitress smiles at Saul and asks Saul what school he goes to and Saul says the name of the school and the waitress says she went there, too, but a long time ago. The waitress smiles at me. The waitress and I are probably the same age, but the waitress looks her age, so I don't feel an affinity with her. I don't look the same age as Darius or Saul or Alondra, either, but I feel more of an affinity with Darius and Saul and Alondra than I do the waitress. I look like I'm between the ages of Darius and Saul and Alondra and the waitress. Most of the time Ellie seems happy about this. Sometimes Ellie makes a point of saying, "At least I have friends my own age." Most of the time when Ellie says this it's because Saul is paying me more attention than her. I have friends my own age, but most of them are busy with things like families and spouses and careers, and I'm not busy with any of those. Most of the time Ellie is OK with this, like when I spend my Friday nights driving her and her friends to the movies and IHOP. Like now.

At the movies Saul sat next to me, and Darius sat next to Ellie, and Alondra sat next to Darius. During the previews, Saul leaned over to me and said, "We have to see that one and that one and that one," and Ellie got pissed and said, "Shut the fuck up, Saul," but Saul doesn't ever shut up. Saul said, "And that one and that one," which was all of them, and then the movie started and I was holding my palm out for Sour Patch Kids and taking sips of Saul's Mountain Dew, just like I used to with Adam.

Saul and the waitress are still talking, and in my head I'm trying to get Alondra's story straight so I don't fuck shit up for her when her dad gets here. No one ever wants to go home so no one ever tells me when they have to be home, so I'm always having to lie to people's parents, which I don't really mind but I'd rather not have to deal with, either.

After the waitress leaves, I go to the bathroom to check my phone. I check to see if Adam has texted me, but Adam hasn't texted me so I put on some lip gloss and go back out to the table and sit down and try not to think about why Adam hasn't texted me.

I open my backpack and take out my camera and set it in my lap. I wait for a candid moment and then snap a picture of Darius and Saul and Alondra. The camera spits out a picture and everyone reaches for it and as they do I snap another picture. Then Ellie and Alondra are posing and Saul and Darius are telling me they don't want their picture taken. They pull the hoods of their jackers up over their heads and slouch in the booth and do a bad impression of people not wanting their picture taken. I take another picture and stuff it down in my bag before they can grab it and put the bag between my knees and grab the last cheese stick.

"Fuck you, Ellie's Mom," Saul says.

"Fuck you, Saul," I say. I stuff the cheese stick in my mouth and smile real big with my mouthful of cheese and Ellie says "disgusting" and I smile bigger and think about asking Saul to take my picture but then I'm wondering again why Adam hasn't texted me, so I don't.

Earlier I went with Saul to Kmart.

    Saul is Ferris Bueller here.

    You get what I mean?

    Saul is someone you don't say no to.

There are probably a million reasons why Adam hasn't texted me, but let's begin with the most obvious and glaring reason, which is: Adam's new girlfriend, Stacy. You've probably seen Stacy and her Mary Lou Retton, all-gum smile on *Oprah* or the cover of *Sports Illustrated* or on a billboard somewhere in the middle of fucking nowhere. She's young and perky and about ten years ago a shark ripped both her arms off while she was surfing and now she's famous and goes from school to school teaching kids like mine about perseverance, something I could use a lesson in myself. I haven't had any near-death experiences or anything even as close to horrific as a shark making a meal of my arms, and I can't seem to muster the energy to take a few pictures and call it an art show. Mostly I sit around surfing the Web with a couple glasses of wine from the box in my fridge or deleting the few pictures I do manage to take in some sort of nightly self-defeating ritual. Recently I spent three hours Googling "prosthetic hand sex" trying to figure out if Adam's new girlfriend can give him a handjob because that's one thing I was always good at, one thing Adam really seemed to enjoy. But I don't even know for sure if Stacy wears a prosthetic hand. Probably she just gives really good blowjobs, which depresses me even more to think about, because I've always been rather insecure and self-defeating when it comes to blowjobs, too. Mostly I just stuck to the hand or moved straight to fucking. Which is another thing I think about more than I should: Stacy's limited range of mobility during sexual intercourse. Or: the inexhaustible number of positions she can get herself into with the use of her prosthetic arms, if she has them. Mostly I just want to think of her lying motionless on her back with her big, all-gum smile. This doesn't really gel with her persevere-in-the-face-of-adversity public image, but it's the way I choose to think of Stacy: flat on her back, counting the minutes until Adam's off of her, writing the next motivational speech in her head.

Saul was the first boy Ellie brought home who didn't refer to me as a cougar or a MILF. Maybe that's why I let him get away with so much. There are probably other reasons, but it's hard to think of them off the top of my head. Off the top of my head, I'm thinking about Adam and the numerous ways I fucked us up. Numerous way number one: allowing myself to believe he'd never fall for someone like Stacy. Numerous way number two: allowing myself to believe he'd never fall for anyone but me.

And sure as shit Alondra's dad comes swaggering in the place and soon enough I'm out of my body, watching myself lie to this man who appears from my vantage point in the booth to be at least six foot five. Yes, I say, she was at my house doing homework after basketball practice, even though she was in the movie theater being pelted by candy with Ellie and me.

"Her dad's black. He'll beat her," Darius had said half an hour earlier when Alondra's dad called and bitched her out for not already being home. "You don't want her to get beat, do you?"

"Of course not," I said.

"White people get beat, too," Ellie said, and I squinted my eyes at her hard, like, *Hello! I'm sitting right here.* And also, *What the fuck?*

"Yeah, but not like black people," Darius said, and Alondra nodded and poured two more packets of artificial sweetener into her coffee along with an Irish Cream creamer, and I wanted to object. I could bring to mind a myriad of household items my mother had incorporated into my punishments. But I had exhausted those stories long ago, and so I checked my phone again, in some sort of self-punishing ritual, and reapplied my lip gloss for the hundredth time.

But now Alondra's dad has come and gone and I'm searching my plate of fries for the soggiest one I can find to pelt at Darius and Saul is sitting next to him pouting because I'm not currently pelting him with fries. I'm not talking to him currently, either.

"What about me, Ellie's Mom?" Saul says.

But I ignore him and throw another fry at Darius instead and now Saul looks like he's going to cry and I have to admit, it feels kind of good when you realize you still have the power to make another human being sad, even if that other human being is fourteen and you're thirty-nine.

Reason number two why Adam hasn't texted me: Jimmy, the twenty-five-year-old Guido with a Mohawk I left Adam for six months ago, in one of those my-life's-pretty-fucking-safe-and-fantastic-currently-so-let's-kick-it-in-the-nuts-until-it's-coughing-blood-and-doubled-over-on-the-sidewalk, preemptive midlife-crisis moments. Naturally things didn't work out with Jimmy. Why would anyone in her right mind believe things would work out with Jimmy?

Ellie and Alondra climb in the back, and Darius and Saul spend two and a half minutes in the parking lot arguing over who's going to sit in the front seat, same as usual.

"Come on, dog."

"No way, man. I called shotgun."

"Dog, you sat in front on the way here."

"I don't care, man. I called it."

And I know what you're thinking. You're thinking: *what an asshole.* You're thinking: *how pathetic.* You're thinking: *maybe if just one time she'd gotten laid in high school* . . . And I'm not going to argue you. I'm not going to deny I'm flattered by the attention. I'm not going to pretend anyone at my twenty-year class reunion had a clue who I was. I'm merely going to ask you to take a harder look at your own life, to write down every petty thought, to examine every questionable motivation. Then I'm going to ask you to spend five minutes with a fourteen-year-old of the opposite sex. And not one of the insecure, unattractive losers, but one of the cool ones, one that's cooler than you were in high school, one that's cooler than you are now, one that knows more about music and cracks funnier jokes and smokes better weed. Then spend five minutes with your average forty-year-old and try not to shoot yourself in the face when all they have to talk about is colon cancer screenings and Sarah Palin and how we can all live greener. I may be an asshole, but I'm not trying to waste my time figuring out how to spend another four point five years on this planet. And I'm sure as shit not trying to talk about Sarah Palin.

A month ago I met Saul's mother at a restaurant for a glass of wine. Saul's mother is in her fifties and a gynecologist. Both Saul's parents went to Ivy League schools. Saul's mother is less outright elitist in her presentation than Saul's father, but you still get the feeling she knows she's slightly better than you. The woman who watches Saul and his sister after school had caught Saul and Ellie smoking pot in Saul's bathroom a few days before. We were supposed to be meeting to talk about that, but mostly we talked about Saul.

"His father's convinced he's going to get a girl pregnant," his mother said.

"Really?" I said. I didn't think Saul was the least likely boy I knew to get a girl pregnant, but he was way down on the list. Darius, Stephen, Diondre, Matt . . . they were at the top.

"I imagine he's dated pretty much every girl in the eighth grade," she said.

"Oh, I don't think so," I said. I'd only known of one girl Saul had dated. He'd broken up with her six months earlier, and she was still obsessed with him. But I didn't mention this. I was being careful not to offer any new information. My alliances were with Saul, though I tried not to make this obvious either.

"So you think he'll go to college?"

"Oh, yeah. Saul's very driven. He might screw around a little, but I don't see him letting that get in the way of his overall vision."

"Huh. Well, that's good to hear."

I smiled and took the last drink of my wine. I couldn't imagine anyone ever doubting Saul. Ever.

The first time Ellie had dinner at Saul's house, Saul's mother looked at Ellie across the dining room table and said, "Why does your mother like Saul so much?"

Ellie told me later that she laughed and said, "Because he's my best friend and he's really funny."

"Saul's funny?" his mother asked.

Ellie wasn't sure if she was joking or not. Saul's mom wasn't smiling. Neither was his dad.

"Yeah," Ellie said. "Saul's a laugh riot."

On the drive home, Saul called me.

"What's up, Ellie's Mom," he said.

"Your parents think you're going to get a girl pregnant," I said.

"Really? What else did she say?"

"They're going to drug-test you."

"Oh, yeah, I already knew that. Want to buy me some synthetic urine off the Internet?"

"Not really, Saul."

"It's cool. Don't text my mom anymore, though. She'll make you not cool."

"All right," I said. "I have to go though," I said. "Almost home," I said.

"Peace," he said.

Reason number three why Adam hasn't texted me: this wasn't the first time I left him for another man. The first time I thought I was in love with his best friend. Of course it turned out I wasn't in love with him, either. It took me six years and two breakups to realize I was never going to be in love with anyone except Adam.

Alondra's dad lives way the eff out in BFE, and I'm wondering why the hell he didn't just take Alondra with him when he was at IHOP an hour earlier and save us all a trip. It's late November and raining and I'm having a hard time reading the directions I wrote down on a napkin back at IHOP and Darius has to take a piss and I have to take a piss and Alondra has to take a piss and we're almost out of gas and Saul's ten minutes shy of being late. I pull the car to the side of the road and Darius walks one way into the cornfield and Alondra and I walk another and the field is wet from so much rain and I start to slip but catch myself. I haven't squatted to piss in a long time and some of the backsplash hits my jeans and my underwear is damp when I pull them back up, but at least I don't have to piss anymore and neither does Darius and neither does Alondra.

"You guys could have used my dad's bathroom," Alondra says as we pile back into the car, shaking the water from our hair, but we're afraid of Alondra's dad and so probably is Alondra.

I pull down the road and the directions now are fresh in my head and one turn later we're in Alondra's dad's neighborhood and five minutes after that Saul is in the front seat next to me and we're singing along to Lil Wayne's *Carter II*, because now that I know Saul cares, I'm talking to him again same as usual.

Reason number four why Adam hasn't texted me: I started texting him back. Three months ago, when things were still hot and heavy with Jimmy, Adam would call and wake me up at three in the morning to ask me if I knew how much I sucked or if I knew how much he thought I sucked and if I thought there was a difference. (My answers: no, yes, maybe?) Once I broke things off with Jimmy and started texting and calling Adam to tell him I knew exactly how much I sucked (a lot!), he stopped texting and calling me, which was around the time Ellie first brought Saul home. The thing about fourteen-year-olds is they always text right back.

Saul lives in an oversized brick house in a neighborhood populated by oversized brick houses. Like I said before, Saul's mother is a doctor. And like I didn't say before, his father is a professor of linguistics at the university in town. Once a week Saul sees a therapist. Apparently, Saul has anger issues, though you'd never know it if you never heard him talk to his dad.

On the drive back from Alondra's, Saul's phone rings.

"Dad, shut up. No, Dad. Shut the fuck up. Why don't you ask Mom about that, OK, Dad? I'll be home when I'm home. Jesus."

"Everything OK?" I say.

Saul laughs. "Yeah, everything's fine."

I realize I'm now *that girl* in the movie, the one who only wants her ex back because he's finally met a nice girl and is happy. I mean, I'm *not* that girl, but I'm aware that's how it appears. Also, I'm not entirely convinced Adam is "happy." Nor am I convinced Stacy is a "nice girl." Just because she had her arms ripped off by a shark doesn't make her automatically and forever a nice girl. And handing her a get-out-of-being-a-bitch free card just because she's hand-job-challenged isn't exactly treating her like everyone else. Treating her like everyone else means assuming she's a frigid bitch because she's sleeping with, or presumably sleeping with, the love of my life. Treating her like every-one else means *fuck her*, I'll do whatever it takes to get Adam back. Which is why I sent Adam the pictures I did two days ago and why I said his name repeatedly on the voice-mail message I left him while masturbating last week. It's all about equality and treating people with respect. I'm just trying to give Stacy every benefit of the doubt I'd want to be given.

At Kmart, Saul grabbed a cart and followed me up and down the aisles. Ellie was back home in her bedroom with Darius. I'd been texting them from the kitchen for fifteen minutes that we were ready to leave before Saul said, "Come on. Let's go." Saul was standing closer than normal, close enough I could tell he wasn't wearing deodorant or cologne.

I texted Darius from Kmart. "Remember," I said, "Ellie's not Muffin." Muffin is Darius's girl. Ellie has a boyfriend. Not Darius, another kid.

"And Saul's not Adam," Darius said.

"No shit, Darius," I texted. "Thanks for the reminder."

None of this would be happening if Adam and I hadn't broken up.

I wouldn't be spending my Friday nights driving around town with a car full of fourteen-year-olds if I hadn't met Jimmy, is what I'm trying to tell you. My life would probably look a lot like yours right now if I were still with Adam, is what I'm saying. But I'm not, so what the fuck. That's how I'm choosing to look at it anyway: *so what the fuck?*

Walking through the aisles with Saul, I was acutely aware of the other shoppers and their relationships to the people they were shopping with: fraternity brothers, teenagers on dates, parents with babies, newly weds, Saul and me.

"They probably think you're my mom," Saul said.

"Yeah," I said. "Probably."

Though I wasn't convinced that was what they were thinking. I wasn't convinced that was what Saul was thinking either.

"Buy me these," Saul said. He was wearing his shit-eating grin and holding up a six-pack of some energy drink I wouldn't buy for Ellie.

"OK," I said. "But you better not drink them all in one night. And no letting Ellie have one."

Saul nodded and dropped the cans in the cart. Saul is Ferris Bueller here. I'm everyone else in the movie.

* * *

Darius doesn't want to go home. We pull into the apartments where he stays on weekends with his mom, and he refuses to get out of the car. No one ever wants to go home, so we do a lot of idling in cars. We idle a while, listening to a new Jay-Z song, until the radio station goes to a commercial, and then I'm done idling. I don't want to go home, but I don't want to sit in this parking lot anymore either. My stomach is starting to cramp from sitting upright for so long, and on account of all the fries and cheese sticks I ate at IHOP.

"Come on, Darius," I say. "It's time to go home."

"No, I don't want to."

"Darius, your mom's probably worried about you."

"That crackhead ain't my mom. You're my mom."

"Come on, Darius," I say.

Darius and I go back and forth like this another three rounds and then Saul says Darius can stay at his house and Darius says, "no shit?" and then I pull back out onto the road. I make a right and another right and a left and now we're idling in front of Saul's house and still no one wants to get out of the car.

"OK, boys," I say.

"Come on, Ellie's Mom," Saul says. "One more time around the block."

"No, Saul," I say. Sometimes I have to pretend to be Ferris Bueller's sister here or we'll never get anywhere, we'll always just be idling.

After we leave Saul's house, Ellie gets in the front seat. "I don't want to go home yet," she says, and I make a right instead of a left off Saul's road and the next thing you know we're downtown driving through the lights and singing along to Eminem because no one's waiting for us at home and the house seems so big now with just the two of us in it.

Four years ago when we first started looking for houses, Adam came with us. We'd been living together for three years in an apartment with Ellie when my father died and fucked everything up. We looked at six or seven houses together and then something happened and it was just Ellie and I looking. And then something else happened and Ellie and I were moving into this house and I was giving Adam money for an apartment across town.

Now if that time comes up, Adam says, "I can't believe I didn't take the money and run." I gave him a large lump sum. Fifty grand. "I guess I was too in love with you to leave then," he says, and this is something he's good at now, making comments that seem offhand but make a steady hum in my brain at night along with the fridge and the A/C.

When Ellie and I get home, we sit in a pair of black leather chairs off the kitchen and open our phones. Ellie is probably texting four or five different people and Adam still hasn't texted me so I have no one to text. I could do something else, for example, read a book, but sitting across from Ellie while she texts I feel lonelier than normal and normal is pretty bad. I look through my contacts. I consider texting Jimmy, but that would be a grand-scale mistake. And as I'm looking, a text comes through and for a quarter of a second I'm hopeful it's Adam, but of course it's not. Of course it's Saul. And soon it becomes apparent both Ellie and I are texting with Saul, which should probably be strange but for some reason isn't. I even say this out loud.

"If some other mother and daughter were texting Saul, we'd think it was weird," I say.

"Yeah," she says, her eyes still on her phone. "For us it's perfectly normal."

"Saul wants McDonald's," Ellie says.

"Yeah," I say. "He just told me, too."

And because neither of us can say no to Saul and neither of us has anything better to do, we're back in the car and driving to the only McDonald's still open at one in the morning and ordering two number nines because, even though he hasn't said as much, Darius is probably hungry, too.

Saul's house is for the most part dark, and we pull to the curb and wait for Saul to appear in the driveway.

"Text him again," I say. And while Ellie is texting, I notice a figure standing in Saul's bedroom window. I know it is Saul's bedroom window because I've been in Saul's bedroom. It's Saul's bedroom, but it isn't Saul.

"Don't look up," I say, and of course Ellie immediately turns and looks up even though I told her not to.

"Fuck," she says, because we both know it's Saul's dad and Ellie is scared shitless of Saul's dad.

106

"Where the fuck is Saul?" I say. "What the fuck is taking him so long?"

It takes five more minutes for Saul and Darius to come out of the house and the entire time Saul's dad is standing there watching us and even though I'm half sure I'm not doing anything wrong I feel as though I am.

Saul comes around to my side of the car, and I roll down the window and hand him his food.

"Your dad's been watching us the whole time," I say.

"Oh, shit," Darius says, taking the drinks from Ellie.

And Saul says, "Don't worry about it." He's smiling, but at the same time he looks pissed. Later Darius calls Ellie and tells her how Saul went off on his dad as soon as they got in the house. "What the fuck were you staring at Ellie's Mom for, Dad? Leave my fucking friends alone," Darius tells her Saul said.

On the way to Kmart, Saul told me his dad used to drink wine with Saul's mother in the evenings but that lately he's been drinking Scotch alone.

"Maybe I've completely misjudged my parents' relationship," he said.

"They've known each other since they were in the eighth grade," he said.

"Sort of like you and Ellie," I said.

"No," he said. "It's completely different."

And I wasn't sure if he meant because he and Ellie would never end up married or because if they did he would never leave her to drink alone.

"My mother used to drink Scotch," I said. "I don't know what my father drank."

Neither of us said anything else after that and then we were at Kmart where most of the people probably thought we were mother and son and Saul begged me for a Nerf gun and I couldn't say no.

Last week when I came to pick Ellie up from school, Darius found me in the parking lot.

"Look what my dad did," he said, pulling back the collar of his shirt and showing me the marks on his neck. "Yeah, my dad and I got in a fight. He broke three of my ribs and slammed my head into the wall."

Darius was bouncing up and down in front of me as he said this. He has a habit of rocking in chairs, bouncing on his feet. The only time I ever saw him sit still was the night he fell asleep in the movie theater. Later Ellie told me he'd been drunk, which made sense. It was a comedy, the hit movie of the summer. And Darius fell asleep ten minutes in. He'd snored on my shoulder, but a light snore, like a toddler or a pug.

Two days after showing me his cracked ribs, Darius showed up at school with marks on his face. "Gang initiation ritual," Saul told us later. I didn't say anything to Darius when I saw it. I made him waffles after school same as always. But when he wasn't looking, I couldn't help staring at the marks. He was rocking in his seat so it was hard to get a steady look.

When we get back from dropping the McDonald's at Saul's, Ellie says she's tired and takes her phone with her up to bed. I watch her go up the stairs wishing she wouldn't. As soon as she's out of sight, I begin worrying about her because even though it feels like she's telling me everything, like she's telling me too much, there are still things I don't know. As soon as she's behind closed doors, I'm powerless to help.

Two months earlier she came downstairs on a Sunday morning in a short-sleeved shirt, and when I handed her a plate of bacon, I noticed the marks on her arm. I waited until she was out of the room to text Saul.

"I'm picking you up in an hour," I said. "We need to talk to Ellie."

After that there were no more marks on her arms.

"Saul's the only person I would want you to tell," Ellie said later, and I said, "I know."

Saul had said, "Ellie, you can't do this ever again," and Ellie had nodded and I could tell by her face and the way she was looking at Saul, like he was someone she couldn't say no to, like he was someone she couldn't disappoint, that she meant it in a way she might not have meant it with me.

Sometimes I don't know what we would do without Saul, whom I would call, what, if anything, they would say.

Reason number five why Adam isn't texting me: he's currently in Hawaii with Stacy. A surfing competition or shark hunt or some shit. According to a mutual friend, he's there eight days. I pour half a glass of wine, and then I sit on my bedroom floor and stare at my phone. I'm not sure if Adam can receive texts while he's in Hawaii, though we're still on the same family calling plan and I'm still paying his phone bill so I could probably find out if I really wanted to, but I don't. I open my phone and start to type a text. I get halfway through it and then close the phone and then open it again and start typing the same thing all over again. I finish the text and stare at it a while and close the phone without sending it. I do this three more times and then I close the phone a final time and lie on my bedroom floor with my cheek pressed to the carpet. I glance at the clock and subtract three hours and imagine what Adam and his girlfriend are doing currently. I text Saul and then I text Ellie. Want to go to a graveyard, I ask them both, and then Ellie and I are back in the car on our way to Saul's. I park a block away this time and wait five minutes and then Saul and Darius are back in the car with us and I've forgotten about Adam and his girlfriend for the moment. My phone is still on the floor in my bedroom, next to the indentation left from my cheek.

I park the car in an abandoned motel lot across the street from the graveyard. The motel's been torn down for years, since before we moved to town, but the sign's still there. I stand in the grass where the motel used to be, imagining the rooms and the people who stayed in them. In my mind someone famous stayed here once, a country music singer, Waylon Jennings or Hank Williams Jr. or Patsy Cline. I lift the camera from where it hangs around my neck, take a picture of the sign, then turn the camera toward Ellie. But she's too quick for me. She shields her face behind her hand, and I end up with one more in a series of similar photographs of Ellie with different backgrounds, this one an abandoned parking lot and sleet.

Darius and Saul are halfway across the highway, and Ellie and I have to run to catch up. We walk past the caretaker's house, and I whisper-yell at the boys to be quiet. I don't want to be caught walking through a cemetery at two in the morning with three fourteen-year-olds, even though it was my idea. I think how Adam would shake his head if he could see me now. You wish you were a teenager, he would say, and maybe he would be right, though in my defense I would say I'm just lonely, and I would be right, too.

We're in the back of the cemetery now so it's OK to talk in normal voices. Saul and Darius are trying to open the door of a mausoleum, and Ellie and I are reading headstones, sorting out families who lived a hundred years ago and had too many kids and not enough money. We always find at least one person to mourn. The last time it was a four-year-old girl named Eleanor who died in 1923. There was a lamb on the top of her grave, and we tried to figure out what had caused Eleanor's death: typhoid or measles or diphtheria. Ellie's busy studying a row of long-deceased brothers when another headstone catches my attention. It's situated between a tree and a lamplight, and I think I can make out what looks like a Pac Man etched into the stone. I walk closer, and Ellie notices and follows. I get close enough to read the engraving, and it's a boy of fourteen, born the same year as me, Matthew Elwood Rucker. The Pac Man is above his name and a golf club is beside it and instantly I can see this boy, a ninth grader at my school, the victim of a school bus accident or leukemia or alcohol poisoning or self-inflicted gunshot wound, take your pick. It's the saddest grave I've seen yet, but probably only because I instantly visualize him as every boy I had a crush on back in high school, and then, almost as instantly, I visualize him as Saul or Darius.

I sit on the ground and Ellie sits down next to me, even though the ground is cold and mostly mud, and we don't talk, we just stare at the grave, at Matthew Elwood Rucker, age fourteen, who probably had the high score on Pac Man at whatever burger joint in town his family frequented and played golf on the school team. And at some point Darius and Saul stand behind us and stare too. Darius and Saul, who are never still, stand behind us, and the sleet picks up and lashes our faces and we pull our hoods tighter and nobody says anything and no one moves.

And then suddenly Darius is on the run again, bolting from the cemetery back to the car and we are chasing him, Saul and then Ellie and then me, and Darius looks back, doesn't see the car, and the car brakes and then swerves, and Darius keeps running, has no concept of his vulnerability, does not understand how close he came.

I get in the driver's seat and turn on the radio and everyone's quiet for a minute and I think of how a friend of mine told me recently that he read a poll in which 70 percent of parents said they would not have children if they had it to do over again. My friend is (happily) married and childless (by choice). I wanted to ask him how many people he thought would still get married if they had it to do it over again, but it seemed like a shitty question to ask so I said, "Really?" and left it at that.

110

At home Ellie goes upstairs for a second time tonight and I don't want her to go this time either but not because I'm worried about her but because I'm worried about myself. I don't want to be left alone. The first five years of her life we slept together every night, but she was a different person then and I guess so was I.

I want to text Adam, to tell him people change, but it's not the sort of thing you can tell a person and also I'm not convinced I have. There's a difference between not wanting to be left alone and change, he would say, and what could I say to that?

I'm adapting to my surroundings, I would say.

I sleep on the floor of my closet now, I would tell him.

I know how much I suck, I would say.

I'm trying to do something about that, I would tell him.

In the morning Ellie comes downstairs in a long-sleeved shirt, and I fight the urge to check her forearms. I remind myself to ask Saul about this later.

"How did you sleep?" I say. I am standing at the stove cooking bacon, and the dogs are waiting at my feet for the pieces I burn.

"OK," she says. She has her phone in her hand. She is texting someone, probably Saul. "Adam texted me," she says. "I forgot to tell you."

I don't look up from the bacon. I am thinking about how if Adam were still here, I wouldn't tell him about Ellie's arms. Then I question that instinct, consider whether it's good or bad. I bite a piece of bacon. I can't decide.

"He said he'd just seen two dolphins jumping in the ocean and that they'd reminded him of me. He said, 'Remember when you wanted to be a marine biologist? I do!' "

"Did you tell him you want to be an actress now?" I say

"No," Ellie says. "I'll tell him later."

I want to tell her to tell him now. I want one of us to be in constant communication with Adam. But texting Adam back is low on Ellie's list of priorities currently, so I let it go. I stare at the bacon sizzling in the pan and try not to think of Stacy standing next to Adam on the beach, watching the dolphins jumping in the ocean. The last time Adam and I were on a beach together, we were in the Cayman Islands and I didn't want to take the boat out to feed the stingrays. I was afraid of getting seasick, so Adam and Ellie went without me.

"Are you sure there isn't a part of you that still wants to be a marine biologist?" I ask Ellie. "Remember the stingrays in Cayman? You really liked those stingrays."

"That was years ago, Mom. I barely remember that."

And I don't know why but something about her barely remembering that trip, the stingrays and dolphins and turtles, makes me sad, like maybe she barely remembers Adam, all the nights he carried her up the stairs to bed and the bowling league they belonged to and the song she dedicated to him at her third grade talent show. But I still remember every guy my mother slept with, even the ones who only lasted a couple weeks and didn't spend any time getting to know me. They're all still here with me, and so I figure it's the same for Ellie with Adam. I figure she's bluffing and hope Adam is, too.

I break a piece of burnt bacon in two and drop the two halves on the floor and watch as the dogs lick them up off the floor and then I lay four more slices in the pan and wait for them to sizzle. I wait to burn them, too.

The last time I saw Adam was a Saturday morning five months ago. The night before he'd come back to take Ellie to a baseball game. It was after midnight when they got home, and I was waiting up with a pair of Manhattans when they did. Ellie went to bed, and Adam and I took our drinks to the basement and put in a movie but didn't watch it. I drank my drink sitting on top of Adam, facing him, and the music from the DVD played in a loop and Adam was already seeing Stacy by this time so he let me kiss him but wouldn't kiss me back. I kept telling Adam I was sorry and Adam kept saying, "Look, this isn't us. We're not us anymore." But he didn't push me off him. He didn't send me upstairs when it was time for bed either. We slept on our sides on the pullout in the office, and I kept waking up to remind myself I wasn't alone on my closet floor.

In the morning before he left, I made eggs and bacon, and Adam said the smell of bacon reminded him of his grandfather.

"Didn't your parents ever make bacon?" I said.

"I guess not," Adam said.

"Didn't we?" I said.

Adam shrugged his shoulders.

"I guess not," he said.

I couldn't remember why we'd never made bacon. I sat in the leather chair and watched Adam eat the breakfast I'd made him and then Adam was gone and for hours the house still smelled like bacon. I went downstairs and made up the pullout and tried to take the DVD out of the player but I couldn't remember which button to push. It was still playing in a loop and I had to call Ellie down to help me because Adam was gone and Ellie was the only one left who knew how to work the remote.

At noon we pick up Saul and go to the mall. It's three weeks before Christmas, and Darius has been banned from the mall for shoplifting or racial profiling or both, so we drop him at his mom's on the way. At all four corners of the mall are the Christmas trees the Salvation Army puts up every year, and the trees are covered with pieces of papers that say something like baby girl or teen boy and the wish list of each child: MP3 player, Barbie doll, socks and underwear, coat. Each of us takes a tag from the tree. Saul takes a boy his age and Ellie a girl her age and I take a card that says infant boy.

Right before Adam and I broke up, we were talking about having children. I made an appointment to have my IUD removed, and then, the day before my appointment, I got cold feet and cancelled. But by then Adam and I had already picked out names: Clementine and Hank. Now those names are on headstones in my mind. I see them and try to figure out how the children died: typhoid or measles or diphtheria.

We shop for Ellie's child first: hair accessories and a Justin Bieber calendar and pajamas with penguins. Then we go to the sporting goods store and buy Saul's kid a football and a basketball and sweatpants and a jersey. By this time Saul and Ellie are tired and complaining. I give them money for the food court and go by myself to the baby clothing store. I am unused to shopping for a boy. I start at the front of the store and work my way back. I pick out onesies with puppies and crocodiles and sleepers with bunnies and bears, I grab baby books and a stuffed pig and a blue blanket covered with stars and half-moons. Of course Adam and I would have been happy with a healthy baby of either gender, but secretly we'd both wished for a boy; Hank, our little cowboy or baseball player or astronaut; Hank, with his mother's excitability and eyes and his father's patience and reliability. The clothing store has their goods arranged by theme: pirates and sharks up front, airplanes and trains in the middle, and in the very back, a section of blankets and

113

pajamas and coats decorated with cowboys and cowboy gear: horse-shoes and hats and lassos. On a hanger over a pair of miniature cowboy dungarees is a miniature cowboy shirt with snaps down the front just like the ones Adam wears, and suddenly I'm remembering a cowboy-themed birthday party for Adam a few years back at which, upon the completion of the birthday song, I ripped Adam's shirt open with one quick yank of his snaps.

I take the tiny cowboy shirt down from the wall and carry it with the bundle of clothes and toys already in my arms to the register and pay, and when I'm outside the store, I pause for a second, remove the cowboy shirt from the bag and fold it neatly into the bottom of my purse. I walk to the food court and find Ellie and Saul and Saul sees me first. Saul stands up, says, "What'd you get, Ellie's Mom?" I show them everything except the cowboy shirt. The cowboy shirt stays hidden in my purse.

Back home the house still smells like bacon and Saul and Ellie say they're going for a walk and probably they're going to get high. I watch them walk down the driveway, and then I shut the door to my bedroom and open my bedroom closet. There is a blanket and a pillow on the floor and I nudge them out of the way with my foot and open a drawer in the back of the closet. The drawer is filled with postcards and letters and manila envelopes addressed to me from Adam. Most of the post-cards are from three years ago: Salt Lake City, the Grand Canyon, Yo-semite; a road trip Adam took during our first breakup, when I was still his "baby girl" and "sweetheart" and "honey." I remove the cowboy shirt from the bottom of my purse and place it gently atop the postcards and envelopes. I tuck it into the drawer and zip my purse and back out of the closet without having looked too closely at anything with Adam's handwriting.

Two hours later I'm sitting on the couch in the basement and Alondra is on my left and Saul is on my right and Ellie is next to Saul and Darius is next to Ellie. We're watching 8 Mile and I'm thinking, "This is the life you have chosen," and it's not the best life but it's not the worst either. A psychologist would have a field day with my life, but how many psychologists' lives resemble anything you'd want to know anyhow?

Halfway through the movie I get up from the couch and go upstairs to get my camera. My bedroom wall is filled with photographs I've

114

taken with my Polaroid over the last six months: Saul and Darius wrestling on the kitchen floor, Saul and Ellie sitting on Saul's skateboard in our driveway, Darius standing on our pool table, Darius jumping off our roof, Alondra and Ellie posing in their bathing suits in Ellie's bathroom mirror, Saul and Ellie listening to music on Ellie's bed, Darius and Saul smoking cigarettes in the cemetery, Ellie and Alondra and Darius and Saul walking through the parking lot toward me after school, Ellie with her hand over her face, Ellie with her hand over her face, Ellie with her hand over her face, Saul sitting on my bed, Saul sitting on his bed, Saul in my car.

And as I'm leaving my bedroom, camera in hand, I glance down at the floor where my phone rests on the carpet. There are three new texts and one is from Saul asking me where I am and one is from Ellie asking me to bring chips and one is from Adam asking me if Ellie got his text.

I text Ellie back "k" and text Saul back "one sec" and then I go to text Adam back but I don't know what to say. I text "yes" and I know I should text something else but I don't know what that something else is or what that something else is is too much to fit in a single text or what that something else is is something Adam doesn't want to hear or something he thinks he doesn't want to hear or something I've already said and keep on saying and saying and saying.

The last time Adam was here I begged and cried and pleaded with him to kiss me back. I was really sobbing and I had to keep wiping at my eyes and nose and mouth with the sleeve of my shirt and then suddenly, amidst all that crying and begging, I had a moment of clarity. Suddenly I saw the scene played out as though it were being videotaped. I sat back on my heels and looked up at Adam. I wiped my eyes some more and said, "Please don't tell *her* about this. Please, please, don't tell her." And Adam looked back at me and said, "I never tell anyone anything, you know that," which made me sob even harder knowing I was the only person Adam had ever really told anything.

And as I'm staring at the screen of my phone, at the word "yes" I've typed into Adam's text, another text comes through. It's Saul. "Hurry up," he says. "You're missing the best part."

And you know how there are those moments in your life when everything's real shitty, so shitty you come up with a whole new philosophy to go with the shittiness, a whole new set of morals, a whole new code of ethics, because suddenly it seems like nothing at all you do or don't do matters and the shittiness is like a freedom you never knew you had? Yeah, well, that's all bullshit, too. Wait thirty seconds and those moments pass and you're right back where you started, fucking shit up.

I stare at my phone. One more minute and Saul will be up here grabbing me. One more minute and Ellie will be calling me about those chips.

I click off Saul's text back to Adam's. The word "yes" is still there. I stare at it one more second before hitting send. I stare at it, visualizing the word flying through the air over the Midwest, over California and the ocean, all the way to Hawaii. I visualize the beach, the water, the openness of Adam's face as he reads it. A little hint of a smile or smirk. A little moment of satisfaction. *I'm still here. I'm still here. I'm still here.*

I leave the phone on my bedroom floor. I grab a bag of chips and go downstairs. I'm curious what Saul thinks is the best part. Every part of *8 Mile* is the best part. Every part.

Nominated by America Short Fiction

LAST CALL

by SAEED JONES

from MUZZLE MAGAZINE

Night presses the gunmetal O of its open mouth
against my own & I can't help how I answer.

He is the taste of smoke, mesquite-laced tip
of the tongue. Silhouetted, a body always

pulling away, but shirt collar in my fists,
I pull him back. Need another double-black

kiss. I've got more hunger than my body can hold.
Bloated with want, I'm the man who waits

for the moon to drown before I let the lake
grab my ankles & take me into its muddy mouth.

They say a city is at the bottom of all that water.
Oh, marauder. Make me a drink. I'm on my way.

Nominated by Muzzle Magazine, David St. John

THE HEALING POWERS OF THE WESTERN OYSTERCATCHER

by HOWARD NORMAN

from SALMAGUNDI

BOB EDWARDS
Morning Edition (NPR)
12-16-2003

Bob Edwards, host:

Imagine leaving home for the summer and while you're away, a terrible event occurs in the place you've left behind. That was the experience of some Washington neighbors of NPR special correspondent Susan Stamberg. Her Tuesday series, No Place Like Home, continues.

SUSAN STAMBERG REPORTING:

Novelist Howard Norman, his wife, poet Jane Shore, and their teen-age daughter spend their summers in Vermont. This year they loaned their DC home to an acquaintance and her two-year-old son. This past July, in the dining room of that house, the woman committed suicide and took her little boy with her.

Ms Shore: At first, I was thinking, and we were all thinking as a family, if we could actually go back home, and if we could actually live in the house, because it had been violated.

Stamberg: So how was it? How did you then, Howard Norman, arrive at the idea that you, in fact, would go back to the house?

Mr. Norman: I think that happened fairly quickly, actually, we agreed relatively quickly that this was visited upon us, that it wasn't something whose source was our life, and that you don't let someone else's demon, if you will, chase you out. I came down a couple of days early, and I will say that it was a powerful feeling to step into the house. The sense of relief at seeing the familiar life was quite astonishing, really, because one doesn't always like where one's imagination goes and the projection of it.

Stamberg: And so it was so much more terrifying to think about it while you were out of town than to go back to what still looked like your house.

EDWARDS: The time is 29 minutes past the hour.

Truth be told, I scarcely knew Reetika Vazirani, and scarcely knew Jehan, either. So if the word *healing* is applicable to working through the consequences of an act of unspeakable brutality, it wouldn't be associated with grieving. Grief is reserved for loved-ones. In this situation, healing was about other imperatives, such as reclaiming the violated interior spaces of heart and home; wanting to gain some perspective, in order to temper, if not erase, the harrowing images of what a person, Reetika Vazirani, suffering the consuming rages and ravages of depression, was capable of doing to her child and to herself, let alone what she visited upon my house.

Years earlier, and just days after we'd begun living in that former house, I was attaching a mezzuzah to the frame of the front door, when Monsignor Duffy, of the Church of the Blessed Sacrament, whose rectory was next door—the church itself was across the street—dropped by to ask if I'd lecture his Catholic Book Club on the subject of "both real and delusional guilt in the novels of Graham Greene. I'd like a Jewish writer's perspective on a Catholic writer's philosophy, played out in the actions and thoughts of his characters." I told him that my lack of comprehension of this subject could only fail his book club.

The church bells ring every fifteen minutes, seven a.m. to seven p.m., and of course more frequently on Sunday mornings, Christmas, Easter, and around weddings and funerals. I soon developed an antagonistic relationship with those bells. A friend described me as being like Quasimodo in *The Hunchback of Notre Dame*, up in the bell-tower clamping his hands over his ears. The thing was, I was trying to get some writing done, each morning needing uninterrupted hours in a row, but the bells constructed never-changing allotments of time, often imposing a sense of anxiety into potentially meditative intervals, let alone punctuating the silence.

While some neighbors no doubt synchronized their hearts to this metronome, to me it caused a kind of arrhythmia. Jehan liked the bells, but they didn't always let him settle into a good nap, wrote Reetika Vazirani in a journal. Anyway, just now I'm thinking of something my therapist said: "Filicide strikes the deepest chords."

Essentially, I wish I didn't have this to write about; every word will come out awkwardly and not suffice. But the fact is, the medical examiner determined that on July 16, 2003, Reetika Vazirani, a poet and forty years old, stabbed her son in the neck, chest and forearm, damaging his blood vessels, lungs and heart. Therefore, this was not, as Kabir wrote, "a gentle transport into the next world," and of course at that moment, too, a father, Yusef, lost his son—you wake up, as Rhavi Galib wrote, to find a demon standing on your heart. Next Reetika Vazirani, really by any definition, more gently transported herself.

How to talk about such a thing? Here I take as much inspiration as I possibly can from what Yasunari Kawabata wrote: "When speaking of those who take their own lives, it is always most dignified to use silence or in the least restrained language, for the ones left most vulnerable and most deeply hurt by such an occurrence can feel oppressed by the louder assertions of understanding, wisdom and depth of remorse foisted upon them by others. One must ask: who is best served by speculation? Who is really able to comprehend? Perhaps we must, as human beings, continue to try and comprehend, but we will fall short. And the falling short will deepen our sense of emptiness."

And yet I found that sometimes I could not use restrained language.

"Reserving judgments is a matter of infinite hope," F. Scott Fitzgerald wrote. Still, I had to subscribe to some initial ways of looking at what

120

had happened. To that purpose, the most incisively spiritual thing I read was a response to a journalist that poet Rita Dove gave: "She couldn't find her way back to herself." And the most ethically useful thing was offered by David Mamet, who had driven over to our farmhouse: "If you are walking down the road and you look up ahead and see a house on fire, if you are a good person you don't wish for it to be someone else's house." The altruism of this felt meaningful, but I said to David that given the waking nightmare of a child-murder, and the bewildered sobbing in my farmhouse, it was very very difficult to feel much like a good person. He stayed for dinner to talk about it.

The summer had just been going along. Then on July 16, my family and a friend, Alexandra, had been to Montpelier, a twenty minute drive from the farmhouse, for dinner at a restaurant. It was a balmy evening and I remember pulling the car up to the house in dusky light and seeing a kestrel heliotroping over the slope of a dandelion field, half way between the garden along the cobblestone wall and my writing cabin. Once inside the house, I lingered in the kitchen while Jane and Emma went upstairs to watch a movie. I'd intended to carry coffee and chocolate mints upstairs. That's when I noticed the message light blinking on the telephone situated on the wall next to the pantry. It was one of those machines capable of archiving far more messages than one would normally receive during just a few hours away from home. I pressed the button, put the receiver to my ear and heard, "You have fifty-three messages." I got a bad feeling—I immediately poured a shot of Scotch—: this could not be good news. Then, after hearing five police messages and one from friends, I went upstairs. Telling Jane, and aware that in the telling I would *cause* sadness, was like gasping for air. We waited until the next day to sit down with Emma and say what had happened.

Our dear friend Stanley drove up for a visit. Emma's pal Caitlin flew up and stayed for a week. Many wonderful people called from all over the place. It was a shocking irony to find out that, in Washington DC, hearing the initial report of the incident in the distracted way we all take in local television news, a few people thought at first it was us who'd been murdered; in the face of this, my desperate stupid little joke was, well, if that had been the case, I wouldn't have answered the phone, would I have? I supposed I wanted to hear the relief in their laughter. But of course we were confused, discombobulated, our lives thrown radically off-kilter, and for weeks and weeks we had terrible, insomniac nights. The days allowed for more distraction; errands, house projects, Emma's Shakespeare rehearsals, city friends up for a visit, walks up the dirt road, swimming, attempting to write, the ten thousand things of quotidian life. But on some very basic level, an air of eerie if abstract preoccupation pervaded and much of the emotional dimensions of familiar life had become unfamiliar; we were self-consciously aware of our need day by day to calibrate, adjust and maintain our equilibrium. We were careful about it. There were friends and laughter on those days. But at the same time, we held an ongoing vigil against despair, and as resourceful as we were, we knew we were amateurs up against a monstrosity. Falling apart, gathering life together, falling apart, gathering.

This odd thing happened with television in Vermont. I can far more understand it now, but at the time it was working on an altogether perplexing level. Jane started to watch episode after episode of *Law and Order*, mornings, afternoons, night. These dramatic procedurals provided background visuals and voices (which sometimes felt like voice-overs to our own life, because to hear what the characters were saying, our silence was required) on the second floor of the farmhouse. I'd come and go, taking in snippets of dialogue and becoming generally apprised of plots and able to recognize the principal detectives, so splendid at portraying sanctimonious and brilliantly analytical scolds. Years later, when discussing this—and I paraphrase here—Jane said that she was working on hope, and her thinking was that if she relentlessly exposed herself to the sheer plentitude and commonality of murder, it might somehow serve to anesthetize the pain of an individual homicide and "make things a little better." In episode after episode of *Law and Order*, the unifying reason for suspension of disbelief was that, with few exceptions, the murder was solved and the perpetrator brought to justice. Yet in messier real life outside of television there had been the perverse miscarriage of justice in Reetika Vazirani's taking the life of her son so as to "save him from a terrible world," a verbatim quote of the helter-skelter logic she advocated to herself more than

122

once in notebooks. Viewing line-ups of episodes of *Law and Order* went on for some time, until Jane realized that she'd begun to "re-traumatize" herself and so for the most part stopped it.

But Jane wasn't alone in trying to find some medium for ad hoc yet persistent investment in the possibility of allegory helping out a little. Because over the next six months, I watched at least thirty times the classic cinematic treatise on child-murder, *M*, directed by Fritz Lang and starring Peter Lorre. This only served to transfer the real-death images, for example those in the police photographs taken in our dining room, to the cinematic horrors of child-murder in the German expressionist film, *M*. Not much help there at all, really.

Emma had turned fifteen that April, 2003. A wonderful pleasure to be with. She was just a regular teen-ager, though I also knew her as having big appetites for life, and remarkably poised. Naturally, when the murder-suicide took place, that poise was shattered; but she got right to dealing with it, because the very next morning, she asked to go rowing at the cottage on East Long Pond I'd rented for the summer. And that's what we did. She took up the oars and rowed herself and me the mile or so circumference of the pond; and whether consciously or not she rowed with fierce concentration and pacing, her face flushed with exertion, her arm and leg muscles straining, and I mean without cease, until we returned to the dock. Once we had overturned the row boat on land and had begun to walk up the wooden steps of the cottage, she said, "I won't develop the photographs I took of Jehan. But they should be developed. That little boy's family should have them."

I felt right then, and feel the same way now, that this seemed entirely consistent with Emma's dignified comportment, and that it showed a lot of self-knowledge, too. I'd seen Emma at work in various darkrooms and could see she loved knowing her way around dark rooms, and that she already had given herself to a kind of parallel life in photography, that is, apart from school and the vexations and challenges of teen-age sociology in general. I can't really say if at that age she'd started thinking of herself as a photographer, but I knew that for her photography was definitely a passion. Her photographs of Jehan had been originally taken as a fifteen year old goofing around trying to entertain a two year old boy—they'd only just met—and now all of a sudden the photographs had become eulogistic portraiture. And so, driving home from

123

East Long Pond, as we spoke a little more about the photographs—because Emma wanted to—it became evident to me that Emma knew how to protect herself, in the crepuscular light of a darkroom, from having to see a child's innocent face float up in the solvent of a developing bin. "No way," as she put it. "No way." And I thought: *my daughter's going to be okay.* In the end I delivered the negatives to Andrew, one of Emma's photographic mentors, whom she'd apprenticed to and who had encouraged her to attend a summer class at the Maine Photographic Workshops. I'd included the instructions, on a professional and personal basis, that after he'd developed the negatives he was under no circumstances, at Emma's insistence, to let her see them lying around his studio. Andrew finally sent the photographs to Reetika Vazirani's mother and step-father, who never responded.

I feel it is important to say again that I scarcely knew her. I didn't at the time and don't now care to be informed about her biographical details; I've had quite enough of her life, which so violently intersected with my family's. We were friendly but not friends. I admired some of her writing and even published three of her poems in an issue of CONJUNCTIONS that I edited. For a month or so in advance of her taking up residence in our house in Washington, my wife had spoken with her on the telephone. My understanding is that Reetika Vazirani had called to ask about teaching jobs, but also indicated that most aspects of her life remained unresolved, including where she might live during the summer. We had been used to letting writers stay in the house. So it was characteristic of Jane's empathy to finally suggest that Reetika Vazirani and her son Jehan might consider doing just that. No big deal, really. We were going to Vermont anyway, and it would be good to have someone look after things. From us it could be a *mitzvah*—a gift. Personally, I had only spoken with Reetika Vazirani once before, at the Breadloaf Writers Conference, and the topic of discussion on that occasion had been restaurants in Middlebury. The second time we spoke was when she stopped by to discuss housesitting.

On that visit, I had no sense of her taking any measure of the house at all; in fact, we kept to the living room. We sat drinking tea while Jehan watched a children's video. After exchanging pleasantries, she said, "A lot of writers said you were away in the summer, and we met once, remember?" Perhaps skeptical, certainly a touch edgy, I said,

"Oh, a lot of writers *who?* " She reeled off a dozen or so names, and I thought to myself, *I don't know any of them.* So I admit that any initial discomfort may have been predicated on the fact that she was so deftly able to opportune the sponsorship of a very loose-knit literary community. But the thing was, when she started in on her domestic travails, I didn't grant much leeway. I felt that asking for a roof over one's head is difficult enough without having to test out various reasons. Besides, the most important reason was upstairs watching a video in my daughter's room.

How could I know? How could I know, that the simplicity of our verbal contract—while living in our house you take care of it—might obfuscate future malevolence? Hindsight, of course, is powerfully suggestive and self-indicting but cannot change what happened. Yet it has often occurred to me that had I let this weary-looking, jittery and singularly accomplished woman with the lovely smile, whose intelligence I was, on the surface, beginning to enjoy, indulge in an hour or so of what I later understood to be a fugue state of exhaustion, fuming anger, self-pity, emotional claustrophobia and God knows what else, I most likely would not have, at least in so perfunctory a manner, muted my protective instincts. I would have heard something alarming. In one breath I say, *How could I know?* and in the next breath say, *I should have known.*

Anyway, when she and I were done talking, I served more tea and brought out some carrot cake. We laughed over the photographs in a biography of Groucho Marx I'd been reading. Emma walked in the door, home from school, and immediately went upstairs to hang out with Jehan; she showed him her collection of key chains and took those photographs of him. I remember, even without any noticeable register of incipient concern, that I felt some relief when they left. I watched through the front window as they walked over to look at The Church of the Blessed Sacrament like tourists. Then I turned away and went up to take a nap, or talk with Emma, or started dinner, I cannot remember. Yet at the same time, I was quite pleased, I believe especially on Jehan's behalf, but for both of them, really, that for a few months they'd have a cozy house where life could be lived, a playground nearby, a thousand books, a writing desk, light-filled rooms, classical CD's in stacks, a rectory of Irish and south-Asian priests next door.

From my mouth to God's ear, I wish I had said, "No—terribly sorry but this housesitting situation isn't possible."

It has to be said that Reetika Vazirani had left a telephone message for Jane's best friend Jody, to the effect that she was "in trouble," and to get to the house as soon as possible. Jody scarcely had known Reetika Vazirani either; but Jody had a key to the house. Given the proximity of the time the message was left and the deciphered time the murder-suicide took place, apparently Jody's job was to discover the bodies—can you imagine?—which Jody eventually did, and quickly alerted neighbors; police and paramedics arrived. In a matter of hours yellow crime-scene tape festooned both back and front porches like a garish Halloween prank. And as the investigation began, news spread, and demons began to stand on a lot of hearts.

At the very end of August I flew down and stepped into the house at about five-thirty in the evening. I had asked friends in advance to take down the three early 20th century Dutch portraits and an enormous photographic portrait of the actor Willem Dafoe, composed by Chuck Close, from the dining room walls. The grim expressions on the Dutch faces had always struck me as judgemental in a fashion almost approaching satire, and I was convinced that these anonymous personages were *witnesses* and we shouldn't have to run any risk of seeing horror reflected in their eyes. Jehan had been freaked by the big face of Willem Dafoe and that photograph had already been taken down.

On the other hand many gifts had arrived to redeem the walls. Antonin Kratochvil had sent one of his photographs. Jake Berthot had sent one of his exquisite drawings of trees. Kazumi Tanaka had sent her woodcut of Japanese cranes lifting from a pond. My friend Elizabeth had sent a photograph of the wild coast of British Columbia she had taken.

I opened a lot of windows, put a vinyl album of Chopin's Nocturnes on the old-school record player, and stood for a moment at the entrance to the dining room, looking at the new shellacked floorboards I'd ordered to replace the blood-stained boards. I looked at the house plants university colleagues had delivered. I set my Olivetti manual typewriter on the dining room table. Facing the corner of the dining room where the bodies had been found, I began typing letters. I wrote William in Hawaii, Stuart and Caren in Michigan, Rick and Rhea in Vermont, Bill and Trish in Vermont, Alexandra in Vermont, David in California, Mr.

and Mrs Malraux in Paris, Peter in Long Island, Jerry and Diane in California, my old ornithology professor Dr. Cleveland in Vancouver, Michael in Toronto, Deborah in Woodstock, New York, Michael, a portraitist of birds in St. Johns, Newfoundland, my college friend Richard in Florida, Mona in Paris, my mother Estelle in Michigan.

I do not fully understand why I went on such an epistolary binge—all told perhaps thirty letters, the briefest five single-spaced pages, and some upwards of twenty pages. Naturally, besides the fact that letters had always helped organize my emotions, I trusted that my friends would tolerate moodiness, outright despair, exhausted humor, philosophical nonsense and everything else. I was drinking espresso after espresso; letters were stacking up next to the typewriter; I switched from Chopin to Bach's compositions for cello and works by Kodaly, all performed by Janos Starker, and with these selections obviously was not seeking ebullience but rather an accompaniment to melancholy. Sleep was out of the question. Letter after letter after letter.

I think it was right around 3:00 a.m., with cicadas whining in the enormous Tulip Poplar tree in the front yard, which especially during high winds I had always felt was too close to the house, that I suddenly was famished and—quite surprised to have an appetite at all—decided on spaghetti, which in any season I considered comfort food. Even with the heat and humidity still coming in through the nighttime screens, I started to boil water in a big pot and thaw out some spicy meatballs stored in the freezer-compartment of the refrigerator. I opened a bottle of red wine. The recipe would be makeshift. I emptied a can of tomatoes, tomato paste, spices into a sauce pan.

All of this had great possibilities, I felt, and then, as the saying goes, *right out of nowhere*—this is impossible to capture—I "felt" something was terribly wrong in the house. Not that something terribly wrong *had* occurred; needless to say, I already understood that. No, the definite sensation, but with an indeterminate source, was of something occurring. *In-progress.* What is more I had suddenly contracted a blistering headache. What else could I do but question my own exhaustion: was I thinking clearly? What trick was my mind playing? No matter, no matter, I stopped cooking and—again I cannot pinpoint the reason—was drawn upstairs to my third-floor attic study.

Once the desk lamp had been switched on, I immediately noticed a novel on the floor; I cannot recall the title but the author was Penelope Fitzgerald. How odd, I thought, because whenever I left for the summer, I would without fail clear my desk, papers filed, pencils in a jar, everything neat and clean and in its own place. Yet here was a novel on the floor. I picked it up and absent-mindedly flipped through some pages; I stopped at an arrow pointing from a passage Reetika Vazirani had underlined to her comment in the margin: *How could she write sentences like this? She should he pilloried on the t.v. news. It can't be forgiven.* I thought to myself, this might otherwise be laughable, evidence of a critical mind in high dudgeon, an exasperated bitchiness; yet given the circumstances I had to sit down.

Turning the swivel chair to the desk, I went through the pages of the novel, discovering underlined sentence after underlined sentence, as well as seemingly endless comment, some tactful and erudite, most expressing over-the-top outrage and dismissal of all worth. The inventory of suggested punishments for "poor sentences" was truly mindboggling.

Sitting there I happened to glance at the bookended line of upright black notebooks I had filled, and tucked in among them was a much smaller, squarish notebook. As I eventually discovered, this was one of thirty-three 3" x 5" black notebooks that Reetika Vazirani had hidden throughout the house. Ultimately they required a macabre sort of treasure hunt whose negative reward was a gut-wrenching and permanently regretful reading experience. In that first notebook alone, the iconography of Medusa-heads, gargoyles and clearly identifiable Hindu Gods and demagogues, some devouring children—let alone succinct rehearsals of the murder of her son by name in writing—were so grotesque that all I could manage was to stumble down to the second floor bathroom and vomit for a good half hour.

Given all this, it may sound preposterous to even suggest, let alone report that anything could be in the least solacing, even desperately so, while I lay there on the cold tiles (themselves soothing to the touch). But there, atop magazines and books on a small shelf, was a much larger-sized blue notebook, a journal, and I opened it up at random and read:

> You have given me the greatest gift, to be led into a house full of light & comfort, paintings, photographs, cd's, tea, books books books I am at peace now.
>
> This has been the greatest gift of all – to make a home like this

Perfectly suited for Jehan and me Two rooms to grow into
(top floor)

5:30 up
6:30 Yoga
8:00 breakfast
read & write
1:00 lunch
laundry
4:00 Jehan napped till 7:00
squandered most of the time piddling
(a good day)

. . . which at first glance seemed a direct address to my family, but may
have been a generalized prayerful declaration, I just cannot know.

In that blue notebook (whose paper-clipped note cynically read: *Save
for Howard*) were theological and fantasy-erotic musings, literary quo-
tations, accounts of dreams, arguments with a certain *Gremlin* (both
sides of their dialogue recorded), professional to-do lists, domestic
to-do lists. And a lot of obsessive consideration given to her "roller-
coaster experience of the humiliating vicissitudes and elusive rewards
of a writing life—"my ambitions are poison." To her quoting of
Borges, "Life is truthful appearances," she added, "I prefer untruthful
appearances."

Recovered a little, a little less dizzy and gotten to my feet, I reasoned
that, if there is one such small black notebook, there might be others,
and if there are others, I had better try and locate them. I started out
frantically and without design, moving through familiar rooms but
motivated by something, to say the least unprecedented let alone
completely alien to my sensibility, and felt within minutes that I was
more or less ransacking my own house. I sat on Emma's bed (where
Jehan had slept), taking deep breaths and understanding the need to
ratchet things down to a slower, more methodical pace—and then got
down on my hands and knees and found a notebook under the mattress
of my daughter's bed. The specific hostility put into that placement

sickened me all over again. I went down to the kitchen to drink a glass of ice water. When I opened the freezer compartment, there was a notebook; I hadn't noticed it earlier, there amidst the cartons of sorbet, sticks of butter, containers of pasta and bottles of vodka. But I just hadn't seen it.

I extended my search to the living room, where I found a notebook between two big books about Matisse. And inside the piano bench were three notebooks fastened together by a rubber band. Soon upstairs in the guest room, I found a notebook under a New Testament Bible she had borrowed from a neighbor. In the utility closet a notebook waited on top of the vacuum cleaner.

I cannot bear to complete this search in writing here, except to say that I saw and read enough in the first six or seven notebooks to be more than convinced that I did not want to know what was in the rest. In time—and I will come to it later in this writing—I realized that certain of the written passages found in these notebooks were forced into my memory. It was as if they had immediately graffitied themselves on a blank wall in my brain. I don't know how else to say it. These obscene mnemonic insistences were in the form of sentence fragments and every sort of bizarre nonsequitur, each with its resident sense of poetic compression and disconnect: *I have a devotional nature but my eye pencil draws tarantulas; I'm a chameleon selling my face; God is at the height of pretentiousness and balloon-faces shouldn't suffer that; take Pratma's Himalayan valium in order to talk in rectangles; flee from the post-traumatic muse-snatcher; Yoga didn't dispel biting trees; Lord I'm an unlucky detective; sleep in the kitchen but running low of jars to fill with unhappy days; nobody but me realized Buddha came back as a drawer; all gratitudes are now Gremlins buying organic for the church*—and: *inevitably I will derange my sanctuary.*

Did I suspect more notebooks might be found? There is absolutely no rhyme nor reason to the fact that I didn't. I could have been quite wrong and my family may have suffered for it. I had the notebooks on the living room couch. It was light out. Through the window I noticed a few neighbors walking past, on their way to the bus, or metro, or to the local Starbucks for a coffee, or breakfast at the diner. I wrapped the notebooks in five separate groupings inside newspaper Scotch-taped shut. I hated these notebooks, I'd never hated anything so much in my life; I was deeply embittered by them, I was shaking. I took them outside and burned them to ash in the garbage can in the alley that separated the rectory and the house. Peering through a window in the rectory, the Indian priest (in whom Reetika Vazirani had confided her mental precariousness; oh, had he only blessed Jehan with an intervention) watched the proceedings. A gaggle of kids on their way to Lafayette Elementary stepped right up to near the garbage can. One boy said, "That's a pretty cool idea," as if I'd started a bonfire on a lark, and his buddy said, "Yeah, maybe I should toss in my stupid take-home quiz!" They walked off down the block laughing and talking. Unnerved but also definitely relieved I sat on the porch and listened to the staccato cooing of the pair of mourning doves that, sitting close next to each other, were often seen on the telephone wire. And when I went back inside the house, it felt as if I had reclaimed the very air, just a little— the light was so lovely against the pastel floral patterns of the living room's overstuffed chairs and sofa. Half an hour of dreamless sleep; I woke to a hopeful sense of lessened sorrow.

Before Jane and Emma returned I had sent a message to an ornithologist friend travelling in arctic Canada around Hudson's Bay to tell her what had happened. She sent a message directly back to inform me that a Quagmiriut-Inuit shaman named Petrus Nuqac, whom I had known decades earlier, was "still very much at work." Much to my astonished gratitude, two days later Petrus Nuqac routed by mail-plane and jet liner from Churchill, Manitoba to Winnipeg, to Toronto and then to Washington, D.C. This was a remarkably arduous passage especially considering that Petrus had never before boarded an airplane of any sort, let alone left the arctic. Having traveled and sat in airports much of a day and night, he arrived by taxi to the house at about 11:00 a.m. Roughly seventy years of age, he was wearing blue jeans, a white shirt, shoes and socks, and a light brown sports jacket, "like a European" as he put it. His red-brown face was deeply furrowed. He had some English and I had some Inuit and we could communicate nicely. After I served him scrambled eggs with lox, potatoes, black coffee, we went out onto the front lawn. On lunch break five or six girls from the parochial school, each wearing a uniform of plaid skirt, black shoes, white blouse, stood on the sidewalk out front, curious as all get-out, to watch Petrus ceremoniously bury a caribou shoulder bone (how had he managed to get such a thing through customs?) traditionally used to fend off malevolent spirits, in the ground and chant forcefully in a high-pitched voice. Then Petrus and I sat on the front porch for a couple of hours. A young parochial school boy, probably detouring over from some assigned errand, stood on the first step leading up to the porch and said, "I heard you're an Eskimo?" Petrus walked right up to him and shook his hand and said, "It took me three airplanes to get here from Canada." I then called a taxi. And Petrus, carrying no luggage except a change of clothes in a plastic bag, went directly back to National Airport.

Later in the autumn, Rabbi Gerry Serota, along with Jody and other close friends, gathered in the dining room, and while there were no forms of exorcism in Jewish religion appropriate to this occasion, Gerry had chosen compelling and beautiful Talmudic and Old Testament passages to read, and firmly instructed us to "not let someone else's sickness drive you from your own home." That is just how he put it and I was grateful for his candor. It went pretty well, given the stressfulness and tears, and not a little resurrection of unease, and it was nice to then have some food and drink in the living room and laugh it up a little. What Petrus and Gerry had offered was poignant and necessary; we'd take every form of blessing we could get. That night I went back to typing letters at the dining room table.

There's a superstition influential in parts of Nova Scotia, that if you want to keep unwanted ghosts out, and wanted ghosts in, you place a scissors cross-wise so that it locks an attic window shut. Seven or eight hours after the rabbi's house-blessing I went up to the third-floor study and fixed a scissors cross-wise in the small window, it being the topmost window of the house.

Such strange things in the aftermath. For a month or so after moving back to Washington, D.C., each time I arrived home from my university teaching after dark, as I walked up the steps, I would experience a formal hallucination; through the dining room window I would see a shadow-woman and shadow-boy in the midst of what resembled a Balinese puppet-play, at once beautiful and tremendously disturbing. And what is more, I would always arrive at the very moment when the woman raised her closed fist high above her head and slow-motion arced it down upon the boy as he reached out for her. Then the boy would fall from view. To my great surprise, after a few times seeing this I more or less got used to it. And then in March or April of 2004,

132

roughly six months after the murder-suicide, these shadow-figures were, permanently as it turned out, gone from behind the window, as if the house itself had banished them.

Naturally, in private Jane and I spoke about moving – who would not?—, maybe renting a different house, judiciously trying to give full voice to the best financial and psychological reasons. And yet try as we might, mostly we talked around it. I think that it was very difficult and painful not only to speak about what had happened, but to admit having been blown so far off familiar navigated courses in life. What is more, our responses to this murder-suicide had revealed some aspects of our individual natures that were surprisingly different, not opposed to each other, exactly, but quite different. In every vital sense, we were on the same page. But I suspect, too, we were loath to credit that sordid and pernicious act as necessitating anything but our perfect togetherness in order for us to endure. In the end this too would pass; still, since July 16 each day had required that we fend off estrangements from familiar life, even if they couldn't all be named.

When we convinced each other that doing the radio broadcast with Susan Stamberg would, among other things, exhibit to our friends that we were doing okay, we in fact both had deeply rooted reservations, but mutual encouragement was more important. No regrets there at all, none. However, when I listened to the interview, I heard the contrast between Jane's pointillist honesty and my own impressionistic decorum. I recognized Jane's intimate use of house/body metaphor and my own reliance on ancient parable and literary quotation to articulate what I myself could not. During that interview and in life in general, I was so afraid of self-inflicted despondency that I would outsource all useful insight to others, rather than claim ownership of any original thinking on how to feel things deeply and say things clearly enough for myself. I started to feel beaten down; all of my reasoning and emotions were generic. However, I did know one thing: out of some ridiculously misguided attempt to remain stoical, I was making myself sick, habituated as I had become to keeping so much sadness, let alone seething anger toward Reetika Vazirani, in a kind of parenthetical regard. I should better have stood on the coast of Nova Scotia and screamed.

On the far more healthy end of the spectrum, Jane was able to dignify her own feelings, a woman whose house was so violated, and pay honest and forthright attention to her concern that all this pain might have lasting effects on trust and love and even destroy parts of one's very soul and even something between us. And come to think of it, the first time I listened alone to our radio interview, I no doubt tried to determine if we ourselves were okay. And I thought, well, yes and no.

As for the wisdom of the ages stuff, my therapist said, "For all the lovely altruism of that proverb you keep referring to, *If you are walking down the road and see someone else's house on fire*—all well and good, Mr. Norman. But in fact it was your house that was violated. You aren't victims, nor are you suggesting anything of the sort—but it was your house. If you want to rely on a platitude, why not try, *No good deed goes unpunished*, and see what connection to the truth that provides."

An unforgivable thing had happened. Yet though we were definitely in emotional limbo, life moved on and life moved on; we had book parties, Emma's sleepovers, dinners, a number of literary-work sojourns apart, Jane and I, saving-grace periods of time in Vermont, a slow slow return to normal life. But the thing was, since our house—our actual address—was made so public, it meant that quite a lot of people we had never met knew where to send mail. In the old life, when any letter would arrive, I opened it right away, but after the murder-suicide, I pretty much came to dread the mail; if a letter had an unfamiliar return name or address, I'd hesitate, sometimes for days, even weeks. One night, looking in a desultory way at a bunch of letters in a basket on my desk, it occurred to me I was treating each day as if I'd been away on work, or vacation, and had arrived home to face a lot of mail. I tossed all of those letters out unopened.

Dozens and dozens of communications—emails, letters, telephone calls—located our house; and some people even posted their treatises on what had happened there on-line. I could only imagine the types of dialogues in full cacophony throughout the extended literary community. This was human nature, I suppose, the human condition. Speculations, hear say, eulogies, recriminations. I tried to look at all this opinion—(as best as I could tell) from knowledgeable friends of the poet, but also sympathetic acquaintances, arm-chair psychologists, hagiographers—as a kind of choral arrangement, a tremendous singing out of innumerable and very conflicted condolences. After all, the phenomenon of artist-murderer, historically speaking, has always been a magnet for all manner of inquiry and debate. But in the end I felt that not only was this public outpouring of emotion inevitable, but an attempt to compose the fullest, if still fragmented biography possible of Reetika Vazirani's life and put it to rest. Still, I feel obligated to express my dumbfoundedness that Jehan was so seldom mentioned. Though novelist Percival Everett said, straight from the heart, "Why couldn't she have at least let her son live? I am still angry because there were so many ways not to hurt the child. I am sick with the knowledge that his sweet life is over."

I must say, many of these communiques contained what often felt like a malignant sort of presumptuousness, like there was some sort of shared conviction that my family somehow needed or wanted to collate other people's lettered, and unlettered, opinions into meaningful comprehension of the childhood, upbringing, failed relationships, ambitions and secrets of this near-total stranger, Reetika Vazirani, or that we had a kinship fascination—always dubious—about the equations between art and madness. It would have been better had many of those people folded and tucked their opinions into self-addressed envelopes and sent them to themselves; years later, they might then read what they originally thought and determine, with perhaps less dissembling, if they had changed their minds.

However, I would also say, even given the sporadic and modest attention I paid to such things, that on the whole, these communiqués fell into recognizable categories of regard: a popular sentiment among them was that Reetika Vazirani's cultural bifurcation (her primary family left Pujab in 1968 when she was six) had somehow mutated into a full-blown bi-polar condition. About the so-called (in her own journal) "immigrant condition"—a transitory heart—Reetika Vazirani's sister, Deepika, thought that in her writings her sister "—magnified her experience. Maybe she needed a compelling, even fashionable subject. Whatever the reason, Otherness became an enduring theme." And a lot of people felt the need to suggest that Reetika Vazirani was somehow fatally trapped between viciously contending elements—there was sheer ambition ("Create a buzz around yourself—that's what I did."), there were money-worries intensifying the difficulties of single motherhood, and there was antecedent madness—her own father had committed suicide. And add to all that her despair about her relationship with Jehan's father, a distinguished poet who lived apart from her and her son.

Perhaps most predictably, literary ambulance-chasers had all sorts of insights about Reetika Vazirani's lines and stanzas, some even suggesting that, when they were closely deciphered, what would come to light was that her writing all along had exhibited, as one correspondent put it, a "posthumous aspect," as if it consisted of pre-dated keenings from the afterlife. However, no poetry is written posthumously, it is only published so, and to suggest that she had clairvoyant powers in retrospect is, sorry, plainly stupid. No, Reetika Vazirani haunted her own writing in real-time; she was no ghost at the typewriter, but held her pen in a living hand.

A number of crazies came out of the woodwork. For example there was the woman who, in a telephone call, claimed she was representing The British Sylvia Plath Society and wanted to "drop by for a little chat." In yet another telephone call the leader of a "Hindu Prayer Circle" inquired as to the possibility of holding their monthly meeting in our house. A doctoral candidate at a college in Brooklyn—again on the telephone—said that her thesis was on "creativity and suicide," and asked if she could take photographs of our dining room and, in addition, if we might provide photographs "from—you know, before. Just so I can have a mode of comparison." A minor performance artist from southern California sent an invitation to attend a performance of *Medea*, in which she somehow played all the parts. And then there was the time I picked up the telephone and heard a woman say, "Hello, I'm a teacher and scholar from Pakistan. And I'm writing about what V.S. Naipaul called forensic memoir." I immediately hung up. What could she possibly have wanted? A letter arrived asking us to vacate our house for an evening so that a group who held seances "specializing in artists" could carry out its mandate. The producer of a television show about paranormal activity found me having a cup of coffee in the café at Politics & Prose bookstore, and was all excited to set up a camera and lighting crew in the dining room of my house: "We're the least invasive of any of the programs in our field."

More and more and more and more .To the point where I wondered, my goodness, what sort of world do we live in? But, really, what did I know for sure? What did I really know? Perhaps only that this thing had been visited upon us; that my deepest sympathies lay with my wife and daughter; that next on my hierarchy of sympathetic response were friends and family who felt deeply for us; and I knew that violence of this nature had occurred through the millennia, in countless numbers of houses, in countless cities and villages, and unfortunately in our house, too. I also knew that no single fact could possibly provide any—my most despised word—closure; but it might allow for perspective.

A year went by.

I think I can honestly say, that for the most part I did not allow myself to expect life to contain, for quite some time to come, as much joy as one previously felt, and believed that to expect otherwise would almost require a new category of optimism. The scaffolding, the framework for joy, had been rebuilt; it was rickety; I hadn't dared to climb up on it yet. When I use the word "joy" here, I mean a reliable, compelling and, yes, at times even transcendent duet between a melancholy natural to my character, and irony. It's just my own definition, of course. So that, when I sat up late into the night and thought about it, I realized that over the previous year, in the main when joy arrived, it was more a simulacrum. Almost recognizeable as joy but not quite. I thought, well, at least I noted the problem, the frustration, the longing to change this condition. As early as age nineteen, on my first visit to Point Reyes National Seashore, I discovered that watching shore birds was a trusted way of transforming a simulacrum of joy into, at least by my lights, authentic joy. And now I wanted joy back, pure and simple, because if you don't have it, you start to experience what Keats called "a posthumous existence." I was terribly afraid of this.

One of my favorite writers, Akutagawa Ryūnosuke, asked, "What good is intelligence if you cannot discover a useful melancholy?" I've personally found that melancholy can often be an intensifying element in humor and, conversely, that humor can, as Ryūnosuke suggests, make melancholy more useful in refining a philosophy of life.

And so in early July of 2004 I traveled out to California to look at shore birds. Jane stayed in Vermont, still shell-shocked but writing poems again—living her life. Emma was taking a zillion photographs, and she would soon have friends staying in the farmhouse, while they rehearsed *Hamlette* (a female-centered and outlandishly comic version of *Hamlet*) to be performed in Craftsbury Common, Vermont, where, all summer, a new steeple and steeple bell were being installed in the Methodist church.

From the San Francisco airport, I drove a rental car north on Route 1, past Muir Woods, stopped for lunch in Stinson Beach, and then continued on to Olema. I set up at The Olema Inn and by two o'clock was at McClure's Beach near Pierce Point Historic Ranch, all of which is part of the Point Reyes National Seashore. To put it in spiritual terms, to me Point Reyes is heaven on earth; for thirty-some years I had consulted field guides to birds, tide pools, beaches, wildflowers, insects, weather with the devotion others may feel in relation to the Bible.

Throughout that first afternoon at McClure's Beach, the heat was counterbalanced by sea breezes, whitecaps glinted in the sun and the sea alternated between blue-grey and blue, depending on how the light presented it. In small flocks and individual presences, flying in, flying off, skittering along the beach. I saw sandpipers, dowitchers, surfbirds, willets, tattlers, turnstones, plovers; at times they made for a riotous neighborhood of birds; then, as if a cross-wind had erased all life, the beach was suddenly bereft of shore birds. I loved as I always have loved watching sanderlings hustle about and forage with their bills as if trying to stitch in place the wavering margin between tide and beach, a margin which soaks away with every wave. (I wondered once if this was the inspiration for invisible ink.) And high aloft over the cliffs hawks and vultures were kiting the thermals. Late afternoon I saw an enormous charcoal-hued and zeppelin-shaped cloud drop a curtain of rain, and this was spectrally backlit with light from the farther sea. And soon a flock of pelicans flew straight out of that rain, as if it was an ancient form of bathing. The pelicans arrived and congregated on the beach, bellying out individual hammocks of sand, muttering, bickering, bill-clacking, and then all at once shut down all utterances, tucking into themselves for a communal nap.

I spent the next couple of hours mucking about the tide pools, taking in the sun, not doing much at all, trying not to think, trying not to think, and then in the light of early dusk a western oystercatcher landed on a small rock island and emitted its characteristic piping whistle, *quee-ap quee-ap wee-o*. This bird is dusty black and has pale legs, a bright orange bill and a rim of orange-red around its eyes. And as I watched this oystercatcher probed every nook and cranny, concentrated every use of its bill, poking, jabbing, laboring to pry up the most tenaciously adhesive of mollusks.

Slowly the exhaustions of travel, the drowsiness from sun and sea air accumulated and I almost fell asleep standing up, though, noting the condition of the tide, I walked back up from the water thirty or so yards and dozed off, only to be woken in late dusk by a cacophony of upwards of at least fifty sea gulls. There were three different species of gulls and all had been drawn to a dead dolphin. The dolphin, now dull skinned and splotched with sand, must have tumbled in while I was asleep. At their rapacious scavenging the gulls were surprisingly unfazed by a rather tall woman, dressed in a dark green rain slicker, blue jeans, laceless hiking boots, her dark blonde hair tied at the top of her head in a dreadlocked mop, standing not more than five feet away from the dolphin. She was working a tripod camera. Now and then, as I watched through binoculars, I saw a gull feign a skirmish with the photographer, hovering mid-air, cough-shrieking like a rusty well-pump, and yet the woman merely went on adjusting her lens, taking photographs of the dolphin, jotting something in her notebook tied by a string to her belt. I watched this until most of the daylight was out over the sea and the cliffs threw shadows on the beach, and then I set out for the trail back up to the gravel parking lot. At the top of the rise, when I turned to look back, there was just enough light to see that many gulls were taloned to the dolphin, wildly flapping their wings as if trying to lift the dolphin and carry it away to a secret lair for the night; their squalls and cries echoed up the beach, as the photographer finally packed up her equipment. She lit a cigarette.

I drove back to the Olema Inn, seeing a bobcat scatter across the road into the tall, dry grass and weeds, and hawks perched on fence posts as the night came on fully. I had a mango salad at the inn's restaurant, then sat in jeans, tee shirt, light sweater and loafers on the side porch, drinking a glass of wine, watching swallows and the occasional bat zigzag and careen after insects. In the cooling night air the fragrance of a nearby stand of eucalyptus was deeply—and familiarly— stirring, and I felt gratified that the day had gone as it had. Then, at around 8:30 a claptrap 1960's Volvo, with two hubcaps missing and a faulty muffler, pulled into the parking area, and when its driver crouched out I saw that it was the photographer. She carried her tripod camera and a leather satchel, her boots slung around her neck, and she was barefoot. When she stepped up to the porch I said, "You were with that dolphin, right?"

"Oh, that was you," she said. "Yeah, I noticed somebody up the beach. I was annoyed. I prefer to be out there alone. I'm usually out there alone."

"Join the club."

She reached out her hand for me to shake and said, "I'm Halley, last name's spelled S-h-a-g-r-a-n—pronounced chagrin."

I laughed and introduced myself. "Does your last name explain why you're drawn to sad sights like that dolphin?"

"Wow, that's pretty funny," she said. "And pretty personal. But you know what? That dolphin was definitely not a sad sight for me."

"How so?"

"Because—death happens in nature and I like to take pictures of it. The way I look at it, the beaches are always full of such news, natural history news I call it. The dolphin was like an obituary from the sea. There's hundreds a day."

"Interesting, how you put things."

"Interesting or not, that's my thinking. Know what else? I don't mind calling myself a nature photographer. I don't mind if somebody buys a photograph of mine because they enjoy nature. That's cool. Life for me has a spiritual affirmation and so does death. That was an ear-full, huh?"

"I'd like to see some of your work."

"I only use black-and-white film. And you know what?—and I can't verify this—I only dream in black and white, I'm pretty sure. My husband Sonam says that in a past life I was color blind. He tends to say stuff like that. He's a Buddhist. I mean a Tibetan Buddhist. I mean a born-and-raised in Tibet Buddhist."

"Did you meet in Tibet?"

Halley sat on the bench beside me; an acrid whiff of what had to be the dolphin snapped in my nostrils, and when Halley noticed me noticing this, she said, "Yeah, well, I was just going up for a bath. But to answer your question, no, we didn't meet in Tibet. But we got married there. No, I'd been teaching an introduction to photography class on the U-C Berkeley campus. Sonam was late for a lecture he was giving in physiology, he'd got lost trying to find the lecture room, and he wandered in. I was in the dark room and one of my students sent him in to get directions from me. but I didn't know where his lecture room was, either. He had the wrong part of campus, I told him that much. But that's how we first met. After that he came to the dark room, like, twenty days in a row or something."

"Thanks for telling me. It's a good story."

"Sonam and I live in Mendocino, but I'm photographing here at Point Reyes so often, it's sort of home-away-from-home, right? My husband has a medical practice that keeps him very busy."

"What kind of medicine does he practice?"

"Regular old general practitioner, though I guess that's kinda rare these days, huh? He went to medical school in London. A lot of people hear that my husband's Tibetan and right away they figure he's into some kind of freaky-deaky medicine. And sure, he tells patients to try alternative medicines of all sorts if they want. Of course he does. And he's even studying serious acupuncture. But he'd always wanted just to put out a shingle like in a Norman Rockwell painting, you know? Except our little family joke is, Norman Rockwell never painted Tibetans."

"What does Sonam think of your photographs—that's personal, I know."

"Why not ask him yourself? You could have dinner with us."

"That's nice of you, but the restaurant here's a bit pricey."

"How about that little white clapboard place near the turn-off to Inverness?"

"Pretty late for dinner, isn't it, or not?"

"How's nine o'clock—they serve till nine-thirty. Come on. Sonam will be pleased. He says I'm an antisocial hermit. *Hermitesse.*"

With obviously long-practised dispatch Halley unraveled her dreadlocks into a waterfall of hair and said, "I'm surprised a sea gull didn't fall out."

I went up to my room to put on a pair of socks and grab a jacket. My notebook was open to four lines of the Robert Frost poem, "A Servant To Servants"—*He says the best way out is always through/ And I agree to that, or in so far/As I can see no way out but through/ Leastways for me*—which I had xeroxed and taped to a page. . . . *the best way out is always through* had become a kind of talisman along the journey between the murder-suicide and, so far, this very moment in Room One of the Olema Inn. I read through the lines again and went down to my car.

It was interesting having dinner with Halley and Sonam. Every table in the place was occupied; the menu was in French and English, and we had a waitress who alerted us to her limited tolerances, after a long night of waiting tables—"If any of you are in the mood to practice your French, I'm not." Sonam ordered in French and so did Halley, but I did not have the language. Our table was on the slatwood veranda near a eucalyptus tree. Sonam was fifteen years older than Halley and at least five inches shorter. He was neatly dressed in grey jeans, starched white shirt, penny loafers. He had a handsome face, short-cropped, black hair, and sported round tortoise-shell glasses. "Halley thinks I look like Mr. Moto in these specs," he said. We chatted about this and that; Sonam asked what sort of books I wrote, and when our food arrived, Halley said, "Sonam, our new friend here asked me what you thought of my photographs."

Frowning in an exaggerated way, Sonam said, "Well, do you mean my opinion of her technical skills and the aesthetic quality of her pictures? Or what it's like to have a house full of—let's see: seagulls torn to shreds, festering whale carcasses, seals with hollowed-out eye sockets, ummm, let's see, what else? Oh, yes, there's an eviscerated bobcat, vultures poking their heads inside a mule deer—and Halley told me you saw her hanging around a dolphin today."

I set down my fork and stared at my food as if I'd lost my appetite. "Maybe I shouldn't have asked the question," I said, and there was laughter all around.

"Actually, Halley sees herself as a—darling, how do you say it? A chronicler of transitional states."

"Meaning," I said, "you think the dolphin was on its way to being reincarnated."

"Yep, transitional could mean that," Halley said. "But it could also mean just turning into organic stuff, you know? Food for beetles. Seagulls turning it to shit that drops on your windshield. It's all pretty straightforward, don't you think?"

"As for the artistic part," Sonam said, "I'm her greatest admirer."

"By the way, what were you doing out there today?" Halley said. "Are you a birder, God help us. Probably not the sort I hate, because you had those cheap-o field glasses."

"No, not that sort of birder, if I understand you correctly. Though I'd love a better pair of binoculars, that's for sure."

I suppose I could have delicately alluded to, even in a way that might more honestly address Halley's question but at the same time indicate my discomfort in dwelling on the subject, the haunting incident that had occurred in my house. In turn I could have said that I'd come out to Point Reyes to get lost and found in shore birds, to walk every trail until I could hardly walk another step, to empty out physically and mentally, then get filled again. But for goodness sake, if the best way out was always through, it didn't mean one couldn't afford taking a moment away from the effort; besides, I thought that to foist all that bleak reference on these kind, interesting folks at our candlelit table, with a full moon rising, during such a get-to-know-each other meal, would be, as we said in the 60's, too heavy. Still, I'd had a little too much wine and said, "Out at McClure's Beach, I wanted to be invisible, just for a few hours, sit out there on the rocks, all that sun and big waves, and sit right next to an oystercatcher, and it would look up every so often, sensing something was there, but then go about being an oystercatcher again"— and I don't know what got into me, but I added, "amen."

My little existential riff had the effect, as is sometimes the case when something of staggering pretentiousness, or insufferable sentimentality, however genuine, is spoken; it caused an eyes-cast-to-table silence for a moment. Sonam ordered espresso for himself and Halley.

"You know," Halley said, "I might have two or three photographs of oystercatchers. Sonam, would you mind looking in my studio when you get home tomorrow. You know, the photographs are filed away in alphabetical order. If you find oystercatchers, bring them back Friday so our friend here can have a look."

After dinner I sat back on the porch of the inn; the late night air drew out the fragrance of eucalyptus even more intensely; I thought of Nabokov's phrase, "memory perfume." The inn's resident, almost lynx-sized cat, Truffle, bounded up onto my lap, a very well-fed animal, and settled in nicely; she allowed me to comb her back with my fingers, and whenever I made the effort to lift and set her down, she dug in with her claws; I quickly understood that this cat would decide when she was through with me. Mulling it over, I was not so sure that I wanted to see photographs of dead oystercatchers, just when I was becoming so engaged with the oystercatcher I'd seen at McClure's Beach and hoped to see much of during the next ten days. Perhaps Sonam wouldn't locate the photographs. I hoped he wouldn't.

But sitting in the eucalyptus breeze, feeling Truffle's growl-purr roll in a kind of gentle, seismic wave head to tail, nothing to do but wait for the familiar, advanced signs of insomnia, I thought hard and with some uneasiness, about why I had been so willing to subscribe to Halley's reductionist philosophies of life and death, and why I couldn't muster up a more natural-to-my-character caustic, or at least probing response, if not in actual conversation then in private consideration. Of course we'd really just met, but that was not it. I think maybe Halley's platitudes were solacing, in the way a landscape can be solacing—if you are fortunate and willing, you live inside it with perfect equanimity.

At dinner I'd been impressed by Halley's phrase "eddies of wet feathers" to describe what she was reminded of when she looked at her photograph of a dead crow she'd recently developed in a dark room in Pt. Reyes Station. When I went back up to my room about 2 a.m., the photograph itself was leaning against my door. Taped to it was a note: *See the moon? It's about 1:30 a.m. now and in an hour I'm heading out to McClure's Beach. Sonam may or may not go with me. Nobody's supposed to be out there at night but you can only see certain things at night. So that's where I'll be—since you seem interested in my work. By the way, oystercatchers sometimes are active at night, if there's a big moon and so on, little known fact. But I've seen that. Halley.*

Generous invitation, I thought, and sat down on the overstuffed chair, switched on the floor lamp and looked at the photograph. I saw the eddies; three stilled whorls of black feathers on the crow's mangled body, each as if sculpted by a water-spout. Studying the photograph, I went from being almost repelled by the eerie vortexes to imagining what a mercy it must have been for that bird to blink out of consciousness, let alone perish, all evidence indicating ("Almost every bone was broken," Halley had said) that the crow had been tumultuously storm-tossed, spun and plummeted to the ground. In other words, I was beginning to see things from Halley's point-of-view and in that was some reprieve, because I was so goddamn sick and tired of all my own morbid distress about life and death, this painful dislocation of the soul.

I set aside the photograph, took up my paperback collection of Frost's poems and read through the entirety of "A Servant to Servants" (whose narrator admits: *yes, I've been away. The state asylum*) and while reading heard mourning doves, which I'd never heard before at night. Just in the past five minutes my new education in birds—Halley's experience of seeing oystercatchers, and my hearing the doves—made for interesting speculations about the role of moonlight in extending the diurnal activities of birds on into the nighttime hours. I fell asleep in my clothes cross-wise on the bed.

Now, I'm more than aware that relating a dream makes most people's eyes glaze over with incredulous boredom so that they begin to morph into the figure on the bridge in Edvard Munch's "The Scream." But the dream of mine I want to tell illustrates Rilke's idea that "the unspeakable is quite capable of intervening on any normal day of waking, breathing in the hours, and dreaming." Anyway, my dream was set in a Chinese restaurant in the North Beach section of San Francisco; I recognized the location because, looking out the window, I saw City Lights Books. Sonam, Halley and I had just completed a feast; bowls, plates, chop-sticks, glasses and tea cups were on the table. Sonam and Halley read their fortunes and shared them with each other; Halley looked at me and said, "Same old, same old." Suddenly, out of nowhere, an ancient-looking hag with beautiful cat's eyes—I think they were Truffle's, the Olema Inn's cat—threw herself onto our table. Shocked, frightened, Halley and Sonam pushed back from the table. The old woman clamped my face between her hands (the texture was like sandpaper) and shouted, "I BEG YOU DON'T READ YOUR FORTUNES! DON'T READ YOUR FORTUNES!" Definitely I was aware of being puzzled as to why she used the plural fortunes, since there was only a single fortune cookie remaining in the porcelain bowl. Then, in a phantasmagoric locution, a squalling flock of sea gulls flew in, lit on the hag's shoulders and carried her off out the door and in the direction of the ocean.

The restaurant, absent waiters, cooks, other customers, was now fog-ridden and cold. For some reason I snapped open my fortune cookie; a bunch of fortunes sprang out as if a heart attack surprise from a jack-in-the-box, each one caught by the tongue of a magnificently painted dragon on the ceiling. A wooden ladder with wheels presented itself; I climbed it to the top rung and read the fortunes, dragon mouth to dragon mouth. As it turned out they were not the sardonic witticisms or pre-fabricated proverbs we generally associate with fortune cookies. Instead, they were—and I comprehended it right then and there in the dream—replications of entries in those 3" x 5" black notebooks Reetika Vazirani had tried to hide, or hide in plain sight.

I startled awake in the bed at the Olema Inn, sweating with a terrible headache—the knowledge of what those fortune cookies contained having crossed over into consciousness. The bedside alarm clock read 3:50 a.m.; I could hear the voice of an owl, but that lovely sound did not prevent me from feeling disoriented near to the point of weeping; my thoughts were frazzled, and I said to myself, "Look, you can't help where your mind goes in sleep." The telephone on the table rang; it was the front desk, the night-clerk reporting that my next door neighbors in Room Two had lodged a complaint about "loud talk—even screaming." I apologized but did not say that I had obviously had a nightmare. I thought the best thing would be to drive out to McClure's Beach. To see what Halley Chagrin might be up to. To extend the day and evening that was so rudely interrupted, take in the night air, the moonlight.

Half way on my drive to Pierce Point Historic Ranch, I experienced a reprise of the all-too-familiar cramped tightening of gloom in my stomach, a minor attack of nausea, the sense of a threaded pulse, and had to immediately park in a turn-off along the road. I got out and stood leaning against the car, taking in as deep breaths as I could. What was this? What was happening? The moon was so beautiful out over the ocean. There was a strong wind off the sea, a shushing whisper of it in the conifers close-by to my right, and far off in the distance to my left, the constellation of lights and vague outline of a behemoth freighter slowly moving north.

Headache notwithstanding, I got back in the car and drove slowly, and when I got to Pierce Point Historic Ranch and again parked in the lot, I took up an industrial flashlight, got out and followed the flashlight's long and wide beam down the path to McClure's Beach. At the end of the path I saw that moonlight seemed literally to be flooding the beach, but there was no sign of Halley, and I hadn't seen her car anywhere in the vicinity of Pierce Point Historic Ranch, either. I walked on the beach toward the cliffs. Sprawling, tentacled Medusa-bulbs of kelp lay here and there—you can actually slip on them. I walked close past the dolphin, which, on quick inspection by flashlight, had been considerably picked apart though there was certainly more for the carrion gulls at first light.

I continued on to the stretch of beach between the cliffs and the archipelago of small rock islands where I'd seen the oystercatcher. Feeling on my skin the cold balm of fog, I ventured out onto a peninsula of coral-jagged rock and stood there, hoping the sea breezes would move straight through my head ear to ear, taking those horrid fortunes with it. And that is when I heard the oystercatcher.

Was it the same one? I thought it must be, since oystercatchers are solitary and territorial birds. While at first I couldn't locate the oystercatcher in the gauzy, spectral light, I continued to hear its plaintive *quee-ap quee-ap*. And after ten or so minutes I saw the bird itself, and seeing it, recognized the ventriloqual talents of the beach at night—the

146

oystercatcher *sounded* like it was further north than it actually was. I moved twenty or so yards up from the peninsula, huddled in a rain slicker and blanket on dry sand beneath the cliffs, where I stayed the rest of the night, the oystercatcher appearing and disappearing, until the mist burned off and the world—with its ocean light, pelicans flying in formation low to the water, and seals bobbing off-shore as background and its dead dolphin foregrounded—for the time being stood in repose and as yet free of gulls.

Roughly an hour after dawn broke the oystercatcher flew off but was back within the hour. Where had it gone? The oystercatcher began to work its rock island again. I watched its frantic industriousness, its fluttering up a foot or two and back down, its preening, and then Halley showed up with her camera and notebook.

Postcards, telephone calls, the poems of Robert Frost kept me connected to Vermont but by and large I felt a resident, for those ten days, in Point Reyes National Seashore. I had even taken to wearing a tee shirt with my favorite painting depicted on it, Milton Avery's "California Landscape/Seascape," with its enclave of house and outbuildings situated above a steep-cliffed horseshoe shaped inlet, surrounded by fields of tawny brown and yellow dry grasses. And during the next eight days—and all through two nights—I accompanied Halley Shagran on her photographic traipses, along beach and trails, through wetlands and woodland, all of which had been, after all of my many visits to this preserve, as familiar as the palm of my hand. Yet as she narrated her own past experiences, railed against local anti-conservationists, imparted all sorts of zoological and botanical information, I came to see these old familiar places in a new light. "Let's face it," she said, "I take photographic autopsies and never run out of subject matter." I even became affectionately accustomed to her off-beat humor. Simply put, I came to feel that by being so artistically absorbed in it, Halley didn't fall under death's spell but cast her own spell on death. I watched her photograph gulls, pelicans, weasels, seals, sea lions, fox, kestrel, mule deer, axis deer, butterflies, beetles, cattle, each animal discovered in its final posture, stage of decomposition, with its fixed stare, agonized or oddly peaceful expression, its corporeal disarray. All of which eventually would be depicted in black and white, like negatives of creation itself, in the photographs Halley developed late into most nights in the darkroom at Point Reyes Station.

My best estimation is, that separate from my time with Halley, I watched my oystercatcher roughly fifty hours on that visit. The oystercatcher's existence offered me a hypnotic passing of time, vicariousness (its connection to the sea), focus, distraction, sorrow, laughter, tears, all helping to move me *through* and escape the grasp of servitude to the fixed notion that only pain and sorrow are real truths, and that joy especially exists only to be subject to doubt. That is, at least in some provisional way, after all those hours in the realm of the oystercatcher, I was feeling joy as opposed to a simulacrum of joy, and that might just warrant use of the word *healing*. Maybe or maybe not. On my last afternoon at McClure's Beach I thought that when the spirit of this wonderful oystercatcher transitions, I hope it becomes an oystercatcher.

As I write this in August of 2010, in a house in Inverness, California, in the early morning hours, with deer nibbling apples fallen from a remarkably craggy tree, a flock of pelicans in view sky-high over Tomales Bay, a stack of letters on the dining room table, a manual typewriter there, too, and having had a breakfast of orange juice, cranberry scones and coffee, I'm reading the posthumously published collection of poems, *Radha Says*, written by Reetika Vazirani. I notice that many of the poems utilize, as part of their narrative strategy, a broken-line form, caesuras imposing what Igor Stravinsky called "the exigencies of an interval." In part what he meant was that silence between musical notes contains as much complexity, as much earned and rendered feeling, as the notes themselves. You could argue that the same idea applies to Morse Code delivering a condition of alarm.

Certainly I am the farthest thing from a poet; still, I subscribe to what W.H. Auden thought, that truly original poetry is the purest air language can breathe, and to sully that air by "melodramatizing the abject soul" makes fraudulent claims on the reader's heart. And I subscribe to what Zadie Smith wrote: "No geographic or racial qualifications guarantee a writer her subject. Only interest, knowledge and love will do that." And I am recalling what Alfred de Vigny wrote: "A calm despair is the essence of wisdom."

With these devoted beliefs and assertions like sentinels, vigilant, posted near at hand—as though standing just yards away on the wooden veranda of this house—I struggle and re-read, struggle and re-read.

Finally I detect faint suggestions of joy in many of the persona poems, with their voices of the 19th Century Urdu poet Ghalib and the Radha of Hindu epic, though I also find much theosophical misanthropy. I suppose that I experience this whole collection as a libretto for the staging of a garish mytho-opera, with each poem an evocation of real suffering. But more down-to-earth, while reading I kept picturing a woman in India; perhaps a poet, perhaps not. She stood in a room in a house, on a woven rug, an heirloom tapestry tread upon by children and adults—possibly representing the sheer fabric of daily life—that was worn threadbare, definitely unraveling.

My sentinels on the veranda are shooed away; be gone!—and sitting at the round glass-top table, in bare feet in the sun now, I am daydreaming the peacefulness of my farmhouse in Vermont, its gently curving road up to my neighbor's mail-boxes, mountains seen in the distance. I think of the wetlands near Port Medway, Nova Scotia, thunderstorms and fishing trawlers on the horizon. What to look forward to today? Well, for one thing, I will not leave this house; let the world arrive as it will; read the entirety of *The Apple Trees Of Olema* by Robert Hass, who lives just up the road, a lifetime of poems containing such indispensable human sadness and joy, and which are as sanely associative as the finest of Cezanne's paintings, and strike the deepest chords. There is a cleansing light over Tomales Bay after a night-long rain. A boy named Jehan's death seven years ago was not the fault of poetry. I close my eyes; there's the oystercatcher, just arriving to the same archipelago as always. It flies off, it returns. It flies off, and after a long time, during which I worry over its fate, it returns.

Nominated by Salmagundi

CRANES, MAFIOSOS AND A POLAROID CAMERA

by NATALIE DIAZ

from SPILLWAY

Kearney, Nebraska Crane Trust

I had a few days left of my stay at the crane sanctuary
in Kearney, Nebraska, when my brother called. It was 3:24 a.m.
It's me, he said. *It's your brother.* He had taken apart

another Polaroid camera and needed me to explain how
to put it back together. His voice was a snare drum, knocking
and quick. He was crying. I didn't want to wake the other visitors,

and I knew he'd keep calling, hour after hour, day after day, lifetime
after miserable lifetime, until I answered. I slid out of bed.
Half-sprinted half-leapt the hallway, into the common kitchen area.

Just tell me what to do. You know what to do, he pleaded.
I should know how to help my brother by now. He and I have had this
exact conversation before—if I love him, if I really love him,

why haven't I learned to reassemble a Polaroid camera?
Instead, I told him about the sandhill cranes, the way they dance—
moving into and giving way to one another, bowing down,

cresting and collapsing their wings, necks and shoulders silver
curls of smoky rhythm—but he didn't believe me. My brother believes
the mafia placed a transmitter deep within his Polaroid camera,

150

but he can't believe in dancing cranes. *You think this is a joke?*
he whispers. *These are fucking Mafiosos I'm talking about.*
You're probably next. He hung up on me. When the light went dead,

I caught my reflection in the sliding glass door—I was standing
in a strange kitchen, in front of a sink, in my underwear—
I have skinny legs and big feet. I resemble a crane.

That dawn, another writer aimed her digital camera at the sky
until the last of an island of late rising cranes lifted into the metallic
air—I couldn't take my eyes off the barrel of lens, the fast trigger

of her finger against the black skeleton of the camera. I wondered
what it would look like cracked open to its upside down mirrors
and shiny levers, how many screws there were, how many lantern–lit

cranes might come unfurling out of that cage. I wondered
what she and I would look like if the darkened chambers of our bodies
were unlocked. What streams of light might escape us and reveal

about the things we collect and hide, and is there a difference
between aperture and wound. Mostly, I wondered where my brother
keeps getting those goddamned Polaroid cameras.

Nominated by Spillway, Susan Terris

GOD OF DUCKS

fiction by TINA LOUISE BLEVINS

from THE GETTYSBURG REVIEW

The Saturday that Cindy walks out, they have made twelve hundred biscuits. They have laid forty-three portions of roast beef into plain white ramekins and baked them in groups of three until, even through the dish room's fog of warm water and half-eaten steak fries, the humble, peppery scent of bubbling gravy reaches their noses. Deftly they navigate the small space they share, covered in sweat and flour, their hair restrained by law, by white nylon nets. Chuck has to wear one to cover his beard and mustache. It is like having a second beard over the first, a white atop the gray. The biscuit cutter is industrial and outlines many biscuits at once; it is the size of a cookie sheet and has compartments, a stainless-steel honeycomb. Cindy is crying as she cuts the dough, wiping the sides of her latex gloves across her cheeks and leaving smudges of flour. Chuck wonders what she is thinking. When he gets off work, he always smells of butter and chicken stock. The smell lives deep inside his skin where soap doesn't reach, and sometimes he stands on the bathmat still glistening from his shower and looks in the mirror, grips the pale, soft mounds of fat around his stomach and thinks, I look like a dinner roll. I'm a biscuit with a dick.

"Goddamn rednecks," says Cindy. "Fuck this job."

"It's not the world's only job, you know," says Chuck, who has been at this restaurant twelve years.

"I can't get another job." Cindy wipes her nose on her sleeve. "My teeth are too jacked up."

It is true: Cindy is barely forty years old but has fewer than ten teeth remaining. Certain consonants become distorted as they slide past her gums, so that she sounds drunk when she talks. Some people at the restaurant do come to work drunk, and it took Chuck several weeks to realize Cindy wasn't one of them. Sobriety makes her a desirable employee in his book, though he supposes it might be a shock to see her at the grocery store checkout, or to hear her mangled country slur on the other end of a sex line.

"Your teeth aren't that bad."

"Your eyes are going, honey," she says. "Or else you're a nice guy, after all." She smiles a little then. Chuck thinks she could probably get a job in a haunted house, but that would only be seasonal.

Cindy makes it through three more roast beefs. If Bart hadn't come back to the cooking area, she might have made it through to the end of the shift. She would have gone home and smoked a joint and put up her aching feet, and by five the next morning, she would have been ready to come in again. But Bart rounds the corner by the salad cooler, wearing his shirt that is peach from one angle and pink from another. He is trying to grow a beard, and stubble covers his face like a spice rub.

"Hey, Cindy," he says. "Did you see we're out of biscuits?"

"Who do I look like, Stevie Wonder?"

Bart's eyes go narrow. "Excuse me?"

Chuck hunkers down over his kettle of green beans and tries to make himself seem smaller. It's no easy task.

Cindy has started crying again. "I said, you think I look like some blind-ass motherfucker? Biscuits are in the oven, and they can stay in there till they burn the place down for all I care!"

She is yelling now. Waitresses and dishwashers and grill cooks hover, not quite out of sight. Bart's entire face is red, his chest heaving, shirt flashing peach-pink-peach-pink. "Okay," he says. "In the office. Now."

"You go in the office. You go in the office and rub one out all over your fancy-ass paperwork. Fuck you. Fuck your biscuits." Cindy turns toward the kettle, peels back her lips in a quivering, decaying grin. "Bye, Chuck, honey. Jesus bless you and Margo."

And then she is gone. She has retrieved her purse from the break-room lockers and walked out into the evening sunlight. The front-porch vista has opened itself in front of her: motel windows with curtains just

153

parted, where travelers consult the local yellow pages; gray crisscross of town roads; cement roofs of gas stations; bulge of green mountains rolling down to the interstate as far as the eye can see. The air must be fresh. It must be a warm, humid afternoon. Chuck will have to pre-cook all the next morning's bacon himself.

Margo is fat. She is not a little fat; she is not fat like the women in diet pill commercials, who beam with pride as they hold up old pants only three sizes larger than their new pants. She does not pull out her wedding dress and cry when she sees how small it is. She is properly fat, her stomach hanging out from under her shirt grandiose and un-apologetic, her rear end so wide the toilet seat leaves red marks down the edges of her buttocks when she takes her "morning constitutional." She was fat when Chuck married her; in their wedding photos the fat on her arms covers her elbows like an overbite. Chuck does not mind this, nor is he ashamed to go out in public with her. Most of the people in this town are fat, anyway. He is a fair size himself, and he likes that his wife is a good cook. He does not want to cook when he is at home.

"You won't believe what happened this morning," Margo says. She is standing in front of the stove talking to Chuck, who is sitting on the living-room couch. The trailer is a '78; half of it is one room, and everything is wood paneled. On the walls are a plaster peacock, shelves of angel figurines, and a portrait of Margo's parents in horn-rimmed glasses.

"What happened?" says Chuck. He is reading *TV Guide*.

"The police came and arrested all those people in that blue trailer next door." She turns to look at him, lowers her voice. "They had a *meth lab* in there. Can you believe it? They could have blown us all to kingdom come."

"Trash," says Chuck.

Margo picks up a spatula and flips the fried squash. The sizzling spikes, then returns to a constant. "I just thought they had a lot of friends stop over."

Chuck smiles into the *TV Guide*. "I guess we could have got us some meth if we wanted."

"Charles!" Margo says, but then she laughs. "I could probably ask Randy for meth. I'm pretty sure I could." Randy works with Margo at

154

the KwikMart. Neither Margo nor Chuck has ever done drugs, not even marijuana.

"Cindy walked out in the middle of lunch."

Margo is peeping into the oven to check the tuna casserole. "No!" she says, straightening up and letting the door snap shut. "Was it that bad today?"

"It did suck, yeah." The cat, brown and also fat, jumps onto the couch. Chuck rubs its head, and it begins to purr. "She was crying a lot," he says. Once, Chuck went into the walk-in cooler and slammed frozen tilapia fillets against the wall until his fingers were numb, then told Bart he had accidentally dropped them. But at least he has never cried at work.

"That poor woman," says Margo, who has never met Cindy. "What will she do?"

Chuck lets the *TV Guide* lie open in his lap, stares at the peacock on the wall across from him. "I don't know," he says. "She's got a terrible mouth on her."

"Well surely she can keep quiet when she needs to."

"You don't understand," he says.

They eat dinner on the front porch, which is a concrete slab with two plastic lawn chairs and a doormat in the shape of an apple. Across the grass of their yard and behind a low wooden fence sits the blue trailer, yellow police tape wrapped around the railing of its leaning rear porch, back door hanging open to reveal the beige edge of a washing machine, a wood-paneled corner leading into a dark hallway. Weeds sprout skyward from the edge of the roof, and at the bottom of the back steps is a ceramic bear, paint chipping off its back.

"Don't they teach you how to close doors in the police academy?" says Chuck.

"They've got a washer," says Margo. She does laundry in town at the Launder-Land.

"They don't have it anymore."

"I guess not."

Chuck eats the tuna casserole; under the slick of egg noodles and cheddar cheese, he can taste Worcestershire sauce, chili powder, something tomato based. "Did you use Campbell's for this?" he says.

"Their tomato was on sale. I know you like the mushroom."

"It's okay," he says.

Twilight comes over the yard, and they linger, sipping glasses of milk.

The doorway of the other trailer becomes dark, police tape hanging vivid in the bluing like a crooked square halo. Chuck thinks about everything he will have to do in the morning since Cindy will not be there. It will be the day for making stuffing; he will have to begin the morning's bread like usual, then drag the day-old bread from the freezer and break it down for mixing with sage and poultry seasoning. He will have to bake extra muffins for the Sunday morning church crowd. There will be the meatloaves, the potato casserole, the roast beefs, the chicken soup, and so on. He will have to rub baking potatoes with shortening and sprinkle them with salt. His hands will be greasy, and he will wipe them all over his apron, and because there is no one to talk to, he will talk to himself, he will grumble and complain, he will sing the chorus of "Idiot Wind" under his breath as the whir of the bread machine fills the air.

Chuck has been in the restaurant business more than forty years. He has worked at bars and diners and strip clubs and family restaurants. He has cooked everything from manicotti to country ham to specialty fudge. Except for a period in '84, when he moonlighted as a janitor after the baby died, Chuck has only ever worked in food prep. He took his first job at sixteen, grilling for a diner on Court Street called Simon's. Chuck did burgers there, and catfish fillets, and pots of pork barbeque that masked the smell from the persistent cloud of second-hand smoke. When Kennedy was shot Chuck saw a man watch the news on the TV over the bar until the ash that hung from his cigarette became a fragile gray arc as long as a pinky finger. He thinks of the cigarette now, when he is sixty-two. Something has burned away and left the shape of him.

It is a hard week without Cindy. Wednesday night he gets behind on biscuits; waitresses with bottled red hair round his corner and argue with him. Thursday he drops a pan of raw beef on the floor, this time truly by accident, and has to file a food cost report. Over the weekend a woman who usually works in the dish room is assigned to help him, but she has not cooked for almost a year, and she ruins six batches of cornbread. Monday is his day off, but he has to come in anyway, because someone else is sick or just hungover. His eyes feel like he has dipped them in flour and put them back into their sockets.

"Chuck." It is Bart. His shirt is yellow today. He has given up on the beard and nicked himself shaving. There is a boy wearing an apron with him. "This is Luke. He's our new backup cook. Luke, Chuck'll be training you. He's been here since the restaurant opened."

Chuck shakes hands with Luke, who grins. He has all his teeth, which have braces on them. His hair is blond and curly, and one of his ears is pierced. Bart pats Chuck on the shoulder and walks back around the corner to the office, looking at something on a clipboard. Luke scratches his nose. "Hey," he says.

"How old are you?" says Chuck.

"Eighteen."

"Ever worked in a restaurant before?"

"Nope."

"Ever baked biscuits before?"

"Nope."

"Ever used an oven?"

"I've made frozen pizzas." Luke grins again, a grin that pretends to be sheepish but is confident underneath. He is not ashamed. From below his apron comes a buzzing sound, and he reaches into his pocket and pulls out a cell phone. He slides a keyboard out from under the screen and begins to type with his thumbs.

"There's no texting except in the break room," says Chuck.

"Hold on."

It is either hold on or tattle to Bart, so Chuck holds on. Luke laughs under his breath as he types, mutters something Chuck cannot hear.

"So what are you gonna do when you drop that thing into a kettle of collard greens, mister?" says Chuck.

"I won't hold it over a kettle of collard greens."

"The woman who worked here before you, Cindy? She could have bought a month of groceries for what that little gadget cost."

Luke pushes the keyboard in and puts the phone back in his pocket. He looks interested now, to a degree. "What happened to her?"

"She quit."

"Why?"

Chuck shrugs. "This place is a hole. Why did you come here?"

Luke pats his pocket. "I got phone bills. Payments on my car. My girlfriend wants to go places all the time."

Chuck has met Luke before. Not Luke specifically, but boys like Luke, and girls too. They pass through kitchens and dish rooms and grill lines in a never-ending flow, their numbers swelling in the summer and during the holidays, dwindling in Septembers and Januaries. They are putting in their time, sometimes out of real need, sometimes at their parents' insistence; this job, this series of hours spent scraping grease and exchanging dirty jokes, mopping up food scraps and peeling potatoes, this is their initiation to toil. After their stint they depart to fulfill their choice; they graduate from trade schools and universities. They go to their offices, salons, and workshops, leaving behind the world of the restaurant, pouring around it the salt of their joy like a spell cleaving dark and light.

"So was she hot?" says Luke.

"Who?"

"Cindy."

"She had nice teeth," says Chuck.

Luke is a decent worker, but he is not very bright. Chuck tries to explain to him that they must bake the cornbread at a different temperature than the one in the manual, because the manual is written for lower altitudes. Luke's corn muffins do not rise in golden mounds, but lie flat and hard, slide over the rims of their compartments and burn.

"How should I know what the fuck sea level is?" Luke is not angry. He is just using language. He spits the word out from around his braces, making it thick.

"From high school, you would think."

"I don't remember anything from high school. What is it?"

"It's the level of the sea," Chuck explains.

"We're nowhere near the sea."

"It's—it's just a unit of measurement, Luke. It measures how high up a place is. We're in the mountains, so that means we're high up, and we have to change our baking temperatures."

"Why?"

"Because of the air pressure."

"How can air have pressure if it's not inside a tire?"

"I don't know! It just does. It's science."

"Science fucking sucks."

The phone is a constant presence. Luke types with one hand while he stirs kettles with the other. If he is dicing onions, he will let the knife lie on the cutting board while he turns away from Chuck to pull out the phone, the backs of his bent elbows shaking ever so slightly from the movement of his thumbs. After a week, Chuck stops saying things about it, but he is baffled. He does not understand how Luke could have so much to talk about with his friends, or his girlfriend, or whomever he is texting. Chuck imagines having a cell phone, texting Margo while she is at home or at the KwikMart. "Out of BBQ today, shipment in tmrw. Burned finger on pan!" And she to him: "Randy says can get u-know-what lol."

Sometimes he and Luke work in silence, or with Luke singing along to the radio, which plays pop songs Chuck does not know. Luke dances when he sings, or half dances, moving his head up and down and tapping his feet, pivoting now and again as he moves across the aisle between the kettles and the steel table. He is never fatigued. He bounces and smiles. He thinks everything is funny. Sometimes, if the radio is tuned to the country station, they talk instead. Chuck tells stories he thinks Luke will like. He tells him about working at Love Shack, the strip club, and about a stripper named Daphne who got grabbed by a drunken lawyer, put her stiletto heel straight through his eye, and never went to jail for it. He tells Luke about the time he caught a grill on fire, how the grease flames towered six feet and set off all the sprinklers in the restaurant. Children were running and laughing as their parents tried to get them out the door while the manager told everyone to remain calm. Chuck used the fire extinguisher, which got chemical dust all over everything. In the dining room, half-eaten slices of toast grew wet like croutons in soup.

Luke is impressed. He says, "That's so badass!"

"It wasn't badass, mister. Somebody could have gotten hurt. I got fired."

"That sucks."

What Chuck does not say is that now, twenty years after the fact, he does tend to think of the grease fire as somewhat badass.

He also learns things about Luke. Luke's girlfriend's name is Kaleigh, and they have been dating for almost a year. Luke wants to be a pilot, but Kaleigh thinks he should become a pharmacy technician because the school is not so long. Luke's father is a jewelry salesman for a chain store, and his mother is dead. Every autumn his father takes him hiking, and they sprinkle a little more of his mother's ashes out into the New River Gorge.

"You can see the bridge from Long Point," Luke says. "She always had a picture of the bridge on her desk at home." He chops the celery

159

more neatly than usual, dividing the stalks with short, even cuts, with great attention.

Chuck tells Margo about Luke. Today, Luke jammed his finger on the mixer. Today, Luke pulled out his phone and showed me a picture of his dog. Luke was late, Luke gave me some lip, Luke made the beef stew too floury and it had to be thrown away. Luke told a joke, let me see if I can remember it.

One night she says, "I'm glad you made a friend."

"He's not my friend. He's a punk."

"He sounds like a nice boy to me." Margo puts Chuck's feet up on the couch and rubs them with her big fingers, hands him the remote control so he can watch *Law & Order*.

"He's all right, I guess."

She says, "I think you like him."

The cat is sick. Chuck gets up one morning to find it squatting in the bathtub, growling low in its throat. He picks it up and sees there is urine on the bottom of the tub; the urine has red in it, he tells Margo. He brings her into the bathroom and points. The next day the cat will not eat. It squats in the tub, in the sink, on the kitchen counter. Margo picks the cat up when it squats and takes it to the litter box, but it will not go.

"What's wrong, Petey?" she says. "Do you hurt?" The cat looks up at her with its round yellow eyes, its eyes like the yolks of eggs.

That night they wake up because the cat is howling. It sounds like it is dying, its cries filling the dark trailer, rising sharp above the sound of the ceiling fan in their bedroom. The windows are open, and when Chuck sits up in bed, he thinks cats must be fighting in the yard. He stumbles across the room and looks outside, where the dim, green shadow of lawn meets the woods at some invisible line. His feet ache deep in the arches; he shifts his weight between them, sees nothing.

"It's Petey!" Margo says, crawling out of the bed, her breasts swinging low beneath her white cotton nightgown.

They go into the living room, where the cat lies on the floor. Margo reaches down to pick it up, but it shrieks when she touches it. Chuck steps barefoot into vomit. Margo wrings her hands, paces back and forth across the carpet. She shakes Chuck by the shoulders.

"What if he's dying?" she says. "What if he is?"

"Should we call the vet?" Chuck says, peering around her to where the cat twitches its feet and moans. He looks at the clock on the wall. It is 3:50. He has to be to work by five.

They decide that Margo will take the cat to the all-night clinic in Lewisburg. She ties her hair in a ponytail and puts on her pink sweat suit. They wrap the cat in an afghan and nestle it in the front seat of the Cougar. As Margo gets behind the wheel, she is crying. She waves at Chuck as the Cougar passes the fence, pale star of her hand afloat in the dark. He stands in the yard in green boxers and no shirt, watching the taillights disappear over the hill. The first of the dew beads on his slippers. Across from him the door of the blue trailer is hanging open again, though now the police tape is gone. Chuck walks over to the fence and rests his elbow on one of the posts, squints into the laundry room of the trailer. Beyond the beige splotch of the washer is the corner to the hallway; there are no pictures on the wall beyond the laundry-room door.

He remembers the hallway of the house he grew up in. The bathroom was at the far end of it, and when he was a boy, he sat on the toilet and stared at the corner by the bathroom door. He knew that something was tiptoeing down the hall toward him, something he couldn't see. He could hear its footsteps, soft and quickening in his ears. The footsteps were his heartbeat, but he only understood this later. He crosses the yard and goes back inside his own trailer.

It is now too late to go back to sleep, and Chuck sits at the table with his coffee, wonders if the cat will die. It is possible they are too old now for a new cat. He remembers there are old cats at the shelter too; perhaps they can take home another old cat instead. If Petey lives, Chuck thinks, maybe they should get another cat anyway. That way, when one of the cats dies, it will not be the only cat they have.

At eleven o'clock Bart comes to the prep area to tell Chuck he has a phone call. Chuck walks to the front vestibule, where the phone receiver lies on the counter next to a waitress keying an order into a computer. Her hands flash over the touch screen: sirloin, baked potato, salad. Chuck wonders if he needs to put more potatoes in the oven. People eating steak get angry so easily. He learned this lesson in '77, courtesy of a bank teller's fist.

It is Margo on the phone. She says that Petey has a urethral obstruction, and that he must stay at the clinic for catheterization. It will take at least two days, she says. She and Chuck must take the money from the Folgers can under the stove. If Petey does not have the catheterization, he will die. Chuck knows she is holding the phone to her ear with her shoulder while she wrings her hands. He says they will pay for the catheterization.

He rubs more potatoes with shortening.

"What's catheterization?" says Luke.

Chuck repeats what Margo explained. "Oh hell no," Luke says and covers his mouth with his hand.

"It's just like using a straw, I guess."

"Oh hell no."

Chuck works on beef noodle soup for the dinner shift while Luke cuts biscuits. The radio is on the oldies station. Kaleigh is mad at Luke because he called her an asshole. Chuck has never used that word for a woman, even in his head. He wonders why. It is natural to call a man a dick, but both women and men have assholes.

"She won't give me head until I apply for pharmacy school," Luke says.

"Well," Chuck says, "I guess you have to decide whether you want to get sucked off or fly airplanes." He is happy to have someone with whom he can say "sucked off."

"I want both."

"You'll have to grow out of that, mister."

Luke presses the honeycomb cutter into the rolled dough and begins to place the biscuits on a pan. "She'll get over it," he says.

"Can't you just apply and then tell her you didn't get in?"

Luke shakes his head. "Everyone gets into pharmacy school. If I'm not smart enough to count how many pills go in a bottle, I'm not smart enough to be a pilot."

"You seem smart to me," says Chuck. He would not ride in a plane flown by someone who did not understand air pressure, but this seems like a mean thing to say. He tries to think of something else. "Maybe you should be a vet," he says.

"And stick a straw up a cat's wang? No way."

"They're charging me an arm and a leg for it, though. I could get at least ten cats for the price of keeping this one."

"Then why do it? Isn't your cat totally old?"

Chuck remembers a night more than twenty years ago when he woke up to the sound of screaming. He ran down the hall of the trailer and into the main room to find Margo standing in her nightgown, holding a carton of Neapolitan ice cream. She scooped it out and flung it on the

162

walls, the floor, the furniture. Ice cream sat melting on the seat of his recliner, left streaks of pink, brown, and yellow down the pleated fabric of the lampshade. Margo threw ice cream at him as well. Drops lingered in the hair on his chest.

"We had a baby that died once," he says. "My wife gets upset over sickness."

"Oh." Luke has just taken some finished biscuits out of the oven. He stands in the middle of the aisle holding the pan and looking at Chuck. "I'm sorry."

"It's okay."

"Was it a boy or a girl?"

"Sarah. She died from SIDS."

"What's SIDS?"

"It's when a baby dies for no reason."

"Oh." Luke sets the pan of biscuits on the counter and begins to brush them with a butter mixture. They glisten gold under the fluorescent lights. "My mom got hit by lightning," he says.

The Lion's Club carnival has come to town, and Chuck takes Margo there to keep her from worrying over Petey. The carnival is set up on the campus of the community college; red-and-white striped tents perch over trampled grass and the clay dirt of a softball field. There is a carousel, a gravity wheel, and a long plastic slide children ride down on sheets of burlap. Every booth plays a different song, and the mixed music rises above the tents, where a Ferris wheel turns a bright-bulbed circle through the sky. Chuck and Margo eat hot dogs and nachos at a picnic table. The chili on the hot dogs is made by the Methodist church and needs more cumin.

"You can ride the rides if you want," says Margo. She is too fat for most of the rides.

"Can you ride the bench on the carousel?"

"Probably."

They finish their hot dogs and ride the carousel, both of them sitting on the bright blue-and-yellow bench. Chuck watches the hooves of the horses move up and down in front of him. Gum is stuck on the hoof of one, and dirt is stuck on the gum. He looks away from the horses and out over the carnival grounds. A dunking chair, a cotton-candy booth, and a beanbag toss swing by him in a repeating loop. Parents stand outside the metal gate of the carousel and wave at their children on the horses. A man throws a burger wrapper toward a garbage can and misses. On his third time around, Chuck sees Luke buying a blue cotton candy for a girl who must be Kaleigh. She has long brown hair with chunky blonde highlights and is wearing a pink knitted cap. She is pretty and petite, just like Chuck imagined she would be. Luke pulls off a tuft of the cotton candy and puts it into Kaleigh's mouth. He leans in to kiss her, but the carousel turns too far for Chuck to see the kiss. He finds himself hoping that Luke will see him. He wonders if it would be strange to say hello.

By the time the ride ends, though, Luke and Kaleigh have left the cotton-candy stand. It would definitely be strange to go looking for Luke, so Chuck decides not to. Since they cannot go on any more rides, he and Margo visit the game booths. They play a game of bingo but do not win any money. Chuck plays the football toss and wins a keychain with the mascot of a local school's team on it. They buy a funnel cake and eat it next to the moon bounce, then they go into a tent where children are standing on stools and reaching into a large tank. The tank is shaped like a ring and made of metal; it is open at the top, and water flows around it in a loop. Floating on the water are dozens of plastic ducks in bright colors: pink, yellow, orange, green, and red. The object of the game is to lift the ducks out of the water and see what is written on their bellies. If the belly has a smiley face, you win a prize. If there is a frowny face, you win nothing. The more money you spend, the more ducks you get to pick up. The more smiley faces you get, the nicer your prize.

Chuck remembers that the Folgers can under the stove is now empty, but he still buys five dollars' worth of ducks. Margo makes her way to the side of the tank, where children part for her girth. She picks up the first duck: a frowny face. The second duck is the same. Chuck feels a tap on his shoulder and turns around.

"Hey," says Luke.

"Where's Kaleigh?" says Chuck, and when Luke looks surprised, "I saw you buying cotton candy earlier. That was Kaleigh, wasn't it?"

Luke laughs and says, "Yeah, it was. Did you think you got me in trouble?"

Chuck is startled. "No! I wouldn't get you in trouble."

"She met some of her friends. They went to do something, I don't know. Whatever girls do." Luke is casual, but there is a tenseness about his face that suggests he is still not getting sucked off. "Playing the ducks, huh?"

"Margo is," Chuck says. Margo turns around at the sound of her name, and Chuck introduces her to Luke. He looks amused but not displeased, as if he had gone out to eat and been presented with a much larger portion than he expected.

"I've heard nice things about you," he says, shaking Margo's hand.

"And Chuck tells me all about you," she replies, smiling at Chuck over Luke's shoulder. Chuck feels his face go red.

"Good stuff, right?"

"Very good stuff, Luke."

"You winning?"

Margo shakes her head. "I got all frowns." She holds up the fifth duck, on the belly of which is a sad face drawn in Sharpie.

Luke grins. "You're just not listening to the ducks," he says. "Watch." He hands a ten-dollar bill to the man who runs the game. Chuck moves closer to the tank to watch. Luke shakes his shoulders, closes his eyes, and holds his hands palms down over the motorized river of ducks. He spreads his fingers and wiggles them, then stands perfectly still for several seconds before reaching down into the water and grabbing a pink duck. He opens his eyes and turns the duck over: a smiley face.

"Luck!" says Margo. She is laughing.

"No way," says Luke, setting the duck on the edge of the tank. "Watch." He performs the same silly ritual, and this time lifts a green duck, also with a smiley face. Chuck wonders if it is possible to cheat at this game. He does not see how it could be done. There is no reflection off the bottom of the tank. Luke's third duck also has a smiley face. He must be very lucky.

"I am the god of ducks," he says.

Now Chuck is laughing too. Children are abandoning their own ducks and watching the three of them. The man who runs the game is shaking his head and beaming. He also does not seem to believe Luke is cheating. Margo and Chuck stand on either side of Luke, and she looks at Chuck over Luke's shoulder again, her dark brown eyes nearly lost in the laugh lines of her face. A feeling comes up in Chuck's chest, stiff and aggressive, similar to heartburn but pleasant. Luke's sixth duck is the first frowny, and gathered children and parents groan in dismay. Chuck reaches up to pat Luke on the back. The fabric of Luke's T-shirt is soft and warm. "You'll get the next one," Chuck says.

Out of ten ducks, Luke gets smileys on seven. He receives a stuffed blue kangaroo, which he tucks under his arm as he pulls out his phone to read a text message. It is from Kaleigh; she is waiting at the car. Chuck wonders how they can be off again. They seemed so close at the cotton-candy stand. Then again, he thinks, it has been a long time since he was eighteen. He may have forgotten what it was like.

Luke gives the kangaroo to Margo. "I hope your cat gets better," he says.

"What a sweet boy," says Margo later, as they walk across the field to their car. Squashed paper cups and burger wrappers dot the ground. Dozens of vehicles are parked on the grass in rows like typewriter keys. Chuck and Margo get into the Cougar and roll down the windows, Margo holding the kangaroo on her lap. She scratches its stiff ears and squeezes it, making the plastic bead stuffing crinkle.

Chuck drives them home over twisting double-lined roads, the summer air filling the car and moving their clothing. When they reach the railroad track, the light is flashing, and the striped barrier moves toward the road in a slow arc. A freight train hauls its black length across their path, and Chuck rolls up his window to dull the rumble. In the glow of the streetlight outside her own window, Margo further examines the kangaroo. She reads the tag to see how it should be washed. She runs her fingers over the blue belly to see if the pouch really opens and emits a soft sound of surprise when it does. Reaching her hand inside the pocket, she pauses and makes a confused face, then pulls something out.

"Chuck," she says. He glances over and sees that she is clutching a folded twenty-dollar bill. She looks like she is going to cry.

"What a sweet boy," she says, hugging the kangaroo to her chest and staring at the boxcars full of coal as they cross the road in steady, clanking succession. Chuck reaches over the gear shift and puts his hand on Margo's arm. She takes one of her hands off the kangaroo and places it on top of his hand. Together they look in front of them. They wait for the train to pass.

The catheterization is a success. Petey must stay at the Lewisburg clinic for another day of observation, then he can return home. Margo calls Chuck at the restaurant at ten o'clock to tell him the news. Even though they are short on money, they decide they will celebrate by eating dinner at Hal's Barbeque. Margo is so happy that Chuck becomes happy. He hums as he squeezes the meatloaf blend from its plastic freezer tube into the greased steel pan. Luke is scheduled in at noon, and Chuck is eager to thank him for the twenty dollars, and to tell him that Petey is fine.

But Luke does not arrive at noon. Occasionally he is late, so this must be one of those times. Chuck begins to mix the biscuit dough himself, so that Luke will not get in trouble. Maybe Luke is late because he and Kaleigh have reconciled, and they are lying in bed smiling and touching each other. Luke is brushing Kaleigh's hair away from her ear and kissing it, whispering about how he will fly her away in a plane. Up above the mountains and across the sea, they will go, until they are soaring over Europe, over castles and cathedrals, over the kinds of things people like them almost never get to see. Chuck thinks this is a clever tactic. If it turns out the two have not reconciled, he will tell Luke to try it.

Chuck waits until twelve-thirty, but then he is unable to wait any longer. He has gotten the biscuits into the oven, but he cannot make cornbread and roast beef at the same time. He goes to the office and tells Bart that Luke is not there. Bart looks in the computer for Luke's father's number, and Chuck returns to the beef. He portions it and spoons the gravy on top, tucks a square of aluminum foil around the rim of each ramekin. He puts the first three ramekins into the oven and the rest into the walk-in refrigerator. When a quarter hour has passed, he returns to the office. Bart is sitting at his desk with the back of the phone receiver pressed against his lips. A series of shrill, demanding beeps from the earpiece indicate the connection is severed.

Chuck knocks on the open door, and Bart looks up but does not put down the receiver. "I spoke to Luke's aunt," he says.

"His aunt?"

"Uh-huh."

Chuck hesitates. "Is Luke sick?"

"Luke's, um . . ." Bart lowers the receiver and looks down at it in his hand like it is foreign and confounding. Moving very slowly, he hangs it up, then rubs his smooth cheeks and adjusts his glasses. "Luke's dead, Chuck."

The sudden onrush of adrenaline throws off Chuck's center of balance; he grabs the edge of the office door and leans into it, dizzy. Bart's shirt is lilac. The phone is white. The dry-erase board says, "The customer is always first." Chuck digests these facts to remain in place. He hears himself say, "What?"

Bart clears his throat. "He and his girlfriend were hit by a semi-truck on Route 19 last night. The driver was drunk."

"What about Kaleigh?"

Bart shakes his head. He clears his throat again and puts the palm of his hand against it as if he were choking. He closes his eyes for longer than a blink, then opens them again. "I guess I'll, um . . . I guess I'll get someone to come in and help you, if I can."

Chuck leaves the doorway and heads down the server aisle toward the prep area. He stops in front of the coffee machine because his legs feel like noodles. Beside the coffee burners is a steel pan filled with mostly melted ice, and inside that pan is a smaller one filled with plastic one-serving creamers. Some of the packets have fallen out of their pan, and Chuck watches them bob in the icy water. He thinks of the ducks. He goes back to the prep area and begins to make the cornbread batter, stirring the bacon grease into the big steel bowl, feeling the mix grow thick and resist his arm. He pulls the whisk out of the bowl and stares at it, then somehow it slips out of his hand and hits the floor with a spatter of yellow gunk. Chuck bends down to pick it up, and then he is on his knees, and he is crying.

He bends all the way down to the floor, until his face is inches from the scum of grease and flour that always coats it. His tears leave dark round dots in the places they fall. Ripping through his chest is a jagged confusion; he does not understand what he is crying about. Even though he is sad about Luke, the happiness at Petey's recovery has not gone away. Both are present in him like separate spices, and suddenly there are other flavors too, spices he cannot identify, mingling and building inside him until he can no longer pick out the taste of one over another. He sobs into the floor, the sound of it muted by the restaurant's constant din of shouting and dish hoses and sizzling meat. He will not die on Route 19; he will never be hit by a drunk driver. He knows it as surely as he knows a thousand recipes. He will die here, baking biscuits, of a stroke or a massive heart attack. He will hit the floor on his back, gasping then going still, and flour will trickle over him like pollen, like early snow, like the ashes of Luke's mother drifting down into the New River Gorge.

"God has a reason for everything," says Margo that night at Hal's Barbeque, where they have still decided to eat dinner. "We can't see His whole plan, but all the pieces fit together in the end."

Chuck has heard her say these things before. The idea itself does not make him feel better, but somehow the fact that she is still saying it does. It is nice to know that if the world were to burn, Margo would say God knew what He was doing. Chuck has never thought very much about God; even now, when such thinking would be understandable, he finds it does not hold his interest. He is paying attention to the barbeque in his mouth, tracing its history all the way back to the pig as it lies in the sun, to tomatoes bulging on some faraway vine, to vinegar and even mother of vinegar, bacteria grabbing hold inside wine and cider.

He lifts his cup of sweet tea with a serious face. "To Luke," he says. "And Kaleigh." Margo lifts her cup to tap it against his. "And also to Petey," Chuck adds.

They cannot afford dessert, so they go home and eat popsicles on the porch. Margo slips her bloated feet out of her flip-flops and wiggles her toes over the concrete. A stretched, distorted shadow wiggles back at her in the lengthening light. She sucks on the popsicle, which is red, white, and blue. "Do you want to have sex?" she says.

"Okay."

They go inside to the bedroom. They undress separately, then Margo takes all the clothes to the hamper in the bathroom. She returns and sits down on the bed next to Chuck, the mattress creaking beneath her. Fat is gathered in rolls along the sides of her back, and between them just over her spine is a thin, smooth furrow of tighter skin. Chuck moves his rough fingers up and down this furrow, then moves to cup each roll individually. The fat fills his hands, rests its weight in them; he massages, then moves his fingers deep between the rolls, where body heat has gathered and covers his hands with a reassuring warmth.

They lie down side by side and kiss for a while, then Chuck moves down the mattress and places a hand on each of Margo's knees. He spreads his arms, and her legs move apart, thighs hanging heavily around his head as he moves it toward the tiny slip of hair visible beneath the swoop of her stomach. This part is his favorite, the finding. On Margo's body everything is exaggerated, thighs and stomach and vulva all engorged, all playful and hiding the part Chuck is looking for, the one he knows is tender and swelling, waiting for his mouth to discover it. This is the kind of sex they prefer now. It is nice, and not as athletic.

It does not take Margo long to come. She has always come easily and with relish, and this time is no different: the bed trembles as she thrusts into his face, groaning as loudly as she wants to. Her body rumbles and

169

flaps, the rolling boil of her pleasure absorbing Chuck like a particle of salt. When she has cooled she does as much for him, taking him into her mouth with the same enthusiasm she gives to her favorite foods, tracing his shape over and over with her tongue, sucking until he thinks maybe he will have that heart attack here instead, he will die here in bed with his wife, and she will have to make him decent before the ambulance arrives.

When he finishes she says, "You taste good." She smiles and wraps her arms around him until they have both caught their breath.

They lie together until they begin to get cold. They say I love you, then Margo goes to take a shower. Chuck puts on a T-shirt and a pair of boxers, gets a bottle of beer out of the refrigerator, and takes it out onto the front porch. He stands on the edge of the concrete slab, looking over the twilit yard. It is a chilly evening for August; it is the first night that fall has come into the air, breathing its shy and restful promise into the summer heat. Things will get easier in the restaurant after August. Children will go back to school, and families will stop traveling. People will save up their money for Christmas and will not go out to eat. Someone will still have to replace Luke, but Chuck will not see that person as much. They will work only one to a shift and see each other in passing.

Across the yard, the door of the blue trailer is standing open. Chuck steps off the porch in his bare feet and walks across the grass, climbs over the wooden fence with lumbering effort, and passes the chipped ceramic bear on his way up the steps of the back porch. He stands in front of the yawning doorway, sticks his head a short distance inside. A musty smell greets him, and beneath that is an acridness he cannot place. Though he saw them come in and out, he did not know the people who lived here. He wonders now who they were, and where they came from. They were cooks too, although they cooked meth. Chuck thinks about Cindy and wonders what has happened to her. He thinks about Bart, who works sixty hours a week at the restaurant and has to wear a tie every day. He thinks about Luke's father, who has lost his family to accident. And he thinks about Luke and Kaleigh, who are in a funeral home at this very moment, perhaps getting makeup applied to their faces or having their hair arranged.

Light is leaving the yard, and Chuck stands on the porch as night enters the trailer, expanding unseen inside the empty rooms. Curiosity visits him, and he imagines going inside, exploring in darkness the emptied space of his neighbors. He stands for a moment with his hand on the threshold, then he reaches for the knob and swings the door shut, pushing all his weight against it until he hears the muffled latch. He climbs back over the low fence. He walks back across his own yard.

Nominated by The Gettysburg Review, Alice Mattison

THE ULTRASOUND

by DAVID HORNIBROOK

from DUNES REVIEW

What does it matter life
   in other galaxies. Even the moon

gathers what it
   loves but never quite pulls it close enough.

It is cold in the waiting room, my wife
   is tired,

doesn't want to read magazines,
   shifts in her seat. I wonder

what it is like to enshrine a life,
   halo yourself around something nameless.

I only know what it is like to live.
   The issue

of *Discover* I'm reading says
   there are holes so deep that nothing,

even light,
   can escape. Say a star enters & we

theorize about where
        it goes.

We go where the nurse leads us.
        My wife wants to choose the room but she can't

& I don't
        remember in which grade I first

learned about gravity.
        She lies down on a bed now & lifts her shirt,

gathers it just below her breasts.
        A woman spreads gel across the planet

surface of her belly.
        My eyes are pulled to the monitor.

A landscape contorts before them, a universe
        expands, contracts, I can't tell which.

Turbulence within a cloud of space dust
        causes a knot to form, the dust around it

collapsing. My eyes cannot escape
        the motion the monitor reveals,

or is it
        just the wand

brooding over the face of the water.
        The hot core at the heart of a collapsing cloud

will one day become a star.
        After a while everyone leaves us alone.

Several days later one of the women
        returns. Her gaze attends

to the space around us. She asks
for us to step out into the hallway.

We don't know how to get there.

Nominated by Laura Kasischke

LORRY RAJA

fiction by MADHURI VIJAY

from NARRATIVE

What happened was that my older brother, Siju, got a job as a lorry driver at the mine and started acting like a big shot. He stopped playing with Munna the way he used to, tossing him into the air like a sack of sand, making him sputter with laughter. When Amma asked him anything, he would give her a pitying look and not answer. He stopped speaking to his girlfriend, Manju, altogether. He taunted me about playing in the mud, as he called it, breaking chunks of iron ore with my hammer. With Appa especially he was reckless, not bothering to conceal his disdain, until he said something about *failed drivers who are only good for digging and drinking,* and Appa wrestled him to the ground and forced him to eat a handful of the red, iron-rich earth, shouting that this was our living now and he should bloody learn to respect it. Siju complained to the mine's labor officer, Mr. Subbu, but Mr. Subbu dismissed it as a domestic matter and refused to interfere. After that, Siju maintained a glowering silence in Appa's presence. When Appa wasn't around, Siju sneered at our tent, a swatch of blue plastic stretched over a bamboo skeleton. Never mind that he was being paid half a regular driver's salary by the owner of the lorry, a *paan*-chewing Andhra fellow called Rajappa, because Siju was only fourteen and could not bargain for more.

Never mind that Rajappa's lorry permit was fake, a flimsy transparent chit of paper with no expiry date and half the words illegible, which meant that Siju was allowed to transport the ore only to the railway station in Hospet and not, like the other drivers, all the way to port cities like Mangalore and Chennai, where he'd run the risk of arrest by border authorities. Never mind that the mine's lorry cleaners, most of whom were boys my age, called him Lorry Raja behind his back and imitated his high-stepping walk. None of it seemed to matter to him. And, as little as I wanted to admit it, he *was* a raja in the cab of that lorry, and moreover he looked it. His hair was thick and black, and a long tuft descended at the back of his neck, like a crow's glossy tail feathers. His nose was straight, and his eyeballs were untouched by yellow. His teeth remained white in spite of breathing the iron-laden air. He seemed, when he was in the cab of that lorry, like someone impossible and important, someone I didn't know at all.

The ore went to the port cities, and then it went onto ships the size of buildings. I hadn't seen them, but the labor officer, Mr. Subbu, had told us about them. He said the ships crossed the ocean, and the journey took weeks. The ships went to Australia and Japan, but mostly they went to China. They were building a stadium in China for something called the Lympic Games. Mr. Subbu explained that the Lympic Games were like the World Cup, except for all sports instead of just cricket. Swimming, tennis, shooting, running. If you won you got a gold medal, Mr. Subbu said. India had won a gold medal in boxing the last time the games were held.

The stadium in China would be round like a cricket stadium, except ten times bigger. Mr. Subbu spread his arms out wide when he said this, and we could see patches of sweat under the arms of his nice ironed shirt.

The whole world worked in the mines. At least that is what it seemed like then. There was a drought in Karnataka and neighboring Andhra Pradesh, and things were so bad people were starting to eye the mangy street dogs. Our neighbor poured kerosene on himself and three daughters and lit them ablaze; his wife burned her face but escaped. Then came the news of the mines, hundreds of them opening in Bellary, needing workers. And people went. It seemed to happen overnight. They asked their brothers-in-law or their uncles to look after their plots and their houses, or simply sold them. They pulled their children out of school. Whole villages were suddenly abandoned, cropless fields left to wither. Families waited near bus depots plastered with faded film signs, carrying big bundles stuffed with steel pots and plastic shoes and

176

flimsy clothes. The buses were so full they tilted to one side. There wasn't enough space for everyone. The people who were left behind tried running alongside the buses, and some of the more foolish ones tried to jump in as the bus was moving. They would invariably fall, lie in the dust for a while, staring up at the rainless sky. Then they would get up, brush off their clothes, and go back to wait for the next bus. For months my family watched this happen. We didn't worry, not at first. Appa had a job as a driver for a subinspector of the Raichur Thermal Power Plant, and we thought we were fine. Then there was the accident, and Appa lost the job. He spent the next few weeks at the rum shop, coming home long enough to belt me or my brother Siju or Amma. After that was over he cried for a long time. Then he announced that we were going to work in the mines. All of us. Siju, who was in the seventh standard at the time, tried to protest, but Appa twisted a bruise into his arm and Siju stopped complaining. I was in the fifth standard, and to me it seemed like a grand adventure. Amma said nothing. She was pregnant with Munna then, and her feet had swollen to the size of papayas. She hobbled into the hut to pack our things.

Within a week, we squeezed onto a bus that was leaking black droplets of oil from its heavy bottom, and Appa bought us each a newspaper cone of hot peanuts for the journey. I flicked the burnt peanuts into my mouth and watched as the land slowly got dryer and redder, until the buildings in the huddled villages we passed were red too, and so was the bark of the trees, and so were the fingers of the ticket collector who checked the stub in Appa's hand and said, "Next stop." We lurched into a teeming bus station with a cracked floor, and I asked Appa why the ground was red, and he told me this was because of the iron in it. While Appa was busy asking directions to the nearest mine that was hiring, and Amma was searching in her blouse for money to buy a packet of Tiger biscuits and a bottle of 7Up for our lunch, Siju came up to me and whispered that, really, the ground was red because there was blood in it, seeping up to the surface from the miners' bodies buried underneath. For months I believed him, and every step I took was in fear, bracing for the sticky wetness of blood, the crunch of bone, the squelch of an organ. When I realized the truth I tried to hit him, but he held my wrists so hard they hurt, and he bared his teeth close to my face, laughing.

That afternoon, just about a year after we had come to the mine, I was working an open pit beside the highway, along with a few other children and a handful of women. I squatted by the edge of the road, close enough that the warm exhaust from the vehicles billowed my faded T-shirt and seeped under my shorts. The pinch of tobacco Amma had given me that morning to stave off my hunger had long since lost its flavor. It was now a bland, warm glob tucked in my cheek. Heat pressed down on my skin, and there was a sharp, metallic tinge to the air that made me uneasy. The women, who usually laughed and teased each other, curved their backs into shells and hammered in silence. The children seemed more careless than usual because I kept hearing small cries whenever one of them brought a hammer down on a thumb by accident. The horizon to the west was congested with a dark breast of clouds, but above me the sun blazed white through a gauze sky. The monsoons were late, too late for crops, but I knew they would hit anytime now. Over the past week, furious little rainstorms had begun to tear up the red earth, flooding various pits, making them almost impossible to mine. I remembered that during the last monsoon, a drunk man had wandered away one night and fallen into a flooded pit. His body, by the time it was discovered, was bloated and black.

Lorries crawled in sluggish streams in both directions on the highway. The ones heading away from Bellary were weighed down with ore, great mounds wrapped in gray and green tarpaulin and lashed with lengths of rope as thick as my ankle. The empty ones returning from the port cities rattled with stray pebbles jumping in the back. The faces of the lorry drivers were glistening with sweat, and they blared their horns as if it might make the nearly immobile line of traffic speed up. Now and then a foreign car, belonging to one of the mine owners, slipped noiselessly through the stalled traffic. I recited the names of the cars, tonguing the tobacco in my mouth: Maserati. Jaguar. Mercedes. Jaguar. Their shimmering bodies caught the sun and played with it, light sliding across their hoods, winking in their taillights. The mine owners lived in huge pink and white houses on the highway, houses with fountains and the grim heads of stone lions staring from the balconies. I looked up as a sleek black Maserati went by, and in its tinted window I saw myself, a boy in shorts and a baggy T-shirt, crouching close to the dirt. And standing behind me, the distorted shape of a girl. I stood up quickly, hammer in hand, and whirled around.

Manju flinched, as if I might attack her with it. A few days before, I had seen two kids get into a hammer fight over a Titan watch they had found together. One of them smashed the other's hand. Later I found a small square fingernail stamped into the ground where they fought.

"I'm not going to hit you," I said.

Her slow smile pulled her cheeks into small brown hills sunk with shadowy dimples. She smoothed down the front of her dress, which was actually a school uniform. It had once been white but was now tinged with red iron dust. It wrapped around her thin body, ending below her knees and buttoning high at her throat. Her hair spilled in knotted waves down her back. She and her mother had arrived at the mine around the same time as we had. Her mother was sick and never came out of their tent. I didn't know what was wrong with her. For a while Manju had been Siju's girlfriend, saving up her extra tobacco for him, nodding seriously when he spoke, following him everywhere. Then he had stopped speaking to her. The one time I asked him about it, Siju leaned to one side, curled his lip, and spat delicately into the mud.

"Hi, Manju," I said. We were the same height, though she was a few years older, maybe fifteen.

"Hi, Guna," she said, and squatted at my feet. I squatted too and waited for her to do something. She picked up the piece of ore I had been working on and gave it two halfhearted taps with her hammer. Then she seemed to lose interest. She let it fall and said, "He came by already?"

"No," I said.

I liked Manju. Whenever journalists or NGO workers came to tour the mines, Manju and I would drop our hammers and prance in circles, shouting, "No child-y labor here!" According to the mine owners, it was our parents who were supposed to be working. We simply lived with them and played around the mine. The hammers and basins were our toys. The journalists would scribble in their notepads, and the NGO workers would whisper to one another, and Manju would grin widely at me. Then, after we found out about the Lympic Games, we had contests of our own. Running contests, stone-throwing contests, rock-piling contests. The winner got the gold medal, the runner-up clapped and stomped the dirt in applause. I liked playing with Manju because I almost always won, and she never got angry when she lost, like the boys sometimes did.

"Manju," I said now. "Want to race? Bet I'll get the gold medal."

But she just shook her head. She stared up at the lorries. She was thin, and the bones at the top of her spine pushed like pebbles against her uniform. I wanted to reach out and tap them gently with my hammer. One of the lorry drivers, a man with a thick mustache, saw her watching and made a wet kissing sound with his lips, like he was suck-ing an invisible straw. His tongue came out, fleshy and purple. He shouted, "Hi, sexy girl! Sexy-fun girl!" My cheeks burned for her, and I could feel the weight of the women's gazes, but Manju looked at him as if he had told her that rain was on the way. I busied myself with filling my *puttu* with lumps of ore. Each full basin I took to the weigh-ing station would earn me five and a half rupees. On a good day I could fill seven or eight *puttus*, if I ignored the blisters at the base of my thumb.

I felt the other workers looking at us, the frank stares of the children. I carefully shifted the glob of tobacco from my right cheek to my left.

"You shouldn't be playing those dumb-stupid games anyway," Manju said.

"No?" I said cautiously. "Why not?"

Manju said, "You should be in school."

I didn't know what to say. It had been two years since I sat in a class-room. I had only vague recollections of it. The cold mud floor. Sitting next to a boy called Dheeraj, who smelled of castor oil. Slates with cracked plastic frames. The maths teacher who called us human head lice when we couldn't solve the sum on the board. All of us chanting in unison an English poem we didn't understand. *The boy stood on the burning deck.* The antiseptic smell of the girls' toilet covering another, mustier, smell. Dheeraj giggling outside. Then three, four, five whacks on the fleshy part of my palm with a wooden ruler, and trying not to show that it hurt. *The boy stood on the burning deck whence all but he had fled.*

"You used to come first in class, no?" Manju said. A gray gust of ex-haust blew a wisp of hair between her teeth. She chewed on it. Her face was whiskered with red dust.

"How do you know?"

"Siju told me," she said, which surprised me. "Siju said you got a hundred in every subject, even the difficult ones like maths. He said you shouldn't be wasting your potential here."

I had never heard him say anything like that. It sounded like some-thing an NGO worker might say. I wondered where he had heard the phrase.

"But, Manju," I said, "I like it here."

"Why?"

I was about to tell her why—because I could play with her every day

180

and because the mine was vast and open and I was free to go where I liked, and, yes, the work was hard but there was an excitement to the way the lorries rumbled past, straining under their heavy cargo—but right then Manju dropped her hammer.

In a strained voice she said, "He's coming."

Siju's lorry looked no different than any of the others, except that it had been freshly cleaned. It had an orange cab, and the outer sides of the long bed were painted brown. The bed bulged with ore, like the belly of a fat man. Siju was clearly on his way to the Hospet railway station. The back panel of the lorry was decorated with painted animals—a lion and two deer. The lion, its thick mane rippling, stood in a lush forest, and the two deer flanked it, their delicate orange heads raised and looking off to the sides. Siju was especially proud of the painting, and I knew he stood over his lorry cleaner each morning, breathing down the boy's neck to make sure that all the red dust was properly wiped off the faces of the animals. His insistence on keeping the lorry spick-and-span was part of why the lorry cleaners made fun of him.

He must have seen us squatting there by the highway, but he kept his eyes on the road. I raised my hand and waved. When he didn't respond, I said, "Oy, Siju! Look this way!"

He swiveled his head toward us briefly.

Manju's big eyes followed him.

Then one of the women working nearby, a woman with a missing eye whose eyelid drooped over the empty socket, spat out her tobacco with a harsh smack and said to Manju, "Enough of your nonsense. Go sit somewhere else. Leave those boys to do their work."

Manju didn't answer, so the woman said more loudly, "You! Heard me? Go sit—"

Manju picked up a pebble and flung it at her. It hit the woman on the shoulder, and she yelped.

"Soole!" the woman hissed.

Manju turned her thin face to the woman. "Soole?" Manju's voice trembled. "You're calling me a soole? You old dirty one-eyed monkey."

I looked at Manju, afraid to speak. She picked up my ore and began hammering at it.

"Manju—" I began. I thought she was going to cry, but then she looked up. "I wish you had a lorry," she said. "Then you and me could drive to China."

Later I took my full *puttu* to the weighing station. On my way I passed Amma working with a group of women at the base of a slope. I stopped to watch her. She was shaking a sieve, holding it away from her body, a red cloud billowing around her. Dark pebbles of ore danced and shivered in the wide shallow basin. A few feet away Munna, naked except for an old shirt of mine, crawled in aimless circles. If he got too far or tried to stuff a fistful of dirt into his mouth, Amma or one of the women would reach out an arm or a leg and hook him back in. When Munna saw me, he stretched out his short arms, ridiculous in their baggy sleeves, and screamed with delight. Amma looked up. She put down the sieve and straightened her back. She was as small as a child, her hands barely bigger than mine. The other women glanced at me and continued working. The muscles in their forearms were laid like train tracks.

"How many?" Amma called up.

"Three," I said. I held up the *puttu*. "This is the fourth one." There were still a few hours of daylight left. A few hours before the red hills of Bellary turned black and the day's totals were tallied and announced by the sweating labor officer, Mr. Subbu, and no matter the numbers, how high or how low, the workers would be expected to cheer.

With her eyes on me, she put a hand inside her blouse to touch the small velvet jewelry pouch she kept there. Whatever jewelry had been in there was pawned long ago. I knew that now it contained a few hundred rupees, two or maybe three. This was what she had saved, in secrecy, for months, money that Appa overlooked or was too drunk to account for. It was for me, my school fees, and she liked to remind me it was there. She eyed me, her lower lip hanging open. I knew she was debating whether to speak.

"Guna," she said finally. "Tonight, when Appa comes—"

"Have to go," I said. "Lots of work. It's going to rain later."

She sighed. "You don't want to go back to school?" she asked. "You don't want to study hard and get a proper job?" She lowered her voice. "Such a clever boy you are, Guna. Such good marks you used to get. You want to waste your brains, fill your head with iron like a *puttu*?"

I made no reply. I remembered what Manju had said about my potential, and I saw myself flinging the entire contents of the *puttu* in Amma's face, iron flying everywhere, scattershot.

Amma was keeping half an eye on Munna, who was trying to climb into the sieve. "Did Siju get a trip today?" she asked.

"You're asking about Lorry Raja?" I said.

"Don't act like those lorry-cleaner boys. He drives well."

I hopped from one foot to the other, balancing the *puttu* like a tray. "Lorry Raja tries to turn on his indicators and turns on the windshield wipers instead."

"Guna!" Amma said.

"Lorry Raja is always combing his hair in the rearview mirror."

One of the women working next to Amma laughed. She had large yellow teeth and a gold stud in her flared nostril. Amma glanced at her, then at the ground.

Encouraged by the woman's laugh, I added, "Lorry Raja's lorry doesn't even go in a straight line." I waggled my palm to show the route Siju's lorry took.

Amma scooped up Munna before he overturned the sieve. She sucked the edge of her sari's *pallu* and scrubbed his cheek, which was, like her own, like mine, red with iron dust. The dust mixed with our sweat and formed a gummy red paste, which stuck to our skin and was almost impossible to get off without soap and water, of which we had little, except for whatever dank rain gathered in stray pits and puddles. It was easy to tell who the mine workers were. We all looked like we were bleeding.

Amma put Munna down, and he began to try to crawl up the slope to me. She held her small body very straight and looked at the other women. "Siju is the youngest driver on-site," she announced loudly. The other women, even the one who laughed earlier, took no notice.

"Only fourteen and already driving a lorry." Amma was breathing heavily, and under her red mask she was flushed.

Munna slid back down the slope and landed on his bottom. He began to wail, his toothless mouth open in protest and outrage.

"He's your brother," Amma said.

We looked at Munna. Neither of us moved to pick him up.

"I know," I said.

I registered my fourth load at the weighing station and emptied my *puttu* into the first of a line of lorries waiting there. The weighing station was marked off from the neighboring permit yard by a low wall of scrap metal: short iron pipes and rusted carburetors and hubcaps that sometimes dislodged and rolled of their own accord across the yard, stopping with a clang when they hit Mr. Subbu's aluminum-walled shed. This shed, a square, burnished structure three times as big as the tent we lived in, was the labor office. Complaints were lodged there, and labor records were written down in a big book. How many laborers worked per day; how many *puttus* they filled; how many laborers were residents at the mine camp; how many were floaters, men and women who arrived by the busload in the mornings and stood in a ragged line, waiting to be given work. Mr. Subbu would come out of his office and point at random, and those who were not chosen would shuffle back to the bus depot on the highway, where they would take a bus to the next mine to try their luck. Those who stayed were given a hammer and *puttu*. Most of them, used to this routine, brought their own. During the day Mr. Subbu's shed could be seen from anywhere at the mine. All you had to do was look up from your hammering, and there it was, a sparkle on the rust-colored hillside. His maroon Esteem was parked outside, a green, tree-shaped air freshener twirling slowly from the rearview mirror. I noticed the greenness of the air freshener because there was not a single green tree near the mine; they all bore red leaves.

Mr. Subbu stood in the shade thrown by a backhoe loader, drinking a bottle of Pepsi. He was wearing a full-sleeved shirt with the top button undone, and I could see the triangle of a white undershirt and a few black tangles of hair peeping from the top. He sweated profusely, and there were large damp patches on his chest and lower back, and two damp crescents in his armpits, which swelled to full moons when he raised his arms.

I stood there, watching him. One of the workers, a young woman with two long braids, came up to him to say something. Mr. Subbu listened with his head bent. Then he put his hand on the girl's shoulder and replied. The girl stood so still that her braids did not even swish. When he finished speaking, he let his hand fall, then she turned and walked away. There had been a rumor in the mine camp about one of the new babies, and how it had Mr. Subbu's nose, and the mother, a rail-thin woman called Savithri, had been forced to sneak away from the camp at night before her husband came for her with the metal end of a belt. I had heard Appa call Mr. Subbu shameless and a *soole magane*, but something about the way he stood all alone in his nice clothes seemed lonely and promising. And as I stood there watching him, it occurred to me suddenly that he might be able to help me. My heart beat faster, and I pictured myself standing in the shade with him, talking, him smiling and nodding.

I went over to stand by him, my empty *puttu* thudding against my thighs. He finished the Pepsi and threw the bottle under the backhoe loader, all without paying attention to me. Then he wiped his mouth with a handkerchief.

"Taking rest?" he said. He had seen me around the mine, but he didn't know my name, of course. There were hundreds of children running everywhere, and under that coat of red we must have all looked the same to him.

"Yes, sir," I said. "Only five minutes," I added, lest he think I was shirking.

"Very good," said Mr. Subbu.

His eyelids drooped, and he nodded his head slowly. I waited for him to offer me a Pepsi, and when he didn't, I kept standing there. I wondered what a man like that thought about. I looked out over the mine, the land cut open in wide red swatches. Compared to the mine, the plain beyond seemed colorless, the trees sitting low to the ground, hardly different from the bushes, whose woody stems bore patches of dry leaves. In the distance there were hills that had not yet been mined, and they looked impossibly lush, rising and falling in deep, green waves against the sky. And the sun, the sun was a white ball that tore into everything, into the blistered skin on the backs of my hands, into the body of the backhoe loader, into the yawning red mouth of the mine.

I cleared my throat. Mr. Subbu's mouth parted and closed, parted and closed. Long strings of spit stretched and contracted between his lips.

"Sir," I said.

Mr. Subbu's eyes snapped open. "Hm?"

"Sir, I want to ask something."

He looked at me. I took a deep breath and held his eyes. They were not unkind eyes, only a little distant, a little distracted.

"I want to become a driver, sir. Lorry driver," I said, speaking quickly.

Mr. Subbu seemed to be waiting for more, so I continued, "I know driving, sir. My father taught me. He was the driver for the subinspector of the Raichur Thermal Station, sir. He drove an Esteem, sir, just like yours." And I pointed to the maroon car that was parked outside his shed.

I didn't think of it as a lie. When Appa had driven for the subinspector, I had sat in his lap whenever the subinspector was in a meeting or on an inspection tour or at the flat of a woman who was not his wife. I would hold the Esteem's steering wheel, dizzy from the musky odor of the leather upholstery, while Appa drove us slowly around the streets of Raichur, his foot barely touching the accelerator, whispering in my ear, "Left, now. Get ready. Turn the wheel slowly." And his hands would close over mine, swallowing them, and I would feel the pressure of his fingers and respond to them, pulling as he pulled, inhaling the spice of the cheap home-brewed *daru* that was always on his breath, waiting for those moments when his lips brushed the back of my head, and we would guide the car together, the big maroon bird making a graceful swoop and coming straight again. "Expert," Appa would whisper warm and rich into my hair as I frowned at the road to hide my pleasure. "So young and already driving like an expert."

I said nothing about the accident, about how Appa had been drunker than usual, how he had shattered the knee of the woman, how he had cried later because of the noise the woman made—a resigned sigh, *oh*—before she fell.

Mr. Subbu's fingers kneaded one another.

"Please, sir," I said.

"How old are you?" he asked.

I paused. "Thirteen," I said, rounding up.

"Thirteen," Mr. Subbu said. He squinted out into the sun, and then he pointed to the one of the workers moving over the surface of the red, undulating plain. The sun shrank him into a black dot, no bigger than one of the pebbles I filled my *puttu* with. "See him?" he asked.

"Yes, sir," I said. And together we watched him for a while.

Then Mr. Subbu said, as if posing a maths problem, "What is he doing?"

"Working," I said.

"Exactly," said Mr. Subbu. "Smart boy. He's working."

I watched a lorry wind its way to the bottom of a hill, heading to the highway, on an uneven road sawn into the hillside. Behind it trailed a hazy red cloud.

"Work hard, and you will get whatever you want," Mr. Subbu said, his voice louder than necessary, as if many people had gathered to hear him. "That's the best advice I can give you, my boy. Your father would tell you the same thing." And he touched me on the shoulder, a fatherly touch, at the same time pushing me lightly so that I found myself back in the sun again.

Instead of going back to the site beside the highway, I went to find Appa. Half-hidden behind a mound of earth, I watched him being lowered into a pit, a rope tied under his arms and passing across his bare chest. He had taken off his pants and wore only a pair of frayed striped boxer shorts. He carried a long-handled hammer like an extension of his arm. The loose end of the rope was held by three men, who braced their feet to hold the weight of Appa's body. And then the earth swallowed him, feet first.

I often came to watch him work like this, when he didn't know I was there. I would count the seconds he was down in the pit, listening for the steady crash of his hammer, muffled thunder. I would wait, alert to the slightest sound of panic, the faintest jerking of the rope. I knew that no matter how many times one did a job, the worst could happen the next time. And just as the waiting became unbearable, and I was about to run into the open, to give myself away, he emerged, red-faced, dangling, gasping like a man being pulled from water.

They untied him, and he began rubbing his skin where the rope had cut into him. One of the men said, "Nice weather down there?" and Appa said, "Sunny like your wife's *thullu*." The man laughed. Appa said, "One day I want to tie up that bastard Subbu and send him down there." The other man said, "He'd get stuck, first of all. Second thing is he's too busy putting his fat hands all over girls. What else you think he does in that office all day?"

"Fat bastard," Appa said. He raised his hammer and brought it down once, hard. Then he lifted it again and let it crash down, and then he did it again, the rise and fall of the hammer all part of the same smooth motion. I could feel the impact of each blow travel through the ground between our bodies, from the muscles in his arms to the muscles in my legs, connecting us.

"Thank god I have only sons," Appa said, and the man laughed again.

When I returned to the site beside the highway, Manju had disappeared. The ground where she had been squatting was scuffed. I crouched over it and tried to make out the marks of her bare feet. A few women were still hunched over, their hammers clinking in rhythm. The woman with the missing eye pulled a pinch of tobacco from a large gray wad and handed it to me. I took it and chewed on it slowly. The bitter tobacco juice flooded my mouth.

The woman watched me chew. "Want to know where that girl went?" she asked.

I tried to imagine what could have happened to her eye. I wanted to apologize for Manju throwing a stone at her, but I was angry at the woman for calling Manju a *soole*.

"She probably went back to her tent," I said.

"Take another guess," the woman said. "Shall I tell you?"

"No," I said.

"Smart boy," she said.

Then she leaned forward and lowered her voice. "Listen to me. That girl is not nice. Okay? Not nice. You should stay away from her."

"Excuse me," I said. "I have to work."

For the next few hours I worked without stopping. I pounded the ore with my hammer, the blows precise, never faltering, the ring of metal against metal filling my head. Sweat poured down my wrists, and I had to keep wiping my hands on my shorts. Lorries ticked by on the highway, marking time. Siju's lorry did not drive past again. After a while the women stood up and stretched their backs. They flexed their fingers and curled their toes in the dirt. The one who had given me the tobacco smiled, but with just one eye her smile looked insincere. They took up their full *puttus* and their hammers and walked off in the direction of the weighing station. As they walked, I noted their square backs, their strong thigh muscles showing through their saris, their strange bow-legged gait, their gnarled feet caked with dirt. None of them owned shoes except for the odd pair of rubber or plastic sandals. Manju had been right, I thought. They looked less like women and more like monkeys, the muscular brown monkeys that would swarm our village outside Raichur. They were fearless and feral, those monkeys, grabbing peanuts from children's hands, attacking people with their small, sharp teeth. A pack of them would sit on top of a low, crumbling wall, chattering and picking lice from each other's fur, in the way that these women scratched their armpits and laughed in low, coarse voices.

The day ripened into purple and then rotted into black, the air sagging with the smells I never noticed when the sun was there to burn it all away, the stench from pools filled with stagnant water and buzzing with mosquitoes, the sweet whiff of shit drifting from the field we all used, furtively or defiantly, even the women and girls. I registered my last load of iron and returned to our tent, where Amma was preparing the coals for dinner. Clouds pressed down on the camp, our city of plastic tents, and we could hear the voices of the men coming down from the top of the rise where they gathered to drink after work every evening.

I could hear Appa's voice above the others, his laugh the loudest. Amma glanced up every now and again, her face a shining red circle of worry in the light of the coals. I held Munna on my lap, and he blinked sleepily into the coals. When we heard Appa's singing, the notes warbling as he came down the rise toward us, Amma glanced quickly at me and began blowing at the coals. I pressed my nose into Munna's neck and smelled his sour baby smell. The coals pulsed brightly every time Amma blew, her cheeks puffed with the effort.

"Guna, the *paan*," Amma hissed, and I rummaged in a plastic bag for the battered shoe-polish tin in which we kept a stock of crumbled areca nut and a small stack of betel leaves.

"Wipe Munna's nose," she ordered, and I used Munna's sleeve to wipe away the shining thread of mucus that trickled out of one nostril.

"Guna—" and that was all she had time to say before Appa ducked his head under the tent and collapsed among us, creating a confused tangle of arms and legs. Amma smoothly moved out of his way and began pressing balls of dough between her palms and pinching the edges until the dough became round and flat, and she laid them over the coals to bake. She stared at them intently, as if they might fly away. Appa leaned on his elbow. He was no longer stripped down but was wearing his torn T-shirt that said *Calvin Kline* and his faded pants rolled up to his knees. In January he had smashed his hammer into the large toe of his left foot, and it had healed crooked, like a bird's beak.

"Supriya," Appa said, drawing her name out. *Shoopreeya.*

Amma said nothing.

"So serious you look," Appa said. His face seemed to contract and expand, and his *daru*-scented breath filled the tent. "Not happy to see me? Not even one smile for your husband? Your poor husband who has been working like a dog all day?"

Amma bit her lip so hard the bottom of her face twisted. She picked a baked roti off the coals with her bare fingers and laid it on a sheet of newspaper. Appa hiccupped.

I held out the shoe-polish tin. Appa took it, popped it open, and sprinkled some areca nut on a betel leaf. He folded the leaf into a neat square and began chewing it. Red juice came out of the side of his mouth. I watched it trickle down his chin.

"Guna," he said then, his mouth red and wet. "How many *puttus* today, Guna?"

I was about to say eight when I caught sight of Amma's face, looking engorged and pleading in the light from the coals. Without taking her

189

eyes off the rotis, she slipped a hand into her blouse and touched her breast where the velvet pouch was.

I said, "Six."

"Six," Appa repeated. "That's all?"

"Yes," I said. "Sorry, Appa." I waited for the sting of the slap.

But instead he reached out and slowly caressed the side of my face. He ran his hand from the top of my head down my cheek, over my chin, and to the soft spot on my neck, where my pulse had begun to race. His hand was like sandpaper, covered in scabs and blisters, some that had burst and scarred, some that were still ripe. I felt every bump and welt against my skin, every dip and hollow. It was as if he were leaving the living imprint of his hand on my face.

"No, no," he said in a rich voice, his singing voice. "Don't say sorry. I should be sorry. I should be the one saying sorry. It's because of me you are here. All of you. It is all my fault." His voice trembled on the edge of a cliff, and his eyes were so dark.

I felt a pricking behind my eyes. My face was humming. There was a heaviness to my limbs. I wondered if this was what he felt like when he was drunk.

"My fault," Appa said. "I'm a bad father."

Appa held out his hand, and I dropped my wages into it. All of it, even the eleven rupees I had just lied to him about. Appa's palm closed around the money, and he dropped it into his pocket. I tightened my arms around Munna. I didn't dare look at Amma.

I heard her body shift. She let out a breath she'd been holding.

"That is his school money," she said.

Appa didn't turn to look at her.

"That is his school money," she said again. "We said this year he would go back. You have to keep some of that for tuition fees."

He said, "You're telling me what to do? In my own house you're telling me?"

Black spots appeared on the rotis, each accompanied by a small hiss.

"You're just one man," Amma said, staring at the spots. "How much *daru* will you drink?" She paused. "I should have had a daughter."

"What bloody daughter?" said Appa. "Why you want a daughter? You want for me to pay dowry? Some snot-nosed fellow comes and says, I want to marry her, and I have to go into my own pocket and lick his bum? No, thank you."

"Daughters help their mothers. And you'd drink all of her dowry anyway," muttered Amma.

190

I thought he was going to caress her too, the way his hand went out, but then I saw he was pinching her, clamping down on the fleshiest part of her waist, right above her hipbone, the strip of bare skin between the top of her petticoat and the bottom of her blouse. She flailed, her mouth open without screaming. One of her hands caught Munna on the side of the head, and she kicked a stray coal so close to my foot that I could feel it scorch my toe. I drew my foot back and waited for Munna to cry, but he didn't.

When Appa let go, there were two semicircles of bright red on Amma's hip, the skin slightly puckered. She was moaning softly but did not let the rotis burn. She picked them off and put them on the newspaper. She was breathing hard through her teeth.

"Supriya, you know what problem you have? You don't smile enough," Appa told her. "You should smile more. A woman who doesn't smile is ugly."

Then Amma's gaze traveled beyond the coals, beyond Appa's prone form, and I turned to see Siju standing at the entrance of the tent. He looked fresh. His hair was combed, of all things. He stood there, watching us, and suddenly I could see us through his eyes, the picture we presented, me with my toes curled in, Munna swaying with sleep in my arms, Appa reclining on his elbow, Amma hunched over the coals. I saw what he saw, and then I wished I hadn't seen it.

"What you think you're staring at?" Appa said. "Sit down."

Siju picked his way to an empty spot between Appa and me. As soon as he sat down, the tent felt full, too full. We were too close together, fear and anger flying around like rockets.

"Where did you go today?" Amma asked Siju. To my surprise, he didn't turn away like he usually did but looked at her with a distant sort of sympathy, as if she were a stranger he had made up his mind to be kind to.

"Hospet," he said.

"Hospet," Amma repeated gratefully. "Is it a nice place?"

With the same careful kindness he said, "Actually, I've never seen a dirtier place."

"What the hell you were expecting?" Appa said, trying to provoke him. "All cities are dirty. You want to eat your food off the street, or what?"

Siju ignored him, and I could sense Appa stiffening.

"How many trips did you get?" Amma asked.

"Trips!" Appa snorted. "He drives that bloody lorry ten kilometers to the railway station. Ten kilometers! How do you call that a trip?"

Siju began to massage his feet. Amma put another roti on the coals. Appa glared at them both, their exclusion of him causing the pressure inside to build and build.

"So? How many?" Appa said. His head swiveled slowly in Siju's direction. "How many *trips?* Your mother asked a question, can't you hear? You're deaf or something?"

"Three," said Siju curtly.

"Don't talk like I'm some peon who cleans your shit. Say it properly."

"Three," repeated Siju.

"You're listening, Supriya?" drawled Appa with exaggerated awe. "You want something to smile about? Your son got three trips to the bloody railway station in a bloody lorry. *Three trips!* What you want a daughter for? With a son like this?"

His glassy gaze never left Siju's face. Amma laid the last roti over the coals.

"Bloody lorry driver thinks he's a bloody raja," muttered Appa.

I pinched Munna under the arm, hoping to make him cry, hoping to create a distraction, but he wouldn't. I pinched again harder, but he sat still, a soft, surprisingly heavy weight on my lap. One of the coals popped, and my heart jumped. I remembered the way the manager of the thermal station had come to our house after Appa's accident. Spit flew from the manager's mouth as he screamed, landing lightly on Appa's face, and I remembered how Appa didn't wipe it off. I remembered the way Appa had said, "No, sir. Sorry, sir. No, sir. Sorry, sir," like he didn't understand the words. Like they were a poem he had memorized. That night he went and lay down on the road, and when Amma went to bring him back in, he said, "Supriya, leave me alone! I deserve this." And I remembered the way she held his head, speaking to him softly until he dragged himself up and followed her back inside.

Now he waited to see what Siju would do.

For a second I thought he would hit Appa. Then he shrugged. "Being a bloody lorry driver is better than hammering bloody pieces of iron all day." He looked at me as he said this, and I looked away.

Amma used her finger to smear the rotis with lime pickle, rolled them into tubes, and handed them to us. She held her arms out for Munna, slipping her blouse down her shoulder, baring her slack breast with its wine-colored nipple. Munna latched on, his black eyes shining in the semidarkness, unblinking, gazing at us. The roti was warm and tasted of smoke, and the pickle was tart, the lime stringy and tough. I thought only about the food, about how it was filling my mouth, sliding tight down my throat, unlocking something. It was always this way. The food loosened something in all of us, a tightly wound spring uncoiling. I felt myself starting to relax. Food could do this, and warmth, and the approach of sleep. There were these moments of calm, when no one spoke, and there were only the coals and the insistent flapping of the plastic tent and the mumble of other families and the sky hanging low.

Then Siju, leaning toward me, spoiled it all by saying, "I have something to say to you."

I swallowed quickly. "I don't want to hear anything," I said. We kept our voices down because Appa seemed to have fallen asleep. He was snoring lightly.

"Listen just one second."

"Oh-ho, Lorry Raja wants to say something," I said.

"Don't "

I put my fingers in my ears and chanted, "Lorry Raja! Lorry Raja!" I knew it was silly, but I wanted to keep this fragile peace, to clutch it tightly in my fist like a precious stone.

"Guna, listen!" Siju said, louder than he had intended.

"What's the racket?" said Appa, coming out of his doze.

"Nothing," said Siju.

"Nothing," I repeated.

Appa closed his eyes again. Amma was still breast-feeding Munna, her head bent in contemplation of his placid sucking.

"That monkey woman called Manju a *soole*," I said quietly.

Siju picked at a scab on his knee.

"What are you two talking about?" Amma asked.

Before Siju could reply, I said, "Manju. *His* girlfriend."

"The girl whose mother is sick?"

I nodded.

"Poor thing," Amma said. "Maybe I should go see if I can do something."

But then Munna fell asleep, still making halfhearted sucks at her nipple, and her eyes went soft. She brushed her hand against the tuft of hair sticking up from his red-stained forehead.

"Don't bother," Siju spat. "*She* knows how to get what she wants."

"I'm going to see if she's okay," I said, standing up. To my surprise, Siju stood up too.

"I'll come with you," he said.

"No!" I shouted.

"Yes," said Amma. "Both of you go."

"Siju," Appa said. He was still in that reclining position. His calves under the rolled-up pants were like polished cannonballs. I remembered the way I had seen him earlier that day, bare chested, bent at the waist, his long-handled hammer making smooth strokes, crashing against the ground. He was not a big man or a tall one, but he was a man who broke iron for ten hours every day.

Siju looked at him for a long moment, then nodded and reached into his pocket. He brought out a set of folded notes and pressed it into Appa's outstretched palm. Appa tucked it into his pocket, where my own wages nestled. He hummed something tuneless and closed his eyes.

Amma was watching us both. "Here," she said. "Take something for them." She made me wrap two rotis in newspaper. "Come back before it rains."

"You don't have to come if you don't want to," I told Siju as we picked our way through the maze of tents. "I won't tell."

Instead of answering he was quiet, which made me nervous. A rat the size of my foot ran across our path and disappeared into the blackness to our right. The rats were a problem in the camp. They got into our food, chewed holes in our blankets, bit babies as they slept. Last year a baby had died from a rat bite. I thought of Munna asleep, of the whole camp silent, a ship of blue plastic afloat on these hairy black bodies that moved and rustled under it, restless and hungry as the ocean.

Manju wasn't in her tent. From inside came the loud, ragged breathing of her mother. Siju raised his eyebrows at me and jerked his chin in the direction of the tent's opening. I shook my head; I could just make out the shadowy figure wrapped in a blanket, smaller than a person should be. Then Manju's mother coughed, a colorless wheezing cough, like wind passing through a narrow, lonely corridor. I took an unconscious step backward.

"She's not there," I whispered.

"Smart fellow," Siju whispered back.

"So now what?"

"We go back to our tent."

"*You* go back," I said. "I'll wait for her here. She must have gone to the toilet."

Siju gave me a long, searching look. "Guna," he said. "Just forget her."

"No!" I almost shouted. I felt the start of tears, burning in the ridge of my nose. Before I could stop myself, I said, "She wants me to take her to China."

"What?" His voice was flat.

"In my lorry," I said. I knew I was babbling. I squeezed the rotis and felt the warmth seep through the newspaper. "She said if I could drive a lorry, I could take her to China. To see the Lympic Games. I asked Mr. Subbu, but he said no. He said if I work hard I'll get what I want."

Siju let out a long breath. "You asked Subbu?" he said. "That fat bastard? You asked him?"

"Yes," I said.

"My god." My brother shook his head. "Come with me," he said.

Mr. Subbu's Esteem was still parked outside his aluminum-walled shed. The shed was directly under a single lamppost, whose light cast it in a liquid, silver glow. The lamppost was connected to a generator, which growled like a sleeping dog. We crept up to the backhoe loader, which was just outside the shoreline of light.

Siju put his hand on my shoulder. "Not too close," he said.

"Why are we here?" I asked. He put a finger on his lips.

We waited, partly hidden by the massive machine. I leaned against it, and the cold of its metal body was a shock. Siju was standing behind me, very close. There was a strange calmness to the whole scene, the glowing shed, the purring of the generator, the still air.

And then, with a movement so smooth and natural that I forgot to be surprised, Manju stepped from Mr. Subbu's shed. She stood there for a moment, her uniform and thin legs perfectly outlined in the light of the lamp, her face lifted like one of the deer on the back panel of Siju's lorry. Then she turned and looked straight at us. I jumped, but Siju's hand was on my shoulder again.

"Be still," he whispered.

But Manju had seen us. Her uniform seemed even bigger on her frame than it had earlier in the day. She was floating in it as she came over to us. Her feet were soundless in the dirt. As soon as she was level with the backhoe loader, Siju stepped out and pulled her behind it. She put her hands on her hips and looked at us for a long time without speaking. Behind her, the lamppost snapped off, plunging everything into darkness. Then the headlights of Mr. Subbu's Esteem came on, and the car floated away, as if borne on an invisible river.

"So," Manju said. As my eyes adjusted slowly, I noticed that her eyes were swollen. She had been crying. I thought of the shed, of Mr. Subbu's hands kneading each other, of the cold bottle of Pepsi, of the way he'd put his hand on the shoulder of the girl with the braids. I thought of the woman with one eye saying, *That girl is not nice.*

"How long have you been standing here?" Manju asked.

"Relax," said Siju coolly. "Guna felt like taking a walk."

"A walk," Manju repeated. She looked at me quickly, accusingly, and I felt a spike of guilt. "And you just walked this way," she said.

Siju shrugged. "That's how it happened."

I said, "We came to give you these rotis." I pressed the newspaper-wrapped rotis into her hand. She looked at them as if I had done something meaningless.

"Let's go back to the tent," I told Siju. I wanted to get away from Manju's raw, swollen face. Her tears had made clear channels in the red paste on her cheeks.

"Just one minute," Siju said. He leaned in close to Manju so that his face was barely inches from hers. He smiled. It was not a nice smile.

"Guna told me you want to go to China," he said.

Manju looked at me, puzzled. I closed my eyes. "What?" she said uncertainly.

"Still want to go?"

He had made a copy of the lorry key. In Hospet. He had waited in the lorry while a shopkeeper fashioned a new one, which was raw and shining and silver. It made me uncomfortable to look at it.

In the lorry yard, the smell of grease and diesel strong in my nose, I whispered, "Mr. Subbu will throw you out if he finds out. Appa will kill you."

"Shut up," Siju said in a normal voice. "Mr. Subbu! Appa! You think I care? Come with us or stay here and shut up. Your decision."

He climbed into the high cab of the lorry. He reached over and held a hand out for Manju, who held it indifferently, as if she were being

196

asked to hold a piece of wood. He let me struggle in by myself. When I had shut the door, he inserted the shining key into the ignition.

"They're going to hear us," I said.

"No, they're not," he said grimly. He turned the key and started the engine.

It sounded like thunder rolling across the plain. I closed my eyes and waited for a shout, a light shining in our faces, the relief of discovery. But no one came. The city of tents stayed dark, except for the glimmer of burning coals. The sky answered with thunder of its own.

Siju did not turn on the headlights, and the lorry drifted out of the yard, past the weighing station, past the permit yard, rounding the perimeter, the camp turning silently on its axis like a black globe, the dirt road invisible.

"On your marks," I heard Siju say. He sounded calm. "Get set. Go."

And then I felt the pressure release, the lorry pick up speed, and we were driving downhill, and there was wind rushing in through the windows, filling my lungs. I could feel Manju's shoulder against mine, and there were Siju's hands curled on the wheel, and the floorboard thrummed under my feet, and I was suddenly awake, wide awake, filled with the cold night air.

Siju flipped on the headlights, and I saw that we were no longer within the boundaries of the mine, we had left it behind, and trees flashed by, their lowest branches scraping the sides of the lorry. There was no time to feel anything. All I could do was keep my balance, keep my shoulder from slamming against the door. We hurtled past rocks that were big enough to jump off. Siju drove leaning forward, without slowing for anything, and the lorry bounced and jostled, and its springs screeched, and in the yellow beam of the headlights I saw the ground jump sharply into focus for an instant before we swallowed it. The hills in the distance were getting closer, and I wondered if Siju intended to drive to the top of them, or even beyond. I wanted him to. I wanted him to drive forever. As long as he kept driving, we would be safe.

But then he stopped, let the engine idle fall into silence. We were in the middle of the plains, far enough away from the mine to seem like a different country. The ground stretched away on every side. The trees provided no orientation. They simply carved out darker shapes in the darkness. Siju took his hands off the wheel and ran them through his hair. Manju's chest rose and fell under the uniform. She stared straight

197

ahead, through the grimy windshield, even after we had been sitting there in silence for minutes.

"Gold medal," I heard Siju whisper.

I opened and closed my mouth, each time to say something that crumbled and became a confused tangle of words.

"You shouldn't have brought Guna," Manju said. The sound of my name made me shiver, as if by naming me she had made me responsible. For this, for the three of us, here. As if whatever happened here would be because of me.

"Why not?" Siju said. "He deserves to come, no? You know, he even went to Subbu today and asked if he could be a lorry driver. All because of you. Sweet, no? Bastard said no, of course. I could have told him not to waste his time; Subbu has his fat hands filled with your—"

"You think I like this?" she said. She spoke to the windshield, to the open plain. "Begging for money? Sir, please give money for medicine. Sir, please give money for surgery. Sir, Mummy's coughing again. Doctor says her lungs are weak. Sir, please give money for doctor's fees. You think it's nice to stand still and let him do whatever he wants? And he gives too little money, so every time I have to go back. You think it's a big game?"

I could tell that Siju was taken aback. "You could work—"

"Fifty rupees per day!" Manju said. "Even if I work all day and night, it would not even be enough for food. Sometimes you're so stupid. Even Guna is smarter than you." After she said this, she seemed to collapse. I could feel her shoulder sag against mine.

"Manju," I said. For no reason other than to say her name.

Siju sat in silence for a while. Then he made a strangled sound in his throat, like he was coming to a decision he already hated himself for. He opened his door and jumped out.

"Come on," he said to Manju.

I made a move to get out.

"No, you stay here," Siju said.

"But—" I started to say.

"Guna, just stay here," Manju said. She sounded tired.

I bit down on my lip. Manju put her arm around my shoulders and pulled me close. I could smell metal in her hair. It was the most vivid thing I had ever smelled. It was a smell that had a shape, edges as solid a building. And then for no reason I thought of our neighbor's wife, the one who survived after her husband tried to burn them all. She lived in the temple courtyard after that, and the priests fed her.

Sometime she would take dried pats of cow dung and put them on her head like a hat and stare at passersby, the skin of her cheek rippled pink. I don't know why I thought of that woman just then, but I did. And while I was remembering her, Manju was sliding away from me, into the driver's seat, her legs stretching to the ground. She dropped with a little grunt.

I heard them walk around the lorry, heard the clink of the chain and the rusted creak as the back panel was lowered. I felt the vibrations of their movements come to me through the empty lorry bed. A scraping noise, and I knew Siju was spreading a tarpaulin sheet across the back. Through the metal, through the fake leather of the seat, through the cogs and gears and machinery, I could feel their movements, the positioning of one body over another. I heard Siju say something in a low voice. I don't remember hearing Manju reply.

And then I didn't want to hear any more, so I listened instead to the whirring of insects in the bushes, the nighttime howls of dogs from the villages whose fires hung suspended in the distance, the wind that traveled close to the ground, scraping dry leaves into piles. The darkness made it vast, vaster than the mine, which in the daytime seemed so large to me. It was different in every way from the camp, where the sounds were either machine sounds, lifting and loading and dumping and digging, or people sounds, eating or snoring or crying or swearing at someone to shut up so they could sleep.

A light wind brushed my face, carried the smell of rain. Tomorrow the work would be impossible, the ground too wet to dig, the ore slippery and slick, the puddles swollen to ponds. The men would slide around, knee-deep, and curse. The children would push each other, making it into a rough game. The lorries would get stuck, their wheels spinning, flinging mud in all directions, and we would have to spend an extra hour digging them out. There would be red mud in the crooks of our elbows, in our fingernails, in our ears. The coals, in the evening, would refuse to light.

For a second I couldn't move, as if the coming days and weeks and months and years were piling on top of me like a load of ore, pinning me against the darkness, and then I found myself slipping into the driver's seat and taking hold of the shining key, which stuck out of the ignition like a small cold hand asking to be grasped. I tried to remember what to do, what I had seen others do. I carefully pressed the clutch. I needed to slide forward to the edge of the seat to do it. I turned the key, and the lorry rumbled to life. I waited for a second, holding my breath, and then in a rush I released the clutch and stomped on the accelerator. The lorry bucked, then jumped a couple of feet, and my temple hit the half-rolled driver's-door window. I put my finger to my skin, and it came away wet with blood. The engine stammered and died, and everything went back to silence.

Siju wrenched open the door and dragged me out of the cab. He grasped two handfuls of my shirt and shook me.

"What's wrong with you?" he said. "What kind of idiot are you?"

When I didn't answer, he let go of my shirt. His pants were unzipped, and I looked at the V-shaped flap that was hanging open. He saw me looking and said, "What?"

"Nothing."

"Just say it, Guna."

"Nothing," I said.

He zipped his pants.

"Then get inside," he said. "We're going home."

"What about Manju?" I asked.

"She wants to sit in the back."

"It's going to rain," I said. "She'll get wet."

"Just get inside the bloody lorry, Guna," Siju said. "Don't argue."

Inside the cab I hugged my body and tried to stay awake. The cold air was still coming in, and I wanted to roll up my window, but Siju had his open, his elbow resting on it, head leaning on that hand, the other guiding the lorry. He was driving slowly now, taking care to avoid the bumps and dips in the uneven ground. We passed a rock, ghostly white, that I didn't remember from the journey out. From the corner of my eye, I looked at him, my sullen brother. Not a raja but a fourteen-year-old lorry driver in a Bellary mine.

"What's going to happen now?" I asked.

He drew his hand inside. "What's going to happen to what?"

To everything, I wanted to say. But I said, "Manju's mother."

He let a few moments go by before answering. And when he did, what he said was, "Come on, Guna. You're smart. You know."

"We could have given her the money from my school fees," I said.

"For what?" He sounded like an old man. "So she can die in three months instead of two?"

After that we didn't talk. The trees fell away, and the ground became smoother. The camp came into view, almost completely dark, just a few remaining fires that would burn throughout the night. Siju parked in the lorry yard and jumped out. I stayed sitting in the cab. A few drops of rain fell on the windshield and created long glossy streaks as they traveled down. The camp would wake to find itself afloat. The rats would come looking for dry ground. Munna would need to be nursed. Amma would put her hand behind his soft downy head to soothe him. Appa would bail out the water that pooled in the roof of our tent. Amma would tie an old *lungi* of Appa's to two of the bamboo poles to create a hammock for Munna that would keep him above the reach of the rats. Manju's mother would shift to a more comfortable position and wait for the rain to stop. There didn't seem to be a reason for any of it, a logic that I could see. There was repetition and routine and the inevitability of accident. Tomorrow Mr. Subbu would drink a Pepsi, and we would dig for iron.

I heard Siju say my name, and I heard the panic in his voice. It was raining in earnest now, the windshield a silver wash. I pushed open the door and nearly fell out. My feet sank into the soft mud. Siju was standing at the back of the truck, the back panel open. His hair hung draggled around his face, and drops of water clung to the tips. He pointed wordlessly to the lorry bed. I forced my eyes to scan the entire space for Manju, but she wasn't there.

We stood there for what seemed like an hour, though I knew it was less than a minute. I pictured her walking across the plains, her face directed to some anonymous town. She would walk for hours, I knew, and when she got tired, she would sleep exactly where she stopped walking, her arms shielding her face from the rain. I imagined her curled up on the ground. I imagined that her hair would plaster her cheek. I imagined that her uniform would be washed back into white, a beacon for anyone watching, except no one would be.

Over the following months Siju began sucking diesel out of the lorries and selling it back to the drivers at 20 percent below pump prices, and by the time the monsoons ended, he had earned enough money for one year of school fees for me. He gave it to Amma without telling me, and I never thanked him directly. We had spoken very little since the night of the lorry ride. I watched him closely for a while, worried that he would disappear too, but he came back night after night, sometimes after we had all fallen asleep, never smiling, never saying much. I knew he took the lorry out sometimes, but he never took me with him again.

He stopped swaggering, and the lorry cleaners seemed disappointed. I went to school in the mornings and returned to the mine afterward.

The next August, after the flooded pits were starting to dry out again, Mr. Subbu arrived at the mine late one afternoon and announced that he was giving everyone the rest of the day off. He smiled at the responding cheer. Then from his Esteem he brought out a small color television and a white satellite dish and hooked them up to the generator, setting them on a rickety table with the help of the one of the laborers. He fiddled with the antenna until a picture flickered on the screen.

We all gathered around to watch the magnificent round stadium in China fill with color and light and music and movement. We watched graceful acrobats and women with feathers and children with brightly painted faces. We watched glittering fireworks and slender athletes in shiny tracksuits and flapping flags with all the shades of the world. We watched as the stadium slowly filled with red light, and thousands of people arranged themselves into gracious, shifting shapes in the center. Thousands more gathered in the seats, their faces reflecting the same awe we felt. We watched, all of us, in silence, stunned by the beauty of what we had created.

Nominated by Narrative

ORIGIN

by SARAH LINDSAY

from POETRY NORTHWEST

The first cell felt no call to divide.
Fed on abundant salts and sun,
still thin, it simply spread,
rocking on water, clinging to stone,
a film of obliging strength.
Its endoplasmic reticulum
was a thing of incomparable curvaceous length;
its nucleus, Golgi apparatus, RNA
magnificent. With no incidence
of loneliness, inner conflict, or deceit,
no predator nor prey,
it had little to do but thrive,
draw back from any sharp heat
or bitterness, and change its pastel
colors in a kind of song.
We are descendants of the second cell.

Nominated by Poetry Northwest, Maura Stanton

THE DEAD

by STEPHEN DIXON

from BOULEVARD

Bartok's dead. Britten's dead. Webern's dead. Berg's dead. Górecki's dead. Copland's dead. Messiaen's dead. Bernhard's dead. Beckett's dead. Joyce is dead. Nabokov's dead. Mann's dead. Bulgakov's dead. Pinter's dead. Ionesco's dead, de Ghelderode's dead. Berryman's dead. Lowell's dead. Williams is dead. Roethke's dead. Who of the rest of the greats isn't dead? The past century. The start of this century, Bacon's dead. De Kooning's dead. Rothko's dead, Ensor's dead. Picasso's dead. Braque's dead. Apollinaire's dead. Maybe all the greats are dead. So what am I saying? Soon I'll be dead. My last brother will be dead. My two other brothers are dead. Robert. Merrill. My last two sisters will be dead. Madeleine's dead. My parents are dead. My wife's dead. Her parents are dead. Their relatives in Europe are long dead. My two best friends are dead. I lie on a hospital bed. I can't get up. I can't turn over. I'm stuck to the bed by wires and tubes. I can't get comfortable and I feel so hopeless and I'm in such pain that I almost want to be dead. I ring for the nurse. Usually someone responds. This time no one answers. I wait. I don't want to antagonize them. I ring again. What will I say? "Make me dead?" "Yes?" "Pain medication, please." "I'll tell your nurse." "I need it badly." "I'll tell your nurse." She comes. "Pain level on a grade from one to ten?" "Nine." I want to say "ten" but there's got to be a pain worse than mine. She gives me the medication through my I.V. I fall asleep. When I awake I begin to hallucinate. Too much pain medication, they've said. What can I do? It's the only way to stop the pain and sleep. The room's become a prison cell. Bars on my windows and door. Then it's an asylum cell. No bars; just extra thick glass. People pass. I hear low voices. "This," they say, and "That." I've got to get out of here. I yell for help. People keep passing my room both ways but no one seems to hear me or turns to my glass door. They all wear white doctor outfits. Gowns. Robes. Whatever they're called, but very white and clean. Lab coats, maybe. Hugging clipboards to their chests. "This," they say. "That." Then some muttering and they're gone. "Help," I yell. "I need help. I'm going to defecate in my bed." They continue to walk past. "OK," I say, "I'm going to shit in my bed." Dummy, I think; the nurse. I ring for her. I can barely manage the little box. The summoning device. Whatever it's called. The thing that turns the TV on and off and raises and lowers the two ends of the bed. I don't know what anything's called anymore. Not even what brought me in here. Bowel interruption. Obstruction. Even if I got the right term, two operations after I got here, I don't even know what it is. "Yes?" "Thank God. Pain medication, please." "I'll tell your nurse." She comes. "It should be no more than every four hours. But we're ten minutes away, so close enough." "Thanks. And it must mean I've slept most of the last four hours. That's good. More I sleep, the better. And I think I need changing." She looks. "You're imagining it. Do you need to go now?" "No. I don't want to sit on it for the next hour. And I haven't eaten anything for days, so there's probably nothing there." I fall asleep. I dream I'm being devoured by lions. I fight to get out of the dream and wake up. So what was that all about? Literary lions? Ah, who cares for interpretations. I close my eyes and hear voices. I open my eyes and see people in white smocks walking past, all of them holding clipboards. "Build," they say. "Don't build." "Then cut." "OK." I've got to get out of here. Dreams, awake, there's always something to be afraid of. The doctor the other day, who was just a resident making the rounds and not even my regular doctor, who said he read my X-rays and I might have to have a bag outside my stomach to collect my shit. If I'm to die, and I'd want to if I had to have one of those bags put in, let me die in my own bed with a big overdose of whatever we got there or they send me home with. And if I'm to live, I need a less frightening room. I want to call my daughters but I can't find my cellphone. They recharged it today and said they put it in a place I could easily reach, but I don't see it. I feel around me. There's the summoning device. A handkerchief. A pen. I'll say I know it's late but I'm going crazy and you have to get me another room. "It's the drugs. But without them I'm even in worse shape. I'm probably not making much sense," I'll say, "but I'm hearing voices. Other people's voices. And seeing people walk past my room who are either dead or intentionally ignoring me, but they never answer my cries for help. If I don't get another room, I'll pull all the wires and tubes out of me, even the Foley, no matter how much that might hurt, and escape." But don't scare them. Or wake them up. They've been so good to you, flying in from different distant cities and staying in your room eight to ten hours a day. Reading to you, though you didn't want to tell them you didn't want to be read to. Holding your hand and doing things like putting damp washcloths on your forehead, though you didn't want those either. Angels, you've called them; so let your angels sleep. And you're not in that much pain now. Comes more often than it goes. And the muttering voices have stopped and no one's walking past your room but the regular nurses and aides, who'd come if you called out for them. Try to sleep. Time will go faster. I pull the covers up to my chin. I'm warm but not too warm. I'm comfortable. My body feels normal. I fall asleep. I dream I'm in Tokyo, where I'd always wanted to go, but got there without having to take a plane. I wake up and it's the beginning of daylight. Dusk. Dawn. What's it called again? I should know. That one's so easy. Words are what I do. But I'm in pain again, which always makes me confused. I ring the call button. That's what it is. Call button, call button; remember it. "Yes?" "Pain medication, please." "I'll tell your nurse." A different one comes. "Hi. I'm Martha. Your tech's Cindy. The new shift." She erases from a white board on the wall the names and phone extensions of the previous nurse and tech and with a marker writes their own. "You slept poorly, your last nurse said. Lots of agitation and talk. Like you wanted a hot thermal bath. Sorry, fella. We don't have that here. And how dragons were out to get you and something about your arms being cut off at the elbows by a sword. And you perspired something awful. She had to wipe you off." "I don't remember any of it. Well, dreams." "Because of all that, I want to hold off giving you the pain medication as long as I can. Still hurting?" "Level nine or eight." "Think you can tolerate it for another half hour? And you could use a fresh gown." She takes off my wet one and puts a new one on. "Anything else you need?" "My cellphone." "You've been sleeping on it," and she pulls it out from under my arm. She goes. Poulenc's dead. Prokofiev's dead. Mahler's dead. Granados is dead. Did I say Bartok's dead? Pärt's not dead. Who else isn't dead? Tanizaki's dead. Solzhenitsyn's dead. Hamsun's dead. Borges is dead. Conrad's dead. Konrad's not dead. Did Lessing recently die? The Italian writer whose first name starts with a D and who in one book wrote too much like Kafka is dead. Kafka, of course, is dead, Cummings is dead. Stevens is dead. Auden's dead. Yeats is dead. Pollack's dead. Leger's dead. Kandinsky's dead. Malevich is dead. Moore, Maillol and Matisse are dead. My pain isn't dead. I shit in my head. I mean in my bed. Suddenly it came. I piss into a catheter, so there I'm OK. I want to clean myself up in the bathroom. I want to drink a glassful of ice water. I want to stand up and walk out of here. I press the call button. "Yes?" "I'm sorry, but I need serious cleaning up. And I presume new bedding and a new gown and my bed remade. I'm lying in slime. I'm sweating like a pig. I need the thermostat lowered. Please have someone come right away." "I'll tell your tech." A young woman comes. Almost a girl. She has a new gown for me and sheets and washrags and a basin of water. "Oh, I see you already have my name on your board." "You're the tech? I'm sorry for the mess I made." "I'm actually a nurse in training but a tech today. So let's have a look. Roll over on your side." I grab the side rail and pull myself up. "I don't know where it came from. I haven't eaten for a week. Nor drunk anything. All the nourishment and liquid I get comes from ice chips and what's in those bags. And this time it's not my imagination and I did defecate?" "In abundance. Won't take a minute." She takes off my gown, wipes and washes and dries me and shakes a can of baby powder over my behind. "Smell's nice, doesn't it. It's one of my favorites." "This must be awful for you. Cleaning up an old man. It made me hesitant to even call for you, but I had to. I'm locked in here." "Don't worry. I'm used to it. And when I become a full-fledged nurse in a year, I'll mostly have a tech doing it for me. You have an abscess in your anus. Has your doctor or one of your nurses spoken about it?" "Nothing." "It must hurt and you don't want the infection getting worse. Tell them." She puts a new gown on me and then changes the sheets with me in the bed. "It's a wonderful profession, nursing. Look at the good work you do. I had to go into one that helps no one." "And what's that?" "Writing." "I don't read much myself. I'm more interested in the sciences." "Good for you. Keep at it. Every man should have as a wife one who is or once was a nurse. That's not a proposal. I was just thinking. Once you get sick the way I did, it'd be so comforting to know I could be taken care of like this by my wife, but at home. My wife's dead." "I'm sorry." "Two years and a month. Greatest loss of my life." "I can imagine. There, you're as clean as new. And you smell nice too." "Thank you again. As I said, you do wonderful work. Can you give me something for my pain now?" "The nurse will have to do that. I'm not allowed. Ring for her." "If I have another accident, and you never know, I hope it's another tech who takes care of it. I'd hate for you to have to do it again. Once, at least in a short period of time, should be enough." "Honestly, I'm good with it. I'm on for twelve hours and it's one of the things I'm here to do." She goes. I ring. "Yes?" "Pain medication, please." "Your nurse is very busy with another patient, but I'll tell her." "Isn't there another nurse who can give it to me?" "It's very busy out here. Sometimes it gets like this, patients who need immediate attention all at the same time. I'll get you a nurse soon as I can." Hemingway's dead. Faulkner's dead. Paley's dead. Sebald's dead. Lowry's dead. Camus's dead. Eliot's dead. Mandelstam's dead. Akhmatova's dead. O'Neill's dead. Williams is dead. Miller's dead. Hopper's dead. Giacometti's dead. Klee's dead. Miro's dead. Sheeler's dead. Soutine's dead. Arp's dead. Sibelius is dead. Strauss is dead. Hovhaness is dead. Vaughan Williams is dead. I have to shit again. I need a basin. Whatever that thing is to put under me in bed. It's comparable to a urinal, but for the behind. Not a chamber pot. I ring. Nobody answers. I ring and ring. "I told you, sir. All the nurses on the floor are tied up with other patients. One will attend to you soon as she can." "But this is for a bowel movement. I don't want to do it again in my bed. All I'm asking for is that thing that goes under me while I'm lying here." "A bedpan?" "A bedpan, yes. You can get a tech to do it. But not the same one; Cindy. She already did it once, and expertly, but I made a mess and I don't want her to go through that again." "You don't get a choice, sir. If she's available, I'll get her. And if not, someone else." If it wasn't for my daughters, I'd like to be dead. But I can't have them going through their other parent dying so soon after the first. A different tech comes, gets the bedpan out of the bottom drawer of my side table, "Raise yourself," and puts it under me just in time. "At least this time I'm not making a big mess in bed for you to clean up as I did with my regular tech." "There's always something that makes life look a little brighter. Think you're done?" "No." "Ring for me when you are. It's a crazy house out there today, worse for the nurses than the techs, so one of us should come." "Thanks." Bergman, Fellini, Antonioni, Kurasawa, Kieslowski—all dead. And Babel. How could I have left out Babel? Babel's dead.

Nominated by Boulevard

From THAT ONCE WERE BEAUTIFUL CHILDREN

by CLAUDIA RANKINE

from PLOUGHSHARES

My brothers are notorious. They have not been to prison. They have been imprisoned. The prison is not a place you enter. It is no place. My brothers are notorious. They do regular things, like wait. On my birthday they say my name. They will never forget my name. What is that knowledge? Is it sadness?

The days of our childhood together were like steep steps into a collapsing mind. It looked like we rescued ourselves, were rescued. Then there are these days, each day of our adult lives. They will never forget our way through, these brothers, each brother, my brother, dear brother, my dearest brothers, dear heart—

Your hearts are broken. This is not a secret though there are secrets. And as yet I do not understand how my own sorrow has turned into my brothers' hearts. The hearts of my brothers are broken. If I knew another way to be, I would call up a brother, I would hear myself saying, my brother, dear brother, my dearest brothers, dear heart. On the tip of a tongue one note following another is another path, another dawn where the pink sky is the bloodshot of struck, of sleepless, of sorry, of senseless, shush.

Those years of and before me and my brothers, the years of passage, plantation, migration, of Jim Crow segregation, of poverty, inner cities, profiling, of one in three, two jobs, each a felony, boy, hey boy, accumulate into the hours inside our childhood where we are all caught hanging, the rope inside us, the tree inside us, its roots our limbs, a throat sliced through and when we open our mouth to speak, blossoms, o blossoms, no place coming out, brother, dear brother, that kind of blue.

The sky is the silence of brothers all the days leading up to my call. If I called I'd say goodbye before I broke the goodbye. I say goodbye before anyone can hang up. Don't hang up. My brother hangs up though he is there. I keep talking. The talk keeps him there. The sky is blue, kind of blue. The day is hot. Is it cold? Are you cold? It does get cool. Is it cool? Are you cool?

My brother is completed by sky. The sky is his silence. Eventually, he says, it is raining. It is raining down. It was raining. It stopped raining. It is raining down. He won't hang up. He's there, he's there but he's hung up though he is there. Goodbye, I say. I break the goodbye. I say goodbye before anyone can hang up, don't hang up. Wait with me. Wait with me though the waiting might be the call of goodbyes.

Nominated by Maxine Scates

TOUCH

by STEVE ADAMS

from THE PINCH

When you receive bodywork what most people won't tell you and what you may not tell yourself is that the experience is personal. How could it be otherwise? Fears and issues are often bound in injuries, and some injuries are more personal than others. There you are, depending on the particular practice, lying naked under a sheet, or exposed in your underwear, or in sweatpants and a T-shirt, relinquishing your body to someone who begins as a stranger. We all have our polarities—male, female, gay, straight, bisexual and all the blends and permutations between, and one may be more comfortable working with some types over others. A straight male may avoid an attractive female practitioner because, worried over controlling his responses, he can't relax with her. A woman may find she more easily trusts another woman. There's nothing wrong with this. You're the one lying there vulnerable. Still, in my experience the individual practitioner supersedes the type. Some are just better than others, or match up better with you, regardless of everything else including how you view yourself. With some it is an art form, and you are their material. As in dance, you can come to know your partner quite well. As with a very good dance partner, you can travel to a place neither of you would arrive at alone. And you will think of them years later, wonder at what transpired between you.

Injuries break boundaries. They reshape us, emotionally and physically. Sometimes they create doorways and humble us to the point where we can step through.

This is a love story.

One morning in Austin about fifteen years ago, I woke to find my right testicle had suffered a trauma overnight and was fixed rigidly to the base of my member. When I prodded it the pain was so severe it brought sweat to my eyelids. After I recovered I stood and examined myself in the mirror. There it hung, or more accurately, didn't, torqued an inch above my left as if it had tried to retract itself into my body for safety, and in failing clung on for dear life.

I had no idea what might have caused the reaction. I thought I must have injured it while sleeping and hoped if I gave it a few days it would recover. But I discovered, day-by-day, that the most basic things I took for granted—running, riding a bicycle, driving for more than a few minutes (my right foot extended and held to the gas pedal), walking more than fifty yards at a stretch, wearing jeans or boxer shorts—could, and usually would trigger a relentless, tidal pain to spread from that part of my body and engulf me as I tried to fall asleep at night. I'm also convinced the male body releases some sort of fear hormone when the testicles are threatened. As if the crippling pain wasn't enough to convince you to protect these oblong carriers of your bloodline, a completely separate dose of raw, undefined terror rages through your system. At night I would lie on my back in bed immobilized, unable to rest on either side or my stomach without setting off the response, looking at the ceiling fan as it spun in the dark room, and trying to convince myself that yes, I would be able to have sex again someday.

As it turned out I would, but not for several years. Along the way to recovery I visited doctors and urologists (they had no answers), a chiropractor (some relief lasting for no more than twenty-four hours), learned to drive my car relying on cruise control whenever possible, and switched from boxers to briefs for the support and from jeans to baggy pants or shorts to reduce constriction. What finally saved me was running across an old friend who'd just started teaching Pilates. A few days after I began working with him I went to a practitioner of deep tissue massage. As traditional forms of medicine had failed me, I was looking elsewhere, anywhere. Almost overnight everything changed. Though I was far from 100%, I found myself able to, among other things, drive my car normally or walk a quarter mile without suffering pain, terror, and flopsweats all night long. Soon that right testicle began to shift back toward its proper position. As near as I can tell by what helped and what didn't, my physical problem seemed to lie with knotted or strained tissue where my right gluteus maximus met my upper thigh, and how that troubled an L-3 vertebra. Nerve stuff. It expands radially. Point X affects Point D.

Whatever. I was just happy I was improving and had a means to deal with it. The means took me to and through a series of bodyworkers. It took me to Jonah.

I moved from Texas to New York City for the third time in my life in 1998 chasing dreams and memories and hopes, but really satisfied with nothing more than living under that skyline again. I had my physical therapy down rote. I owned a Pilates mat and barrel and knew a solid routine. I now could walk, run, ride a bike, and yes, have sex again, provided I attended to my Pilates twice a week and visited a good bodyworker every month or two. Upon arriving, finding that bodyworker was one of my highest priorities.

Jonah was referred to me through a mutual friend. There are many terrific forms of bodywork, but Jonah's was shiatsu. He worked out of a martial arts studio on 14th Street. I followed him into a small space partitioned by a bamboo screen. He was maybe 5' 10", an inch taller than me with curly brown hair starting to recede and a dancer's body. He spoke softly, asked me what was going on, and I told him about my injury in shameless detail. He nodded, then I lay before him on the mat, one stranger to another. He lit a scentless candle. He circled a hammer around a small ancient-looking hand gong and the tone flowed out like water. He closed his eyes and went to work.

It was over a year before he dropped his first overt clue he might be gay. I'd just scored a rent-stabilized apartment in Greenpoint, Brooklyn, and wanted to find a bicycle I could ride in my neighborhood. I asked him for recommendations. He was a runner as well as a bicyclist, and he guided me to a small shop on 10th Avenue run by a man from Puerto Rico. "I remind him of Celia Cruz," Jonah told me proudly, if somewhat shyly. "Tell him Celia Cruz sent you." Which surprised me. I didn't think Jonah looked like Celia Cruz at all.

After he moved from that first studio, I visited him in a room he rented in a chiropractor's office. For a short period afterward he took the subway to the Upper West Side and the apartment I was subletting. My small, green parrot adored him, trilled and puffed up and rested on one leg while Jonah worked on me on the floor of my living room. Finally he chose to use his own apartment. He told me he'd decided to cut back on his clients so he could do better, more focused work, and since we would be in his home he wanted to be picky about who he brought into it. I was glad to have made the cut but hardly thought about it. I only consider it now. Some clients exhausted him, he said, but I clearly didn't, even with whatever worries I brought in. Before we began a session, I'd sit on the mat, and he'd listen as I described where my body hurt, where it was tight, what was happening emotionally in my life since the last time he saw me. By his way of thinking, it was all connected. Then I'd lie down, he'd dim the lights, press the CD player to play ambient music (this, I think, was one of his systems for timing a session), and start. He'd lay his hands (they were always surprisingly warm) on my belly, close his eyes, and I'd begin to float away. He once explained that the belly informed him of where to go next, what part of the body he should address. I can only describe his state as a kind of trance. If moments later I realized I'd forgotten to tell him about a pain somewhere and blurted out the oversight he always looked startled at my voice, maybe at the fact that I was even in the room with him. But he'd recover, nod and say "okay," then close his eyes and we'd begin the float again.

I'm almost ashamed of how little I paid him. When once I asked him if I should pay more he told me that he wanted to keep his price down so I could afford to come often. The sessions lasted an hour and a half, and usually two. This was, I realized fairly quickly, not about the money for him. It was a spiritual practice. It was how he served. When once I asked him how else he paid the rent he told me offhandedly he did some teaching at Circle in the Square and also something called "clown therapy" for hospitalized children with the Big Apple Circus in New York, as well as for another group in Germany where he spent half the year with his partner. Jonah never gave me that much detail. I think part of that was his natural instinct to keep boundaries in place with clients, but more so I think he just didn't like to talk about himself. He was a body person and that's where he spoke first, and possibly best, through his hands and movement, while each session I'd blather to excess about politics, my writing, or a woman who'd hurt my feelings. He'd fly back and forth between Germany and the U.S. When he was gone I visited other practitioners working other disciplines.

From Jonah's perspective there wasn't anything out of the ordinary about what we did. He was a theater artist from Canada, a specialist in movement, physical acting, mime, and shiatsu, cobbling together a meaningful life and meaningful relationships in Germany and New

York City. Our friendship that developed over the eight years before he died was simply a logical and natural experience. He was a healer. It's what he did. But for me, going once every month or two to a gay man's apartment and giving over my body to him was a foray into new territory, and one I only wish I could return to.

Shiatsu is a relatively modern Japanese form of massage therapy derived from ancient Chinese principles. It's practiced through loose clothing. Its system follows the same meridians as acupuncture, but instead of needles, fingers press, and often deeply. Its intention is to unblock energy flow, release knotted musculature, stretch and loosen connective tissue, and create a harmonic relationship between internal organs. The practitioner may also stretch the body as he moves and breathes with his client. Jonah said he liked to work with me because it grounded him. He considered what we did a form of dance.

Jonah's apartment was on West 45th Street between 8th and 9th Avenues across from the Hirschfield Theater. My sessions there allowed me a personal foothold in what was not long ago called Hell's Kitchen. He'd taken the apartment in the late '70s and held onto it ever since. It was one of those old New York apartments where you felt the presence of generations who'd lived there before you. The paint on the windowsills was layered so thickly the windows didn't close right, and there you could see the different colors the apartment had been painted through the years cracking in spiderwebbed patterns. The bathroom door I shut when I changed into my sweatpants and T-shirt didn't close completely either because of the paint. Inside, a metal chain hung from the lightbulb in the middle of the ceiling as an on/off switch. The heavy, rounded porcelain sink and toilet came from eras back, and the bathtub sat off the floor on brass feet. Like many New Yorkers, Jonah kept the unscreened window cracked open in winter and summer, and through it came yells and sometimes the sound of bottles breaking from the homeless shelter across the alley. I would peer out, breathe the air drifting in as I watched the bodies shift through windows across the way, listen to them talk and laugh and argue, and think *this is a real New York apartment*.

The only time our relationship faltered was in 2004 after Bush won the election. My body was tied in knots at the loss, and I dragged it to Jonah so he could disentangle it as he always did. From the beginning of our session I could talk of nothing else. Finally I lay on the mat and he did his thing. Usually I would leave a few minutes after a session, but afterward we began talking again. He looked directly in my eyes and calmly, but clearly and with anger, pain, and no small amount of alarm described how the extreme right wing had used fear and hatred of gays to whip up the electorate against the Democrats. And he'd thought it wouldn't work, but it did. Jonah had moved to New York from Canada and become a U.S. citizen because he'd believed in this country. He'd wanted to be part of it. And now he wondered why. Why had he become an American? There seemed a trace of accusation in his voice.

It was palpable how exiled he felt. Even though my party had lost, I was still part of the straight world, while he belonged to the "disease" the extreme right so publicly wished to excise. Also I was native born. He was seeing me for the first time as "other," as "different." Or at least I thought he was, so of course he began to look "other" to me. Didn't he know I felt cast out too?

I could've told him he and I were on the same list, that if they got him they'd get around to me. I could've quoted the line, "First they came for the Communists . . ." But I hadn't any words, and any words would've come up short. I stood, ready to leave, and gestured toward the mat. I said, "Well, clearly I don't have a problem with it." He looked up at me, not responding, taking in my gesture. He turned to the mat; that bed, of sorts. I think it was at that moment he considered what a great distance a straight boy from Grand Prairie, Texas, might travel to come to a point where he could lie beneath him and trust him implicitly with his body. What happened on that mat, as well as my feelings for him, were hardly casual.

The last time I saw him was shortly after Katrina ravaged New Orleans. I'd decided to fly down to witness the disaster and spend some money, as that city so badly needed it. Jonah was about to return to Germany to be with his partner and do his clown therapy in one of their hospitals. As I got to my feet I told him I was going down that weekend to New Orleans to put flowers on Marie Laveau's grave. I felt a need to mourn, to ask forgiveness, to bring an offering, and I knew of no better place than the grave of the voodoo queen of New Orleans. I saw Jonah's eyes widen in recognition at the name.

He'd recently stitched and restitched me back together as I went through a lengthy and particularly devastating breakup with a woman. Tears had run down my face as he'd worked on me, and he'd extended the sessions until he was satisfied I'd recovered enough to face the

216

subway. During that time he showed me a picture of his partner, Michael, who was younger than him and stunningly beautiful. At the time I thought, *Way to go, Jonah!*

As wonderful as New York can be, you don't last there without help. I felt lucky to call him my friend. I don't know why, but as I stood at his door that night ready to leave, I had a subtle but unwavering feeling I might never see him again. An unlikely phrase popped into my head: "Don't ever die." But that is a horrible curse to lay on someone, so I substituted, "Don't ever retire."

A few months later, when it seemed time for him to be back I was overcome with concern. It was irrational, I knew, but I couldn't shake the feeling. I began to wonder how I would find out if he were to die. Would I wander by his apartment and see if his name had been taken off his mailbox? It dawned on me we shared no friends, no family who could inform me. I experienced a sense of vertigo. To calm myself I decided to send him an email casually asking how he was doing. He responded within a day telling me he'd developed a health issue and was being treated in Germany. Oddly, this made me feel relieved. I'd reestablished contact and my intuition had not been entirely off. He said he had a tumor in his pancreas but was doing well; he just hated the nausea from the chemo. He said he'd be back, recovered in New York.

I happily took him at his word. After all, he was the health professional and should know. Still, something pressed me in my response to tell him I'd been planning, should I ever run across him on the street in Times Square, to introduce him to my friends only as "my shiatsu angel." Years earlier when I'd told him I always staked out a spot at Spring Street to witness the annual Halloween parade, he'd informed me he would be participating as "Johnny Angel." Bright-eyed and excited, he'd asked me to look for him, and I did, but he was lost in the myriad bodies and costumes.

In his next email he said he was making progress and he and his partner would be flying to New York soon. He was planning on teaching classes that fall. Again, about the time I expected him back my anxiety over his health, along with my fear of his disappearing swarmed me. I decided to call his apartment, carefully removing any note of concern from my voice, and left a message saying I was wondering if he was back and how he was doing and to give me a call. I left my number.

When I listened to the phone message from his partner, Michael, the following day saying Jonah had passed, I was only surprised by the degree I'd been expecting it. Michael's voice was clear and measured, with just a trace of an accent. I called Jonah's number and Michael picked up. I told him I was sorry for his loss. He said Jonah had been improving and they actually thought he was going to recover. But after they came back he suddenly took a turn, and within a couple of weeks was gone. Before he died Jonah had told him to let me know. There was going to be a memorial service at Circle in the Square the next night in the downstairs theater where *The Spelling Bee* was then running.

They say it's only when someone dies you fully know who they are. Death is the final page of the final chapter, and like a finished novel its total shape only comes into view at that moment. There were certain things I knew about Jonah. I knew he had a beautiful, younger life-partner. I knew he'd been my friend for eight years, supporting me during my hardest times in this city. I knew his loss would affect me structurally, on a foundational level. I knew he'd loved New York, as I did, had come here from another culture, as I had. And the last time I saw him I had known on some deep level it would be the last time I would see him. What I did not know was who he was to others.

Making my way down the deep, three-tiered stairwell to the theater lobby was like slowly dropping into an ocean: ten steps down, a small landing; ten steps down, another landing; ten steps down, the floor and its blue carpet textured with tiny red dots. Three of the walls were white. The fourth, behind the stairwell, was red. Enormous, round, white pillars held up the ceiling. People swirled over the carpet greeting each other, smiled as they recognized a face, hugged a friend. I felt self-conscious. I knew no one. Unmoored as I was I searched for an anchor and spotted a small table where they'd created a shrine with a number of Jonah's personal objects. Beside it an easel displayed a photograph, a headshot of Jonah as I'd never seen him. Wearing a white doctor's smock, his makeup was minimal, like a mime's, and instead of smiling he looked serious. Too serious. Comically serious. On the end of his nose was a bright red rubber ball. He was "Dr. Know-Nothing," his clown doctor character. I pictured him scurrying mute around sick children's beds like something out of the Marx Brothers, putting his stethoscope to the television, taking the lampshade's temperature, sending up the real doctors and their bewildering, frightening behavior to the kids and giving them something to laugh at while he made a sane comment about that sterile, insane place. So this is who he was to sick children, I thought. A sign on the table said, "Take something." I wanted to rake away a bagful of the objects, but stopped myself. I spotted a tiny patterned incense plate I'd seen every time I'd visited him. I carefully tucked it away and walked toward the entrance of the theater.

At the door a small, somber looking woman wearing a red clown nose handed me a program along with my own red clown nose. Inside I chose a seat up high, far back and to the left of the stage. The seats were covered in red fabric. Silver numbers were stamped to seat bottoms. I recognized Michael up front by his blond hair. The bleachers down to the left were packed with what I correctly assumed were his students. Friends and family filled the lower center and right bleachers. The rest flowed into the risers above. I estimated over two hundred people had come. Many were wearing their noses. I rolled the soft foam ball in my fingers and tried it on.

The gay and theatrical communities have a lot of experience with memorial services. They know what they're for and how to make them work. There was a small group of friends present who had bonded with Jonah when he arrived in New York in the '70s, and one of them ran the show, was the stage manager and host. An official from a hospital stepped to the microphone and talked about what wonderful work Jonah did there and how he would be missed. A group of Jonah's fellow clown doctors spoke of him with the gravity of soldiers speaking of a fallen comrade. The head of the theater school at Circle in the Square talked of the great loss to his school, and stated that the legendary physical acting course Jonah developed and taught over the years would be renamed, "The Jonah Course." What was evident was that my Jonah, my quiet personal friend, was a dynamic figure in theater and in the world of clowns. The guy was a star, and I'd never known.

The group of students beside the stage sang, "You've Got a Friend," in harmony. A dancer presented a movement piece. People were coming and going onstage. Lost in my emotions, I found it hard to keep up with it all. One young woman wanted to thank Jonah for giving her her "clown name" when he'd seen the defining trait in her movement and emotional makeup one day during class. Another student, who apparently hadn't even taken his class, wept as she spoke because now she never would. Professors stood and talked about Jonah's sense of humor and the practical jokes he was always playing on them, which surprised me as he'd been so serious with me. When the host paused to ask if anyone else needed to say something, I had an urge to speak, but I wasn't a relative, I wasn't part of any of these extended families, and didn't know what to say except *you don't know me but I loved him too.*

And of course that opening passed as quickly as it appeared; the host was now gesturing toward Michael, coaxing him onto the stage.

It took him a moment before he got to his feet, then he walked up the steps to the microphone. His first words were, "I don't want to be standing here." His last were, "Goodbye, Love." In between was everything else I can't remember. I only remember thinking that grief must give us these brief moments of strength he demonstrated, a window of time so we can say what we must say with some dignity and clarity before falling apart.

The lights went down as through the speakers Diana Krall sang Joni Mitchell's "A Case of You," and a video on a screen showed a sequence of slides—Jonah onstage with a group of actresses, Jonah dreamy-eyed in the late '70s with a full head of curly hair, Jonah and Michael on their wedding day. Afterward, we were asked to put on our clown noses. The room was suddenly filled with bright red balls stuck in the middle of hundreds of faces. It was almost funny. Then the clowns sang a song, and the memorial was over. The lights came up. People rose to their feet as if out of a dream. Some moved toward the exits, some toward the family by the stage. I knew if I left I'd take the emptiness I felt with me, so using the chance to give my condolences to Michael, I made my way down to the floor. Everyone there seemed filled with love and an odd joy. Unsure as I was whether it was proper for me to approach Michael or what I would say to him, my legs still propelled me his way. I felt smaller than everyone around me. He was very tall. I hesitated, then touched his arm. "Michael?" I said. He turned and smiled down at me as if he knew me but couldn't place me. "I'm Steve."

"*Steve*," he said with such warmth I can still hear his voice. He took me in his arms like I was a lost creature come home. He held me like he needed me. I don't know if I've ever been more grateful. Then he turned; Jonah's sister was watching, and he tried to introduce me. "This is Steve," he said, searching for words. "One of Jonah's . . ."

I looked at her. I didn't know what to say or how to say it. How could I describe it? "He was my shiatsu guy," I managed. She nodded, then Michael joined her as they made their way through other well-wishers and friends to carry on the responsibilities of burying a loved one.

I headed from the theater down Eighth Avenue toward 42nd Street where I was meeting friends for a show at B.B. King's club. I didn't want to go but I already had a ticket. I cradled the red clown nose in my hand inside my jacket pocket. At 45th Street I paused and looked down the block toward the building where Jonah had lived, then continued on.

At the club I met my friends wearing the clown nose. They didn't know how to respond to it and neither did I. Everyone in the place was intent on having a good time, and why shouldn't they? But I felt separated. I kept putting on the clown nose and taking it off. The waitress did her best to ignore it. *Is he trying to be funny?*

The next morning I laid out my Pilates mat and began my workout. I remembered Jonah telling me we were like dance partners, and I saw an image of a pair of professional ice skaters where the male is clearly gay and the female is straight. There is nothing sexual between them, but there is something physical. The bond is undeniable. They go on with their other lives before and after the dance. They meet on the ice.

I knew that what happened between myself and this man would be non-repeating. The circumstances couldn't be replicated. I was a different person now. Like a first best friend, a first kiss, a first pet, I would never feel this kind of intimacy again. I found my fingers pressing the same pressure points on my feet and along my shins that Jonah would press. It was then I began to cry. The truth was, more than anything, I would miss the way he touched me.

Nominated by The Pinch

LATE ORACLE SONNET

by DAVID ST. JOHN

from THE KENYON REVIEW

1) Up late last night up late now this morning
2) *The new clover whitening the hillside*
3) The glass empty on the zinc counter
4) Also the white thimble of coffee awaiting you
5) *The cello she once painted turquoise & black*
6) Nobody cares nobody moves nobody thinks
7) *The spray of iris sprawled across the sofa*
8) The windows are blank with last night's rum
9) *The rhinestones suckled in the lead of the day*
10) The comfrey & the feldspar & the drying mud of night
11) *The columns made entirely of white dust*
12) That terrible taste that horrible taste
13) *The anise seeds lodged in the teeth of the corpse*
14) The opal ink scrolling the single page of her skin

Nominated by Susan Terris, Mark Irwin

WINGS

fiction by LORRIE MOORE

from THE PARIS REVIEW

Should he find he couldn't work it there would still be time enough.
— Henry James, *The Wings of the Dove*

The grumblings of their stomachs were intertwined and unassignable.

"Was that you or was that me?" KC would ask in bed, and Dench would say, "I'm not sure." They lay there in the mornings, their legs moving at angles toward each other, not unlike the ashes she could see through the window outside, the high branches nuzzling in the late March breeze, speaking tree to tree of the thrilling weather. Her dreams of eating meals full of meat, which caused her teeth to gnash in the night—surely a sign of spring—left the insides of her cheeks bloody and chewed, one saliva gland now swelled to the size of a raisin.

Shouldn't they be up and about already? Morning sun shot across the ceiling in a white stripe of paint. She and Dench were both too young and too old for this close, late-morning, bed-bound life, but their scuttled careers—the band, the two CDs, the newsletter (turned e-letter turned abandoned cyber litter) on how to simplify your life (be broke!), the driving, the touring, the scrambling, the foraging in parks for chives and dandelions, the charging up of credit cards, the taking pictures of clothes and selling them on eBay ("Wake up!" she used to exclaim to him in the middle of the night, sitting up in bed, "wake up and listen to my IDEAS!")—had led them here, to a six-month sublet that allowed pets. Still in their thirties, but barely, they had bought themselves a little time. So what if her investments these days were in pennies, wine corks, and sheets of self-adhesive Freedom stamps. These would go up in value, unlike everything else. Beneath her bed was a shoe box of dwindling cash from their last gig, where they'd gotten only a quarter of the door. She could always cut her long, almost Asian hair again, as she had two years ago, and sell it for a thousand dollars.

Now, as she often did when contemplating wrong turns, she sometimes thought back to when it was she had first laid eyes on Dench, that Friday long ago when he had approached her at an afternoon sound check in some downtown or other, his undulating tresses not product-free, a demeanor of arrangement and premeditation that gussied up something more chaotic. Although it was winter, he wore mirrored sunglasses and a thin leather jacket with the collar turned up: 150 percent jerk. Perhaps it was his strategy to improve people's opinions of him right away, to catch an upward momentum and make it sail, so when the sunglasses came off and then the jacket, and he began to play a song he had not written himself, he was on his way. He lunged onto one knee and raced through a bludgeoning bass solo. At the drums he pressed the stick into the cymbal and circled it, making a high-pitched celestial note, like a finger going round the edge of a wineglass. He smacked the tambourine against his head and against the snare, back and forth. When he then approached the piano, she stopped him. "Not the piano," she said quietly. "The piano's mine."

"Okay," he said. "I just wanted to show you everything I can do." And he picked up an acoustic guitar.

Would it be impossible not to love him? Would not wisdom intervene?

Later, to the rest of the band, whose skepticism toward Dench was edged with polite dismay, she said, "I don't understand why the phrase 'like an orchestra tuning up' is considered a criticism. I love an orchestra when it is tuning up. Especially then."

From the beginning, however, she could not see how Dench had ever earned a living. He knew two Ryan Adams songs and played guitar fairly well. But he had never done so professionally. Or done anything professionally that she could discern. Early on he claimed to be waiting for money, and she wasn't sure, when he smiled, whether this was a joke. "From whom? Your mother?" and he only smiled. Which made her think, yes indeed, his mother.

But no. His mother had died when he was a teenager. His father had disappeared years before that, and thereafter for Dench there was much moving with his sisters: from Ohio to Indiana to California and back again. First with his mom, then with an aunt. There was apparently in his life a lot of dropping in and out of college and unexplained years. There had been a foreshortened stint in the Peace Corps. In

Swaziland. "I'd just be waiting at a village bus stop, reading a book, and women would pretend to want to borrow it to read but in truth they just wanted a few pages for toilet paper. Or the guys they had me working with? They would stick their hands in the Porta-Potties, as soon as we got them off the trucks: they wanted the fragrant blue palms. I had to get out of there, man, I didn't really understand the commitment I had made, and so my uncle got a congressman to pull some strings." How did Dench pay his bills?

"It's one big magic trick," he said. He liked to get high before dinner, and seemed never without a joint in his wallet or in a drawer. He ate his chicken—the wings and the drumsticks, the arms and the legs— clean down to their purple bones.

And so, though she could not tell an avocado plant from flax (he had both), and though she had never seen any grow lights or seeds or a framed license to grow medical marijuana from the state of Michigan, KC began to fear he made his living by selling pot. It seemed to be the thing he was musing about and not saying. As she had continued to see him, she suspected it more deeply. He played her more songs. Then as something caught fire between them, and love secured its footing inside her, when she awoke next to him with damp knots in the back of her hair like she'd never experienced before, the room full of the previous night's candles and the whiff of weed, his skin beside her a silky calico of cool and warm, and as they both needed to eat and eat some more together, she began to feel okay that he sold drugs. If he did. What the hell. At least there was that. At least he did something. His sleepy smiles and the occasional flash of a euro or a hundred-dollar bill in his pocket seemed to confirm it, but then his intermittent lack of cash altogether perpetuated the mystery, as did his checks, which read D. Encher, and she started to fear he might not sell drugs after all. When she asked him straight out, he said only, "You're funny!" And after she had paid for too many of his drinks and meals, as he said he was strapped that week and then the week after that, she began to wish, a little sheepishly, that he did sell drugs. Soon she was close to begging. Just a little sparky bark, darling.

Instead he joined her band.

It had been called Villa and in the end it had not worked out—tours they had paid for themselves with small-business loans, audiences who did not like KC's own songs (too singer-songwriter, with rhymes— calories and galleries—of which she was foolishly proud—dead and wed), including one tune she refused to part with, since briefly it had been positioned to be a minor indie hit, a song about a chef in New Jersey named Jim Barber with whom she'd once been in love.

Here I am your unshaved fennel
Here I am your unshaved cheese
All I want to know is when I'll—
feel your blade against my knees.

Its terribleness eluded her. Her lyrics weren't sly or hip or smoky and tough but the demure and simple hopes of a mouse. She'd spent a decade barking up the wrong tree—as a mouse! Audiences booed—the boys in their red-framed spectacles, the girls in their crooked little dresses. Despised especially were her hip-hop renditions of Billy Joel and Neil Young. (She was once asked to please sing down by the river, and she'd thought they'd meant the song. She told this sad joke over and over.) Throughout the band tours she would wake up weeping at the edge of some bed or other, not knowing where she was or what she was supposed to do that day or once or twice even who she was, since all her endeavor seemed separate from herself, a suit to slip into. Tears, she had once been told, were designed to eliminate toxins, and they poured down her face and slimed her neck and gathered in the recesses of her collarbones, and she had to be careful never to lie back and let them get into her ears, which might cause the toxins to return and start over. Of course, the rumor of toxins turned out not to be true. Tears were quite pure. And so the reason for them, it seemed to her later, when she thought about it, was to identify the weak, so that the world could assure its strong future by beating the weak to death.

"Are we perhaps unlovable?" she asked Dench.

"It's because we're not named, like, Birth Hearse for Dogface."

"Why aren't we named that?"

"Because we have standards."

"Is that it," she said.

"Yeah! And not just 'Body and Soul' as an encore. I mean we maintain a kind of integrity."

"Integrity! Really!" After too many stolen meals from minibars, the Pringles can carefully emptied and the foil top resealed, the container replaced as if untouched back atop the wood tray, hotel towels along with the gear all packed up in the rental truck whose rear fender bore one large bumper sticker, with Donald Rumsfeld's visage, under which read DOES THIS ASS MAKE MY TRUCK LOOK BIG?—after all that, she continu-

226

ally found herself thinking, If only Dench sold drugs! On hot summer days she would find a high-end supermarket and not only eat the free samples in their tiny white cups but stand before the produce section and wait for the vegetable misters to come on, holding her arms beneath the water in relief. She was showering with the lettuces.

She and Dench had not developed their talents sufficiently nor cared for them properly—or so a booking agent had told them.

Dench took offense. "You forget about the prize perplexity, the award angle—we could win something!" he exclaimed, with Pringles in his teeth.

The gardenia in KC's throat, the flower that was her singing voice—its brown wilt must be painstakingly slowed through the years—had begun a rapid degeneration into simple crocus, then scraggly weed. She'd been given something perfect—youth!—and done imperfect things with it. The moon shone whole, then partial in the sky, having its life without her. Sometimes she just chased roughly after a melody—like someone kicking a can down a road. She had not hemmed in her speaking voice, kept it tame and tended so that her singing one could fly. Her speaking voice was the same as her singing one, a roller coaster of various registers, the Myrna Loy-Billie Burke timbre of the Edwardian grandmother who had raised her, a woman who had trained at conservatory but had never had a singing career and practically sang every sentence she uttered: "Katherine? It's time for dinner" went flutily up and down the scale. Only her dying words—marry well—had been flat, the drone of chagrin, a practical warning: life-preserving but with a glimpse of a dark little bunker in a war not yet declared. "Marry well" had been uttered after she begged KC to get a teaching certificate. "Teaching makes interesting people boring, sure," she had said. "But it also makes boring people interesting. So there's an upside. There always is an upside if you look up."

Dench's own poor mother couldn't leave him—or his sisters—a dime, though he had always done what she said, even that one year they lived in motels and he obligingly wore a nightgown identical to his sisters' so that they might better be mistaken for a single child, to avoid an extra room charge, in case the maid walked in. His young mother had died with breathing tubes hooked right to her wallet, he said, just sucking it all up. Dench made a big comedic whooshing sound when he told this part. His father's disappearance, which had come long before, had devastated and haunted her: when they were out for dinner one night his father announced that he had to see a man about a horse, and he excused himself, went to the men's room, and climbed out the window, never to return. Dench made a whooshing sound for this part of the story as well.

"I can't decide whether that is cowardice or a weird kind of courage," Dench said.

"It's neither," KC replied. "It has nothing to do with either of those things."

Motherless children would always find each other. She had once heard that. They had the misery that wasn't misery but presumed to be so by others. They had the misery that liked company and was company. Only sometimes they felt the facts of their motherless lives. They were a long, long way from home. They had theme songs hatched in a spiritual tradition. There was no fondling of the gold coins of memory. The world was their orphanage.

But when they moved in together he had hesitated.

"What about my belongings?" he asked.

"It's not like you have a dog who won't get along with mine," she said.

"I have plants."

"But plants are not a dog."

"Oh, I see: you're one of those people who thinks animals are better, more important than plants!"

She studied him, his eyes large with protest or with drugs or with madness. There were too many things to choose from. "Are you serious?" she asked.

"I don't know," he said, and turned to unpack his things.

Now she rose to take the dog for his daily walk. She was wearing an old summer dress as a nightgown, but in the mornings it could work as a dress again, if you just tossed a cardigan over it and put on shoes. In this risky manner, she knew, insanity could encroach.

The sublet she and Dench were in now was a nice one, a fluke, a modern, flat-roofed, stone-and-redwood ranch house with a carport, in a neighborhood that was not far from the hospital and was therefore full of surgeons and radiologists and their families. The hospital itself was under construction and the cranes bisected the sky. Big-jawed excavators and backhoes worked beneath lights at night. Walking the dog, she once watched as an excavator's mandibled head was released and fell to the ground; the headless neck then leaned down and began to nudge it, as if trying to find out whether it might still be alive. Of course there was an operator, but after that it was hard to think of a creature like that as a machine. When a wall was knocked down and its quiet secrets sent scattering, the lines between things seemed up for grabs.

The person who owned their house was not connected to the hospital. He was an entrepreneur named Ian who had made a bundle in the nineties on some sort of business software and who for long stretches of time lived out of state—in Ibiza, Zihuatanejo, and Portland—in order to avoid the cold. The house came furnished except, strangely, for a bed, which they bought. In the refrigerator they found food so old it had dust on it rather than mold. "I don't know," said Dench. "Look at the closets. This must be what Ian was using. With hooks this strong maybe we don't need a bed. We can just hang ourselves there at night, like bats."

With Dench she knew, in an unspoken way, that she was the one who was supposed to get them to wherever it was they were going. She was supposed to be the GPS lady who, when you stopped for gas, said, "Get back on the highway." She tried to be that voice with Dench: stubborn, unflappable, keeping to the map and not saying what she knew the GPS lady really wanted to say, which was not "Recalculating" but "What in fucking hell are you thinking?"

"It all may look wrong from outer space, which is where a GPS is seeing it from," Dench would say, when proposing alternatives of any sort, large or small, "but on the ground there's a certain logic."

There were no sidewalks in this wooded part of town. The sap of the stick-bare trees was just stirring after what looked like a fierce forest fire of a winter. The roadside gullies that would soon warm and sprout Joe Pye weed and pea were still just pebble-flecked mud, and KC's dog, Cat, sniffed his way along, feeling the winter's melt, the ground loosening its fertile odor of wakened worms. Overhead the dirt-pearl sky of March hung low as a hat brim. The houses were sidled next to marshes and sycamores, and as she walked along the roads occasionally a car would pass, and she would yank on Cat's leash to heel him close. The roads, all named after colleges out East—Dartmouth Drive, Wellesley Way, Sweetbriar Road (where was her alma mater, SUNY Buffalo Street?)—glistened with the flat glossy colors of flattened box turtles who'd made the spring crossing too slowly and were now stuck to the macadam, thin and shiny as magazine ads.

HOSPICE CARE: IT'S NEVER TOO SOON TO CALL, read a billboard near the coffee shop in what constituted the neighborhood's commercial roar. Next to it a traffic sign read PASS WITH CARE. Surrealism could not be made up. It was the very electricity of the real. The largest part of the strip was occupied by an out-of-business bookstore whose plate-glass windows were already cloudy with dust. The *D* was missing from the sign so that it now read BORERS. In insolvency, truth: soon the chain would be shipping its entire stock to the latrines of Swaziland.

Cat was a good dog, part corgi, part lab, and if KC wore her sunglasses into the coffee shop he could pass for a seeing-eye dog, and she for a blind person, so she didn't have to tie him to a parking sign out front.

The coffee shop played Tom Waits and was elegantly equipped with dimpled cup sleeves, real cream, cinnamon sticks, shakers of sugar. KC got in line. "I love this song," the man in front turned to say to her. He was holding a toddler and was one of those new urban dads so old he looked like the kidnapper of his own child.

She didn't know what she felt about Tom Waits anymore: his voice had gotten so industrial. "I don't know. I just think one shouldn't have to wear goggles and a hard hat when listening to music," she said. It was not a bad song, and she didn't feel that strongly about it, only sorry for her own paltry tunes, but the man's face fell, and he turned away, with his child staring gloomily at her over his shoulder.

She ordered a venti latte, and while she was waiting, she read the top fold from the uppermost paper in the stack below the shrink-wrapped CDs by the register. When she finished, she discreetly turned the paper over and read the bottom fold. This daily, fractured way of learning the front-page news—they had no Internet connection—she had gotten used to. Be resourceful! So their old newsletter had advised. This way of bringing Dench his morning coffee (she drank her half while walking back, burning her tongue a little) and getting the dog a walk was less resourceful than simply necessary. Sometimes she missed the greasy spoons of old, which she had still been able to find on the road when the band was touring and where a single waitress ran the register, the counter, all the tables, calling you "honey"—until you asked for soy milk, at which point all endearments ceased.

Now she walked back via Princeton Place, a street she didn't usually take, but one that ran parallel to her own. Taking different routes fortified the mind, the paper had said today. This street contained a sprawling white-brick house she had seen before and had been struck by—not just its elegance and size but the magical blue sea of squill that spread across its sloped and wooded lot. She had once seen two deer there, with long tails that flicked like horses' and wagged like dogs'. Only once before had she seen a deer close-up, along the road's edge on Dart-mouth. It had been hit so fast it had been decapitated, and its neck lay open like a severed cable bundle.

Cat nosed along the gullies and up the driveways, whose cracks were often filled with clover.

She stared at the wings of the white-brick house which were either perfectly insulated or not heated at all, since there was still unmelted snow on the roofs. Suddenly an elderly man appeared by the mailbox. "Howdy," he said. It startled her, and his stab at gregariousness belied his face, which bore a blasted-apart expression, like a balding, white-haired Jesus on the cross, eyes open wide and worried, his finely lined mouth the drawstring purse of the aged and fair.

"Just getting my newspaper," he said. "Nice dog."

"Hey, Catsy, get back here." She tried to pull the leash in but its automated spring was broken and the leash kept unspooling.

The man's face brightened. He had started to take his paper out of its plastic sleeve but stopped. "What's the dog's name? Cathy?" He did not scrunch up his face disapprovingly when he failed to hear what you said, the way deaf people often did. But he did have the recognizable waxen pee smell of an old man. It was from sweat that no longer could be liquid but accumulated like scaly air on the skin.

"Uh, Cat. It's part family name, part, um, joke." She wasn't going to get into all the Kathcrines in her family or her personal refrigerator-magnet altar to Cat Power or the general sick sense of humor that had led this dog, like all pets, to be a canvas upon which one wrote one's warped love and dubious wit.

"I get it." He grinned eagerly. "And what's your name?"

"KC," she said. Let that suffice.

"Casey?"

"Yes," she said. A life could rhyme with a life—it could be a jostling close call that one mistook for the thing itself.

"We live the next block over. We're renting."

"Renting! Well that explains it."

She didn't dare ask what that explained. Still, his eyes had a wet dazzle—or an amused glint—and were not disapproving. Cat started to bark loudly at a rabbit but then also turned and started barking at the man, who took a theatrical step back, raised the paper over his head, and pretended to be afraid, as if he were performing for a small child. "Don't take my crossword puzzle!"

"His bark is worse than his bite," KC said. "Get over here, Cat."

231

"I don't know why people always say that. No bark is worse than a bite. A bite is always worse."

"Well, they shouldn't make rabbits so cute or we wouldn't care if dogs ate them. Why are rabbits made so cute? What is nature's purpose in that one?"

He beamed. "So you're a philosopher!"

"No, not really," she murmured, as if in fact she thought she might be.

"I think the rabbits are probably only accidentally cute to us. Mostly they're cute to each other. The purpose? More rabbit stew for everybody."

"I see. So you're a sort of Mr. McGregor kind of guy. I was always scared of Mr. McGregor!" She smiled.

"Nothing to be scared of. But it does seem of late that there is some kind of apocalyptic plague of rabbits. Biblical bunnies! Would you like to come and finish your coffee inside?"

She didn't know what to make of this invitation. Was it creepy or friendly? Who could tell anymore? Very few people had been friendly to them since they'd moved here two months ago. The man's tea-stained teeth made a sepia smile—a dental X-ray from the nineteenth century.

"Oh, thanks, I really should be going." This time the leash caught and Cat came trotting toward her, bored and ready to move on.

"Well, good to meet you," the old man said and turned and walked back toward his house, with its portico and porch and two stone chimneys, its wings that stretched east and west and one out back smaller and south-facing, with a long double sleeping porch she could barely see. Over here on Princeton Place things seemed bigger than they were on Wellesley Way. She hated money, though she knew it was like blood and you needed it. Still, it was also like blood in that she often couldn't stand the sight of it. This whole let-them-eat-cake neighborhood could use a neat little guillotine.

"Good to meet you," she said, though he hadn't given her his name.

"Here's your coffee," she said to Dench, who was still in bed.

"Yum. Tepid backwash."

"Hey, don't complain. You can go next time and bring me back half."

"I'm not complaining," he said in a sleepy stretch.

She took a brush sharply to her scalp and began brushing. If she waited longer with her hair she might get twelve hundred. She threw it back and arched from her waist. Only in the mirror could she see her

Decatur tattoo, put there one night in Britannic Bold in the crook of her neck, when they were playing in Decatur and she wanted to be reminded never to play there again. "That's a strange way to be reminded," Dench had said, and KC had said, "What better."

"Was there a big line at the coffee shop?" Dench asked, smacking his lips.

"No. I stopped and talked to some guy. Cat is going up every driveway that ever had a squirrel or rabbit dash over it."

"Some guy?"

"Geezer."

"Hey, this backwash is good. There's something new in it. Were you wearing cherry ChapStick or something?"

"Have you noticed that there are a lot of people with money around here?"

"We should meet them. We need producers."

"You go meet them."

"You're cuter. Of course, time is of the essence in these matters."

She loved Dench. She was helpless before the whole emotional project of him. But it didn't preclude hating him and everything around him, which included herself, the sound of her own voice—and the sound of his, which was worse. The portraits of hell never ceased and sometimes were done up in raucous, gilded frames to console. Romantic hope: From where did women get it? Certainly not from men, who were walking caveat emptors. No, women got it from other women, because in the end women would rather be rid of each other than have to endure themselves on a daily basis. So they urged one another into relationships. "He loves you! You can see it in his eyes!" they lied.

"Casey!" The old man shouted the next morning. He was out in his front yard pounding together something that looked like a bird feeder on a post.

"Hi!" she said.

"You know my name?"

"Pardon me?"

"Old family joke." He still seemed to be shouting. "Actually my name is Milt Thahl."

"Milt." She repeated the name, a habit people with good memories supposedly relied on. "They don't name kids Milton anymore."

"Too bad and thank God! My father's name was Hiram, and now that

I'm old I find my head filled up with his jokes and stories rather than very many of my own, which apparently I've forgotten."

"Oh," she said. "Well, as long as you don't actually come to believe you are your dad, I suppose all is well."

"Well, that may be next."

"Probably that's always next. For all of us."

He squinted to study her, seemed to be admiring something about her again, but she was not sure what. No doubt something that was a complete mirage.

"Nice to see you again," he said. "And you, too," he said to the dog. "Though you are a strange-looking thing. Its like he's been assembled by Nazi veterinarians—a shepherd's head, a dachshund's body, a—"

"Yeah, I know. Sometimes he reminds me of the dog in *Invasion of the Body Snatchers*."

"Hmmm?"

"The remake."

"The remake of what?"

"*Frankenstein!*" she yelled. His deafness could give her a heart attack. Perhaps this was nature's plan for old people, to kill each other in an efficient if irritating fashion.

She could feel the heat leaving the coffee and entering her hand. "He's like a dog made in Frankenstein's lab!" Sometimes she hated the dog. His obliviousness to the needs of others, his determined, verbally challenged conversation about his own desires—in a human this would indicate a severe personality disorder.

"Oh, he's not that bad," said Milt. "And wouldn't we like his energy. In tablet form."

"That would be fantastic."

"But you're young; you wouldn't need something like that."

"I need something." Was she whining? She had never made such an announcement to a stranger before.

"In lieu of that, come on in and have a blueberry muffin with me." Again, the lines between neighborliness and flirtation were not clear to her here. She knew in this community you had to do an extroverted kind of meet and greet but she had heard of divorced soccer parents wandering off from their children's games and having sex in the far parking lots of the park, so the guidelines were murky. "And while you're at it you can help me with the crossword puzzle."

"Oh, I can't. I have to get home. Lot of things to tend to."

"Well, it's not ten to. It's ten past."

"To tend to," KC repeated. Perhaps his deafness had exhausted all the other neighbors and this accounted for his friendliness to her. On the other hand, no one seemed to walk around here. They either jogged, their ears stuffed with music, or they drove their cars at murderous speeds. One old man could not have single-handedly caused that. Or could he have?

"Hmmm?"

"Gotta get home."

"Oh," he said and waved her on.

"Maybe tomorrow," she said out of kindness.

He nodded and went back to work.

She stopped and turned. "Are you making a bird feeder?"

"No, it's a book nook! I'll put books inside and people can help themselves. Like a little library. Now that the bookstore is closed. I'm just adjusting the clasp."

"How lovely." It was a varnished pine angled to look like the ski chalet of a doll.

"Giving the old guy a thrill? Good idea."

"What's wrong with you?"

"I'm just saying," said Dench in a hushed tone. "He's probably loaded. And gonna keel soon. And . . ."

"Stop." This was the grifter in Dench, something violent in the name of freedom, like his father who had fled through the men's-room window. "Don't say another word."

"Hey, I'm not talking about murdering him! I'm just saying you could spend a little time, make him happy, and then the end result might be, well . . . we'd all be a little happier. Where's the harm?"

"You've really gone over to the dark side." He could be shameless. Perhaps shamelessness kept bitterness at bay. Not a chance Dench could ever be bitter. Bitterness came when one had done the long, good thing and then gone unrewarded. Dench would never operate that way. She, on the other hand, had been born with a sort of pre-bitterness, casting about for the good and unacknowledged deed that would explain her feelings—and not coming up with it. So instead a sourness could beset her, which she had to appease and shrink with ice cream and biographies of Billie Holiday.

"Hey, wasn't it you who wrote, 'Get your hands on some real meat?'" Now he began to sing. " 'An old shoe can be made chewy like game /

but it takes a raftload of herbs and it's just not the same.' You wrote that."

"That was a love song to a chef. Before I knew you."

"It's good. It's got existentialism and culinary advice." His eyes avoided hers.

"You're pimping me. Is this what you call your 'talent for life'?" He had once boasted he possessed such a thing.

"It's a working view."

"You'd better be careful, Dench. I take your suggestions seriously."

He paused and looked at her, sternness in one eye and gentleness in the other. "Well, my first suggestion is don't take my suggestions. And there's more where that came from."

"There's a smell in the house. Yeasty and sulfuric. Can you smell it?" She looked at Dench with concern, but he seemed to have none.

"The Zeitgeist."

"Something rotting in the walls."

"Meat or shoe?"

"Something that died in the winter and now that it's spring is decaying in the floorboards or some crawl space or one of the walls of this room."

"Maybe my allergies are acting up. But I think I have smelled it along this side of the house, on warmer days, out there trying to get better cell-phone reception. A cabbagey cheese smell: goaty with a kind of ammonia rot."

She reached for a sip of Dench's coffee.

"He probably has adult children."

"Probably," said Dench, turning away and then looking back at her to study her face.

"What?" she asked.

"Nothing," he said.

Dench's sexiness, his frugal, spirited cooking (though he was no Jim Barber), his brooding gaze, his self-deprecating humor, all had lured her in. But it was like walking into a beautiful house to find the rooms all empty. In those beginning years she often saw him locking eyes with others, as if in some pact. At times he glanced at her with bewildering scorn. There was, in short, little conversation of tender feelings. Just attachment. Just the power of his voice when it spoke of things that had nothing to do with them. When it churned round and round on its loop about his childhood, parental misdeeds, and rages at his lot. Intimacy was not his strong suit. "Clubs and spades," he joked. "Not diamonds, not hearts. Red cards—I just see red. They throw me out of the game every time."

"Shut up and drink your beer."

Where were the drugs?

He required a patroness but had mistakenly auditioned for her. If she possessed fewer psychic wounds than he had hoped for in a woman her age, or at least useful different ones, he would attempt to create some. But she was less woundable than he might think. She had not had a father who had to see a man about a horse. She, in fact, had had a father who'd been killed by a car named after a horse. Along with her mother. A Mustang! How weird was that? Well, she had been a baby and hadn't had to deal with it.

Her grandmother had almost never mentioned her mother. Or her father. They had been scurrying across a street to get home, holding hands, which had fatally slowed them down.

Where were the drugs?

Patience was a chemical. Derived from a mineral. Derived from a star. She felt she had a bit of it. But it was not always fruitful, or fruitful with the right fruit. Once she had found a letter in Dench's coat—it was a draft in his writing with his recognizable cross-outs, and it began, "It has always been hard for me to say, but your love has meant the world to me." She did not read to the end but stuffed it back inside the coat pocket, not wanting to ruin things for him or the moving surprise of it for herself. She would let him finish his composing and choose the delivery time. But the letter never arrived or showed up for her in any manner whatsoever. She waited for months. When she finally asked about it, in a general way, he looked at her with derision and said, "I have no idea what you're talking about."

Inside the old man's house, wide doorways led to shaded rooms; corridors to stairways to more corridors. Whole areas of the house were closed off with ivory quilts hung with clipped rings from fishing spears—to save on heating, she quickly surmised. There were stacks of reading material—a not uncozy clutter of magazines, some opened and abandoned, and piles of books, both new and used. On top of one was a dried-out spider plant that looked—as they used to say heartlessly of all their dying spider plants—like Bob Marley on chemo. She recognized the panic at even a moment's boredom that all these piles contained, as well as the unreasonable hopefulness regarding time. In a far room she spied a piano, an old Mason & Hamlin grand, its ebony surface matte with dust, and wondered if it was tuned. Its lid was down and stacks of newspaper sat on top.

"Don't mind the clutter, just follow me through it—the muffins are in the kitchen," he said. She followed his swaying gait into the back of the house. Beneath the wisps of white hair his skull was shiny and his scalp had the large brown spots of a giraffe—if only they weren't signs of looming death they would look appealing and whimsical and young people would probably want them—give me a liver spot!—as tattoos. Smaller versions freckled his hands. "I keep hoping this clutter is charming and not a sign of senility. I find myself not able to tell."

"It's like a bookstore or a thrift shop. That kind of clutter is always charming."

"Really?"

"Perhaps you could go all the way and put little price tags on everything." A shaming heat flushed her face.

"Ha! Well, that was partly the idea with the book nook out front. That I could put some of this to use. But feel free to add your own. All contributions welcome." The muffins were store-bought ones he had reheated in a microwave. He had not really made them at all. "I shop sparingly. You never know how long you've got. I don't even buy green bananas."

"Very funny."

"Is it?" He was searching her face.

"Well, I mean . . . yes, it is."

"Would you like some coffee, or do you want to just stick with your own?" He signaled with his head toward the paper cup she still held, with its white plastic top and its warted brown vest made of recycled paper bags. She saw that it was instant coffee he meant, a jar of Nescafé near the stove. He turned the burner on and gas flamed into the blue spikes of a bachelor's button beneath the kettle.

"Oh, this is fine," KC said. What did she care if Dench got no coffee today? He would prefer this mission of neighborly friendliness, would he not?

They sat down at his table, and Milt placed the muffin on a plate in front of her. "So tell me about yourself, " he said, then grinned wanly. "What brings you to this neighborhood?"

"Do I stand out that much?"

"I'm afraid you do. And not just because of those tattoos."

She only had three. She would explain them all to him later, which is what they were for: each was a story. There was *Decatur*, the vow never to return there. There was also a *Moline* one along her collarbone—a vow never to return there, either. The *Swanee* along her bicep was because she liked the chord ascension in that song, a cry of homesickness the band had deconstructed and electrified into a sneer. It had sometimes been their encore. When there was one. It was also a vow never to return there. She mostly forgot about all these places until she looked into a mirror after a bath.

"My music career didn't work out and I'm subletting here. I came back to this town because this is where I used to visit my grandmother in a nursing home when I was young. I liked the lake. And she was in a place that looked out onto it, and when I went to see her I would go into a large room with large windows and she would race over in her wheelchair. She was the fastest one there with the chairs."

He smiled at her. "I know exactly the place you mean. It's got a hospice wing in it called Memory Station. Though no one in it can recall a thing."

KC stuffed the muffin in her mouth and flattened its moist crenellated paper into a semicircle.

"What kind of music do you play? Is it loud and angry?" he asked with a grin.

"Sometimes," she said, chewing. "But sometimes it was gentle and musing." Past tense. Her band was dead and it hadn't even taken a plane crash to do it. They'd hadn't been able to afford to fly except once. "I'll come by and play something for you sometime."

His face brightened. "I'll get the piano tuned," he said.

There was that smell again, thawing with the remnants of winter, in their walls. This was the sort of neighborhood where one could scarcely smell a rancid onion in a trash bag. But now this strange meaty rot, with its overtones of Roquefort.

"What do you really think that is?'" KC asked Dench through the bathroom door. The change of seasons had brought new viruses and he was now waterboarding himself with a neti pot.

"What?"

"The smell," she said.

"I can't smell anything right now—my nose is too congested."

She peeked into the bathroom to see him leaning sideways with the plastic pot, water running down his lips and chin. "Are you disclosing national security secrets?"

"The netis will never learn a thing from me," he said.

"You can take a book or leave it. There is a simple latch, no lock." The honey-hued hutch might indeed attract birds if it didn't soon fill up with books and the clasp were not shut.

"Let's see what you have in there already." She moved in close to him. His waxy smell did not bother her.

"Oh, not much really." An old copy of *The Swiss Family Robinson* and one of *Infinite Jest*. "I'm aiming for the kids," he said. He had put up a sign that said, "Take It or Leave It Book Nook: Have a Look." Like a community bicycle, you could take one and never have to bring it back. Dench himself had a community bike from several communities ago. "Now that the bookstore has gone under, and with the hospital so close, I thought people might need something to read."

There was something antique and sweet in all this—far be it from her to bring up the topic of electronic downloads.

"Probably there is a German word for the feeling of fondness one gets toward one's house the more one fixes it up for resale."

"Hausengeltenschmerz?" said KC.

But he was thinking. "My wife would have known."

His wife had been a doctor. He told KC this now as she ate another muffin in his kitchen. It had been a second marriage for his wife, so there was a bit of sunset in it for them both: he had been stuck in his bachelor ways and hadn't married until he was sixty.

("Bachelor ways!" Dench would seize on later. "You see what he's doing?")

"She was a worldly and brilliant woman, an oncologist devoted to family medicine and public-health policy," said Milt.

There was a long silence as KC watched him reminisce, his face wincing slightly while his mind sifted through the files.

"I never got on with her daughters much. But she herself, well, she was the love of my life, even if she came late to it and left early. She died two years ago. When it came it was a blessing really. I suppose. I suppose that's what one should say."

"I'm sorry."

"Thank you. But she was brilliant company. My brain's a chunk of mud next to hers." He stared at KC. "It's lonely in this neck of the woods."

She picked off a moist crumb from the front of her jacket. "But you must have friends here?" and then she put the crumb quickly in her mouth.

"Well, by 'neck of the woods,' I mean old age."

"I sort of knew that, I guess," she said. "Do you have friends your age?"

"There are no humans alive my age!" He grinned his sepia teeth at her.

"Come on." Her muffin was gone and she was eyeing the others.

"I may be older than I seem. I don't know what I seem."

She would fall for the bait. "Thirty-five," she said, smiling only a little.

"Ha! Well, that's the sad thing about growing too old: there's no one at your funeral."

She always said thirty-five, even to children. No one minded being thirty-five, especially kindergartners and the elderly. No one at all. She herself would give a toe or two to be thirty-five again. She would give three toes.

He looked at her warmly. "I once studied acting, and I've kept my voice from getting that quavery thing of old people."

"You'll have to teach me."

"You have a lovely voice. I take note of voices. Despite my deafness and my tinnitus. Which is a nice substitute for crickets, by the way, if you miss them in the winter. Sometimes I've got so much whistling going on in my ears I could probably fly around the room if it weren't for these heavy orthopedic shoes. Were you the singer in your band?"

"How did you know?" She slapped her hand down on the table as if this were a miracle.

"There's a way you have of wafting in and hitting the sounds of the words rather than the words themselves. I mean to clean off this piano and get you to sing."

"Oh, I'm very much out of tune. Probably more than the piano. As I said, my career's a little stalled right now: we need some luck, you know? Without luck the whole thing's just a thought experiment!"

"We?"

"My musical partner." She swallowed and chewed though her mouth was empty. He was a partner. He was musical. What was wrong with her? Would she keep Dench a secret from him?

Dench would want it. "What can I get for you?" she had asked Dench this morning, and he had stared at her balefully from the bed.

"You have a lot of different nightgowns," he'd said.

"They're all the dresses I once wore onstage." And as she got ready for her walk, he said, "Don't forget the coffee this time. Last time you forgot the coffee."

"It's good to have a business partner," Milt said now. "But it isn't everything."

"He's sort of a genius," she lied. Did she feel the need to put Dench in competition with his dead wife?

"So you've met some geniuses," Milt smiled. "You're having fun then. A life with geniuses in it: very good."

She lived with so much mockery this did not bother her at all. She looked deeply into his eyes and found the muck-speckled blue there, the lenses cut due to cataracts. She would see the cut edges in the light.

"Do you think Ian would miss a few of his books?"

"No one misses a few of their books. It's just the naked truth. Look at the sign down the road."

The missing *D* of the bookstore: perhaps Dench had stolen it for himself, stashing it under the bed; she didn't dare look.

"Old Milt has a little book nook—I thought I'd contribute."

"I see."

"I'd only take a few. I can't donate my own since they all have the most embarrassing underlinings. In ink." Plus exclamation points that ran down the page like a fence by Christo. Perhaps it was genetic. She had once found an old copy of *The House of Mirth* that belonged to her mother. The word *whoa* appeared on every other page.

"Come here. Lie on top of me." His face was a cross between longing and ordering lunch.

"I'll squash you. I've gained five pounds eating muffins with Milt." He grabbed her hand but she gently pulled it away. "Give me some time. I'm going to cut out the sweets and have a few toes removed."

She had put on a necklace, of freshwater pearls so small they were like grains of arborio rice decorating the letters of *Decatur*. She combed a little rat's nest into the crown of her hair to perk it up. She dabbed on some scent: fig was the new vanilla! As she went out the door, Dench said, "Win them with your beauty, but catch them off guard with your soul." Then there was the pregnant pause, the instruments all cutting out at once—until he added, in a chilly tone, "Don't even bother with my coffee. I mean really: don't bother." After that she heard only her own footsteps.

"I brought you a couple books," she said to Milton. "For your nook."

"Well, thank you. Haven't had any takers yet, but there's still room." He looked at the titles she had brought: *Collapse: How Societies Choose to Fail or Succeed* and *Lady Macbeth in the Gilded Age*. "Excellent."

They once again went inside and ate muffins. Forget coffee: this time she had not even brought the dog.

She began to do this regularly, supplying Milt with more of her landlord's books. He had taken to looking so happy to see her, his eyes brightening (blue, she had read once, was the true color of the sun) so much she could see what he must have looked like when he was young. He was probably the bachelor that all the old ladies were after. He had the look of a gentleman, but one who was used to the attention of women, even as the uriney smell had crept over him. "Here we are: two lonely fools," he said to her once. It had the sound of a line he'd said before. Nonetheless, she found herself opening up to him, telling him of her life, and he was sympathetic, nodding, his peeled-back eyes taking on a special shine, and only once or twice did he have to lean forward disconcertingly to murmur, "Say that again?" She didn't mention Dench anymore. And the part of her that might consider this and know why was overshadowed by the unknowing part, which she knew in advance was the only source of any self-forgiveness. Ignorance ironically arranged for future self-knowledge. Life was never perfect.

When she twice stayed into the afternoon to fix Milt something to eat and once stopped by later to cook a simple dinner, Dench confronted her. "What are you doing?"

"He's a frail old man on the outs with his stepdaughters. He could use someone to help him with meals."

"You're fattening him for the kill?" They were looking into the abyss of the other, or so they both probably thought.

"What the hell are you talking about? He's alone!"

"A lone what?"

"A lone ranger! For Pete's sake, what is wrong with you?"

"I don't understand what you're pretending."

"I'm not pretending. What I don't get is you: I thought I was doing what you wanted."

He tilted his head quizzically the way he sometimes did when he was pretending to be a different person. Who are you doing that head-tilt thing for, she did not say.

"I don't know what I want," he said. "And I don't know what you're doing."

"You know exactly what I'm doing."

"Is that what you think? Are we always such a mystery to ourselves and to others?"

"Is a disappointment the same as a mystery?"

"A disappointment is rarely a mystery."

"I'm starting to lose confidence in you, Dench." Losing confidence was more violent than losing love. Losing love was a slow dying, but losing confidence was a quick coup, a floor that opened right up and swallowed.

Now he lifted his face beatifically, as if to catch some light no one else could see. His eyes closed, and he began rubbing his hands through his hair. It was her least favorite thing that he did in the head-tilting department.

"Sorry to interrupt your self-massage," she said and turned to go and then turned back to say, "and don't give me that line about someone has to do it."

"Someone doesn't have to. But someone should." The muttered snark in their house was a kind of creature—perhaps the one in their walls.

"Yes, well, you're an expert on should."

It broke her heart that they had come to this: if one knew the future, all the unexpected glimpses of the beloved, one might have trouble finding the courage to go on. This was probably the reason nine-tenths of the human brain had been rendered useless: to make you stupidly intrepid. One was working with only the animal brain, the Pringle brain. The wizard-god brain, the one that could see the future and move objects without touching them, was asleep. Fucking bastard.

The books she brought this time were *Instinct for Death* and *The Fin de Millennial Lear*. She and Milt stood before the nook and placed the volumes inside.

244

"Now you must come in and play the piano for me. At long last I've had it tuned." Milt smiled. "You are even allowed to sing, if you so desire."

She was starting again to see how large the house was, since if they entered through a different door she had no idea where she was. There were two side doors and a back one in addition to the front two. Two front doors! Life was hard enough—having to make that kind of decision every day could wear a person out.

She sat down at the piano, with its bell-like sound and real ivory keys, chipped and grainy. As a joke she played "The Spinning Song" but he didn't laugh, only smiled, as if perhaps it were Scarlatti. Then she played and sang her love song to the chef, and then she did "Body and Soul" and then her version of "Down by the River," right there inside the house with no requests to leave and go down by an actual river. And then she thought that was probably enough and pulled her arms back, closed her mouth, and in imitation of Dench closed her eyes, lifted her face to the ceiling, and smoothed back her hair, prepping it for the wigmaker. Then she shook her arms in the air and popped her eyes open.

Milt looked happier than she'd ever seen him look. "Marvelous!" he said.

No one ever said *marvelous* anymore.

"Oh, you're nice," she said.

"I have an idea! Can you drive me downtown? I have an appointment in a half hour and I'd like you to come with me. Besides I'm not allowed to drive."

"All right," she said. Of course she had guessed that soon she might be taking him to doctor's appointments.

Instead, she drove him in his old scarcely used Audi, which she found stored in the garage with a dust cloth over it, to his lawyer's. "Meet my lovely new friend, Casey," he said, introducing her as they were ushered into the lawyer's gleaming office and the lawyer stared at her skeptically but shook her hand.

"Rick, I would like to change my will," he said.

"Yes, I know. You wanted to—"

"No, now I want to change it even more than I said before. I know we were going to leave the house to the Children's Hospital, which was Rachel's wish, but they're doing fine without us, their machinery's over there tearing things up every day on that new wing. So instead I'd like to leave everything, absolutely everything, to Casey here. And to make her executor as well."

Silence fell over the room as Milt's beaming face went back and forth between pale-feeling KC and pale-looking Rick.

"Milt, I don't think that's a good idea," KC said, clutching his arm. It was the first time she had actually touched him and it seemed to energize him further.

"Nonsense!" he said. "I want to free you from any burdens—it will keep you the angel you are."

"It hardly seems that I'm the angel."

"You are, you are. And I want you and your music to fly untethered."

Rick gave her a wary look as he made his way slowly behind a mahogany desk the size of a truck flatbed. He sat down in a leather chair that had ball bearings and a reclining mechanism that he illustrated by immediately beginning to bounce against it and spin slightly, his arms now folded behind his neck. Then he threw himself forward onto a leather-edged blotter and grabbed the folder he had in front of him. "Well, I can get Maryanne to change everything right now." Then Rick studied KC again, and in a voice borrowed from either his youth or his son, said to her, "Nice tats."

She did not speak of it to Dench. She did not know how. She thought of being wry—hey, Villa is back! And this time it's an actual villa—but there was no good way. She had been passive before Milt's gift—gifts required some passivity—and she would remain passive before Dench. Besides, the whole situation could turn on a dime, and she half hoped it would. God only knew how many times Milt had changed his will—so she would try not to think of it at all. Except in this way: Milt had no one. And now he had no one but her. Which was like having no one.

Dench appeared in the bathroom doorway as she was cutting bangs into her hair with nail scissors. "I thought you were growing your hair," he said. "I thought you were going to sell it."

"It's just bangs," she said, threw down the scissors and brushed past him.

She began to take Milt to his doctor's appointments. "I've got reservations both at the hospice wing where your grandmother was and also right there," he said as they passed the Heavenly Sunset Cemetery.

"Do you have a good tree?"

"What?"

"Do you have a good space beneath a strong tree?" she said loudly.

"I do!" he exclaimed. "I'm next to my wife." He paused, brooding. "Of course, she has on her gravestone 'Alone at Last.' So I'm putting on mine 'Not So Fast.' "

KC laughed, which she knew was what he wanted. "It's good to have a place."

At the doctor's, sometimes the nurse, and sometimes the physician's assistant, would walk him back out to her and give her hurried and worried instructions. "Here is this new medicine," they would say, "but if he has a bad response we'll put him back on the other one." Milt would shrug as if he were surrounded by a gaggle of crazy relatives.

Once, a nurse leaned in and whispered, "There's a fear it may have spread to the brain. If you have any trouble on the weekend, phone the hospital or even the hospice. Watch his balance particularly."

One morning, KC took another of Ian's books to Milt's book nook and, not seeing the old man outside, she worriedly tied Cat to the book-nook post, went up to the main door, and knocked. She opened it and stepped in. "Hello? Good morning? Milt?"

Out stepped a middle-aged woman with an authoritative step. Her heels hit the floorboards and stopped. She wore black slacks and a white shirt tucked into the waistband. Her hair was cut short—thick and gray. It was the sort of hair that years ago, when it was dark, wig-makers would have paid good money for. She stood there staring for a long time and then said, "I know what you're up to."

"What are you talking about?"

"One of his Concertos in Be Minor. How old are you?"

"I'm thirty-eight."

"I wonder if he knows that. You look younger."

"Well, I'm not."

"Hence your needs."

"I don't know what you mean."

"No? You don't?"

"No." Denial, when one was accused, was a life force and would trump any desire to confess. An admission of guilt would knock the strength right out of you—making it easier for your arms to be twisted behind you and the handcuffs put on. It was from Dench, perhaps, that she had learned this.

"Shall we sit?" The pewter-haired woman motioned toward one of the sofas.

"I don't think that's necessary."

"You don't."

"No, besides, I was just walking my dog, and he's still tied up outside. I was just checking on Milt."

"Well, my sister has taken him to his doctor's appointment, so he won't be needing you today."

In bed, KC lay next to Dench, staring at the ceiling and smoking a cigarette, though they were not supposed to smoke inside. Cat lay on the quilt at the foot of the bed, doing his open-eyed fake sleep. They were carnies at the close of Labor Day. She stared at her Hammond keyboard, which right now had laundry piled and draped over it in angles.

"What illness do you suppose Milt actually has?" Dench asked.

"Something quiet but wretched."

"Early onset quelque-chose?"

"I don't think I can go on visiting him anymore. I just can't do it."

Dench squeezed her thigh then caressed it. "Sure you can," he said.

She stabbed out her cigarette in a coffee cup then, turning, rubbed her hand down along Dench's sinewy biceps and across his tightly muscled stomach, feeling hounded back into his arms, which she had never really left, and now his arms' familiarity was her only joy. You could lose someone a little but they would still roam the earth. The end of love was one big zombie movie.

"Do you realize that if you smoke enough you will end up lowering your risk of uterine cancer?" she said.

"That's a bad one," said Dench. "The silent killer. Especially in men."

"What did you do today?"

"I worked on some songs about my slavery-oppressed ancestors. I'm blaming the white man for my troubles."

She thought of his father. "Well, in your case it's definitely a white man."

"For most people it is. That's why we need more songs."

"Life! It's a hell of a thing, isn't it."

"I wouldn't have voted for it." She kissed him on his shoulder. "Wouldn't it be lovely just to fly out of here and live far away on a cloud together?"

"To be birds and see Gawwd!"

"Yes! We could be birds in a little birdhouse that had books and we could read them!" she exclaimed.

Dench turned his head quickly on the pillow to stare at her. "Perhaps we have that already," he said. "But darlin', we ain't seeing God."

"Because God is off in some cybercafe, so tired from all those biblical escapades that now he just wants to sit back and google himself all day." She pulled her hand away from Dench, since he had not reciprocated with his own. "If he's not completely deaf to our cries, he's certainly deaf in one ear."

"For sure. Not just the hardware of the inner ear but the hairs and jelly further in: all shot."

"You're a strange boy."

"You see? We're getting past the glaze and right down to the factory paint here."

She let a few days go by, and then she resumed her stopping at Milt's on her coffee runs. Because summer was creeping in she was now bringing Dench iced coffee, but invariably the ice cubes would melt, and she would just drink the whole thing herself. Milt still heated up his muffins but often needed her to drive him to doctor's appointments as well as to other places, and so she ran his errands with him, watching him greet the salespeople, the druggist, the dry-cleaning girl, all of whom he seemed to know. "I'm so glad my wife's daughters are gone," he said at one point as they were driving home. "I dread the house with them there. I'd rather just return to the cave of my own aloneness!"

"I know how you feel."

"You have no idea," he said and leaned in to kiss her on the cheek before he got out of the car. "They are as cold as they come. I mean, even the ice on Mars melts in springtime!"

Once she took the old man swimming. They went to a beach farther north on the lake, at a state park on a weekday when there was no one there. "Don't look!" he squealed as he took off his shirt and limp-jogged into the water, where he was safer than he was on land. He was not in bad shape, merely covered with liver spots, and his stomach was only slightly rounded and his breasts about the size of her own.

"How's the water?" she called to him. A line of silver at the water's edge sparkled in the sun. The sky was the deep belligerent blue of a hyacinth.

"Expect the unexpected!" he called back. She could see he'd once been a strong swimmer. His arms moved surely, bold, precise. Of course, when you expected the unexpected, it was no longer unexpected, and so you were not really following instructions. As she approached the water she saw that the silver line along the sand was the early die-off of the alewives: washed ashore gasping and still flipping on your foot as you walked. The dead lay in a shiny line up the beach, and if one of the fish had died closer to the waves it caught the light like the foil of a gum wrapper. Another putrid perplexity of the earth. She dove out anyway—to swim among the dying. She would pretend to be an aquarium act, floating among her trained, finned minions; if she imagined it any other way it was all too sad. She bobbed around a bit, letting the olive waves of the lake crest up and wash over her.

They picnicked back on shore. She had brought cheese sandwiches and club soda and difficult peaches: one had to bite sharply into the thick, fuzzed skin of them to get to the juice. They sat huddled in their separate towels, on a blanket, everything sprinkled with sand, their feet coated in it like brown sugar.

"Too bad about the dead fish," Milt said. "They'll be gone next week, but still. So may I!"

Should she say, Don't talk like that? Should she, in her bathing suit with her tattoos all showing, feign a bourgeois squeamishness regarding conversations about death? "Please don't talk like that," she said, peach juice dripping down her chin.

"Okay," he said obediently. "I'm just saying: even Nature has her wickednesses." He took out a flask she didn't know he carried and poured her a little into a paper cup. "Here, have some gin. Goes in clean and straight—like German philosophy!" He smiled and looked out at the lake. "I was once a philosopher—just not a very good one."

"Really?" The gin stung her lips.

"Terrible world. Great sky. That always seemed the gist." He paused. "I also like bourbon—the particular parts of your brain it activates. Also good for philosophy."

She thought about this. "It's true. Bourbon hits a very different place than, say, wine does."

"Absolutely."

"And actually, red wine hits a different place from white." She sipped her gin. "Not that I've made an intense study of it."

"No, of course not." He rinsed gin around on his gums.

Back at his house he seemed to have caught a chill and she put a blanket around him and he grabbed her hand. "I have to go," she said.

A sadness had overtaken him. He looked at KC, then looked away. "Shortly before my wife died she sat up in bed and began to shout out the names of all the sick children who had died on her watch. I'd given her a brandy, and she just began reciting the names of all the children she had failed to save. 'Charlie Pepper,' she cried, 'and Lauren Cox and Barrett Bannon and Caitlin Page and Raymond Jackson and Tom DeFugio and little Deanna Lamb.' This went on for an hour."

"I have to go—will you be okay?" He had taken his hand away and was just staring into space. "Here is my number," she said, writing on a small scrap of paper. "Phone me if you need anything."

When he did not reply she left anyway, ignoring any anguish, locking the door from the inside.

Perhaps everyone had their own way of preparing to die. Life got you ready. Life got you sad. And then blood started coming from where it didn't used to come. People revisited the deaths of others, getting ready to meet them in the beyond. KC herself imagined dying would be full of rue, like flipping through the pages of a clearance catalogue, seeing the drastic markdowns on stuff you'd paid full price for and not gotten that much use from, when all was said and done. Though all was never said and done. That was the other part about death.

"I had the dog all day," complained Dench, "which was no picnic. No day at the beach."

"Well I had Milt. He's no kiss for Christmas."

"I don't know what I'm supposed to think about all the time you spend with him. "

"According to you, you never know what to think."

"It just seems to me that if things are going to take, they shouldn't take so long. By the way, I've found out what that odor is."

"Really?"

The smell, even with the warm weather ostensibly drying things out, was still in the walls. There was the occasional scurrying of flying squirrels in the attic. It was surprising that Cat didn't jump up and start barking.

"The rot of a bad conscience."

"I really doubt that."

"Well, let me show you." He opened the hatch to the crawl space that constituted the attic. He pulled down the folding ladder and motioned for her to climb it. "Take this flashlight and move it around and you'll see."

When she poked her head into the crawl space and flashed her light around, she at first saw nothing but dust and boxes. Then her eyes fell on it: a pile of furry flesh with the intertwined tails of rats. They were a single creature like a wreath, and flies buzzed around them (and excrement bound them at the center) while their bodies were arrayed like spokes. Only one of them still had a head that moved and it opened its mouth noiselessly.

"It's a rat king," said Dench. "They were born like that, with their tails attached, and could never get away."

She scrambled down the ladder and shoved it back up. "That is the most revolting thing I've ever seen."

"They're supposed to be bad luck."

"Put the door back down."

"A surprise for Ian. I did phone the pest-removal place, but they charge a thousand dollars. I said, 'Where are you taking them, Europe?' We may just have to burn the house down. It's completely haunted."

"Really."

"We could work up plausible deniability: What kerosene can? Or, Many people are known to go shopping while cooking pot-au-feu."

She studied Dench's face as if—once again—she had no idea who he was. Having found the rat king he now seemed to be the star of a raucous horror film. He was trying to be funny all the time and she no longer liked it, as if he were auditioning for something. Soon he might start telling Milt's jokes: *I keep thinking of the hereafter: I walk into a room and say, What am I here after?* She only liked Dench's Jesus jokes, since in them Jesus was sort of an asshole, which she thought was perhaps a strong possibility, so the jokes seemed true and didn't have to be funny, and so she didn't have to laugh. "Don't ever show me anything like that again," she said.

Cat came up and started to hump Dench's leg. "Sheesh," said Dench, as KC turned to leave, "he's had his balls cut off and he still wants to date."

Summer warmed all the houses. Most of them did not have air conditioners, Ian's and Milt's included. She took Milt one evening to a nearby café, and they had to dine outside, at a wobbly metal table near the parking lot, since the air within was too slicing and cold. "I think I would have liked that cold air when I was about seventeen," he said. "Now I feel the heat is good for the old bones."

They ate slowly and although the food clung to his teeth, KC did not alert him. What would be the purpose? At some point, good God, just let an old guy have food in his teeth! They ate squash soup with caramel corn on top—molar wrecking.

"You know," he said, chewing and looking around, "people get fired from the barbershop, a restaurant closes, this is a slow town and still things change too fast for me. It's like those big-screen TVs: all the bars have them now. I can't watch football on those—it feels like they're running right at me."

KC smiled but said nothing. At one point he said loudly of his custard, "The banana flavor doesn't taste like real banana but more like what burped banana tastes like."

She glanced over at the next table. "I kind of know what you mean," she said quietly.

"Of course old people are the stupidest. It's the thing that keeps me from wanting to live in a whole facility full of them. Just listen to them talk: listen to me talk. It's like, I've been walking around with this dumb thought for forty years and I'm still thinking it, so now I might as well say it over and over." He again sang the praises of his wife, her generosity and social commitment—"She went to clinics in India all the time!"—and then turned his attention to KC. "You are not unlike her, in a way," he said. Behind him the sun set in the striped hues of a rutabaga.

"I can't imagine," she said. Instead her mind was filled with wondering what the neighbors must think.

"Your faces are similar in a way. Especially when you smile!" He smiled at her when he said this, and she returned it with a wan one of her own, her lips in a tight line.

When she walked him back to his house the crickets had started in with their beautiful sawing. "Tinnitus!" Milt exclaimed.

But this time she didn't laugh, and so he did what he often did when he was irritated: he walked with his most deaf ear toward her so that he could stew in peace. She noticed him weaving and knew that his balance was off. At one point he began to tilt, and she quickly caught him. "An old guy like me should wear a helmet all the time," he said. "Just get up in the morning and put it on."

He then turned and peered through the dusk at her. "Sometimes at home I think the ringing in my ears might be the phone, and I pick it up, hoping it might be you."

She helped him into his house—he took the front stairs with greater difficulty than he used to. She turned on the lights. But he switched them off again, and grabbing her hand sat in a chair. "Come here and sit on my lap," he said, tugging her firmly. She fell awkwardly across his thin thighs and when she tried to find her footing to stand again he braced and embraced her with his arms and began to nuzzle her neck, the *u* and *r* of *Decatur*. His eyes were closed, and he offered his face up to her, his lips pursed but moving a little to find hers.

KC at first let him kiss her, letting their lips meet slightly—she had to be obliging, she had to work against herself and find a way—and then his rough and pointed tongue flicked quickly in and out and she jolted, flung herself away, stood, switched the lights back on, and turned to face him. "That's it! You've gone off the deep end now!"

"What?" he asked. His eyes were barely open and his tongue only now stopped its animal darting. She swept her hair from her face. The room seemed to whirl. Life got you ready. She had once caught a mouse in a mousetrap—she had heard the snap and when she looked it seemed merely to be a tea bag, a brown mushroomy thing with a tail, then it began flopping and flipping and she'd had to pick it up with a glove and put it in the freezer, trap and all, to die there.

It was time. "You're completely crazy!" she said loudly. "And there's nothing I can do at this point but call the hospice!" Words that had waited in the wings now rushed into the crushed black box of her throat.

His face now bore the same blasted-apart look she'd seen when she first had met him, except this time there was something mangled about the eyes, his mouth a gash, his body slumped in banishment. He began silently to cry. And then he spoke. "I looked him up on—what do you call it—Spacebook. His interests and his seekings."

"What are you talking about?"

"Good luck," he said. "Good luck to you and your young man—I wish you both the best."

"It's done."

She sank against the door. She had waited all night for the hospice people to come and carry Milt off the next morning, and then she had signed some forms and promised to visit, promised to come help him with the crossword puzzle, and, taking the keys of the house, she had locked it, then walked hurriedly home.

Dench was putting his cell phone away. He looked at her worriedly and she returned his gaze with a hard glare. He then stepped forward, perhaps to comfort her, but she shoved him off.

"KC," he said. And when he cocked his head as if puzzled and tried in forgiveness to step toward her again, she made a fist and struck him hard across the face.

Her life in the white-brick house was one of hostessing—and she poured into it all the milk of human kindness she possessed. There were five bedrooms and one suite turned entirely over to the families of children at the hospital whose new pediatric wing was now complete. She had painted the walls of every room either apricot or brown, and she kept the crown moldings white while she painted the ceilings a celestial blue. Every morning she got up early and made breakfast, a ham-and-egg bake that she served in a large casserole in the dining room, and although she made no other meals she made sure there were cookies in the front room and games for the siblings (who also played with the dog). She sometimes attempted music in the afternoons, sitting at the piano while people tried to smile at her. She wore high collars and long sleeves and necklaces of blue slag to hide her tattoos. She left magazines for people to read but not newspapers, which contained too much news. She maintained the book nook, stuffing it with mysteries. In the summer, she opened up the sleeping porches. She watched the families as they went off in the morning, walking their way to the hospital to see their sick children. She never saw the sick children themselves—except at night, when they were ghosts in white nightgowns and would stand on the stairwell landings and recite their names and wave—as she roamed the house, thinking of them as "her children" and then not thinking of them at all, as she sleeplessly straightened up, but she would hear of their lives. "I missed the good parts," the mothers would say, "and now there are no more good parts." And she would give them more magazines for flipping through in the surgery lounge, in case they grew tired of watching a thriving aquarium of bright little fish.

Tears thickened her skin the way cave memory and brine knitted the rind of a cheese. Her hair was still long but fuzzily linted with white, and she wore it up in a clip. There were times looking out the front windows, seeing the parents off on their dutiful, despairing visits, when she would think of Dench and again remember the day he had first auditioned raucously for their band, closing with some soft guitar, accompanied by his strong but inexpressive baritone, so the song had to carry the voice, like a river current moving a barge. She had forgotten now what song it was. But she remembered she had wondered whether it would be good to love him, and then she had gone broodingly to the window to look out at the street while he was singing and she had seen a very young woman waiting for him in his beat-up car. It had been winter with winter's sparse afternoon stars, and the girl was wearing a fleece chin-strap cap that made her look like Dante and also like a baby bird. KC herself had been dressed like Hooker Barbie. Why had she put this memory out of her mind? The young woman had clearly driven him there—would she be tossed away? bequeathed? given a new purpose by God, whose persistent mad humor was aimless as a gnat? She was waiting for him to come back with something they could use.

Nominated by The Paris Review, Lydia Conklin

SELF-PORTRAIT WITH EXIT WOUNDS

by OCEAN VUONG

from ASSARACUS

Instead, let it be the echo to every prayer
drowned out by rain, cripple the air

like a name flung inside a sinking boat,
let it shatter the bark on the nearest kapok

and through it, beyond the jungle's lucent haze,
the rot and shine of a city trying to forget

the bones beneath its sidewalks, through
the refugee camp sick with smoke and half-sung

hymns, the shack lit with the final candle, the blackened
faces we held between our hands and mistook

for brothers, let it past the wall, into a room brightened
with snow, a room furnished only with laughter,

Wonder Bread and mayonnaise raised
to cracked lips as testament to a triumph

no one recalls, let it brush against the new-born's
flushed cheek as he's lifted in his father's palms

wreathed with fishgut and cigarettes,
burrow through that wall where a yellow boy

soaks in blue television flood, the boy
who cheers as each brown gook crumbles

on the screen where Vietnam burns perpetually
in the mind's blown fuse, let it whisper

in his ear—before sliding through, clean
like a promise, and pierce the painting of fruit

above the bed, enter the cold supermarket
where a Hapa woman who wants to shout

Father! At every white man possessing
her nose, may it sing, briefly, inside

her mouth, before laying her down between
the jars of tomato and blue boxes of pasta,

the deep red apple rolling from her palm,
let it drill a hole in her throat and into

the prison where a father watches
the moon until he's convinced it's the last wafer

God refused him, and let it enter the wood
where a man is slumped at a desk lit only

with night's retreat, trying to forge an answer
out of ash pressed into words, may it crack

that stubborn bone above his heart—blood
and blood seeping through an epic

of blank pages, but if for nothing else, let it soar
like a kiss we've forgotten how to give

one another, slicing through all the burning rooms
we've mistaken for childhood, and may it go on

to circle the earth, warping through seasons
and years before slamming back into 1968,

to Hong Long Bay: the sky replaced
with fire, the sky only the dead look up to,

may it find my grandfather, crouched beside
the Army Jeep, his blond hair flickering

in naplam-blasted wind, pin him
down to the dust, where mother and I

will crawl out from history, that wreck
of shadows, tear open his olive fatigues

and clutch that name hanging from his neck,
that name we press to our tongues as if to relearn

the word for *live*, let us carry him home on our backs,
bathe his cooling body in salt and jasmine and call it

good, but if for nothing else, let me believe
as I weave this death-beam like a blind woman

stitching a flap of skin to her daughter's ribs,
let me believe I was born for this—as I cock back

the chamber, smooth and slick, like a true
Charlie. Like I could hear the song drowned out

by rain as I lower myself between the sights
and pray—that nothing moves.

Nominated by Assaracus

RELIQUARIES

by PAUL ZIMMER

from THE GEORGIA REVIEW

reliquary \ 're-lə-, kwer-ē \ n. {Fr reliquaire, from ML reliquaiurium, from reliquia relic + Larium-ary—more at relic}: a casket, shrine, or container for keeping or exhibiting relics (remains, leavings, of a deceased person)
— *Webster's Third New International Unabridged*

The Prague Book

I have traveled to Europe at least forty times across a handful of decades, but I never had occasion to visit Prague, the great diamond of Bohemia with its "fairy tale" skyline, a city that centuries ago was planned to rival Paris and Rome.

In 2005 the Metropolitan Museum of Art in New York brought together a magnificent exhibit called *Prague: The Crown of Bohemia, 1347–1437*, and I read ecstatic reviews of it in the *New York Times*. In 2011 the museum offered the hardcover catalogue of the exhibit at a wonderful sale price I could afford, and so I bought it. When I opened the package, I was stunned immediately by the portrait of St. Luke on the book's cover, a reproduction of a painting by Master Theodoric in Holy Cross Chapel at Karlštejn Castle. St. Luke holds a sacred text which spills over onto the angled edge of the tooled golden frame, and he riveted me with his large, gray eyes. In fact he looked directly and inescapably at *me*. A cream-colored ox, apparently Luke's traditional symbol, whispers benignly in his ear (perhaps telling Luke a few of my secrets).

At the bottom of the frame is a rounded hole that puzzled me. The book says it is "a compartment for a relic," so St. Luke's finger bone or toe or perhaps a piece of his shinbone had originally been placed there. The painting had been a reliquary until someone made off with the relic.

260

The arrival of the exhibit catalog was a significant recent moment in my life. It is a beautifully produced collection of remarkable paintings, illustrated books, alphabet designs, tombstones, sculptures, and sacred objects of all sorts . . . but I was most struck by its emphasis on reliquaries.

For instance, an arm of gilded silver, studded with gems and semi-precious stones, rises from a beautifully crafted four-steepled church. The rising arm has a thin open grate through the metal up its inner length. This reliquary contains the arm bone of St. Vitus (290–303), the patron saint of the cathedral where it is deposited.

One reliquary bust made of gilded silver, cameos, intaglios, pearls, and rock crystal contains the arm of St. John the Baptist. John is an imposing, regal figure; over his shoulders is draped a cloak of gold that looks like a camel hair coat. Another bust, dated 1355, is quite strange: it shows an aesthetic, very thin, unidentified man wearing a jeweled crown; in his chest is a long, elaborate opening through which, even in the catalogue photograph, I can see some sort of bone capped at each end with gold.

A striking copper repository bust might portray Count Matthew Csák, a lord of upper Hungary in the fourteenth century, but the book says it could also be St. Ladislas. In either event the top part of the reliquary head has been sawed off, so the potentially identifying attributes of either Csák or Ladislas are now gone.

The Prague book is a wonder to me. I sometimes keep it propped up on a table in our library so that the eyes of St. Luke are on me when I am working.

The Splinters

Usually the cabinet in the sacristy of St. John the Baptist Church in Canton, Ohio, was kept locked, but it was open that morning almost seventy years ago when I caught a glimpse of the reliquary inside. When later I asked Eugene Aspell about the splinters displayed in the golden receptacle, he informed me in smug, reverential tones, "They are pieces of St. John the Baptist's shinbone. Every church in the world that is named for St. John has some of these in its sacristy."

Aspell was *head-altar-boy-in-charge*, and his family's house was a block away from the parish. It had a big cross next to its doorbell, there was a small holy water font just inside the door, and all the pictures on the walls were decorated with palm fronds.

Mr. Aspell, Eugene's father, who owned a large clothing shop, seemed to be permanent president of St. John's Men's Club, and Aspell's mother was chief officer in that club's feminine counterpart, the Women's Sodality. Aspell was the smartest kid in our grade school, an ecclesiastical prodigy who, through his unquestionable piety, was even able to ward away the playground bullies, who gave him wide berth, committing their atrocities on me and other children in far corners of the yard.

Aspell was even envisioned by some of his admirers to be a potential candidate for canonization. I sometimes suspected he was already scheming about the miracle he would be required to perform. When he prayed, Aspell did not bend down over his clasped hands like the rest of us, but spread his slender hands open like lilies at his sides as he raised his rapt face to the altar. This was impressive, I must admit— but still, I didn't always believe everything Eugene Aspell said.

I had heard school rumors about the fabulous gilded repository in the sacristy cabinet. I had but one peek at it; Aspell, in his sanctity, claimed to have seen it many times while he performed privileged tasks in the vestry. When I questioned him carefully about this, he assumed his religious "mystery" look and gazed at me with pity and forgiveness for my probing.

Altar boys were not allowed to come into the vestry proper until the mass was beginning and the procession being formed. The one occasion when I was able to see the holy splinters, I was putting on my surplice in the altar boys' cloak room when Mrs. Denke, the housekeeper in the priest residence, came hurrying through to bring a message to Monsignor Animus. On an impulse I followed behind her into the vestry because I was a nosy kid and wanted to have a look around.

The room was crowded with priests, deacons, novitiates, acolytes, and assorted thurifers for a Palm Sunday solemn high mass; for a moment no one noticed me lurking behind Mrs. Denke's considerable presence, so I managed to slip all the way into the room. The big ornate wall cabinet was open, probably because special objects were needed for the service, so I got a good look into it.

The gilded reliquary was on the top shelf. What looked like splinters of some sort were displayed against white cotton or cloth pressed into a round piece of glass. Gold encircled the glass and radiated from the relic, the entirety resting on an elaborate base studded with green and blue jewels.

Mass was to begin in five minutes, and Monsignor Animus was annoyed by Mrs. Denke's interruption as he finished straightening his spangled chasuble. The monsignor always seemed to be irked by something. Then he noticed me standing behind her gawking, and his face suddenly turned the color of uncooked hamburger.

"Zimmer! What are you doing in here?" he rasped. Monsignor Animus was gray, holy, ancient, and considerable. His glower was a ray gun. I knew if he wished he could forever damn me all the way to hell in an instant. Whenever he looked at me my urine grew warm and urgent. I had sneaked into sacred territory and was caught out, breathing heavily as the retinue of clergy and sub-clergy all turned to look at me. Eugene Aspell was in the room, preparing for the important job of bearing the bannered cross. He looked away from me.

Finally I managed to respond: "I thought Mrs. Denke was motioning for me to follow her, Monsignor." It was the best I could do, and the old priest found my response totally inadequate. He reached out with both hands and I winced, thinking he was going to shake me by my ears, but he grabbed my shoulders and squeezed hard, then turned me around abruptly and marched me in disgrace out of the vestry and back into the altar boys' dressing area, where he turned me around so he could drill me with his ray.

"I'd send you home right now, Zimmer, if we didn't need you to fill out the procession service." He shook his finger in my face before he hurried back into the sacristy to finish robing. "We'll talk about this later," he snapped over his shoulder.

Lord, God! Could I admit to Monsignor Animus that I'd slipped into the room because I wanted to gawk at the splinters of St. John's shin? Doubtless this was a major desecration, perhaps even a mortal sin, a violation of some privilege given only to priests and a few elderly nuns . . . and Eugene Aspell. Would I be struck blind? It was probably a mortal sin! In any event, I felt sure that it was damningly serious. Perhaps Jesus would forgive me—but never Monsignor Animus.

Then, somehow, I was granted my own miracle. I spent weeks cringing and hiding at school, certain the fires of hell were about to be ignited around me. But my violation was never mentioned again. Apparently the incident slipped away into the deeper creases of Monsignor Animus' ancient brain. Perhaps he just had bigger Friday fish to fry, or was just letting me stew in my own guilty juices. Or perhaps it didn't really matter at all.

When I was a kid I had my very own hallowed turf, an untended vacant lot just down the street from my family house on McGregor Avenue. Here I built hideaway huts of orange crates, stashing childhood objects and burying personal treasures such as dead bugs and spiders after placing them in tobacco tins. Here I conducted my private rites of youth.

I very much liked these times when I could be alone—as I like being alone now with these words and paper. With my Dad's sickle I cleared small isolated patches in the high weeds, areas that were concealed and known only to me, some of them tucked up against the tan concrete garage building that ran beside the field all the way back to the alley behind. When I was on the outs with my playmates (which was not infrequently, because I was the only Catholic kid in the neighborhood) or feeling moody, I would go to my pagan place to hide, meditate on little boy things, and renew myself. I wasn't wanking off or looking at dirty pictures, I was just being by myself. No one knew I was there, and I recognized early that this kind of aloneness is a rare thing in this world, and to be cherished if you desire it.

One summer someone posted a FOR SALE sign on a wooden post at the street end of my sacred ground, and this violation disturbed me. The *cheek* of some adults! I decided to eliminate the threat. Late one warm morning when I was certain I was not being observed, I knocked the sign over with my father's hatchet, took it back into the high weeds of the lot, and buried it under some loam and dirt that a colony of ants had turned up.

Several weeks later another wooden sign appeared. I waited two days and, when I was certain the coast was clear, dispatched it in a similar way. One day a larger steel sign on a metal post had been hammered deep into the ground—a Nazi-like violation of my sacred ground. A sticker affixed to the reverse side of the sign stated, WARNING: REMOVAL OF THIS SIGN IS A VIOLATION OF THE LAW!

Bullshit! What was the Law to someone who had already committed a mortal sin? This required even sturdier action. But how? One evening at dusk I tried to shake and dislodge the metal sign, but only succeeded in cutting one of my fingers open.

Well, I thought, how much risk was I willing to take to protect my hallowed ground? This would require brave action beyond the law of land or church. I appropriated one of my father's heavier screwdrivers and slipped down the street one evening just after sunset. But strain as I might with my twelve-year-old hands, the bolts kept turning on the other side of the steel post, and I could not remove the screws.

I pondered my father's toolbox some more and selected a crescent wrench and a larger screwdriver. One evening just at dusk I violated the civil law—as I had violated church law. With my bony hands aching, I finally managed to remove all the nuts and bolts just as my parents started calling for me in the early dark. I hustled the sign away and momentarily covered it with leaves, then ran home.

My parents were angry with me for violating their curfew and wanted to know where I had been. I would not lie, but I would not tell them. It was *my* secret. I was grounded for a week—but protecting my place was worth the punishment. The offending sign was gone and I had triumphed. No one ever had the temerity to post another sign on my restricted, sacred patch again during my tenure.

The Dog

When I was seventy five years old, our wonderful dog—our perfect dog—Sheba died at the age of seventeen. My grief overwhelmed me, memories rolled, and I staggered with sadness, crying like a chastened child. My wife Suzanne and I loved her too much, perhaps, and waited too long to have her put away. Sheba had done all she could do and was ready to fall over by the time we finally took her to the veterinarian. (I weep again as I write this.) The doctor was very kind to all of us and gave Sheba the fatal shot as Suzanne and I placed our hands on her.

The vet said, finally, "Her heartbeat has stopped now." We fell away from touching Sheba and reached to hold each other. The doctor waited until we had gathered ourselves again and asked, "How do you want me to dispose of her? You can have the body to bury, or we can take care of it here. We can also have her cremated and you can have the remains."

Neither of us had given this any thought. Burying Sheba in the fields she loved seemed the thing to do, but I had had a heart attack and surgery not long before and was in no shape to be swinging a pick or shoveling—which would have only prolonged our grief anyway.

Both of us wish to be cremated ourselves when we die—so why not our beloved dog? "It will be $200," the veterinarian said. In our sadness we would have given $2,000.

A few days later an office assistant called and said Sheba's cremated remains were ready for us to pick up. I don't know what we expected, but the ashes were not in a sack or a paper box; they were in a wine-colored vessel, not much bigger than a large soup can—a fancy enameled cylinder decorated with golden interwoven curlicues. The vessel was not sealed—apparently in case we wanted to scatter Sheba's ashes. I opened it. Yes, ashes to ashes, dust to dust. But Sheba's ashes did not smell of death.

I closed the can again and for a while put it on a bookshelf over my desk in the library. For weeks, each time I looked up and saw it, I would have a small meltdown. Still, Suzanne and I did not feel we wanted to scatter Sheba's ashes, preferring to keep them in one place.

We decided to bury the can of ashes in our yard. I got a spade from the barn and managed to dig a small hole between two trees. I found a large flat stone and asked our daughter, who does sculpture and happened to be visiting, to chisel an "S" on it. I placed the can of Sheba's ashes in the hole, filled it in, and dragged the flat rock over it.

The rock is still there. After first writing this passage I left my desk to walk out into light flurries to look at Sheba's reliquary. I brushed the snow off so I could see the S.

In summer when I run the John Deere mower around our yard, I have to fiddle my way around the stone between the two trees, but I always do this happily. Sometimes I scatter grass clippings across the stone with the mower. I always look down and think of Sheba, sometimes saying hello to her aloud, and this gives me strange comfort.

Familia de Delcausse

Some years ago, traveling with my family in rural France, we stopped in a lovely small town built across some hills. We took a walk, looking for grand houses, monuments, or churches, trying to take in the aura of the place. Turning a corner that gave onto an open market area, we saw a small domed temple in the midst of a centuries-old graveyard on a rise above the square, and we ambled up the hill to inspect it.

France has many such cemeteries; the weathered gravestones heaved this way and that around a large, memorial temple with a rusted gate of iron bars across the entrance. We peered into the shadowed recesses at a niche where a statue of the Virgin Mary sublimely gazed down at the infant Christ in her lap. She was surrounded by dusty mourning wreaths and by cloth flowers arranged in porcelain vases. Two huge candlesticks, now encrusted with pools of cracked wax, had been placed on each side of the virgin.

A heavy padlock was clamped to a hasp on the bars across the entrance. Someone had placed two pots of begonias, wilted long since, on the steps leading up to the barred entryway. A bronze plaque over the arched threshold was ornately inscribed, FAMILIA DE DELCAUSSE, 1816.

Napoleon's wars had finally ended in 1815. Perhaps this monument signified a renewal of religious fervor in France. Were Delcausse family members buried beneath the shrine, or was this just a pretentious display of wealth and devotion? The place held latent forces—there seemed to be remote spirits in the shadows, an ancient perspective which eluded my grasp, and yet somehow I sensed its significance.

Looking into this dim space I could make out a tarnished bronze urn with a curved glass plate embedded in its side, through which I could barely see a gray/brown object. I took off my bifocals and put them back on. Perhaps it was some family keepsake, a piece of jewelry or consecrated object. I shivered when I realized I was looking at a bone in the urn. I felt sure of this—perhaps it was a bone of the Pater Familias Delcausse, or some saintly family member.

St. Augustine

Many years ago, when I was twenty, I met a young man several years older who remained my good friend until he died a few years ago. He was a man who had studied religion a long while and came within a year of being ordained a Catholic priest. He left the seminary for intellectual and personal reasons, but retained his religiosity into his early middle age—when he lost it somewhere in the mire of the Korea/Nixon/Kennedy assassination/Vietnam/Johnson/pill era.

I am not in the slightest sense a practitioner or scholar of religion; when I met my friend I had already begun drifting away from Roman Catholicism, already doubting many of the beliefs that are required of the faithful. My friend, who wanted me to make a balanced decision about religion, hovered nervously about and gave me books to read: a copy of the New Testament, *The Imitation of Christ*, *The Diary of a Country Priest*, *The Seven Storey Mountain*, the writings of St. Thomas Aquinas, and *The Confessions of St. Augustine*. With some difficulty I lurched through the latter two. The Augustine confessions particularly mystified my fidgety twenty-year-old psyche, and ultimately I abandoned my reading.

Continuing to wonder, as I always have, about the origins of the curious human inclination to hang on to the corporeal parts of the saintly dead, I was directed back to Augustine's *Confessions* through an interesting new book by Andrea Nightingale, *Once out of Nature: Augustine on Time and the Body* (University of Chicago Press, 2011). A review of it sent me back to my now-yellowing, sixty-year-old copy of *The Confessions* in an attempt to trace some history of the reliquian custom.

Much of Augustine's book remains opaque to me, but Nightingale in her book about him says that Augustine, "By a daring feat of imaginative inversion, applied to the relics of Saint Stephen in Hippo . . . insisted that 'the region of the living' was to be found where one would least expect it—'in the dust of the dead.'"

In *Confessions* Augustine wrote:

> . . . my mind gave over to question thereupon with my spirit, it being filled with the images of formed bodies, and changing and varying them, as it willed; and I bent myself to the bodies themselves, and looked more deeply into their changeableness, by which they cease to be what they have been, and begin to be what they were not; and this same shifting from form to form, I suspected to be through a certain formless state, not through a mere nothing; yet this I longed to know, not to suspect only.

He then goes on to address God: "Thou wert, and nothing was there besides, out of which Thou *createdst heaven and earth*; things of two sorts; one near Thee, the other near to nothing; one to which Thou alone shouldest be superior; the other, to which nothing should be inferior."

I lack a scholar's rigor or the ability to fully comprehend Augustine's meaning in "to which nothing should be inferior," but I believe that a basic key to the reliquian tradition is in this last phrase, in which he "bends himself to the bodies themselves" as they "begin to be what they were not, a formless state to which nothing would be inferior."

Morose Inclinations

Not only saints' particulars are venerated in reliquaries. Several years ago a reliquary was purchased by a collector at an auction in Florence.

In it were a right thumb, a finger, and a tooth preserved in a slender case created of wood and glass and topped with a carved bust. When the new owner consulted with scholars about his recent acquisition, the contents were authenticated as being the remains of Galileo Galilei. They had been taken, along with another finger and vertebrae, during his reburial in 1737, almost one hundred years after his death, by some Florentines who wished to remember the great scientist as a counter-saint, a martyr for the cause of science.

The creation of reliquaries and the collecting and preservation of human remains represent a sort of morose inclination which has extended through the world to this day, not always for worshipful purposes: Egyptian mummies, shrunken heads, two-headed babies preserved in formaldehyde by circuses, scalps taken in the "Indian wars," the body of Ted Williams preserved in liquid nitrogen at minus 320 degrees Fahrenheit, trophy body parts taken by soldiers as souvenirs in wars, Lenin's tomb, the preserved bodies of popes, Einstein's brain— we remain strangely fascinated.

The Turtle

My parents never allowed me to have a dog or cat, resisting my most inspired supplications. This deprivation was mostly my mother's doing because she'd been raised in country places and remembered how dogs dragged mud and filth onto the rugs of a cleaned house.

But once, to my great excitement, I convinced her to allow me a small dime-store turtle, which I kept one summer on our shaded back porch in a wooden box stuffed with grass clippings. His name was Murgatroyd and he had a rough American flag decal on his shell. (This was in 1945.) I swatted flies and plucked ants and beetles for Murgatroyd all summer, and I gave him dried turtle food and water in jar lids.

I tried to play with my pet, tried to get him to grip a twig with his mouth or chase a BB, but he was never interested and remained coldly indifferent. I couldn't tickle him, and if I tried to pet him he pulled his head into his shell. He had no ears, so it did not seem sensible to sing songs to him, as I would have to a cat or dog.

I'd place him in the palm of my hand, hold him close to my face, and look at him for a brief while each day, believing he looked back at me, but he never blinked acknowledgment nor made movement enough to acknowledge my presence.

Murgatroyd ate very little, despite my best efforts to keep him fed—

269

and one day, after several months, he did not move anymore. The only pet I'd ever had—dead in a very short time. I purloined one of my mother's canning jars, stuffed it with cotton from my Boy Scout first aid kit, slipped in Murgatroyd's corpse, and screwed down the lid, then bore him down the street to my sacrosanct lot. With my mother's garden trowel, I buried him between two trees-of-heaven in a very secret place beside the old cement garage. I piled some special rocks over his burial place, one of which I had chiseled a rough *M* on, and I said some sacred turtle words over the little reliquary.

I went on to other things that summer: pea-shooter fights, Monopoly, Cleveland Indians radio broadcasts, jungle comics, Ouija boards, endless baseball catch with my mates. Then early autumn came, and I had to face the ordeal of school again.

Not until the following spring, when the vacant lot was greening up, did I put my secret hideaway in order again and visit the place of Murgatroyd's interment. Solemnly I unpiled the stones on his grave and dug up his reliquary. It was somewhat dimmed by its year in the ground, but I cleaned it off so I could see the turtle's body, which seemed to have collapsed a bit and turned a darker green. I studied the corpse through the glass and—of course—finally could not resist the impulse to unscrew the lid. That was my first smell of death, and I fell back. How malodorously we all die! Somehow I got the lid screwed back on, and without further study or ceremony reburied the jar and piled the rocks back on top.

I did return the following summer when I was fourteen, my last year as an altar boy, and the last in my sacred field. I dug up Murgatroyd's reliquary and looked in through the grungy glass at his remains, reduced considerably now to a small black husk. I did not unscrew the reliquary lid again, but carefully reburied it and replaced the marker stones.

More than six decades have passed. A few years ago I was invited to give a reading of my poetry at one of the colleges in my hometown. My parents are long gone, but I took the time to drive through our old neighborhood in Canton, past our house, which looked reasonably well tended. But, down the street, a rather large house stood on the lot of my sacred ground next to the seemingly indestructible cement garage. I paused my car to look along the garage wall toward the place of Murgatroyd's burial.

No, I did not presume to knock on the house door and ask the owner if I might look for my turtle's reliquary. I am a strange-looking, bent, hoary old man now. Looking for a dead turtle's grave? They would probably have called the police.

But as I gazed down the garage wall I fancied the jar might still be there—being close enough to the old concrete to have survived the bulldozing when the house was built—and I felt certain that there might still be a bit of Murgatroyd in that durable canning jar, even after all this time—something not sacred and superior, but "to which nothing should be inferior."

Nominated by Stephen Corey, Gary Gildner

LISTENING TO VIRGINIA

by JEFFREY HARRISON

from THE HUDSON REVIEW

To the Lighthouse on CD

Driving around town doing errands,
I almost have to pull to the side of the road
because I can't go on another minute without
seeing the words of some gorgeous passage
in the paperback I keep on the passenger seat . . .
but I resist that impulse and keep listening
until it is almost Woolf herself sitting beside me
like some dear great aunt who happens to be a genius
telling me stories in a voice like sparkling waves
and following eddies of thought into the minds
of other people sitting around a dinner table
or strolling under the trees, pulling me along
in the current of her words like a twig riding a stream
around boulders and down foaming cascades,
getting drawn into a whirlpool of consciousness
and sucked under swirling into the thoughts of
someone else, swimming for a time among the reeds
and glinting minnows before breaking free
and popping back up to the surface only to discover
that in my engrossment I've overshot
the grocery store and have to turn around,
and even after I'm settled in the parking lot
I can't stop but sit there with the car idling

because now she is going over it all again
though differently this time, with new details
or from inside the mind of someone else,
as if each person were a hive, with its own
murmurs and stirrings, that we visit like bees,
haunting its dark compartments, but reaching
only so far, never to the very heart, the queen's
chamber where the deepest secrets are stored
(and only there to truly know another person),
though the vibrations and the dance of the worker bees
tell us something, give us something we can take
with us as we fly back out into honeyed daylight.

Nominated by The Hudson Review, Ted Deppe, B. J. Ward, William Wenthe

ICONOGRAPHY

fiction by AYŞE PAPATYA BUCAK

from THE IOWA REVIEW

Soon there will be a girl who will not eat. Some will call her the Turkish Girl; others, the Starving Girl.

Like most, I will read about her, see her decline and rise on the news. I, like many, will find her beautiful, though I won't know why.

It will happen, simply, like this:

One day she wakes feeling full, and so she skips breakfast, then lunch, then dinner, and she wakes the next day so hungry she still doesn't eat, the pain so exquisite that it feels true. It feels exactly like her.

But that truth is little known.

Most think she got the idea from the news, from the hundred and one Turks, including teenage girls, who died protesting the government's treatment of those imprisoned for their politics. Others think it was Gandhi. Or Thoreau, whom she read for her freshman seminar at her American university, or Kafka in European Lit the next semester. Some blame websites, call it an eating disorder. Some call it misguided idealism, student politics overrunning common sense, the fault of a twenty-four-hour fast sponsored by the Students for a Sustainable Society (which she joined on her way to the dining hall one night). Actually, there is no evidence that she participated in the fast, as it was an honor system kind of thing, and in fact she forgot to starve that day, which was weeks before her own fast, and in fact that day she not only ate three meals but also shared a sausage pizza with her roommates around nine p.m., three hours before the fast, which she forgot to begin, was to end.

Before she will be the Starving Girl, she is not even *the* girl, but merely a girl, an international student at an expensive American university, not terribly political, not terribly religious. Not even terribly Turkish.

First she fasts in silence. Nobody notices. Then they ask if she is losing weight. You look great, they say. And then, you look thin. And then, do you want my ice cream, pasta, cereal bar, bagel, Diet Coke? And finally they call university administrators, who call her parents, who fly in, as soon as they can, from Ankara where they run a hotel near the Atatürk mausoleum, which they are forced to leave in the hands of their assistant manager, who takes the opportunity to allow all of his distant relatives from the East to visit for free, with the result that one impressionable cousin removes her headscarf at the foot of Atatürk's statue, refuses to replace it despite the quiet insistence of her parents, and ends up leaving her family for good. The Starving Girl's parents would be affected by this story, by their implicit participation in the splitting of a family, but they, because of their own troubles, never hear it.

Never does the Starving Girl think of herself as anything but hungry. It is the others who give her act drama and meaning, which, in the end, she is happy to accept.

The American university moves her to the student health center while they wait for her parents. Nobody, even she, is exactly sure how long it has been since she has eaten. At the health center, her professors, her roommates, her friends, and a number of strangers are brought in one at a time and then in groups. They ask her to eat. The president of the American university asks her to eat. Her roommates ask her to eat. The nurses ask her to eat. The president, the roommates, and the nurses together ask her to eat. What do we need to do to make you eat? they ask.

Change everything, she says.

It is the first thought that comes to her mind.

The next day the president of the American university brings in a boy who lived in a tree for nearly two years and who is also an alumnus, and he asks her to eat. You need to live so you can spread your message, the tree boy says. My death is my message, the Starving Girl says. My hunger is my message. She smiles a little smile as she says it. Or so the alumnus tree boy will write in his memoir years later.

Can you be more specific? the president of the American university asks. About the message?

It is a very political university. They do not mind political actions as long as they have meaning and nobody is seriously hurt.

I hunger, the Starving Girl says.

For what?

For everything to be different.

The tree boy gets angry. Not everything should be different. Some things are really great. Some things need to stay exactly the same, he says.

The Starving Girl looks at him and again she smiles. It may be that she is too weak to speak; it may be that she has nothing to say. Or maybe she finds him funny. I wouldn't like to say.

Because of the visitors—the friends and strangers—most of campus hears about the Starving Girl, and so a reporter, who is in the Starving Girl's European Lit class in which they read Kafka and who is also from the university newspaper, comes to interview her.

What is it that you are trying to say? he asks.

She leans in closer to him, sliding along her bed, and looks into his face, but she does not answer.

Do you resent the contribution that food growers are making to global warming? he continues. Is it the pesticides? The cattle farts? The trucks and planes that move food millions of miles every day? People's need to eat tomatoes all year long, as if summer were eternal?

Could you repeat the question? she says, and they both laugh.

But really, he says. Doesn't that stuff bother you?

Of course, she says, just above a whisper. Everything bothers me.

Is it the fattening of the poor? The fast-fooding of the nation? The Starbucking of the city? The drive-through, drive-by habit of eating that allows us to graze all day until our hearts explode with oversatiation and implode with alienation?

It's everything, she says.

That is where it really begins. "Student Protests Everything" is the headline of the article picked up by the *New York Times*.

The Starving Girl's parents are temporarily detained when first the Turkish government and then the American take them in for questioning, first for leaving the country, and then for entering.

The reporters come, and at first she is just another idealistic teenager put into the spotlight before she has the skills to handle it. It is part of her initial charm. She quietly says things like: I'm not a role model. I'm not trying to change anybody's behavior. I'm doing this just for me. She was always soft-spoken and on the verge of thin. But then one day she stops talking, just as she had stopped eating, and becomes something more.

The students camp in front of the student health center at night and carry signs saying "It's Everything" during the day. They would continue with their coursework—it's a good school after all, the students practiced multi-taskers—but the faculty take a bus to Washington and camp in front of the White House, and so classes are cancelled.

Soon there are articles speculating about the Starving Girl's love life, and reporters ask her opinion, which she does not offer, on many different world matters.

Bono comes to visit.

It all happens very quickly.

Soon the world is split between those who want to feed her, those who want to join her, and those who are afraid.

In Turkey, she becomes first a symbol of the East—the sacrificial martyr—and then a symbol of the West—the liberal protestor—and finally, yet one more point of interpretation and argument.

In a midnight visit, the president of the American university tells the Starving Girl how proud he is of her—this may be a real chance, he says, for not just the nation but the world to change—but the only way to keep this thing going is if she does not die and so won't she please eat. It would be their secret. The president is an exceptionally tall man, an advantage when speaking to crowds, but now he tries to round his shoulders in, to bend at the knees, to get closer to the Starving Girl. He crouches down by her bed, puts his hand on hers, and has to resist pulling it away when he feels how cold her fingers are.

No secrets, she says, speaking for the first time in days. But I will take some water.

For just a moment the president of the American university wants to call her a stupid bitch, even though he is not the kind of person to think, let alone say, such a thing. Look what this is doing to me, he thinks. He straightens in a bolt, yanks his hand out of hers when her fingers tangle with his, and leaves without remembering to bring her water.

Inside the Starving Girl's mouth, the soft palate, the uvula, the tonsils, the anterior and posterior pillars are all dry. The nurses have been teaching her anatomy, with the hope that it will connect her to her body. And in some sense it has. Now when she is bored, she reads herself like a textbook, cataloging her parts and how they feel.

A doctor who is famous for talking on television and who happens to be Turkish comes in and explains what will happen to her body if she continues to refuse food: the ache, the muscles burning as they deteriorate, constricting in on themselves, the disintegration of her organs, the blackening of her sight, the elimination of her hearing, the bleeding under her skin.

I can live with that, she says, her voice a quiet croak. She is disappointed when the doctor does not deliver the obvious comeback: not for long you can't.

In fact, with each day, the sensations of her body are a mystery, awe-inspiring in their intensity. The Turks were among the first to infect a person with a disease in order to prevent it. They knew sometimes you had to be sick in order to live. The Starving Girl does not know this intellectually, but in her body she does. She thinks, in her long dying, she is completely alive. And strangely happy.

Finally the Starving Girl's parents arrive, and at first, like the university, they refuse to force her to eat. They take her from the student health center into their room at the local hotel and let her lie in bed and watch cable television. They have heard that watching television leads to eating. Their daughter has changed since coming to America; they think maybe they need to treat her like an American. But they do not know the Starving Girl is only watching the shifting lights on the screen as if they were an unending Fourth of July display.

Sometimes she drinks water with sugar from the hotel's in-room coffee station. She can still stand and walk to the bathroom if she takes her time.

When she wakes at night with her mother beside her and her father on the cot the hotel had rolled into the room and unfolded like a hospital bed, the Starving Girl thinks of what will happen when she dies. Her mother will wash her body alone, not even looking at it as she works her hands and washcloth underneath the sheet that shrouds the body, no longer recognizable by touch. For the Starving Girl it is a beautiful memory.

For years, her cheeks held a roundness that was not matched by any other part of her body. When she was a young girl, her mother would cup her fat cheeks and say, Baby. Sometimes she did it even when the girl was a teenager. Sometimes her father did it. Baby, they would say.

At first her parents do nothing but suggest room service, chocolate from the mini-bar, pretzels from the vending machine on the third floor. Then they bring in *manti* and *lahmajun*, the Starving Girl's former favorite foods, from the closest Turkish restaurant, which is more than fifty miles away. The restaurant's chef, when he hears who the customer is, volunteers to travel to the hotel and cook fresh in their kitchen, but her parents say there is no reason to come; she will not eat. She is no longer hungry.

And how would you describe hunger? We live as if we know what we want, as if we are capable of deciphering the signals our bodies send out, but what if we are wrong? I may say hunger feels like illness, but how can I know how it felt to her? Or what if hunger is an illness that eating covers but doesn't cure? Could eating be one more drug that masks the disease?

Most of the time, she is in a state between fantasizing and dreaming. Newspaper headlines float in front of her, captioning a future in which hundreds, then thousands of students join her fast, followed by the elderly, then the overworked, the immigrants, the stay-at-home parents, their toddlers, the teachers, the small business owners, the used book sellers, the hedge fund brokers, the CEOS, residents of the West, of the South, of the East, until finally no one is eating. It is a hunger strike so large that everything changes, and for at least a year, ours is a world in which everyone helps each other, and the worst things that happen are the kinds of arguments you have when you are tired but that can be solved when you are rested again.

It is not a future she invents; she believes it is the future come to her. And maybe it is.

What is the word, she asks her mother in a whisper. Her mother waits. The Starving Girl points a finger into her upper arm, like she is shooting herself. Inoculation, her mother says, and the girl nods. I am the inoculation, she says. I am the little bit of sickness that stops the disease, she says. Her mother shakes her head, but her daughter has already closed her eyes. I am the spotlight, the Starving Girl says with her eyes closed, and it is as if she has shut them against her own bright light.

When finally the Starving Girl cannot rise without help and wets the bed, then lies without comment on the damp sheets until her mother slides in next to her and says, what's this—only then do her parents call the president of the American university again. They do not know who else to ask for help. The president suggests an eating disorder clinic that will take the girl in, lock her in, feed her one way or another. If it is a choice between saving the world and saving his student, he will save his student, he tells the administrative assistant who is in the room when he takes the call. The president offers to arrange a ride to the clinic. The Starving Girl's mother does not want to say yes—she is ashamed of her inability to care for her own daughter, to convince her to live—but she does say yes, as does her father. What else can they do? They do not want to be parents to a martyr; it is not an honor they would choose.

So that afternoon, just as the first of a convention's-worth of pharmaceutical sales representatives is checking in at the front desk, the Starving Girl's father carries her through the halls of the local hotel, down the elevator, and staggering through the lobby, into the waiting car arranged by the president.

She is not light; she is heavy.

The pharmaceutical sales representative and all those in the hotel lobby that day are the last to admit to seeing her or her family. Later, they comment on how the father seemed as if he might fall, and how he refused their help, which in truth they did not offer.

There will be a dispute over what happens next.

Some say the Starving Girl is cured by the clinic, is either unbrainwashed or brainwashed, depending on your point of view, so that she eats and maybe forgets her hunger. She returns to the American university under a different name and graduates and returns to Turkey, or she returns to the American university under a different name and graduates and stays in the U.S. Or she returns to Turkey under a different name without graduating. Or she stays in the U.S. under a different name without graduating. In any case, she blends back in with the rest of us.

But some say the car she is riding in is intercepted by the Students for a Sustainable Society, who held the first twenty-four-hour fast, and who have been holding a sympathy strike of their own, though they alternate days of not eating, as death is not part of the sustainable message, and the Students for a Sustainable Society take the Starving Girl to an undisclosed location where they offer her a choice: eat or don't. We don't mind either way. Some say that given this freedom, the Starving Girl eats. Some say she doesn't. Some say her beauty and her hunger inspire all of the Students for a Sustainable Society who took her to the undisclosed location to stop eating, and they all die, unseen and unfound forever. Others say the Students and the girl start a revolution so underground that few people even know the effects of their actions, which are many.

Some say she moves to Canada.

Some make jokes.

Others say other things.

One story is this:

The car does not take her to an eating disorder clinic. It takes her to a secret location set up by the government underneath another secret location, where her parents are immediately disappeared. They last see their daughter with her eyes closed and her head tilted against the window of the limo, a small smudge of fog on the glass where her breath hits it, the only sign that she is still alive. They are taken from the car—forcibly in the case of her father, who was brought out first, and docilely in the case of her mother, who was second—by two men who are neither tall nor short, large nor small, dark nor light, wearing clothes that are instantly forgotten and expressions that are cold in that they are blank. The men take the Starving Girl's parents to another car, a black sports utility vehicle, and that is the last that is known of them, though years later it is believed by many that an elderly woman who surfaces at a Tibetan monastery with no memories of her past is actually the Starving Girl's mother.

The Starving Girl, who cannot anymore remember if she is a person, is placed underground in a room that looks like a hospital room but is not. The government keeps her alive while they decide whether or not they prefer her to die. There she floats, a body adrift without its mind, and a mind adrift without its body, for several days, until the doctor who is assigned to care for her, a man who has never married and never had children but has always longed for both marriage and children, and who is believed to be working for the government but isn't, brings in a select group of journalists, celebrities, and intellectuals, all of whom he was once a doctor for, to meet her during the night.

Her skin is tight in places, sagging in others. Her bones show. Her hair is mostly gone. Her fingers twitch. And she smells.

I am the only one to touch her. I kneel next to her bed and encircle her wrist with my thumb and forefinger. She does not move.

"What do you want?" I ask loud enough for the others, clumped together across the room, to hear.

Some believe she does not answer. Others believe she says, "Get up." Others insist it is, "Give up."

I know what she said. But I will not tell you. This is your story, not mine.

The doctor asks the select group of journalists, celebrities, and intellectuals what he should do. Should I save her? he asks. Or do I maintain my cover and see what else the government gets up to?

The group is silent, thinking the same thing, until finally one of them, the oldest and most famous, a woman with a sheath of bright white hair that she has pulled back in a slick ponytail, says it: You should let her die.

The others look to me as if, having touched her, I have some special say. My fingers tingle where they touched her wrist. Maybe it is her action that allows our inaction. Maybe her action was so large it left no room for ours.

Remember: an absence of action is an action, just as an absence of belief is a belief.

Remember: it is easy to love and hate her, both. To believe "get up" and "give up" are simultaneously sensible options.

And so she dies.

This is the kind of thing that can happen when you give up your body. Others do what they want with it. And your body is more of you than you perhaps imagined—with her body went her intent, her words, her self.

She's mine now. And yours, too.

The headlines are huge.

But that is not the only way. Here is another:

At the eating disorder clinic, where she is delivered without incident, the Starving Girl meets many girls and older women, too. We don't talk much. Meals—when so many others socialize are too fraught for us. Many of the girls eat in their rooms, with only a counselor present. Even when we are together in the dining room, it's an unspoken rule that nobody speaks. Talk is usually in the shared bathrooms or late at night with our roommates, and mostly that is the whispered swapping of strategies for when we are clear of this place.

We did not know she was coming, but when she arrived, it was obvious she was special. There were photographers outside—we could see them from the windows. And the staff whispered together. Finally somebody saw her, recognized her from the news. She was for us a hero. She hid her disease in plain sight: hunger strike.

At first she was in the medical ward. They called her by a different name, but we knew it was her. We decided to strike, too. Just as soon as we were on the outside. She was an inspiration. Even when she told us not to, when we watched her gain weight, when we watched her family visit and leave smiling and finally one day leave with her, walking on her own, we all knew we would strike. She could have said anything, and it wouldn't have stopped us. She had given us the idea, created the cause, and each of us waited, eating our half portions, gaining our single digits, eating just enough, saying just the right things to move to our freedom. She ate, but she left the rest of us hungry. And you have to understand, hunger for us was proof that we were alive. Our future strike glowed inside each of us, something to live for, even if it would kill us. I do not exaggerate. Inside of us, she glowed.

Really, there are so many ways this story could end. Remember, it has not happened yet. But here is my last:

I help the Starving Girl and her parents into the car, then slide in behind the wheel. Her mother sits in front, while she and her father sit in the back.

"Please," her father says as he straps on her seatbelt and then his own, and the Starving Girl looks at him gently.

"Without you, I would not be able to live," he says.

He is not one to beg.

She pauses. Then finally she says, "Okay."

And instead of saving the world, she saves him.

Nominated by The Iowa Review

TALLAHATCHIE

by SUSAN B.A. SOMERS-WILLETT

from ORION

for Emmett Till

In the mirror this river made of you
waxes a mother's wish: *I want the whole world
to see what they did to my boy.* In the casket,
you whistle, stuttering. You reek under glass. So
this is what a river will do, carve and swell
just like a woman, singing a glossy blues.
Lord knows, your face—it sorrows across my page.

Lord knows your face. It sorrows across my page
just like a woman singing a glossy blues.
This is what a river will do, carve and swell.
You whistle, stuttering. You reek under glass, so
to see *what they did to my boy.* In the casket
waxes a mother's wish. I want the whole world
in the mirror this river made of you.

Nominated by Orion, Aimee Nezhukumatathil

FATHER OF DISORDER

by JESSICA WILBANKS

from RUMINATE

My anger, when it comes, grows from my chest outward. It's as if my heart turns into a witch's cauldron, simmering my blood until it rages its way through my veins, blushing my neck, quivering my hands, and pulsing itself into my formerly peaceful thoughts.

This used to happen to me quite often when I was cooking dinner for a man I loved very much. I'd be washing carrots idly, chopping garlic, and then that heat would get to pumping. I'd clench my lips closed and concentrate on the chopping, until this man—a very good man whose own blood ran lukewarm—would ask me for a spatula or something, and then all holds were off.

I can still see this man's face, surprised at first, like a toddling child walking blithely through the park, thinking he's holding his father's hand before looking up to see a stranger. Of course this man took my anger into himself, thinking maybe his desire for a spatula was wrong, that he was wrong, him instead of me, simply because I was fiercer and more furious. But this man was not a dormouse, so then his own blood finally charged him up with adrenaline and fury, and we would fight over the food we were cooking.

It seemed to me when one prepares a meal in a swirl of rage, some of that rage must disperse into the food, so that when we ate hours later, after our blood was running at a more reasonable temperature, our previous heat dissipated into the meal. This is very likely a misinterpretation of the law of entropy, which states that energy tends to flow from being highly concentrated into places where it has the freedom to move.

Later, when we lay beside each other in bed, our bodies were still hot to the touch. We edged away from one another, cocooning ourselves far into the separate corners of our king-sized bed until it seemed like we were sleeping alone.

I am not the only one who struggles; my brothers also have a share in the family anger. One of them batters the ocean with it in his morning surf sessions. When he visits our parents there's no ocean available, so he's always slipping out to meet a friend or pick up groceries. If there isn't a car around to take him away, he straps on his sneakers and hits the trails, running until his heart is too tired to beat anger into him.

Another of my brothers is too gentle to ever let his anger out. He gave himself over to addiction instead, and only methadone brought him back. On his visits home for Christmas he drinks the vial of pink liquid in the morning and then nods off on the couch for much of the day, eyelids fluttering, holding my mother's dark-colored cat in his lap. When he wakes up in the late afternoon he bakes chocolate chip cookies and smiles at us, but while he's sleeping, I sometimes see a certain expression in his face, and I know then that in his sleep his anger goes to meet him.

Meanwhile my father nibbles on something in the kitchen, hums softly, asks me if I want a cup of coffee. I sit on the porch with him for a while as he tells long stories about the dogs and asks me questions about my life. His eyes are clear and steady, his mind is quiet, but the caffeine revs me into impatience. I start thinking about all the things I have to do when I fly back home, and when my father tries to tell me a joke I've heard a thousand times before, I thrum my fingers against the side of the porch and interrupt him with the punch line. He turns quiet, and I don't look up to meet his eyes.

II

When my brothers and I were growing up, a whole series of rented farmhouses rocked on the axes of my father's moods. It didn't take very much to get him thundering like some Old Testament prophet—maybe my brother had refused to wear socks to church, the dog had gotten into a neighbor's chicken coop, or we had slammed the door hard enough to wake the baby. Or sometimes his moods had nothing at all to do with us. The heat had just started rattling around in his head, and my father had to do something to get it out.

Whenever we saw his storms forming, my brothers and I sought small spaces, tucking ourselves into the fold of the long closet under the attic stairs, breathing in that mothball smell, and running our fingers along the mottled plaster. Or we'd slip out the front door and make for the weedy strip of gravel under the tall boxwoods that lined the front of the house. If his thundering reached a particular level, we'd run for the empty silo in the barn next door and curl up at the bottom, watching the swallows cut into the blue circle of sky above us.

But sometimes he'd spy an ankle as we ran by him, glimpse a curl of my hair from under the boxwoods, and then he'd rush after us, all the while yelling—we were bad, we would always do the wrong thing if presented with a choice, there was no way to right us, not even the rod would right us, though he would certainly try to right us, and we would sink lower and lower with every shout, as if his voice was a post-hole digger driving us down into the ground.

After a while my father would retire, spent, to occupy himself with something else that needed fixing. He'd get to banging wrenches around under the car, trimming his roses, building a pen for the ducks, and after a while he'd call us over to show us a praying mantis or teach us how to change the oil on my mother's car. We'd approach gingerly until we were satisfied that his anger was finally sleeping at the bottom of his mind. We were too young to be anything but grateful his rage was gone—we were especially too young to wonder where it went.

During these episodes my mother would look on from the four-paned window in the parlor. She was slower to forget my father's fits, and so she'd simmer there for a long while as my brothers and I gathered around my father again, tipsy with joy, passing him tools and laughing uproariously when he attempted a joke. My mother was no longer young, and she had stopped trusting my father a long time ago. She had also made it through high school chemistry; she knew that when a hot pan cools, its heat doesn't just disappear. The law of entropy prevails. That heat had to go somewhere, and even then my mother suspected the air hadn't just taken it up and blown it away from us.

III

The word *entropy* was coined by Rudolf Clausius, the sixth child of eighteen, born in the German town of Köslin to a Lutheran pastor and his wife. In all known photographs, Clausius is sharp-faced and unsmiling, a wintery beard masking his thin lips; but students and friends frequently referenced his kind and sympathetic nature. As a young man Clausius dabbled in history before moving on to focus on mathematics and physics. His doctoral dissertation was an unsuccessful but ambitious attempt to explain the blue of the sky by day and the red of sunrise and sunset.

Prior to the publication of Clausius' ninth scientific paper, "On Several Convenient Forms of the Fundamental Equations of the Mechanical Theory of Heat," there was no such thing as energy. Heat was thought to be a discrete substance called caloric, a weightless, colorless gas that made things hotter when it seeped through them. Caloric was not thought to operate whimsically, though, heating substances according to some inner drive, but was rather governed by a series of laws. One popular scientific book, *A Guide to the Scientific Knowledge of All Things Familiar*, written in 1840 by Rev. Ebenezer Cobham Brewer, explained the substance this way:

Q. What is heat?
A. The sensation of warmth.
Q. How is this sensation produced?
A. When we touch a substance of higher temperature than ourselves, the warmer substance keeps parting with its heat, till both are of equal temperature.
Q. What is that "stream of heat" called, which flows thus, from one body, to another?
A. CALO'RIC. Caloric, therefore, is the matter of heat, which passes from body to body; but HEAT is the sensation, of warmth, produced by the influx of Calo'ric.

Caloric theory was serviceable for a time. It explained why the ground froze when an icy wind blew by it, as well as the slow melt of snow when warmed by the sun. The notion reigned unchallenged until Nicolas Carnot, a young upstart from France, published a paper pointing out that when one bores holes in cannons immersed in water, the water boils without cooling the cannon. Carnot's findings baffled the scientific community until Clausius published a paper positing that the reigning notion of heat was incorrect, and should be replaced by a concept he called energy.

The twin axioms of caloric theory, updated by substituting heat with energy, mutated into what is now known as the second law of thermodynamics, unchallenged now since 1865. Energy can be transformed from one state into another, but can never be destroyed, and energy tends to flow where it is crowded to places where it has the freedom to move.

It doesn't seem like a coincidence that Clausius reached the pinnacle of his career prior to the death of his wife, who passed away during the birth of his sixth child. After her death, Clausius devoted himself almost entirely to fatherhood, collapsing into bed after long days of fathering his brood without a helpmeet. Years later, he published various papers and eventually returned to teaching—holding examinations from his sickbed right up until his death—but some historians are baffled that the promising scientist played only a minor role in the blizzard of scientific advances following his discovery of entropy. One historian called Clausius' lack of further achievement "strange, even tragic." His brother's memoirs are mum as to whether or not Clausius regretted his choice to devote himself to fatherhood, whether the scientist lay awake at night with cannons and equations on the brain, closing his eyes to thoughts of how all of the energy that might have gone into his scientific projects had instead been dispersed into the care and feeding of six lively youngsters. His brother simply wrote that the great scientist "was the best and most affectionate of fathers, fully entering into the joys of his children."

IV

Time proved my mother was right to worry about us, at least based on the diagnoses my brothers and I fielded as we maneuvered adolescence: Alcohol Abuse (2), Anorexia Nervosa (1), Attention Deficit Disorder (3), Bipolar Disorder (1), Depression (2), and Substance Abuse (2). The sheer quantity of clinical language that has attached itself to my brothers and me is somewhat troubling, but I'd like to think we're decent people. It's true none of us have owned homes, produced masterpieces, birthed children, or found love—instead we live paycheck-to-paycheck in second-rate cities, waiting tables, teaching other people's children, mowing lawns, and installing concrete countertops in other people's kitchens.

My mother sees our father as the Great Undoer, the progenitor of all our trouble, a volcanic force that turned us from sweet, tow-headed

290

children into sarcastic adults. Tears spring to her eyes when we tell stories about the time that the police hauled my father away after he punched my brother, the time my father broke a wooden spoon on my brother's thigh, the time my father slept in a tent for two weeks before letting his anger drop and speaking to us again. It troubles her even more that my brothers and I frequently recount these stories while sitting around the kitchen table laughing ourselves into near-seizures, beers in one hand and cigarettes in the other, hooting with glee as we mimic the way my father's eyes get to darting when he's about to blow.

From our limited positions, it's hard to trace these far-away stories to our various disorders, but my mother peers far above our heads and finds gossamer threads there. She traces them through a maze of twenty years, all the way back to my father, who's still holding those four threads in his hands. In my mother's eyes, my brothers and I are overgrown marionettes dangling at the end of those lines, all of our reactions linked to the jerks and shakes he gave them long ago. Our plaster heads are pivoted toward our father; our felted ears perked for whatever words might be coming out of his lips.

V

Maybe it's because I don't want to be a marionette, but I've always felt that when I lift my arms, I do so out of my own volition. Each of my parents would disagree, but while my mother believes my father's anger sent his offspring skidding down the path toward destruction, my father submits to a different theory of predestination. He sees the world not as a blank canvas, but rather a Calvinist chessboard in which the moves are already prescribed by God. Whenever he feels it's necessary, he trots out all sorts of evidence from the onionskin pages of his well-thumbed Bible—evidence supporting his claim that the various loves and hurts and sins which will move our lives are already written invisibly in the air. My father believes we have little choice in the matter of our own fate, and that conviction seems to be a great relief to him.

At fifteen, I resisted this doctrine. My God was clean-shaven and delighted to let me roam through my life on my own two feet. Unfortunately for all of us, my fifteenth summer fell around the time when my father's rages pivoted away from material triggers—leaving toys in

291

the grass to catch on the blade of the lawnmower—and toward more ideological triggers—whether or not a young person may tell another young person to shut up, or, even more dangerously, whether or not one has free will.

My brothers and I usually avoided being corralled into vehicles with our father, but that summer, close proximity was unavoidable. I had a job baby-sitting for a pair of rambunctious boys in the same Virginia town where my father commuted daily, and so every weekday morning I joined my father in the cab of his ancient pick-up truck. The ride would start out well enough—the truck hiccupped down the long dirt-packed driveway while my father sipped his tea, commenting quietly on the weather—but around the time we hit the shiny asphalt of Route 4, he'd toss his teabag on the floor of the cab and begin to survey everyone in our family, charting his approval or disapproval of their choices. Somewhere around the long swoop down to North Beach, the road cut through a series of steep hills and the conversation turned into a bull ride.

One day his mind started whirring at an even higher speed, lurching and thumping like the laundry in our second-hand dryer, and my father began arguing that his temper was not his fault, he had no choice in acting the way he did, and couldn't do better if he tried. I thought this was ridiculous and said so; I said we were all responsible for ourselves. My father began hollering, but instead of trying to follow his trail as I usually did, through faulty logic resting on stray bits of Scripture, I turned my head to the truck's filmy window, and began eyeing a nearby barn that had crumpled into a field. My father's voice became distant and the red left on the barn took on a special sheen. I studied the scene with a vague, journalistic excitement until it was out of my eyeshot; it was surprising to me how easily my father's voice faded.

I think it bothered him most of all that I had turned away from him, crossing my scrawny arms, preparing to wait out this tempest. My usual reaction when faced with the force of his temper was to take on his energy, either matching the cycling of his mind and arguing with him, or, more frequently, busting into tears. Either way there was a dispersal. This time, though, I refused it, which meant the heat was left in him, and so of course he had to do something to release the pressure.

My father abruptly changed lanes, the better to reach the right-hand side of the road, where he stomped on the brakes and stretched across the bench seat until he reached the door handle. He pushed the door open, despite its creaks of protest, and then with the commuters roaring past us, he ordered me out of the truck.

The sound of the truck peeling away broke me out of my reverie, and I started crying, cars whizzing by me as if I was invisible. Nowadays concerned suburbanites would have snatched me up in minutes, offering sliced oranges and a cell phone, but back then it was not an unusual thing to see a teary teenager loping alongside Route 4. I cried for a while as I walked, but soon became bored and started imagining I was really alone and wouldn't be able to call my mother when I reached the gas station another half mile south.

An hour or so later I was tucked back into the family bosom, but that night I imagined the ease of departure—how I might hitchhike the hour-and-a-half to D.C., buy a Greyhound bus ticket with my babysitting money, and make it to the Carolinas before morning. The possibility of distance had slipped into my blood like a unshakeable virus, even though I would be eighteen before I left, and when I did leave it was my father who drove me toward New England and my college years in that same pick-up truck.

VI

I tell a revised version of that story every Christmas, to the endless amusement of my brothers. The licentious nature of memory leads me to erase the sneakers I had on and substitute high heels, sending my former self trooping through trailer parks and across algae-filled drainage ditches, looking for a phone so I could call my mother. Some Christmases a trucker offers that humiliated girl a ride to Philadelphia, a man hocking peaches by the roadside sells her a Ball jar of warmish water for fifty cents, and a mangy dog follows her for miles despite her comic attempts to shoo it away.

Even my sober mother chuckles at these retellings, while my father, nestled in the middle of his offspring, smiles and shakes his head as if reminded of the behavior of a long-forgotten uncle prone to half-baked stunts. Time's arrow has done its work on him, frosted his beard and thinned his hairline. A stroke last spring cut him down a little more, thickening his tongue and gimping his right leg. His rage hasn't completely disappeared, but his body no longer supports it—the words that stung when they came from a black-bearded, sun-stained man fall flat when they slur out of this old man's mouth. In the play of our lives he has become King Lear—still the titular character, but limited to serving as a catalyst for the activities of the next generation.

My father's not the only stranger at the table. I hardly recognize my raucous, hairy brothers, whose speech is littered with words that would have blanched the children they once were. Even stranger than their adult bodies and habits is the knowledge that at any moment, we are all free to walk away, to fly back to our individual sets of rooms in far-away cities, jingle our keys in the lock, nudge the door open, and enter a quiet space marked with only our own smell, delightfully free of other Wilbankses.

It wasn't always like that. Our family used to be an entirely closed system. For much of our childhood, we were home-schooled by our mother. Aside from our trip to church on Sunday mornings, my father was the only one who had any sort of communion with the outside world, and even then it was a tentative sort of communion, since he worked for himself as a bricklayer, doing small jobs for individual homeowners. My father liked to say that we had everything we needed under our own roof, but this meant that when his rage left him and ricocheted around the house, there was nowhere for it to go. If a door could have opened into our family, my father's anger might have exploded outward, but as it was the house was shut up tightly for our own protection.

The pieces of our world desperately want to move, to flow, to exchange. Hot pots cool down immediately—the atoms in that hot pan are vibrating rapidly and want nothing more than to mix their energy with the cooler, slower atoms, dispersing the heat and creating less of an extreme. It is simply the way of the world. There's no way to stop this process—the more something is pressurized, the more likely it is there will be a violent explosion when it finally manages to make an escape.

VII

An endless stream of philosophers, poets, and psychologists have mistakenly equated entropy with disorder rather than dispersal, but fortunately for science, there is a certain physicist, now in his nineties, who is on a one-man crusade to set the matter straight. Dr. Frank Lambert has devoted his twilight years to a letter-writing campaign urging textbook publishers to move away from "the cracked crutch of disorder" when teaching entropy. He has been largely successful, pointing out that just as the dispersal of sugar into coffee is not a chaotic process, entropy is energy's way of evening itself out. No one would argue that a suitcase, once unpacked and put away, makes a house less orderly than before. While some might find a degree of apocalyptic excitement in the idea that our universe is rapidly becoming more and more chaotic, Dr. Lambert points out that entropy in its truest form is a little less exciting. In the end, all hots and colds will fizzle out, sweet and bitter will combine, and everything will become somewhat lukewarm.

I appreciate Dr. Lambert's efforts, but it's hard to shake my original conception of entropy, which is closer to the Marvel Comics version. In that universe, Entropy was the son of Eternity and one of the Seven Friendless, a motley crew of near-deities who have been around since the beginning of creation, each of whom contain a force absolutely necessary for the world to move forward. Entropy was light blue with a tiny head, painted half-black and half-white like a hybrid sort of mime, his head sitting atop the bulging upper-body of a typical superhero. Entropy's purpose was merely to undo, and he did it all too well. There came a time in which he had destroyed everything around him, and then all was nothingness and there was nothing left to destroy. This must have been a strange moment for Entropy—the whirring in his head was finally over and all was quiet and peaceful. But instead of being content with the void and the destruction he caused, Entropy decided to try his hand at creation. Urged on by Captain Marvel and Rick Jones, Entropy took a cue from his father's example and came up with the big bang, thus restarting the engine of time and turning into his father, Eternity. The destroyer of worlds became the creator of worlds.

There are some Marvel fans who question this story, typing in all capitals during their late nights on the Marvel message boards, pointing out that if Entropy becomes Eternity and the world begins again, then Entropy doesn't exist anymore, so how can the world exist without disorder? How can time start back on itself, again and again, forever, if Entropy is missing?

I see their point, though I like to think even Entropy itself can change his mind, that the future is not yet written and can still surprise us. And yet a world without entropy is impossible. Even Dr. Lambert would agree. Without entropy, he'd say, ice would never melt, sugar cubes would never fall apart in coffee, and spices would never soak into the rich broth of a pot of chicken soup.

VIII

The Reverend Ebenezer Cobham Brewer, the author of *A Guide to the Scientific Knowledge of All Things Familiar*, was known to be a chatterbox. One scribe put it more delicately, writing that the man "was never adverse to opening his stores of knowledge to anyone with whom he might converse." Throughout his life Brewer developed the habit of writing down various questions he had about science, and when he eventually attempted to find the answers to his questions and published those pages, he found a vast audience throughout Europe.

Brewer's popularity might have come from his enthusiastic (though often misguided) treatments of scientific principles, as well as his willingness to tackle the theological implications of those discoveries.[1] The enormous technological and scientific advances of the 1800s had shaken the Church's hold on society and led to a great deal of anxiety for a deeply religious public. But for Brewer, an ordained minister, scientific laws did not necessarily contradict theological precepts.

Brewer's guide is thus littered with references to God, who in his wisdom gave fur to the beasts of the field and "robes of feathers" to the birds of the air (section XIII), made animals and vegetables dependent on one another (section XVIII) and ensured that grass and other vegetables are excellent radiators of heat (section XVI). Throughout the Guide, Brewer is candid about the limits of scientific theory—when asking himself what one should do to keep safe from lightning, he solemnly advises his imagined reader to ". . . draw his bedstead into the middle of his room, commit himself to the care of God, and go to bed; remembering that our Lord has said, 'The very hairs of your head are all numbered.'" While his contemporary Charles Darwin made no attempt to fuse evolutionary theory with theological precepts, Brewer's reasoned and rational catechism frequently crescendoed into a burst of religious fervor.

> Q. Shew the WISDOM of GOD in making polished METAL and woolen CLOTH BAD RADIATORS of heat.
> A. If polished metal collected dew as easily as grass, it could never

---

[1] *Brewer cannot be blamed for including mistaken information about caloric theory in his volume, as the Guide was published prior to Clausius' paper on entropy, but his other mistakes were legion. Legend has it that when Brewer asked a scientist to proofread the Guide prior to its publication, the scientist advised him to burn the book rather than publish it.*

be kept dry, and free from rust. Again, if woolen garments collected dew as readily as the leaves of trees, we should be often soaking wet, and subject to constant colds.

Q. Shew how this affords a beautiful illustration of GIDEON'S MIRACLE, recorded in the book of Judges, vi. 37, 38.

A. The fleece of wool (which is a very bad radiator of heat) was soaking wet with dew: when the grass (which is a most excellent radiator) was quite dry.

Q. Was not this CONTRARY to the laws of NATURE?

A. Yes; and was, therefore, a plain demonstration of the power of God, who could change the very nature of things at his will.

I have left much of my childhood devotion behind me, but I still find myself appreciating Brewer's breezy subversion of newly ironclad scientific laws. There are indeed laws governing the natural world, and I have seen evidence of them. And yet it seems beneficial to think that every once in a while, there is the possibility of interruption, the opportunity for things to shift.

IX

Every evening, when my father's pick-up wound through the hills and around to whatever farmhouse we rented at the time, he'd use the last bit of daylight to try and eke out some more green from his garden. He liked nothing more than to walk around the yard inspecting his plants, turning up leaves to detect the presence or absence of fruit. Only when my family moved the last time did he stop planting a garden. Maybe he was tired of leaving his hard-earned fruits to the next tenants. Instead, he poured himself into the hundred or so potted plants dotting the rim of the wide southern porch. He planted jasmine and gardenias for their lingering, musky scent, brilliant blue puff-ball hydrangeas, gawky, over-eager black-eyed Susans, savory herbs, and the delicate peonies my mother loved. His trees were all in five-gallon buckets with holes drilled in the bottom; they lived out their lives root-bound and doomed to a stunted height with delays in flowering.

During my time in college, two of my brothers were motoring through adolescence and squealing their tires up against my father's rage. Often I dug through the falsely cheery tone of my mother's weekly phone call to try to find out the real story of how everyone was doing. At some point during my sophomore year of college she didn't try to hide the anxiety in her voice. Apparently my middle brother had developed the habit of throwing his cigarette butts lazily off the porch, and one morning, my father had found one in a prized gardenia pot. Smoke poured out of his ears, I would imagine, like a real-life Yosemite Sam, and he went on a rampage, knocking his beloved plants off the wide porch and onto the ground. My father didn't stop until all of the plants were up-ended, and then he took off in the truck. While my mother shut herself up in her bedroom and prayed for deliverance, my youngest brother, Joshua, went out on the porch and stood there for a long time. He must have been eleven then, and I suppose he started with what was closest to him, righting the pots that were still whole, consolidating the plants whose pots had shattered, sweeping and raking spilled soil into manageable piles.

"I lost some," Joshua told me the next day on the phone, as I squatted on the stairs of my apartment in Western Massachusetts, sucking on a cigarette. "The jasmine is just not gonna make it."

Who knows where my father slept that night—his truck, maybe—but when he came home sometime in the late morning, he sat in the cab for a while. The view from the driveway is such that he must have seen the porch just before he lumbered up the hill to the house, stopping to feel the leaves of a hearty tomato bush that had made it through the previous day's drama without being much worse for wear. When he finally opened the screen door, he looked at my mother, who shook her head, and then at my two oldest brothers, who refused to meet his eyes. I wasn't there to see the look on Joshua's face when my father came in, but my mother told me he was sitting on the couch, reading *Architectural Digest*. I guess my father reached for him, to hug him, maybe, or thank him for putting things in order. But Joshua looked up from his magazine and shrugged. "I didn't do it for you," he said. "I just like plants."

My father nodded and headed into the kitchen, and Joshua went back to reading *Architectural Digest*.

X

The principle of emergence is better known as the-whole-is-more-than-the-sum-of-its-parts. It dictates that in some living systems, astonishingly complex patterns develop out of simple interactions between its members. Emergence, one physicist admits, works "uncomfortably like magic." An individual termite never intends to build a mound, and yet, year-by-year, the mindless motions of many individual termites accumulate into a thirty-foot tower of termite saliva and excrement, a tower that gives the termites the humidity their fragile bodies need to survive.

In the same vein, family systems theorists believe families are more than a collection of individual hands and laps and minds. Instead they are a mysterious assemblage capable of producing their own weather, just as wind, warm ocean waters, humidity, and the Coriolis effect work upon each other in order to form a hurricane. Those therapists who subscribe to family systems theory believe a damaged part of a family— a parent or child—can only be healed in the context of the family itself. The individual cannot be parsed out and treated alone, but rather must be viewed as a mere strand in a web of emotional dependencies. As a result, their practice focuses on identifying the near-chemical reaction occurring when all of these discrete personalities combine in the home, a reaction similar, perhaps, to the slow simmer of individual vegetables, meat, and spices in a pot of boiling water.

The difference between the family and the individual is the difference between that murky, flavorful pot with its slow, rolling broth, and the still life on the countertop, where garlic and onion share space with celery, carrots, tomatoes, and chicken. There on the countertop, in the late afternoon light, the carrots are in a state of utter carrotness, unpolluted by the onion's musk or the celery's surprising richness—all the ingredients are still whole.

Beside the kitchen table where my brothers and I tell old stories on our rare visits home, a splotched photograph dangles from the refrigerator from some greasy old magnet. It's a black-and-white family portrait, taken by my father on the self-timer. In it he is looming to the rear of the family, glaring into the camera. Meanwhile my mother looks doubtful. She holds us tightly, and now I know why—the heat was being turned up on the stove.

Central to the second law of thermodynamics is the concept that time's arrow always moves in one direction. Entropy always increases; energy will always disperse into a place where it isn't so crowded. There is no restorability, and neither is there a rabbit-trail back to the time when my father's rage was still stuffed inside his own head, when my mother believed holding us tightly could help, and my brothers and I were still smiling with that pure, buck-toothed joy unique to children.

That old snapshot dangles above our heads as my brothers and I each take a side of that square kitchen table. We are entirely different people now, long-limbed adults prone to stray fits of temper or laughter. We'll never be that particular family again, but it's no tragedy that soup subsumes its ingredients and simmers them into a new creation. At least that's what I tell myself.

Nominated by Ruminate

YOUR BODY
DOWN IN GOLD

by CARL PHILLIPS

from SUGAR HOUSE REVIEW

You can make of the world's parts something
elemental, you can say the elements mean
something still worth fucking a way forward for:
maybe the dream coming true; maybe the dream,
true to form, coming undone all over again—
you can do that, or not, while a sail unfurls,
or a door

        blows shut . . . So it turns out there's more
of a difference between love and deep affection
than you'd have chosen. So what? Remember
the days of waking to disasters various, and of
at least in part your own doing, and saying
aloud to no one *I have decided how I would*
like to live my life, and it isn't

                     this way, and
how you actually believed it: you'd change,
the world would? Man with a mourning dove in
one eye, rough seas in the other, lately the light—
more than usual, it seems—finds us brokenly. I say
let's brokenly start shouldering the light right back.

Nominated by Sugar House Review, David Baker,
Martha Collins, Elizabeth Powell, Lloyd Schwartz

THE PIECE NEED NOT BE BUILT

by ANDREW ZOLOT

from AMERICAN CIRCUS

> *It is not generally a failure of execution but a collapse of taste—of critical and creative instinct—that brings an art to eclipse. The error in the artist, which perhaps was only momentary and experimental, is echoed with approval by his admirers and a shoal of imitators, and gregariousness and snobbery complete the corruption. ("We understand this art, which the ordinary person can only gape at: we are distinguished people.") So the flock gathers sheep. But poetry has never fallen so deep into this bog as painting and sculpture have, and I believe is now pulling out of it. Poetry must use language, which has a resistant vitality of its own; while sculpture (for instance) may sink to fiddling with bits of wire and tin trinkets.*
> *—Robinson Jeffers, "Poetry, Gongorism, and a Thousand Years"*

The artist standing at the end of Jeffers' thousand years and looking back in nostalgia may walk the whitewashed halls of the Museum of Modern Art and ask why his museum has been transformed from a verdant promenade of marvelous portals to a warehouse for collected trash and preschool geometry. He might ask, quite rightly, why art has been stolen away from the eye and heart by the pesky brain, he might comment on its hijacking by the academic complex, and he might cry in despair for the future of love in a world of driftwood barbed wire sculpture.

Is it in poetry that salvation lies? Is it language that will beat back the tides of relativistic pseudoart and reclaim the mystery of artistic shamanhood, the weaver of dreams, and the savior of men's souls? Here, now, please read this fairly representative excerpt from a placard accompanying an art installation at the Museum of Modern Art:

"The work comes into existence at the moment he articulates an idea with words, a phrase that also becomes the title of the work. That work can be displayed as written language or as the physical manifestation of the described action but, as Weiner states, 'The piece need not be built,' either out of text or out of material—the decision rests with the 'receiver upon the occasion of receivership.'"

Were one to avoid looking at any of the art in the museum and simply read the descriptive literature—which this particular placard laughably implies would be equivalent experiences—she would sense the decay of the art in the decay of the language used to describe it. Nobody would call the vast majority of the works on the contemporary and modern floors of the Museum of Modern Art beautiful. The language used to describe art has been sterilized in the last hundred years to reference "space" and "acts" and "processes."

It is somewhat ironic that the most moving piece of art on the lower floors of the MoMA is not accompanied by any placard or affective literature. I refer, to the Museum of Modern Art's "Coat Check," an exhibit installed by the Board of Trustees as part of the museum's renovation that ended in 2004. The structure of the exhibit is one of complex and intricate comment on art and its housing, and I will take a moment to lay out its ideological and physical components. Contrary to Weiner, however, I suggest that to truly experience Coat Check one must go see it in person.

Coat Check is the first piece of art one encounters at the MoMA. It is also the last. This is, of course, assuming one has brought a coat at all, or is accompanying somebody who has a coat and wants to check it. As the likelihood of wearing a coat is tied directly to the weather, Coat Check is a vibrant piece of art in the winter months and a decidedly mute comment on absence in the summer. One component of the genius here is Coat Check's reversal of the implied characters of the seasons. Winter, the season of loneliness, flushes Coat Check with energy and conversation. Summer, season of warmth and freedom, makes of Coat Check a ghostly and quiet monument.

Coat Check is one of those rare pieces that has "capacity," i.e. the length of one's engagement with the piece is proportional to the number of other patrons trying to access it. Depending, then, on the time of year, Coat Check will involve different time commitments. If the line to see Coat Check is long, anticipation is built up as a function of standing in the winding, cordoned-off line. In the summer Coat Check is quite sad in its neglect from the patrons, but this is countered by the speed with which one gets through the ordeal. So Coat Check, in its ingenious layout, parallels the human inclination to dwell on happy moments and rush to forget sadness.

But of course the meat in the pie is the checking of the coat, and here Coat Check, unlike many of the less interactive pieces in the MoMA, really earns its keep. Behind a row of windows trusty museum employees stand ready to transfer your coat to the installation. You are prompted to forfeit your coat in return for a piece of plastic with a number on it corresponding to your coat's place in Coat Check. Your coat is then placed on a large, rotating system of hangers and carried off into the darkness. Coat Check is a chameleon, its vestments changing with the fashions and whims of the museum's patrons. On any average day, it is black and gray, but can be enlivened by a red trench coat or yellow parka at any moment. It is the intersection of machine and man, the utility of a storage space replenished hourly by the furs and wools of New York City's cultured patrons.

As I mentioned before, Coat Check is the first installation one encounters at the museum, and it is the last. There is an implied circularity, that one must end up at Coat Check by virtue of having started there. If you bring no coat, then this contingency is avoided, your visit to the museum shortened. Coat Check's dynamics are only reinforced by your decision re: coat, and in capturing your decision either to *be* or *not be* part of Coat Check it represents the true universality of any great art.

That Coat Check brackets a visit to the museum in an act of communal art-building—the creation of a rotating mosaic of clothing—inevitably promotes the notion of replacement. The coat, distilled to an idea, is one of protection. In Coat Check, the coat is stripped from your body. You are left vulnerable and must seek shelter deeper in the museum among the artwork. And when you've had your fill, you return to Coat Check to trade your heart for your sleeves.

Unlike the rest of the pieces and installations at the MoMA, Coat Check is shrouded in silence: there are no placards, no discussions about its merits, no docent on hand to wax on the Board's intentions or artistic inspirations. It is in this understatement that Coat Check comes out as the real winner at the museum. In this era when art is described by words that mean nothing, better to shut up and simply be something.

Nominated by American Circus

THE MONSTER: CLASSIFICATIONS AND EXPLANATIONS

by SUSAN SLAVIERO

from TREELIGHT

How to track the monster

Press your sternum to the ground and lift your eye to the rent in the bloodgrass. Seek unnatural leavings. curdled meat in a coconut shell, hexagonal eggs, a shallow grave dug behind a dead girl's ear. The brush will be freckled with burgundy. It will show patches of blight that suggest salt, or a nuclear detonation. Suckberry. Belladonna. The signs are nebulous. There will be a notable absence of rabbits.

How to recognize the monster's lair

Probably a hive, pink and ugly. It might be necrotic. Look for stone tables littered with the husks of deboned Jezebels with rosemary in their hair. Or perhaps you will notice a book of rare poisons in the cupboard with the spoons and tea towels? The walls will be chalky, the mirrors painted black. You will find paper cups filled with pointed teeth, grommets behind the brickwork, boiling pots of rattlesnakes and witchvine.

How to know the monster when you see it

If it's a parasitic bloom with the powers of telepathy, you're probably being digested already, even if you think you're in a warm parlor. If you're lucky, it will be a masked killer baying at a kitchen clock and you're the one holding the gun, but it isn't always this easy. The monster might have a proboscis or a circle of eyes on its bare back that swivel in unison. Consider the possibility that it will be hideous, but know that a beautiful cluster of heads is as deadly as it is hypnotic.

How to know if you are the monster

You will know you are the monster if you begin to make your own monsters. These are the homunculi living in the bones of your cheek that make you itch and hunger for fat mugs of milk or maybe you just think you are hungry. Maybe you are lonely. Maybe you will sew yourself a mate out of mannequin limbs and furry rodents you catch with your feet. Maybe you are the unsympathetic character in a horror movie who lives alone and keeps mounds of termites in the basement for nefarious purposes. You will never quite believe you are the monster, even when they find you sleeping in a nest of newspaper with a fresh heart in your pocket.

No. Not even then.

Nominated by Treelight

DON'T LET THEM CATCH YOU

fiction by MOLLY PATTERSON

from THE IOWA REVIEW

No one knows what the kidnapper looks like, but everyone knows he is strong and fast. He waits at bus stops and in the woods. He has a car and there's a long rope coming out from it that you can't see because it's made of a special material that's invisible. And the rope has a loop on the end of it. When you step into the loop, he drags you in like a fish.

Then he drives away with you, and no one ever sees you again.

At piano, I play "Tarantella" worse than before. "Did you practice this week?" Mrs. Duncan asks.

I say yes, but I didn't because our keyboard broke. Last time it happened, Uncle Mike fixed it. Now he's in Afghanistan again, and I don't know who will fix it.

Mrs. Duncan asks how many times I practiced. I tell her one hour every day, and she shakes her head.

Outside, I stand on the front porch. Mrs. Duncan's house is bigger than ours. We don't have a front porch—only two steps that go up to the door, and when you open it, you're in the living room and Brandy's magazines and sweaters are all over the floor, and Mom will yell at her for leaving her crap everywhere.

Mrs. Duncan's front yard has a little black tree as tall as the top of the windows. It's November, so the ground is gray and brown.

Inside, Anne Fontaine is playing "Russian Dance." It sneaks through the windows and the keyhole in the door. It swirls around on the porch like a little tornado of leaves. Anne is one and a half years older than me. She has long, lemony hair with lots of clips and barrettes. Her mother takes her everywhere in her silver car.

I wait a long time.

Brandy doesn't come.

My sister is supposed to pick me up, but she never does what she's supposed to because she's fourteen. She doesn't care about anyone except her new boyfriend, who is three years older and wears gel in his hair like the Russians. He smells like cigarettes and Cheetos and squints when he looks at me. He doesn't ever say anything, except to Brandy. When he talks to her, he puts his hand on her neck and moves his lips close to her ear.

"Kaitlyn," Brandy told me the first time her boyfriend came over, "if you tell Mom that Chaz was here, I swear to God I will break every bone in your right hand."

She chose that one because I'm left-handed and she wouldn't want to have to help me do things like writing and eating. But that would make it so I couldn't play piano anymore. Brandy hates that I'm so good at piano. When Uncle Mike left for the army, he got Mrs. Duncan to start giving me lessons. He didn't get anything at all for her.

It was after he left that Brandy started dating Chaz. I don't tell Mom that he comes over because I'm good at keeping secrets. Even Brandy's secrets. Even though she doesn't do what she's supposed to, like coming to Mrs. Duncan's to walk me home from piano when there's a kidnapper driving around looking for girls who are all alone.

It's getting late. Anne Fontaine finishes playing "Russian Dance" and moves on to a song I don't know. Her mom will get here soon to pick her up. I don't want her to ask why I'm all alone. Anne will stand next to her in her watermelon raincoat, and her mom will shake her keys in her hands. Both of them will look at me like I'm a lost dog they have to help, but only because it's the right thing to do, not because they want to.

I don't need their help. I need my sister to come get me. But she isn't here, and that means I have to start walking home by myself.

It happened like this: a girl got off the bus. Her friends waved good-bye to her from the windows. They would see her tomorrow; tomorrow was Thursday. She started walking and the bus drove off. Then she disappeared and no one saw her again.

Brandy told me the girl went to another school in our district. She told me the kidnapper took the girl away in his car.

"Did someone see it?" I asked.

308

Brandy looked at me in the mirror. Her eyes were gooped with mascara. It was after school and it was four o'clock and there wasn't anything good on TV. Just shows where people sat on couches and cried or stood in front of a judge and yelled about money. Brandy was getting ready for Chaz to come get her. She was sitting in front of the mirror in our bedroom and her make-up was spread out on the floor around her. Her stuff always takes up more space than mine. "Of course not, stupid." She went back to putting on lip gloss.

"Then how do you know?"

"Everyone knows. It's on the news."

Brandy doesn't watch the news. Whenever the news is on, she's always out with Chaz in his lizard-green car. She isn't supposed to leave me alone when Mom is gone. But she always does anyway.

"Maybe they'll find her," I said.

"No, they won't."

"They could."

Brandy shrugged. The phone rang and she gave me a dark look. "Go watch TV or something."

I went. Brandy doesn't care that it's my room, too.

It's nine blocks to our house and you have to cross Olive, which has four lanes and stoplights and a lot of cars. I don't like it because the people sit in their cars and watch when you run across in front of them. Sometimes they're alone and talking to themselves. Sometimes they're arguing with the person in the passenger seat, and when they turn to look at you, their eyes are squinted up so that only the black parts show.

I look up the street in the direction I have to go. There aren't any cars coming.

One block, two blocks. I watch my feet on the sidewalk.

A week ago, our teacher took us down to the gym for a school assembly. We sat on the floor and listened while the principal told us about Stranger Awareness. Strangers, she said, can be people we know. "Is the mailman a stranger?" she asked, and we all answered yes. "That's right," she said, and then she told us that while not all strangers are bad, we should never go anywhere alone with a stranger.

But if the kidnapper catches me, I won't have a choice. He'll put me in the back of the car, and we'll drive a long way to his house on top of a waterfall, somewhere in Italy or maybe Japan. He'll have gel in his hair, and he'll smoke cigarettes and tell me how I will never get away, not ever. He'll tell me that he chose me out of everyone because he knows I am the most talented piano player in the world and he wants someone to play music for him for the rest of his life.

But when I play, he'll become sad. He'll howl and beat his head with his fists and cry. It's too beautiful! he'll weep. You're too wonderful to keep alone in a house on top of a waterfall! And then he'll know that he has to set me free.

But maybe I won't go back home when he lets me go.

Somewhere behind me, a car door slams. I turn around. A bright red bird flies from one side of the street to the other and disappears inside a bush.

There are cars parked all along the side of the street. They have wet, dark-looking leaves pasted on their windows that look like big hands pressed against the glass from the inside.

Did the kidnapped girl sit in the backseat or the front?

At Olive, I have to wait for the walk sign. A dirty red car with three men in it pulls halfway into the crosswalk. Two of the men are fat, and one is skinny. There's loud music with screaming voices coming from the car. The driver is one of the fat ones. His tiny eyes are buried deep in his face. His two friends are talking, but he follows me with his eyes.

When I get to the other side, I start running, and I don't stop again until I reach home.

Locked.

The house is dark. Brandy isn't there.

We have a key hidden in a secret place because sometimes my sister forgets to bring hers. I can get it, but I don't want to go inside alone. Inside, it's hard to breathe because the air is heavy. Sometimes the basement door is open and I have to shut it, and when I walk past a mirror or a window, I get afraid that my reflection will start doing something different than me.

Brandy doesn't care about any of that. Once, she asked Mom why she didn't give me my own key. I was in the living room watching reruns on TV. They were in the kitchen yelling at each other.

"Because then you'd think it was okay to leave her alone. You do remember that your sister is eight years old."

"She's *seven*," Brandy said. "Jesus, Mom, you don't even know how old your own daughter is?"

I heard the refrigerator door slam and all the jars rattle around.

"I have my own life, you know," Brandy said in a loud voice.

"Jesus Christ!" Mom said. "What do you want me to do?"

"Why don't you get a fucking babysitter?" Brandy yelled. She stomped in from the kitchen and went to our room. Mom came in with a can of Coke in her hand. She looked at me and then at the TV. "Turn that thing off," she said and went back to the kitchen.

The next day, Brandy left me alone for the first time. She was gone for two hours. I spent the whole time sitting next to the front door, so I could open it and run out if I heard footsteps coming up from the basement. "See?" she said when she got back. "That wasn't so bad, right?" Chaz pulled away in his car, and Brandy watched him go. Then she pulled the front door closed behind her and took a king-sized Snickers bar out of her hoodie. "This is for you," she said, holding it out in front of her. "For being a decent sister and not ratting me out."

"I don't want it," I said. My stomach felt spiky from being nervous and scared.

Brandy frowned. "Don't be an asshole. Chaz spent money on this." When I didn't say anything, she set the candy bar down on the TV and went to our room. "Just don't whine to Mom," she said over her shoulder. "I'm warning you."

When I got hungry, I ate the whole candy bar and then felt sick.

Standing on the steps, I squint at the houses across the street. Their windows are filmy, like crocodile eyes. I can't tell if anyone is looking out.

We keep the key hidden under a rock. But I can't let anyone see me get it. If a thief knew where it was, he could come in the middle of the night and tiptoe right up beside my bed. He would wave his hands over my face. I'd be fast asleep; I wouldn't even know he was there. Then he'd pick me up and squeeze me until I couldn't breathe or yell, and he'd jump out through the window and run away.

At the side of the house is a bush that comes up to my waist. I pick up the big rock behind it.

The key isn't there.

I push my fingers around in the dirt. It's crumbly and cold and smells like the inside of the fridge when there's food rotting inside. My fingers get dirty and I don't find anything.

It's getting dark. Nighttime is when the thieves come out, and prisoners who escaped from jail. Cars drive by with thumping music, and the people inside them laugh too loud. At night, there are crazy people who could run up to you from behind and push you down on the ground.

Not even for any reason.

Just because you are alone.

I squat down behind the bush. Lucky for me, it's a magic bush that makes me invisible. Even though there aren't any leaves, when I go behind it no one can see me. I just disappear.

A long time goes by. I watch cars drive past. Some of them are neighbors who park and get out and go into their houses. A skinny, streaky cat comes out from behind the corner of a house. A man I don't know walks down the sidewalk real slow with a gym bag swinging at his side.

The way he walks with big, lazy steps makes me scared of him.

There are other people besides kidnappers you have to watch out for.

Finally, the green car comes down the street. It stops in front of our house. My sister stares out the window with a bored, angry look on her face. Chaz turns off the engine, and they sit there for a while without speaking. After a few minutes, Brandy looks at him and says something, and they both get out of the car.

That's when I stand up and become un-invisible.

"Holy fuck!" Brandy yells when I come out from behind the bush.

"I'm locked out," I say. "My legs hurt and I'm cold."

"Where's the key?"

"I don't know."

Brandy folds her arms. Her mouth gets flat, like whenever Mom yells at her for something. "You better not've lost it. Mom'll freak out."

"I *didn't* lose it. It's supposed to be there and it's not."

Chaz says to her, "You've got your key, right?"

"I'm not an idiot," she answers. She sticks her fingers into the front pocket of her jeans. Chaz runs his hands down her sides and says something into her ear. She shakes her head a little.

I want to tell Chaz to stop touching my sister.

"I'm hungry," I say.

Chaz looks at me. His hands are still frozen on Brandy. My sister opens the door, and I follow the two of them inside.

I get a bag of chips from the kitchen. It's an almost-full bag. I decide to be nice and share with Brandy and Chaz. But when I go in the living room, there's no one there. The TV is on with the volume up really loud, and the door to the bedroom is shut. I don't like that the TV is on with nobody watching it.

I stand at the back of the room, eating potato chips out of the bag.

On the TV, a fat woman wearing a lot of eye make-up is standing in a bright kitchen stirring some sauce in a pot. "Mm," she says, dipping her head so the steam from the pot goes right up in her face. "That sure does smell good." She widens her eyes, which are already big and surprised-looking because of the make-up. I glance at the door to the bedroom, then back at the screen. "You'll just have to take my word for it," says the fat woman with a wink, and she's looking right at me.

"Brandy," I say, going up to the door. I rattle the knob, but it's locked. "Brandy, come out here."

"Not now," my sister says from somewhere on the other side of the door.

I turn to look over my shoulder. The remote control is sitting in the middle of the couch. I don't want to go over and get it alone. The fat woman's face isn't on the TV, but her voice is still talking. There's a picture of her hands picking up little bowls of spices and tilting them so the camera can see. "Just for a minute," I say.

I hear Chaz mumbling something. After a second, my sister says, "Not right now, K. Just watch TV."

I stand with my ear to the door, trying to hear them talking. I don't care what they're talking about. I just want them to come out of the room. The two of them can sit on the couch together and I'll sit on the chair and they don't even have to look at me at all. We can just watch *The Simpsons* and laugh at the funny parts, like Brandy and me used to do with Uncle Mike when he came by for dinner.

"Kaitlyn, I can see your feet under the door," Brandy says, and now she sounds annoyed. "Just go the fuck away for once."

I feel my face twisting up like a balled-up tissue. I'm thinking about the way Brandy didn't come get me from piano and how she left me locked out of the house in the cold. I'm thinking how unfair it is that she yells at me for no good reason. I'm thinking that I hate hate hate hate hate my sister. Looking at the door, I imagine I can see Brandy's stupid face pasted across it. I pull back my arm and hit it with the palm of my hand as hard as I can. "Fuck you, Brandy!" I yell, and then I cross the living room fast and run out the front door.

I am a swooping owl, a fast train. Nothing and no one can catch me.

I run down the sidewalk all the way to the end of the street, then turn the corner and keep on running. A street goes off to one side, and I run down that. As long as I keep moving, I don't care where I go.

A car passes by me and doesn't slow down. I know it's not the kidnapper. The kidnapper is already stopped and parked, waiting somewhere for me to show up.

And if I meet him, I'll just take my chances and get in his car.

Uncle Mike once told me a stranger might be an angel in disguise. When he e-mailed us from Afghanistan, he said, "Don't worry, I got an angel watching over me here."

It's almost all the way dark now. I've run a long way, and I'm starting to get tired. I slow down to a walk just to catch my breath.

At one of the houses, a man in a too-big T-shirt is standing on the top step smoking. He watches me walk by. He doesn't wave or nod, but his eyes squint up like he's trying to figure out why I'm there. I don't like how he stares without saying anything. I start to walk faster. When I look back, his body is turned a little. He's still watching me, but now he's talking to someone inside the house.

In a second, he's going to stamp out his cigarette.

He's going to come down the steps to the sidewalk.

He's going to start chasing me, and I don't know where to go.

I stop moving. My heart's beating so fast I think I'm going to be sick. I want to run, but my legs feel like they're filling up with ice.

Down the street, a car turns the corner and starts driving toward me. It's so dark I don't see what color it is until it goes under a light. The next second, it stops and the window comes down.

Chaz leans across the seat. "What're you doing all the way over here?"

"I got lost."

"You want to get in?" Chaz asks.

I look back, and the man has gone into his house. But he might come out again. He might just be waiting until I'm alone. "Okay," I say, because suddenly I'm tired and I don't want to have to run from anyone else.

Chaz reaches over to open the door, and I climb into the front seat.

We don't go on the streets that take us back to the house. Instead, we get on the highway. "You like Burger King?" Chaz asks, and I say yes. "I'm hungry. You hungry?"

Everything he says is a yes-or-no question.

At the drive-through, Chaz orders two Whoppers for himself and gets me a Kids Meal. "You want the burger?" he asks.

"Chicken fingers," I say.

"Yeah, with ranch sauce, right? That's what Brandy always gets."

I get mad thinking about Brandy. I don't want him to talk about her. "Barbecue sauce," I tell him.

We eat in the car while he drives. I don't know where we're going, but I don't ask. I'm just glad to be somewhere warm, and I have French fries and chicken fingers to eat, and I don't have to worry about strangers because I'm already with one. He holds the burger with one hand and drives with the other. It reminds me of how Uncle Mike drives, sitting way back in the seat. Chaz flips through the stations on the radio, using the hand that holds the burger. I eat my Kids Meal and get barbecue sauce all over my fingers.

When I'm done eating, I stuff all the trash in the white paper bag. I stare out the window at the telephone poles flashing by and then my eyes close. It's like falling off the top of a tall building. I'm asleep way before I get close to the ground.

When I wake up, everything is slow and heavy. It feels like all around me, instead of air, there's a big sponge. Like I shouldn't open my eyes yet because I'm still supposed to be asleep.

It's quiet. The car isn't moving. Chaz's hand is on my leg.

It's barely resting there. More like it's floating just above it. I turn my head, but he isn't looking at me. He's watching his fingers crawling up my leg like he doesn't know yet what they're going to do.

"It's okay," Chaz says. Now his other hand is in his lap, moving. "It's okay."

I don't think he's talking to me.

When we get back to the house, Chaz reaches across me to open the door.

I get out of the car. My whole body feels itchy and light. I don't want to go into the house with Chaz and see my sister, but I don't want him to drive away, either. "Aren't you going to come in?" I ask.

He shakes his head and looks through the windshield. "Don't worry," he says, "I'm not going to tell Brandy what you did."

As I'm walking up to the house, I hear the car drive away.

Inside, Brandy is sitting on the couch. It's completely dark in the living room, except for the light from the TV. My sister doesn't look at me. She keeps watching the TV, where there are some trees and a lot of police cars, and a man's voice is talking as a photo flashes on the screen. It's one I've seen a few times while flipping through the channels. It's of a girl with brown hair wearing a Cardinals T-shirt, smiling so big her eyes are almost closed. Her teeth are short and wide, like they don't fit her mouth. "They found that kidnapped girl," Brandy says, and she looks over at me. Her eyes are wide and empty, like she doesn't know who I am, or doesn't care. "She's dead," she says and turns back to the TV.

I don't want to watch anymore. I don't want to look at the picture of the girl. She was alive before, and now she's not, and nothing can change what happened.

There's nothing else to do, so I go over and sit at the keyboard. I try turning it on even though I know it's broken. No sound comes out when I press the keys. No one is going to fix it until Uncle Mike comes back, and I don't know when that will be. I duck to look at the tangle of cords at the back of the keyboard, and that's when I see the spare key lying against the wall, almost hidden in the carpet. I remember a few weeks ago when Brandy couldn't find her own key at the bottom of her backpack. "Here, go put this back," she'd said when we got in the house, throwing me the spare key as she ran to the bathroom. But I hadn't put it back right away, and then I'd forgotten.

I pick up the key. I run the teeth along the palm of my hand. All I can think is that I have to bury it again, so no one knows it's my fault it got lost.

Nominated by The Iowa Review

THE SEPARATION/ RETENTION

by KWAME DAWES

from HUNGER MOUNTAIN

It should be as African as possible . . .

August Wilson

How African can it possibly be to dance
to the flattened palms on a wooden table,
to be belly full of fried chicken and sweet
potatoes, to be blood dizzy with sugared
tea, to be shuffling on the creaking boards,
to be circling around a round fat conjure
man calling out the dip and spin, a man
whose gift and calling is to bind
lost and fleeing souls—how African
could it be to shuffle like this into
a frenzy, to lose decorum in the waist,
to sweat, to abandon the pressure
of your daily worries, to forget the long
road ahead of you, to make your
body release all the mourning
in your heart for what you have
left behind; to make a pattern
of twists and turns that batter
down every longing; every need
you have for a touch, every
hunger unmet, how African could
it be? Only the long gash
of forgetting: the shame of remembering,
the empty space where language
was; the transition of self

and meaning into the lowest form
of ignorance, only the stiff collar
of a preacher's sermon against
the hand rising up inside of you,
only the fear of spirits on dark
dusty roads, only the burden
of your grandmother's smell,
like the smell of a deep forest;
the yellow of her eyes, the heaviness
of her tongue, the gutturals she speaks
into the night; only the dread
of that; the fear of losing yourself
to something beyond you, yet
deep inside of you, only
the auctioneer's scatology, only
the commerce of your labor,
only this seductive love called
America with its cold breath
on you despite its promises of warmth,
only these could make it impossible
to be African. How African can
this juba dance be, how African?

Nominated by Hunger Mountain, Marvin Bell

WRITING & PUBLISHING A MEMOIR: WHAT THE HELL HAVE I DONE?

by ANDRE DUBUS III

from RIVERTEETH

It was early September at a college in upstate New York. The maples in the quad were still in full bloom, and the grass was clipped and dozens of young men and women walked along the paved pathways, carrying books and backpacks, a cell phone in one hand, their iPod in the other, many of them with an earbud in one ear so they heard music on that side of their head while they carried on conversations on the other. I was there to give a talk to the entire incoming freshman class, all of whom had been sent a copy of my memoir, *Townie*. By nightfall it had begun to rain, and I'd just eaten dinner in a room of raised panels and deep carpet with twenty or so members of the faculty. Many carried umbrellas as we hurried across campus to the hall where I would give my talk.

Like many published writers, I give a lot of talks. Sometimes to crowds, sometimes to small groups. Sometimes I'm nervous beforehand, other times I'm not. Tonight, I was nervous. Over five hundred eighteen-year-olds had just read all about my youth, and now I was expected to say something important to these young people, something that might inspire them as they began their first tentative steps into their college years. I was anticipating the kinds of students I often encounter on campuses across the country, a baseball-cap wearing, gadget-addicted mix of earnestness and glazed distraction, of intense desire for something real and helpful and a standoffish world-weariness that comes not from the world itself but from far too many cyber-simulations of it. Whenever I'm in their presence, I feel a deep need to give them something worth showing up for, a story or a quote or a line of thought and feeling that comes from years of trying and failing and trying again to write truly about human beings—in this case, myself.

But when we village elders stepped into the cavernous hall, nearly every seat taken by a young man or woman from various parts of the country, some from other parts of the world, something strange happened. We started walking down the aisle and I heard, "Hey, that's him." "Lookit, there he is." And then came applause, loud and sustained, then a few kids were standing up, and the applause grew louder. What *was* this? I kept moving to the front, but I was glancing around at these young faces. In so many of them was an expression of acknowledgment and recognition, many of them peering around others to get a closer look at me. And then it became clear what was happening; they weren't clapping for the middle-aged author of a book they'd been required to read; they were clapping for the boy and violent young man I'd been; they were clapping for the kid who'd grown into the man walking up to the stage to greet them; they were clapping not for Andre, the writer, but for Andre, the main character in a story called *Townie*. I may as well have been Jake Barnes or Harry Potter or Captain Queeg. And as I waited to be introduced, I stood there feeling as if I'd lied to them in some way, that I had somehow misrepresented myself. But had I? Yes. And no. Not at all.

In my hometown of Haverhill, Massachusetts, the mill town where I grew up and the setting for *Townie*, I'm told it's referred to as "The Book."

"Hey, have you read The Book?"

"You shittin' me? I'm *in* The fucking Book."

Just weeks after it was published, I was to give a reading at the Haverhill Public Library. Over five hundred people showed up. The librarian introduced me, and there was enthusiastic applause, a few raucous whoops and shouts from the rear of the room. I looked out over the crowd and took them in. Many were my age, in their late forties or early fifties. Behind aging skin and hair and a few extra pounds, I recognized a face here, the eyes of another there, people I hadn't seen in over thirty years, when we'd all attended the same high school with its undercover narcs and drug dealing, its high-achieving jock kids from across the river, the leather-wearing, pony-tailed losers like me on the mill side, the kids or grandkids of immigrants from Ireland and Italy, Greece and Puerto Rico and the Dominican Republic. And there were older men and women there, too, the parents of those of us who grew up in the shadow of the Vietnam War and Watergate and Nixon flying away from the presidency in his helicopter, an echo image of what so many of our own fathers had done, though they'd driven away in Chevys or hopped a bus or just hit the road with a thumb out.

I thanked everyone for coming, then I read a few brief passages and took some questions. Mostly, though, the audience offered comments, and mostly these were words of thanks for telling our story. "Our story." I liked hearing this and was grateful for their gratitude, but I was also confused by it. I knew what they meant, that I'd written about that in-between generation we were members of; ten years younger than the Vietnam baby boomers but ten years older than Generation X, we were kids who grew up listening to early Aerosmith on eight-tracks in Z28s, drinking Haffenreffer tall boys and smoking angel dust. We grew our hair to our waists and carried pints of Southern Comfort in our Dingo boots like Janis Joplin, but the party had moved on years ago and so we were left wearing costumes, having sex too young, drinking too much, fighting in barrooms and in the street, our broke single mothers too overwhelmed to do much about it. I knew what they were thanking me for, but still, wasn't *Townie* essentially *my* story?

Years ago I read an interview with the writer Janet Burroway, in which she says that when readers go to the novel, what we're really saying to it is this: "Give me *me*." Most of us know this to be true. If the writer goes deeply enough into her characters and their stories, then they'll go deeply enough into us too, their own natures resonating with ours, like an easterly breeze moving wind chimes on a porch we'd never even known about. But with creative nonfiction/memoir, the breeze seems to be even more direct, the wind chimes closer to the front door of the house in which we live.

"Hey, don't tell me, but I know who the Murphy brothers really are. The Pecker Street gang."

The man who said that wore a dark sweater and Dickie work pants, broken capillaries blooming across his upper cheeks. He was my age, and looked pleased with himself, and I liked him right away.

"You got it," I said.

"Andre." A woman was raising her hand from the crowded center of the room. She had short gray hair and a plump, warm-looking face, her eyes lit with a street-savvy light I wouldn't want to mess with: "Now when I want people to know about my life, I just have them read your book. But what do you think of what the mayor's saying about it?"

Just days before, the Mayor of Haverhill had written on his Facebook page that I was "embellishing details" and that Haverhill had never been the tough mill town I wrote about in *Townie*. If this were a novel, his words wouldn't have bothered me at all, but this was a memoir, and when that word is printed beneath the title of a book, the contract between its writer and the reader is this:

> *Dear Reader,*
>   *Everything you read in this book happened, at least to the best of my memory, which like everyone's is seen through a deeply subjective emotional lens. Still, I have tried to be loyal to the facts as I remember them, which isn't always the truth, but it is my truth.*

I was on tour when I heard about the mayor's postings. I called him and told him I was concerned, that a charge like that against a memoir could very well undermine the authority of that book. And I had not "embellished." He apologized and told me he'd only begun to read my book that morning, that he'd been reacting to published reviews and interviews which referred to 1970s Haverhill as a "depressed crime-ridden mill town."

"But Mr. Mayor, it *was*."

"Not in my neighborhood."

"Where'd you live?"

"Riverside."

"Well, I lived across from the Avenues. A much different neighborhood."

We talked a while longer. The mayor said he'd read the first hundred pages of my book, and he could see I wasn't writing so much about the town as I was about my boyhood and my family. In fact, he said, it was clear to him that I hadn't called Haverhill any of those things the newspapers were calling it, and he had to admit, there were parts of our city then, especially the bars along the river of an almost entirely boarded-up downtown, that were pretty rough.

"In fact, when I was a young lawyer, my first clients were drug dealers from near where you lived."

"Thank you."

322

"And my wife did remind me that I took boxing lessons to defend myself then."

"That's all I'm saying."

But the mayor, who has worked diligently to make downtown Haverhill a much more vibrant place than it was forty years ago, had every right to worry about how it was being described by the national press now. I told him I would make sure to mention things are different today. He promised to stop posting charges of embellishments on his website.

I told the woman in that library crowd that I respected the mayor, and now that he'd begun to actually read my book, he was taking back what he wrote about it.

A man standing near a window raised his hand. He looked over six feet tall and well over two hundred pounds, and he wore a black beret and a black sweater and black pants. He was my age or younger, but he was leaning on a cane. His goatee was wispy and just beginning to gray.

I called on him.

"You know your friend Cleary? Your best friend when you were kids?"

His voice was reedy and restrained, like he was trying to hold back an emotion that wasn't all good.

"Yeah? What about Cleary?"

"He was my brother."

Cleary, always clowning and stealing and drinking and getting high, the son of a hopelessly alcoholic mother and distant father, my best friend when I was thirteen, fourteen, and fifteen, stabbed to death at age twenty-five by the common-law wife he used to beat.

"Mark? Is that you?"

He nodded, and I left the podium and walked down the side aisle to Cleary's younger brother I hadn't seen in years. I hugged him and he hugged me back, and then the crowd began to clap, and I walked back to the microphone and told them just who he was.

Later, at the book-signing table, he asked me to inscribe a copy to their father. Mark told me how happy his old man was to hear that his oldest son, dead far too soon, had made it into the pages of a real book, that his son would live on now, that he wouldn't be forgotten. On the title page of the book, I wrote how much I loved and missed his son, and I wrote his son's real name and wished the father well, and signed my own.

But a week or two later, I received an email from Mark's girlfriend

323

telling me Mark's father had read the book and that he was very, very upset. And why wouldn't he be? How could I not have thought of this earlier? I described his son as having been a wife-beater in his last days; I described how deeply alcoholic his mother had been, this woman who died of her disease not long after her oldest child had been stabbed to death; I wrote how absent he, the father, had seemed to me during those years. My God, what had I *done*?

I'd written as truly of that time as I could, that's what I'd done, but my intention never was to hurt anyone. Ever. These things rarely happen when what you write and publish is fiction.

Not long ago, my sister Suzanne walked into my kitchen holding up three or four stapled sheets of paper.

"Andre, have you seen this interview? It's one of the guys from your book. He says he's gonna kill you."

It was like hearing that a character who dies violently at the end of your novel has risen from the fictive dead to have a word with you. Or that a character you've worked hard to make three-dimensional and real is angry because she's just not likable enough, and now she's on talk shows saying so.

"Let me see that."

My sister handed over the interview pages. I put on reading glasses and sat down. I don't usually read much of what people write about me or my work. It's not that they have nothing valuable to teach me; quite often, I'm sure they do. I avoid it because writing daily is challenging enough without having a flurry of voices in your head, most of them negative, telling you what you do wrong and even sometimes right. I've come to believe that if there's any single enemy to human creativity, it's self-consciousness, and while criticism can of course be instructive, it almost always comes after the fact, when it's too late to do anything about what has apparently failed, so over the years I've found that true and sustained artistic growth comes solely from the sweet and not-so-sweet daily labor of writing itself.

But I had to read this, especially once I'd read the title: "Maligned Character in *Townie* Challenges Andre Dubus." This comes from a blog dedicated to "Book and Author Information," and it's a sit-down interview with one of my "characters," who the interviewer (GTC) describes as "Devin Wallace, a tall, beefy man now sitting next to me in a dim and ominous place, stinking like hot panties and stale perfume, near where Wallace fought the future author thirty years ago."

GTC: Dubus writes that he changed everyone's name except those in the immediate family. What's your real name?
DW: None of your business.
GTC: Okay, no problem. Have you read *Townie*?
DW: Obviously. That's why you're here.
GTC: Why's that?
DW: To let people know what a prick Dubis is.
GTC: I believe he pronounces his last name Duh-BYOOSE.
DW: We don't go for that French shit around here.
GTC: I can see why Dubus decided to get ready.
DW: Ready for what? To become the biggest sucker puncher in history. Even Dubus admits it, the half that isn't fiction. He says he ran over and hit a guy sittin' behind his steering wheel and who wasn't even lookin'. And he kept hittin' the guy. Come on.
GTC: The guy'd been nudging the bumper of a limousine where Dubus' girlfriend was riding.
DW: Girlfriend? Sounds like he went out with her four years and didn't get anything. Or he's lyin' since she's one of those Muslims.

You may have noticed that I've put quotation marks around the word *characters*. Why? Because these are actual people, aren't they? This is nonfiction, right? Isn't Devin Wallace the same man who beat me up so badly one night thirty years ago he almost killed me? In fact, later in his interview, he even corroborates exactly what I wrote about him in *Townie*:

DW: Look . . . I weighed at least two-fifty and he must've been about one-sixty. When we got outside, I went right after him and stuck my head into his chest and drove him into the frozen sidewalk. He couldn't lie about that with a hundred witnesses around us, yellin' for me to kill him. I punched his face until he grabbed my wrists and then I grabbed his hair above each ear and started slammin' his head into the concrete and he was lucky the police came and pulled me off.

Here's that same scene from *Townie*:

He feinted away from it, his head ramming into my chest, and I was lifted and there was the back-slap of pavement, a weight on my sternum. The first punches were almost a surprise, hard and fast from the right and left, sparks behind my eyes. I opened them, and there he was on my chest. His face was in shadow, and it was hard to breathe and he kept punching and my hands grabbed both wrists and wouldn't let go.

"*Kill him, man. Fuckin' kill 'em.*"

There were more words out there in the air around us, men's voices, then Jeb's. "That's my *brother.*" His hands on the shoulders of the one on me, but then other hands pulled him away and there was yelling, had been for a long time, from the one on me who had a handful of hair on both sides of my head, my fingers still locked around his wrists, and he began to lift my head and slam it back down, lift it and slam it, the concrete beneath me felt like a betrayal . . .

One dictionary definition of the word "memoir" is this: "a record of events written by a person having intimate knowledge of them." Certainly "Devin Wallace" and I had intimate knowledge of that particular fight, and it was gratifying for me to read that his memory of it dovetailed precisely with my own. Or did it? Maybe his own recollection of that fight was shaped by my having written about it in *Townie*. Maybe he only remembered it after having read about it. But even if that was the case, why was he so intent on showing what a "prick" I was? Because he truly thought I'd been "the biggest sucker puncher in history"? This is coming from a man who freely admits that he had ninety or a hundred pounds on me and still he straddled my chest, grabbed my hair, and began slamming my head against the concrete again and again. But later in the interview, there's a clue about what might really be bothering him:

DW: Don't you just love the way Dubis spends pages settin' up his excuses? He claims he spent the day paintin' inside a closed room and his brain was stewed and his balance was so bad he shouldn't have been drivin' and he could barely see. Then, in the bar, he says a pretty lady named Hailey told me to fuck off 'cuz I was hasslin' her and had "predatory" eyes. That's bullshit. She wanted me and Dubis was jealous.

Predatory eyes. That's probably what pissed him off more than any-thing. But they *did* appear predatory to me, at least in my memory of that scene thirty years later. And even if there was nothing predatory about his eyes, his behavior certainly was; the college girl he was hitting on was telling him no, and he was ignoring her no. But I had a hunch it was something else that was making "Devin" want to kick my ass again three decades later: I had written my story, and he had not writ-ten his. Now mine was recorded in some way, and his was not. Why did I get to have this happen? How did I get to be the main character in a book, and Devin Wallace, who was still drinking in those same bars on that same dirty river and had story after story to express about his own life, why would his go untold?

And then there are my "truths" versus other people's "truths." Some of my childhood friends look back on that time and place much differ-ently; one is Jimmy Quinn, a "character" in the book. His real name is also Irish, with a two-syllable first name and a one-syllable last name. By the time he was sixteen, he had a reputation as being a very tough and dangerous kid, a guy who'd easily beaten up grown men. He was over six feet tall and just under two hundred pounds, and he was hand-some, even with a chipped front tooth. For many years in my youth, he was the only kind of guy I wanted to be, one who could defend himself and anyone he was close to. A few weeks after the book came out, my publisher forwarded to me an email from him, and we began to cor-respond. I hadn't seen or spoken to him in years. He wrote to me that he was reading the book and that he especially liked the parts about him. Every few days, I'd get a new email from him telling me where he was in the story and what he thought of it. He told me about his life now, about his wife of many years and their three nearly grown chil-dren. I enjoyed these emails, and was struck by how reflective he'd gotten, how he was no longer that kid I remembered, though I heard that he still occasionally got into fights downtown and consistently came out ahead, the way he always had.

In one of his last emails to me, he told me that when he looked back on all those house parties and bar fights and street fights, even the one at the high school when he got stabbed and almost died, that he couldn't stop laughing at all the fun we'd had.

"Why was your book so *dark*?"

What could I say to this? He was the oldest of nine kids. They all lived with their mother and father in a big house on Main Street. He was an athlete who played football and baseball. Other boys respected him, many feared him, and most girls were drawn to him. We both lived in the same depressed town, but for him it was a playground. For me, it was just one more manifestation of the home I lived in—unsafe, unclean, wild, gray, and unhappy.

I wrote all of this back to him, and there was the strange sense that I was writing not to the man still living in Haverhill, Massachusetts, just nine miles from where I was raising my own family, but that I was writing to Jimmy Quinn, the young, handsome brawler in my book: Jimmy Quinn, the character.

He wrote back: "I thought you were going to say that. Makes sense."

The following Christmas, a woman from the Haverhill Chamber of Commerce asked me if I'd be willing to sign some books at an outdoor booth at their "Santa Stroll" through downtown. I told her I would, then promptly forgot about it. The night I was supposed to be there, my friend walked by and saw my booth unmanned and heard I wasn't coming. "No problem," he said. "I'm Jimmy Quinn. I'll sign 'em."

I heard he signed quite a few like this: "Merry Xmas! Best wishes, Jimmy Quinn."

I had never planned to write a memoir in the first place. It was the summer of 2007, and I had just delivered to my publisher my novel, *The Garden of Last Days*. I was contracted to follow this up with a collection of personal essays, a form I respect deeply. My wife and I are blessed with three children (Austin, 19, Ariadne, 17, and Elias, 15), and when our sons were very young, they began to play baseball. This was a sport I knew nothing about and had never followed or played, but because they were interested in it, I became interested in it, too. Now, years later, because of them and their years on the mound as Little League and Senior League and high-school pitchers, I've become a devoted fan of baseball. I began to write an essay about this, and the question fueling it was: how as a kid did I miss this game I now love so much? What was I doing instead? These questions led to what ultimately became my accidental memoir, *Townie*.

But in those first drafts I was hiding something. Somewhere, sometime I'd read this from a writer whose name escapes me: "If you're going to write a memoir, you should be able to sue yourself for libel."

Because so many years had passed since my youth (I was turning fifty writing the book), I felt there was enough emotional distance that I could write honestly about my own flaws—my early paralyzing fears and physical cowardice, my rage and eventual violence perpetrated against others, etc.—but I was not prepared to write about my family. Wasn't that *their* story to tell? Who was I to shine a light on their privacy?

My editor at my publishing house told me that she knew very little about my family, but it felt to her that I was leaving out some significant details about having grown up with them. I told her I was and why. (I did not tell her what, precisely, I was leaving out, that my younger brother was suicidal and had been sexually abused by his female special-education teacher for six years in our house, that my older sister had been gang raped and was selling drugs, that my younger sister was isolated and deeply depressed, that my exhausted, over-worked and underpaid mother was just barely holding on with her fingernails, that my father was largely absent.) She told me that whatever I was leaving out, it was all part of my story, too, and that if I couldn't write completely honestly, then this shouldn't be a published book.

A few days later, I told a friend—a gifted and accomplished novelist—my dilemma. He told me that if it were him faced with the same challenge, he'd ask himself this: Am I trying to settle any scores with this book? If the answer was yes, he wouldn't write it. Or he might write it, but he wouldn't publish it. If the answer was no, then he'd go ahead and write it. I knew then I wasn't trying to settle a score with anyone. I wasn't angry at my parents. (Though there were years when I had been, when I felt they could have taken better care of us four kids than they had, but the decades had fallen away and then came my belief that we all get out of bed each day trying to have the best day we know how to have, which is not the same as the best day we can have, and that's where all of us have room to grow, and so by the time I began writing *Townie* I had largely forgiven my parents.) I did not even feel sorry for the boy I'd been or the childhood I'd had. Certainly, there are far worse out there, generation in and generation out; I simply felt pulled to try and capture that time, that early-1970s mill town, growing up with a low-income, single mother and all that entailed, as truly as I possibly could.

Months of revision later, I had written the last line and knew this was a much more honest book. I had gone into my house and revealed whatever I felt it was important to reveal. For years I'd thought that the reason I'd become an effective fighter was this: I was the bullied boy who learned how to throw punches that then became fueled by all the pent-up hurt and rage of the victim. But opening those doors back to my family taught me how wrong I'd been: I couldn't stop my younger brother from wanting to die; I couldn't protect him from the grown woman suffocating him; I couldn't save my older sister from getting raped or keep her from selling drugs or hanging with scumbags who didn't love her and never would; I couldn't talk my little sister out of putting a padlock on her bedroom door and her heart; I couldn't lift my exhausted mother off the living-room floor where she'd fall asleep every night after her fourteen-hour days; I couldn't get my father to call or come over more than the brief times we saw him on Sunday afternoon or every fourth Wednesday night; and I could not stop myself from believing that, as the oldest son, all of the above was my job. It was every bit of this that I'd been putting into my fists in those fights.

And there was more, too. I, like many young men, had turned my hurts and disappointments into rage and aggression. My brother had turned his inward and become depressed. I had become homicidal. He had become suicidal. This alone seemed an important note to hit in my memoir, and after I'd written it in, I was not going to give my brother, or any of my family, veto power. (I'd done that once with a personal essay about the birth of my daughter. In it, I had written briefly about my brother's first child, born out of wedlock, and after Jeb had read the manuscript, he said, "You can write about your own life, but leave me the fuck out of it." At the time, over twenty years before I'd write *Townie*, I didn't even question whether he was right or not; I assumed immediately that he was, and I cut those references to his first child. Later, when the essay was published, Jeb read it again and said, "I should've let you keep that in. The essay was better with it.") So now I was simply going to warn my family of what to expect, and I started by giving my sister, Suzanne, a copy of the manuscript that she would then pass around to the others.

Suzanne finished reading it in two days, and she surprised me by saying she had the exact same emotional memory of those years, and then she said: "But did you have to put in the part about my selling drugs? I have a pretty important job, you know." I do know. My sister has become a national leader in the prevention of domestic violence, and right now she's working closely with the Obama administration. I said to her, "Honey, you were *sixteen*. Besides, it gives you street cred!"

My younger sister, Nicole, responded next. She told me her childhood had been too shitty for her to want to visit it again and so she will continue to read my fiction, but not this. I told her I understood that completely.

At this point, the manuscript was still at my sister's house, and the actual book was moving into production. It was time to tell my brother and mother what was coming.

I was pretty worried about Jeb, probably because of what had happened with that essay years before, and because sexual abuse and attempts at suicide are deeply personal and entirely his business. And yet it was part of my story, too, and I felt compelled to keep the few pages I'd written about him. I'd wanted to meet in person to talk about this, but Jeb was working on a restaurant he'd designed down in Salem and couldn't get away.

One afternoon, sitting in my truck outside the grocery store, I called his cell phone. When he finally answered he sounded tired and distracted, and I could hear the sounds of construction behind him—men's voices, a drill bit whirring into wood or concrete, the pop-pop of a nail gun.

I told my brother I'd finished this accidental memoir thing.

"Yeah?"

"And I—"

"What, brother? Just say it."

"I've put in your sexual abuse and suicidal years. It seemed like a lie if I didn't."

I heard only those construction sounds, nothing else. And it occurred to me that my brother could be so unhappy about this that he might sue me to try to stop it.

"Jeb? You there? Are you okay with this?"

"Well, brother—" I could hear him draw deeply on a cigarette. "I would never want to step on anyone else's tube of paint."

My eyes filled up, and I was thanking him, and he interrupted me and asked me if I could at least make it clear somewhere in the book that he's *not* that fucked-up boy anymore? That he's a very successful designer?

"I mean this could hurt my business. I've got my *kids* to think about."

I promised him I would, and the following morning I wrote an acknowledgements page about him and the rest of my family, each of whom *is* doing well all these years later.

My mother was next, this woman who stayed and raised us and did the best she knew how, this woman who—like so many before and after her—could very well have crumbled and descended into alcoholism and drug addiction, verbal and physical abuse of us, who could have driven away, even for one night, but never did. She was the absolute last person I wanted to hurt in any way, yet in *Townie*, I'd described a woman who had essentially given up being the one in charge, someone who felt to me and my siblings less like a mother and more like an older sister rooming with us and surviving any way she could.

I seemed to pick a moment to tell her when I didn't have to look her directly in the face. We were in my truck driving up the highway to an academic conference on the masterful work of her dead ex-husband, my father. I was behind the wheel, and she was in the passenger's side. We were each sipping from cardboard cups of hot coffee, though I needed no extra jolt.

"Mom, you know I just finished writing a, you know, a—"

"I know, honey, your memoir."

"Yeah, well anyway, there's a part in it about you and how—I don't know—you kind of, you know, gave up for—"

She reached over and squeezed my forearm.

"Don't you *dare*—" (Oh, fuck, I already had; what was I going to do *now?*) "Don't you dare not write anything because you're worried about me. You write your story, damnit. It's your story, and you should write it the way you need to write it. Besides, honey, I'm too old to give a shit what people think about me anyway."

I laughed and wiped at my eyes and thanked her. We began to talk about other things, then soon we were seated side by side at a conference on the work of my dead father, the one I was most worried about reading my memoir, even though he'd been dead twelve years.

I had naively assumed—semi-consciously—that because he hadn't lived with us, I wouldn't have to write about him much at all. But as I wrote my way back into those years, I learned otherwise. The word "to remember" is the opposite of dismember and means "to put back together again." As I was putting back together the years of my growing up, my father's absence in our daily lives became a major presence in the book.

For a while, a few weeks or a month, I resisted it. I knew that if I were to continue writing as honestly as I possibly could, I wouldn't be able write about him in the most flattering light. He had wonderful qualities: he'd been immensely gifted, a true and humble artist, generous, funny, attentive to the suffering of friends. But as a young father, he also had been largely AWOL, and it hurt me to know that my writing was already showing this; I loved him, I missed him, I was proud of the art he had created with his time on earth, and I did not want to betray him.

Years earlier, when I'd just begun to publish my fiction, my father and I did a reading together in New York City. I read first and then it was his turn. As he wheeled himself up to the microphone, there was boisterous applause, and a woman sitting next to me leaned in and asked: "Was he just the *perfect* father?"

What could I tell her? That no one is? That it was my mother who raised us, not our father? That when he was around, he really wasn't? But she was clearly doing what I'd seen so many other readers of my father's work do; she was confusing the writer with his beautifully wise writing, the flawed artist with his nearly flawless art. I think I smiled and nodded and turned my attention towards my father, who'd begun to read.

People who read his stories tend love them to a degree bordering on worship. Art of this caliber can change lives. The last thing I wanted to do was to paint my father in such a way that I might somehow damage that nearly sacred relationship between his devoted readers and—not *him*—but his work. But neither could I idealize him in any way; in *Townie*, I was trying to stay as loyal to my subjective memory of those years as I could, and in those years, my father was a deeply flawed one.

But if my father's own art sought to do nothing else, it sought to illuminate truths, and all my writing life I'd been trying to do the same thing. So I held my nerve, stepped into my fears, and tried to capture my father as he'd been.

I was in a bookstore in Ohio on the paperback tour for *Townie*. A Catholic priest sat in the front row. After my reading and talk and a few questions from others in the audience, the priest raised his hand. He was wearing his Roman collar and looked to be in his late sixties. He also looked troubled. The section I had just read showed how oblivious our father had been to the kinds of lives we children were living on the other side of the river from where our father wrote and taught. The priest said: "But your father wrote so insightfully about children in his fiction. How could he have missed this about you kids?"

"My old man, if he were here, would be the first to tell you that the writing is larger than the writer."

"But what about everything he wrote about being a man of faith?

How could he have written those things and then behaved so consistently badly?"

I may have quoted D. H. Lawrence: "It is not I who writes, but the wind that blows through me." The conversation continued, and I could see that this priest was no less troubled. Then he said this: "In the midseventies I was a stock broker on Wall Street, then I read you father's novellas, and I—" He paused, seemingly unsure about whether or not he should continue. "I quit and joined the seminary and became a priest."

"And now that you've read my memoir," I said, "you're wondering if the man whose work put you on your path was a fraud."

The priest half-nodded and said no more.

I told him and the others gathered there that my father was no fraud, that his work was genuine and authentic and far wiser than he, a mere man, could ever have been. I told that priest he should never think otherwise. He seemed semi-comforted, but that night, lying in my hotel room wide awake at three thirty in the morning, I kept seeing my own death and possible reunion with my father, and what did I see? I saw him sitting before me, his trimmed beard as white as it had been in life, and he looked hurt and confused. He looked betrayed.

In his essay "The Magic Show," Tim O'Brien argues that successful characterization in fiction is not a pinning-down process, an act of "nailing" a character, but quite the opposite. The deeper we go into character, the darker and more mysterious it gets. In this sense, he asserts, we are all unknowable. *Townie* is not fiction, but when I wrote it, I was using tools I try to use as a novelist: sensory detail, direct dialogue and real-time scenes, essential brushstrokes that make more textural and alive a moment. In the earlier part of the book, when I was a young boy, I tried to write deeply from that perspective, without judgment or commentary. As I got older, I allowed the voice to change, but again, I tried to stay emotionally who I'd been at the time. And one of the things I had been was largely fatherless, something that came as a surprise to the older me writing all this.

I was giving a talk at a university on the West Coast. Afterwards, a big, gray-haired man in a red sweater stood in the audience and said, "I read your book, and I think your old man was a friggin' prick. How come he never took you guys to a *ball* game, for Christ's sake?"

Hearing this was like getting slapped across the eyes. I took a breath.

I sipped some water. I did not believe my father had been a prick, but what I had written, and no one else, had given this man standing in the audience—all of whom were now looking at me to see how I would react—this picture of my father.

I told the big man in the red sweater what I truly believe, that the book is out of my hands now and he's entitled to any emotional reaction he may get from it. (I did not tell him, but I'd been thinking it, that his story with his own father might be resonating here, too.) "I don't think my old man was a prick, though."

"Then why didn't he take you guys to a game? Why didn't he ever call you on the phone or take a drive over to your house on a weekday?"

I told him the truth. "I don't know. He'd have to tell you that, and he's not here to defend himself."

The man sat down, and I was relieved the next question had to do with one of my novels.

Again, late that night, I lay in my hotel bed wondering just what I'd done. I'd been hearing that the reviews of my book were positive, but many of the reviewers went after my father for having "abandoned" us. But had he? In the town where I now live, I know a woman whose husband drove away ten years ago, leaving her to raise their five kids alone: no phone calls, no visits, not one penny in child support. The last she's heard, he's living somewhere in Japan. Now that's abandonment. My father never did *that*. But I also had to stand by my remembered portrait of him, the very one that got that man and many other readers, apparently, to dislike my father. That he simply had not been present for much of our growing up. But he'd been so much more in life than this absent father I'd painted; by describing him only through the eyes of his oldest son who'd needed him, hadn't I reduced him in some elemental way? Hadn't I done the opposite of making him a mystery? Hadn't I nailed him and nailed him badly?

Man, I hoped not. I sure as hell hoped not.

A Barnes & Noble on the Upper East Side of New York City. A handsome middle-aged woman raised her hand and said: "I guess I like your new book, but you don't seem to know much about *women*. There's hardly any in there."

A few people laughed, a few others looked uncomfortable for me. I laughed too, then told the woman that that's because *Townie* is a memoir, not an autobiography. If it were my life story—and who wants to read the life story of some fiction writer from Haverhill, Massachusetts?—then it would have three hundred pages about all the women in my life, but it's a memoir, a memory of a time in my existence that has a shape and narrative arc of its own, the way so many moments of our lives do: my young mother and father divorced; we lived in poverty and my mother was left to raise the four of us as best she could; we moved from one cheap rented house to the next, and I was always the new kid and I got bullied till one day I began to fight back till that was all I ever seemed to do, and I was on a road that would either get me killed or put in prison; and it was my finding creative writing that put me on a more peaceful and constructive path.

This *is* my story. I did not make it up. Nor did I put in any moments that did not happen in my life, but still, there's the vaguely shameful feeling that I've cast in stone something that should stay fluid, our ever-evolving and changing memories of who we and the people we love really are. And walking up to the podium of that stage of that college in upstate New York, the cavernous hall filled with applauding young people, I wanted to tell them that I was glad I had written my story, that I was grateful to them for reading it, but please don't confuse me with that Andre in the book; he's a character, and I'm real. That was then, and this is now.

But then they stopped clapping and the hall grew quiet. I could hear the rain on the roof and against the windows, and I could see so many of their faces—expectant, slightly wounded, hungry for something helpful, many masking this hunger, and I felt the younger Andre, the only one they knew, descend into my legs and arms and chest and face. Then we were both stepping toward the microphone, and together, we began to speak.

Nominated by River Teeth

A SUMMER GARDEN

by LOUISE GLÜCK

from POETRY

1

Several weeks ago I discovered a photograph of my mother
sitting in the sun, her face flushed as with achievement or triumph.
The sun was shining. The dogs
were sleeping at her feet where time was also sleeping,
calm and unmoving as in all photographs.

I wiped the dust from my mother's face.
Indeed, dust covered everything; it seemed to me the persistent
haze of nostalgia that protects all relics of childhood.
In the background, an assortment of park furniture, trees and
    shrubbery.

The sun moved lower in the sky, the shadows lengthened and
    darkened.
The more dust I removed, the more these shadows grew.
Summer arrived. The children
leaned over the rose border, their shadows
merging with the shadows of the roses.

A word came into my head, referring
to this shifting and changing, these erasures
that were now obvious—

it appeared, and as quickly vanished.
Was it blindness or darkness, peril, confusion?

Summer arrived, then autumn. The leaves turning,
the children bright spots in a mash of bronze and sienna.

2

When I had recovered somewhat from these events,
I replaced the photograph as I had found it
between the pages of an ancient paperback,
many parts of which had been
annotated in the margins, sometimes in words but more often
in spirited questions and exclamations
meaning "I agree" or "I'm unsure, puzzled—"

The ink was faded. Here and there I couldn't tell
what thoughts occurred to the reader
but through the bruise-like blotches I could sense
urgency, as though tears had fallen.

I held the book awhile.
It was *Death in Venice* (in translation);
I had noted the page in case, as Freud believed,
nothing is an accident.

Thus the little photograph
was buried again, as the past is buried in the future.
In the margin there were two words,
linked by an arrow: "sterility" and, down the page, "oblivion"—

"And it seemed to him the pale and lovely
summoner out there smiled at him and beckoned . . ."

3

How quiet the garden is;
no breeze ruffles the Cornelian cherry.
Summer has come.

How quiet it is
now that life has triumphed. The rough

pillars of the sycamores
support the immobile
shelves of the foliage,

the lawn beneath
lush, iridescent—

And in the middle of the sky,
the immodest god.

Things are, he says. They are, they do not change;
response does not change.

How hushed it is, the stage
as well as the audience; it seems
breathing is an intrusion.

He must be very close,
the grass is shadowless.

How quiet it is, how silent,
like an afternoon in Pompeii.

4

Beatrice took the children to the park in Cedarhurst.
The sun was shining. Airplanes
passed back and forth overhead, peaceful because the war was
over.

It was the world of her imagination:
true and false were of no importance.

Freshly polished and glittering—
that was the world. Dust
had not yet erupted on the surface of things.

The planes passed back and forth, bound
for Rome and Paris—you couldn't get there
unless you flew over the park. Everything
must pass through, nothing can stop—

The children held hands, leaning
to smell the roses.
They were five and seven.

Infinite, infinite—that
was her perception of time.

She sat on a bench, somewhat hidden by oak trees.
Far away, fear approached and departed;
from the train station came the sound it made.

The sky was pink and orange, older because the day was over.

There was no wind. The summer day
cast oak-shaped shadows on the green grass.

Nominated by Philip Levine, Jessica Roeder

DONATE!

fiction by JACK LIVINGS

from A PUBLIC SPACE

Yang had come home from the factory for lunch. The courtyard was covered in brown peach blossoms, exactly as it had been when he'd left that morning. He was standing beneath the old peach tree, debating how best to punish his daughter, who hadn't even touched the broom he'd left leaning against the trunk for her, when the earthquake hit. The branches above him shivered and dropped petals and twigs on his head. Must be something big up there, he thought, tearing around after a pigeon. He was looking up, hoping to spot a yellow weasel, which would have been good luck, when suddenly the tree shook off its remaining petals and he found himself staring directly into the sun. He felt unsteady on his feet, as if, in the middle of choppy seas, he'd decided to stand up in his rowboat for a better view. He threw his arm around the tree's rough trunk just in time to catch himself from toppling over backward. His stomach churned. Across the courtyard, a terra-cotta roof tile landed with a thunk on the packed earth. The mahjong players who congregated outside his neighbor's gate, an excitable bunch to begin with, were yelling like madmen; the public toilet attendant, a Korean War vet in his seventies, reliving a nightmare of American shelling, cried out for the mahjong players to take cover. Horns wailed on Fuchengmen Street as traffic locked up. Dogs yelped. A windowpane popped. A single clay flowerpot tipped over and fell from its perch by the front gate, landing with a thud-crack against the pavers. Wind chimes clattered in the still air. Yang crouched down and felt around on the ground in front of him, trying to steady himself with his free hand. The broom fell over and whacked him on the shoulder, and he saw his wife coming toward him from their bedroom, waving her arms and shouting. At first he couldn't make out what she was saying over the storm of noise in his ears.

"Bing Yang! It's an earthquake!" she was saying.

He looked down at the fresh blanket of pink petals on the ground. "Are you hurt?" he said.

"I'm fine," she said. "It's only tremors. Nothing serious."

"You know my inner ear is unhealthy," Yang said.

"Watch the horizon," she said.

"I'm doing what I can," he shouted, annoyed.

"Be calm."

He looked up at her with the eyes of a wounded animal turning to its predator.

"What?" she said.

"Help me up?" Yang said.

Gong crossed her arms. "Get up yourself. You're fine. Given any thought to Little Li?"

"Do I look like I've had time to make a phone call?" His knees cracked as he stood, and a wave of light-headedness washed over him. "Where's my phone?" he said.

Gong waggled her cell phone at him. "She already sent me a text. They're evacuating to the soccer field. The epicenter was hundreds of miles from here. This isn't such a big deal. It's over."

Yang moved away from the tree and swept flowers off his shoulders, bits of bark from his shirt and trousers. Gong reached out and brushed some blossoms from his hair. Yang fished around for his phone and dialed his daughter.

"You've evacuated?" he said when she picked up.

"What?" she said. "We're on the soccer field."

"Did the school collapse?" he said.

"Yang!" Gong shouted. "Leave her alone."

"I'm asking serious questions here," he said. His daughter was laughing, but not at anything he'd said. She was fourteen, a cipher to him.

"Bing Li," he said, "come home right now." He made a face at his wife. "And when you get here, sweep up these peach blossoms like I told you."

Gong grabbed the phone away from him.

"Hey!" Yang said.

Gong put the phone to her ear. "Little Li, stay put. Don't move a muscle until your teachers tell you to. Good-bye." She sighed and crossed her arms.

"Well, let's go see what this is all about," Yang said. "And you can rub this knot out of my shoulder." The broom's blow, glancing enough, had hit the site of an old injury.

"Who in heaven did I offend to get stuck with you?" she said, laying her hand on his back.

"Clearly you're cursed from a former life," he said, giving her a weak smile.

When Little Li arrived home from school, the first thing she did was ask Yang for a donation.

"My class is sending money to the victims," she said.

"How do you know about victims?" Yang said. "What victims?"

"Daddy. I'm not five."

"Yes. Sure," he said. He turned the television back on.

"It'll be a miracle if anyone survived. And this isn't the end of it," she said. "After Tangshan in 1976, the aftershocks were five-point-zero on the Richter scale, and they kept coming back for months and killing more and more people." She shook her head.

"You weren't even alive in 1976."

"And you were still a peasant in 1976," she said. He didn't respond.

"Daddy, there's not a building left standing in some villages. Everything's collapsed."

"Such unshakable optimism," he said. "Who told you this? Your teachers?"

"What would they know? They've been teaching all day. I got texts. Ming Weilin's cousin lives in Sichuan. He told her everyone's dead."

"Everyone's not dead," he said. "The administration organized the donations?"

"No. We did it ourselves while we were waiting."

"That's very industrious of you," Yang said, pulling a ten-yuan note from the roll in his pocket. "Let this be a seed that grows tall."

"Okay," Little Li said. "Embarrassing."

"You're welcome."

"Mama," she called. "Mama, I need money for the earthquake victims."

"Hey," Yang said. "That's a family donation. Ten kuai family donation," he shouted after her as she crossed the courtyard, bound for her parents' bedroom, dragging her feet through the peach blossoms.

"Zhou Hao's dad gave him fifty kuai when he came to pick him up," she shouted back. "Mama! I need money! Daddy's being a tight-ass!"

"Watch your mouth," he muttered. On the TV, rescue workers in red jumpsuits and hard hats stood precariously atop slabs of gray rubble. A scene of unimaginable destruction, the newscaster said, and Yang thought, If it's unimaginable, why am I looking right at it, genius? The camera zoomed in on a woman covered in gray dust, clawing at chunks of concrete, desperately plunging her bare hands into the tangle of rebar, glass, jagged planks of wood, stone. She was digging for her child. Her teeth were bared in anguish. The camera remained on her until Yang had to cough down the ache in his throat and look away.

"Come here," he called hoarsely.

After a while, Little Li slouched back in.

"Here." He pulled a hundred-yuan note from his pocket and closed her hands around the crumpled paper.

"That's more like it," she said. She looked at the TV, which was replaying images of the mother digging in the rubble. "Nobody's alive in there. That woman must be suffering from post-traumatic stress disorder. She's going to end up in an asylum."

"Her child is buried."

"She looks ridiculous."

Without understanding what he meant to do, Yang jumped up from his chair, violence coursing through him. He had never before raised his hand to her, and Little Li flinched. When Yang lowered his hand and looked away, Little Li reassembled herself and set her face to register disregard. There was a tear in the corner of her eye, and her cheeks were flushed. Yang was vibrating with anger, unable to look at his daughter, unable to defuse. Breathe, he told himself.

"Keep your comments to yourself," he said. A spasm bit into his shoulder when he reached for his jacket. "And help me get this on." The spasm widened into a bright, electric grip gathering up the muscle in his shoulder. He made a face.

He chased the sleeve around with the tips of his fingers, unable to gain purchase on the nylon lining, flapping his arm weakly.

"Do you need some medicine?" Little Li said.

"No," he responded, too sharply, he realized, but there was nothing to do about that.

Little Li dipped her head. She reached for the jacket, taking it by the collar as she exhaled in exasperation, her hip cocked at an angle of supreme impatience. Yang wondered when she had become this person.

She gave the jacket a weak shake.

"Do I need to take my donation back?" he said, wincing as he guided his other arm in.

"No," she said, holding the jacket still. "You look weird when you make that face."

"I wouldn't wish this on my worst enemy," he said. "I'm going to the hospital."

"Really?" she said, dropping her guard and turning toward him.

"To give blood," he said.

"For your back?"

"Are you serious?" he said.

"No."

"To donate," he said.

She pondered this, then said, "I don't have to, do I?"

"No," he said, "You're too young."

"Oh, good." She picked up the remote and skipped through the channels. "When is this going to be over? It's just the same old rubble." She was testing the waters and waited for her father to laugh, but he didn't. "It's been two hours already. Mama!" she called out into the courtyard. "What if the earthquake is still on tonight? What am I supposed to do about *Lovely Cinderella*?"

She cocked her ear, and hearing nothing, shouted, "Dad's going to the hospital to give away his blood!"

"You don't have to make it sound like a crime," Yang said.

"Then why were you trying to sneak out of here without telling Mom?"

Gong came shuffling across the courtyard, moving as though underwater, every step weighted, a diluted, slow-motion replay of the actual event.

"Did you take pills?" Little Li asked her mother.

"I'm fine," she answered, holding Little Li's eyes for a moment.

"Okay, so he's giving his blood away for free," Little Li said, opening her mouth wide in an imitation of shock.

"Your father and the rest of the Revolutionary Guard," Gong answered. "Take off your jacket and sit down. Wait for them to issue a formal request and then you can get a little credit. You, of all people, running to the rescue. They'll drain you and then a doctor will say they need a kidney and you'll say, Where do I sign? Just wait for Old Gao to come around asking for volunteers. If you do it through her, maybe she'll mind her own business for a week."

They lived near the Forbidden City in an ancient hutong neighborhood. Most of their neighbors were Chinese yuppies whose boredom with the practical elements of Communism, like work groups and neighborhood committees, was a source of wonder to Yang. He'd grown up in the countryside in the late sixties and early seventies, and as a child he'd pulled yams next to intellectuals sent down for reeducation. He respected the party's ability to whip citizens into a storm that could flatten everything in its path. These days, when a yuppie butted heads with the neighborhood committee over a plan to install a bathroom in his three-hundred-year-old home, he bribed a cadre in the municipal government who directed the committee to issue a variance.

The rest of Yang's neighbors were foreign executives, Swiss and Germans who levitated above the quaint diktats of local governance. The neighborhood committee's power, such as it was, had concentrated in seventy-five-year-old Gao Lin, a woman who had fought off real estate moguls and the municipal government when they'd tried to evict her from her house, a gold mine to whomever could sell it out from under her. None had succeeded, and her gate now bore a white plaque marking the house a cultural and historical treasure. Her family dead and gone, she was the last soldier encamped behind crumbling fortress walls. When she went out, she shuffled around the hutong like a shrimp on its tail, stopping to take note of infractions and issue tickets, which she pinned to her neighbors' heavy wooden gates. She fined them for improper bicycle parking and for failing to sweep their entrance stones. She fined them for neglecting to report their neighbors' infractions. No one bothered to pay the tickets or remove them, and when a breeze blew through the hutong, the papers rustled like leaves. The rain pulled them down, and she replaced them with tickets for littering.

She was hard as nails, and none of the Chinese left in the neighborhood would have tried to have her removed from her post. Even the municipal-level cadres were slightly afraid of her.

"When she comes around I'll tell her I've already donated blood. They'll give out certificates," Yang said.

"She'll talk you into giving another pint," Gong said.

"Are you watching this?" he said, pointing at the television. "I'll gladly give another pint."

"Don't have a heart attack," she said. "We lost a clay pot and some flowers from the tree. This could have been a lot worse."

By the time Yang got to the bus stop, the news had hit the evening papers, but most people were staring into the middle distance, looking to Yang not unlike a bunch of unplugged televisions. At the hospital, he had to pay a scalper one hundred yuan for a ticket to cut the admit line and, once inside, he searched four floors before he found someone who could direct him to the proper department for donations.

When he announced his desire for his donation to go to Sichuan, the volunteer behind the desk, a young woman wearing heavy black glasses and a white paper nurse's hat, told him that per regulation, all donations would be apportioned according to need. "Local injuries are our immediate concern," she said. "People were hurt inside city limits and the suburbs. Fifteen people were injured on the Fifth Ring Road."

What a robot, Yang thought.

"There's real carnage down in Sichuan," he said.

"There have been no reports of casualties."

"Give me a break," Yang said. "The province is a graveyard. It's a disaster zone."

"The central office for disaster response has issued no such statement," she said.

"I'd prefer this donation should go to Sichuan," Yang said.

"For the earthquake?" the woman replied.

"For the snowstorm," Yang said.

"There's no need for that," she said sternly.

Yang sighed. He could keep arguing, which inevitably would cause the volunteer to leave her post for a break that lasted until he gave up and left, or he could acknowledge that the woman on the other side of the desk maintained unassailable power. "I understand," he said. "The blood goes where it's needed most. I just want to help." He palmed a twenty and offered his hand. She looked up, and without pretense plucked the bill from it.

"It's rare to meet someone as civic-minded as you," she said. "I'll ensure your donation goes to Sichuan." She wasn't much older than Little Li, and he took a hollow satisfaction in having bent her to his will.

He filled out some paperwork and she directed him to an exam table covered with green paper. An orderly wearing large silver headphones came and swabbed his arm, then slipped in a needle. "Relax and be cool," the orderly said. "I'll check on you in thirty."

"Where's everyone else?" Yang said.

The orderly pulled one of the cups away from his ear and said, "Whassat?"

"The other donors?" Yang nodded at the empty exam tables around him.

The orderly crinkled his brow and released the earphone, which snapped back with a muffled pop. He disappeared into the hall.

Yang lay back on the table. He'd grown up in a farming village, his only possessions two blue Mao jackets, one stuffed with cotton for the winter, the other without cotton for warmer months, and a family of wooden frogs that fit into the palm of his hand. In 1980, a migrant work program brought him to Beijing, where he bored holes in door hinges and small gauge gears at a state-run metal-stamp factory. Twenty years later, he had become co-owner of the factory. He was worth twenty million yuan, but most of his neighbors assumed he was a schoolteacher with a patrilineal claim to his hutong house. This aggravated his wife to no end. They'd paid cash for the house. It put Gong in a murderous state of mind when a neighbor asked her husband about his employment and he ducked his head and chuckled like a mountain hermit. "Metals," he'd say, if pressed. She had given up trying to explain to him that to be rich was glorious and there was no shame in having means. Even total strangers felt a sense of relief and pride in the presence of success.

Yang looked down at the tube, dark, almost black with his blood.

His parents were still alive and though they accepted his money, they wouldn't move in with him. They were perfectly happy living like two turtles under a rock out in Xianghe. There was no way he and Gong could ever be so content in each other's company. Someone would have to surrender first.

A while later, the orderly returned and with surprising care slipped out the needle, affixed a bandage, bent Yang's arm up at the elbow, and placed a rice cake and a cup of juice on the exam table next to him. He picked up the blood bag and left without a word.

Yang was nearly home when he realized he hadn't asked for a certificate to prove he'd donated. He gave it a moment's thought and kept walking.

It was the first thing Gong asked about. She made a strained face before he'd had a chance to answer.

"There must be a name for it," she said.

"For what?" he said.

"This psychological disorder of yours."

"They were very busy. You should have seen the line. There was no time to fill out certificates."

"Sometimes I think you go out of your way to oppose me."

He peeled back the gauze to show her the petal-shaped bruise in the crook of his arm.

"Show that to Old Gao when she comes around."

"What's the big deal?" he said.

She opened her mouth to speak, then stopped herself.

"There's no way to know how many were hurt," he said. "How many children are dead?"

"Be quiet," she said very softly, almost as if addressing a voice in her head.

"In the larger view, a pint of blood isn't much, but it's something," Yang said. "It's part of a philosophy of, well, compassion."

"Don't you dare say I'm not compassionate," she said.

"I didn't," Yang said.

"Why don't you show some compassion for your family before you help total strangers?"

"You have no sense of logic," Yang said.

"And you do? You'd rather remain anonymous than do a simple thing I asked of you? How's that logical? Could you have done one simple thing to make my life easier?"

"A certificate makes your life easier? Your life is hard?" Yang said. "Do you go hungry? Does Little Li cry because the stones cut her shoeless feet?"

"Stop making fun of me," she said.

Yang shrugged, and he felt, high on the left trapezius, a seizure of the muscle exactly where the broom had struck it.

"I have to lie down right now," he said.

"Did you even bother to ask for a certificate?" Gong said.

Oh, why did she have to ask, Yang thought. There was no point in trying to answer. Unanswerable questions led to evasions. He didn't reply.

"Go lie down," she said.

This was the standard procedure to preserve his back, which would cripple him for days if not accorded the proper respect. The method, part traditional medicine, part common sense, required him to lie perfectly still for hours, staring at the ceiling. Normally Gong would bring him the radio or read him a book, but two hours passed before she entered the room.

"I'm sorry," he said.

"You better be," she said. She set a steaming cup of water on the table and emptied a packet of Yin Qiao San into it. Yang's nostrils flared at the scent, but otherwise he was still as a corpse. Gong lowered herself to the edge of the bed and leaned in, her lips on his ear. "Behave like a child and I'll treat you like one."

"Hm," he said, closed his eyes, and reached up to touch her cheek. The thorny fist in his back clenched tighter. He could beat the pain if he drank the herbs and remained as still as possible. He gently laced his fingers together to form a bridge across his chest. In through the nose, out through the mouth. He tried to visualize old paintings of sleeping philosophers soaring out over vast canyons, borne up in their dreams by mystical forces, but the image of the mother digging in the rubble kept coming back to him. He stayed there until he fell asleep.

The next morning he awoke at dawn and slid out of bed. There was still a finger of pressure against his shoulder blade, but the sharp wire of pain had left his body. Gong didn't stir. Her lips were parted and her braids lay splayed out at right angles on the pillow.

The sky was pinking over the roof on the other side of the courtyard, and he stopped to look in on Little Li. Her sheets were in a pile on the floor, and she was strewn across the bed as though she'd crashed through the roof. Yang feared for what her life would bring.

He set out for the post office, stopping to pick up an egg-and-scallion crepe from a street vendor he knew, and still arrived before the doors were opened. Bicycle postmen streamed out of the alley adjoining the building. By the time the doors opened at eight, he was surrounded by a crowd of early birds balancing parcels in their arms. They all went inside together and assembled in a rough line, each one ready to dash for the window should this tenuous civility break down. In February the year before, the government had declared the eleventh of every month Queuing Day, an attempt to reduce the scrums that formed wherever people congregated to wait their turn at a window. It was May, and as the summer Olympics got closer, rhetoric had increased, and people did their best to satisfy the rules, but no one expected the newfound order to survive once the foreigners had gone home.

Only one window was open, and Yang kept eyeing a wooden table set up in the corner of the lobby. When it was Yang's turn, he told the clerk what he was there for and she called into the back, then directed Yang to the table. Another postal worker struggled through a door with a steel voting box he held to his chest. He crashed it onto the wooden table, the steel biting into the wood, the metal table legs scraping across the stone floor. The worker settled into the chair behind the table, sighed, and motioned for Yang to step up.

"Donations for the Red Cross?" Yang said.

The employee behind the table nodded mournfully. Yang wondered if he had lost relatives in the earthquake. Or maybe he'd merely gotten into character when his boss told him to man the donation box. Some people were like that. Given a chore, there was no limit to what they'd do to succeed. Yang had planned to give three hundred, but he stuffed one thousand yuan into the slot and left without a word.

While he'd been waiting inside, the PLA had erected three green canvas canopies on the sidewalk, each one bearing a poster-board sign with blood types. A young man in fatigues and a Red Cross armband ran up to him.

"Sir, what blood type?"

"I've just made a donation," Yang said.

The young man narrowed his eyes. "Blood?"

"Money. To the Red Cross," Yang said, pointing at the soldier's armband. "I gave blood yesterday."

"You gave blood yesterday?"

"At Beida. Beida Hospital."

The soldier leaned in to Yang like a prosecutor trying to catch a witness in a lie. "At Beida Hospital?"

"That's what I said."

"Whole blood or plasma?"

"What do you mean?" Yang asked.

"Which did you donate?" the recruit said, his voice rising. "Blood or plasma?"

Yang wasn't entirely sure, but he said, "Whole blood."

"Good. You can donate plasma."

Yang pulled up his sleeve to show the bruise.

Glancing down at Yang's arm only long enough to confirm that it was, in fact, an arm, the recruit said, "You're the picture of health. Why are you trying to wriggle out of this? Don't you care about your comrades in Sichuan?" People were staring. Comrades? Who used that word any more?

"Where do I go?" Yang said. The recruit grabbed his arm and pulled him over to an officer in a lab coat, then double-timed it back to the sidewalk.

"Quite a trapper you have there," Yang said.

"Blood type," the lab coat said.

All business, Yang thought.

The lab coat had to stick his arm four times to get a vein, and by the time the needle was in, Yang was ready to strangle the stonefaced bastard. An hour later, he was unceremoniously dismissed, his right hand pressing a hunk of gauze to his arm, the left clutching a bean cake. He couldn't stop yawning and his stomach was an empty pit, and he got in line at the nearest noodle shop. The TV was going in the corner, scenes of rubble, children's backpacks, more footage of distraught mothers throwing themselves against blank-faced fathers. Yang tried not to watch.

A construction crew was hunched shoulder to shoulder around the shop's flimsy linoleum tables. They parted to allow Yang a place without breaking the shoveling motion of their chopsticks. Yang nosed into his bowl.

The heat from the smooth porcelain warmed his fingers, and after he'd eaten most of the noodles, he began to feel more like himself. He wished someone would turn off the television, and he tried to tune it out as he ate, but it was hard to ignore. Then his phone began to ring.

"Better get it," his neighbor said, smiling. "Might be the office." Some other guys laughed. It was an offhand remark, but Yang understood its meaning, and it set his teeth on edge. The men sharing the table with him wore dusty canvas jackets with heavy gloves jammed into the chest pockets, and here he was in a button-down shirt and pressed trousers. But his arms were as sinewed as any man's at the table. He made a fist. He could teach anyone there to operate a thirty-ton H-frame press. He hadn't forgotten.

The phone stopped, then started up again.

"Sounds urgent," the construction worker said.

Yang backed away from the table to take the call.

It was Gong. "Back's better?" she said.

"Ah, it's better, thanks."

"Where are you?"

"On my way to work." On a normal day he'd have been at the factory since just after dawn, plowing through production logs and calling customers.

"Where are you?"

"Noodle shop," Yang said.

"You sound funny," Gong said.

Yang knew the construction workers were listening. "On my way," he said, and hung up. Then, as a precaution, he turned the phone off.

The TV droned on over the slurping of noodles. Back in the kitchen, the cook was whipping a rope of dough through the air, strands multiplying as he strung the noodles like yarn on his fingers, then a twist and smack against the counter and into the boil. The cook's arms were loose, extensions of the noodles themselves, and he proceeded through the operation with so little apparent attention to what he was doing that Yang felt no shame in staring. There was an automatic quality to his movements, the thoughtless perfection of repetitive motion, the perfect state, Yang thought, of doing without thinking. All his life, thinking had gotten him in trouble. When he'd acted on impulse, he'd always been rewarded.

He hadn't noticed that one of the construction workers was standing next to him.

"This is sick stuff, eh?" the man said, pointing at the television.

"Yeah," Yang said, still watching the cook.

"I'd have expected better from Yao Ming. But he probably eats white bread and speaks English at home," the man said.

Yang nodded absently. "Now," he ventured slowly, "what is it that Yao's done?" he said, only just then turning to see that the basketball star was on-screen.

"Cheap bastard's only pledged five hundred thousand yuan to the relief effort."

"I see," Yang said.

"He's going to miss five hundred thou like I'd miss a fen."

"True," Yang said. "He's in a hard position."

The man cocked his head and took in Yang's clothes and shoes. "I don't see what's so hard about it," he said. "But I guess you guys have got to stick together."

"I haven't played ball in years," Yang said, but the construction worker didn't laugh. He hadn't meant to defend Yao, but Yang suddenly felt that he'd rather be misunderstood. "What a man does with his money is his own business," Yang said.

"How much have you given?" the man said.

Yang looked back at him blankly. He presented both arms and pulled up his sleeves.

"Blood?" His mates turned around and Yang was aware of their eyes on him.

"You look like you might be good for five hundred thousand," one of them said.

"I've already made my donation," Yang said, moving toward the door. "I've done my part."

"Keep walking, asshole," someone shouted as he hustled out the door. "Say hi to Yao Ming for us."

Yang walked back to the post office and donated another two thousand yuan.

Then he caught the 451 bus to the industrial park in Fengtai District, where his factory was located.

His partner, Rabbit, a middle-aged number cruncher whose round black glasses would have been more at home on a French painter, met him at the industrial park gate. Rabbit seemed always to be bathed in light sweat, no matter the temperature, which made customers nervous, but he was good under pressure and had an elephant's memory. His hair was neatly combed in the front but in back looked slept on. Every day he wore the same brown tie that, with the perennial bags beneath his eyes, gave him the harried air of a salaryman who'd barely survived his latest bender. Yang and Rabbit had known each other since childhood and Yang recognized that it was all a ruse, Rabbit's mannered fumbling, the rumpled bedsheets he called clothes. Rabbit was a hard, calculating man. He'd worked the same fields as Yang in the days when school had consisted of memorizing passages of revolutionary poetry. In another life, he'd have become a professor of mathematics, but history had conspired against him. Yang understood the machines and tended to customers and Rabbit kept the books and dealt with the men on the floor. He had the common touch.

"What's the good word?" Yang said.

"Come on, come on," Rabbit said, holding Yang's arm as they walked toward the factory. "You picked the wrong day to leave for lunch, pal. You should have seen this place. The lights were swaying like a fat lady's tits. I can't believe you weren't here. Sounded like a tank battalion rolling through the place. The boys were scared to death. Zone Chief Zhou's been calling for you."

"What's he want?"

"Donations. The zone committee's hitting up the workers when they leave at the end of shift, and the workers' union has a separate donation drive. These guys' danweis are pushing for donations, and their kids all came home from school yesterday asking for money. It's chaos in there. There was a fistfight in the locker room this morning—one of the Huis said that he'd donate five kuai but no more because none of his people lived in Sichuan, and Brother Chu—you know Chu Pi, from Baiduizi— he slams this Hui against a locker and next thing you know, Brother Chu has a broken nose and half the room's standing on top of the Hui. This isn't good. We're going to end up all over the papers."

"Idiots," Yang said, quickening his pace. "I thought Chu Pi had some sense."

"He claims it was his patriotic duty," Rabbit said. "Meanwhile, we're losing ten thousand an hour while they're standing around waving their dicks at each other." Rabbit pushed through a pair of heavy fire doors and looked over at Yang. "You hear about Yao Ming?" he said, a wry grin on his face.

"I heard," Yang said.

"Cheap bastard," Rabbit said as he pushed through another pair of doors and they hustled down shit alley, past the men's toilets and the men's locker room, through another pair of fire doors that opened to the factory floor. The space was heavy with silence. Lit like a subway car and as long as a soccer field, the factory floor usually vibrated slightly. Searing noise forced everyone to wear ear protection, but without the mechanical thrum that marked time twenty-four hours a day at full production, the workers' voices advanced and receded like winking stars in the black sky.

Yang and Rabbit climbed the metal stairs to the platform outside their office. Yang rapped his ring against the metal railing until the workers milling around below turned their faces upward, most squinting as if looking into the sun. A couple of the guys took off their hard hats.

"Where's Brother Chu Pi?" Yang shouted, surveying the crowd.

"At the hospital," someone shouted back.

Yang nodded. "Gentlemen," he began. He had no idea what he was going to say to quell the men's spirits. This made about as much sense as trying to talk away the rain. Yang heard the purring of an air compressor and somewhere in the thermoforming area, the tinging of cooling metal. He cleared his throat and began again. "Gentlemen, our country is suffering. We are lucky to have been spared—" he stopped, aware that among his men there would be those with relatives in the south. "Those of you who are concerned for your families—I am concerned for your families, too. Don't ignore the fact that our factory is still standing and we have our lives. We can help best by keeping production high."

355

Some of the men clapped weakly.

"That is the best thing for China. Maintain production," Yang said, drawing out the words.

"Why?" came a voice from the back.

"Isn't it obvious?" Yang said. But it wasn't obvious even to him, and at that moment he caught a whiff of his own woolly sweat wafting up, and found himself considering a wild notion: he should bus the entire workforce to Sichuan to aid in the recovery effort. But by the time they got there, the men would have been drunk for two days. They'd have beaten each other to a pulp and would get off the bus in worse shape than the quake survivors. "If we fight about small things," he shouted, "we miss opportunities to help. This is not about fighting. This is about helping."

Rabbit pushed his glasses up onto his nose, leaned over the railing, and shouted, "And you're all going to help run this factory out of business if you don't get your lazy asses back to work, and then where will you be?"

A wave of laughter went up from the men. Rabbit had a way with them. A balled-up rag flew out of the crowd. Rabbit snatched it from the air and dramatically shook his fist at the men. "Get back to work before we call in the riot police on you assholes," he said.

"What are you going to do to aid the victims?" someone shouted.

"We're doing plenty," Rabbit shouted back.

"This isn't funny! We're making personal donations," the worker shouted, "so where's yours?"

Another man said, "My wife's factory is covering her personal donations!"

Rabbit looked at Yang, who smirked at the man's obvious lie.

"We should be compensated for our donations!" another man shouted.

Yang held up his hand. The men quieted down. The year before, the factory had sent one hundred thousand yuan to the Yunnan quake relief effort, and one hundred thousand to flood relief the year before that. But this one felt different. Yang had to find the right balance: a donation large enough to calm the men, but not so large as to make it look like he had money to burn. The men complained endlessly about their wages and suspected that untold riches were piling up in vaults beneath the factory, money withheld from them expressly to scuttle their chances for advancement in the world. What if he fired them all on the spot, sold the factory to the highest bidder, and settled into a quiet life of mahjong and cold beer? And why was it his duty to compensate the men for their donations? It was the damned ingratitude that got him. How dare they hold his feet to the fire.

"Beijing Number Seven Peony Metal Fabrication, Limited, will match the donations of any and all employees," Yang said slowly, his eyes searching for any man willing to return his gaze, "and above that amount will donate three hundred thousand yuan to the relief effort."

That ought to shut them up, he thought. People only think of themselves, even when they believe they're helping others. It's every man for himself. Then he heard the applause. The men's faces, turned up to him like a band of starving children he'd fed from his own kitchen. Some were waving their hard hats. Amazing, he thought. But by tomorrow they'll have found a reason to turn against me. Three hundred thousand won't be enough. He turned abruptly and went into the office, the men's cheers still audible after he'd closed the door, like an ax chopping at him, breaking him up into pieces they'd throw on a fire to warm their rough hands. He fell into his leather chair and closed his eyes.

That was how Rabbit found him when he returned to the office after laying some more brotherly abuse on the men.

"Finally, you've died from stress," Rabbit said. "Now your daughter's treasures will be mine."

"Soon enough," Yang said without opening his eyes. "I'm down two pints to the Red Cross."

"What a patriot. Hope you got a receipt."

Yang opened his eyes a touch, but Rabbit had concerned himself with a towering sheaf of invoices, his fingers playing up and down the jagged ridge of paper.

"What word from the proletariat?" Yang said.

Rabbit didn't respond immediately. The office was arranged so that he sat with his back to Yang. It wasn't spacious, but was large enough for their two desks, both heavy wooden Qing dynasty knockoffs, their chrome-and-mesh swivel chairs, several banks of file cabinets, and three boxy modular chairs for visitors. A small refrigerator stocked with kimchi and beer hummed against the wall.

Rabbit's fingers hovered at a corner of paper protruding from the stack before pincering an invoice, which he held close to his face, his upper lip retracted from his incisors as he peered over the top of his glasses. "It's fine," Rabbit said. "You know how people get. They say they're worried about their relatives, but mostly they're worried about their own skins, and they just want to get on with it."

Yang sighed and closed his eyes again. "Three hundred thousand," he said.

"It's enough. You're still a rich man no matter how much you give away," Rabbit said. He quickly added, "But no one thinks you're holding out."

"The men know I'm not a public speaker," Yang said.

"Don't worry about it. The rich always have trouble communicating with the poor," Rabbit said, dropping the page to his desk, satisfied with his inspection.

"I'm not the only rich one around here," Yang said.

"Appreciate that," Rabbit said. "The difference is, I don't feel like I owe the men anything."

"What's that supposed to mean?" Yang said.

"You've done well for yourself, that's all. Admit that you don't speak the same language anymore."

"What? I'm supposed to live in a shack and eat fried rice?" Yang said.

"No," Rabbit said. "Just the opposite. You have to admit that you don't live in a shack and you can't expect them to treat you like you do. It's time for something new. You're the boss. You're not one of them anymore. Your schedule's not twelve on, twelve off. Work, eat, run home to screw and catch some sleep. You split for lunch and you don't show up until noon the next day." Rabbit fixed his eyes on his friend. "You should have been here yesterday. You know what it sounded like? The cargo bay of a ship in a storm, creaking and groaning and everything sliding around. But the men, silent as a tomb. They were petrified, and where were you? They're your responsibility, for better or worse. That's how it is. You were absent in their time of need. You abandoned your children in their darkest hour."

Yang picked at the button of his shirt before responding. "Where would I be without you?" he said.

Rabbit searched Yang's face, but finding only the same pair of sad black eyes he'd known for forty years, he nodded and went back to his paperwork.

For several days, Yang came to work and sat in his chair. The zone chief called five, six times a day, but Yang declined. At first, Rabbit would get on the line and placate the zone chief, but eventually the chief refused to speak to him. It had gotten personal. Day after day, there Yang sat, placid as a frog in the mud. Maybe it was a calculated act of rebellion, but Rabbit couldn't understand for the life of him what his partner stood to gain by antagonizing the chief. The chief could make real trouble for them. Rabbit's own patience was wearing thin. He had enough problems trying to keep the men on the floor organized without having to play nursemaid to Yang.

During this time of silence, Yang came to understand the crisis in his own way: the workers would be satisfied by nothing less than strips of flesh from his back. The country would take nothing less than everything he had. Zone Chief Zhou was leaving messages at all hours on his cell phone. He was cursing Yang in new and creative ways, threatening to shut the factory down. Yang smiled as he listened to a message from the chief degrading his mother.

On the third day Rabbit lost it. "Did you have a stroke? Have you gone nuts?" he shouted at Yang.

Nothing.

"I'm calling a psychologist if you don't pull it together!" Rabbit yelled.

Yang smiled.

"I'm serious, you asshole!"

At home it wasn't much better. The first night Gong had paced around her husband, consoled him. The next night she screamed at him. Then she sat across from him, gnawing at her lip.

"You're under a lot of pressure," she said. "I understand. But that doesn't mean you have to act like a mental patient. You can't just hole up like this. Rabbit's been telling me what's going on. I don't want to wind up living on the street. I won't." She waited for a glimmer of recognition, a sign of concern. He gave her nothing. "You call back the zone chief and you do what he wants," she said. "You do exactly what he tells you to do. Why, on top of everything else, are you trying to bring the government down on our heads?"

She tilted her chin at him, waiting for an answer. When none came, she answered for him. "You are. You're trying to ruin us."

Yang got up and turned on the TV.

"You think this is a good example for Little Li?" she said. His smile cracked just a hair. Gong threw up her hands and left the room.

The news from near the epicenter of the earthquake in Beichuan County, deep in the Longmen Mountains, was horrific. Seven thousand dead in the town of Yingxiu, population nine thousand. In Dujiangyan, southeast of the epicenter, fifty children would be entombed in the rubble for weeks before workers could exhume them. Their parents encamped atop the concrete slabs, fighting with police to watch over the bodies of their children, singing them songs at dusk, telling stories to the rubble. Some had already been imprisoned for their defiance. Starving dogs and cats wandered over the wreckage, nosing into the rubble until rescue workers ran them off. Hundred-foot lengths of asphalt road had sheared off mountainsides and slid into valleys, sweeping away hamlets with no more pause than a drop of water rolling down a windowpane.

Yang considered the loneliness of dying beneath a slab of concrete, in the dark, mouth caked with dust and stone. He'd tried to be good, to do his duty, but what had he changed?

Newscasters sobbed as they reported on missing children reunited with their parents. Yet that was not what his countrymen concerned themselves with. The day after the quake, he saw in the *United Daily News* the total amount of donations by the ten richest people in China. In one day, 32.5 million yuan. And still, public outrage swelled. It was as though the benefactors had shat on the victims' graves. No donation was enough.

Chief Zhou had ordered a massive sign erected outside the zone gates listing, by order of size of donation, the twenty-seven companies located within. The names were in blocky script on a grid, framed on either side by cascading yellow and red bunting, the board rising to a height of two stories above the sidewalk. Included was each company's phone number and the exact amount, to the fen, donated to the earthquake victims. Passersby stood in front of the sign and dialed the listed companies, yelling indignantly at whomever picked up. If they couldn't get through, they pinned angry notes to a smaller comment board on the opposite side of the gate. The first-place company got as many calls as the last-place company, Yang's Beijing Number Seven Peony Metal Fabrication.

In the end it was the office secretary, a young cousin of Rabbit's, who ripped the phone cord from the wall and refused to answer any more calls until something was done. Rabbit went to Yang.

"I'm withholding your paycheck until you call the chief and sort this out," he said.

"So what?" Yang said.

"Just call the man," Rabbit said.

"I don't want to."

"Fine. I'll tell the men you're withholding our donation."

"So? They can read the sign," Yang said.

"They're under the impression the zone chief is putting the squeeze on you for a kickback. You want me to tell them that you're keeping the money for yourself?"

360

"You'd kick your own mother in the balls," Yang said.

"My mother keeps her balls in a jar on the shelf, my friend, right next to yours."

Chief Zhou's office kept him on hold for five minutes while Yang listened to a tinny recording touting the zone's commitment to aiding the victims of the Wenchuan earthquake. The voice also reminded him that the zone was accepting applications for factory space, which could be modified to meet tenants' needs.

"Hello?" the chief said when he finally came on the line, as if he'd just run into the office and hadn't been sitting there fuming, fantasizing about various methods by which to kill Yang, the entire time.

"Chief Zhou, it's Bing Yang, Beijing Number Seven Peony Metal Fabrication."

"Bing Yang. Good to hear your voice. How have you been?" the chief said. His tone was calm and collegial, and if Yang hadn't known the man was exercising every muscle in his body to keep from reaching through the handset to crush his throat, he'd have thought it was a courtesy call.

"It's been busy, Chief. I'm sorry I couldn't return your call sooner."

"Busy man, Yang."

"Busy."

"Yang, let's cut the bullshit."

"Bullshit cut, Chief," Yang said.

"I'm urging you to make a donation through the industrial zone. You've seen the board. It's a disgrace. You're one of only two companies who haven't helped the victims, and Beijing Heavy Transmission Eight is liquidating its holdings as we speak, so I might as well take them off the board entirely. Don't tell me you're broke, too."

"Oh, no sir, Chief. We've had better quarters, but we're okay."

"Good. So, how much will it be? They found a little girl alive in Beichuan, did you see that? Buried four-and-a-half days."

"Amazing. It's a testament to the human spirit, Chief."

"I agree, Yang. So, how much?"

"Well, Chief, I've prepared a donation of three hundred thousand," Yang said. "We may end up bankrupt, yet."

Chief Zhou didn't laugh. "That's fine, Yang. That might be enough to help me forget your behavior so far. When should I expect it?"

"Whenever you're ready to massage my scrotum," Yang said. Across the office, Rabbit gasped and made waving motions with his arms.

Yang waved back.

"What?" yelled Chief Zhou.

"Just cutting the bullshit, as requested."

"You son of a bitch!" Chief Zhou's voice shook. "Three days you keep me waiting? I've got cadres from the Central Committee up my ass about this, and you're wasting my time with this? What have I ever done to you?"

Rabbit was pale, his breathing shallow.

"Let's avoid conflict, Chief," Yang said, holding the receiver away from his ear. "Why don't I just write a check to your personal account and we'll be done with it?"

Rabbit made a choking sound.

"You fucking hick," Chief Zhou sputtered. The line clicked and he was gone. Yang set his handset back in its cradle.

"Oh, oh, oh," was all Rabbit could say. He kept wiping his brow with a handkerchief.

"What's he going to do?" Yang said. "Add another zero to our tally on the big board? My conscience is clean. We'll give three hundred thousand directly to the Red Cross and we'll match the men's donations. I've given my own blood. Why is everyone so interested in draining my accounts?"

Rabbit stared at him. "You've lost your mind. Your wife's already calling me in tears. I'm running your customers for you. Okay, my friend. That's one thing. But now you're messing with the party. Chief Zhou is going to drop a bomb on us."

"He just wants his cut," Yang said.

"No shit. And he wants to keep his head attached to his shoulders. If he doesn't get a donation from every company, in two weeks he'll be driving a dump truck in Xinjiang, spending Friday nights at the mosque."

"You're a party member," Yang said. "Can't you have him brought up for self-criticism for trying to collect bribes? Doesn't that go against 'Love and respect honest labor and thrift'?"

"When did he ever solicit a bribe?"

"Come on!" Yang said.

"You have to have proof," Rabbit said. "You're putting me in a terrible position. Let's make the donation together. We'll pull it from operating expenses, no cost to you or me. Deal? It's a business expense. It's an operational expense," Rabbit said.

"And then how much does Zhou kick back to you?" Yang said.

Rabbit's face fell. "You're going to ruin us both," he said.

"Right," Yang said. "I'll let you sort this out. I'm going home."

Yang opened the office door, the whine of the factory flooding in around him, and clanked down the stairs.

He passed his bus stop, intending to use the walk to the subway to clear his head, but when he got there he passed the entrance without giving it a second thought. His mood had begun to lift. It had been days since he'd exerted himself physically, and as he walked, effortlessly cutting through crowds, weaving around food vendors and CD pirates, he began to formulate plans for daily exercise routines that would get him back to peak condition. He'd once been a distance runner, in his teenage years, and from his distinction on the track he'd made connections that took him to Beijing. It had been the start of everything.

He worked himself into a state of exhilaration, awash in beneficence at the thought of tightening his laces at the edge of a track, joining the other early morning runners. He could turn everything around by donating more than any other company. He and Chief Zhou would have a good laugh about it afterward, and Rabbit would shake his head in admiration, as if to say, you sly old fox, I should have known you were up to something. He'd buy presents for Gong and Little Li in apology for his bad behavior.

By the time he turned into his hutong, he'd laid out a plan for reconciliation that involved a banquet at the Kunlun Hotel and presents at everyone's setting. He would draw the people he loved into his orbit.

When he rounded the final corner, he saw Old Gao outside his gate, writing a ticket. Her back was to him, and Yang shuffled his feet and coughed to alert her to his presence. Her arm paused its scribbling motion, so he knew she'd heard him, but when he came up beside her, she flinched and said, "You startled me!"

"I'm sorry, Mrs. Gao," Yang said.

"Here," she said, holding out the ticket.

"I see." He studied her long, swooping strokes on the paper. She had quite beautiful script and he wondered if she'd been an intellectual in her former life. "Improper disposal of garbage," he read aloud. "Thank you, Mrs. Gao."

"Don't be smart," she said. "Bing Yang, it's lucky I've found you. The neighborhood committee is receiving donations for the earthquake victims. Some of these foreign ghosts have given more than we Chinese," she said, waving her arm in the direction of his German neighbor's compound. "It's a point of national pride, and I know we can count on you."

Yang's jaw began to ache. He felt his mood disintegrate like a stone wall crumbling to powder.

Then Old Gao said, "Mr. Bing. You're crying," as if to scold him for his breach of etiquette. When he didn't reply, she moved away from him, cane tapping rapidly, and called out over her shoulder, "You'll bring a donation when you can."

Yang pushed open his gate and went into the courtyard. Little Li had finally swept up the petals, but he felt no sense of pride in her obedience. He dabbed at his eyes with his sleeve and lowered himself onto a bench across from the denuded peach tree. It was late afternoon, pigeons and starlings circling above, their cries filling the courtyard as they looped over his house. Every once in a while a pigeon would flap down to attach itself to a limb, make some cooing noises, then fly back up to rejoin its kit. The light faded, and Yang stared at the tree for a long time, until its uppermost branches were only black outlines against the purple sky. He thought that if he had an ax, he would chop it down, but he didn't, so he sat, folding and unfolding the garbage ticket and trying to recall what it had been like to be poor.

Nominated by A Public Space

THINGS TO THINK ABOUT

by SCOTT BEAL

from THE COLLAGIST

—for Zoe

Not fire. Not fire cascading in blue jewels
      from the stovetop gas jets, not tentacling
the tile, not fire creaking up the stairs, trying on the clothes
      in your closet. Not fire twining like ivy
up your mother's bones. Saying not fire,
      though, is the same as saying fire, nebulas
of gasoline, starbursts in the soapdish,
      magma running in the gutters.

You've never seen a blaze not caught
      behind a grill or sunk inside a circle of stones,
never seen a spark catch a curtain
      or race along a fuse but in your head
dust is gunpowder and your body wrapped in sheets
      a mummy in a furnace, so if you're not thinking
about Athena being born wearing armor,
      of the clank when she lands on her feet

and turns, armed, to face her father's gaping brain,
      think of snails at the shell wash,
a burger joint in the basement.
      Think of cloudboats or whaleboats

or a sun with no fire in it, just continually opening
        daffodils pouring nectar over the planets.
Think of things you can send in an envelope,
        things you can lead on a leash.

Think of what the sun could be made of
        if it wasn't fire, not fire licking its chops,
breathing in your ear as you sleep,
        saying shh, don't wake up, it's all in your head,
and it is, the fire, it's all in your head,
        you can kill it with a thought, so think
of all the things you could build a bridge from
        for your tubful of plastic people,

think of the plots of puppet shows for pandas,
        think of when you and I used to dance
to Mr. Jack, how we stomped and thrashed around the purple
        swivel chair as a voice screamed Fuck! You! Pig!
though you were three and didn't catch it
        and your memory of those years is burnt clean,
everything burns, everything will,
        but if you let that thought overtake you as you lie

in the dark we're half ash already,
        so think of the bridge you'll build
and the township waiting for your people on the other side
        with turquoise pools and a lean-to
made of picture books, think of the fabulous animals
        with whom they'll talk about the view
across the river of the smoking quarry they have left behind,
        its veins of charcoal, its glorious ores.

Nominated by The Collagist

THE FIELD MUSEUM

by ROGER REEVES

from THE CINCINNATI REVIEW

It is customary to hold the dead in your mouth
Next to the other dead and their failing trophies:
Quetzal, starthroat, nightjar, grebe, and arctic loon:
This ash for my daughter's tongue, I give without
Sackcloth or sugar: the museum closing,
The whale falling from heaven due
Upon our heads at any time: our haloes already
Flat as plates and broken about our ankles:
How often can you send a child to meet a ghost
At the river before the child comes back speaking
As the river, speaking as the pedal-less red
Bicycles half-buried in its bank, speaking bolt oil
Spilling down the legs of a thrice-trussed bridge
Just after a train lurches toward a coast covered in smog:
The river must be thick with this type of body:
A daughter bearing bird names on her lips, cutting
Her ankles on cans that resemble her mother's tongue.

Nominated by The Cincinnati Review, Maxine Scates, Diane Seuss, Philip White

A PORTRAIT OF THE WRITER AS A RABBIT

by SABINE HEINLEIN

from THE IOWA REVIEW

Unlike rabbits, the stereotypical German is stationary, predictable, and consistent. She plans ahead, stays close to home, and doesn't risk awkward jumps. But rabbits and I—we are *übermütig*.

Composed of the German preposition *über* (beyond or above) and *mütig*, which derives from the noun *Mut*, or courage, *übermütig* is commonly translated as *carefree, coltish*, and *slaphappy*. But none of these translations captures the adjective's condescending quality. A German who is overly courageous isn't a hero. A German who fails to consider where her jumps will land her is conceited and presumptuous.

Rabbits and I live in the moment; we have a hair trigger and aim high. A truly happy rabbit doesn't take into consideration the powerful strength of her springy hind legs. When she is exuberantly joyful, she puts on "binkies," a series of Jerry Lewis jumps that land her in unforeseeable places. As a result, she bumps into walls and against chairs and slides across hardwood floors. Watching my pet rabbits do their binkies, the stereotypical German in me wants to call out, "Be careful! Don't forget how strong your hind legs are! Don't be *übermütig*!" But instead I stand back, applaud, and feel inspired.

The binkies are, of course, a form of joyous practice that saves lives in treacherous situations. With their unpredictable jumps and jolts and their ability to suddenly reverse direction, rabbits often manage to fool and escape their pursuers. A well-performed binky can be the difference between life and death.

Staying where I grew up would have killed me. My little Bavarian burrow was stultifying. I devoured the stories passing strangers brought to our home, but there were never enough.

My parents often called me *übermütig* as a child.

"You are *übermütig*!" My father would say when I jumped on the couch and ran around the fireplace, skidding on the tiled floor; when I let myself dangle from his elk trophies and climbed on the steel sculptures in the yard.

"This will end in tears!" my mother would warn. And often it did. Tears of embarrassment and anger, because whenever I did fall, my parents would say, "I told you so! You shouldn't have been so *übermütig*!"

As a child I enjoyed digging and dangling, jumping and skidding, but hated the guilt it brought on. I wanted to free myself from my family's fears and from Germany's enervation. We rabbits are masters of escaping enclosures; if necessary we fit into the tightest spaces and can jump up to several times our height.

I got Nils when I was sixteen and didn't know who or what I was (although I was good at pretending I knew). Nils was a small, skinny rabbit, four pounds at the most. He had black, velvety fur and black, beady eyes.

After high school, Nils and I left the German South of our childhood to Hamburg in the far North. In the late afternoons I sat on the piers and watched the sun disappear behind the ships that headed out of the harbor. This was when I knew that there was only one place else to go. While it would soon be night in Hamburg, the day had just begun in America. I wanted to be where Br'er Rabbit fishes with his predators and where Bugs Bunny dresses in drag. I wanted to see the world the way rabbits do: their eyes, positioned strategically on the sides of their heads, allow for an almost 360-degree panoramic view.

While I figured that in New York my rabbity idiosyncrasies would be welcome, I didn't know what to do about Nils. He was a moody and sensitive rabbit and had already had his share of moves. Afraid that he wouldn't survive a transatlantic journey, I decided to stay put awhile.

Nils was home when I returned from parties and soothed me when I was lovesick. Exasperated with family, friends, and myself, I burrowed my face in his fur. When everything around me was new and unsettling, Nils was there. His binkies brightened starless nights; Nils showed me how to fully enjoy the moment while staying on guard. Most importantly, he taught me to sit down and work. When I paced up and down with pursed lips, he stripped off the wallpaper and chewed on my rugs. But when I sat at my desk to read and write, he calmed down and rolled up into a ball by my feet. The writing of my first stories was accompanied by the sound of him crunching his teeth, the rabbit's equivalent to a cat's purring.

Nils traveled with the summer sun that lit my Hamburg apartment, his tiny black figure melting into the black carpet. After three hours of sunbathing, his fur was scorching like a cast-iron pan. To keep Nils comfortable on the dreary gray days that dominate the German North in the fall and winter, I bought him a white lambskin rug. This lambskin became his passion. He would pluck and pluck at it until he accumulated a large white beard. Then he would sit behind his beard in a corner, like a department store Santa Claus. Thanks to Nils it was Christmas 365 days a year.

Nils lived much longer than I had expected, and it wasn't until after I finished school that I went to New York City for a visit. My first two weeks there only confirmed what I already knew: New York was where I belonged. As if my longing competed with his life, Nils suffered a stroke after my return.

At age eleven, Nils was suddenly unable to move his hind legs. I put him on his lambskin, and his large round eyes, still black and shiny, sank deep into mine.

It seems implausible now, how the old, cranky vet kept refilling the syringe, pumping more and more poison into my four-pound rabbit. As the drug finally began to work, Nils started crunching his teeth. "A reflex," the vet said, dismissively. But I read that cats often purr as they are being put to sleep to either calm themselves or their owners. Maybe it was Nils's last attempt to reassure me that life would continue without him.

The vet asked me to take Nils to the waiting room to give the euthanasia time to work. As I sat on my plastic folding chair, cradling Nils in his lambskin, I sobbed uncontrollably.

"What do you have there?" a woman with a cat in a crate said. My voice contorted by tears, I responded, "A rabbit. He's dead."

"A *what*?" the woman screeched. "A monkey?"

"A rabbit!" I tried again. Sorrow and tears had turned the German *Hase* into an *Affe*.

Friends and family thought it exaggerated that I suffered so much over the death of a rabbit. (In Germany, there are rules to everything. A relative's death warrants one year of suffering; a dog's death a week; and a rabbit's death one day at the most.) But I felt as if with the rabbit, something inside me had died. I am my rabbit. My rabbit is I. There are few people I can understand and who can understand me, but rabbits and I can relate to each other.

Now that my last German rabbit was gone, I had to move on and away. In New York, I thought, I would become who I couldn't be. I was terrified of my future, but nothing could now hold me back. Rabbits and I are anxious yet curious by nature. We are sensitive and hard-bitten. While we are easily startled, we are drawn to explore new, treacherous territory once the imminent danger has passed.

In the wild, rabbits can survive for months on nothing but branches and roots. Yet they can smell bananas, by far their favorite food, from a distance of two hundred feet. I found the rabbit's versatilities well worth pursuing, but knew that I still had a lot to learn. I had to adapt to my new environs.

After a couple of months in New York, I couldn't stand my rabbitless life any longer. I was stuck and needed a teacher, a friend, a playmate. One rainy day I walked past a pet store in the East Village, where, confined to a small terrarium, sat a large, gray rabbit. The raindrops on the store's window made the rabbit's fur sparkle. Clearly, he must be a treasure, I thought. Hoping to make myself whole again, I bought the poor beast. In a spurt of hope—hope for a sunnier sky, a sunnier life—I named my first American rabbit Sunshine.

A handsome lagomorph with very large ears, one floppy and the other pointing straight up to the sky, Sunshine was a prelude to a whole new learning experience. Not only did I learn more about rabbits; through him I discovered America.

"When are you going to eat him?" my visitors would ask, and astonished by Sunshine's large size they would add, "Do you even own a pot that big?!"

Being a hunter's daughter, I didn't mind their jokes. What I minded was that my American guests would usually follow their jokes with a morbid childhood experience. "One-day-I-came-down-to-the-basement-and-my-rabbit-was-dead" was a standard. Other varieties included, "I-had-a-rabbit-as-a-child-but-he-died-after-only-eight-days," and "My-rabbit-was-mauled-by-our-dog." American rabbits didn't seem to last nearly as long as German rabbits. (I began to fear for my life.) What *did* I know about my new country? What did my new country know about me? Nothing, really. We were strangers to each other.

In America rabbits are commonly sold in pet stores as Easter gifts for children and then quickly discarded—dropped off in public parks and shelters because people are appalled at their obsession for chewing on wood and rubbery things. The same rabbits that are common house pets in Germany are considered an "exotic species" here. Rabbit health isn't routinely taught in vet school, and the few rabbit-savvy, "exotic" vets in New York charge far more for treating rabbits than their colleagues charge for treating cats or dogs.

When I came to New York in 2001, Rabbit, Rescue & Rehab, a local advocacy and rescue group, operated out of private homes in New York and knew of only two rabbit clinics in the city. (Today RRR occupies a small room in East Harlem's Animal Care and Control, and its list of rabbit-savvy clinics in New York has grown to a meager four.)

It is true that the health requirements and drug sensitivities of rabbits differ widely from those of dogs or cats. But calling them "exotic" seemed exotic to me. Like humans, rabbits have adapted to nearly every corner of this world. The swamp rabbit has waterproof fur; he can swim and dive across rivers and hide underwater from predators. The desert cottontail eats cacti and satisfies his need for water by drinking the dew on plants. The brush rabbit can climb trees, and the marsh rabbit makes up for his missing tail with extraordinarily broad feet that help him move over soggy terrain. Most notably, these habitually shy and quiet creatures have adapted to us—our small New York apartments, our big, sudden movements and booming voices.

One of the rabbit's "exoticisms" is that he has a very delicate digestive system. To prevent his system from shutting down, he has to eat constantly. His guts have to be in constant motion. Sunshine, for example, *inhaled* one large romaine lettuce head, several pieces of broccoli, a carrot, a bowl of oatmeal, and a bucket of hay per day. While this made it easy for me—my rabbits and I have always shared our fridge and pantry—it also meant a considerable strain on my budget, particularly considering the costly veterinary care. I soon began growing dandelion, basil, and carrots in my meager Brooklyn backyard.

Rabbits commonly go into "stasis" if stressed, fed inappropriately, or not fed often enough. They can die within twenty-four hours if they don't eat. It's likely that the "rabbit-in-the-basement" died because his

372

or her needs were neglected. None of this strikes me as particularly exotic.

Yet the perceived exoticism of rabbits coincided with my observation that Americans tend to perceive deviations from their individual experiences and needs as exotic. (Germans, on the other hand, consider deviations as *inept*, which isn't any better. The label of exoticism and ineptitude both alienate "the other.")

To Americans, I was exotic. "Sabine? And you pronounce the *e* at the end? That's exotic!"

"Well, actually, Sabine is possibly the most common name for German girls born in the mid-seventies," I would respond. (My parents weren't particularly creative.) "And we Germans—like Italians, Romanians, Russians, Spaniards, etc.—pronounce each and every letter of a word." Now I sounded not only exotic, but also blunt, insensitive, pissy even. At the beginning, I did not understand the American way of making conversation and the principle that it is always better to have *something* to say than *nothing*.

I began to identify with Sunshine's exotic status. I had to remind myself how exotic I must appear to those for whom Germany was a small land that lay sleepily on the globe's back side. It takes years to become an integral part of a new country, and it takes years for the new country to become a part of you. Your body absorbs its new territory much more effortlessly than your soul. Adapting without losing yourself is the main challenge.

I decided to join three rabbit groups and learned that what the American public misses in terms of rabbit expertise and compassion, its rabbit lobbyists more than make up for. In America, there is an A for every Z, a hug for every blow, and plenty of chatter for every stutter. You can either be pragmatic, or you can go overboard. American rabbit enthusiasts tend to do the latter.

Hats off to the House Rabbit Society, and for Etherbun and NYCbuns, two Yahoo groups dedicated to the well-being of lagomorphs. Thanks to them, thousands of rabbits that would have been euthanized are alive today. Never mind that some group members are a bit crazy and militant. For example, a forum discussion about a rabbit's intestinal tumor kept numerous members awake until finally enough prayers were said and pictures of the rabbit's autopsy were posted. A woman's one-line help request sparked more than a dozen outraged replies over several days: "My husband HATES the rabbit and has said if she is still in the house after the new year, he will give her to a chef who cooks rabbits," she wrote on NYCbuns. Some members offered to drive the husband "out to the wilderness and leave *him* there."

The employment of baby rabbits in a "Sweet Millions" lottery commercial ignited outrage as well. Sweet all right, but were the baby bunnies treated humanely? Does a rabbit suffer when squeezed into a teacup and forced to ride a small carousel? And, more importantly, can a rabbit learn how to ride a little unicycle?

Sunshine had better things to do than ride a unicycle. As if trying to make up for the months he had spent in his tiny terrarium, he was a daredevil at binkies. Rain, snow, or shine, at seven o'clock in the morning he would scratch on the fridge door and demand his morning carrot. Once his white lips had turned emergency-vest orange, he jumped up on the window ledge, squeezed through the bars, and bounced into the backyard. There, he raced around the mulberry tree and ricocheted off the fence and onto the wooden benches. Sometimes, in the middle of his jolt, his behind jerked up as if he had suffered a seizure. Then his front legs touched down like a tornado. Chased by an imaginary pursuer, Sunshine zigzagged through the yard. To my surprise, he—the prey—enjoyed being pursued.

For rabbits, life and death are invariably intertwined. It is the powerful strength—and volatility—of their large hind legs that unifies these antipodes. A frightened rabbit sometimes commits suicide in his last moments of life: if he is caught by the wolf, the coyote, or the unkind human, he can jerk his hind legs so violently that he breaks his own back.

After his morning workout, Sunshine would return to the apartment for a hearty brunch. While he ate, he shit, and while he shit, he ate. Rabbits love to cross lines and do things we humans keep strictly separate. (In this case, their line-crossing makes it easy to litter box-train them. Just put some hay into their litter box, and they'll get the idea.)

Carrot-binkies-eating-shitting was Sunshine's routine for a couple of years, until one day he returned from the yard and refused to eat his second breakfast. I grew worried when around noon he only briefly nibbled on some radish greens and then hid in a corner. By evening it was clear that something was seriously wrong.

What I experienced on Sunshine's last day of life now seems emblematic of my first years in New York. Despite an abundance of ingenious *stuff*—duct tape and Goo Gone still blow my mind—a lot was still missing. There was no pet supply store or vet in my Brooklyn neighborhood, and it took me years to find things like needles and thread. See, we Germans are organized. Each town has at least one major department store within walking distance where one can find anything, from sewing material, cosmetics, and pet supplies, to clothes, cigarettes, books, and Boston lettuce. The departments and their most common items are neatly listed on maps near the escalators. How is it possible that in the greatest city in the world one has to visit three or four different stores and neighborhoods to find the stuff one needs on a daily basis? How was it possible that on a Tuesday night at six p.m. there wasn't a single rabbit vet in all of New York who would see Sunshine?

The large animal hospital by the Fifty-Ninth Street Bridge said they didn't have a rabbit specialist on duty but could try to keep Sunshine alive until the next morning when their specialist returned. The other rabbit-savvy vet had already left her office.

In the middle of the night, Sunshine's eyes began to tear a thick, milky substance. Although still breathing and sitting up straight, he looked like he was already gone. At two in the morning, Sunshine suffered a seizure and died.

The next morning I dug a grave under the mulberry tree behind the old wooden benches where Sunshine had done his binkies each morning. Placing his limp body into the hole, I was once again astonished by the enormous size of his two hind legs.

It is not a coincidence that Americans lack an appropriate word for *übermütig*—and that Germans lack a translation for the English word *reinvention*. But how can one reinvent oneself without being *übermütig*? *If you fall down, pick yourself up and dust yourself off*, Americans say. From there I assume one is to walk a different route to avoid falling over the same obstacle twice. In Germany, the proverb *Cobbler stick to your lasts*, which is hardly known in the U.S., still enjoys great popularity. The Germans' lack of flexibility and their animosity to changes in habits and roles had threatened to suffocate me. In New York I wasn't admonished to stick to my lasts, but I was forced to adapt and unearth what I had in me. Neither one was easy.

Around the time I realized that I needed to loosen up and play, I discovered my kinship with Beatrix Potter. Potter bought her first rabbit, Benjamin Bouncer, at a London bird store and smuggled him into her room in a paper bag. About her second rabbit, Peter Piper, she said, "He was clever at learning tricks, he used to jump through a hoop, and ring a bell, and play the tambourine." Peter Piper is also said to have had a penchant for buttered toast.

Potter recognized the rabbit's ability to alter himself. In *The Tale of Peter Rabbit*, she showed how her protagonist "squeezed under the gate," skillfully portraying the rabbit's capacity to shrink and stretch parts of his body. Rabbits can be doughy, shapeless lumps one moment and delicately squeeze through fences and into cracks and crannies the next. A rabbit, Potter reminds us, can morph into anything; he can even become dinner: "Don't go into Mr. McGregor's garden," Mrs. Rabbit says to her children. "Your father had an accident there; he was put in a pie by Mrs. McGregor."

This was an encouraging book! Just keep on changing!

Epilogue
A few years into my time in New York I fell in love with Giovanni García-Fenech, a Mexican whose maternal ancestors had come to the New World via Italy and Malta. *Fenech* is the Maltese word for rabbit. The family's coat of arms bears a grinning white rabbit on a green lawn. Naturally, Fenech and I soon got married.

Seven years ago we adopted Teddy from the House Rabbit Society. Teddy is a master of reinvention, and we never grow tired of observing his appearances. He has muddy brown fur with blond patches and looks like a stuffed animal that has been washed with too much soap and too much love. Like Margery Williams's Velveteen Rabbit, it is love that has made Teddy real. The only thing we know about Teddy's previous life is that his owner gave him up because he had to go fight in Iraq. This soldier must have treated Teddy nicely. Why else would he be so addicted to cuddles?

Teddy is old now and very arthritic, but he still plays charades. Sometimes he hunches up and stretches his neck like a turkey. In these moments I am sorely tempted to play along and slip paper frills around his ankles. But I know that as soon as I opened the oven door, Teddy would morph into a loaf of bread, a sack of potatoes, or a Volkswagen Beetle or disappear behind the radiator like a roach.

Because we couldn't keep pace with Teddy's insatiable need for attention, we adopted Pooka. She is sweet and loving, but, unlike Teddy, she's an independent traveler and free spirit. Pooka was named after a line in the movie *Harvey* ("A fairy spirit in animal form . . . [t]he Pooka appears here and there, now and then, to this one and that one. A benign but mischievous creature"). With her white fur and large black rings around her eyes, Pooka mostly resembles a panda bear. Sometimes she looks like a Goth whose mascara is running after a good cry. After two hours of binkies and biting our ankles, she turns into a drowsy subway rider, her little head slowly sagging to the side as she dozes off. If a fire truck drives by with its siren blaring, she briefly erects herself and shakes her head in a failed attempt to stay awake. Then she slumps back down in slow motion, leaning on Teddy's shoulder.

I have learned to see the world through my rabbits, but I still wonder who created these odd creatures. And who or what makes me? I am neither superstitious nor religious, but I still regard rabbits as *someone's* caprice. God is said to have rested on the seventh day—but I suspect it was on that day that He created rabbits, those little useless creatures with their disproportionate legs and ears, their *übermütig* binkies, and their prowess to transform into anything, even a lost girl's soul.

Nominated by The Iowa Review

THERE WERE SUCH THINGS

by W.S. DI PIERO

from ZYZZYVA

I knew the words would be waiting for me,
how various sounds play in the mouth and mind,
each time a different estero in my heart
like your bracelet's lost coral scale, your bone hairpin,
the lipstick smudge sliding off torn tissue
a special event each time, thing by thing,
word by word. I knew these creatures, as before,
would be waiting in their familiar names,
in *dowitcher, willet, whimbrel* and *coot*
or *snipe* or *curlew*, that I could speak and speak.
Where were you that day? Why weren't you with me?
But what waited there was something else.
Muscling nonstop around each other,
dingy leopard sharks shadowed the shallows,
the light dying on their silty backs.
They seemed to be themselves the moving waters.
They were the swimming absence of the words
they drove away, part of the new vocabulary
of exclusions, of what might have been birds,
symmetric in their bones like umbrellas,
the feather and flesh of what was now elsewhere.

Nominated by Jane Hirshfield, Gary Short

LIKABLE

fiction by DEB OLIN UNFERTH

from NOON

She could see she was becoming a thoroughly unlikable person. Each time she opened her mouth she said something ugly, and whoever was nearby liked her a little less. These could be strangers, these could be people she loved, or people she knew only slightly whom she had hoped would one day be her friends. Even if she didn't say anything, even if all she did is *seem* a certain way, have a look on her face, or make a soft sound of reaction, it was always unlikable—except in the few cases when she fixed herself on being likable for the next four seconds (more than that was impossible), and sometimes that worked, but not always.

Why couldn't she be more likable? What was the problem? Did she just not enjoy the world anymore? Had the world gotten away from her? Had the world gotten worse? (Maybe, probably not. Or probably in some ways but not in the ways that were making her not like it.) Did she not like herself? (Well, of course she didn't, but there was nothing new in that.)

Or had she become less likable simply by growing older—so that she might be doing the same thing she had always done, but because she was now forty-one, not twenty, it had become unlikable because any woman doing something at forty-one is more unlikable than a woman doing it at twenty? And does she sense this? Does she know she is intrinsically less likable, and instead of resisting, does she lean into it, as into a cold wind? Maybe (likely) she used to resist, but now she sees the futility, so each morning when she opens her mouth she is unlikable, proudly so, and each evening before sleep she is unlikable, and each day it goes on this way, she getting more unlikable by the hour, until one morning she will be so unlikable, inconveniently unlikable, that she will have to be shoved into a hole and left there.

Nominated by Noon, Kim Chinquee

THE STORY

by B.H. FAIRCHILD

from THE YALE REVIEW

It has no name and arrives from nowhere,
eager for new adventures: the murmur and cries
of the crowded streets of Istanbul or Rome
or Brooklyn, the blazing eyes of the last gray wolf
deep in a cave in New Mexico, the sob of the wind
between the disks of an abandoned tractor
on the high plains, the homeless man chasing
his runaway grocery cart down Sunset Boulevard,
a young woman looking out from the front porch
of a duplex in Enid, Oklahoma, waiting for the mail.

It has, as they say, a mind of its own, bearing
secret knowledge, truths from another world,
transparent and untranslatable, luminous
and cryptic. It arrives almost silently, only
the slight crush of lawn grass beneath its sandals,
a surprise even though you have somehow
expected it. Your hands, rough and calloused
from the toils of the imagination, reach out
to gently shake its narrow shoulders, to tousle
its well-combed hair silvered by moonlight.
Where have you been? It says nothing, of course,
walks to the far corner of the room, and begins
to pray. After waiting for hours, you offer it
coffee and a slice of pecan pie, then more coffee.

When it leaves, you follow close behind in fear
and a traveler's anxiety. *Where can a story end?*
If it arrives from nowhere, where can it end?
But then, as you pass through familiar streets,
past the clapboard houses, the pomegranate tree
just coming into bloom, the blue Buick parked
by the curb, you understand, for there is your mother
among the bird cries of the porch swing, reading
a letter from a small island somewhere in the Pacific.
There is the front door with its torn screen,
the voices of a soap opera from the radio, the creak
and whisper of cottonwood branches overhead.
This is where the story ends. And now you know,
this is also where it begins, and you lean
into the light, put the pen to paper, and write.

Nominated by The Yale Review, Ted Deppe

CONSEQUENCE

by ERIC FAIR

from PLOUGHSHARES

I enter my name into a search engine. There are 3,700 results. The word torture appears in most of them. I read the blogs. I read the comments that follow. I find more blogs. I pretend those don't bother me either. I check e-mail, thirty-eight new messages.

> *Mr. Fair, I'm not at all sure why you have your panties in a twist. It seems clear that you were a willing participant, as a civilian contractor, in the interrogation process in Iraq. This is old news.*

I navigate back to the opinion page of *The Washington Post*. The comments section is still growing. More than eight hundred now. I read the new ones and some of the old ones too. I read my article again. I check e-mail, fifty-seven new messages.

> *Eric, your words are empty and hollow. I do not accept a single one of them. But let me offer you a suggestion if you want to do the honorable thing: kill yourself. Leave a note. Name names. Until that day, I hope you never sleep another hour for the rest of your life.*

I keep pretending not to be bothered. Then I drink. In the mornings I pretend to have slept. I watch Sarah drive off to work. We both pretend our marriage isn't suffering. During the day I pack boxes; we are moving to Princeton. I'll be studying at the seminary, pursuing ministry in the Presbyterian Church. I hope no one there reads the article.

The admissions office calls. I speak with the Dean. "I can't get most students to read a newspaper let alone appear in one," he says. "Maybe your time in Iraq will become part of your ministry."

I enter the seminary's administration building to file paperwork for my veterans benefits. I am early. The office is closed. Other students wait with me. I avoid them. I look at the pictures on the walls. They are black and white, taken during the Civil War. There is a grainy photo of Brown Hall with a blurred image of a student walking across the quad. I wonder if he is a veteran of Antietam or Gettysburg. I wonder if he knew Andersonville or Camp Douglas.

I enroll in a summer language class. I study Greek in order to read the New Testament more effectively. It reminds me of the Army. I studied Arabic in order to interrogate Arabs more effectively. I settle into a life of muggy morning walks to class followed by chilly afternoons in the seminary library. I arrive on campus in the early morning, review my homework, attend class, eat lunch, and then spend the rest of the afternoon memorizing verb charts and case endings. I return home in the early evening, tell Sarah about the day, eat dinner, watch the news, get drunk, and read e-mails with subject lines like Iraq, interrogation, and torture.

Mr. Fair

I still have a .45 caliber 1911. I suspect you know the firearm. I'd loan it to you gleefully if you get really depressed. And I'd happily take whatever legal consequence might come my way for having done so. You'd be doing the world a favor by removing yourself from the gene pool.

With revulsion at the subhuman you and others like you surely are.

I get to know my fellow students. There is a children's book author from Boston, a mathematician from Los Angeles, a youth worker from Kansas, an actor from New York City, and a former NFL lineman from Florida. One is a recent graduate from college. One has been traveling in Europe. One is middle-aged. One is retired. There is not a single veteran among them.

I say nothing about Iraq. I mention in passing that I'd served in the

Army, worked as a police officer and then gone on to consult for the U.S. government, but I never mention the words Iraq, contractor, interrogator, or Abu Ghraib.

As Greek consumes my mornings and afternoons in Princeton, Abu Ghraib dominates what remains of my day. I return home to the apartment and field phone calls from reporters in Philadelphia, filmmakers from Norway, psychologists from Boston, authors from the world of academia, lawyers from Amnesty International, and investigators from the Department of Justice.

Someone tells me to speak with a lawyer. The lawyer tells me not to speak with anyone. He tells me not to antagonize the government. He tells me to be honest. He tells me he will keep me out of prison. He tells me to focus on Greek. He arranges a meeting.

I tell my professor I am sick. I put away verb charts, participles, and lexicons, board a train for Washington, D.C., and meet with Department of Justice lawyers and Army investigators in the shadow of the U.S. Capitol. I disclose everything. I provide pictures, letters, names, firsthand accounts, locations, and techniques. I talk about the hard site at Abu Ghraib, and I talk about the interrogation facility in Fallujah. I talk about what I did, what I saw, what I knew, and what I heard. I ride the train back to Princeton. I start drinking more. Sarah takes notice. I tell her to go to Hell.

I sit for my final Greek exam in August. It is a passage from Paul's letter to the people of Thessalonica.

> *You yourselves know, brothers and sisters, that our coming to you was not in vain, but though we had already suffered and been shamefully mistreated at Philippi as you know, we had courage in our God to declare to you the gospel of God in spite of great opposition.*

I am not one of the believers in Thessalonica. I am one of the abusers at Philippi.

There is a break before the start of the fall semester. The campus is quiet. I spend time alone in the seminary library. I read Karl Barth and Reinhold Niebuhr. I read C. S. Lewis and Dietrich Bonhoeffer. I read Kurt Vonnegut. I pretend I will make a good Presbyterian pastor someday.

The semester begins. I enroll in a preaching class. One week we study poetry. I memorize a poem and perform it in front of other students.

The professor asks me to read lines over again. My pace is too fast. I haven't stressed the right words. "Like a devil's sick of sin." It still isn't right. I say it again. "Good," he says. "Bring that energy to the pulpit."

I make new friends. None of them read newspapers. I join a flag football team. I agree to volunteer as a referee. I show up for a game, don my striped shirt and blow the whistle. Players from both teams are furious. I am a terrible referee. One player is particularly incensed. He approaches me, grabs my shirt, pulls me toward him, and then shoves me to the side. "See, see, this is what they're doing. They can't do this. It's called holding!"

In Fallujah I am grabbing a detainee, shoving him to the side, moving him through a line of Iraqis who have just been taken from the battle-field. Some are still bleeding. One is missing part of his face. We are processing them, sorting them into groups for future interrogation. Well-dressed ones to the right, shabby looking ones to the left, faceless ones to the medic. The well-dressed ones are likely men of influence. The shabby ones are the pawns. But the shabby ones never seem to understand directions. They just stand there looking dumb. So we grab them and shove them and push them.

I return to the apartment after the game and find Sarah. I tell her about the student who shoved me. I tell her I will kill him. I am angry. I am yelling. I am yelling at Sarah. Thirty minutes later I am still angry. I am still yelling at Sarah. I say something terrible. I leave to buy whiskey.

> *Mr. Fair, I am a former WWII vet. You think you saw hell, well pal let me tell you that you haven't seen anything that bad. Don't be ashamed, you did your job. What you saw was no worse than some college fraternity initiation ritual. Have a good life and sleep well from now on.*

I visit the seminary chaplain. She directs me to the office of student counseling. There is a questionnaire with multiple-choice questions.

I elaborate on additional sheets of paper. The head counselor calls the next day. She will see me personally. We meet. We talk about terrible things. She tells me I am smiling. She calls it a defense mechanism. I tell her more terrible things. I ask her if she thinks I am a terrible person. She smiles. She says no.

I meet with a PhD student from South Africa. He is working on his dissertation and wants to talk to me about forgiveness. He tells me about the Truth and Reconciliation Commission that followed apartheid. Men were granted amnesty in return for their confessions. He believes we should consider the same thing in this country. He thinks I would be a good candidate for such a process. The other option, he says, is Nuremberg-style trials. He doesn't think that's a good idea. But there must be consequences, he insists. Forgiveness requires consequence.

In the spring I appear on "Radio Times," a PBS radio program out of Philadelphia. I skip a class on systematic theology and drive into the city. Calls are taken from listeners. Many have questions about my motivations for going public, some want to know what can be done to prevent future abuses, and others think I haven't gone far enough. Some ask about torture, others about seminary. Someone wants to know what I think about Dick Cheney. The last caller is screened by the producer during a brief promotional break. He is angry. The producer wants to know if I am comfortable fielding his questions. I accept. He asks me if I believe in Hell.

The hour is up. The interview ends. I am the first of two guests that morning. The next hour is about to start. I remove my headphones, gather my notes, and move out of the way. The producer meets me outside the studio and thanks me for my time. She leads me out a back door to the guest parking lot. It closes and locks behind me.

Eric, I hope you burn in hell for the rest of your life, you son of a bitch. You're a piece of shit.

Later that Spring, I attend a conference entitled No2Torture at Columbia Seminary in Georgia. The conference is attended by notable members of the antitorture movement within the Presbyterian Church. The speaker list includes Lucy Mashua, a torture survivor from Kenya. She has endured female genital circumcision, forced marriage, and then additional abuse for speaking out. She is there to speak for the victims of torture. I am there to speak for those who tortured them.

We break into small groups. Each group has a large placard placed on the wall in front of a table to identify its purpose. My placard reads "Victims and Perpetrators." Lucy, the victim, sits across from me. We are surrounded by other participants who want to hear what Lucy and I have to say. We say nothing. A photographer approaches. We stand for a picture. People gather to watch. Someone says it is a vision of Heaven: victim and torturer hand in hand. We are not hand in hand.

I sit and listen to the speakers. They talk about torture. They talk about the Roman Empire and the early Christians. They talk about Just War and The Doctrine of Last Resort. They talk about Nazis. Then I am introduced. I read my article. They applaud.

> *Mr. Fair, You should be tried for treason. I hope that terrorist in your dreams catches up with you and reminds you that he is there to kill Americans including you. You have disgraced the uniform you once wore.*

Back at Princeton, I interview for a summer internship. A church is looking for someone to run its youth program and preach on a set number of Sundays. We talk about my background, my education, and my interests. They ask about my first year at Princeton. I try to talk about class, but they read newspapers, so they ask about Iraq. They say I should preach about war. We talk about interrogation. They are interested. They ask more questions. I am tired, so I answer them.

I talk about Abu Ghraib. I talk about the detainees. None of them would cooperate. None of them would work with us. None of them would tell the truth. They all pretended to be farmers or mechanics or fishermen. They pretended to be drivers or cooks or clerks. No one was Republican Guard. They all hated Saddam. They all supported America. No one was hiding weapons in their backyards or explosives in the irrigation canals. None of them knew anything about the teams of men burying artillery rounds in the highway. They insisted it was all a misunderstanding. But the rockets and mortars kept coming. Incoming rounds killed detainees, melted their bodies into a mash of blood and pus. IEDs killed our friends.

And so we deprived detainees of sleep, or made them stand for long periods of time, or shoved them or grabbed them or manipulated their diets. We blared loud music, kept them cold, kept them lonely, kept them scared. It made some of them cooperate. Maybe it would work on others too.

Then I went to Fallujah. It was worse. More people were dying. My friend was standing next to a car. It detonated. He disappeared. They found parts of him the next day. We detained and deprived and grabbed and shoved and isolated and abused as best we could.

I grew weary. I went back to Baghdad. It was quiet there. I thought about where I'd been. I thought about what I'd done. I quit. I went home. I applied to seminary. I published an article in *The Washington Post*.

The interview ends. I return home. The nightmares are waiting on me. I dull them as best I can. The church calls the following week and offers me the job.

Near the end of the semester, a BBC camera crew follows me around for the day. "Act normal," the producer says. I stand in front of smart-looking buildings. I sit at a desk and pretend to read. I sit with a friend at lunch and pretend to have a conversation. I enter the chapel and pretend to pray. The crew sets up chairs on the main quad for an interview. I am illuminated by two large spotlights. In the background, the senior class sits for its graduation picture. I see them pointing at the lights.

Eventually, I quit.

In Iraq I attend chapel. I recite The Lord's Prayer, take communion, and say The Apostles' Creed. The Chaplain offers a benediction.

> *May The Lord bless you and keep you.*
> *May the Lord make his face to shine upon you, and be gracious to you.*
> *May the Lord lift up his countenance upon you, and give you peace.*

I go to work. I review the next interrogation. It will be the youngest brother again. He frightens easily. I tell him I will protect him. I tell him he will remain anonymous. I cover his head with a burlap sack. I muzzle his father and brothers with strips of duct tape and file them into the room. I tell him a confession will free his family. It won't. It works. I remove the sack. He cries.

I pretend not to be bothered.

Nominated by Joan Murray

THE LIT CLOUD

by MEI-MEI BERSSENBRUGGE

from DENVER QUARTERLY

1

I come to a rock by water to watch the sun set.

Sun lights a gray cloud above me, with so many rooms and convexities.

When I look up again, it's a scrim of lighting effects.

There's no volume to the object.

I watch sunset in late summer, trying to quiet myself, to open my heart, desiring relatedness; it comes as metaphors of weather.

To work with the metaphor, it's first visualized, then energized to this gray transparency expression in a shaman.

My cloud forms from earlier humidity, temperature change, thermal currents becoming manifest.

There's a mutual need for presentation between sky and inner self.

I receive from the cloud a sense of dignity for my fervent desire to express it.

Sunset is translating energy, and my spirit wants to gain space from time.

Place and time are like a crystal bridging between my intent and evening weather, to reflect into being an image, potential, as you also reflect.

Because everything I perceive is in place in gold light, its relating to me is intrinsic.

2

To work with weather, she suggests something without form but force, wind or water, which manifests movement.

So I immerse myself in moving light and reflection, diffuse like yellow of rugosa.

I imagine other intuition or destiny of sea, land as filters through which the metaphor forms.

I equate hope with intuition.

Weather is an emanation of the conscious life force of space, producing undulating waves.

The luminous field of being has a pulse.

When sun hits the void, the present, a volume, it seems like a war, like a dance.

There's pressure change, obstruction, energy surges in earth's field, just like the etheric field of an individual.

This stress reality can be altered by expanding our filters to accommodate any possible weather as the state of harmony.

That permeates twilight.

Each day the sun sets one minute earlier.

I connect my being here at the repeating point of sunset to its different times.

Sun shines through woods as I walk, angles in air, like fault lines in the crystal.

Its circular movement is a linking of threadlines, reflecting into being something that was an idea, an image, then everything around becomes a reflector in gold of time passing as motion manifesting.

Spirit refers to this cloud image or scrim awareness within what is forming.

It directs energy into ley lines by law of its being and how it's organized toward us for expression.

My intuition to come here draws from a repository of dreams I don't remember or haven't yet dreamed, which are ley lines.

Imagination, description, hormonally draws me to imbalance, stress, the urge for an external connection to discharge polarity, for internal security.

Like trees, mist, loons, I contribute to the expression of the place where I wait.

A small hickory seeming to have dropped its leaves all at once reflects a blaze of light from the ground, and birches crowding near guard the circle from diffusion

The tree's spirit remains in one place.

But if connection forms with a human it can become mobile, even verbal, and extend the range of its awareness, for example, by giving away a branch or as here.

4

Afterglow casts gold horizontality across water, yellow seaweed, rose sky.

Why does it fill me with happiness, with liberty?

Weather moves through us in fluid systems of air, water, molten rock, even solid rock, earth and her elements, just as thoughts adjust and change, bringing precipitation and shade, cold across granite.

Oncoming weather is announced by signs and received by us as a communion of awareness.

I hurry through woods to the water, anguished, lonely, inadequate to my work.

That place is a portal, a rabbit hole of inspirited orientation.

I attend to the portal effect, sun doubling in a cloud reflection, array of filament recordings, and I'm attended as a portal myself.

I intend hope, loving faith, then seeing aligns with limitless gold spreading the sea with warmth, the way a film unifies with light and motion.

My being becomes focused and transformative, like a river in rain.

Then I widen my sight for more facets of exposure of shoreline to the turbulence of storms.

Experience, perception, emotion, strength and fatigue interpenetrate with multiplicities of oncoming weather and star repetition, occupying the same sunset.

The cloud is passionate according to creative principles of motion, counterforce, exchange, as I also experience symptoms.

Here, a dragonfly at the end of day shifts to an idea that's worked into being.

Raven is a courier, shifting and creating mid air.

I notice a strip of grass sloping back from my ledge, a foot tall with green blades and spreading panicles of purple flowers a low violet cloud!

Nominated by Denver Quarterly

THE READER

fiction by ROBERT COOVER

from CONJUNCTIONS

Without a reader of his own, he creates one in a story he calls "The Reader." He decides that she is sensitive, intelligent, discerning, appreciative, widely read—in short, his perfect reader—and she is also exquisitely beautiful with an endearing smile and a loving, compliant nature. She professes to adore his writing, written specifically for her to read, which encourages him to believe she adores him too. Well, of course she does, it's his story, how could she do otherwise? So, she loves him, adores him, but necessarily in the abstract, as a reader loves the absent writer, alive or dead, lacking the circumstances to express her love more directly, which is his plight as well. He writes a poem inspired by her, brilliant in concept and powerful in its execution, and she reads it, adores it, clasps it to her breasts. Having designed them himself, he knows everything about those breasts. When she presses the poem to them, it's as though his hands are there too, his lips. But they are not. He can't touch them, though he knows she longs for him to do so. Because he loves her and wants her to be happy, he invents a handsome young man to keep her company, himself genteel, highly literate, of a warm and generous nature. This development in his story happens during a visit one morning to his local bookstore. As he sits there in the worn leather chair where he always sits, having a second cup of coffee, browsing yesterday's newspapers, and taking notes in his little blue notepad, he decides that this is where the two will meet, and they do. She is reading one of his books. The young man has also read it. It is their shared affection for the author that brings them together. The man takes another of the author's books down from the shelf and remarks on its narrative subtleties, its irresistible lyricism, its nobility of purpose. She is awed by his intimate knowledge of a book so dear to her. Soon they are naked. Love blooms between them. She is happy. But he who has brought all this about is not. In fact, writing about them, he suffers a terrible surge of jealousy at the very moment the young man kisses her breasts. Never mind that this man also loves his writing, he's gone. Hit by a truck. A tragedy. She is deeply sorrowed, being a sensitive person, but too bad, he was not right for her. She knows that now. So he enters the story himself. Or someone bearing his name and likeness does. They meet in the same bookstore. He is sitting at a table, giving a public reading to a packed, admiring audience and, at the moment she first sees him, she forgets her grief and falls desperately in love with him. It is total surrender. He may do with her as he pleases. First, of course, he has to introduce himself. She does that for him by handing him a book to sign, telling him that it is her favorite of all he has written, and the greatest book she has ever read. He smiles up at her, catching the lovelight in her eyes, his own eyes perhaps reflecting it. It is, he says evocatively, a mere trifle compared to the book he is working on now. She gasps in recognition of the revelatory moment, her hand at those breasts where his will soon be. Perhaps she intuits that the new book is for her and for her alone. Would you like a cup of coffee, he asks in a seductive manner, returning the signed book to her, or perhaps a glass of wine? No, thank you, says the woman sitting in the worn leather chair opposite him with a book in her lap, staring at him with something between curiosity, concern, and alarm. He apologizes, explaining that he is an actor; he is auditioning for a play and was practicing his lines. It's called "The Reader," he says when she asks, as he leaves the bookstore, intending never to return. The reader has also left the bookstore. She is in the apartment of the famous writer she has just met, which is to say, his own apartment, or one much like it, though cleaner and more elegantly furnished, with famous etchings on the walls instead of pages torn from magazines. She is admiring his vast library (not much room for etchings actually). Have you read all these books? she asks. All those in this room, yes. The unread ones are in the bedroom. May I see them? Of course. She picks one up from the stack on his bedside table. By now she is naked again. She does this so easily. The writer in the story is also removing his clothes. As is he himself, less gracefully perhaps than the other two. But what next? He has his hero and heroine naked in a bedroom together, and they're excited, he's excited, but the story is going nowhere. Her radiant beauty, all the more dazzling with her clothes off, has made him forget who she is. Should she be reading something? The book she has picked up, he sees, is a science fiction novel about creatures from outer space, which does not seem promising. He decides to put his clothes on again and go back to the bookstore. Luckily the chair he prefers is unoccupied and the same woman is in the chair opposite. It is all quite convenient, and he wonders for a moment if he is in a story someone else is writing. The woman asks him if he got the part for which he was auditioning and he apologizes and explains that really he is a writer, not an actor. He had been trying to invade the thoughts and feelings of his characters and became so intensely engaged with them that he got carried away and started speaking their lines out loud, but was ashamed to say so. She finds that quite amusing and says she knows how it can happen. He asks if she is also a writer and she replies that, no, she is only a reader, but she has often heard writers talk about getting confused as to what was real in their lives and what was imaginary, and sometimes something like that happens to her as a reader. He asks her if she has ever felt like she was living in somebody else's story. All the time, she says. But I'm never the main character, she adds with a sad smile. She recalls the line he spoke aloud about going for a glass of wine, and asks if that offer is still on. Soon they are both naked, lying on a mattress in her apartment, each with a glass of red wine on the floor beside them. It seems to him that it has happened as easily as in the story he is writing. She is not beautiful and the book she has been reading is a cheap romance, but he is grateful to her. The love felt between the writer, the one who is like himself and bears his name, and the beautiful reader has been consummated, and now the story can move on. She is still deliriously in love, of course, but what about him? On the one hand, he knows that he owes it to his public to remain true to his craft, undistracted by wives and lovers, and on the other, she *is* his public. The beautiful reader turns toward him with a dreamy smile. I am so honored, she whispers, and his heart melts. As am I, he murmurs, yet he understands that something has been broken between them. You are beautiful, he adds, but— and his heart aches to say so—you have ruined my story. Her smile does not change. She seems not to have heard him. Well, of course, it was not the writer in his story who said this, it was he himself. The woman lying next to him has risen, perhaps offended. She is already dressing. If you have any money, she says, I'll go buy us a pizza. He untangles his cast-off pants and fishes around in the pockets, realizing that he is indeed very hungry. In his creative throes, he has forgotten about eating.

While he's on his hands and knees doing that, she whops his behind. See what else I can ruin, she says with a crooked grin and swats it again. Mushrooms, pepperoni, sausage, extra cheese, and garlic? Great. He hands her a bill and, with a wink, sinks back on the mattress. He will leave his writer and reader to their own uncertainties. This is how a story ought to end.

Nominated by Conjunctions, Joyce Carol Oates

ISLANDS

by YUSEF KOMUNYAKAA

from POETRY

for Derek Wolcott

An island is one great eye
   gazing out, a beckoning lighthouse,
searchlight, a wishbone compass,
   or counterweight to the stars.
When it comes to outlook & point
   of view, a figure stands on a rocky ledge
peering out toward an archipelago
   of glass on the mainland, a seagull's
wings touching the tip of a high wave,
   out to where the brain may stumble.

But when a mind climbs down
   from its high craggy lookout
we know it is truly a stubborn thing,
   & has to leaf through pages of dust
& light, through pre-memory & folklore,
   remembering fires roared down there
till they pushed up through the seafloor
   & plumes of ash covered the dead
shaken awake worlds away, & silence
   filled up with centuries of waiting.

Sea urchin, turtle, & crab
   came with earthly know-how,
& one bird arrived with a sprig in its beak,
   before everything clouded with cries,
a millennium of small deaths now topsoil

& seasons of blossoms in a single seed.
Light edged along salt-crusted stones,
    across a cataract of blue water,
& lost sailors' parrots spoke of sirens,
    the last words of men buried at sea.

Someone could stand here
    contemplating the future, leafing
through torn pages of St. Augustine
    or the prophecies by fishermen,
translating spore & folly down to taproot.
    The dreamy-eyed boy still in the man,
the girl in the woman, a sunny forecast
    behind today, but tomorrow's beyond
words. To behold a body of water
    is to know pig iron & mother wit.

Whoever this figure is,
    he will soon return to dancing
through the aroma of dagger's log,
    ginger lily, & bougainvillea,
between chants & strings struck
    till gourds rally the healing air,
& till the church-steeple birds
    fly sweet darkness home.
Whoever this friend or lover is,
    he intones redemptive harmonies.

To lie down in remembrance
    is to know each of us is a prodigal
son or daughter, looking out beyond land
    & sky, the chemical & metaphysical
beyond falling & turning waterwheels
    in the colossal brain of damnable gods,
a Eureka held up to the sun's blinding eye,
    born to gaze into fire. After conquering
frontiers, the mind comes back to rest,
    stretching out over the white sand.

Nominated by Poetry

CONFESSIONS OF A RECOVERING ENVIRONMENTALIST

by PAUL KINGSNORTH

from ORION

SCENES FROM A YOUNGER LIFE # 1:

I am twelve years old. I am alone, I am scared, I am cold, and I am crying my eyes out. I can't see more than six feet in either direction. I am on some godforsaken moor high up on the dark, ancient, poisonous spine of England. The black bog juice I have been trudging through for hours has long since crept over the tops of my boots and down into my socks. My rucksack is too heavy, I am unloved and lost and I will never find my way home. It is raining and the cloud is punishing me; clinging to me, laughing at me. Twenty-five years later, I still have a felt memory of that experience and its emotions: a real despair and a terrible loneliness.

I do find my way home; I manage to keep to the path and eventually catch up with my father, who has the map and the compass and the mini Mars bars. He was always there, somewhere up ahead, but he had decided it would be good for me to "learn to keep up" with him. All of this, he tells me, will make me into a man. Needless to say, it didn't work.

Only later do I realize the complexity of the emotions summoned by a childhood laced with experiences like this. My father was a compulsive long-distance walker. Every year, throughout my most formative decade, he would take me away to Cumbria or Northumberland or Yorkshire or Cornwall or Pembrokeshire, and we would walk, for weeks. We would follow ancient tracks or new trails, across mountains and moors and ebony-black cliffs. Much of the time, we would be alone with each other and with our thoughts and our conversations, and we would be alone with the oystercatchers, the gannets, the curlews, the skylarks, and the owls. With the gale and the breeze, with our maps and compasses and emergency rations and bivy bags and plastic bottles of water. We would camp in the heather, by cairns and old mine shafts, hundreds of feet above the orange lights of civilization, and I would dream. And in the morning, with dew on the tent and cold air in my face as I opened the zip, the wild elements of life, all of the real things, would all seem to be there, waiting for me with the sunrise.

SCENES FROM A YOUNGER LIFE # 2:

I am nineteen years old. It is around midnight and I am on the summit of a low, chalk down, the last of the long chain that winds its way through the crowded, peopled, fractious south country. There are maybe fifty or sixty people there with me. There is a fire going, there are guitars, there is singing and weird and unnerving whooping noises from some of the ragged travelers who have made this place their home.

This is Twyford Down, a hilltop east of Winchester. There is something powerful about this place; something ancient and unanswering. Soon it is to be destroyed: a six-lane motorway will be driven through it in a deep chalk cutting. It is vital that this should happen in order to reduce the journey time between London and Southampton by a full thirteen minutes. The people up here have made it their home in a doomed attempt to stop this from happening.

From outside it is impossible to see, and most do not want to. The name calling has been going on for months, in the papers and the pubs and in the House of Commons. The people here are Luddites, NIMBYs ("not-in-my-backyard" grumblers), reactionaries, romantics. They are standing in the way of progress. They will not be tolerated. Inside, there is a sense of shared threat and solidarity, there are blocks of hash and packets of Rizlas and liters of bad cider. We know what we are here for. We know what we are doing. We can feel the reason in the soil and in the night air. Down there, under the lights and behind the curtains, there is no chance that they will ever understand.

Someone I don't know suggests we dance the maze. Out beyond the firelight, there is a maze carved into the down's soft, chalk turf. I don't know if it's some ancient monument or a new creation. Either way, it's the same spiral pattern that can be found carved into rocks from millennia ago. With cans and cigarettes and spliffs in our hands, a small group of us start to walk the maze, laughing, staggering, then breaking into a run, singing, spluttering, stumbling together toward the center.

SCENES FROM A YOUNGER LIFE # 3:

I am twenty-one years old and I've just spent the most exciting two months of my life so far in an Indonesian rainforest. I've just been on one of those organized expeditions that people of my age buy into to give them the chance to do something useful and exciting in what used to be called the "Third World." I've prepared for months for this. I've sold double glazing door-to-door to scrape together the cash. I have been reading Bruce Chatwin and Redmond O'Hanlon and Benedict Allen and my head is full of magic and idiocy and wonder.

During my trip, there were plenty of all of these things. I still vividly remember *klotok* journeys up Borneo rivers by moonlight, watching the swarms of giant fruit bats overhead. I remember the hooting of gibbons and the search for hornbills high up in the rainforest canopy. I remember a four-day trek through a so-called "rain" forest that was so dry we ended up drinking filtered mud. I remember turtle eggs on the beaches of Java and young orangutans at the rehabilitation center where we worked in Kalimantan, sitting in the high branches of trees with people's stolen underpants on their heads, laughing at us. I remember the gold miners and the loggers, and the freshwater crocodiles in the same river we swam in every morning. I remember my first sight of flying fish in the Java Sea.

And I remember the small islands north of Lombok, where some of us spent a few days before we came home. At night we would go down to the moonlit beach, where the sea and the air were still warm, and in the sea were millions of tiny lights: phosphorescence. I had never seen this before; never even heard of it. We would walk into the water and immerse ourselves and rise up again and the lights would cling to our bodies, fading away as we laughed.

Now, back home, the world seems changed. A two-month break from my country, my upbringing, my cultural assumptions, a two-month immersion in something far more raw and unmediated, has left me open to seeing this place as it really is. I see the atomization and the inward focus and the faces of the people in a hurry inside their cars. I see the streetlights and the asphalt as I had not quite seen them before. What I see most of all are the adverts.

For the first time, I realize the extent and the scope and the impacts of the billboards, the posters, the TV and radio ads. Everywhere an image, a phrase, a demand, or a recommendation is screaming for my attention, trying to sell me something, tell me who to be, what to desire and to need. And this is before the internet; before Apples and Black-Berries became indispensable to people who wouldn't know where to pick the real thing; before the deep, accelerating immersion of people in their technologies, even outdoors, even in the sunshine. Compared to where I have been, this world is so tamed, so mediated and com-moditized, that something within it seems to have broken off and been lost beneath the slabs. No one has noticed this, or says so if they have. Something is missing: I can almost see the gap where it used to be. But it is not remarked upon. Nobody says a thing.

WHAT TOOK HOLD

It is nine-thirty at night in mid-December at the end of the first decade of the twenty-first century. I step outside my front door into the farm-yard and walk over to the track, letting my eyes adjust to the dark. I am lucky enough to be living among the Cumbrian fells now, and as my pupils widen I can see, under a clear, starlit sky, the outline of the Old Man of Coniston, Dow Crag, Wetherlam, Helvellyn, the Fairfield Horseshoe. I stand there for ten minutes, growing colder. I see two shooting stars and a satellite. I suddenly wish my dad were still alive, and I wonder where the magic has gone.

These experiences, and others like them, were what formed me. They were what made me what I would later learn to call an "environ-mentalist": something that seemed rebellious and excitingly outsiderish when I first took it up (and that successfully horrified my social-climbing father—especially as it was partly his fault) but that these days is almost de rigueur among the British bourgeoisie. Early in my adult life, just after I came back from Twyford Down, I vowed, self-importantly, that this would be my life's work: saving nature from people. Preventing the destruction of beauty and brilliance, speaking up for the small and the overlooked and the things that could not speak for themselves. When I look back on this now, I'm quite touched by my younger self. I would like to be him again, perhaps just for a day; someone to whom all sensations are fiery and all answers are simple.

All of this—the downs, the woods, the rainforest, the great oceans, and, perhaps most of all, the silent isolation of the moors and mountains, which at the time seemed so hateful and unremitting—took hold of me somewhere unexamined. The relief I used to feel on those long trudges with my dad when I saw the lights of a village or a remote pub, even a minor road or a pylon, any sign of humanity—as I grow older this is replaced by the relief of escaping from the towns and the villages, away from the pylons and the pubs and the people, up onto the moors again, where only the ghosts and the saucer-eyed dogs and the old legends and the wind can possess me.

But they are harder to find now, those spirits. I look out across the moonlit Lake District ranges, and it's as clear as the night air that what used to come in regular waves, pounding like the sea, comes now only in flashes, out of the corner of my eyes, like a lighthouse in a storm. Perhaps it's the way the world has changed. There are more cars on the roads now, more satellites in the sky. The footpaths up the fells are like stone motorways, there are turbines on the moors, and the farmers are being edged out by south-country refugees like me, trying to escape but bringing with us the things we flee from. The new world is online and loving it, the virtual happily edging out the actual. The darkness is shut out and the night grows lighter and nobody is there to see it.

It could be all that, but it probably isn't. It's probably me. I am thirty-seven now. The world is smaller, more tired, more fragile, more horribly complex and full of troubles. Or, rather: the world is the same as it ever was, but I am more aware of it and of the reality of my place within it. I have grown up, and there is nothing to be done about it. The worst part of it is that I can't seem to look without thinking anymore. And now I know far more about what we are doing, We: the people. I know what we are doing, all over the world, to everything, all of the time. I know why the magic is dying. It's me. It's us.

HOW IT ENDED

I became an "environmentalist" because of a strong emotional reaction to wild places and the other-than-human world: to beech trees and hedgerows and pounding waterfalls, to songbirds and sunsets, to the flying fish in the Java Sea and the canopy of the rainforest at dusk when the gibbons come to the waterside to feed. From that reaction came a feeling, which became a series of thoughts: that such things are precious for their own sake, that they are food for the human soul, and that they need people to speak for them to, and defend them from, other people, because they cannot speak our language and we have forgotten how to speak theirs. And because we are killing them to feed ourselves and we know it and we care about it, sometimes, but we do it anyway because we are hungry, or we have persuaded ourselves that we are.

But these are not, I think, very common views today. Today's environmentalism is as much a victim of the contemporary cult of utility as every other aspect of our lives, from science to education. We are not environmentalists now because we have an emotional reaction to the wild world. Most of us wouldn't even know where to find it. We are environmentalists now in order to promote something called "sustainability." What does this curious, plastic word mean? It does not mean defending the non-human world from the ever-expanding empire of *Homo sapiens sapiens*, though some of its adherents like to pretend it does, even to themselves. It means sustaining human civilization at the comfort level that the world's rich people—us—feel is their right, without destroying the "natural capital" or the "resource base" that is needed to do so.

It is, in other words, an entirely human-centered piece of politicking, disguised as concern for "the planet." In a very short time—just over a decade—this worldview has become all-pervasive. It is voiced by the president of the USA and the president of Anglo-Dutch Shell and many people in between. The success of environmentalism has been total—at the price of its soul.

Let me offer up just one example of how this pact has worked. If "sustainability" is about anything, it is about carbon. Carbon and climate change. To listen to most environmentalists today, you would think that these were the only things in the world worth talking about. The business of "sustainability" is the business of preventing carbon emissions. Carbon emissions threaten a potentially massive downgrading of our prospects for material advancement as a species. They threaten to unacceptably erode our resource base and put at risk our vital hoards of natural capital. If we cannot sort this out quickly, we are going to end up darning our socks again and growing our own carrots and other such unthinkable things. All of the horrors our grandparents left behind will return like deathless legends. Carbon emissions must be "tackled" like a drunk with a broken bottle—quickly, and with maximum force.

Don't get me wrong: I don't doubt the potency of climate change to undermine the human machine. It looks to me as if it is already beginning to do so, and that it is too late to do anything but attempt to mitigate the worst effects. But what I am also convinced of is that the fear of losing both the comfort and the meaning that our civilization gifts us has gone to the heads of environmentalists to such a degree that they have forgotten everything else. The carbon must be stopped, like the Umayyad at Tours, or all will be lost.

This reductive approach to the human-environmental challenge leads to an obvious conclusion: if carbon is the problem, then "zero-carbon" is the solution. Society needs to go about its business without spewing the stuff out. It needs to do this quickly, and by any means necessary. Build enough of the right kind of energy technologies, quickly enough, to generate the power we "need" without producing greenhouse gases, and there will be no need to ever turn the lights off; no need to ever slow down.

To do this will require the large-scale harvesting of the planet's ambient energy: sunlight, wind, water power. This means that vast new conglomerations of human industry are going to appear in places where this energy is most abundant. Unfortunately, these places coincide with some of the world's wildest, most beautiful, and most untouched landscapes. The sort of places that environmentalism came into being to protect.

And so the deserts, perhaps the landscape always most resistant to permanent human conquest, are to be colonized by vast "solar arrays," glass and steel and aluminum, the size of small countries. The mountains and moors, the wild uplands, are to be staked out like vampires in the sun, their chests pierced with rows of five-hundred-foot wind turbines and associated access roads, masts, pylons, and wires. The open oceans, already swimming in our plastic refuse and emptying of marine life, will be home to enormous offshore turbine ranges and hundreds of wave machines strung around the coastlines like Victorian necklaces. The rivers are to see their estuaries severed and silted by industrial barrages. The croplands and even the rainforests, the richest habitats on this terrestrial Earth, are already highly profitable sites for biofuel plantations designed to provide guilt-free car fuel to the motion-hungry masses of Europe and America.

What this adds up to should be clear enough, yet many people who should know better choose not to see it. This is business-as-usual: the expansive, colonizing, progressive human narrative, shorn only of the carbon. It is the latest phase of our careless, self-absorbed, ambition-addled destruction of the wild, the unpolluted, and the nonhuman. It is the mass destruction of the world's remaining wild places in order to feed the human economy. And without any sense of irony, people are calling this "environmentalism."

A while back I wrote an article in a newspaper highlighting the impact of industrial wind power stations (which are usually referred to, in a nice Orwellian touch, as wind "farms") on the uplands of Britain. I was e-mailed the next day by an environmentalist friend who told me he hoped I was feeling ashamed of myself. I was wrong; worse, I was dangerous. What was I doing giving succor to the fossil fuel industry? Didn't I know that climate change would do far more damage to upland landscapes than turbines? Didn't I know that this was the only way to meet our urgent carbon targets? Didn't I see how beautiful turbines were? So much more beautiful than nuclear power stations. I might think that a "view" was more important than the future of the entire world, but this was because I was a middle-class escapist who needed to get real.

It became apparent at that point that what I saw as the next phase of the human attack on the nonhuman world a lot of my environmentalist friends saw as "progressive," "sustainable," and "green." What I called destruction they called "large-scale solutions." This stuff was realistic, necessarily urgent. It went with the grain of human nature and the market, which as we now know are the same thing. We didn't have time to "romanticize" the woods and the hills. There were emissions to reduce, and the end justified the means.

It took me a while to realize where this kind of talk took me back to: the maze and the moonlit hilltop. This desperate scrabble for "sustainable development" was in reality the same old same old. People I had thought were on my side were arguing aggressively for the industrializing of wild places in the name of human desire. This was the same rootless, distant destruction that had led me to the top of Twyford Down. Only now there seemed to be some kind of crude equation at work that allowed them to believe this was something entirely different. Motorway through downland: bad. Wind power station on downland: good. Container port wiping out estuary mudflats: bad. Renewable hydropower barrage wiping out estuary mudflats: good. Destruction minus carbon equals sustainability.

So here I was again: a Luddite, a NIMBY, a reactionary, a romantic; standing in the way of progress. I realized that I was dealing with environmentalists with no attachment to any actual environment. Their talk was of parts-per-million of carbon, peer-reviewed papers, sustainable technologies, renewable super-grids, green growth, and the fifteenth conference of the parties. There were campaigns about "the planet" and "the Earth," but there was no specificity: no sign of any real, felt attachment to any small part of that Earth.

THE PLACE OF NATURE

Back at university, in love with my newfound radicalism, as students tend to be, I started to read things. Not the stuff I was supposed to be reading about social movements and pre-Reformation Europe, but green political thought: wild ideas I had never come across before. I could literally feel my mind levering itself open. Most exciting to me were the implications of a new word I stumbled across: *ecocentrism*. This word crystallized everything I had been feeling for years. I had no idea there were words for it or that other people felt it too, or had written intimidating books about it. The nearest I had come to such a realization thus far was reading Wordsworth as a teenager and feeling an excited tingling sensation as I began to understand what he was getting at among all those poems about shepherds and girls called Lucy. Here was a kindred spirit! Here was a man moved to love and fear by mountains, who believed rocks had souls, that "Nature never did betray the heart that loved her" (though even then that sounded a little optimistic to me). *Pantheism* was my new word that year.

Now I declared, to myself if no one else, that I was "ecocentric" too. This was not the same as being egocentric, though some disagreed, and while it sounded a bit too much like "eccentric," this was also a distraction. I was ecocentric because I did not believe—had never believed, I didn't think—that humans were the center of the world, that the Earth was their playground, that they had the right to do what they liked, or even that what they did was that important. I thought we were part of something bigger, which had as much right to the world as we did, and which we were stomping on for our own benefit. I had always been haunted by shameful thoughts like this. It had always seemed to me that the beauty to be found on the trunk of a birch tree was worth any number of *Mona Lisa*s, and that a Saturday night sunset was better than Saturday night telly. It had always seemed that most of what mattered to me could not be counted or corralled by the kind of people who thought, and still think, that I just needed to grow up.

It had been made clear to me for a long time that these feelings were at best charmingly naïve and at worst backward and dangerous. Later, the dismissals became encrusted with familiar words, designed to keep the ship of human destiny afloat: romantic, Luddite, NIMBY, and the like. For now, though, I had found my place. I was a young, fiery, radical, ecocentric environmentalist, and I was going to save the world.

When I look back on the road protests of the mid-1990s, which I often do, it is with nostalgia and fondness and a sense of gratitude that I was able to be there, to see what I saw and do what I did. But I realize now that it is more than this that makes me think and talk and write about Twyford Down to an extent that bores even my patient friends. This, I think, was the last time I was part of an environmental movement that was genuinely environmental. The people involved were, like me, ecocentric: they didn't see "the environment" as something "out there"; separate from people, to be utilized or destroyed or protected according to human whim. They saw themselves as part of it, within it, of it.

There was a Wordsworthian feel to the whole thing: the defense of the trees simply because they were trees. Living under the stars and in the rain, in the oaks and in the chaotic, miraculous tunnels beneath them, in the soil itself like the rabbits and the badgers. We were connected to a place; a real place that we loved and had made a choice to belong to, if only for a short time. There was little theory, much action, but even more simple being. Being in a place, knowing it, standing up for it. It was environmentalism at its rawest, and the people who came to be part of it were those who loved the land, in their hearts as well as their heads.

In years to come, this was worn away. It took a while before I started to notice what was happening, but when I did it was all around me. The ecocentrism—in simple language, the love of place, the humility, the sense of belonging, the *feelings*—was absent from most of the "environmentalist" talk I heard around me. Replacing it were two other kinds of talk. One was the save-the-world-with-wind-farms narrative; the same old face in new makeup. The other was a distant, somber sound: the marching boots and rattling swords of an approaching fifth column.

Environmentalism, which in its raw, early form had no time for the encrusted, seized-up politics of left and right, offering instead a worldview that saw the growth economy and the industrialist mentality beloved by both as the problem in itself, was now being sucked into the yawning, bottomless chasm of the "progressive" left. Suddenly, people like me, talking about birch trees and hilltops and sunsets, were politely, or less politely, elbowed to one side by people who were bringing a "class analysis" to green politics.

All this talk of nature, it turned out, was bourgeois, Western, and unproductive. It was a middle-class conceit, and there was nothing worse than a middle-class conceit. The workers had no time for thoughts like this (though no one bothered to notify the workers themselves that they were simply clodhopping, nature-loathing cannon fodder in a political flame war). It was terribly, *objectively* right wing. Hitler liked nature after all. He was a vegetarian too. It was all deeply "problematic."

More problematic for me was what this kind of talk represented. With the near global failure of the left-wing project over the past few decades, green politics was fast becoming a refuge for disillusioned socialists, Trots, Marxists, and a ragbag of fellow travelers who could no longer believe in communism or the Labour Party or even George Galloway, and who saw in green politics a promising bolthole. In they all trooped, with their Stop-the-War banners and their Palestinian solidarity scarves, and with them they brought a new sensibility.

Now it seemed that environmentalism was not about wildness or ecocentrism or the other-than-human world and our relationship to it. Instead it was about (human) social justice and (human) equality and (human) progress and ensuring that all these things could be realized without degrading the (human) resource base that we used to call nature back when we were being naïve and problematic. Suddenly, never-ending economic growth was a good thing after all: the poor needed it to get rich, which was their right. To square the circle, for those who still realized there was a circle, we were told that "social justice and environmental justice go hand in hand"—a suggestion of such bizarre inaccuracy that it could surely only be wishful thinking.

Suddenly, sustaining a global human population of 10 billion people was not a problem at all, and anyone who suggested otherwise was not highlighting any obvious ecological crunch points but was giving succor to fascism or racism or gender discrimination or orientalism or essentialism or some other such hip and largely unexamined concept. The "real issue," it seemed, was not the human relationship with the nonhuman world; it was fat cats and bankers and cap'lism. These things must be destroyed, by way of marches, protests, and votes for fringe political parties, to make way for something known as "eco-socialism":

411

a conflation of concepts that pretty much guarantees the instant hostility of 95 percent of the population.

I didn't object to this because I thought that environmentalism should occupy the right rather than the left wing, or because I was right-wing myself, which I wasn't (these days I tend to consider the entire bird with a kind of frustrated detachment). And I understood that there was at least a partial reason for the success of this colonization of the greens by the reds. Modern environmentalism sprang partly from the early-twentieth-century conservation movement, and that movement had often been about preserving supposedly pristine landscapes at the expense of people. Forcing tribal people from their ancestral lands, which had been newly designated as national parks, for example, in order to create a fictional "untouched nature" had once been fairly common, from Africa to the USA. And, actually, Hitler had been something of an environmentalist, and the wellsprings that nourished some green thought nourished the thought of some other unsavory characters too (a fact that some ideologues love to point to when witch-hunting the greens, as if it wouldn't be just as easy to point out that ideas of equality and justice fueled Stalin and Pol Pot).

In this context it was fair enough to assert that environmentalism allied itself with ideas of justice and decency, and that it was about people as well as everything else on the planet. Of course it was, for "nature" as something separate from people has never existed. We are nature, and the environmentalist project was always supposed to be about how we are to be part of it, to live well as part of it, to understand and respect it, to understand our place within it, and to feel it as part of ourselves.

So there was a reason for environmentalism's shift to the left, just as there was a reason for its blinding obsession with carbon. Meanwhile, the fact of what humans are doing to the world became so obvious, even to those who were doing very well from it, that it became hard not to listen to the greens. Success duly arrived. You can't open a newspaper now or visit a corporate website or listen to a politician or read the label on a packet of biscuits without being bombarded with propaganda about the importance of "saving the planet." But there is a terrible hollowness to it all, a sense that society is going through the motions without understanding why. The shift, the pact, has come at a probably fatal price.

Now that price is being paid. The weird and unintentional pincer movement of the failed left, with its class analysis of waterfalls and fresh air, and the managerial, *carbon-über-alles* brigade has infiltrated, ironed out, and reworked environmentalism for its own ends. Now it is not about the ridiculous beauty of coral, the mist over the fields at dawn. It is not about ecocentrism. It is not about reforging a connection between overcivilized people and the world outside their windows. It is not about living close to the land or valuing the world for the sake of the world. It is not about attacking the self-absorbed conceits of the bubble that our civilization has become.

Today's environmentalism is about people. It is a consolation prize for a gaggle of washed-up Trots and, at the same time, with an amusing irony, it is an adjunct to hypercapitalism: the catalytic converter on the silver SUV of the global economy. It is an engineering challenge: a problem-solving device for people to whom the sight of a wild Pennine hilltop on a clear winter day brings not feelings of transcendence but thoughts about the wasted potential for renewable energy. It is about saving civilization from the results of its own actions: a desperate attempt to prevent Gaia from hiccupping and wiping out our coffee shops and broadband connections. It is our last hope.

THE OPEN LAND

I generalize, of course. Environmentalism's chancel is as accommodating as that of socialism, anarchism, or conservatism, and just as capable of generating poisonous internal bickering that will last until the death of the sun. Many who call themselves green have little time for the mainstream line I am attacking here. But it is the mainstream line. It is how most people see environmentalism today, even if it is not how all environmentalists intend it to be seen. These are the arguments and the positions that popular environmentalism—now a global force—offers up in its quest for redemption. There are reasons; there are always reasons. But whatever they are, they have led the greens down a dark, litter-strewn, dead-end street where the rubbish bins overflow, the light bulbs have blown, and the stray dogs are very hungry indeed.

What is to be done about this? Probably nothing. It was, perhaps, inevitable that a utilitarian society would generate a utilitarian environmentalism, and inevitable too that the greens would not be able to last for long outside the established political bunkers. But for me—well, this is no longer mine, that's all. I can't make my peace with people who cannibalize the land in the name of saving it. I can't speak the language of science without a corresponding poetry. I can't speak with a straight

413

face about saving the planet when what I really mean is saving myself from what is coming.

Like all of us, I am a foot soldier of empire. It is the empire of *Homo sapiens sapiens* and it stretches from Tasmania to Baffin Island. Like all empires, it is built on expropriation and exploitation, and like all empires it dresses these things up in the language of morality and duty. When we turn wilderness over to agriculture, we speak of our duty to feed the poor. When we industrialize the wild places, we speak of our duty to stop the climate from changing. When we spear whales, we speak of our duty to science. When we raze forests, we speak of our duty to develop. We alter the atmospheric makeup of the entire world: half of us pretend it's not happening, the other half immediately start looking for new machines that will reverse it. This is how empires work, particularly when they have started to decay. Denial, displacement, anger, fear.

The environment is the victim of this empire. But the "environment"—that distancing word, that empty concept—does not exist. It is the air, the waters, the creatures we make homeless or lifeless in flocks and legions, and it is us too. We are it; we are in it and of it, we make it and live it, we are fruit and soil and tree, and the things done to the roots and the leaves come back to us. We make ourselves slaves to make ourselves free, and when the shackles start to rub we confidently predict the emergence of new, more comfortable designs.

I don't have any answers, if by answers we mean political systems, better machines, means of engineering some grand shift in consciousness. All I have is a personal conviction built on those feelings, those responses, that goes back to the moors of northern England and the rivers of southern Borneo—that something big is being missed. That we are both hollow men and stuffed men, and that we will keep stuffing ourselves until the food runs out, and if outside the dining room door we have made a wasteland and called it necessity, then at least we will know we were not to blame, because we are never to blame, because we are the humans.

What am I to do with feelings like these? Useless feelings in a world in which everything must be made useful. Sensibilities in a world of utility. Feelings like this provide no "solutions." They build no new eco-homes, remove no carbon from the atmosphere. This is head-in-the-clouds stuff, as relevant to our busy, modern lives as the new moon or the date of the harvest. Easy to ignore, easy to dismiss, like the places that inspire the feelings, like the world outside the bubble, like the people who have seen it, if only in brief flashes beyond the ridge of some dark line of hills.

But this is fine—the dismissal, the platitudes, the brusque moving-on of the grown-ups. It's all fine. I withdraw, you see. I withdraw from the campaigning and the marching, I withdraw from the arguing and the talked-up necessity and all of the false assumptions. I withdraw from the words. I am leaving. I am going to go out walking.

I am leaving on a pilgrimage to find what I left behind in the jungles and by the cold campfires and in the parts of my head and my heart that I have been skirting around because I have been busy fragmenting the world in order to save it; busy believing it is mine to save. I am going to listen to the wind and see what it tells me, or whether it tells me anything at all. You see, it turns out that I have more time than I thought. I will follow the songlines and see what they sing to me and maybe, one day, I might even come back. And if I am very lucky I might bring with me a harvest of fresh tales, which I can scatter like apple seeds across this tired and angry land.

Nominated by Orion

WAYS TO BEGIN
A POEM

by RACHEL ROSE

from SONG & SPECTACLE (Harbour Publishing)

1.

Begin at the source. Open the book of thyself,
contentious one, thy book in four chapters, four scrolls.
Rise on your own yeast. Spill your villanelles'
hot vowels. You will not go
blind. Though imagine what you might see
if you did.

2.

Begin with a friend (a writer) playing a board game
at a party. Question: something found in a desk
that starts with J. His answer: Jizm. Haiku the difference
between men and women. Stray red leaf.

3.

Begin with seed, then. The way we touch each
other. Flipped: a car on fire after a game involving men
in padded suits. Brute mob drenched in fuel. Saltpeter.

Fertilized papyrus
of undecipherable texts. Ink licked to language,
stanza after stanza of buttons popped. Terza rima
of nipples, navel, quilt washed in light.

Outside bombs dismantle a station. Somewhere else
not here. Begin again, please. Pantoum communion.
To be written, to be folded into shapes
suited to the poem. Smell of a river waiting for salmon.

Not here. Begin again, please. Pantoum: come
inside my body. Joy of song without words
suited to the poem. Smell of a river waiting for salmon.
Silhouette of your form against a torn white curtain.

Poem of thy creases. O where have you been, sweet
reeking ballad monster? Pray
that tomorrow will know by heart
today. Begin by holding hands
under the table. A hip kisses a tambourine.
A troubadour is condemned for her troubles.
Our love meets in the ruins of a castle
full of ravens. We

buy daffodils, we play the cello badly but with joy.
We grow yellow tomatoes. We let them cut us open,
we put children in the garden. Remembering the loneliness
of the lunch room, we decide not to have children.
If the form can be found, there may be salvation.
There are lilacs. Lilacs have form. It is quiet

but for the poem's gasp. We bone thrust until we bruise
apart. Naked in the kitchen, we slice chanterelles for dinner,
add a fistlump of butter, crushed sage. Fragrance enters
your hair. My own. Is there one god, or many? Evening star
sings forth a thousand more in the pale green mosque
of the sky. Stretch marks. Two lemons on a table. Still life.
Begin with the body, poisoned to save the body.
Tragicomedy. The form.

Nominated by Harbour Publishing

IN COLORADO
MY FATHER SCOURED
AND STACKED DISHES

by EDUARDO C. CORRAL

from POETRY

in a Tex-Mex restaurant. His co-workers,
unable to utter his name, renamed him Jalapeño.

If I ask for a goldfish, he spits a glob of phlegm
into a jar of water. The silver letters

on his black belt spell *Sangrón*. Once, borracho,
at dinner, he said: Jesus wasn't a snowman.

Arriba Durango. Arriba Orizaba. Packed
into a car trunk, he was smuggled into the States.

Frijolero. Greaser. In Tucson he branded
cattle. He slept in a stable. The horse blankets

oddly fragrant: wood smoke, lilac. He's an illegal.
I'm an Illegal-American. Once, in a grove

of saguaro, at dusk, I slept next to him. I woke
with his thumb in my mouth. ¿No qué no

419

tronabas, pistolita? He learned English
by listening to the radio. The first four words

he memorized: In God We Trust. The fifth:
Percolate. Again and again I borrow his clothes.

He calls me Scarecrow. In Oregon he picked apples.
Braeburn. Jonagold. Cameo. Nightly,

to entertain his cuates, around a campfire,
he strummed a guitarra, sang corridos. Arriba

Durango. Arriba Orizaba. Packed into
a car trunk, he was smuggled into the States.

Greaser. Beaner. Once, borracho, at breakfast,
he said: The heart can only be broken

once, like a window. ¡No mames! His favorite
belt buckle: an águila perched on a nopal.

If he laughs out loud, his hands tremble.
Bugs Bunny wants to deport him. César Chávez

wants to deport him. When I walk through
the desert, I wear his shirt. The gaze of the moon

stitches the buttons of his shirt to my skin.
The snake hisses. The snake is torn.

Nominated by Maxine Scates

HOUSEBREAKING

fiction by SARAH FRISCH

from THE PARIS REVIEW

Nothing is lost, and all is won, by a right estimate of what is real.
    —Mary Baker Eddy, Science and Health with Key to the Scriptures

Seamus lived in Wheaton, Maryland, in the last house on a quiet street that dead-ended at a county park. He'd bought the entire property, including a rental unit out back, at a decent price. This was after the housing market crashed but before people knew how bad it would get—back when he was still a practicing Christian Scientist, still had a job and a girlfriend he'd assumed he would marry. Now, two years later, he was single, faithless, and unemployed. The money his mother had loaned him for a down payment was starting to look more like a gift, as were the checks she'd been sending for the last year to help him cover the mortgage. His life was in disrepair, but for the first time in months he wasn't thinking about any of that: he was sitting out back on a warm spring day with a woman. Her name was Charity, and she was a stranger.

Earlier that afternoon Seamus had been weeding by the driveway, and she'd stopped to ask him if the cottage in the backyard was available to rent. It was already rented, but soon they were on his deck, talking and sharing a six-pack Charity had been carrying and that she confessed she'd planned on drinking alone.

She wore cutoffs and a backpack—a faded green thing cinched around her waist. She had yellow hair, dark eyes, and a broad, easy smile that made it seem as if she would be perfectly comfortable anywhere but was especially pleased to find herself there, with him. He wasn't a drinker, but in her presence he drank one beer and then another. By the third beer, he both wanted her desperately and suspected that no good could come of it—that to hunger for what you could touch was to invite disaster.

Charity lived in Arlington, with her ex-boyfriend and his aging mother. They'd been together ten years, she said, and the breakup was a rough one. She was trying to find a place as far away from them as possible but still on the Metro. "I just need to be out of that house," she said, offering Seamus the last beer.

He said he was already drunk.

"You're pretty tall for that," she said. "You must not drink a lot."

"I used to be a Christian Scientist." He regretted the words as soon they were out of his mouth. People mixed Christian Science up with Scientology, or said things like, Is that the religion where you don't believe in doctors?—as if he had refused to acknowledge doctors' very existence.

Charity said that she'd had a Christian Science friend in high school; the religion had always reminded her of Buddhism. Buddhism had always reminded Seamus of Christian Science, and he said so. "Only Christian Science is unrelentingly positive. The world's a harmonious place."

"I imagine that's a hard view to maintain," Charity said, "once you start looking around,"

Yes, he said, it was.

Even after Seamus stopped taking care of his house, he had kept up the exterior for his tenants. Now, in the late-afternoon light, he could see how pretty the backyard looked: the little brick pathway that led to the blue and white cottage tucked back among the trees, beyond that the woods, shimmering green and gold in the late-afternoon sun.

"My ex's house has the gravitational pull of a black hole," Charity said. "I can't believe I'm still here."

"Congratulations," Seamus said. Then he asked her to stay for dinner.

For months Seamus's friends had been telling him he was depressed, and as soon as he stepped into his kitchen he saw what they meant: shades drawn, empty takeout boxes piled in the trash, the refrigerator looming in the dim light like a grimy white thumb. A year ago, he used to cook every night, but now all he could find was a package of ground beef rotting in the crisper and a can of pumpkin sitting inexplicably on the bottom shelf. In the freezer he located a month-old chicken and a stick of butter that he had bought one afternoon in a bout of hopefulness so brief that it had passed by the time he got home.

He defrosted the chicken in the microwave, sliced butter and stuffed it under the skin, and slid the whole thing into the oven to roast. When he turned around, Charity was standing so close behind him that he almost jumped. She had on her backpack. "I should leave."

"Don't."

"I'm kind of a mess right now. You don't need that."

"Don't tell me what I need," he said, surprised by how forceful he sounded. She looked surprised, too, but when he reached out and pulled her toward him, she grinned.

He almost cried when he saw her body. He was dizzy with longing and something that felt like fear. Afterward they lay in the dimming light of the room, her arm across his chest, her breathing slowing until he thought she was asleep. It occurred to him that for all those years when he'd believed there was no life in matter, he'd never had to contend with something that felt this good.

They lay in silence until her phone rang. She dug it out of her cutoffs and silenced it. "I don't want to go back to that hellhole," she said.

"Stay here till you find a place," Seamus heard himself say.

"I didn't mean it like that." She looked embarrassed, as if he had accused her of something.

"Everybody needs help."

"It seems like a bad idea," she said, quietly.

Seamus said he was trying to be more open to bad ideas.

When she accepted, it was with such obvious relief that he wished he'd offered the instant they'd met. Soon the smell of roast chicken filled the house, and they got dressed and returned to the kitchen, where they tore apart the bird and finished off the last of the beer, piling the bottles, sweaty with chicken fat, into the recycling.

On the couch after dinner, they talked about real estate. Seamus said he wasn't comfortable being a landlord because he didn't like living off somebody else's work. His tenants—Irene and Claudia, a lawyer and her ten-year-old daughter—were rarely at home, and he hated charging a single mom to rent a place she didn't use. He said that his mother was helping with the rest of the mortgage while he looked for work, and he'd begun to dread their weekly phone conversations because he found it so hard to admit, yet again, that he hadn't found a job. His mother would tell him what she always did: he was secure in the arms of unconditional Love; the Lord would provide. When her checks arrived in the mail, he put them immediately into envelopes so he didn't have to stare at the numbers, or her signature, or the Bible verses she always wrote in the memo lines.

His mother was a third grade teacher, and he knew that the money was most likely coming from her new husband, a Republican who owned rental property all over Honolulu. He didn't tell Charity about the husband.

"It's been humbling taking money from other people," he said.

Charity said she thought it was nice that he could admit that—that there was a time when Greg and his mother had provided for her, and she'd also found it humbling, especially because she'd been on her own for a few years by then.

She had her bare feet up on the coffee table. There was a streak of dirt on her calf that he hadn't noticed in bed. She told him she'd grown up in Bridgeport, Connecticut. Her mother had died when she was twelve. She'd gone to live with an aunt, then at fifteen moved to D.C., where she'd lived with her father for six months before he'd gotten a job as a construction worker overseas. A year later she met Greg at the restaurant where she waited tables. He was twenty-four at the time and had initially acted as both a boyfriend and mentor. He'd encouraged her to move in with him and his mother, pushed her to quit her job, to finish high school and then college. They became her replacement family, she said. Sometimes they still made her feel like a child. "It wasn't until the last couple of years that I realized how overbearing he was. He was furious when I decided to go to business school, and even madder when I took the job in public relations."

"You work in PR?"

"It's an exclusive firm. We only take clients who can demonstrate a total absence of social conscience."

"That's not what I expected," he said, suddenly awkward. "I imagined you were a teacher or an artist."

"You're looking at Weekend Charity. Wait till you see me in a suit."

He asked why she'd chosen to work with her company, and she shrugged and said that she'd mostly taken the job to piss off Greg. "We do PR for the Chamber of Commerce, the biggest lobbying group against climate-change legislation. He can't stand that."

"He's an environmentalist?"

"He calls himself 'pro–Earth life.' He says either you're for humans living on the planet or you're against it."

She crossed her feet. Outside the sky was dark, a single light on in the cottage.

"Half our clients are scrapping the planet for parts," she said.

"That's terrible."

424

"But the people aren't all bad, and I enjoy a lot of the work. Plus it's not like there's anything else out there."

"Tell me about it," Seamus said.

Charity said she'd turned down only one project. Her boss had asked her to write a press release for Halliburton after the news broke that a group of its employees gang-raped a coworker and locked her in a shipping crate. "I said no way, and they gave it to another woman. Now she's a VP. She's so smug about it I could punch her in the face."

That night they slept together in his bed, the window cracked open, the smell of the woods carried in on the wind: dampness and new growth, the early spring. Seamus drifted off with Charity's head on his shoulder and woke sometime before dawn to find her sleeping heavily on her stomach, her arms out and back bare and pale in the gray light, the white sheet twisted around her waist as if she'd lashed herself to the bed.

His last job had been in the tech department at a human-rights nonprofit in D.C. He was still a practicing Christian Scientist at the time, but even then he struggled to understand how so much suffering could exist in a world governed by a set of harmonious natural laws. He tried not to dwell on the stories his coworkers told, but sometimes he'd come home too upset to even pray. He would feel better only after going to church, or on the rare occasions his girlfriend convinced him to attend a Wednesday testimony meeting.

He'd been with the organization for a couple of years when his boss asked if he would go on a trip to Pakistan to document civilian deaths from U.S. drone attacks. The videographer had come down with shingles. Seamus had always assumed his first trip out of the country would be somewhere in Europe—visiting castles, staying in hostels, sleeping on trains. "I have some experience in video," he said.

"I don't know how much you'll be able to film," his boss said. "But given the area we think it's probably a good idea to have a man along."

Three days later Seamus found himself sitting in a row of blue vinyl airport seats on a layover in Doha, Qatar, a city he'd never heard of in a country he'd never heard of, his Bible and *Science and Health* stashed in his carry-on along with the Islamabad travel guide.

The woman he was traveling with was in her midfifties, with silver hair cut bluntly at the jaw, so straight it could have been ironed. Her name was Melinda. She had pale green eyes, translucent and eerily unyielding, the backs of them like the marbled walls of an antique swimming pool. She was a mother of three.

"They're around your age," she said. "My eldest is a lawyer. My middle son is a writer."

"It must be nice to have brothers."

"They're good support for each other."

He asked what her youngest son did.

"He's dead. He was murdered when he was fifteen."

"I'm sorry."

Melinda nodded, looking away.

A friend of Seamus's mother had a three-year-old daughter who drowned in a river at a family reunion. Seamus remembered the woman weeping at their kitchen table, saying that losing your child was like being sliced and gutted, then made to walk around as if you were whole. His mother had taken the woman in her arms, but even then (he was only ten) he could see she didn't quite know what to do. He had watched the woman weep, wondering why his mother didn't say the things she always said when he cried: God was Love, they were all safe in His loving arms.

Melinda had bent down and was rummaging around in her carry-on. She pulled out what he thought would be a photo but turned out to be a map of Pakistan.

"This is where we're going," she said, running her finger along a region labeled *Federally Administered Tribal Areas.* "Did you do the reading?"

"I did," he said. She looked pleased and a little surprised, so he felt compelled to give her a full report. He told her how un-American the whole thing seemed: an intelligence agency killing hundreds of civilians in a non-combat zone of a country that was supposed to be an ally; the CIA director denying the existence of the program; the "double tap" policy of firing two missiles in the same spot, the second strike carefully timed to incinerate first responders—health-care workers, neighbors searching for children in their beds. Even the malicious and weirdly boyish names of the aircraft themselves—*Predator and Reaper drones*, the *Hellfire missiles* they carried—had unnerved him, as if the government could barely contain its glee at the prospect of murdering people by joystick.

"Seems pretty American to me," she said. "But I suppose you know that."

"There's knowing and there's *knowing*."

"That's why we're hoping for video."

Seamus made a point from one of the readings, that the civilian deaths and constant terror caused by hovering drones must be working against U.S. interests in the region.

"I hate that argument," Melinda said. "People have a right to life outside our political agenda."

He knew she was right. They passed the rest of the layover in silence.

In Islamabad they spent a few days getting ready. The sprawling flatness of the city surprised Seamus: its broad parkways and trees planted in rows, the scattering of high-rises downtown, like enormous outdated computer chips turned on their ends. Parts of the city seemed like shabbier and sweatier versions of Denver. He couldn't help feeling disappointed. On the streets people stared.

"They don't see a lot of Westerners?" he asked Melinda.

She laughed—the first time he'd heard her laugh. "Not a lot of guys your size around here."

She'd been crammed into an airplane seat next to him, but the idea of her thinking about his size felt oddly like a violation.

Melinda had arranged for them to travel illegally, with two Pakistani human-rights workers as their guides. On the second day Seamus and Melinda met the men in the hotel lobby. They were younger than Seamus expected, in their late twenties. They clearly considered Seamus the leader of the trip and directed most of their conversation to him, even after he announced that Melinda was in charge. Melinda seemed unsurprised by this state of affairs. She watched quietly as they spoke. Every now and then she asked a question that never would have occurred to Seamus. (Will we be allowed to film? *Not always.* How can we interview women if our translator is a man? *You can't.*)

The men dispensed a lot of advice: Say you're British, not American; Don't play the radio in the car; If you see a woman, turn your eyes away, and whatever you do, never touch a woman, not even to shake hands; The same man who is your enemy and intends to redress a wrong by shooting you dead is honor-bound to protect you when you set foot in his home, even at risk of harm to his family.

One of the men began explaining how to handle expensive camera equipment in such an impoverished area, and then stopped, saying to Seamus, "But you must be experienced filming in these kind of conditions." Seamus couldn't bring himself to correct him.

Later Melinda and Seamus went shopping for supplies at Jinnah Super—a two-story, open-air structure with rows of tiny stores—then stopped for a burger and fries at a food stall. While they ate, Melinda told him about women's rights in the tribal areas: honor killings, men throwing acid on young girls' faces whom they suspected of learning to read.

She had once documented an honor killing in Jordan involving a young woman whose aunts had escorted her into an open field so her little brother could shoot her in the back of the head. "The family seemed quite proud," she said.

Seamus imagined the aunts walking one on either side of the girl, stepping silently away as the boy appeared from behind.

Melinda finished off her burger and started on the fries. "It's hard to separate it all out. I'll have to remind myself we're there for the drones."

Seamus's left foot had been itching since he got off the plane, and now it ached. He leaned over and removed his hiking boot. A small red recess the size of a dime had appeared on the arch of his foot. He pressed it with his thumb, and pain rippled up his ankle.

"What's that?" Melinda asked, her green eyes on his face.

"I don't know."

"It's probably the boot."

Seamus recognized in her voice a judicial finality. Exonerated: the country, the city, the climate. At fault: Seamus—for having worn hiking boots to a city that (as she had said twice since they arrived) was one of the most cosmopolitan in South Asia.

Neither of them mentioned the foot again, and the rest of the day he limped along behind her, trying to ignore the pain. Back in the hotel room that evening, he stripped off his sock and found the infection had eaten away at his flesh; the hole in his arch was hot and red and almost twice the size it had been earlier that afternoon.

He got out his books and opened *Science and Health* to one of his favorite quotes—"Divine Love always has met and always will meet every human need." He had once believed that the material world was a dream, his own sensations and experiences shadow puppets on a curtain: projections of that infinite unknowable space where all broken things were in fact whole, where the world existed as it always had and always would, in love and infinite unity. Back then he could live in the dream, even enjoy the dream, but he knew that what he saw was not real, and he should work to recognize the harmony and perfection of all things. When he was sick or injured he prayed to know that he was healthy and whole, and then sooner or later he would become healthy and whole again.

He put down the book and lay back, closing his eyes. The pain in his foot was hot and frightening—a much bigger pain than he would have expected from a small crevice of inflamed skin. It disoriented him, as did the tiny, dank hotel room, and the knowledge that he was halfway across the world from home, his only companion a woman he hardly knew. He thought if he took a painkiller he might be able to pray without distraction, but he didn't have one and didn't want to bother Melinda. He turned out the light and lay a long time staring into the shadows. Soon the day's final call to prayer sounded over the tinny loudspeaker. While thousands of people washed their faces and forearms and feet and pulled out their mats, Seamus closed his eyes and tried to sleep.

The next morning he couldn't stand on his foot.

Later he wondered what would have happened if he hadn't agreed to let Melinda take him to the doctor. Maybe he would have been able to heal himself through prayer, as he'd been able to a number of times before, or maybe the foot would have gotten worse and he would have flown back home—back to his job and girlfriend and state of mild but workable confusion about the nature of the world and his place in it. Instead he found himself standing outside a large house, near the foothills on the edge of the city.

The doctor was a friend of Melinda's, a middle-aged Dutch expat. "You're a lucky man," he told Seamus. "I know people who'd pay good money to travel with this lady."

They followed him upstairs, past a servant on the landing, and entered a room that reminded Seamus of an ad in a magazine— a study with a leather couch, French doors, a balcony that looked out over a sparkling pool, and beyond that, the green rolling hills north of the city. The doctor sat Seamus down on the couch and gently lifted his bare foot into his lap, walking a pair of plump dry fingers along the arch.

"Is it infected?"

"No. Just the worst case of athlete's foot I've ever seen."

Melinda stood looking out over the balcony, her shoulders squared and prosaic beside the French doors. Seamus examined her back for signs of laughter.

"A topical cream and an oral antifungal should take care of it," the doctor said.

Afterward, a servant brought them tea around a small table, and the doctor and Melinda talked about their years working at an NGO together in Bangladesh. Eventually Melinda said, "We better get to the pharmacy before it closes."

Seamus had taken medication only once—antibiotics when he was a child, which he took for a chest cough that turned out to be pneumonia—and only after his mother realized that her overwhelming fear had prevented the infection from healing. Now, back in the tiny hotel room, he took out his texts and copied down a couple of his favorite lines:

God changeth not and causeth no evil, disease, nor death;

That I may dwell in the house of the Lord all the days of my life, to behold the beauty of the Lord, and to inquire in His temple.

The air conditioner sputtered beside him, pumping damp air into the room. He could hear the TV in Melinda's room next door and a bus idling heavily in the street below. He stared at the words on the page. Then he took the medicine. By the time he woke up the next morning his foot had already started to heal.

Sunday morning Seamus woke to find Charity sitting on the edge of the bed. "I'm running over to Virginia to pick up some work clothes," she said. "I'll be back this afternoon—unless Greg chains me to a radiator."

Seamus asked if she'd like him to go with her, and she shook her head. She was joking; she really wasn't worried. Greg was like a child; she could always stick him in a time-out if he got out of hand. As soon as she was gone, it occurred to Seamus that she might be making her escape, and he had no way to reach her; he didn't even know her last name. Still he went about his day as if he'd be seeing her in a few hours. He spent most of the morning cleaning the house, and in the afternoon he shopped for groceries, buying meat and vegetables and vodka and tonic because Charity had mentioned it was her drink—feeling sheepish and giddy at the checkout as he watched the bottles shuttle down the belt to the register.

Charity arrived at six, wearing an old sweatshirt of his that he hadn't realized she'd taken. She was carrying a large duffle.

"You're back," he said.

He must have sounded surprised because she laughed. "It looks great in here."

He put the steaks on the grill out back and came in to start on the salad. She made them both drinks and leaned on the counter, watching while he worked.

"You're a bear of a man," she said. "Do you love women?"

He'd been drinking too fast and he was sweating. He said he was raised to love everybody.

"Good. Because from what I can tell when a guy says he loves women, he just means he likes cunnilingus and feeling in control."

"Sheesh," he said, embarrassed for them both.

They stayed talking at the table long after dinner. Seamus asked about her ex-boyfriend, trying to keep his tone casual.

"It just took me a while to realize our relationship was dead," she said, "and even longer to move out. He's not an easy person. He manages a Verizon store, but he makes his real money breaking into houses. He doesn't believe in government or owning things. He says the laws are designed by people with power to protect their power. We used to fight about it. Where I come from people work hard for their shit and you're supposed to respect that. I told him stealing stuff out of a house was a violation of a person's intimate space. By then I was getting my MBA, and he said he was offended that me and my vagina were so overly privileged that we were equating taking people's property with rape." She frowned. "As if I had said that—as if not being raped is a fucking privilege."

Seamus, not knowing what to say, made them each another drink.

"In the end I managed to find a place, but on the day before I was going to sign the lease his mother broke her hip. Greg's gone a lot at night and the old lady couldn't stay home alone—and he begged me to stay around and help. So I did. I waited on her hand and foot. Then a week ago I came home early from work and caught her downstairs with her potter's wheel strapped to a dolly, dragging it across the living room." She quickly added, "It was a portable potter's wheel. God knows how she got it on the dolly. Even the portable ones weigh like fifty pounds."

"With her broken hip?"

"They faked it to keep me there. I'm telling you, that house is unhealthy."

Seamus got drunker and drunker as the evening progressed. Charity was drinking, too, but showed no signs besides two patches of pink that appeared on her cheekbones. It was as if she belonged to some other, more resilient species. At midnight he tried to do the dishes. Charity sat on the floor by the stove, hugging her knees to her chest." "Why'd the woman cross the road?" she said.

"Why?" Seamus was having trouble understanding where his wrists ended and his hands began.

"The road? Who let that bitch out of the shipping crate?"

"That's a hideous joke," he said, and she said, yes, it was. Then she said, "You know what Greg told me this morning when I went to get my clothes? He said he'd shoot himself if I left. My mom shot herself. He knows that."

The Seamus who couldn't find his hands found his anger. He came over and squatted beside her. "That asshole," he said, pulling her into his arms, her hair against his face, filled with desire and sadness and the smell of liquor on her, his body no longer struggling against his mind but taking orders from somewhere deep inside.

"It's not about me. I can see that now," she said. "All these years and I was just a foot soldier in his crusade against the world."

After four days in Islamabad, Melinda, Seamus, and the human-rights workers piled into a car and went west, stopping near Peshawar to buy a burqa from a kiosk by the side of the road, and again to pick up their translator, a talkative man in a leather jacket who was soon telling them about how he would have been a doctor if the money wasn't so good in translating. The five of them spent the next couple of weeks together, traveling around the high, dusty mountains in Waziristan, staying with the families and friends of the guides, learning about the damage done by American drones and the Pakistani military. Seamus had imagined he would be out in the streets, filming strangers while they answered Melinda's questions, but now he saw how impossible that would have been. People stayed out of the streets because of the drones, and every time Seamus's party left one house it was to travel to another. The houses themselves were like fortresses, with high walls and towers lined with tiny square windows for rifles. Everywhere they went Seamus was treated as Melinda's superior. During one conversation, their host, a local chief and uncle to one of the guides, dispatched Melinda to the women's quarters to be entertained by his wife. But for the most part, men listened politely while Melinda's questions were translated, then turned to Seamus to give their answers. Seamus sometimes glanced at Melinda for a reaction, but she always looked attentively phlegmatic, giving nothing away.

Melinda wore a head scarf inside the homes, but on the road she was in full burqa, which seemed to make her more silent than usual, so that Seamus sometimes felt as if he were riding beside a bird in a cage that somebody had thrown a sheet over. He was relieved not to have to watch her watching him while he chatted with the other men, but he was also ashamed of that relief. He was always grateful to escape when the car stopped—to be away from her silence and the blue mesh of her veil, to stretch his cramped legs and spit the dust from his mouth. The men would go off in search of directions or food—one of them always staying behind, leaning against the car with the rifle while he talked to Seamus—but Melinda rarely left the back seat, a blue tent of a figure that could have been anyone.

They saw their first casualties in Miranshah, where the group toured a hospital room packed tight with cots of wounded men and children. Seamus had been given permission to film, and he walked around the room with the camera, grateful because he couldn't imagine what else to do with his hands and eyes. He filmed a man who had watched his wife die with their child in her arms, another who had lost both legs. He filmed child after child, covered in bandages, unconscious in their cots or staring into his camera with wide impassive eyes.

Afterward they found a man who identified himself as a Pashtun freedom fighter and agreed to be filmed if he could wear a scarf over his face. The translator stood at Seamus's elbow, speaking into the camera: "They murder us down to the youngest child. If they see Pashtun in a Toyota car they call them Taliban or spy. They call airstrikes onto the vehicle with innocent people in it." By "they" he meant the American and Punjabi devils.

Seamus felt the first twinges of a headache right after they had left the hospital, and it built throughout the afternoon. By evening it was jackhammering at his left eye, and his stomach rolled in his gut. Back at the house where they were staying, he threw up in a bucket and lay down on his mattress. He tried to say a few words of prayer but couldn't make sense of them, as if he were reciting a song in a language he had forgotten. He drifted off into a half-sleep and dreamt briefly that he was in the hollowed-out bone of a dead thing, where a shape he couldn't identify moved in the shadows. He had a word to describe the shape, but even dreaming he didn't know what the word meant, and when he awoke it was gone. The human-rights workers were sitting on the bed next to his, speaking in Pashto. Soon they got up and left. He dozed off again. The next time he woke up, he found Melinda sitting on the edge of his bed, holding a glass of water.

"You're not supposed to be in here," he said.

She shrugged. "I thought maybe you hadn't been drinking enough," she said coolly. "It could be altitude sickness."

He sat up and took the glass from her. "Thanks. I'll be okay."

She was watching him, and he could tell something was bothering her. After what felt like three full minutes of silence she asked, "Did you notice how few women were in that hospital today?" He nodded. "I asked one of the guides about it. He said it was becoming difficult to find female doctors to work in the region, and many female patients didn't come in because it was shameful for them to be touched by male doctors. He used that word," she said. "Shameful."

"But what if they're dying?"

"Seamus, have you ever thought about why two guys with Kalashnikovs offered to show us around Waziristan?"

"Are you saying they're not human-rights workers?"

"I'm not sure it's that simple."

The ever-present film of dust was thicker now, coating his teeth and tongue. "If we can't really know," he said, "then what's all this for?"

She stared at him, her expression unreadable. "You seem really shook up."

His ears burned, and he put the glass to his mouth and drank.

On their last day they visited a town where they had heard there'd been a number of civilian casualties. They were spending the afternoon with a family—cousins of one of the guides—and to avoid attracting attention to their visit, they parked the car a ways from the house. The day was cold, the sky a wide, hollow blue over snow-covered peaks, the streets empty except for a couple of men with rifles who turned their faces away as soon as Melinda came into sight. Seamus shivered under his heavy fleece. The translator pointed to the sky where two black dots hovered a few miles off.

"Smile," Melinda said. "Some guy in Nevada's deciding whether or not to blow your face off."

Soon they had turned a corner, but they could still see the drones and hear the humming.

"That's a sinister sound," he said.

Melinda said he might as well get used to it: "Anything you can do to somebody can be done to you."

The interview was with a father and son who gave Seamus permission to film the conversation. Melinda sipped tea, awkwardly holding the veil up with one hand. Every once in a while she interjected with a question, but mostly the men talked. Behind the video camera Seamus felt useful and strangely detached. A small group of kids gathered at his knees to stare at the machine, scattering when he moved and reconfiguring a few feet away, like minnows at low tide. At some point the men sent the children out and began talking about the latest attacks: a drone had killed ten people at a market, and then dozens more of the victims' relatives, neighbors, and friends later that same day at the funeral. They had lost two adult family members, including an uncle who was a tribal elder and supported the family, and three children. Seventy-three people were killed in all, twelve of them children. Their neighbor's wife had her nose blown right off her face.

When the interview was over, Melinda came over to Seamus and leaned in so close that he could feel her breath on his neck. "Let's get the hell out of here," she said. He looked down at her drawn face and, in a brief flash of vindication, thought, I'm not the only one who's shook up. But then he remembered her murdered son, remembered his mother's friend with the drowned child, and was ashamed.

On the way back to the car, the street was deserted, the wind kicking up dust around them. The guides and translator trailed behind; they seemed to be arguing about something. Melinda walked beside him in full burqa.

"Isn't it odd?" he said. "I mean, if a drone can read a license plate on a car from miles away, how did somebody make the mistake of hitting a funeral full of civilians?"

"Who said it was a mistake?" said Melinda sharply. Then she broke into a jog, lifting the burqa to her knees, exposing her khakis and tennis shoes. Seamus began to run also and in a second he was behind her. Together they jogged through the empty street, past the mud houses shuttered against the world. They were almost at the car when they came around a corner and found a small boy standing in the middle of the street, weeping. At his feet lay the body of a man facedown in the dirt; the back of his shirt was soaked in blood.

The interpreter appeared behind them and politely, as if he were directing them to watch for a step, said, "Please run."

"Get video," Melinda shouted, reaching over and slapping Seamus's hand, a hard, stinging slap—later he would think her hand must have slipped. He pulled the camera from his fleece and pressed record, but the guides had rounded the corner behind them and were pressing them forward with the heft of a small crowd, saying, "Hurry now, it's not safe here." Soon Seamus was running again, the camera in his hand, his breath and footsteps in his ears.

Back in D.C. he watched the footage and discovered the camera hadn't recorded sound. The boy appeared briefly onscreen—a silent flash of his figure, a small face broken with grief—followed by bumping brown hillsides, ground and sky, the high, white mountains on the horizon. Seamus was at his desk, ignoring an inbox stuffed with e-mails about hard drives and software installation. When the video was over, he went online and watched another video—Pakistani soldiers lining up Pashtun men and shooting them in the chest. On the low-quality video it looked clean, almost choreographed—the men in long shirts, standing with their shoulders touching, then dropping into the high, shifting grass. After that he found that he was done for the day, and when he got home he knew he was done for good—that he'd arrived at a jagged slab of stone at the edge of the world, with no ground ahead. He called his boss and left a message on his voice mail saying he quit.

"I lost my faith over athletes foot," he told his girlfriend. She said he was being reductive and flip and she couldn't help him if he didn't tell her the truth. A few months later they broke up. He stopped leaving the house. His friends from church tried to support him, e-mailing him articles from the *Sentinel* on peace and spiritual thinking, stopping by Sunday mornings to offer him a ride. But after a while they seemed to sense his restlessness with their presence, or grew tired of his refusal to go to church or to share what he was thinking or feeling. He saw less and less of them, his days turning so gray and ill defined he could find no language to describe them.

Charity moved in, using his towels, eating his food, riding the Metro into the city to work and in the evenings meeting him out at restaurants and bars, or returning home to the dinner he'd cooked, eating out on the back deck as the evenings grew warmer, the late-evening light fading into the trees. At one point she said she should start looking at apartment listings again, and he said, "Please don't," and they decided—quickly and together—that she should live there. She said she could pay something toward his mortgage. He said he wasn't charging her to sleep in his bed, but in the end she convinced him to let her pay. She wrote the first check on the month anniversary of their meeting and left it on the kitchen counter by the coffee pot. It was four hundred dollars over the amount they'd agreed on, and it embarrassed him so badly he had to leave the house and walk around the block. Back home he found Charity in a deck chair, taking apart the Sunday paper in her lap.

"Your check was too much."

"I hate money."

He said he felt emasculated and she said to get over it; he was living off charity now.

"What?"

"I wanted to make the joke before you did."

"I wasn't going to make that joke."

She wrote him a new check for the correct amount.

A few weeks later they drove to Arlington to pick up Charity's things. It was early evening. The rush-hour traffic was slow through the city and stopped altogether on the bridge. Charity sat in the passenger seat, snapping the door handle as if she might jump out at any moment.

"Stop," Seamus said.

"Sorry. I'm just not looking forward to dealing with Greg."

Then, as if saying his name had rattled something loose inside, she starting listing off details about her ex: he didn't drink milk because it was a quarter pus; at one time he had owned a pet ferret but abandoned it outside animal control because the smell bothered his mother; he talked constantly about climate change and had once woken Charity in the middle of the night to tell her humans were causing the end of the eleven thousand-year-old environmentally stable Holocene epoch, and that Earth's climate had already crossed three of the nine thresholds between now and a planet that couldn't sustain widespread human civilization.

"They're like the nine rings of hell," he said, "except interlocking, so that you don't know when the whole chain will come clattering down."

She said she didn't want to discuss climate change right then, and he accused her of reckless "blindering," which she didn't think was a word. He said she'd see what he meant in a couple of decades—when the superrich bought up what was left of the inhabitable land while everyone else died of extreme weather, starvation, war, and disease.

She told Seamus how, for her birthday, Greg had driven her to an alley in Georgetown in the night, where he had scaled a fence, opened a gate for her, and led her through a backyard to a fancy old house. She was thinking there must be some kind of surprise party when he kicked down the back door. "I was stunned," she said. "I just followed him around the house while he bagged things—you know, emptied out the woman's jewelry box. I was scared we'd get caught and pissed at Greg for putting me in that situation. I kept asking him about the alarm— what if we'd triggered a silent alarm? Later I found out he had a friend at the company."

"He wanted to scare you?"

"Yeah, but I wasn't that scared," she said. "It was weird, I didn't feel that bad, either. It was this huge, spotless house and it felt good watching him fuck it up. You know they had someone waiting on them, cleaning their house every day, doing their laundry, managing their money, making their food. You know nobody in that house was working the night shift while her seven-year-old put herself to bed. And you know what? Their money's probably just as dirty as Greg's. Maybe legal, but dirty. There's a lot of that in this city. I see it all the time. If you've got enough money, you just rig the system so you don't have to break any laws."

Seamus said that watching people screw each other to get rich made it hard for him to believe in a loving, all-powerful God. "Either there's a powerful God who doesn't love us," he said, "or a loving God who has no control."

"Or no God."

"Right," said Seamus. "Or that."

Greg lived in a two-story house with a porch swing and eaves and flowering bushes around the windows. It was not what Seamus had pictured.

"There's not much to carry," Charity said. "I put most of my stuff in storage." Then she asked Seamus to wait in the car. He watched her walk up the front steps, take out a key, and let herself into the house, then he put his seat back and closed his eyes. The night was warm and still, the smell of magnolia drifting through the car window.

"Hey," somebody said near his left ear. He opened his eyes and found a face a few inches from his own. His first impression was that a puppet had popped up over the edge of the car door, all curly black beard and hair and a round, pale face.

"Are you the guy my wife's leaving me for?" Greg said. Under all the hair he looked young and slight, his slender wrists resting on the door, crossed like the paws of a cat. "She didn't tell you? Of course she didn't tell you."

"You're Greg?"

"Welcome to my world," Greg said. Seamus could smell dinner on his breath, beef and onions. "How tall are you?"

Six five.

"What do you do for a living?"

"I'm unemployed."

Greg snorted. "Go figure. She's always looking for a big fucking project."

The screen door banged and Charity came out of the house, a trash bag in each hand. Seamus pushed the car door open, forcing Greg to step back. He walked over to Charity and took the bags from her. "You okay?" he said. She nodded, her face tight. He put the bags in the trunk, trying hard not to feel as if he'd stumbled onto the set of somebody else's life—somebody else's *marriage*.

Greg followed Charity around to her side of the car, but she climbed in, locking the door. Seamus got in, too, and started the car, but Greg ran back around to the driver's side and stuck his head in the window. "Hold on," he said, sounding so miserable that Seamus was tempted to turn off the ignition and say, Let's talk about this. It's hard but it doesn't have to be this hard. But Charity had grabbed Seamus and was digging her fingers into his elbow. He put the car in neutral and let it roll. Greg jumped back, and Seamus slid into gear.

They drove in silence until they reached the dark, empty parkway. "I'm sorry about that," Charity said. "We were common-law. I divorced him a year ago and he knows it."

"What does divorcing a common-law involve?"

"Nothing," she said. "We don't have any shared assets." Then she started to cry.

As the weather grew warmer, they took weekend trips—hiking in the Jefferson National Forest, fishing off a rented canoe in northwestern Maryland—or walked through the woods behind the house, down to the botanical gardens. Sometimes they stopped to watch the kids on the carousel or bought tickets for the miniature train and piled in alongside the families.

During the week, Charity left early and worked late, and Seamus spent much of his day at home alone. He found himself thinking of Greg, replaying their conversation, remembering how young he looked, as if he'd been preserved by some particular rancor that flowed through the veins of people who had always known exactly what to believe and acted accordingly. Seamus was sickened by the idea of Greg and Charity as a couple, although he couldn't imagine them together at anything but a great distance—a set of small, gray figures on a barren landscape, moving far beyond his reach. When Seamus wasn't feeling panicked or jealous, he lost hours on the Internet researching topics in which he had only a peripheral interest—the latest version of the firefighter exam or details on becoming a forensic accountant—or watching old sitcoms:

Family Ties, Mork & Mindy. Sometimes he got back in bed as soon as Charity left the house and spent the day sleeping, masturbating, and sleeping again, waking midafternoon when the sun hit the bedroom windows, worn out and ashamed. It was a beautiful thing, his life with Charity, but he found he had difficulty believing it was real unless she was right there beside him.

"Stand porter at the door of thought," his mother said. She meant, Changing your thinking will change your experience of the world. But he couldn't. His inertia, his *unemployment*, seemed to leak into everything, and he wondered why Charity hadn't grown tired of him yet. One evening, walking through the woods behind his house with Charity, he asked, "Am I your project?"

"Why would you say that? Do I act like I'm trying to change you?"

"No, but you haven't known me that long. What happens when you find out how depressed I am about the world?"

"The world's a fucked-up place. I can't imagine being with somebody who wasn't at least slightly depressed by it."

"Greg said I was your project."

She glanced over at him. "Why didn't you tell me?" No, she said, he wasn't her project—Greg just thought everyone had sketchy self-interested motives for what they did because that was all he could imagine. "*I* was *Greg's* project," she said.

There had been a brief thunderstorm earlier, and bits of pink sky showed through the treetops. A catbird clamored through the bushes, calling after them in a high, cranky voice. Seamus took Charity's hand.

He got worried sometimes, he said, because things seemed so good between them. In Christian Science, romantic love was supposed to bring you to divine love. "Wanting somebody this bad sets you up for trouble. You're not supposed to believe that anything beside God can make or break your happiness."

"You're not a Christian Scientist anymore," she said, her eyes on the path. She looked a little sad.

He started telling her about his trip to Pakistan, about Melinda and the guides and the hospitals—the kid he saw crying in the road over the body. He said he should have helped him: when you come across something like that, you're responsible for helping, not because you're an adult or a human-rights worker or an American, but because you—a sentient creature—happen to be there.

He expected her to say something reassuring, something about how he'd done his best in that moment, but instead she said, "I see what you mean."

He dropped her hand, picked up a stick, and swung it at a bush. He felt disgusted at himself and childishly angry; but it seemed unfair, almost sadistic, the way situations appeared out of nowhere and demanded your immediate response, then afterward provided no way of changing what you did or didn't do. "We're terrorizing families, killing old people and little kids, thousands of civilians. It's evil."

"Christian Scientists don't believe in evil, right?"

He swatted another bush, then examined the end of the stick, where an animal had chewed off the bark. Evil in Christian Science was the absence of good, he said, as darkness is the absence of light.

"My mom shot herself in a dumpster," Charity said. "Out back of the restaurant she managed. I think she was trying to be considerate, not wanting to leave a mess." She said, "Everybody's got that broken-off thing inside them, Seamus. At some point you just learn to live with it."

He bought a portable radio and carried it with him all over the house, then outside to Irene's cottage, where he was doing repairs. He moved through the details of his tenants' life—a pair of child's pajamas with cows and stars, legal briefs in a pile on the kitchen floor—and listened to the news. Soldiers shot people at checkpoints; mudslides devoured towns; rebels and drug traffickers and governments tortured and killed civilians. One morning he heard a scientist talk about climate change and the planet in the decades to come: droughts, hurricanes, floods, wildfires; cities consumed by oceans and deserts. There was hope, she said. Humans already had the technology necessary to meet the world's energy needs. "At this point it's purely a political problem," she said—and Seamus saw Greg's face and felt a stab of jealousy. How unbearable it was that this thieving slip of a man, with his politics and opinions and romantic history, might be right about everything.

In the late afternoons Seamus would start making dinner, and by the time Charity arrived home from work, by the time he'd glimpsed her glossy head in the front hall, he was jittery with anticipation—would walk out, his hands covered in fat or flour or oil, to watch her as she shed her shoes and pantyhose and jacket in a little pile at the bottom of the stairs. One night she came in and stripped all the way down to her underwear. She had the expression of somebody who might punch the next person who asked something of her.

"Is everything all right?"

"Get me out of these clown clothes." She said she'd had a bad day but didn't want to rehash it. "Petty shit."

"Tell me."

She stood there in her underwear, staring at him. Then she said, "Some asshole's been bugging me at work."

Who? Seamus wanted to know. And what did she mean by bugging?

It was just somebody's stupid assistant. He'd been leaving her notes, hanging around her office, asking her out—nothing she couldn't handle. Seamus was about to ask her another question, but she shook her head in a gesture that seemed so exhausted and miserable that he put his arms around her instead. She rested her head on his chest. Then she lifted her face to him and said, "Take your pants off, please. I'd like to have an all-consuming sexual encounter."

Later that night he made her promise to tell him if the guy kept it up. "You can always call me from work," he said. "I'll come right down."

"I know."

The next week she was in Chicago for business. One afternoon he went out back in his pajama pants to water the flowers around the cottage. He was bending over to unfold a kink in the hose when he had the sudden sensation that he was being watched—not the metaphysical watching of a Father-Mother God that he had experienced in his childhood, but a pair of human eyes on him, taking him in. He turned off the hose and checked all around the house; there was nothing. He decided the solitude must be getting to him. It occurred to him in a sort of daydream that if Charity had set up a hidden camera somewhere, if she'd seen the current state of his days, she'd have to leave; no self-respecting woman could do otherwise. He needed a job, any job.

He spent the last day of her absence cleaning the house and applying for jobs. When she came home he asked her if she'd set up a nanny cam. She laughed. "What kind of trouble did you get into while I was gone?" she asked.

"I'm scared that you'll see how depressing it is to be me without you."

Sunday evening he opened his inbox and discovered an offer for an interview. It was at the D.C. branch of a small aerospace company that manufactured plane parts and supplied some defense contractors. He called Charity over and showed her the e-mail.

She was in one of her odd, almost reckless moods that had begun appearing at the end of each weekend.

"I bet those valves are for drones. You're going to make drone valves for a living?"

"It's not entirely clear."

She was leaning on him, her elbow digging into his shoulder, breathing heavily near his ear.

"This is the world we live in," Seamus said. "If I'm going to be a part of it, I have to grow a pair."

She said he had beautiful balls, like gilded twin lapdogs guarding his asshole.

"Have you been drinking?"

"Yup."

He asked why she was drinking alone, and she said she was trying to forget that it was the start of the workweek. "It takes too much carbon to turn myself into work Charity. I'm so fucking sick of blow-drying my hair."

"I don't think anybody would mind if you stopped blow-drying your hair."

She climbed into his lap. "You're very sweet."

He could smell the alcohol on her breath. "Is it that guy, Charity? The one who was harassing you? Is that why you don't want to go to work?"

She leaned back, examining his face so carefully that he wondered if there was something on his nose. "No," she said. "Not that."

"What is it?"

"I told you I didn't want to do this shit forever," she said.

"Well, at this point I think a terrible job is better than no job. I'm doing the interview."

"You go on then," she said solemnly, as if he were announcing a birth or death.

A week later Seamus was in a suit, riding the Metro into the city in the early afternoon. He found a seat in the corner, leaned his head back, and closed his eyes. The car was quiet except the hum of the wheels and the voice announcing the doors opening and closing. He was almost asleep when he felt a tap on his knee. A boy, maybe nine or ten years old, stood in front of him in a rubbery, forest-green raincoat that looked a couple of sizes too big for him. His hand was in front of him, and he was holding a fistful of paintbrushes, which stuck out of his fingers at angles, like twigs he'd scooped off the ground.

"You want to buy some brushes?" he said, staring at a spot just beyond Seamus's shoulder with eyes that looked as if they had a film of algae growing over them. "They're premium art-store quality."

Seamus wondered if the kid had been kidnapped by a criminal ring of some sort, and then, because it seemed like the least he could do, he took out his wallet.

"Three dollars," the boy said.

"All I have is a twenty."

"That's fine."

Seamus handed him a bill, and the boy took it with one hand and then opened his first.

They were, in fact, nice brushes, art-store quality. Seamus picked out a slender one with smooth, golden bristles. The boy dropped the remaining brushes in the pocket of his slicker and turned away.

"My change?"

"Sorry, man," the boy said with a shrug. "Can't change a twenty." He crossed the car and waited by the door, small and upright in the big green coat. Seamus watched him, feeling deflated, knowing he didn't have it in him to chase down a kid in a rain jacket and demand his seventeen bucks back. The train stopped, and the boy hopped off. The doors slid closed behind him. Seamus watched as they pulled away from the station, the platform flickering to darkness. His own reflection appeared on the glass—a ghost Seamus staring back at him, woefully absurd in his suit and tie, like an oak tree dressed for dinner. He leaned his head against the window and allowed the knowledge he'd held at arm's length to settle over him—that this fantasy that he would somehow rejoin the capital's workforce, the industrial-military complex, was just that, an embarrassing fantasy.

As soon as he was above ground, he called to cancel the interview but kept landing in the wrong person's voice mail. He gave up and went inside. He couldn't bring himself to cancel at the front desk, where an older man, who smiled so sweetly that Seamus wondered if he'd mistook him for someone else, wrote down his name and directed him to a chair to wait. So Seamus waited in a small chair by a plant, growing more and more resentful as the minutes passed.

His interviewer, a middle-aged man in a suit, arrived half an hour past the scheduled time. Seamus followed him into an office and sat down on the far side of a large desk. He was feeling petulant in a way he hadn't experienced in years. If only they'd had their receptionist answer the phone, or fixed their shit phone tree, he wouldn't be there. Who thought it was a good idea to have computers answer phones anyways? What did the CIA do when it called to order more parts for their extrajudicial killing machines? Did they get the phone tree, too?

"Imagine an ideal day working for us," the man said. "What do you see yourself doing?"

"Say you get some bad press over all the kids your drones are killing," Seamus said.

The man interrupted to say they didn't manufacture drones, but Seamus couldn't have gotten off the ride if he'd wanted to: "I could design some animated Reaper drones for your splash page—some pretty little graphics of them taking out schools or ripping through family celebrations. We could set it all to an uplifting jingle."

The man sighed. "If you're here as a protester, I'm really not the guy to talk to."

For the first time, Seamus really looked at him. He was older, probably in his late sixties, with the broad, gray head of an aging mastiff. He looked exhausted, as if he'd interviewed dozens of ill-mannered applicants that day.

"I'm sorry," Seamus said. "I realized on the train over that I couldn't work for a weapons manufacturer. I didn't have the guts to cancel."

The man nodded wearily. "Sometimes things get the better of us. I understand."

Seamus said he was sorry again—and again—and then he got up and left as quickly as he could.

On the train home there was standing room only. He was sweating and uncomfortable in his suit, too miserable to be properly disgusted with himself about the interview. He just wanted to be home, curled up with Charity in bed. He anchored himself to a pole in the middle of the car and soon was wedged between another man—who could have been a congressman or a lobbyist if he hadn't been riding the Metro—and a cheerful-looking woman in a red sweater. A young couple occupied the seats below him, the girl, pregnant, resting her hands on her belly. They were arguing. "If you bring up Hider again I'm going to scream," the girl said.

"But what's to say it won't happen again?" the boy said.

"Stalin killed twenty million people."

"Jesus, it's the Holocaust. The fucking *Holocaust*."

The woman in the red sweater turned to Seamus and told him in a hushed voice that still managed to sound cheerily informative that there was no point in having the quantity-versus-quality argument when the basic premises were flawed: Stalin killed six, not twenty, million people, but he was also responsible for the first ethnic killing campaigns in interwar Europe—something people always credited to Hitler.

Her perfume was strong and flowery; Seamus could almost taste it in his mouth. "Excuse me," he said, squeezing past her and pushing through the crowd to the nearest door, the one that divided the cars. It was locked. Panic swelled in his chest and he turned around, pushing back through the clot of people, the crowd of bodies and coats and suits and backpacks and bags, until he was at the exit doors. He stood there for minutes, bracing himself against the cool glass.

An hour later he was above ground under the darkening sky. It was raining, and he walked home with the cars hissing through puddles beside him—past strip malls, Chinese and Eritrean restaurants, the park entrance, onto the dimly lit residential streets of his neighborhood. The rain was soaking through his clothes, and by the time he reached his house, he was wet and exhausted. He turned the key in the lock and swung the door inward. It connected with something on the other side. "Charity?" She was standing right behind the door, wearing her coat. She squinted as if he were slightly out of focus, her lips set in a tight line. "You okay?" he asked. She shook her head.

"I have a problem with Greg."

"Greg?"

She seemed to be vibrating, as if she were struggling to bring herself back to him. "How was your interview?" she asked.

"I'm not taking that job."

"Good," she said. "They subcontract with Halliburton. I looked it up." Then she said she had some business to take care of—she'd be back in a couple of hours. She tried to step around Seamus, but he blocked her. "Excuse me," she said. Her hand was behind her back and he reached out and unfolded her arm, bringing her fist around so the tool she held was exposed between them. It was his toilet auger, a grimy looking thing with a handle and a couple feet of coiled steel wire connected to a pole. The label read CRAFTY TITAN.

"Seamus," she said. "You don't understand."

He put his arms around her and pulled her toward him, the auger between them. "That thing's unsanitary."

She leaned her head against his chest, the smell of her hair filling his nostrils. "He's been stalking me at the office—leaving me nasty notes. I don't need this. You should be able to leave the past behind you, not track it into your new life on your shoes." She stepped back and looked up at him. "I swear I wasn't trying to lie to you, Seamus—I just didn't want to deal."

He didn't know what to say. He asked her what she was planning on doing with his toilet auger.

"There's some shit I need to unstick."

"That's not funny."

She shrugged. "It's kinda funny." Then she said she figured she could whip the shit out of the old lady's legs with the hanging bit. "It's the only way to get to him—through his mother. It used to be me or his mother. Now it's just her."

"I couldn't find a pipe," she said. She reached into her jacket, pulled out a photo, and handed it to Seamus. It was a picture of himself, wearing plaid pajama pants and a T-shirt, watering the flowers in the pots outside Claudia and Irene's cottage. Someone had written across his face in black marker, "Tell your parasitic landlord boyfriend he better watch his foie gras."

"It was on my desk at work," Charity said. Seamus stared at the photo. "See?" she said. "We can't let him get away with this. It'll only get worse."

"How does he know you're paying to live here?"

She shook her head, "He means parasite on society—as in the landlord class."

"But he's a burglar."

"Don't engage with his arguments."

"Aren't you engaging?"

"I'm not engaging, I'm escalating," she said. "I'm raising the stakes so high he can't afford to play."

He laughed a little, although he felt like he might cry. It was all wrong, he said, the photo, the break-ins, the idea of whipping an old lady to teach her son a lesson. Charity glared at the photo in his hands, looking grimly determined. He saw that his only shot at dissuading her was to go along and look for an opening.

"Wait for me," he said.

And after he had changed out of that awful suit and returned downstairs, he found her still there, waiting.

They drove across the city, through the night traffic and onto the bridge, where they sat in more traffic. The Potomac was broad and black below them, the radio playing eighties hits and commercials for mattresses and blustering DJs laughing at their own ignorant jokes.

"All those months I waited on her hand and foot," Charity said. "You should have seen the way she talked to me." She was very still beside him, her face in shadow.

In Arlington they parked a block away from the house and sat in silence for a moment in the dark car. He was sick with dread and something else that it took him a second to identify as desire. He reached over and touched her face in the shadows. Her cheek was cold under his fingers, and she leaned in and pressed her mouth against his. It tasted of something bright and cold, as if she'd been running outside. "You don't have to do this for me," she said.

"I know."

They got out and walked toward the house, Charity carrying the toilet auger on her shoulder as if it were a bat. The ground was dry; the rain hadn't come this far south. At the corner of the yard she said, "I gave him back the key. We'll have to climb in. She leaves her window open, otherwise she overheats—like a pug."

He followed her through the yard to the porch, and then up one of the pillars, which was surprisingly easy to climb. He pulled himself onto the shingles and crouched next to Charity. He was about to say something about how ironic it was that they were breaking into a housebreaker's house—how it shouldn't be that easy—when she put a finger to her lips and pointed to a window.

He found himself standing in a warm little bedroom, decorated as if it were a Victorian-themed movie set: ornate wallpaper, a fireplace, a four-poster bed with a lace canopy, and a thick, oriental rug. A massive woman in a pink bathrobe sat on the edge of the bed. She was in her early sixties, with thin, reddish hair; a large, round face; and the smooth, poreless skin of a small child. Her pink terrycloth robe spread out across the bed in a mountainous landscape, falling open at her legs, exposing a pair of pale thighs. For a moment she looked surprised, but the expression quickly changed to cold amusement.

"I'm here because I won't be treated like this anymore, Mama," Charity said, twisting the auger in her hands. Her voice rose with the last word. Sweat beaded on her upper lip and she was breathing quickly, shifting her weight between feet. She didn't look like a woman who was going to whip the shit out of anyone. Seamus's gut sank.

"Show me what you got there, honey," Greg's mother said, articulating the words as if she were talking to a toddler. She put forward a plump hand.

Charity held out the tool in her hands and walked toward the bed. Greg's mother took the auger between a thumb and forefinger and dropped it onto the rug. Then she grabbed the girl's wrists and pulled her down to kneeling, pressing Charity's face into her lap, stroking her hair. Seamus saw Charity's shoulders shaking. She was weeping in the woman's thighs. The woman raised her eyes to Seamus with a look of humorous tolerance, as if they were fond custodians and Charity their damaged little charge.

"It's okay, baby," she said. "Everything's going to be just fine." She was obscene, Seamus thought—her royal manner, the presumption of camaraderie when she met his eyes, her meaty hand on the girl's head. No, not the girl—Charity.

Charity lifted her face and said, "No, Mama, it's not okay."

And Seamus—who had finally arrived in a world where he was destined to witness but not understand—had to agree.

Nominated by The Paris Review, Maria Hummel

W.C. FIELDS
TAKES A WALK

by PAISLEY REKDAL

from WILLOW SPRINGS

Alone, I march with my ruined mouth, plaid vest
stinking of whisky. Alone, with my little vial of pain
rattling at my leg. People want me
to say something funny and I tell them, *Only privacy
amuses me. You want funny, break a bone
and sing through it.* That's my name plate,
calling card: fat man, drunkard, turnip-
face: rage's endless, hectoring joke.
Fans pretend they can't believe it, insist
it's all a game: they call me Santa
in the gossip pages, they call me Naughty
Chickadee. But it's the lion they like,
roaring and bleeding, their timid fists
rapping at my cage. Fame
means accepting you can be only one story.
I like to stand backstage, jeering at the coal-
scrubbed comics who won't make it,
laughing at their quivering
cheeks, their still-white mouths, and shout,
You don't believe it! The vaudeville girls,
I thought they'd get it, with their champagne
curls, breasts leoparded with sequins. But too soon
they slip offstage to wipe the grease
paint off, unpin their dresses, kiss their kids
and let their figures go. They're tired,

they say. After all those shows. Tired women, tired
like my mother with her German cheekbones,
papery and yellow. At the stores, she could barely
rouse herself to act Camille half the time,
the other half like Garbo. While at home
she never knew what to be, wringing her hands
by the kitchen stove, too sensitive, she said,
to the sad slow beat of my heels
drumming on the carpet. She said
she wanted life to be something *realer*
for herself. Me, I can walk a mile with a nail in my boot
and a smile on my face. I can walk
until the metal drills into my sole.
I shake my vial with its jabbering pills.
I stroke my coat, bathe myself in perfumes of cigar smoke.
I pour whiskey into my whiskey.
Then I pour it down my throat. Once, joking
with the boys by Dempsey's locker, a group
of rotted teeth fell out. And Dempsey winced!
Tried to look away. (I'm proud to say
the space still gapes: I never got a bridge.
Why hide? That gap is me now, all the way.)
Chump, I warned the boxer, *that kind of girlishness
will get you in the end*. And then
I stuck my tongue through that bloody place
and sang The Marseillaise.

Nominated by Willow Springs, Aimee Nezhukumatathil, Donald Platt

OUT OF DATE: THE JOYS OF OBSOLESCENCE

by HAL CROWTHER

from BLACKBIRD

The word itself looks weird and ancient, like something indecipherable scrawled on a cave wall or half-eroded from a decrepit tombstone. The word is "crwth," a Welsh word—in English, where vowels rule, the word became "crowd." The Irish version is "cruit." The musical instrument that goes by these names is as archaic as the lovely Welsh language, and more obsolete. It's a six-string bowed harp or lyre, something like a fiddle until you hear it, that has been traced back to eleventh century Byzantium. The crwth has been played very little, if at all, since the seventeenth century; its history is so obscure that the principal authority cited by Wikipedia is *Musical and Poetical Relicks of the Welsh Bards*, published by Edward Jones in 1784. If you Google "crwth," you'll find this sentence, which more or less defines obsolescence: "Since the art of crwth-playing died out so completely, and since it was an instrument of the folk culture rather than part of the academic musical world, the exact manner—if, indeed, there ever was one exact manner—in which the instrument was traditionally played, like the tunings employed, will probably never be known for certain."

A modest revival of interest in the crwth, part of the original instruments movement, is based largely on conjecture and experimentation. Elsewhere on the internet you can find a video of Sean Folsom—a rubicund American musician who bills himself as Sean the Piper—wearing a Renaissance gown and one of those flat guildsman's hats that looks like a meat pie with a velvet ribbon, solemnly playing and patiently explaining the crwth. Its sound is fetching in a way, at least to me, but distinctly . . . medieval. At this point I confess what may be obvious, that my surname, Crowther, means crwth-player. Crwthist? I'm descended, at some point lost in time, from a musician who played songs now forgotten ("The repertoire of surviving crwth tunes is very small") on an instrument no one now alive knows for certain how to play. Perhaps generations of these forlorn bards roosted in my family tree. People with surnames like Miller or Shoemaker, or the even more antiquated Cooper or Fletcher, remind us in a similar way of lost trades and traditions. But the Crowthers, as I see it, boast the most obsolete pedigree of all. Even the Flintstones seemed less out of date.

As a senior citizen with arthritis and cataracts, peering myopically down the smoking barrel of the twenty-first century, I know that bearing an expired name and representing an extinguished heritage has helped me to understand my life and accept the arc of my own fortunes. I'm no stranger to obsolescence. For twenty-five years I earned a living with an instrument now consigned to an oblivion even more complete than that of the crwth, because there will be no attempt to resurrect the typewriter. Yet this humble machine produced a comforting music of its own. Each year, inevitably and sadly, there are fewer of us who remember the companionable percussion of the Royal, the Olivetti, the Smith-Corona. The atonal but almost syncopated symphony of a big-city newsroom with its clicks and taps and ringing carriages, its tempo as varied as the speed and vigor of the fifty typists, was a sweet sound that will never be heard again on this planet, except in the fitful dreams of old reporters.

Grim electronics and grimmer economics brought an end to all that. But it's idle nostalgia to grieve for the tools of yesteryear. Technology has its way with every profession, more often for the best. Lumberjacks with chainsaws rarely yearn for those crosscut saws their fathers strained to pull; modern fishermen don't dream of hauling nets by hand. It may be sheer coincidence that the rapid disappearance of the typewriter and the rapid decline of journalism seem to coincide. That journalism has declined woefully is a very easy argument to document and sustain, but not without offending sincere individuals whose livelihood depends on its survival, in some as yet undetermined form.

I don't blame young people for tuning out when a bitter graybeard evokes the good old days. Right or wrong, prescient or senescent, it's an unbecoming role he's playing, one I'd rather avoid. Mine is a personal, not a cultural, lament. Anyone who hasn't registered the alarming divorce of broadcasting and professional journalism is simply very young. Yes, I can remember when foreign bureaus and documentaries—and thoughtful objectivity—were the pride of network news departments, and the cable news Punch-and-Judy was less than an embryo. As for print journalism, which seems to be following the Smith-Corona into oblivion, volumes have been published, and will be published (for your Kindle?) to explain what happened to us and why. I have little to add to a front-page story by *New York Times* media columnist David Carr, who chronicled the pitiful disintegration of the once proud and powerful Tribune Company, publisher of the *Chicago Tribune* and the *Los Angeles Times*.

Carr's story, ironically published during national Newspaper Week, acquainted us with Tribune CEO Randy Michaels, a former radio shock jock assigned by billionaire Sam Zell to manage his controlling interest in the failing media giant. According to Carr, Michaels demoralized company headquarters in Chicago with a bizarre infusion of trash-radio culture—misogyny, sexual harassment, profane tirades, raunchy schoolboy humor, sleazy giveaways—that Tribune veterans could scarcely believe, far less tolerate. Carr reported that Michaels introduced himself to his new colleagues at a Chicago hotel bar by getting drunk and offering a waitress one hundred dollars to show him her breasts. "I have never seen anything like it," recalled one eyewitness, no longer a Tribune employee. Carr also claimed that Michaels and an executive cadre of his old radio cronies looted the bankrupt Tribune by paying themselves huge bonuses while the company staggered ever deeper into debt.

Michaels—forced to resign a few weeks later—is a short, fat, bottom-fed individual who looks like the carny selling cheese fries at the county fair. To call him a scumbag is a description, not an insult, since a shock jock is a *professional* scumbag—it's his stock in trade. Anyone who's never heard one of these baboons castrate a pig in the studio or audio-tape a sex act in St. Patrick's Cathedral (both true) is a lucky American indeed. It's no secret that radio is a latrine; we wince because this repulsive huckster hired and fired newsroom personnel for two legendary newspapers that were, within recent memory, among America's most powerful and prestigious. Actually Michaels fired, mostly. More than four thousand Tribune Company employees have been terminated since he and Zell took over in 2008. For newspapers, the hour is very late. For newsmagazines, perhaps even later. *Newsweek*, where I once labored, died a cruel death in the marketplace. It was purchased for a dollar by a ninety-one-year-old stereo tycoon, now deceased, who merged it with *The Daily Beast*, a web magazine run by glitter-monger Tina Brown. ("Beastweek?" one reporter speculated.) *Time* magazine, another employer from my long-ago youth, has suffered similar financial and artistic decay and hangs like a decomposing albatross around Time-Warner's tired neck.

The news about the news is uniformly depressing. If you're tired of hearing that from pundits and disgruntled old newshounds, take it straight from the Kansas Department of Education, which has cut off funding for high school journalism courses after a review of labor-market data. As reported in *Newsweek*, "the state deemed journalism a dying industry unfit for public funds, which are meant for 'high-demand, high-skill or high-wage' jobs." Ouch. It's only Kansas, but it stings. To make the rout more poignant, the first jobs eliminated by the stressed-out, stripped-to-survive print media were the very jobs I used to work. Columnists, book editors, film, drama and fine arts critics— along with investigative reporters, foreign and Washington correspondents and editorial cartoonists—were dismissed as highbrow luxuries for newsrooms trying to get a grip on grassroots America. If I should have the good luck to live another twenty years, I suppose my résumé will provoke as much bewilderment among my grandchildren as if I'd told them I was an itinerant crwth-player. They'll nod and give me a cup of something warm and pat me on my trembling shoulder. ("He said he 'reviewed' books and films for newspapers. Yesterday he muttered something about 'Pogo' and 'Lil' Abner.' Has mama checked his medications?")

But that's in 2030, when we'll all be living underground to escape the heat, and half a billion Americans will own three billion guns. (Not much hunting underground, but lots of stress to trigger domestic disputes.) My guess is that the information revolution will not be a major issue in 2030. I'm trying to process my obsolescence here in 2011, in my first year of eligibility for Medicare. The shock of having spent my professional life in "a dying industry" isn't necessarily the most traumatic assault on my sense of self. No one who wasn't in the work force—or in the world—in 1985 can possibly comprehend the speed or the magnitude of the technological metamorphosis we have just witnessed. Rip van Winkle would have had to sleep two hundred years to wake to the future shock you'd experience if you'd only been napping since the Reagan administration. Those of us who were at mid-life or beyond when the cyber-tsunami struck faced adjustment pressures unlike any in human history.

How did I cope? There's an analogy that appeals to me. Here in Maine where I'm writing, we're menaced by a pack of homicidal drivers, usually males under thirty in big new trucks, who cruise narrow two-lane roads at NASCAR speeds, day or night. If you drive at conventional speed, the cowboy comes up behind you so fast the hairs stand up on your neck. If there's no sane chance for him to pass you, as is often the case on these roads, you have two choices: You can speed up dangerously to increase the distance between your bumper and his, or you can signal a right turn and pull over on the shoulder to let him streak by. The first few times I saw this second maneuver, I wondered whether it represented courtesy or terror. But it is, of course, the right move, even if it goes against your grain. And it's the move I chose, a few years ago, to accommodate the alien technology that came roaring up in my rearview mirror at one hundred miles per hour. I didn't hit the accelerator, though by nature I'm more combative than acquiescent. I pulled off the road and let the monster roll on by. Just where it's going, no one knows and I don't care.

Once you pull over, you forever wear the big *O* for obsolete. You can't hide it. The wired world snickers, your children roll their eyes, preadolescents with fists full of gadgets regard you with wonder, with pity. You become selectively illiterate, because the technology constantly spawns new words and acronyms you have no need or wish to learn. How painful is this excommunication, this life in the ghetto of the left-behind? Personally I like it here. The company and conversation are first-rate, even if most of the neighbors are drawing Social Security. The experience of dropping out of the tech-rat race reminds me of a line in one of my wife's best novels, about a mountain girl in her teens who finds herself pregnant and alone, "ruint" for good according to her parents and her community. A good reputation and a good marriage are now out of reach, but she finds it mysteriously liberating. "When you're ruint," Ivy says, "It frees you up some."

When you're out of date and committed to it, it frees you up some. I honestly doubt that I'll live to regret it. The parade goes by, and it can be highly entertaining as long as you don't have to march, to learn the cadence and keep up the pace. You pick a choice seat on the reviewing stand and watch, unencumbered by performance anxiety, status or public opinion. You don't count anymore, as the marchers reckon it, and as

Janis Joplin once sang in "Me and Bobby McGee," "Freedom's just another word for nothin' left to lose."

Loneliness and self-pity aren't major problems when your obsolescence is more or less voluntary. Smugness—unearned self-congratulation—is more of a threat. I hate to sound smug. I realize I'm very fortunate—blessed—to have had the option to say no. There are talented journalists my age and even older, discarded by the dying industry, who are blogging, friending and Twittering themselves to exhaustion, hoping to catch the last seat on a train that's already disappearing down the tracks. The loss of their self-respect is a personal tragedy; the loss of their gifts and experience is a national one. And of course the option of a life off the grid was never open to Americans who began their careers post-Gates, post-Jobs, post-Silicon Valley. We live in an age when even shepherds and forest rangers are probably wired from hat to boots.

The electronic express keeps rolling, and there's no turning back. "Refuse it," prescient advice Sven Birkerts offered to conclude his Luddite manifesto *The Gutenberg Elegies* (1994), now sounds as dated and wistful as the fight song of a team that lost 70-0. Yet those of us doomed to anachronism by technology enjoy many compensations, not the least of them the knowledge that we're gravely underestimated by cyber-sophisticates who pity us. The rumor that I've been reduced to tears and profanity by the multiple remotes that control hotel TV sets is not entirely unfounded. Mr. Wizard I am not. But the myth that computers and allied appliances are simply too complicated for tired old minds is based on the youthful assumption that everyone *wants* to learn this stuff, that anyone would if he could. The truth is that nearly anyone can if he has to. When circumstances force us to operate these impudent twenty-first century machines, we fossils engage reluctantly but rarely fail. Survival-level computer skills are no neuroscience, nor were they meant to be. A motivated chimpanzee can do this, or even Randy Michaels.

It's not so hard to teach an old dog new tricks—not if his dinner depends on it. But the more tricks he has to turn to fill his bowl, the more he's going to hate you. And you can double the hatred—I speak for an incorrigible minority of old dogs—if he thinks most of your new tricks are stupid. The vices and virtues of the all-wired world merit ferocious cultural debate, but it's hard to sustain a dialogue with young people who've never lived without the glowing screens, the blinking lights, the voices from the ether. Terms of discourse have changed as rapidly as hardware and software, and created the most prodigious generation gap in history. Rising generations—as opposed to sinking ones like mine—can't be expected to grasp how quickly it happened, how it never evolved but exploded. Children born in Nagasaki after 1945 might have the same difficulty forming a clear picture of their city before the bomb. We, the obsolete, are obliged to argue from general principles. The purpose of technology is to make it easier to perform the essential tasks of our lives, tasks that include survival. But what if, instead or in addition, it merely creates tasks and problems for which there was no need, for which no human relevance can be logically demonstrated? What if it merely multiplies entities unnecessarily, in defiance of Occam's razor? How many apps does it take to screw in a light bulb?

Nielsen reports that the average teenage girl in America sends more than 4,000 text messages a month, eight messages for every hour she's awake. By an admittedly rough calculation that's more social messages in thirty days than I've sent (through any and all media) in my entire life, now approaching two-thirds of a century. To me this statistic is as weird as a rumor that these girls roast and eat their pets. Apparently technology has activated some latent psychological, perhaps even genetic tendency toward incontinent interconnection, but I can't imagine what we've gained from it. There's no question that much has been lost—first and worst of all our privacy.

Privacy is the Great Divide. For the civilized—now the obsolete—it's a primary article of faith that the tougher, the more impermeable the critical membrane between public and private, the more civilization flourishes. In the past, this has been one of the few important points of agreement between serious liberals and serious conservatives, and certainly among all the founders and architects of the Republic. Without privacy there's no dignity, and without dignity "freedom" has no meaning. Thirty years ago, you could search in vain for an American who thought privacy was expendable. Yet recently one of the billionaires responsible for the rapid erosion of American privacy—some entrepreneur of the PC, cell phone or social network industries, I can't recall—was asked how we could protect our privacy and replied dismissively, "Get over it." "Get over it," the bastard said, instantly converting my distaste and distrust to fear and loathing.

This is the grim place to which the heedless have marched us. The resistance—scattered, aging—will never produce a twenty-first century Patrick Henry to cry "Give me privacy or give me death." But the death of privacy, like Goya's *Sleep of Reason*, is breeding monsters. What do we make of the handsome Indian-American freshman at Rutgers, with an angelic smile and no history of antisocial behavior, who filmed and then webcast his roommate in a homosexual embrace? He never expected his victim to jump off the George Washington Bridge, but what did he expect? We'll never know what this cherubic Iago was thinking, but just as hard to understand is that webcam/computer installations are standard equipment in freshman dorm rooms. When, why did all this electronic garbage become a generational norm?

A federal court convicted Ashton Lundeby, a seventeen-year-old North Carolina high school student, of masterminding an elaborate internet scheme that involved false reports of bombs planted at universities, high schools and FBI offices. Lundeby and his co-conspirators would call in a bomb threat to the local police, record each emergency response with surveillance cameras and then sell the footage to paying customers online. The Lundeby scheme required so much chutzpah— or criminal innocence—and so much expertise that we shake our heads in awe. But the confluence of electronic wizardry and commercial initiative is bound to remind us of billionaire Facebook entrepreneur Mark Zuckerberg and the bio-movie *The Social Network* that skewered him as a tormented sociopath. I never saw *Avatar*, but Zuckerberg and many of the other creatures portrayed in *The Social Network* were far more alien to me than blue people with tails in 3D. If they are the future, please help me find the door to the past. Hand me my crwth and my bow. Put the meat-pie hat with the ribbon on my head, and point me toward a market town where someone might spare a shilling for a tune.

Criticism from the sidelines, from the happily obsolete, has been ruled inadmissible. If you don't play, who cares what you think about the players? Most of the recent books blaming psychic trauma on cyber-overload, like Jaron Lanier's *You Are Not a Gadget*, have been written by Silicon Valley apostates with second thoughts about the digital revolution. But I don't think any of us from pre-microchip generations have the right to shrug and look away. We—some of us—invented, marketed, and served them this bewildering array of gadgets. And there's ample evidence that something ragged and unclean, something morally unsettling is loose among young people who could be your children and grandchildren, or mine.

Monsters whose obsessions result in crimes and lawsuits aren't isolated cases, unfortunately. They're nurtured in a flourishing internet subculture of bullies, creeps, and clowns. The *New York Times* ran a story about teenagers in an upscale suburb who were using cell phone cameras to record fights, savage beatings and violent stunts that compete for attention on websites like MySpace and YouTube. Many of the quotes in this story by Corey Kilgannon were chilling, jaw-dropping messages from a micro-culture gone mad. "Kids beat up other kids and tape it, just so other kids will see it and laugh," shrugged one seventeen-year-old boy. "Or they just post stupid things they did online so other kids will look at their Web page." His friend added, "Teens always do crazy stuff, but it's just that much more intense and fun when you can post it. When you live in a boring town, what else is there to do?" And another explained, "Kids put their fights online for street cred."

No less disturbing were the expert analyses the *Times* reporter solicited. "A lot of teens have this idea that life is a game and it's all just entertainment," said Nancy E. Willard, who wrote a book on cyberbullying. "In doing this, they're jostling for social position and status, or establishing themselves in a certain social group, or just attracting attention. To them, this is defining who they are and what people think of them. The idea that 'people know my name' is an affirmation of who they are." A role model for many of these suburban exhibitionists was a local man whose videos of himself hurling his body through neighborhood fences, an internet sensation, spawned a national fad. "A week ago, no one knew who I was—now my name has been on every news and talk show," said this idiot, Adam Schleichkorn, now twenty-five. "I don't care that it's for something stupid. I was on Fox News cracking jokes. Maury Povich called me today. So I'm known as the fence-plowing kid. At least I'm known."

You see what I mean by divergent terms of discourse. What does a grandfather on Medicare say to the fence-plowing kid, besides "Jesus Christ, kid"? Mark Zuckerberg, one of the world's youngest billionaires, would be an equally tough lunch date. The infantilization of American culture seems to be an established fact—judge only from Hollywood films, which in the thirty years since I was a film critic have changed their demographic from predominantly adult to predominantly pre-school. Another established fact is the link between the sedentary online life and an epidemic of obesity. But there's a chicken/egg problem with severe psychological displacement. Were Americans already evolving into strange life forms that require more and better electronic toys to mirror and exhibit themselves, or should we hold the toys responsible for their transformation?

Only the most embarrassing old-timers claim that things were better, or that we were better, way back when. To the best of my recall, teenagers of the '50s and '60s were just as cruel and status-conscious and no less obsessed with sex, though we knew a great deal less about it. Adolescent lives weren't better, perhaps, but they sure as hell were different, and the difference appears to be all about context, about expanding identity groups. We lived our lives for a limited audience of parents, siblings, teachers, classmates and neighbors. It wasn't a very attentive or demanding audience, but only one teenager in a thousand—a great athlete, a beauty queen, a musical prodigy—ever imagined a wider, even a national audience. The rest of us accepted our limitations. Academic achievements might lead to opportunities for a richer, more comfortable life later on; catching a touchdown pass or hitting a home run could be converted into immediate status and sometimes even sexual currency, coveted and hard to come by. (Forgive the male point of view—to boys like us in those days, females were another country.)

Hardwired teens of the internet era see all the world as their stage. And sometimes it is. The common dream of online performers is to "go viral" like Adam Schleichkorn, whose original fence-busting video attracted 70,000 viewers. The most hardcore juvenile delinquent of the '50s would have been petrified at the thought of all those eyes. But now we discover a subculture where the natural need for privacy has been reversed, somehow, into a neurotic need for constant attention—attention of any kind at all. In this alternate universe it's better to be disgusting, to be a figure of fun or an object of contempt, than to be invisible. Voyeurs demand, exhibitionists deliver, then they switch chairs. Vicariousness is all.

When did people begin to think of themselves as public offerings, as products they're obliged to market and sell from cradle to grave? A typical teenager of fifty or even twenty-five years ago was alone in his locked room sulking, possibly even reading—possibly even reading something obscene. The typical (?) teenager in 2011 seems to be out filming himself to program his Facebook page or compete for attention on YouTube. This reversal is so radical, we could debate whether "personal technology," in little more than a decade, has altered America's DNA. But the eradication of privacy as a core human value doesn't account for the cruelty, for the internet's "culture of sadism" that the computer scientist Jaron Lanier decries in his book. It doesn't account for the Rutgers atrocity or subhuman video "pranks" like attacking homeless men and beating a thirteen-year-old girl—both popular attractions on websites that encourage this spreading infection.

461

Is it possible that expanding the community immeasurably, from the dozens to the millions, dilutes all the positive aspects of community—compassion, loyalty, mutual support and responsibility? That as the community expands, communality contracts until dog-eat-dog rules again? With the whole anonymous world watching, at least in your imagination, do individuals lose substance, become little more than "viewers"—totaled online as "hits"—and Facebook "friends" you'll never meet? You wouldn't beat or betray a friend, but a "friend" is another matter. This is just a suggestion from the sidelines. No doubt the fence-plowing kid has a different explanation. The blessing conferred on those whom obsolescence has claimed is that we'll never have to compete with "the kid" for the world's attention. If you will, if you do, God help you.

Of course it's a small minority of teenagers who beat up the homeless for publicity and post nude pictures of themselves online. But I'm afraid the majority is too marinated in the culture that breeds this behavior to see how grotesque and pathetic it's become. It takes perspective. If you're still able to take one step off the grid and look back, the view might shake you up, or crack you up. The dividing line between generations is laid down sharply in *The Social Network* when Sean Parker, loathsome founder of Napster, cries out in his cups, "People used to live on farms and in cities, now we'll all live on the internet!" If Parker's outburst chills you as a vision of an ultimate dystopia more depressing than *1984* or *Brave New World*—as the filmmakers intended—you're on my side of the line. If you barely notice it, you're lost on the far side.

Elsewhere the line is not so cleanly drawn. I confess that I laugh at people who buy and prize the Dick Tracy cell phones that do everything but brush your teeth and walk your dog. I also concede that I have extremely intelligent, serious, otherwise discriminating friends who poke away at the silly things with apparent fascination. These converts are not and will not be obsolete, perhaps as a matter of pride? But without dinosaurs like me to remind them, they'd forget what the old order was like. Have I disappointed them? What did I ever do to feed a suspicion I could be seduced by gadgets that invite me to gape at movies, stock reports, spreadsheets, pornography, weather maps and email on a screen half the size of a playing card, like some gorilla mesmerized by a Christmas tree ornament? Which of us is weird?

The last question can't be answered definitively. In the few years since it opened, the high-tech superhighway—ten lanes, no speed limit—has carried most Americans far from their origins, and lured nearly all of us out of our comfort zones. But the highway is littered with accidents, too, and road signs that lead us nowhere. It's mainly an aesthetic decision, finally, to pull off the road and turn off the ignition. It's possible to remain physically and mentally vigorous thirty years after most of your contemporaries have faded away. But I believe that each of us has a kind of cultural expiration date, and there's nothing more pitiful than a person who's exhausted his cultural shelf life and doesn't know it. Think of the sexagenarian who claims to love Eminem. How do you know when you've expired? Maybe when popular culture pushes you beyond contempt into physical nausea. I reached that place a while ago. If you're old enough to remember Jerry Ford and you're not there yet, you will be soon. Unless, of course, you're one of the shell people with no core of sensibility or belief, ever ready to hitch a ride on anything that comes your way.

This isn't a popular song I'm playing, or one you're likely to hear again. But it isn't a dirge. Or a swan song. Obsolete and unashamed, we feel like farmers who got their crops in safely before the hard rains fell. As storm clouds gather, it's a time to walk the fields of stubble with the old dog, the hearthdog, and see, as the Bible says, that it is good. Then comes a long winter musing by the fire—though spring remains a question mark. The past is a flickering daydream, the present is turning ugly, and the future belongs to no one, though the kind of heirs we might have chosen seem less and less likely to inherit. We haven't said "goodbye," we've just said "enough."

In common usage the word "obsolete" has become too pejorative. Many outdated things—Jim Crow, the Vatican, cigarettes, the two-party political system—wear out their welcome but fail to achieve extinction rapidly enough. Yet so much that's obsolete deserved a better fate. We may be the last of our kind, but we flatter ourselves that we'll be missed, perhaps even heeded more in the future than we were in the past. In my research I came across a lovely sentence in praise of the homely, ancient instrument that gave its name to my father's family. With a minor lapse of modesty, I can pretend that the author is speaking of me: "For all of its (his) technical limitations, the crwth has great charm, and is much more than a historical curiosity."

Nominated by Blackbird

MY NEIGHBOR'S BODY

by BECKIAN FRITZ GOLDBERG

from FIELD

What can I do tonight about the wild camels in Australia
whose herds the government will thin by aerial gunning?
The truth is all I do these days is watch the neighbor's hedge
of brooding oleanders sway, heavy with dark red blossom.
They are twelve feet high on his side of the arroyo
and hide his house. I don't know who lives there
but I know he has a truck and listens to the country station.
I can't help what I know and what I don't know
helps me. I stand out on the patio and smoke when I have
     work to do.
The blooms light their deep pink auras. All spring
my neighbor rattles things behind his house, throws
things on top of other things. It echoes. I haven't done
a good day's work since that day in class when I required
every poem henceforth to have in it a jacamar & hereby
have followed policy. It's the least I can do. My neighbor's song
     tonight
rues some faithless woman as he kills the engine, leaves
the radio on until the song is done. I have never seen his body.
I have never seen his faithless wife. I am on the side of
the black oleanders moving their great mind
under the little moon. They are fifteen feet high
and hide my house. It's been good, our not knowing each other.
He won't mind me still out on the patio not telling him
in Egypt once I heard camels call to one another

as they milled about and one by one kneeled for tourists to mount.
It is an ugly cry trapped, I can only say, like
the body of the letter *m* set on fire on their throats. In Cairo's heat
I moved around like royalty with a retinue of children
asking for American dollars. Like royalty I gave sometimes
and sometimes not. The hotel that summer was filled
with engineers working on the underground, work that stalled
each time they hit a buried wall or well of ancient kingdom,
and late afternoons they'd drink with Madam Ariana, the manager,
a Coptic Christian and a true believer
that ketchup was the cause of cancer and that opera
refined the soul. Tonight the moon holds its high white note over
the desert slopes. Here we are. What can we do
about camels in Australia stunned in the warm sheen of
their own blood? Dry yellow petals scatter on the patio.
They do this when they are alone. The world is full of the helpless,
seeing its one hand, the petals mounded briefly at the patio wall.
Their whisper like the guard's pulling us aside in the museum
where they kept animal mummies, mostly ibises and cats.
Their necks were wrung in sacrifice, their bodies emptied, filled
    again,
sewn and wrapped like dolls for gods who looked just like them.
For a dollar, he said, we could touch one. I know
everyone has to make a living. I don't know how my neighbor
does. He has somewhere to go to and somewhere to come back
and isn't that enough? Each day if I say he's happy he is happy.
If I say he is miserable he is. If I say put on a song sometimes
he does. Then I don't get much work done, another iridescent
jacamar lies unwritten. Tonight a hundred living things
chirr in the arroyo, the rest is quiet. Our lives are quiet.
We know what we know. I know my neighbor's body must have fire
like mine. It must have dim soft places no one's touched
for the longest time. I know it must rise sometimes at night
for no reason and then must go somewhere and sit. I don't know
what it is that aches. The body does not know how to speak
for itself. It stands out on the patio in the dark thinking this time
of John-Michael who has tattooed across his chest a line
from a poem he loves. He is brave. Think of the women
who'll face it there, a love no thing or woman will come between,
and turn & some come anyway. They'll know and not know.

There is no language there. The hedge shifts its thick
ocean of leaves in the wind and John-Michael is gone. Light
winks through. My neighbor is home, and if he knew he was
on my mind tonight he'd call the police. For all I know he's a
   cowboy
and would kick me to crap. For all I know he is
the police. For all I know he is lonely and would weep.
Beware of the neighbor. Beware the one who imagines you
in some form other than your own, filled with other desire, empty
of other emptiness. Beware of the one who does not.
You are the gentle camel. You are the rufous-tailed jacamar.
Your blossoms hang open in the dark, riding the black
wave of oleander. And I am kissing my neighbor's full mouth,
tracing
the moon above his left nipple. I am lying against his body,
reaching down and cupping them, gently, in my hand, for didn't we
come helpless into the world, my love, but we came anyway.

—for H.C. and for J.M.B.

Nominated by Field, Elton Glaser, David St. John

PHILANTHROPY

fiction by SUZANNE RIVECCA

from GRANTA

Days before she met the novelist, Cora went to the library and brought home a stack of plastic-sleeved hardcovers with one-word titles like *Heirloom* and *Ruffian* and *Seductress*. Her favourite was an early effort with an unusually loquacious title: *The Illegitimate Prince's Child*. At first it was unclear who was illegitimate, the prince or his child. It turned out to be both. During the Hep C Support Group at the drop-in, Cora read aloud sentences like 'Evelina knew Rolf would never marry her if she revealed her true station, but having been a bastard himself, how could he inflict the same fate on the unborn child inside her?' She regaled the needle-exchange staff with passages from Ruffian, substituting clients' names for the well-endowed hero's. She knew she was being inappropriate but she couldn't stop. She studied Yvonne Borneo's soft-focus author photos and imagined the hilarious incongruity of her vaunted good works – scattering gold pieces to hookers as she was borne down Mission Street on a litter, that sort of thing – and now that the appointed time had arrived for them to meet, she wanted Yvonne Borneo to deliver. She wanted a white mink hat and coat, a thick tread of diamonds across the collarbones, peacock-blue eyeshadow and sharp swipes of blush and impossibly glossy lips: the rigidly contoured, calculatedly baroque opulence of an eighties soap star auditioning for the role of tsarina. And Yvonne Borneo disappointed her by showing up at Capp Street Women's Services in a plain taupe skirt and suit jacket. Her sole concession to decadence was a mulberry cashmere scarf, soft as a runaway's peach fuzz, held in place with a metal pin shaped like a Scottie dog's silhouette.

'Well, you're just a tiny little mite,' was the first thing she said to Cora. Her voice was butterfat-rich but filmy, like an old bar of dark chocolate that had taken on a grey cast.

The novelist/philanthropist was more vigorous than her wax-figure photographs, and at the same time much frailer. She thrust her shoulders back with a martial bearing when she laughed, which was often, but Cora noticed her hands trembling slightly when they weren't clasped in front of her. Her hair was beginning to thin. She was grandly imperious in a merrily half-ironic way. When Cora offered her a slice of red velvet cake, which she'd read was the novelist's favourite, Yvonne said, 'Bikini season's upon us. I daren't indulge!' Yet she didn't flinch at the posted Rules of Conduct, scrolled in silver marker on black paper, hung above the TV in the main lounge, and frequently amended for circumstance. In the past few months, necessity had compelled Cora to add 'NO SHOWING GENITALIA', 'FLUSH THE TOILET AFTER YOU SHIT' and 'DON'T JERK OFF IN THE BATHROOM'. This last rule was intended for the pre-op MTFs.

Yvonne read the rules from top to bottom, and when she was done she ruffled herself slightly, as though shaking off a light drizzle. Then she smiled brightly at Cora.

'Well,' she said. 'Girls will be girls.'

Cora reminded herself that Yvonne Borneo was not easily shocked. How could she be? Her only child, a girl named Angelica, had stepped in front of a bullet train at twenty, after years of struggling with schizophrenia and – it was rumoured – heroin addiction and sex work, although Yvonne had never confirmed this. She focused on the schizophrenia, referring to her late daughter as having 'lost a battle with a significant and debilitating mental illness'. The foundation she established after Angelica's death, the Angel Trust, gave money to provide mental health care for young women who had 'lost their way' and were at risk of suicide.

Angelica had been the same age as Cora. As teenagers in the same Utah behaviour modification programme for troubled youth, they had known each other slightly. Cora was waiting for the right moment to tell Yvonne this. She tried to engineer an interval of quiet, seated intimacy, lowered voices, eye contact. But Yvonne moved too fast and talked too quickly, asking about city contracts and capital campaigns and annual reports, and Cora needed her money – the money from airport book sales and Hallmark Hall of Fame movie rights and the pocket change of millions of frustrated housewives – so badly she could hardly keep the desperation out of her voice. The city cuts had been devastating.

The Department of Public Health's deputy director, who had set up this meeting, warned her to cover her tattoos.

'Even the ones on my face?' Cora had said.

'I forgot about those. OK, just don't say anything about her daughter being a dope fiend.'

In Cora's tiny office, Yvonne lingered a few moments before the Dead Wall, which featured photographs of kids who had overdosed or killed themselves or been stabbed. None of these photos were appropriately elegiac, since the bereaved families usually couldn't be counted on to give Cora a cute school picture or a Polaroid of the deceased with a puppy. Most of the dead were memorialized in the act of flipping off the camera or smoking a bowl.

Yvonne put a hand to her chin. 'It's so sad,' she said. 'Such a waste.'

'Yes,' Cora said.

'Well,' Yvonne said. She sat down, crossing her legs. 'What do you envision the Angel Trust being able to do for you?'

She asked this without real curiosity, her tone silky, keen and expertly measured as a game-show host's. Cora began to sweat.

'Well, first of all, I wouldn't have to lay off any more outreach staff,' she said. Without realizing it, she was counting on her fingers. 'And there are basic expenses like rent and utilities. And I'd love to increase Sonia's hours – she's the psychiatrist – because we're seeing a lot more girls with serious mental illness out there right now.'

Yvonne frowned. 'Well, the psychiatrist's hours, yes, I can get behind that. But as for the layoffs – it's always our preference that my funds not be used as a stopgap for deficits in government funding. My board prefers not to dispense bail-out money.'

And this, Cora told herself, was why she hated philanthropists. Their dainty aversion to real emergency and distress, their careful gauging and hedging of risks, their preference, so politely and euphemistically stated, for supporting programmes that didn't really *need* help to stay open, but sure could use a shiny new foyer, complete with naming opportunity. This was what she hated about rich people: their discomfort with their own unsettling power to salvage and save, the fear of besiegement that comes with filling an ugly basic need, their distaste for the unavoidably vertical dynamic of dispensing money to people who have none. The way they prided themselves on never giving cash to homeless people on the street, preferring a suited, solvent, 501c3-certified middleman, who knew better. For Cora, the hardest part of running the drop-in was not the necrotized arm wounds, the ubiquity of urine and rot, the occasional OD in the bathroom, the collect calls from prison. It was the eternal quest for money, the need to justify, to immerse herself in the fuzzy, lateral terminology of philanthropy. Over the last ten years Cora had learned that donors don't give a programme dollars to save it from extinction; they 'build a relationship' with the programme. They want 'partners', not charity cases. And deep down, they believe in their hearts that people in real, urgent need – the kind of person Cora once was, and the kind she still felt like much of the time – make bad partners.

Cora cleared her throat. 'Well,' she said, 'increasing Sonia's hours won't do much good if we don't have a roof for her to work under, or a way of bringing clients to her.'

She thought she saw Yvonne stiffen. Cora knew she was terrible at diplomacy. When she got angry she preferred to yell; and if she were in front of the Board of Supervisors or the mayor's staff instead of Yvonne Borneo, she would have. But this woman, this sleek, self-made authoress – that word, with its anachronistic, feline hiss of implied dilettantism, seemed made for her – had to be handled differently. She had no civic obligation to stem disease; she helped at her whim. It had to be some little thing that reeled her in, some ridiculous coincidence, some accident of fate. And Cora remembered her trump card.

There was no time to wait for a transition. She opened her mouth and prepared to blurt something out, something inappropriate and apropos of nothing – *I knew your daughter when she was a dope fiend*, maybe – when a pounding on the gate stopped her. Then a wailing. Someone was wailing her name.

Yvonne Borneo perked up so markedly her neck seemed to lengthen an inch. 'Do you need to see to that?' she said.

Cora excused herself and went to the back gate. It was DJ, a regular client who had come to the door and screamed for her plenty of times before, but never when anyone important was present. Cora had once lanced a six-inch-long abscess on DJ's arm – she'd measured it – and when the clinic doctor pared away the necrotized tissue, bone showed through. DJ had started coming to the women's centre at nineteen, freshly emancipated from foster care, clearly bipolar, and Cora had been trying to get her to see Sonia for seven years. She was twenty-six now and looked at least forty.

Today she looked worse than usual, in army pants held together with safety pins and a filthy tank top that revealed the caverns of scar tissue on her arms, the bulging sternum that seemed to twang fiercely under her skin like outraged tuning forks. When she saw Cora, DJ thrust both arms through the bars of the gate, like a prisoner in stocks, and wept.

'You came to see me when no one else did,' she sobbed.

'OK, DJ,' Cora said. 'OK.'

DJ did this a lot: went back and forth in time. She was talking about when she'd been stabbed by a john two years before and Cora had been the only one to stay with her at SF General, eventually securing her a semi-private room and making the nurse give her painkillers. 'Yeah, she's an addict,' she had snapped at the young woman on duty. 'It still hurts when she gets stabbed.'

Sometimes DJ would recount an unknown past assault, or several, quietly sitting in the corner of the needle exchange and saying, 'He raped me, Cora,' while peering through the twisted vines of her hair. 'I know, hon,' Cora would say. 'I'd cut his balls off if I could.' This always seemed to calm DJ down.

After Cora's sister had a baby and the baby got older and began to speak in lucid sentences, its vocal patterns and flattened sense of chronology reminded Cora of DJ: that tendency to recount, repetitively, in the balanced and slightly bemused tones of a person under hypnosis, past events as though they had just happened. No 'I remember this', just 'Mama dropped a plate and it broke', meditatively, with an air of troubled, grieving reflection. It seemed to her that DJ, like the baby, was stuck in some cognitive cul-de-sac and, unlike the baby, would never develop a perspective layered and three-dimensional enough to find her way out.

Now Cora looked into her wet face and said, 'DJ, I've got someone in there. Someone I'm having a meeting with. If you come back in an hour, when I open the exchange, we'll talk. OK?'

DJ gazed at her. 'An hour?' she said hollowly.

'Yeah.'

The girl's face began to twist and shift like there was something behind it, trying to get out. She slumped forward, forearms still resting on the bars of the gate, and moaned. Cora smelled alcohol and urine.

'DJ, please. One hour. I've got someone who might give us money in there, and I can't just leave her sitting in my office.'

DJ slumped on the concrete, fingers still poking through the grates, and muttered, 'OK, OK, OK.'

When Cora returned and apologized to Yvonne, the novelist said,

'Everything all right?' Before Cora could answer, the screaming started again. DJ was now banging her head against the metal bars of the gate and howling, 'I'm sorry, I know there's a rich lady in there, but I need to come in!'

Cora grabbed her ring of keys and hurried down the hall. It was starting to get dark outside but she could see a wet patch of blood on DJ's lip from the banging. When she unlocked the gate, DJ fell against her, almost gracefully. Cora staggered under the weight and struggled to dig her hands into the girl's armpits, hoisting her up to standing. She lost her grip, and they collapsed together on the concrete floor. The crotch of DJ's pants was soaked through. 'It's just so cold,' the girl slurred. 'It's just so cold out there. I keep peeing myself, Cora.'

Cora took DJ's chin in her hands and looked into her eyes. They were unfocused and dilated, but not fixed. She was just very drunk.

'I can't be out there right now.'

She pressed against Cora. They were entangled now on the floor of the hall, and Cora felt a hot dribble of urine slowly, exhaustedly trickle across the floor underneath their bodies. 'It hurts,' DJ said.

'I think you might have a UTI again, hon,' Cora said. 'Remember when we talked about pissing right after you fuck?'

'She's fancy,' DJ said.

At first Cora thought DJ was going back in time again, but then realized she was referring to Yvonne Borneo, who stood in the middle of the hallway in her grey suit, arms at her sides, projecting the deliberate, neutral composure of a wartime nurse – one of her own heroines, perhaps, kindly but remote and weighted with an incurable private grief.

'Is there anything I can do?' she said.

And so Yvonne Borneo helped Cora haul DJ into the bathroom. It was Yvonne who picked through the clothes bin and found clean pants and a sweatshirt, who went and bought three black coffees at the diner down the block while Cora helped DJ shower. And later, it was Yvonne who sat in the needle exchange with Lew, the volunteer, while the on-site nurse gave DJ a dose of antibiotics and Cora spent an hour trying to find her a shelter bed for the night. It was fruitless. There was nothing.

'What if we book a decent hotel room for her and you take her there in a cab, make sure she checks in?' Yvonne suggested.

Cora shook her head. 'If she's going overnight somewhere, it needs to be a place where people know what they're doing.' She looked down at her lap. 'The only option is to 5150 her.'

Yvonne didn't ask what a 5150 was. She said, 'Well, if the alternative is to be on the streets . . .' She trailed off. From the exam room came the sound of DJ alternately screaming and sobbing. The sounds were a kind of last gasp, witless and terrifying as the *crunch* before a piece of machinery breaks down for good. Cora stood up and shut the door to her office.

She made the call. Half an hour later, when the paramedics burst in the front door of the drop-in, four big burly men, louder and stompier than necessary in the way paramedics always are – the way anyone is, for that matter, who comes in the guise of eleventh-hour rescuer – and strapped DJ to a gurney, Cora ran alongside the stretcher and told the girl that things would be OK. But she knew this was unlikely, just as she knew her chances with Yvonne Borneo were blown, because the woman had borne witness to Cora's greatest failure, a failure multiplied by the scores of clients just like DJ: girls who could not change. The part of them that knew how to accept help, whatever that part was called – Hope? Imagination? Foresight? – had been destroyed. And what Cora and her staff did for such girls, day after day, felt more and more like hospice care: an attempt to minimize the worst of their pain until death.

Cora stood in the alley after the ambulance took off. It was Friday night and all the barkeeps along Mission and Valencia were dumping empty bottles into recycling bins. The sound of breaking glass seemed gratuitously destructive, nihilistic. She watched a woman walking down Capp Street in a short swingy coat and heels. A car pulled up alongside her and idled. Some idiot from Marin, thought Cora. The woman and the man in the car conferred for a moment, and the woman drew herself up and hurried down the sidewalk, shaking her head, outraged, as the vehicle pulled away.

When Cora came back into the exchange, Lew was alone.

'Where's Yvonne Borneo?' she said.

'You mean that lady? That narc-looking lady?'

'Yes,' Cora sighed. 'She left, didn't she?'

Lew shrugged. 'She left when the paramedics got here. She looked freaked.'

'Did she say anything?'

'Nope. Maybe *toodaloo* or something.' He flapped his wrist.

Cora sat down. 'She did not fucking say *toodaloo*.'

'No,' Lew admitted. 'She did not.'

The first time Cora saw Yvonne's daughter was in Ravenswood's recreation room. They were both fifteen. She remembered Angelica as tall and big-framed and slumped, with choppy bangs and sidelong, slippery eyes, seemingly beyond nervousness and fear, reduced to the passive, grim spectatorship of an inured captive. There was sympathy in the look she gave Cora, but it was neutered, the retroactive ghost of sympathy you have for your own past, stupid self.

One of the other girls asked how long Cora would be staying.

'Not long,' Cora said, scared. Straining for flippancy. 'Two weeks probably.'

Angelica laughed.

'That's what we all thought,' she said. She spoke in Cora's direction but didn't look at her. Cora tried to snag her gaze but it kept floating away, elusive and directionless. Then Angelica turned to leave the room and that's when she said the chilling thing, head down, so quiet and unassuming she could have been saying it to herself. 'Honey,' she said, 'you are *never* getting out of here.'

That night, her first at Ravenswood, Cora cried and sweated in her bed. Every fifteen minutes an aide came in and shined a flashlight on her. She wasn't allowed to talk to her dad on the phone. 'Can't be a daddy's girl forever,' one of the staff told her cheerfully. A dry-skinned, freckled woman wearing a sweatshirt with a grainy Georgia O'Keeffe flower scanned on the front. 'You have a vagina on your shirt,' Cora told her. The woman's mouth twisted into a tight, hurt smirk. 'You need to grow up,' she said. 'I won't tell anyone what you said this time, but you need to start growing up.'

At night, Cora would watch the snow from the tiny window in the Chill Out Room. She'd discovered that if she said things like *vagina* and *penis* and *fuck* enough, she'd get sent to the Chill Out Room and could be alone and not have to talk to anyone or pretend to be listening. There was no toilet in there, so she tried to limit her beverage intake. The hours stretched on. Cora would sit on the floor, scowling at the aide who came by every half-hour to ensure that she hadn't found an inventive way to hang herself. All the staff on the girls' ward were women, soft and easily hurt but inflexible, vicious in a hand-wringing, motherly way. Turned-down mouths and sad, round faces. If you called one of these women a fucking twat, her eyes would fill up and her voice quaver with genuine injured dignity. Then she would tell you she was very

474

sorry, but you couldn't shower or change your underwear or socks until you apologized and admitted you were wrong. And the terrible thing was, she'd actually *seem* sorry. They were all perpetually cowed by their own brutality, quivering and defeated by the measures they were forced to enact. If Cora was nice to them, they were worse: unpardonably brisk and springy and relieved, presumptuous in their patting and hugging, insufferable in their tentative optimism. Their non-violent and vaguely cutesy demands – that she sing show tunes in the bathroom to prove she wasn't shooting up or purging, that she do three jumping jacks for every swear word uttered, that she participate in a sock-puppet revue dramatizing what she wanted her life to be like in five years – made her want to kill, and she envied the boys, who, it was rumoured, merely got hog-tied and placed in restrictive holds.

When Cora got home after her meeting with Yvonne, she sat on the floor of her living room and did sudoku puzzles for two hours. Then she tried to sleep but couldn't. The apartment was too quiet and she missed her cat, Melly, who had been dead for two weeks. Melly was a soothing, watchful, totemic presence, like a Buddha statue. She had a charming trait of standing on her two back feet for hours at a time, as if this was a restful position, her front legs hanging straight down from her chest, exposing the fur on her stomach, which was wavier and coarser than the rest. Cora and her friends had gathered round and laughed and marvelled and took pictures on their cellphones and praised Melly for being so cute and novel, until the day the vet informed Cora that Melly had advanced bone cancer and the reason she stood on her back feet was that it was the only position that alleviated her excruciating pain. Melly was put to sleep while Cora held her, whispering apologies, and she wanted to get another cat but was afraid of misinterpreting another signal, unwittingly laughing at another decline.

Melly's food and water bowls were still in the kitchen, half full, the water filmed over with bits of fur on the rim, the corners of each room still hoarding tumbleweeds of cat hair. Cora wiped the rim of the water bowl with her thumb. She kept remembering Yvonne Borneo in the bathroom of the drop-in, kneeling on the floor in her taupe skirt, pulling off DJ's army pants with grim, sharpened concentration. In those moments she seemed to have stepped into a transparent sleeve like the plastic sheaths on her novels, an invisible barrier that kept her from getting dirty. Not shying away from the wetness on DJ's pants. Not wincing at the smell. But not registering it, either. At one point, she leaned over DJ, blotting at the girl's bloody lip, and her Scottie-dog pin dinged against DJ's nose. DJ blinked, started, stared at Yvonne as if she hadn't seen her before.

'You're taking my clothes off,' she murmured.

'Yes,' Yvonne said. 'So you can clean up.'

'Oh, God,' DJ moaned. 'Oh, God.' Then she squirmed to one side and planted her hands flat on the floor and vomited, not all at once but like a cat with a hairball, a series of back-arching, rippling convulsions.

'Get it all out,' Yvonne had said.

The phone rang. A man's voice, clipped and high-pitched.

'Is this Cora Hennessey? Of Capp Street Women's Services?'

'Yes,' Cora said.

Someone's dead, she thought. *DJ's dead.*

'My name is Josiah Lambeaux. I'm the personal assistant to Yvonne Borneo.'

'OK,' Cora said.

It was raining. The ride to Yvonne Borneo's house felt needlessly meandering, up and down hills and around curves in the dense foggy dark, the car's lights occasionally isolating a frozen, fleeting image – a hooded man in a crosswalk, head bowed; a shivering sheaf of bougainvillea clinging to a stone wall; peeling layers of movie posters and Lost Cat signs and sublet notices trailing wet numbered tabs, plastered across the windows of vacant storefronts. Josiah drove his dove-grey sedan with the decorous effacement of a dad trying not to embarrass his teenage daughter, and she sat in the back and watched his thin neck tensing, his hands modestly manipulating the wheel with a pointed lack of gestural flair as they entered Seacliff, a hazy Land of the Lotus Eaters perched on the edge of the Presidio's red-roofed orderliness: a mirage of wide, silent streets and giant lawns and strangely permeable-looking mansions, many of them white and turreted and vaporous in the dark, whose banks of windows turned a blind slate toward the bay and its light-spangled bridge. As they turned onto the mile-long, cypress-lined lane leading to Yvonne Borneo's estate, Cora stuck her face an inch from the back-seat window and imagined how hard it would be to run away from this place. Did Angelica break out under cover of night and run the entire mile from the front door to the road? What intricate alarm systems did she have to disassemble before she even crossed the

476

threshold? And once she was free, adrift in this silent, echoing no-man's-land of ghost-houses and yawning boulevards, how did she keep going? Having known nothing but this eerie greensward with its self-contradictory air of utter desertion and hyper-preservation, how did she know where to go, or even how to leave? Cora's own leave-taking, at fourteen, was comparatively easy. She waited until the house was silent and snuck out her bedroom window and climbed the backyard chain-link fence, to the road where her twenty-year-old boyfriend, Sammy, waited in his car. Her father barrelled out the back door after her, chased her across the yard, grabbed the belt loop of her jeans and pulled as she threw herself against the springy fence. She'd been shocked by how easily the fence swayed and shuddered as she clung to it. The change she'd filled her pockets with – pennies mostly – poured out, spattering on the ground and hitting her father in the face and arms. As he clutched her ankle, his eyes were screwed shut against the shower of coins and so he didn't see the foot of her free leg swinging toward him with all the lethal agility of the gymnast she'd once aspired to be, and he could only reel back, shocked, as the heel of her boot stomped down on his face.

She broke his nose. Her poor father who was only trying to protect his little girl from statutory rape at the hands of the druggie boy she adored. The weird sexual territoriality of fathers, some ancient hold-over from the days of dowries and bloody marital sheets. Even then, she knew it was about his ego, *his* deflowered honour, not hers. When Sammy overdosed and she came crawling back home, strung out and incoherent, her father wouldn't let her in the house or even talk to her. He sent her to Utah, where Angelica was.

During the moral inventory phase of the twelve steps, she called her father and apologized.

'I'm sorry I broke your nose and put you through all that worry and mess,' she said.

He seemed dumbfounded. 'I don't even like to think about that,' he said. 'As far as I'm concerned, it never happened. You are what you are now, and that's who my daughter is. You. Not that other person.'

'But I have to make amends, Dad,' she said.

He said, 'You can't make amends for something that never happened.'

As the sedan reached the end of the lane and the house reared up before them, Cora forced herself to take deep breaths. Josiah parked and opened the passenger door for her, and she followed him past a row of topiaries and rose bushes, the heads of the flowers bowed by the rain. The house was a giant whitewashed box of sparkling stone, vaguely French Regency, wrought-iron balconies jutting from huge, blue-shuttered casement windows. As she and Josiah walked to the front door, a series of motion-sensor floodlights clicked on, one after the other, dogging their steps.

Yvonne Borneo was waiting for them in the vestibule.

'Cora!' she exclaimed. 'You made it!'

Then she hugged Cora. She wore silk lounge pants and a gauzy tunic, and Cora, chin pressed against the novelist's dry, soft neck, smelled lily of the valley and starch.

'Thank you for having me,' Cora said. During their embrace, Josiah had vaporized; they were alone in a high-ceilinged foyer of slate and marble.

'You are *such* a tiny thing,' Yvonne said, sorrowfully looking Cora up and down.

Dinner was dished out by Josiah: skirt steak and buttered carrots and parsley potatoes in ceramic serving platters. When he produced a bottle of red wine and plucked Cora's glass by its stem, she held up her hand.

'No,' she said. 'No, thank you.'

'It's an excellent wine,' he said.

'I don't drink.'

She'd been saying this for fifteen years, and the reaction was always the same: a wide-eyed, almost abject solicitude as the implications of the statement were processed. Then an abashed hush. Josiah poured her a glass of water.

As soon as Josiah left the room, Yvonne leaned forward slightly and looked at Cora. A centrepiece of bare black branches sat between them. She gently pushed it aside.

'I wanted to have you over to apologize to you, in person,' she said, 'for leaving so abruptly last night.'

'Oh, no,' Cora said. 'No, I understand. I figured you had to get going.'

Yvonne kept gazing at her. 'It was hard for me,' she said slowly, 'to see someone in that condition.'

'Of course,' Cora said.

'How is DJ?'

'Well, they've got her on a forty-eight-hour hold. So . . .' Cora shrugged. 'I guess at least she's detoxing right now. And maybe she'll have a shelter bed by the time she's out.'

Yvonne looked down. 'I don't know how you do it,' she murmured. 'Every single day. How you don't lose hope.'

Cora surprised herself by saying, 'Oh, I do. I just pretend that I don't.'

Yvonne looked up, staring at her sharply, and Cora had a peculiar sensation of loosening, uncurling and pushing off with a fortifying heedlessness that was liberating and bleak. If she still drank, she would have taken a gulp of wine at that moment. In her mind she saw money, coins and coins of it, running through her fingers.

'May I ask you a question?' Yvonne said.

Cora nodded.

'Why did you leave home?'

Cora had told the story of her downward spiral in front of countless donors. After years of twelve-step testimony she could easily slide into the instructive, talking-points tone this spiel seemed to demand. She always began with a disclaimer: *My parents weren't abusive. Which makes me different from most runaways.* Measured, wide-eyed, absolving everyone of everything. *I made a choice.* And she opened her mouth to say it again, and found that she couldn't.

What she heard herself saying instead was, 'I was in love with an older guy, and I wanted to have sex with him.'

Yvonne's fingers closed around the stem of her wine glass. She frowned.

'And that's why you left home?'

'Pretty much,' Cora said. 'My parents didn't let me date. They were really, really afraid I'd turn into a slut. I mean, *preoccupied* with the possibility I'd turn into a slut. As in, every rule they made revolved around protecting me from that fate. And, um, I wanted to have sex. So.'

Yvonne looked grave and slightly stricken.

Cora kept going. 'And this guy got me into drugs, and then he overdosed and I just went crazy. I kind of wanted to die with him. And I think it was mourning, the whole time I was on the street like that. I could say to you that I was a bad, bad girl and experimenting and rebelling, or whatever, but I really do think it was my way of mourning. And I could say there was one big, defining experience that changed me and made it OK, but there wasn't. It's still not OK. It'll never be OK. I just eventually stopped mourning.'

Yvonne said, 'But you got off the drugs. You made a life for yourself.'

'The other thing was a life too.'

Yvonne looked dismayed. 'But what kind of life? Strung out, on the streets? Addicted to drugs?' She trailed off, toyed with her fork.

Cora laughed, meanly. She was suddenly very angry. She had been waiting, she realized, for this chance since the moment they had met. Since before.

'Believe me,' she said. Her voice was deliberate and low, feeling its way. 'No one would do drugs if they weren't fun. The drugs are what I miss the most.'

She laughed again, this time with disbelief at having said it out loud. But it was true.

Yvonne gracefully nudged her glass aside and cradled her chin in one long-fingered hand.

'I wouldn't really know,' she said evenly.

Cora blurted out, 'I was with your daughter at Ravenswood.'

Yvonne stared.

'I don't know how long she was there. I was only there for a month. That's the way it worked, you know, if your parents couldn't afford to keep paying, they'd get told you were cured. And if your parents were rich enough, you were never cured.'

In the dimness Yvonne's face seemed to tighten into facets, like a diamond, each outraged angle giving off light. And Cora kept going. She couldn't stop.

'That place was, excuse me, a mind fuck. They made up a diagnosis and made you try to fit it. Which may have been what they did to Angelica. Who I only saw once or twice, because I was stuck in a tiny padded room, alone, most of the time.'

Her voice was unrecognizable to her ears: ragged, lashing, corrosive. Almost breaking. When she yelled at City Hall, it was mostly a put-on: she was angry, but she also knew she had to seem sane, galvanizing, in the right. Now she was simply ranting. Ranting at the millionaire who had invited her to dinner. And she couldn't stop.

'I was a junkie when I went in there,' she said. 'Like your daughter. And as soon as I got out, I couldn't *wait* to go do some drugs. I felt *lucky* to be out of that place and doing drugs again.'

She was out of breath. For years she had counselled parents, engineered reconciliations, built bridges for girls to reconnect with their estranged families. Even if those families had made terrible mistakes, like sending their daughters to offshore boot camps, beating them, disowning them for getting raped or pregnant. No matter how awful the parents had been, they clung to Cora; they called her and told her how much they loved their daughters. They said things like, 'You don't have to tell me where she is; just tell her that I love her.' They cried. They listened to her with the chastened raptness of converts. They did what she suggested. And if their daughters came back, or pulled themselves clear and forgave their parents, Cora thanked God she'd been patient, bitten her tongue, refused to say the very things she was now saying to Yvonne Borneo.

Yvonne picked up her napkin.

'Let me stop you right there, please, Cora,' she said. Her voice was calm.

'I still –'

'Please,' Yvonne said. 'Please.'

She waited until Cora became uncomfortable enough with the silence to sit back, with poor grace, and say, 'All right.'

'I think,' Yvonne said, 'I wanted to meet you because I knew something about your past. I knew you were a runaway. And on some level I wanted to see you and find out about you. I wanted to find out why you survived and my daughter didn't.'

She folded her hands and cleared her throat, and when she resumed speaking her voice slackened, sagging with the dead weight of futile certainty. 'It's because she was schizophrenic, that's what you'd tell me. And maybe you'd be right. But let me ask you this. If the situations were reversed, if you had been the one to die, and if Angelica were sitting in front of your parents right now and saying how awful Ravenswood was, what a mistake they made, what would your parents tell her?'

Cora's mouth was parched. The bitten shreds of her lips stuck together when she tried to separate them.

'I don't know,' she said.

Yvonne's mouth stretched into a desolate smile.

'I'll tell you,' she said. 'They'd say exactly what I'm about to. They'd say, "My daughter was an ocean underneath an ocean." And it would be true. I see these girls on the streets, girls like DJ, the girls in your drop-in, and I know every single one of them is someone's daughter. And to their own parents, every single one of them is an ocean underneath an ocean.' She tapped her index figure on the table in rhythm with the words. 'Fathoms and fathoms deep. A complete mystery. My daughter is completely unfathomable to me. And certainly, if I may say so, to you.'

Cora balled her fists under the table. She knew she should be mollified – if this were a TV show, she would be cowed before the unassailable authority of maternal privilege – but she was furious, burning, convinced that nothing had ever made her angrier than this: this artful abdication of responsibility, this consigning of every lost daughter to a communal slag heap of pretty Persephones. She remembered her father's voice on the phone, telling her, 'You can't make amends for something that never happened.' How matter-of-factly he had absolved her of everything. How she wished she could accept his words as a gift and pretend they didn't feel like a swift and brutal erasure of her entire adolescence as though it were some wartime atrocity, a stack of bodies to be buried and sprinkled with lime. He had excised a part of her to the cutting-room floor. And when he reminisced about her growing up, as he occasionally did on her birthday and when he'd been drinking late at night and watching sentimental films on American Movie Classics, he selectively focused on those childhood behaviours that predicted and explained Cora's choice of career. How she'd always had a charitable bent. Defended smaller children from bullies. Brought home injured baby birds. Cried when starving Ethiopians were on the news. A Florence Nightingale whitewash, obscuring the simple fact that she cared about homeless junkie underage prostitutes because she used to be one. She knew what it was like to be Angelica, in a way Yvonne Borneo could never know.

'My parents,' she said, 'would never say that. Because I am not the same person as your daughter. I don't look at what happened to Angelica and think *there but for the grace of God go I*. We're all different. We're all different people!'

She was sputtering now, losing her eloquence, letting herself go in a way she never had before, and in her mind she saw the drop-in shuttered, saw herself somewhere else, working in an art store, maybe, or walking the streets of a strange city, or telling an entirely new subset of people what she used to be and what it meant, giving it a new spin, all the dead and dying girls of the Mission as distant and abstract to her as Bosnian war orphans, as famine victims, far away and someone else's problem, and she remembered how, at the moment the phone rang in her apartment the night before, there was a panicked, nonsensical moment in which she thought, she *knew*, it was Angelica. It was Angelica, calling to tell her something about her mother. To say be gentle with her, because she's in pain. Every moment of the day she's in pain. And Cora lifted her eyes from her plate and said, 'You're not going to give me any money, are you?' When her voice shook, she didn't know if it was with despair or relief.

Honey, you are never getting out of here.

She was dimly aware of the thin and careful form of Yvonne Borneo getting up from her chair and walking around the table. Then there was a hand on her shoulder – experimental, inquisitive, in the manner of a cat testing its balance on some unfamiliar surface.

Cora peered through her fingers. The novelist's face was inches from her own. Her brown eyes were very still and steady. Cora knew she was being shown something, that Yvonne was allowing some skimmed-away sediment to settle and collect in her dark eyes, in the grooves of her face, in the curves of her mouth. The look she gave Cora conveyed neither reproach nor remorse. What did it convey? Cora would never really know. She could only register something old and muddied and orphaned between them, a helpless moat of transference, brimming with the run-off of two people whose primary identities were, in the eyes of each other, not that of philanthropist and beneficiary, or writer and caregiver, but of someone else's mother and someone else's child. And it was this – this ancient ooze of crossed signals, this morass of things unsaid – that made Cora lower her forehead to Yvonne's shoulder and whisper, 'She loved you. I could *tell* that she loved you,' as the novelist stroked her hair the way Cora once imagined her stroking the head of a fox stole, automatically, with the phantom tenderness of a hand toward an object that is not the right thing at all, but is soft at least, and warm.

Nominated by Granta

INTERRUPTING AUBADE ENDING IN EPIPHANY

by MARCUS WICKER

from SOUTHERN INDIANA REVIEW

Could I call this poem an aubade if I wrapped it
in fragrant tissue paper? If I locked this morning

in the mind's safe deposit box and polished it
66 times per day, until a sky's description noted

the number of feathers on a sparrow's left wing
and the crab grass jutting from his uppity beak?

I once wrote a poem about a fruit fly orgy
in a grape's belly. Its crescendoed combustion

was supposed to represent the speaker's feelings
for a wife named Joy. That poem never really

worked out. This poem is aware of its mistakes
and doesn't care. This poem wants to be a poem

so bad, it'll show you a young smitten pair
poised in an S on a downy bed. The man inhales

the woman's sweet hair and whole fields
of honeysuckle and jasmine bloom inside him.

He inhabits a breath like an anodyne and I think
I could call this poem an aubade if it detailed

new breath departing his mouth. I think I could
get away with that. Because who knows what

that even means? Maybe I mean
that's safer than saying it straight

like, *This is about the woman I'll marry.*
How one summer, she hit snooze four times

each sunrise. This is about her smiling
and nodding off, and smiling, and listening

to me mumble into the back of her perfect
freckled shoulder about anything but poetry.

And this morning at my desk, in the midst
of a breath, I remember not every moment

needs naming, I know precisely what to call this.

Nominated by Southern Indiana Review

PAINTING THE SUMMER PALACE OF THE QUEEN

by PHILIP KELLY

from THE SUN

I invade people's lives for a living. At dawn I climb ladders to their second-story windows and fiddle with their locks. I place flammable materials in their garages and wake their sleeping dogs. I meet flannel-robed housewives as they hurry their husbands out the door.

I'm a house painter. I beg hesitant homeowners to paint their sitting rooms Chinese red. To suburbia I bring color wheels and clanking planks and dropcloths as multicolored as Joseph's coat. To a world too busy with rush-hour traffic and the concerns of Wall Street, I bring beauty and color.

I am an artist on a grand scale. I paint the dreams of architects, of builders, of husbands, wives, and children. I fail often enough. I choose the wrong hues; I must darken and reapply a stain; I have fallen fifteen feet onto a carpet of red bricks.

At times I paint palaces.

I bring art books to work. I'll paint a bedroom the color of the lantern light in van Gogh's *Café Terrace at Night*, holding the book up to my happy client's walls. I've brought Goya, Sargent, and Bonnard to construction sites with cement mixers out front. To morning kitchens alive with coffee and popping toasters and kids rushing off to school, I've brought Rubens.

Last year I brought Vermeer to an oceanfront house owned by a family of Germans. Grandpapa had bought the two-story, redwood California cottage in the thirties. Now he was gone, and Papa, his son, was the

486

elderly head of the flock, still with a shock of black hair and ten grown boys of his own and a wife in a nearby nursing home.

Every day, after visits with Mom, a few of the boys showed up at Papa's house unannounced with gruff, shouted greetings. They were all cabinetmakers, fallen from the same old-world tree. They'd shoulder each other about while cooking in the kitchen, joking and laughing, the two family dogs wandering in the forest of legs, hoping for fallen tidbits. It kept Papa going.

Upstairs, painting a bedroom, I had Vermeer's *View of Delft* at hand. When I had counseled Papa to paint his bedroom the color of the yellow house in Vermeer's distance, Papa had nodded. I'd told him how Proust had written of that house, of its yellow color, and Papa had nodded. And when I was done exclaiming my passion, he'd raised a bushy eyebrow and said simply, "You're the painter, painter," and left me to my work.

After a couple of days of seeing me gnaw an energy bar for lunch, this garrulous family adopted me. "Painter, lunch!" they'd call. "Get your ass down here!" We'd sit at the long table and pass dressings and pitchers of juice, and the boys would tell stories and shout at each other and eat platefuls of sausages and sauerkraut, then get quiet as they discussed how Mom was doing. When their pain became too obvious, they'd shake it off and ask, "Painter, why aren't you eating? How's that yellow going upstairs, painter?" Rather than talk of Vermeer, I'd reply, "Fine. Pass the damn sausages."

In the living room two La-Z-Boy chairs faced a window that looked out on the ocean. After lunch Papa sat in one; a son, full of sausages, collapsed into the other. Both draped warm cloths over their eyes, pulled up light blankets, and reclined like mummies laid out for their final rest. Each dog found a lap—Cuddles nestled in one, Buddy in the other—and they were all soon asleep.

As I'd tiptoe up and down the stairs for tools and paint, one or the other dog would half open a sleepy eye, then go back to snoring.

My life as a painter is as simple as a sparrow's: a morsel here, another there, no planning too far ahead. It's the times.

It wasn't always this way. Not too long ago I was booked for years in advance. New houses were hammered into being overnight, and owners of the older ones were spiffing theirs up. There seemed to be no end to the shine Southern California was putting on. They call it a "bubble," but it didn't pop so much as gradually deflate, like an old kickball. Five years ago we heard the first leak of air: a slight *psff*. Now I am booked for only the next two months with absolutely nothing beyond that. The ball is flat. I keep my business cards ready—"Thirty-Five Years Painting Houses by the Sea," they read—hoping to catch the eye of potential customers as I work on the Germans' house on the boardwalk. But I finish the job with no new work on the horizon. When a loyal customer named James calls to ask if I can fly to Hawaii to paint his vacation home, I am on the next plane. I would have flown to India.

I bring a book on Titian with me to Hawaii, where I have come to paint a seven-million-dollar house that looks across a turquoise sea to a distant horizon. I get to live here while I restore its beauty. The plantation-style house is spacious, breezy, comfortable, lived-in—and painted a god-awful mustard yellow, the walls black with mildew. I'll be here two months for sure, on the island of Oahu, where I grew up.

I sleep on the *pune'e*, a large Hawaiian couch, which faces the ocean. I watch the full moon pull itself from the blue water, feel the trade winds rustle my sheet. Two coconut trees cradle the moon. I plan my next day's painting as I fall asleep.

A Pacific golden plover is my constant companion each day. Her feathers tawny and black speckled, she scurries about the lawn, stops, raises a slim leg, and balances in silence—a ballerina with a long yellow beak—then drills the ground for a worm. I watch her from my ladder. It's April now. She'll be here through May, like me. Then she'll fly three thousand miles without landfall to her summer home in Alaska.

When the real-estate ball finally hissed flat, it affected everyone.

My old friend Terry is a builder. His father was one too. Throughout his high-school summers Terry climbed the wood skeletons of buildings and hammered nails. After graduation he went to the University of Notre Dame but still came home in the summers and hammered. Even with a master's in English in his pocket, he continued to work construction. It was his first love. He built houses in Southern California for thirty years or more and then made the leap into the surging tide of commercial real estate: he planned and built a business center—offices to rent, sidewalks, sprinkler systems, a two-story atrium in the foyer.

He threw all he had into it, even mortgaged his house. In the booming economy it was a no-lose venture. It was the times.

I painted Terry's house five years ago. It hadn't been done since he and his wife, Maureen, had bought it. It took me an entire summer to paint it, inside and out—a long, hot Southern California summer.

I worked around Terry, painting the four children's rooms, though the children were all grown and moved out. Bold blue, sage, sunflower yellow. Maureen loved colors, and with belts loosened by the booming economy, she had freedom to turn the house into a jewel box after thirty years surrounded by Navajo white.

One daughter's room was destined for a deep, sensuous rose, but it would have to wait. It had become Terry's office, filled with blueprints and books on various city ordinances, a steel-gray draftsman's stand in the middle. It was the room where he kept his dream. I can still see him bent over the plans for his business center. Construction hadn't yet begun. He appeared like a woodcut of Erasmus: high forehead, full face, small glasses, pen in hand, studying the scroll before him.

Every other weekend that summer, Terry and Maureen would travel to Mexico to build houses for the poor. I was left behind to paint their home and care for their sheepdog, Molly. I'd sometimes enter Terry's office, thumb silently through the pages of a blueprint, and wonder at his courage. His business ventures and generous charity work in Tijuana made my life and career seem so much safer and simpler.

On July 4 I returned from a walk on the beach to see Molly standing on the garage roof, a shaggy, hundred-pound sentinel. I had left an upstairs window open to air out the room, and Molly had scrambled through it. From down the street she looked like a large gray bird. Not sure whether to laugh or cry, I coaxed her in with a cold Fourth of July hot dog.

I think of her often now, in light of what has happened to Terry's dream—Molly the sheepdog, balancing on a rooftop, pondering the future.

For the first week I bleach the Hawaii house with a Hudson sprayer eight hours a day to get rid of the mildew. I protect the red and the yellow hibiscus and the ginger plants that circle the home, but I fail to protect myself and nearly bleach the skin off my arms. I limp to an urgent care in town to be swaddled with gauze and given antibiotics.

I don't tell James, who lives on the mainland, about my mishap. Jobs are scarce; one has to be Superman today. "Thirty-Five Years Painting Houses by the Sea" also means that I am old. After work I walk the soft-sand beaches. I do my push-ups. I never tell a client my age. I have to stay strong to do this work. It's the times. And this is the house I've been given to paint.

I want to paint it white, and I know just the right shade. It's the white of the queen's summer palace. I haven't told James yet. I need to visit the palace first.

One morning I drop from the rugged crown of the Ko'olau Mountain Range into a mist-showered valley where sits Queen Emma Kalele-onalani's summer palace, a pearl in the forest. Known as "foster child of the moon," the palace was used by Queen Emma and her family as a retreat from hot and dusty Honolulu in the mid-1800s. Today it is a local landmark, well kept by the elegant Daughters of Hawaii, a mixture of nineteenth-century-Boston wood siding and relaxed Hawaiian roof lines. A stream bordered by royal palms runs through the grounds. Building and gardens included, the queen's summer palace is about the same size as the home I've been entrusted to paint.

I stand on the porch with a fan deck of white paint swatches in my hand. Charlotte, one of the palace's docents, watches from the lawn. She is Hawaiian, a trace of Tahitian red in her white-gray hair, and descended from royalty; her childhood bed is one of the museum pieces inside.

Charlotte lifts the hem of her muumuu and walks barefoot up the porch stairs. She touches a finger to the paint chip in my hand. "In the morning it's white like this," she says, and I can smell the ginger flowers in her hair.

It took me thirty-five years to come to this royal palace, to choose a color for another palace. I get to play this delicious game because I've given all those years to my trade. I am old enough to have primed doors with linseed oil and waited a week to apply paint; old enough to know about split coats and antiquing, to have learned these things by rote. I've had old Italian guys on job sites tell me, "This is how my father did the wood." I read books on wood finishing and went to school to study colors. I learned that preparation is 75 percent of the job. I learned how to use blowtorches to remove paint, to use "long-oil primers" and other old-world techniques now illegal. Who knows how much skin and lung

I've given to my craft? But each day spent breathing sanding dust and washing my body in paint thinner brought me a little closer to this serene palace porch where I am discussing colors with Charlotte.

"At noon it looks like celery," she says. "In the evening it's the rose of roses."

Charlotte has seen the ghost of the long-ago queen twice. Both times she was descending these porch steps in her white wedding gown.

"This is the white you want."

Thank you, Charlotte. Thank you, Queen Emma. I go home now, to paint.

Terry had hoped one day to build an entire village in Mexico. He had an eye on a hilltop outside of Tijuana. There he'd build small factories that would produce toilets, siding, cabinets, doors, and windows. Homes would occupy the tree-lined streets, with schools and libraries sprinkled about. The residents would work in the factories and send their children to the schools and the libraries. And with the money from this success, Terry would buy another hilltop, and another community would blossom.

But this grand scheme hinged on the success of Terry's venture north of the border. Until his business park was rented out, Terry would continue building single homes in the dense neighborhoods of Tijuana.

It takes only a day to build a house in Mexico. I know because I went there with Terry one spring Saturday to be in charge of the painting, with the help of volunteers from a Catholic high school. We left at dawn for the two-hour drive south.

Terry is laconic, with a wry sense of humor. We talked baseball—I told him I was sorry that, even so early in the spring, the writing was on the wall for his Dodgers—and spoke sparingly of the charity work he had done for twenty years, always getting his whole family involved.

"It helped give my kids an idea of what they had," he said.

When we got there, the volunteers stood in a circle outside an empty shopping center close to the border and said a prayer. Terry stood a bit distant, head down, silent, unsure of public prayer, perhaps. We go way back, he and I, both taught by Jesuits.

When work on the house commenced, Terry was the master builder. The site was on a steep hillside. Across the street in an empty lot were the lumber, the paint, the busload of lost-looking high-school students, and me. We were a haphazard and unconvincing bunch. I went about opening five-gallon buckets and piecing together the brushes and rollers.

A stairway of used tires driven into the dirt slope led up to where Terry stood with the woman who would receive the house. They were discussing where the windows and doors would go. Terry bent down with chalk while the young woman looked proudly out her imaginary windows to the view below: brown-dirt hillsides and dwellings of concrete or bleached wood in need of paint. The streets were chalky cement, dirt, or gray stones cobbled together. The only bright spots were the women in floral dresses on the way to market, red-striped baskets on their shoulders—and, in the distance, a man in a straw hat walking with a bouquet of cotton candy, the pink and blue clouds floating in the dust he kicked up.

I wished we had some blue or red in our color palette, but it was all chocolate brown. Hearing Terry's voice in my head—*It's donated; use it*—I coached the kids on how to paint the siding panels and the two-by-fours while others banged the skeleton of the house together. Terry straddled a beam and some joists, directing the action with a large hammer, pointing with the butt end to give instructions, then bending over to drive in nails with a resounding *whack*.

He patted the woman's children gently on their behinds, moving them like chicks away from the swinging beams. He was tougher on the adults: I heard him say to a photographer recording the event, "Sir, you can stand anywhere on the planet except where you are standing." Then he walked the tightrope of two-by-fours to straighten another corner.

The young woman wore a white dress, delicate and seemingly out of place in the dusty bustle. Her little ones, wearing T-shirts down to their knees and rubber sandals on their feet, alternated between holding her hand and running off. On a hillside across the way, goats wandered, their bleats and bells joining the sounds of saws and hammers.

Her new house went up around her.

In Hawaii in the evening I read my book on Titian, plan my painting for the next day, and watch the plover step demurely about on the lawn. It delights me to read, after a long day, that in the last stages of a work's completion Titian "painted more with his fingers than his brushes." It pleases me to learn, too, that in his later years critics of the master misread his bold innovations as evidence of his faltering powers and failing eyesight.

In the words of a visitor to Titian's home in 1566: "I found him, although he had become extremely old, with the brushes in his hand for painting."

I imagine that I am working for the queen, painting long lines of wood siding, keeping a wet edge, and listening to the wind and the sea murmuring on the reef. I climb the ladder and pull the three-inch brush left to right, then descend and move my ladder, climb and pull again. It is not a baleful repetition; more like a workman's chant.

I talk to the plover as I paint. She stoops to peck, then raises her head to watch me and whistles. I have been painting alone here for three weeks. In another week she may answer.

"The queen would be happy to see this color," I tell the speckled bird. I dip my brush, climb, and pull. I say to the plover, "In the evenings, this white is the rose of roses." I know the queen would love her color. I hope my client does.

The house in Tijuana went up like a toy model: a bedroom, a bath, a family room, and a loft. Terry's own design. I laughed and joked with the high-school kids as we painted. Their hearts were in it, but their young bodies balked at the hard labor. I sensed it was no one's calling, yet they did a beautiful job.

The house complete, the workers and family thanked each other, and the key to the front door was presented in a simple ceremony. The kids could throw their schoolbooks inside before going to play in the streets.

The neighbors watched with good-natured curiosity, as if a circus had come to town and was now pulling up stakes. Terry put away his tools and told me that he and I had one last stop to make before we headed home.

Our destination was in a tightly packed neighborhood close to the center of town, an area of steep, cobblestoned streets and sandwiched homes. Terry had to look at a house in need of a roof, to decide if he would help. The decision would be based on time, money, and need.

We parked on a slope so close to vertical that we had to put rocks behind our tires to keep the truck from rolling. Then we climbed a ziggurat of well-worn, foot-high concrete steps to reach the home. The owners met us at the blue-painted front door: an older couple, short, with the high cheekbones and tight facial skin of Mexico's indigenous people. The man, in a work shirt and jeans, said nothing for the duration of our visit but stood quietly by the open front door, arms folded in a polite manner. It seemed he could have stood there patiently forever. The smell of barbecue and cement filled the Saturday-evening air as the woman of the house led Terry and me around.

The house had two rooms. The entry room doubled as sitting room and kitchen: a gas stove in the corner, pots hanging from nails, a couple of straight-backed, white-painted chairs with seats of straw mesh. The only light was from a small window with a flowered curtain that allowed a peek at the hills of Tijuana.

Terry stepped carefully, inspecting the block walls, knocking firmly on them, as if wondering what exactly was holding up this small *casa*. I did my best to appear knowledgeable and thoughtful but probably looked comical. The woman followed us, as close as a shadow, nervously straightening her white blouse and saying, "Bueno, bueno," each time either of us touched a wall or glanced at the low wooden ceiling. An earnest smile never left her face. She knew this was some sort of test for her little palace, and she would do all she could to make sure it passed.

The bedroom was as dark as a cave. A black-and-white television sat atop a dresser, showing a soccer match. The bed filled the room, and there was the scent of wax candles. Our heads grazed the ceiling as, like a pair of monks, we circled the room, touching the walls and ceiling. "Bueno, bueno," the woman said.

Terry didn't reply but just continued to touch, look, and think.

The three of us backed out of the room and smiled our way to the front door: three very different smiles—Terry's thoughtful, mine hopeful, the homeowner's pleading.

"Gracias, muchas gracias," the woman said at the front door, bowing slightly, and Terry and I made our way to the street, removed the rocks from behind the tires, and backed down the hill to begin our drive to the border.

I offered that it was lucky for the couple that the rainy season was over.

"There will be many more," Terry replied.

As we drove north, I talked around the question I wanted to ask, whose answer I felt I knew: *How did that business-center enterprise of yours finally make out?* Instead I asked Terry how many homes he had built in Tijuana.

494

"Hundreds, Phil." *Hundreds.* I thought of Molly balancing on that roof.

It was almost dark now on the freeway. Traffic was light. We were both tired. Terry wore his Notre Dame ball cap, the faded fighting leprechaun on the bill. He moved his shoulders in slow arcs—he'd had two operations on them and was due for a third.

I asked Terry how he felt the day's build had gone.

"I think it went fine."

The small talk was over: no more Dodgers, no pennant wishes. I asked about his project, the dream that would carry his family, and his charity work in Mexico, into the future.

His worn shoulders gave a slight upward flinch. Bad timing, he said. "I'd be fine moving in with one of my kids, as long as I had work." It was too dark for me to see his eyes. "It would kill Maureen if we had to move out, though. She loves that house." I thought of the children's rooms painted red rose, sunflower yellow, parchment.

Terry turned on the ballgame. I'm not a Dodgers fan, but it felt good to hear Vin Scully's voice. He had called these games through many an economic up and down. We drove home listening to baseball.

Later, on the living-room couch with Maureen and a beer, in a room no longer painted a dated, smudgy white, Terry thanked me for my help. "She'll get her roof, not to worry, Phil," he said of the woman we'd visited.

How many homes, how many roofs over others' heads?

Hundreds.

The plover has flown, beginning her long, uninterrupted journey to Alaska for the summer.

I clean my latex brushes at the bar sink by the pool. It is late afternoon, a Saturday. Terry built a house today in Tijuana, three thousand miles away.

As I clean up, a chameleon watches me from his perch on a jade stone frog. He watches from the corner of his wide yellow eye. We have become late-afternoon partners of a sort.

I sleep on the *pune'e*, listen to the surf, watch the moon-rise. I wake and go back to work.

The trade winds have increased and blow about twenty-five miles per hour. I hold tight to my ladder. The myna birds have discovered the lawn and march about like cocky majorettes. The hibiscus flowers are in full bloom, bursting with yellows and reds, but the bushes them-selves lacerate my skin like a visit from the Spanish Inquisition. I carry band-aids in my pockets. I work my way steadily down the sides, the tired mustard yellow disappearing under my brush. The owner won't be visiting for months. He has given me complete authority on all deci-sions. I wonder what he will think of this color's royal lineage.

In the evening it's the rose of roses.

I watch the chameleon from the corner of my eye. White blossoms loosen and flutter from the tree nearby. A rose-red sac falls from the chameleon's throat. He raises a curious olive-green head and pauses, then does his quick push-ups in the slanting sunshine.

I work till dusk, climbing to close the French windows to within a hair's breadth, clanking my ladders down as quietly as I can. Visitors sit on the front porch next door, swing on the mango-tree swing. There's lemonade and laughter. It is summer.

I kneel on "Thirty-Five Years Painting Houses by the Sea" knees and tidy my makeshift shop. The neighborhood mongrel trots in and pants at my side. "Poi-dog," the Hawaiians call such an animal: "all mixed up." I pet the poi-dog's freckled face.

I'm as poor as a church mouse, having spent all my money, happily, on books and travels. This has both prepared me and left me unpre-pared for these times—these worn, gray, mournful times of colorless economic news.

I tighten the caps on my thinner, acetone, and denatured alcohol to discourage curious children and pets. I scour my brushes with a wire brush, straighten them, and set them bristles-up in a plastic bucket. I ready tomorrow's materials and scratch behind the pooch's ears.

Then I work my way quietly about the house, checking today's prog-ress and folding the Joseph's-coat tarps, making sure the hisbiscus and ginger plants have endured. I dust the windowsills and cover my shop.

The chameleon sits on the frog's head as if it were a throne, and this place were his palace.

Nominated by The Sun

VILLON'S EPITAPH (BALLADE OF THE HANGED MEN)

by FRANÇOIS VILLON

translated by RICHARD WILBUR

from THE HUDSON REVIEW

O brother men who after us remain,
Do not look coldly on the scene you view,
For if you pity wretchedness and pain,
God will the more incline to pity you.
You see us hang here, half a dozen who
Indulged the flesh in every liberty
Till it was pecked and rotted, as you see,
And these our bones to dust and ashes fall.
Let no one mock our sorry company,
But pray to God that He forgive us all.

If we have called you brothers, don't disdain
The appellation, though alas it's true
That not all men are equal as to brain,
And that our crimes and blunders were not few.
Commend us, now that we are dead, unto
The Virgin Mary's son, in hopes that He
Will not be sparing of His clemency,
But save our souls, which Satan would enthrall.

We're dead now, brothers; show your charity
And pray to God that He forgive us all.

We have been rinsed and laundered by the rain,
And by the sunlight dried and blackened too.
Magpie and crow have plucked our eyeballs twain
And cropped our eyebrows and the beards we grew.
Nor have we any rest at all, for to
And fro we sway at the wind's fantasy,
Which has no object, yet would have us be
(Pitted like thimbles) at its beck and call.
Do not aspire to our fraternity,
But pray to God that He forgive us all.

Prince Jesus, we implore Your Majesty
To spare us Hell's distress and obloquy;
We want no part of what may there befall.
And, mortal men, let's have no mockery,
But pray to God that He forgive us all.

Nominated by The Hudson Review

IF THE MAN TOOK

fiction by JOANNA RUOCCO

from NOON

If the man took the teleological view, which he would, he would, of course he would, he would attempt to use the sensations he derived from the penile motions in my vagina to produce orgasm, ejaculating in or near my vagina, thereby terminating the sex act as such.

I would use the convention of assent so that the man could get on with his nocturnal commitments, dog walking or sleeping or watching recorded sports footage, what have you. If the man was having difficulty ejaculating, because of some blockage, or because he was nervous or because he took a pill, a selective serotonin reuptake inhibitor or a nonselective serotonin reuptake inhibitor, I would feel that I had failed in my function as a woman, because I am affected by the pressures in our present society that correlate a woman's value as a woman with her ability to satisfy the sexual desire of a man, even a man for whom she feels no strong attachment. My ego would drive me to make pelvic floor contractions and moans—and the man would eventually ejaculate, ending the sex act by the standards established by our present society, and possibly fertilizing an egg, which I might decide to gestate, for either hormonal or emotional reasons, although it is unlikely that such a fine distinction is possible to make, and finally I would be delivered of one, or even two or three, humans. Could I claim that they consented, these humans, these new humans held up into the air? I could not make such a claim. Every being is born unconsenting. The being is made by violation. It is what we make of Non-Being, more and more humans, born to die, unconsenting—it will be perfectly okay.

Nominated by Noon

ALL-AMERICAN

by DAVID HERNANDEZ

from THE SOUTHERN REVIEW

I'm this tiny, this statuesque, and everywhere
in between, and everywhere in between
bony and overweight, my shadow cannot hold
one shape in Omaha, in Tuscaloosa, in Aberdeen.
My skin is mocha brown, two shades darker
than taupe, your question is racist, nutmeg, beige,
I'm not offended by your question at all.
Penis or vagina? Yes and yes. Gay or straight?
Both boxes. Bi, not bi, who cares, stop
fixating on my sex life, Jesus never leveled
his eye to a bedroom's keyhole. I go to church
in Tempe, in Waco, the one with the exquisite
stained glass, the one with a white spire
like the tip of a Klansman's hood. Churches
creep me out, I never step inside one,
never utter hymns, Sundays I hide my flesh
with camouflage and hunt. I don't hunt
but wish every deer wore a bulletproof vest
and fired back. It's cinnamon, my skin,
it's more sandstone than any color I know.
I voted for Obama, McCain, Nader, I was too
apathetic to vote, too lazy to walk one block,
two blocks to the voting booth. For or against
a woman's right to choose? Yes, for and against.
For waterboarding, for strapping detainees

with snorkels and diving masks. Against burning
fossil fuels, let's punish all those smokestacks
for eating the ozone, bring the wrecking balls,
but build more smokestacks, we need jobs
here in Harrisburg, here in Kalamazoo. Against
gun control, for cotton bullets, for constructing
a better fence along the border, let's raise
concrete toward the sky, why does it need
all that space to begin with? For creating
holes in the fence, adding ladders, they're not
here to steal work from us, no one dreams
of crab walking for hours across a lettuce field
so someone could order the Caesar salad.
No one dreams of sliding a squeegee down
the cloud-mirrored windows of a high-rise,
but some of us do it. Some of us sell flowers.
Some of us cut hair. Some of us carefully
steer a mower around the cemetery grounds.
Some of us paint houses. Some of us monitor
the power grid. Some of us ring you up
while some of us crisscross a parking lot
to gather the shopping carts into one long,
rolling, clamorous and glittering backbone.

Nominated by The Southern Review, Elton Glaser, Bob Hicok

THE WASTE LAND APP

by TESS TAYLOR

from THE THREEPENNY REVIEW

It is a nostalgic poem, so let me start with my own memory of it. Seventeen or so years ago, I came to *The Waste Land* in the way I then came to most poems—high on caffeine, late at night, crouched on the floor of Moe's on Telegraph Avenue, coming to books by finding Berkeley jetsam. I would have been alone, away from friends, perhaps en route to a party, perhaps not. I was comfortable in my aloneness. I had no money, so I wore hand-me-down clothes and bought hand-me-down books. On evenings like the one where I first read Eliot, I collected things I liked—Rexroth, D. H. Lawrence, Dostoevsky, Pound, Levertov. I liked nice books, certainly, but ragged ones, too—the cheaper, more underlined, more battered, the better. I can't say how much I understood of *The Waste Land*—I think I read it because it was Eliot, and I knew I should read him. I was ambitious. A lot of it, not merely the epigraph, was Greek to me, but it was sonic Greek. I bought the collected works for $3. I read them in solitary hunger.

I have a distinct memory of that self and that book, and when, seventeen years later, a publication I quite like asked me to review the new iPad app of *The Waste Land*, it was this memory I had to contend with. When the app—$14 for one poem, displayed on a machine that costs several hundred dollars—emerged ethereally in our kitchen on my husband's iPad, complete with service announcements and jargonish code, I was ambivalent.

Welcome to the new technology. My first impression of receiving the poem was of being on hold. Despite the app's ability to appear in our kitchen via download, getting the "book experience" to work took some faceless proforma code-filled emails to the iTunes support line (the Greek replaced by the daily flarf of 6W9JNTNAKA9E, at your service). This took a day or so, in spurts. How often these days one has to call customer support: we have traded in laying down our lives in coffee spoons for calls to iTunes. Hold music played. Informational menus repeated. TO SPEAK TO X press 3. I missed the clear simplicity of the book, which you can always open. I missed the dusty scent of Moe's. I missed the memory of myself reading.

Still, after some sturm und drang, the app got installed. With a finger tap, I opened it. *What are the roots which clutch?* According to interviews about the app, its publishers, Faber and Touch Press, designed it to put the poem front and center. It felt *sort-of* center: the app opens to a menu of eight kinds of interactive experience, of which just reading the poem is only the first. Tap "poem" and position the iPad in lengthwise direction and clear text appears. I did. But before I could see T. S. Eliot's poem, I saw, once again, my own face hovering in the screen. I was in my own way, yet again. "Can you turn off the lights?" I called to my husband, who was reading the newspaper beside me. "I cannot see the poem."

Glare removed, complaints quelled, coffee beside me, I finally began to read, or rather, to explore my newly mediated book experience. For the next month, as I played with the app, I was impressed, educated, delighted, and grudgingly won over. I liked scrolling around *The Waste Land*. I could see that there was something keen about how the app mixes its medium to suit the poem's message. After all, what is *The Waste Land* but modernism's composite icon, collaged fragments of everything from the King James Bible to the Ziegfeld Follies and working class pub speech to *The Tempest* and back? This is a poem of many voices. Now it's possible to listen to everyone from T. S. Eliot himself (in 1933 and 1947) to Seamus Heaney to Viggo Mortensen comment or read. Heaney is brilliant. Mortensen is comic and flatfooted and overblown. In 1933, Eliot sounds high-toned, like a priggish priest. In 1947, Eliot sounds, quite frankly, a little bored.

This is all interesting trivia. Little by little I became an apologist for my gizmo. It eases new possibilities for scholarship. It offers a richness of modes of encounter. Copious notes accompany the text, and they are available immediately. They flit in and out, depending on how you tilt the screen. If you're reading the app in the horizontal position, the notes scroll alongside the poem, little app-aritions. They helpfully expand at a finger's tap. Want to know how many times the word "dead" appears in *The Burial of the Dead?* Search and find all ten, including the title. Curious what that Greek epigraph might mean? It need not be Greek to anyone. Not only the translation and commentary but also a short micro-history of the Sybil at Cumae pops open. You can read and Google at once, without even Googling. Here is the book made porous. Here is symbiosis between text and Cliff Notes, a permeable membrane between reading and interpretation, a choose-your-own-adventure crash course in Eliot. There is no cumbersome flipping.

As I played, I found myself musing that perhaps *The Waste Land* is especially suited to interactivity. After all, Eliot has never been what you might call accessible. Indeed, *The Waste Land* delights in obscure allusion. It practically shouts, "Get a dictionary! Get an encyclopedia! I demand exegesis!" Because of this, its annotation has always been something of a given. Herein, perhaps, lies the app's genius. What is exegesis if not interactive?

As for the bells and whistles, there were many. Some, like Seamus Heaney's magisterial armchair commentary about his own sense of initial alienation from Eliot, were amazing. Some of them worked backwards to the poem itself—as if one were to watch the cinematic movie history of *Dracula* before reading the book. In one part of the app, Fiona Shaw performs the poem as a one-woman show in a theatrical collage of voices. She wears a mousy sweater and torn Keds while pacing around a shambling shabby-chic country house in Dublin populated by dusty harpsichords and pseudo-Greek statues. It's not a bad setting for a "bitch gone in the teeth/for a botched civilization." Nevertheless, instead of thinking about T. S. Eliot, or his poem, I found myself thinking about Fiona Shaw and her shoes. I thought Fiona looked slightly chilly in her scarf.

There were treasures. Amid all the filmed commentaries, photo gallery, tips, etc. was my personal favorite, something I kept returning to: the facsimile of Eliot's typed pages corrected by Pound's pen. Even wholly dispersed—sent to a hundred thousand shiny ethers—these had an intimacy about them, a revelation of craft. Even technologically rendered, their record of the writing hand, the editing hand, the exploratory scribble—all these clues led back from my disembodied hovering to the thinking bodies that, ninety years ago, made this work.

As I looked at the pixelated scribbles of that first manuscript, I thought about all they represented—the record of an impassioned intimate conversation between two formidable people, two individual minds coming together to think about one grand poem. But even as I looked at these facsimiles, my own newness distracted me. Email popped below my screen into my husband's box. Little text messages appeared. He would be late to dinner. I could control the stereo and change the music. Had we scheduled the diaper delivery? I was not alone on the floor of a bookstore. I was in the great throng—not Eliot's great throng, but my own. And, I admit, I felt too near the banalities of my own life to enjoy the masterful way that Eliot had transformed his.

Though I came to like the app better as I settled into it, I was never wholly at home. I couldn't figure out a way, exactly, to review it as an object or text except to have recourse to a description of my own ambivalence exploring it. Its notes are excellent, its productions learned, its films finely produced, but I still felt thornily lost in the thicket of my own encounter. Was this reading or wasn't it? Is this production and distribution of simultanaeity a significant form of newness? Is this the future of reading or merely one possible future? Is this a mirror of our own distractedness or a tool that can make our reading more accessible?

While thinking about these questions, I came across a 1939 meditation by William Carlos Williams. Armed with his own feelings of what newness should sound like, Williams (never a fan of Eliot) had this to say about Eliot's work: "[The poems are] birds eye foods, suddenly frozen at fifty degrees below zero, under pressure, at perfect maturity, immediately after being picked . . . I am infuriated because the arrest has taken place just at the point of risk, just at the point when the danger threatened, when the tradition might have led to difficult new things. But the God damn liars prefer . . . freezing . . . the result is canned to make literature." I do not want to settle the debate between Williams and Eliot, but in this case merely to steal the image in all its rich problematic promise. How do we make writing and reading experiences that cause us to risk something? Despite its seeming to represent the way the future might take form, I felt that in encountering the app I felt frozen, packaged, arrested, just, just, just at the point of real thought.

In the end, the app provoked confusion and ambivalence, pleasure but also disapproval—not really towards the app, but towards the world that was changing so quickly, towards my uncertainty of what this means. *Make it new*, said Pound, celebrating the onslaught, setting a course for poetry, for art, for modernism. Pound called us then to engage, to respond to change with change, to make forms that make sense of the flux. Then came Eliot, making it new while mourning the dead, mourning the brokenness of his generation. Reading *The Waste Land* again comforted me, not because of its newness, but because of its nostalgia, its grief for all that was broken.

Nominated by The Threepenny Review, Joan Murray

AKHMATOVA

by MATTHEW DICKMAN

from THE AMERICAN POETRY REVIEW

That's right! Now I remember. I was on the beach
looking at Haystack Rock,
putting my finger into the mouths of sea anemones,
their tentacles sweeping over my knuckles, I was whispering
the word *brother*
to one, and the word *sister* to the other
though maybe they were both. I wanted to be close
to another species. I had been reading about the dark windows
Akhmatova looked through
to see if her son had been let out of prison. As I walked around
the shallow pools
feeling like I had done a good job being myself
I heard my third-grade teacher
whisper into my ear
what's wrong with you? You want to be stupid your whole life?
She was a nun and wore, I imagined,
a rosary of barbed wire underneath her white blouse.
No matter how long I put my finger into the natural world,
no matter how often I mistake the flies
above the trash for stars, Akhmatova's son will still be chained
against a wall, the sea will still push
against the rock, and a part of me will be sitting near
a window in homeroom, my head lowered, my skeleton warm
inside my body, my brothers and sisters alive in the salty pools of
   the world.

Nominated by Jane Hirshfield, Mark Irwin

CADIZ, MISSOURI

fiction by ROBERT LONG FOREMAN

from AGNI

I never had much use for Cadiz. I don't mean the port city in south-western Spain, though I've never had any use for that Cadiz, either. The one I have in mind is at the heart of America, and despite the way it's spelled the residents pronounce its name like "callous," its *z* become an *s* that hangs limp from their tongues. If you say it the Spanish way, they correct you.

Whereas the original Cadiz was founded in the ninth century BC by some Phoenicians who settled in the path of a prominent trade route, I cannot imagine why America's Cadiz was built where it was. It was not built on the river, or the interstate. There were no trade routes running through it. You couldn't get a decent sandwich there, at least not on the Saturday I spent exploring it with Charlie, soon after we moved nearby. There was never a reason to go back after the first trip. They had a nice courthouse—I'll give them that—but if you've seen one granite courthouse you've seen them all.

Our Cadiz did not share the longevity of its Spanish namesake. It stood barely a century and a half. The first Cadiz has survived invasions, pirate attacks, and the Franco regime, but its American counterpart was wiped out in minutes by a rogue weather pattern. The town hardly deserved its name.

I would say that I regret not seeing more of Cadiz when I had the chance, but there was nothing to see there except doomed houses. They weren't worth looking at until we found out they were doomed, and by then it was too late.

When a tornado comes to take away your house, your pets, and, your neighbors, it comes as a surprise, but if you live in Missouri you expect one every time the weather looks like it might turn against you, which it does in summer months several times a week. I watch always for the slightest misbehavior of a thunderstorm; I know all the cues for catastrophic weather.

My first thought, every time I hear about a new tornado, is that if one comes to my house I will have to go huddle in my basement. Something I learned when I moved to Missouri: if your basement is old and you don't have a fortune to spend on restorations, a rainy day will flood it waist-high with grime and disease. Ours is a space we never use, a part of our house that serves no purpose, except as a habitat for strange insects.

For if the water in our basement were not a problem, still there would be cave crickets. They are massive and look like spiders; they're often called cricket spiders. With legs thick and black, they don't move until you come close, and when you do they leap across the room. It's terrifying.

So on the morning in July when the rain got suddenly harder than it had been since I woke up, the sky turned slightly green, the warning siren went off, and at the same unlikely time I saw the clouds out my window surge east as if their cloud-lives depended on it, my first thought was not of my impending death, but of the creatures in my basement. I am embarrassed by this, but it is true; in my mind, the threat of physical contact with big insects outweighed the fact of real mortal danger. I froze, hoping I could stay where I was and simply watch the sky restore its recent shade of gray, but for a long minute it only got more green, and soon the green verged on black. The air looked sick, like an ailing cumulonimbus had ruptured and drained bile into the lower atmosphere. I didn't see or hear a cyclone, but if I had it would have seemed an afterthought, a side effect of the Missouri sky, the sight of which was like the sight of a solar eclipse to those who don't know what it is.

If this had been forty or sixty years ago, I would have heard cellar doors slamming over the siren as mothers shuttled their children to safety, but everyone here works during the day, and I seem to be the only one who does it at home.

As it happens, the tornado spared me and the furniture, and my legs were spared getting soaked with cellar water. Within a minute the green dissolved, and the storm behaved again like a typical storm.

When I looked online I heard the news that our neighboring village of Cadiz had just been reduced to eight square miles of shredded houses and overturned cars. The whole town was destroyed in minutes—minutes I had spent fearing the same ruin they suffered, even as they suffered it. Having seen nothing of interest in Cadiz when I was there in person, now—through my TV and computer screen—I could not take my eyes off the place.

I saw semis overturned and crushed in a pile. I saw houses that had been blown to pieces. I saw men and women behold their town inert and ruined, most of them in tears. Worst of all, somehow, were the images of trees that had been cut in half, like arms with their hands lopped off, reaching for the same gray sky I sat under. I read reports of old men and women crushed by the ceilings above their heads, of dogs who helped the living find the dead. I saw no corpses, but hour after hour the death toll rose.

Charlie came home a few hours early. It was a Friday, so we had the whole weekend to spend adhered to our couch, watching Cadiz. We could have driven fifteen minutes and seen the wreckage ourselves, but we thought it better to keep a respectful distance and observe from the same remove as everyone else in the country. At one point Charlie suggested we see how we might help. "Help?" I said, and threw up my hands, as if to make plain how empty they were of lifesaving devices. Meanwhile, out the window, ambulance sirens wailed. We knew, for once, where they were going.

A cave cricket will sometimes get into the house. On our first morning here, the day after we moved in, I saw one crouching in the middle of what was to be our living room. I knew I would have to kill it; Charlie was out getting us coffee from a gas station.

The thing nearest my hands was an open box of some of our books. I had been lining our shelves with them. I threw a French-English dictionary at the creature. It leapt aside to safety, just a split second before the book landed. I threw another, it leapt again. I then spent ten minutes trying to kill it in this fashion. Every time—or almost every time—it saw my literature coming, it jumped out of the way. I threw *Native Son*, *Regarding the Pain of Others*, one of Charlie's old industry reports, and a Kafka anthology, before I finally crushed it with an old copy of *Dune*. I raised my arms above my head and shouted "Yes!" loudly enough to cause an echo. I announced my victory to Charlie, when he returned, with great pride. Nonplussed, he said I was acting as if I'd killed the Wicked Witch of the Midwest. The next time he went out, he returned with glue traps and put them in the corners of our rooms, to catch any creatures that landed on them and to preserve our books, he said, from ever being flung again.

The cave cricket is one of Missouri's best-kept secrets. So is the brown recluse spider—I have killed twelve of them since we moved here. Its venom is so powerful it can rot and blacken your skin with one bite; if you don't get a recluse bite treated you can lose a limb. I have heard they get in your sleeves and bite you when you put your arms through, so I shake out all of my shirts before I wear them.

The space between St. Louis and Kansas City is a death trap. Our town is at the midpoint of fatal Missouri, where if the tornadoes and fauna don't kill you, the heat will. Between May and September, the temperature is usually a hundred degrees.

I try not to complain too much to Charlie; he was equally reluctant to relocate here for his work. Mostly I confine my grievances to conversations with my sister Anne, who is sympathetic enough from her end of the line. She has the luxury of sympathy, living back in Boston in the house where we were raised. She has yet to visit.

Despite the instant demolition of Cadiz, our little city went unscathed. Some trees in town lost branches, but that happens in the average thunderstorm. Some buildings were lost on Route 40, which is the quickest way to get to Cadiz, but they were outside our city limits, and our town suffered no casualties.

It hadn't even been an especially large tornado, but it hadn't needed to be, because with no more than ten thousand residents Cadiz was not a large town. It was more of a suburb, but there is no big city it could be a suburb of.

For this and other reasons, I was surprised to learn from news reports that the people of Cadiz were planning to rebuild. They didn't report this as news, per se; it was something they took for granted, saying things like, "Rebuilding has already begun," which sounds triumphant enough when spoken by a first-string newsman who has never been to Cadiz.

I wondered, having seen the relative squalor of pre-tornado Cadiz, why its people didn't simply abandon the site in favor of moving to our larger city, which, despite its many drawbacks, has sandwich shops and better schools. We have a food co-op called the Farmacy, and a vintage clothing store called Easily Suede—they had no such redeeming things in Cadiz. Many Cadizians commuted to work here in town as it was, but people get attached to their homes, and so they would restore them. In the meantime, they needed places to stay, where they could regroup as the wreckage cleared and essential things, like their hospital and grocery store, were restored to working order.

Refugees from Cadiz began arriving in our neighborhood that Monday. Community organizers—I didn't know we had them—had gone door to door all weekend, asking for volunteers to take in survivors from the dead city.

Some of our neighbors offered one or two of their rooms to those in need. A single mother two blocks down took in an orphaned toddler. The aged, retired Robinsons made an extra set of keys for a young, childless couple, no older than twenty-five, who'd lost their first house and both their jobs. A family of four settled in one bedroom in the home of some Presbyterians up the street.

We took in no one from Cadiz. It was something I talked over with Charlie, the evening of the visit of our community's organizer, an earnest man if I ever met one. He was also a bald man if I ever met one. His forehead wrinkled as he stood on the other side of our screen door, making his pitch, as the news of Cadiz blared from the TV across the room. He didn't want to guilt us into taking someone in, he said, and he could see our house was "pretty small," but he told me who had volunteered so far, and I knew some of their houses were no larger than ours. He said the survivors would only need to be here for "about a week, at most." He left me with his card, which had "Community Organizer" printed across the bottom—killing my theory, developed a minute prior, that our community had not had organizers until Cadiz was razed and people suddenly had something to do.

Charlie and I discussed it briefly, but we both knew we would never let someone else live with us. We like to be alone—with each other, but also without each other. My favorite thing about our house is that it's shaped like a U, so we can get out of each other's sight when we need to. We can each inhabit one end of the U, and with a wall between us we feel like we're by ourselves.

I knew we would make good hosts. We have two bathrooms, despite our house being "pretty small," plus an extra bedroom. But the second bedroom is my office, and the extra bathroom is where Charlie shaves every morning while I blow-dry my hair in the other one. I didn't want to give up these things, and besides, accepting a refugee would be like adopting a child. We wouldn't know we'd gotten a psychopath until it was too late.

Since we moved here, I have been taking morning walks with the neighbor's cat. I didn't coax him into joining me; he followed me around the block on my first trip, and it became our routine. He slinks from bush to tree to fire hydrant as I stride over the pavement. I mostly confine these walks to my little neighborhood, which stands slightly higher than the rest of the town, kept apart from it by a four-lane road with constant, heavy traffic.

After Cadiz, when I took these walks, I would see the newest members of our modest homeless population. A bearded man who always wore the same faded, red T-shirt would sit on his borrowed porch as I went past with the cat and my travel mug full of coffee. I'd watch him from the corner of my eye, but he didn't seem to take notice. He sat alone and stared across the street, looking dazed, like he'd never seen so many houses keep still for so long.

I waved hello to some of the survivors, like an older couple who looked the way I expected a tornado's near-victims to look. It wasn't that they were permanently windblown; rather, they seemed relieved. I always knew when they were near—on my walks, at the supermarket, at the bank—because I'd hear them laughing together as they approached. They behaved as though they knew, now, that they should cherish every day they spent alive, for they recognized how precious life is in this perilous region. But as I told Charlie, I suspected this to be nothing new; they must have lived this way before the storm hit. Charlie took their good cheer as a sign that either they were very religious or had extraordinary homeowner's insurance.

Our favorite refugees were both thirty-three—a little younger than me and Charlie—and like us they weren't from Missouri. I met them on one of my walks with the neighbor's cat. I had just passed the house with the bewildered man on the porch when there came my way a man and woman both dressed in jeans and T-shirts. The man was tall—at least six foot two—the woman half a foot shorter. They had brown hair and brown eyes. They looked younger than they turned out to be. As I neared them, I didn't let on that I'd noticed them, and they did the same. As we got closer, we made eye contact, all of us squinting as if we knew each other from somewhere. As soon as we passed, I turned to say hello. They returned the greeting, and as we stopped walking in opposite directions I said, "My name's Karen," and they introduced themselves as Claire and Jared. I asked, "Are you all from Cadiz," pronouncing it as the Cadizians do, diplomatically. They nodded, and turned around and walked with me for several blocks as we talked. They didn't have a destination, they said, it was just that they had been taking morning walks in Cadiz and didn't want to give up the habit simply because their town had ceased to exist. I could tell they were realistic people. They said they were staying in the neighborhood, and I invited them over that evening, "for drinks."

They came, and together we had a night like I hadn't had since moving to Missouri, one in which you get to know someone with the fullest confidence that you're going to like them as much, if not more, when the evening ends as you did when it started. We sat on our screened-in porch, under the moon and the sound of crickets of the aboveground variety.

Jared was from outside Seattle. Claire was born in Minnesota. Jared and I had the same number of friends as teenagers who eventually died from heroin overdoses; he said it was not uncommon in a place like Seattle, and I said it was "a Boston thing, too." Jared, we learned, liked beer, enough that he and Charlie followed the same beer blogs. Claire shared my love-hate relationship with cooking, in that we both liked the idea of cooking but didn't like to wait for things to heat up—which, said Claire, is at least seventy percent of cooking. I felt as blessed by their company as they must have felt cursed, considering they'd just lost their house and their dog. He had been a Weimaraner, one who went by the unlikely name of Fat Joe. They both cried a little when they mentioned this, and I think Jared drank at least two more of Charlie's IPAs than he would have had they not suffered such a loss a few days before.

I was surprised to see them cry; I had been struck by how the storm hadn't seemed to faze them. Claire said they'd mostly felt guilty about "the whole thing." They had not been harmed, or known anyone who had. "It was scary" Jared said. "Really scary, I mean"—but, he explained, they had just moved to Cadiz a week before. Most of their furniture was still on its way, by freight, to the rubble that had been their rented house—which, added Claire, they hadn't even liked very much.

Claire's tears had come as abruptly as the cyclone, and Jared's followed. I considered reaching across to Claire, putting my hand on her shoulder to comfort her, but despite our moderate social lubrication I

514

didn't know if I knew her well enough to do that. A few minutes later, they said they should get going. They said their host family might worry if they didn't, and so they went.

Perhaps I should have gone through with the hand-to-shoulder contact, I thought in days to follow. I asked Charlie the next morning if I had done something wrong, if I hadn't been responsive enough to Claire's tears. Some people know exactly what to do when someone else in a room begins to cry. I am not one of them. When we didn't hear from them, Charlie maintained that they probably weren't ignoring us on purpose. They had, he said, things on their minds that were bigger than me.

If you looked at certain websites in the weeks after Cadiz, you would never have guessed that a tornado seized the town and emptied it out. On the Cadiz Craigslist page, life carried on. Men, as before, were looking for love, or looking for casual sex, or looking to sell their motorcycles. Women were doing things, too. When announcing furniture for sale, no one mentioned the weather pattern that may or may not have torn the roof from over their heads. The single men weren't looking for replacements for the wives they'd just lost—though when I brought this up with Charlie he said that if this were the case it was the sort of detail likely to be left out of a three-sentence Craigslist ad.

Eerier to me was how the town looked on Google's Street View feature. Touring Cadiz on Google was like traveling one week back in time. According to Google, the courthouse was still standing. The hospital was whole, the trees had their leaves and weren't broken in half, and although the sandwich shops were missing, they hadn't been there before the tornado either. I knew—and Charlie reminded me—that this should not have seemed strange. Google doesn't update its street views on a biweekly basis. Still, on some level I expect a street to look in life the way it looks online. I know I am not alone in this, even if Charlie isn't with me.

I returned to Cadiz often, through Google, retracing the steps I took on my one visit there in person. I skipped my walk with the neighbor's cat on some mornings, in favor of my virtual stroll through the now-missing city. I googled my way past Granny's Gifts, an antique shop, where a woman held a door for a man, both of them frozen in place. Next, on my right, were the coffeehouse and post office. They weren't there anymore, but there they were.

515

I could see people at the wheels of their cars and on the sidewalk. At least one of them must have been recently killed. I kept my virtual walks carefully hidden from Charlie, who, if he had caught me taking them, would have made a remark he thought was very funny.

Near as Cadiz was, and even after much of the wreckage had supposedly been cleared, I was not about to drive there and see the ex-town for myself, despite the curiosity that kept me coming back to pictures of it in ruins. I had spent so much time thinking about Cadiz, and watching it, without venturing in, that to go there now would have been embarrassing, like breaking a deeply uncomfortable silence with an ex-friend who has become a virtual stranger.

Two weeks after our evening of drinks together, we heard again from Claire and Jared. They e-mailed to say they were living in a FEMA trailer beside the wreckage of their rented house, which would soon be cleared by a construction crew, to make room for the next incarnation of their rented house. They said that to access the Internet they had to drive five miles to the nearest Starbucks. They asked if we wanted to meet again.

We did, and while I never went so far as to establish these terms for our friendship, I would spend time with them as long as it meant not going to Cadiz. On a Sunday, we lent them our extra pair of bikes and went for a ride on the Mason Trail. One Saturday afternoon, we took a long drive that ended at the winery on the river, which I was especially glad to do because driving west for twenty minutes to reach it meant getting even farther from Cadiz.

Jared and Claire spent almost none of our time together talking about the tornado that had murdered Fat Joe and two hundred Cadizians. They never volunteered their tale of surviving the storm, and we never asked for it, but they did mention some things they had lost. They waxed nostalgic, not traumatic, as we discussed pre-cyclonic Cadiz. Claire said that although she hadn't been glad to relocate from Philadelphia for the sake of Jared's job, she'd seen some good in the town. They'd had a surprisingly active ceramics scene, she said, though that was gone now.

The thing she missed most was her car. It had been her first car and it had "run just fine" even after all those years of owning it—how many years she didn't say. Now she didn't know where it was. It was probably in a field somewhere, I submitted, to which she nodded, looking away.

More to my liking, our new friends volunteered objections to Missouri as a whole. The way we talked, one would think tornadoes were the least of its problems. Jared said there was a kind of tree they had in Philadelphia—he couldn't say what kind—that he didn't see here. Missing it made him feel like he was "in a foreign country." Claire complained how hard it was to find a decent cup of coffee, a comment that prompted the rest of us to nod vigorously in agreement.

Typically quiet in conversation, this subject matter animated me. I live just a thousand miles from the place I call home, I said, but it feels like not another country but another planet. "There's nothing I recognize here," I said. "The buildings don't look right. It's all so new."

Claire asked, "How old is the oldest building? Not even two hundred years, right?"

Empowered, I told the three of them about the long walk I took the day Cadiz was crushed. I had not yet mentioned it to Charlie, or to anyone else.

I was visited, on the morning of Cadiz's ruin, by a cave cricket. Claire groaned at my mention of it. It was the biggest one I'd ever seen, I said. It was the boldest one, too. Out of nowhere it landed on my desk, so that I leapt backward, sending my chair hurtling to the floor. I knew at once that my workday was over. I knew if I left for a while and came back later it would make itself scarce, creeping under a dresser or behind the stove, sparing me the ordeal of trying to kill it, so I put on my sandals and ventured out.

I had also just had a long talk with Anne, who told me a walk might make me feel better about living here. "Missouri is one of the least polluted states in the country," she said, making this information up. "Breathe the air."

The cat joined me, as usual, but I veered from our typical course to head into town. My feline companion stopped and crept home behind me when I left our niche with its garages and cultivated greenery. I had no destination. There was nothing I wanted to buy. There weren't even nice-looking buildings to see, not like back home, where if I walked in any direction for five minutes I'd at least see an old church to make my trip worth the trouble. Jared nodded at this.

It was mid-morning, and I got as far as the littered four-lane highway, where a man stood at the crosswalk. Despite his location, and the way he looked expectantly out at the cars, he didn't want to cross the street. Many of the drivers thought he did, as they waited through the first half of every green light to let him go. They watched him as the light changed, and continued to watch him after it did. Then, his lack of intention made plain, they drove on, shaking their heads or raising their hands, palms up in disbelief and fury. They'd been faked out, and throughout it he stood perfectly still, with his round glasses and pink baseball cap.

I don't think he knew he was the cause of this confusion and anger. He looked oblivious, which is how he has looked every other time I've seen him. In the daytime, and at night, he wanders through town asking strangers for money, maintaining his characteristic, incongruous expression, not unlike the look of someone who is hard at work on a crossword puzzle. He'll approach and ask, slurring, if we've "got any change," but whereas the average panhandler on the East Coast will put some life into his pitch and claim that he merely needs change for bus fare, or something, this man asks for it as if he's not sure what money is and wants only to hold some to see how much it weighs.

I could sense that my friends expected this story to have a climax, so I pushed on: there is something about this part of the country that seems to cultivate pointless, dull oddities like this man. "He wouldn't last five minutes in Boston," I said. "Here, he's part of the landscape." It was the landscape I found fault with, I explained, not the man—this place without topography, this infernal land that hills forgot.

I told them how I'd looked out at all the cars stopped in traffic and the gray buildings and wondered why any of it was ever put there. I wondered how it was not smashed to pieces long before, and as my friends and husband listened I gathered from the gathering clouds that were their expressions that I had ventured into territory where they would not follow. "It's not that I wished a tornado on Cadiz," I said, looking at Claire's unsmiling face. "I wouldn't wish that on anybody."

And I would never say, I explained, that God had punished the people of Cadiz for anything. "I don't believe in God. But I wonder if—you know—we should take this last tornado as a sign that maybe there are better places to live."

Perhaps my story went over so poorly because we were at the winery, and the wine was okay, and the day was pretty, with the river glittering behind me where I couldn't see it but the others could. The others were looking at the scenery that stretched away from us. I had cast an awkward pall. I knew I could do one of two things: either dig myself a deeper hole, or shut up. Eventually someone praised the wine and we moved on.

I had not told them how, when I got home, the cave cricket had not crept into a hole at all. He was in plain sight, caught in one of Charlie's glue traps. All six of his legs and both antennae were stuck to the surface. He would never come unstuck; to pull him away would have killed him. Cave crickets don't make noise, so he stood there looking lifeless, but very much alive. I didn't know what to do. I wanted to end his life for him, but anything I crushed him with would stick to the trap, and the glue might never come off. I didn't want to throw the trap out. I didn't want to go near him. So I left him there, and I kept an eye on him all that day, and on the day to follow, as he slowly, helplessly died.

I still have not ventured into Cadiz, but I think about it often, even though I've half forgotten the earthquake in Haiti and other tornadoes south of us. It's not because Cadiz is so close, for it might as well be in Pakistan for all the contact I've had with it and all but two of its people. There is something else involved, something more than morbid curiosity, I told Charlie when he caught me watching Cadiz clips on YouTube six months after the storm, and asked why I still paid it such attention.

I didn't tell him what it is, and he didn't ask. It is fear, but not a fear I am used to. It is like a new kind of fear someone at Google invented, a fear I never knew until I moved to Missouri. It stems from the constant threat of tornadoes, but has more to do with these empty landscapes, the Missouri license plates I am still not used to seeing everywhere, and the way our house makes me feel, when I am in it, like I am still outside, no matter what part of the house I am in.

And there is more to it even than that. In those first weeks after the storm, when I looked at images of Cadiz, I felt, in a small way, validated. It was as if my inward impression of Cadiz and its outward appearance had, in the space of a few minutes, been reconciled. Cadiz was so irresistible to me after the storm because, finally, one piece of Missouri looked to everyone else the way it had appeared to me all along.

I would not have admitted that at the time—not even for the purpose of creating awkward moments at wineries. It is the kind of thing Charlie would not understand, and I don't think anyone else would get it either, at least not anyone who lives around here.

Nominated by Maureen Stanton

GETTING BY

by BOB HICOK

from FREQUENCIES (YES, YES BOOKS)

I love the idea of climbing a ladder
carrying another ladder. Of climbing that ladder
carrying a tree. Of climbing the tree
to get closer to where rain
doesn't fall, to touch the asceticism
of the sky, the hem of drought.
As when the woman I love said,
I don't love you anymore, and I decided
to love her for not loving me.
Within a year, she loved me again
for loving her negations. In the same way,
I love the rain for killing itself
before it reaches the grass, I love the grass
for turning brown, I love brown
for being the color of my thirst, I love my thirst
for its willingness to kill me. But this is all
an idea, a man on a tree on a ladder
on a ladder on a planet in a solar system
in a poem that is fighting for its life,
like the city I see when I close my eyes,
or the night of my closed eyes
that falls upon the city, or the people
in the city who look up
and want moonlight, even a quarter moon,
even the word *moon* on a string will do.

Nominated by Yes, Yes Books, David Jauss, Daniel S. Libman, Fred Leebron

IMAGINATION

fiction by SIGRID NUNEZ

from THE SUN

In walked Dick Franz with his look of a warlock. Flowing gray hair, furry eyebrows like mice hunched above his sheer cliff of a nose, black jacket over black shirt, stovepipe legs in black jeans. Without even saying hello to anyone, he darted into the hall bathroom, and before Elsie could stop herself (wait, had she *tried* to stop herself?) she pictured him turning into a little dog—no, a large dog, or at least tall enough to lift its leg and aim into the bowl. Then he was back, man-shaped again, striding into the living room to mingle with the other guests.

Elsie looked out the window behind the sofa, where for the past half-hour she'd been sitting, largely (but not ungratefully) ignored. Her mother was afraid it would rain, ruining her plans for supper outdoors, and although it was not raining yet, the sky was clearly brooding about it. Elsie tried to stop herself from wishing it would rain, but it was useless. After all, the thought had come to her, hadn't it? She hadn't willed it; it just all of its own wicked self came. Of course she knew it was wrong. But how were you supposed to stop thinking something once it popped into your head? Do tell her.

She turned back from the window to find Dick Franz looming. He reached for her hand and he kissed it, which is what Dick Franz did. "I won't say you look gorgeous, because I know you've already heard it to death." The flattery rolled right off her. She had indeed been complimented on her looks that evening a tiresome number of times. When she didn't respond, he wavered, knitting his brows. The mice bumped noses, and it was only by the most athletic effort, one that made her feel as if her chest would literally explode, that Elsie was able to stop

herself from laughing. "*Thank you* are the words you're searching for."
As Dick moved on, Elsie hid her face in her hands.

Two years ago, when she was on the cusp of adolescence, she'd had a crush on Dick, which only baffled her now—as it had baffled her to be told that, in his youth, Dick had been "quite the ladies' man" (by her mother, who also confessed to having been one of the ladies). He was now married to Nick (*Dick* and *Nick*: why was there always something to put her in danger of losing it?), who'd been invited to the party too, of course, but was off somewhere, shooting one of his eco-documentaries. Dick was an architect, like Elsie's mother—in fact, they had met as students together in architecture school. Elsie's father's job was even more boring: market research for electronics.

Her parents liked to call this their "country house," though they were only a stone's throw from their home in the city and there were few places anywhere in that town where, if you listened closely, you could not hear traffic. But for her parents this was one of the charms: an easy commute for them, as well as convenient for their city friends, who could be invited up just for the day—though sometimes guests were invited for a whole weekend. (Never longer. Her father's favorite saying was the one about houseguests being like fish: after three days they start smelling.) This weekend, for example, all the beds would be full. Dick was staying. Also her mother's friend Luane, who was in the midst of a blistering divorce, and, ointment for those blisters, Luane's new, younger boyfriend, Joel.

Her parents gave a party around this time every year, a kind of farewell to summer. Elsie thought a summer house with no beach was, well, not a summer house. But her mother had a vast fear of the ocean for the very good reason that the Pacific had swallowed her big brother (Elsie's uncle), an experienced surfer, when she was still a girl. Luckily she had not grown up afraid of all water, and, sunk into the lush lawn beyond the back porch, like a giant spearmint lozenge, was a pool large enough to swim laps. No one wanted to swim today, though. That week had been unusually cool, and there was no sun.

Most of the guests had driven or taken the train up from the city, but there were several who, like Elsie's family, had second homes in the area, or who lived there year-round—Dr. Lem, for example, who'd moved into the house next door after retiring a decade ago and who even now was wheeling his wife (knocked off her feet permanently by a reckless bicyclist the summer before) to the drinks table. Dr. Lem himself had mild Parkinson's. He braced the wrist of one tremulous hand with the other as he took the glass of ginger ale from the bartender and lowered it into the hands of Mrs. Lem. The little scene lashed Elsie's heart. Old people were so depressing. And everyone here, if not quite as old as the Lems, was old. Elsie's mother had urged her to invite one or two of her own friends. But why on earth would Jess or Paloma—the very idea of Princess Paloma . . . As she watched the bartender pour a glass of wine for Dr. Lem, Elsie remembered earlier overhearing him say to one of the waiters, "What the fuck kind of party is it with no music?"

And besides, she and Paloma weren't getting along so well—not like last summer, when they'd first met, in a lyrical-dance class, and become inseparable. Between then and now Paloma (who had to live in Albany because her father worked for the governor) had done the strangest thing Elsie had ever seen a girl do. It was a reversal of the correct order of things: Paloma's best friends were now all boys. Girls, she had texted Elsie, didn't make good friends. *Cz femalz by natr cnt b trstd.*

Slap in the face! But the indignation that had flared in Elsie had been immediately doused by guilt. Though Paloma didn't know it, Elsie had shared with Jess a few of Paloma's confidences. That her mother had cancer was the biggest one. Elsie had no idea why she'd done this to Paloma. She had no desire whatsoever to hurt her (she loved Paloma!). She just hadn't been able to stop herself. Of course she had known that Jess would never repeat what she'd been told. There, you see? Girls *could* be trusted. Elsie totally trusted Jess.

As usual at these catered parties, whether here or in the city, the waitstaff was young and attractive: The tall, darkly tan bartender, whose features were somehow both tough and angelic. The two female waiters, one blond, the other blonder, each with hair slipping adorably from loose topknots and skin as pink and ivory as a baby's. All actors, you didn't have to ask. This wasn't a party, this was a film about a party, it amused Elsie to think. Tough Angel and Blond and Blonder were the stars. Everyone else was a minor character or an extra. Some kind of thriller. Tough Angel was a fraud; he was actually here to rob the place—or to kidnap Dick, the mad scientist, who possessed some secret knowledge that, if it fell into evil clutches, could be used to destroy the world. Blond was Tough Angel's duped and innocent lover; Blonder, his nemesis. Any moment now the shooting would start. Everyone would scream and scramble for cover, and Agent Lem would leap out of her wheelchair with a gun in each hand and start blasting away too.

But first they had to eat. Her mother was motioning guests toward the dining room, where the table was spread with plates of cold meat and fish and several kinds of salad. People served themselves, then streamed through the kitchen and out to the back porch or onto the lawn. A sky like a trough of curdled milk about to be dumped on them made it seem later than it was. But the rain held off.

Elsie was hungry, but don't expect to see her stuffing her face. No one could accuse her of being anorexic (if only!), but there was no way she was not going to obsess about her weight. That summer she had put on two and a half pounds. (With a lick of satisfaction she had noted that Paloma had put on at least five. Warning: hanging out with boys makes you fat.)

A bowl of olives sat within reach. When she had eaten one, Elsie saw that her mother, famous for doing everything right, had forgotten a small detail. She supposed that she, Elsie, was to blame. ("Your mother's so worried, it's starting to distract her at work," her father said.) She rolled the pit idly between two fingers before tucking it down her neckline, into her bra. Oh, wouldn't *that* be a sick little joke to play on the next boy who wanted to feel her there. She felt herself there, palpating the bump, the outline of which was visible through the thin cotton of her shirt. Was that what it was like? According to Paloma, her mother had sat up in bed one morning, and (mysteriously, given that it didn't hurt) her fingers had gone straight to it: a hard little lump, like a—pit? No, that wasn't it. Like a—

"Oh, Elsie." Her mother's voice was soft, but it affected Elsie like a bark. "Do you have any idea how that looks?"

"Except that no one's looking. And you forgot to put something out for the pearls—I mean, pits."

Her mother looked tired but pretty tonight, with a new short haircut and yesterday's gray streaks now dyed Burnt Cinnamon. Summery and très gamine in her blue-and-white sailor's smock dress and flat sandals. But not, right this moment, happy.

"I'll take care of it," she said. "Why don't you go get something to eat?" Elsie stood. "But first give me that thing." Elsie dug out the olive pit and dropped it into the waiting palm. Her mother closed her fist and waved it under Elsie's nose. "You know, this is a perfect example of what we've been talking about." Though her mother had never hit her, Elsie had no trouble imagining that fist coming at her again and again. Her mother made no secret of the frustration that had been building for months now. She wanted to beat Elsie's brains out. Elsie's father hid his feelings better, but: "I don't think we can accuse your mom of exaggeration here."

"Poor impulse control," they called it. Poor judgment. Saying whatever she felt like without thinking how it would sound. To her math teacher, who, observing Elsie's uncovered yawn, wanted to know if Elsie was bored with geometry: "No way. I love geometry. I'm just bored with this class." And there had been other complaints from school. About Elsie being disruptive, either for talking in class or, more worryingly, inappropriate laughter. It was not just that she laughed louder and longer than everyone else at things that were funny, though that was troubling enough. It was that she laughed when no one else was laughing and there appeared to be nothing funny at all. If you asked her what she was laughing at, she'd tell you nothing, never mind, she couldn't say. Or she'd tell you the pathetic truth: she didn't know. The flip side of this was equally inexplicable bouts of tears, which, again, she either could not or would not explain.

An inventive imagination was a gift of the gods— or a curse if you couldn't control it. Elsie would sometimes start talking, telling a story, say, and get so carried away, piling it on so thick, flying off on so many tangents, that she might as well have been speaking in tongues. If you pointed this out to her, her response would be to clam up.

But the worst thing so far had been the scream. At school one day Elsie had accidentally left her French workbook in her locker and been given permission to leave class to go get it. The lockers were on the ground floor, two flights down. It was allergy season, and as she reached the second-floor landing, she let out a head-scouring sneeze. The stairwell responded with the most awesome, eerie echo. So what would it sound like if she screamed?

Like a girl who'd seen Ghostface, apparently. Those who came running were not amused. The assistant principal was not the least bit understanding. Even Elsie's friends accused her of being uncool.

She got tired of saying, "It just happened," and being told that this would not do. "I wanted to hear what it sounded like" and "I couldn't help it" would not do either. But she was telling the truth. Why couldn't everyone just accept it? Sure, it seemed like a bad idea to her after the fact. Sure, she was sorry—especially now that some kids were treating her like a freak. And she had apologized. Several times. What more did they want? Do tell her.

When her mother found out, she said, "In a situation like that, before you act, you have to take a deep breath."

Actually, she *had* taken a deep breath before screaming.

"*What* are you laughing at?"

"Nothing."

Her mother took a highly ostentatious deep breath herself before starting over. "In a situation like this, you have to take a deep breath and ask yourself, 'What will happen if I do this thing?' And if the answer is 'Something bad,' then you have to show some control. You have to tell yourself not to do it. And if that seems too hard, focus on the consequences. Say, 'Will I be sorry?' Yes? Well, then, why ever do it? And *just don't.*"

Later, during what was basically the same conversation but in a calmer mood, Elsie tried to explain to her parents that, at the time, it had felt almost as if someone was daring her ("What—you don't mean like a voice?" her father interrupted anxiously. "It wasn't like you heard a voice telling you to scream, did you, hon?"), or as if she was daring herself. But hadn't she always had a touch of that particular devil in her? Once, in grade school, she told them, two boys had dared her to eat a pale-blue capsule one of them had found on the ground. There was no way to tell what it was, but Elsie had taken the dare. All three spent the rest of the school day on the edge of their seats. But when nothing happened, they were disappointed. Elsie had kept this episode a secret from her parents, and now, seeing the horror benumb their faces, she wished she had taken it to her grave.

Her mother wanted to believe that school was to blame—everyone knew how stressful school could be. And in fact, though the summer had been far from perfect, there had at least been fewer worrying incidents, and nothing remotely as upsetting as the scream.

This morning, however, things had gone very wrong. Elsie and her mother were having breakfast (her father was sleeping in, as he often did on weekends) when her mother started talking about the party. It was still not too late for Elsie to invite a friend, she said. And she added carefully, "By the way, what's up with Paloma?" She had sensed something was wrong weeks ago, but so far Elsie had kept her in the dark. Now enlightened, Elsie's mother assumed a knowing expression and announced that Paloma's behavior was because of the cancer. (Yes, Elsie had broken her promise to Paloma a second time, but did it matter anymore?) "Mothers aren't supposed to get sick with serious diseases that might take them away from you." Elsie's mother said Paloma resented her mother for getting cancer; she felt betrayed, and now those feelings had become twisted into the subconscious fear that females couldn't be trusted. Attachment to breastless boys was much safer. Did Elsie see what her mother was getting at?

Elsie thought she did, and though she wasn't completely convinced, the explanation gave her some comfort. But then her mother said, "Now, about the party. Can you promise you'll behave? I mean, can I count on you not to do anything perverse?"

It wasn't the first time she had used that word. The first time, Elsie had been annoyed. This time she was enraged. "Think about it, Mom. Do you really want to call your own daughter a pervert?" Elsie knew what a pervert was. A pervert was a flasher. A pervert was the burglar who broke into Jess's house last summer and took a shit in the kitchen sink. A pervert was someone who got off watching a gerbil being trampled by a masked midget in red patent-leather high-heeled boots.

"No, no, no," her mother said. "I told you before, Elsie, you're confusing two different words. *Perverse* doesn't have to mean perverted. It can mean contrary. It can mean just plain difficult."

"Except you didn't say contrary or just plain difficult, did you?"

Ten minutes later they were still bickering.

"This is absurd," her mother said. "Don't you see? *This*, in *itself*, is perverse. Exactly what you're doing right now. Well, I've got a very busy day ahead of me, and I'm not going to sit here and play stupid word games." And for the rest of the day—which had been busy indeed with the arrival of the caterers and the final preparations for the party—they had avoided each other.

Elsie sailed through the dining room, eyes averted disdainfully from all the calories on display. Outside on the porch, her father was holding forth on his favorite topic: the future. Specifically, the future of high tech. He was all "gesture recognition" and "touchless touch screens" and how, sooner than you think, your iPhone wouldn't be in your hand but implanted right in your brain.

Before, when she used to hear her father go on like this, so animated and smart-sounding, Elsie would feel a warm tingle of pride. Now the feeling was more like prickly heat. She had become aware—her mother had *made* her aware—that there was a problem with the way her father talked when he had an audience. "Sometimes I'm afraid he comes across like he thinks he's the only one who knows anything about the subject," her mother had said. Which Elsie could see now was only too true. And, newly sensitized, she had picked up on how, even when the topic wasn't one her father knew a lot about, he still tended to present every piece of information as if it were firsthand, and to repeat others' ideas and opinions as if he'd come up with them himself. "That's his best book," she'd heard him say about a writer she was almost sure he'd never read.

She was heartened to see the people sitting nearest her father looking attentive, seemingly happy to pick at their plates while listening to him run on. Then she noticed Arthur Klaus, one of the partners in her mother's firm, who'd come with his pretty-and-elegant-though-grossly-pregnant wife, Min. At the moment Min was seated on the porch sofa and chatting softly with Luane. Arthur was standing nearby, watching Elsie's father with an ironic, forbearing little smile, as if listening to some child's elaborate tall tale. Elsie scanned the group, measuring people's expressions, and thought she caught something similar on Luane's boyfriend's face. Except that Joel wasn't watching her father. He was looking down, as if taking care that his thoughts not be too readable. He looked a bit puzzled to Elsie—and, she thought, her insides shriveling, a bit embarrassed. She remembered what she'd been told Joel did for a living: he was a computer engineer. He probably knew everything about the subject, and yet, rather than join in, as you'd expect in any normal conversation, he kept quiet. Looking puzzled. Looking embarrassed. Looking away.

She had seen enough. She felt scalded. She had to do something, and in an instant she knew what it would be. Who cared if it was cold? So what if it was about to pour? In her mind she was already enjoying it: a bracing dip, a spell of furious kicking and stroking. Who cared if no one else was going in the pool?

Empty dishes had been cleared from the dining table, and in their place was a cheese platter, a fruit bowl, an apple cobbler, and a chocolate-raspberry layer cake. Elsie folded a large slice of cake in a napkin to take with her upstairs, wolfing down half before she even made it to her room.

The window was open. Elsie lay in bed, watching the billowy white curtain as it kept getting sucked out and blown back in again, like the veil of a dithering bride. She had left the party—had been bounced from it, actually, like a drunk or a crasher (*in my own fckn hse*) before it was over. Now she texted back and forth with Jess while listening to the sounds of the party winding down and waiting for her mother's inevitable knock. Her mother did not knock, though. She walked right in, a breach of family etiquette, which said a lot about her state of mind.

Earlier Elsie had cried herself near delirious, and the sight of her swollen face blunted her mother's anger. Still, the talk must be had. Her mother must vent her anger.

Her disappointment.

Her worry.

Her frustration.

(Mercifully, since not all the guests were leaving, she also had to keep it short.)

"I just wanted to go swimming," Elsie said. And to swim she'd needed to put on her swimsuit, which was what she'd gone up to her room to do. First, she had finished the cake. The disgusting-looking cloth napkin, with its brown and red smears, now lay atop her dresser, catching her mother's eye and making her wince.

Her bikini on, Elsie had grabbed a towel from the hall closet and run barefoot downstairs and out the back door without a glance at anyone (though aware of drawing several glances herself).

Up close, the pool, reflecting a sky like a sheet of tarnished silver, was not so inviting. All she had to do was look at it, and she was covered with goose flesh. She dropped the towel and was about to dip a toe in when, from what felt like every direction, wind blustered into the yard. The water rippled as if an invisible rock had been tossed in. From the lilac bushes rose a loud hiss, and suddenly the bushes were twisting and flailing, like women being strangled. As if in fright, the apple tree dropped its fruit, and the lawn flattened: a threatened animal laying its ears back. A trident of lightning flashed, and between two bursts of thunder Elsie heard her father shouting at her to get away from the pool. She turned and ran.

The first drops came down so big and hard and far apart that it was like a stoning. She had just reached the house when the deluge began. The wind sprayed the rain with wild abandon, driving everyone on the porch indoors.

It was at this point—"obviously"—that Elsie should have gone straight to her room and changed back into her clothes. "We're not prudes, any of us," said her mother. "But how do you think it looked? In the living room, with everyone else dressed, and you prancing around practically naked." (Elsie had left the towel by the pool where she'd dropped it.) "It was . . . it was just"—Elsie braced herself for

529

perverse—"inappropriate. Didn't you even notice that you were making people uncomfortable?"

(Once, after passing two elderly men sitting together on a bus, Elsie had heard one of them say to the other, "It's when they're stacked like that and still just kids that they really ought to be declared a public nuisance.")

The truth was, the only thing Elsie had noticed in the living room was Tough Angel staring at her. What had happened next was hard to explain. She hadn't known how to put it, even to Jess. There was her mother's version: "Then you go strutting up to the bartender and start flirting like mad, putting him in the most awkward position, since he was working and shouldn't even have been talking to you."

It must have been the underwire in her bikini bra, the kind known to set off metal detectors. His stare was a magnet, pulling her to him, and while his hands were busy among the bottles and glasses, those eyes never left her, held her there. And then, like a hypnotist, he made her dance from one bare foot to the other and sway and giggle and swing her long hair. She would not have been surprised if by simply arching an eyebrow he'd been able to levitate her.

There had been some kind of small talk—what grade was she in, did she like school, was she sorry summer was almost over—to which she could hardly remember responding. What she remembered instead was the feeling of her heart capsizing inside her like a little boat. What she remembered was thinking how incredibly, heroically handsome he was, and knowing full well what her mother later presented as if it was news: "He's not a kid, Elsie. He's, like, thirty years old." If an exaggeration, only a slight one. Didn't Elsie realize how inappropriate it was, flirting with a man that age? No. How could she? She had been bewitched. Bewarlocked.

But that Elsie had been humiliated you didn't have to tell her. At a certain moment something behind her had snagged his attention, and a sly look had flitted across his face. Glancing over her shoulder, she saw the two waitresses watching from the dining room, elbowing and clutching at each other. Though they knew she could see them, they made no effort to hide their glee. Bitch and Bitchier. She had turned back just in time to catch Kip, as the bartender had introduced himself, winking at them.

She was cutting quickly across the living room when she saw her father sitting by himself in a corner, checking his phone. She went straight to him and, ignoring his startled expression, climbed onto his

530

lap. She'd wanted a hug, but he kept his arms at his sides, and she could feel him tense all over, the way he might have done had she been the drunk wife of one of his friends.

"Elsie," he began uncertainly. She wanted to speak but was afraid that if she unclenched her throat the tears would gush, never ending. She squeezed her father's neck, but he only grew stiffer. This time she did notice other people: the looks they exchanged with one another, and how they, too, seemed at a loss. "Elsie, please," said her father, still without touching her. She squeezed her eyes shut.

She felt a hand on her back. But it was only her mother. "If you're quite through making a spectacle of yourself," she said, speaking into Elsie's ear, "maybe you could go upstairs. And if you'd do me the favor of staying there so that I can enjoy the rest of my party in peace, I would so appreciate that."

It was odd: the storm had passed, but the air it left behind was heavy and very warm. Even with the window open, Elsie's room was stifling. She could not sleep. Her cotton nightgown stuck to her skin, and no matter how many times she slugged the pillow, it refused to support her head as she wished. Everyone else in the house was asleep. (The insomniac can always tell.)

She tried not to think about Kip (real name? short for—?) but those eyes were indelible, the burning eyes of a wild thing caught in the light of the moon. Thirty: not old enough to be her father, but close. She tried to imagine what she herself might look like at that age. As pretty as she was now? Prettier? (Doubtful.) But suppose she never got there. Suppose she died young. *By her own hand.* The poetic-sounding phrase had always appealed to her. Of course, that was the real reason they didn't live near the beach. Because her mother, famous for being able to see into the future, had foreseen this: her beloved daughter, her cherished only child, walking into the sea.

Awash in self-pity, trembling with the poetry of it all, Elsie swallowed hard.

Two o'clock. Never before had she stayed up this late. But she was not even tired, and to lie itching in that hot bed one minute longer was to lose her mind. Without knowing exactly where she was going—could it be she was sleepwalking?—she got up and left the room.

Passing Dick's door, she pictured him asleep and the mice, liberated between the stroke of midnight and dawn, chasing each other around the room. A dangerous fit of hysterics seized her, but she managed to avert disaster by clamping her hands over her mouth and crossing her legs as tightly as possible. (Still, she leaked.)

Downstairs she hesitated only a moment before heading out the front door.

It was thrillingly dark: her parents considered it a waste of energy to keep on the outside lights (or air conditioning) through the night, and there was no moon. The grass, cool and slick from the rain, poked deliciously between her toes. There was a weight to the darkness that, in spite of the warmth, made her think of snow. Mounds of black snow in the yard, a thick layer over the field separating their house and the Lems' (where, like a low, dim star, an energy-wasting porch light gleamed).

She stood in the middle of the black lawn and looked back, and when she saw that the house had vanished, she felt wobbly, as if she were teetering at the edge of a deep well.

How could it be that she smelled magnolias when the blossoms had died months ago? But the night had turned everything strange: the yard was alien country, and she herself was a different girl from the miserable one of an hour ago, the angry one of yesterday morning. It gave her a giddy sense of power to be prowling around outside while everyone else slept.

She tried a few moves she had learned in dance class. She hitched up her shoulders and shimmied until her nightgown slipped down past her slender hips. When she stepped out of it, she was naked. The night approved, taking her in its arms, touching her everywhere with black-suede-gloved hands.

She walked through the grass, taking high, coltish steps, her whole body fluttering with excitement. She made a large semicircle that brought her around to the back of the house. Here, the black snow was deeper. And she was not alone.

It must be some animal, she thought. It had been on her left and had just now moved across her path so that it was on her right. She couldn't see or hear it, but she knew it was there. She began walking faster.

She lay on her side in the wet grass, stunned, panting. In the dark she had not realized how close she was to the apple tree. She had stepped on an apple, twisting her ankle and falling with her full weight on the joint.

When she got her breath back, she tried to stand, but an appalling blast of pain made her knees buckle. She sat on the ground, her stomach churning. She could not tell if the ankle was dislocated or fractured, or both. All she knew was that she could not walk.

What choice did she have, then, but to crawl? She gritted her teeth as she moved onto all fours. But after going only a little way she stopped. The torture of her foot being dragged along the ground was too much. (The ankle was surely broken.) The struggle, brief though it was, left her covered in sweat and near vomiting. The house might as well have been a hundred miles away.

Elsie was fourteen. So far in her life she had never known serious illness or hurt. She'd experienced pain, of course—headaches, cramps— but never anything so bad that it could not be relieved by aspirin. Still it was not the physical suffering that made her start to sob. It was knowing that she was going to have to scream for help. She would scream, waking the entire house. Lights would blaze on, everyone would come running—and then how on earth would Elsie go on living? Do tell her.

She sobbed a little harder as she imagined her mother repeating something she had said earlier, before leaving Elsie's room: "Are you really that desperate for attention?" How cruel, how unfair life was, Elsie thought bitterly. She had done nothing to deserve this. *Nothing.* And the conviction of her own innocence pierced her.

Tired from holding the same awkward position, she stretched out and rolled gently onto her back. Insects brushed and batted against her. A moth landed like a kiss precisely on her lips. After a few minutes the ground, though rough and hard, did not feel so cold anymore.

And what if, instead of screaming, she was to force herself to lie here like this until morning? Her mother usually woke up early. It was likely that she'd be the first one out of bed. It wasn't impossible that she would discover Elsie before any of the others had a chance to see her. Yes, she thought. It was worth a try. She closed her eyes experimentally (though sleep would be out of the question). After all, morning was not that far off. But was she really that brave? It would be the hardest thing she'd ever had to do in her life. Her entire leg, toes to hip, burned like a log roasting on a fire. Could she really suffer so much pain in silence?

She had forgotten all about the animal. Now a rustling from the trees behind the swimming pool told her it was still there. She pushed herself upright, staring wildly into the dark. She thought of the mountain lions and coyotes and bears that people had claimed to have seen in the area—sightings that were not always believed. But Elsie believed them all (at least, she did now), and she was afraid. There she lay, naked, helpless, injured. Easy prey. Then a twig snapped as if a man's foot had trod on it, at which she felt a scream of hurricane force start to gather inside her.

Unseen, the fox stood with one forepaw lifted, muzzle in the air, sniffing the smell of human fear. Had this been an imaginary fox, a creature of folklore, not just clever but kind, he might at least have gone and fetched the poor girl her nightgown.

Never before in his nocturnal visits to this place had the fox encountered a human being. He rotated his ears as she took a deep breath.

Nominated by The Sun, Jay Rogoff

THE EARTH ITSELF

by TIMOTHY DONNELLY

from POETRY NORTHWEST

To quantify the foolishness of the already long since failed
   construction project, the famous German polymath

undertook to calculate the precise number of bricks
   the Tower of Babel would have required had it ever been

finished. The figure he came up with ran an impressive
   eighteen digits in length, climbing all the way up

to that rarely occupied hundred-quadrillionths place.
   Looking at it now, between loads of laundry, the figure

calls to mind an American telephone number—area code first,
   then the prefix, then the line number, followed in turn

by a trail of eight additional zeroes. I feel a little lost
   through the hypnosis of those zeroes, but I still pick up

the phone and dial that number now. A recording says
   the number I've dialed isn't an actual telephone number

after all. Please try again. I do. Same result. I try dialing
   that trail of zeroes instead. This time the recording says

that the call I'm making might itself be recorded. I hesitate a bit
  at the thought of that, when all this crazy science, all

this poking into mysteries, panting for answers, always
  harder, higher, my phone calls today and the recordings

during laundry, the laundry—it all comes crashing down.
  I don't have time to experiment. I'm hanging up the phone.

But wait, there's more! On my rush back to the laundromat
  I remembered I forgot a part. The polymath figured out, too,

that if the tower had reached its destination, it would have
  taken over eight-hundred years to climb to the top.

What's more, his calculations say the mass of all those bricks
  would have outweighed, slightly, the earth's own mass,

meaning the tower would have used up all the matter of
  the planet it was built on, which is foolish enough, and then

a little more, which is ridiculous, unless the tower is secretly
  just the earth itself, with the added weight of all the living on it.

Nominated by Poetry Northwest

LOVE LIKE THAT

by JUDE NUTTER

from THE BRIAR CLIFF REVIEW

Cannula, from the Latin, means *little reed*,
and how could you not be thinking of the hero, ricocheting
through the forest, tailed by the enemy, then breaking
cover to find himself at the frayed margins of a swamp
where the water parsley and the hemlock are fuming
into the slow fireworks of their umbels, where,
on the first try, he severs a perfect length of reed and submerges –
simply sinks beneath the convenient surface of the water –
to breathe, calmly, through its long, hollow body.
But your mother was drowning anyway, propped up
on a pale talus of pillows, the twin stems of the cannula
looped demurely behind her ears, and you know, now,
that such escapes are not possible; that the burden
of water would be greater than the weight the sheeted
muscles of the diaphragm are designed to overcome.
Her room overlooked the hospital's high-walled garden
with its drapes of ivy from which a single robin kept flying
in red arcs of lament, breaking out from behind
the waxed latches of the leaves. Beyond, a field gone fallow,
and the white needle of an egret marking the river's
open seam, and little hiccups of colour as cars on the ring road
passed a gap in the hedge. She had no use for that garden
with its lavenders and jasmine and Black Knight buddleia.
And you never entered it either because, while she was dying,
you denied yourself the world on her behalf. It was later,

after she had gone into, and locked you out of,
the dirt's still house, and you had driven back to the hospital
with those oxygen tanks that had stood for weeks
like green torpedoes in the garden shed that you heard
from the nurses how on the morning when your mother's lungs
were drained for the last time and you'd sat watching
a robin slipping in and out of the ivy, your father had been told
that he could leave her, now, in that room, with its view
out over the garden toward the private triumphs of the yellow flag
and the bog cotton among the flare of standing water
in the field – it was, after all, close to the end. Or
he could take her home. And that your father had made them
    weep.
Home was the terminus of a long drive west through a landscape
imprisoned by the rain's long memory; mile after mile
of blind, sharp turns and wind-panicked grass until that short,
straight trough between the peaks of the Slieve Mish
where the way is always in shadow,
where the veil between the worlds is thin,
where a King of Munster had once built his ring fort
high on the slopes of Caherconree and then, every night,
set its stones spinning so no one could find its entrance.
Where ravens are busy still, building omens out of their bodies.
And so to arrive at last at a small house on the western edge
of a country, where the land's confident and green repose
finally gives itself up to the tireless, unbuttoning hands
of the sea. We talk about bodies of water, but how
can sunlight enter and unfasten such a body
until it becomes an other life whose grip we walk into
and out of all day at will. And we don't talk enough
about the moment when that light abandons the water
at evening and the sea, turning its back, becomes suddenly
secret and remote. And it's like a door closing.
It's like a heart shutting down. And too much has been said
about the boats casting off from the quay and leaving
the clutch of the harbour; all that tonnage –
blocks and shackles and nets – upheld and under power,
catching and riding the swells. But that's what they do,
those boats leaving the harbour – they head west
toward the hour of such abandonment. And that's exactly

what your father said - your father, his legs shredded
by German bullets when he was twenty, who walks
with a cane and a limp and leaves faint scuffs in the carpets
and the grass of the garden, who cannot lift
even the raked piles of papery sabres blown from the branches
of the cordylines or plastic pots of new-rooted fuchsia
for your mother's grave. He'd said that he wanted to take her
    home;
and that he would take her home, even if he had to carry her.

Nominated by The Briar Cliff Review

THE GENTLEMAN'S LIBRARY, A NOWADAY REDUX

by BILL COTTER

from THE BELIEVER

NOTES TOWARD THE CREATION OF A COLLECTION OF THE MOST IMPORTANT WORKS OF LITERATURE OF ALL TIME, INCLUDING TALES OF CRIPPLING SELF-DOUBT AND POSSIBLE ETERNAL DAMNATION

DISCUSSED: *A Man of Means, Unquiet Coffee Shops, The Definition of Literature, Books That Stop Wars, A Bundling-Up of Existential Drawers, A Turn toward Wikipedia, Considerations of Shelf Space, Olfactory Generalizations, A Long-Suffering Mail Carrier, Pan-Seared Cod, Muttonthumping*

In late 2008 I was offered a position for which I later realized I was not qualified. Since I needed a job, and since no background or credit check was required, and since it paid nineteen dollars an hour and was as close to a dream job as I could imagine, I took it. The task: compile a list of the 1,500 most important works of literature, catalog them, buy them, and install them in my new employer's private library, a tastefully converted attic space filed with empty, dedicated shelves in an old Austin house not far from the University of Texas. JB, my employer, a

An appendix to this essay can be found at *believermag.com/library*.

man of some means, explained that he wished to retire early from medicine, a job of some means, and have immediately at hand all the literature that matters. The Victorians would have classified this a gentleman's library; that's to say, a large number of books, ideally first editions in fine or original bindings, collected according to some principle or subject (genre-definers, Shelley and his circle, *horae*, really big books, unica, whatever), shelved eccentrically in a charming, crepuscular space, then read, one after another, at leisure, until boredom or death ends the endeavor.

JB—late forties, smart, mysterious, inquisitive, enthusiastic, a gentleman—seems unlikely to yield to death or boredom, and so in a couple of decades he will surely be among the most diversely well read persons in town. That his library will have been compiled by one of the most ill-read persons in town is a humiliating personal irony I've withal suffered alone.

The thing is, I hadn't known of my steep deficiency when I started the job. I thought I'd read selectively and widely. After all, I'd finished the Hergé corpus as a boy, devoured a respectable portion of the world's prison-escape literature as an adolescent, read the sci-fi impresario Jack Vance's thinner books in high school, devoured the free galley proofs and advanced readers that were the only perks of my many bookstore jobs, and, during the long summer of 1995, when the greedy, infantine federation of professional baseball players and their owners fucked everybody out of a regular season, I read *Ulysses*, a long, novel-like work composed by an unstable Irishman, only two words of which I remember, the first and last: *Stately* and *Yes*; the rest of the book was a kind of summer-long literary blackout.

The breadth of my reading, combined with my bookselling and book-restoration experience, would, I thought, surely be enough to compile a list unassailable in scope and selectivity. At our first meeting, I told JB I'd have it ready for him in a week or so, an estimate he greeted with delight, as he was anxious to have the library stocked and ready.

A week later, stupefied, I informed JB that it might take closer to a year to put together a passable list. Disappointed—crestfallen—JB asked why. I told him that I hadn't realized there might be more to the project than noting Pulitzer Prize winners, scanning the classics wall at Barnes & Noble, and consulting my dad, the best-read person I knew. I told JB I hadn't realized that the Chinese had produced more than just the *Art of War* guy; the Nigerians, Achebe; the Colombians, Márquez. I told JB I hadn't realized that there lives a woman named

Patricia Grace who was the first Maori woman to publish a short-fiction collection, that a certain Ayi Kwei Armah was the first Ghanaian to produce an existential novel, that one Amos Tutuola was the first Nigerian magical-realist, that something called *El Güegüense*, composed by an unremembered Nicaraguan around 1550, was considered the oldest work of theater in the Western Hemisphere. I informed JB that I'd discovered that *Gilgamesh* is not the oldest known work of literature (four centuries saltier is *The Instructions of Šuruppak*, a work of Sumerian wisdom literature); that the Dark Ages were not too dark to write in; that the European Renaissance of the fourteenth century started in the twelfth; that an Arabian fellow named Ibn al-Nafis wrote science fiction in the thirteenth century; that Margaret Cavendish, a British lady of the seventeenth, also penned sci-fi; that some anonymous fifteenth-century Balochistani literati composed an epic ballad, *Hero Šey Murīd*, a folkloric drama on a par with the best Elizabethan tragedies; that 1989's groundbreaking lesbian children's book, *Heather Has Two Mommies*, was eight years preceded by the Danish *Mette bor hos Morten og Erik*. I told JB that there was simply far too much to learn, so much that it would be impossible to establish the relative importance of individual works; impossible to avoid the unknowing omission of gems and the inclusion of chaff. I did not tell him that deep down I felt the production of his library would be not a yearlong project but an utterly unfinishable one, doomed to imperfection. He might end up with tidy rows of indisputably important works, but they would be everywhere muddied by the miserable daubs of impostors, and everywhere pocked with unforgivable lacunae—books that should be included, except that I don't know where or what the hell they are.

After my melodramatic pessimism died down, we began again. At Spider House, a local coffee joint that plays Social Distortion at eight o'clock in the morning, JB and I met to discuss exactly what his library was to be. What kinds of books, what editions, what. How much time to spend, how much money. Two hours and three cups of pitchy coffee later, both JB and I were surprised to discover that JB wasn't entirely sure what he wanted. I began to get the feeling that he wanted me to tell him.

"I'm not retired yet," he said. "In order to retire early, I must work constantly. Which leaves me little time to devote to the development of the library. That is why I hired you."

You know, I really don't know what I'm doing, I thought, and said instead, "I'll do my best."

JB told me there were a few things he was certain of. One, diversity was to undergird the entire project. That meant all nations, cultures, eras, and genres were to be quarried. Two, all works must be in, or have been translated into, French, English, or Spanish, the languages in which he is most comfortably fluent. Three, books were to be critical editions, not specifically first editions. Four, spend no more than one hundred dollars on any one book.

"Anything else?" I said.

"That's it."

"I supposed we should define *literature*," I said. "And *important*."

"Let me know what you come up with."

JB paid for our coffee and we parted. A homework panic the likes of which I hadn't experienced since junior high seized me by the trachea, dragged me thirteen blocks to my house, placed me before a laptop, and commanded me to define this library.

Literature, I decided, because there was no one else to do the deciding for me, would comprise fiction, nonfiction, poetry, drama, and orature. In other words, everything. To refine this, I came up with exclusions: musical theater, shadow plays, declarations, manifestos, speeches, periodicals, constitutions and bills of rights, statutes and codes, patents, lyrics, broadsides, single poems, single letters, journalism, boilerplate, recensions, revisions, and exegeses of major works, and scientific/mathematical papers published in peer-reviewed journals. Why these? I don't know. But I'm the decider.

But what would constitute *important*? Must a work have won prizes? Conquered best-seller lists? Piqued extremists? Must it have been panned by Kakutani, clubbed by Oprah, criminalized by Congress? Those are all fine things, but ultimately I decided that a candidate work must satisfy at least one of the following criteria (though qualifying per se wouldn't oblige inclusion, since we were limited by our shelf space):

(1) Caused serious and/or lasting controversy, such as Simone de Beauvoir's *Le deuxième sexe*, the Tridentine Council's *Index librorum prohibitorum*, Charles Darwin's *On the Origin of Species*.

Of course, the words *serious*, *lasting*, and *controversy* are all as ambiguous as *literature* and *important*. It is here I realized that striving for objectivity was futile; that this library was going to be shelves and shelves of a literary simpleton's guesses.

(2) Was instrumental in causing or stopping war, revolution, or geno-cide, such as Heinrich Kramer and Jakob Sprenger's *Malleus malefi-carum*, Seymour Hersh's *My Lai 4: A Report on the Massacre and Its Aftermath*, the anonymous *Programa zavoevaniya*.

A little more concrete.

(3) Launched a genre, or is considered its definitive work, such as Jorge Luis Borges's *Historia universal de la infamia* (1935; magical realism), Radclyffe Hall's *Well of Loneliness* (1928; lesbian fiction), Yoshida Kenkō's *Essays in Idleness* (1332; essays—two and a half centuries before Mon-taigne!).

Hopelessly un-concrete. For instance, no less than a hundred differ-ent works are regarded, by one expert or another, as the first novel writ-ten in English: Swift's *Gulliver's Travels*, Sir Philip Sidney's *Countess of Pembroke's Arcadia*, Aphra Behn's *Oroonoko*, Bunyan's *The Pilgrim's Progress*, and a profoundly obscure sixteenth-century work called *Be-ware the Cat* by one William Baldwin.

(4) Had exceptional and inimitable circumstances surrounding its coming-to-be, such as Anne Frank's *Het achterhuis*, Leonora Chris-tina Ulfeldt's *Jammers-minde*, Henry Darger's *History of the Vivian Girls*.

The production of any work of any kind is, in its way, exceptional, and of course inimitable. Still, some twenty books in the library were cho-sen as a result of my interpretation of this criterion.

(5) Markedly changed the understanding of the world, such as Nicolaus Copernicus's *De revolutionibus*, Kurt Gödel's *Über formal unents-cheidbare Sätze*, Baruch Spinoza's *Ethica*.

Every bit of research suggests that many existential drawers were up got in a bundle because of these books.

(6) Was censored, suppressed, banned, or resulted in the author's death, such as Miguel Servet's *Christianismi restitutio*, John Cleland's *Fanny Hill*, Taslima Nasrin's *Lajja*.

(7) Is the foundational work of a religion or movement, such as the *Vedas*, Martin Luther's *Disputatio pro declaratione virtutis indulgen-tiarum*, *The Book of Mormon*.

(8) Has shown great longevity, such as Hesiod's *Theogony*, Eleventh-Dynastic Egypt's *The Tale of Sinuhe*, the Mayan *Codex dresdensis*.

(9) Is prominent within a culture, class, or age underrepresented in mainstream literature, such as David Unaipon's *Legendary Tales of the Australian Aborigines*, Briton Hammon's *Narrative of the Uncommon Sufferings and Surprizing Deliverance of Briton Hammon*, Leslie Feinberg's *Stone Butch Blues*.

Here we go again. Every adjective, and some of the nouns, can be interpreted in so many ways. Underrepresented literature, to me (in light of my previously mentioned ill-readness), amounted to nearly a quarter of the library.

(10) Transcends literary and cultural boundaries, such as Anna Sewell's *Black Beauty*, Robert Burton's *The Anatomy of Melancholy*, Pai Hsien-Yung's *Nièzi*.

(11) Is a perennial subject of discourse, scholarship, or syllabi, such as Xueqin Cao's *Hong lou meng*, J. K. Rowling's *Harry Potter* series, and Thomas Aquinas's *Summa theologica*.

(12) Provides the only substantive account of a period of history that would otherwise have been lost, such as Gregory of Tours's *Decem libri historiarum*, the anonymous *The Secret History of the Mongols*, and Herodotus's *Histories*.

And so, from these foggy axioms, which JB approved, a list could be compiled that required only research, extrapolation, presumption, and guessing, obviating well-readness altogether. I would not have to read books; merely read about them. A relief! I could do this. I could do this on the couch in my underpants. I would consult other lists, then run each title through that first protocol of dilettanti, the variably learned, ever-inflating, ever-infuriating *speculum maius* of the lay: Wikipedia.

A list began to form. Patterns emerged. Numbers mounted. Statistics resolved. Such as: 60 percent of the books were originally written in languages other than English, 7 percent were available only in paperback, 20 percent were by women, 3 percent were by Anonymous (and here I paraphrase Virginia Woolf: "Anonymous was a woman"), Jean-

Jacques Rousseau and Mary Wollstonecraft both had a record four books on the list. Three books had the same title: *The Red Book*. The thirteenth-century mystical poet and juridical thinker Rumi was represented by a five-volume shelf-warper titled *The Big Red Book*; the other two just happened to be the largest and smallest single volumes in the library: the larger by the psychoanalyst Carl Jung, and the smaller, whose title is prefixed with *Little*, by the psycho-Leninist Mao Zedong. Also curious: six books were titled in the interrogative: Albee's *Who's Afraid of Virginia Woolf?*, Nikolay Chernyshevsky's *Chto delat?*, Vladimir Lenin's *Chto delat?*, Judy Blume's *Are You There God? It's Me, Margaret*, Ivan Bloch's *Budushchaya voina?*, and P. K. Dick's *Do Androids Dream of Electric Sheep?* The longest work—not counting the *Ynglè Encyclopedia*—was the *Gesar Epic*, a twelfth-century central Asian chantfable, at some twenty million words. Meanwhile, the longest novel (and the only as-yet-unpublished work in the library) was Henry Darger's aforementioned *The Story of the Vivian Girls, in What Is Known as the Realms of the Unreal, of the Glandeco-Angelinian War Storm, Caused by the Child Slave Rebellion*: 7.5 million words, less than half of Darger's lifetime output, yet five times the length of Proust's infamously wordy *À la recherche du temps perdu*. The shortest work was Lucy Terry Prince's "Bars Fight," a moving ballad at a mere 183 words.

Plenty of exceptions to our forthset charter of axioms ultimately found their way into the library. *Le code civil des Français*, for example, is a code of very civilized civil law so elegantly and economically composed that the entire text of the first edition formed a volume about the size of a hardcover of *Gone with the Wind*. This tidy body directly influenced the civil codes of most European nations, most of Latin America, Saudi Arabia, Egypt, Kuwait, Quebec, and the state of Louisiana. I learned all this from a rare-books dealer who specializes in both French law and returning email queries from total strangers. For many works I came across, I would simply write to the person who'd committed the most scholarship on the book in question, explain the library project, and pray for a return email. Often that prayer was answered.

Another exception: Valerie Solanas's 1967 *SCUM Manifesto*, a radical anarcho-feminist tract that called for the wholesale annihilation of men, either satirically or literally (a close reading will support either interpretation). Certainly the most influential work whose entire first print run of two thousand was by mimeograph. Also excepted: Einstein's letters to Roosevelt, the charter of the nuclear arms race.

Sojourner Truth's "Ain't I a Woman?"—word for word the most pow-erful antislavery speech ever delivered; Emile Zola's *J'accuse . . .!*; the anonymous *Manden Charter*; Columbus's *Carta escrita al escribano de ración de los Señores Reyes Católicos*, announcing the discovery of the New World; Abu Khabbab al-Masri's *Explosives Course*. All exceptions to the exceptions.

And, bucking the no-technical-stuff rule, we included Andrew Wiles's proof of Fermat's last theorem, a 106-page solution to the most famous unsolved problem in mathematics, at least up until 1995. Evidently only two or three people understand it. (It is unknown whether Wiles is one of them.) As such, it has been crowned the most unreadable work in a library swarmy with them.

Perhaps this is a good place to open a brief parenthesis on readabil-ity. As I slowly began to get a feel for the calculus above, it grew clear that some—lots—of the qualifying books might not keep the average reader's attention for very long. Though Chanakya's treatise on polity, Isidore of Seville's *Etymologies*, and the *Annotated Code of Canon Law* might all in fact be un-put-down-able, brief synopses found on the in-ternet suggest they are not, that the mere cracking-open of any of these works would put one to bed, if not kill one outright.

"JB," I said, "I don't know about some of these. Do you really want Paul the Deacon's *Historia Langobardorum*? It looks boring."

"Does it meet the criteria?"

"Kind of."

"Which one?"

"Number twelve."

"Then I want to read it."

And there you have it.

As the statistics and curiosities became more and more compelling, my original wrath and dolor began to subside. Confidence and opti-mism crept in. But so did new loathings, fresh biles, novel peeves. As-cendant among them: the lists of others. Have you noticed that lists of exceptional-in-some-way somethings, like books, really nettle people? That book shouldn't be there, this book should, that list has no large-print YA spiritual self-help proto-horror, this one is all white guys, that one is gender-queer unfriendly, this one left off *The Da Vinci Code*, that one is for losers, this one is for prudes. I know the longer I worked on JB's list, the more annoyed I became with other lists. Yet they were absolutely essential to the entire undertaking: the Modern Library's 100 Best Novels of the Twentieth Century (plus its cognate list for nonfiction); like compilations issued by *Le Monde*, *Time*, the *Guardian*, the *New York Times*, *Die Zeit*, *NRC Handelsblad*, the World Library. Then there's the *Encyclopedia Britannica*'s sixty-volume *Great Books of the Western World*, Thomas Jefferson's list of essential reading, and, most of all, Harold Bloom's *The Western Canon*. Whenever my research dead-ended, whenever a knight's tour of the internet met with oblivion, I went to Bloom, which includes a list of some 1,100 books by 900 authors. The best of the best. At times, I felt like my list was approaching Bloom's in breadth and acumen, but then I'd remember that Bloom had probably read every single book in his list, whereas I'd read about one-tenth of one percent of mine. Maybe not even that many. Definitely S. E. Hinton's *The Outsiders*, though, and some of the books with pictures.

After two years of list-making, during which I took many long breaks (to JB's understandable frustration), it was finally time for the really fun phase of the project, and the one to which I felt best suited, given my vocation as a rare-books dealer and avocation as a collector: buying all the books.

Let me be precise: buying would be only half of this phase of the project, the other half being not fun at all: data entry. In addition to walls lined with books awaiting his retirement, part of JB's vision for his library was an accompanying sortable database in which each work would be cataloged, described, summarized, reviewed, and appended with numerous tags. If, say, JB was in the mood for seventeenth-century Ethiopic philosophy, the ideal database would respond to a search for those three tags by returning 1667's *Hatata*, by Yacob Zera, North Africa's great ethicist. After testing numerous private, downloadable programs and finding them all wanting in one or another serious way, we turned to *librarything.com*, a social-networking site that functions much like Facebook, except that books, not friends, are the social coin.

Though LibraryThing is hardly ideal—it is buggy, slow, unfriendly, and resistant to bulk uploads (and downright impervious to bulk uploads from Macs)—its capacity for data appears to be without limit. And it can be made private so that others cannot pinch your work, slander your tastes, or try to make friends. But best of all, more than one person can work on it at a time, because I couldn't do all the data entry by myself, certainly not within a year. Luckily, Austin filmmaker and fledgling rare-books dealer Joan Hendrix was available for hire. She would soon prove the more agile in all aspects of the enterprise, especially buying, LibraryThing wrangling, and assuaging JB's polite frustrations at my general sloth and incompetence.

JB had had his shelves built long before he hired me. The available space would allow for 1,500 books—hardcovers preferred—calculating, as I did, the average thickness of a single volume at one inch, a dimension dictated by and extrapolated from measuring the books on my own shelves. Well, my estimation was a bit off. I had cleverly accounted for colossi like the *Domesday Book*, Blackstone's *Commentaries on the Laws of England*, and the *Corpus Aristotelicum*, but some works I did not take into account, because I'd never heard of them: Bjørneboe's *History of Bestiality* (three volumes, eight inches of shelf space), the *Obras* of Sor Juana Inés de la Cruz (four volumes, nine inches) ,Wu Cheng-en's *XiYu Ji* (four volumes, eight inches), Moses De León's (attr.) *Zohar* (four volumes, six inches), others, many others. The projected census of the library began to shrink. It was rescheduled to 1,400 books. Then 1,300. Then 1,250. By this time Joan was in full employ and we had begun buying. As more and more books came in, it became clearer that even 1,250 would overtax the shelves. An expansion was necessary. So, in a room with nary an inch of naked wall available for additional shelves, JB called upon Roberto, his carpenter, a Vitruvian sorcerer responsible for much of the exquisite woodwork in the rest of the house, and somehow he conjured up enough extra shelf space to hold the projected 1,250—as long we bought abridgments or microprint editions of the really big books, like the *Oxford English Dictionary*, the *Talmud*, and Churchill's *The Second World War*.

But a new problem emerged, this with the list itself. I began to come across other books, must-haves, no-brainers, imperishable DiMaggios of literature that I missed the first time round. For them to have room on the shelves, I realized it would be necessary to cull the herd. I would revisit books chosen early on in the project until I found one I'd erroneously esteemed, downgrade it to crap, pluck it from the shelves, and, in its stead, install a worthier book. At present there are some two hundred volumes of formerly timeless world literature piled up in my room at home, waiting for mug shots and sentencing to Amazon for recoup.

Wherever possible, Joan and I bought critical editions, or companion volumes, especially for the dense, smartypants stuff like Derrida's *De la Grammatologie* (#1,087), an indigestible French sea biscuit in which something called *deconstructive criticism* is defined; Judith Butler's *Gender Trouble: Feminism and the Subversion of Identity* (#990), a fundamental work on feminism and queer theory written in sentences of record-breaking length; and Joyce's *Finnegans Wake* (#1,235).[3]

The books came from all over. Joan and I purchased most of them through the standard online retail platforms of Amazon, Alibris, Biblio, and AbeBooks. We also bought from private dealers, browsed second-hand shops, rifled thrift stores, photocopied library books, shopped the shelves of friends and relatives. Most online purchases came from American vendors, but 20 percent or so were from abroad, mainly Europe, Latin America, Australia, and Canada, but also a goodly number from India. These last were generally excellent photo-reprints of British Raj-era translations of Indian and other Eastern classics, like the *Panchatantra*, a third-century BCE Sanskrit conduct book in the form of a collection of moralistic animal stories. (At the risk of offending through generalization, I would like to mention that many of the books shipped from India smelled of kerosene. And many books from France smelled of tobacco smoke, German books of coal smoke, Latin American books of the sea, British books of mildew, New England books of road salt.) A handful of books came from space: those with virtual imprimaturs I simply printed out and bound in library buckram.

One ebook was not so easy: the *Liber Juratus Honorii*, a thirteenth-century grimoire, an elegant modern-English translation of which can be found online, and only online. Why not just print and bind as before?, you ask. Because of the following proviso, which forms the web page's incipit:

> Permission is hereby granted to make one handwritten copy for personal use, provided the master bind his executors by a strong oath *(juramentum)* to bury it with him in his grave. Beyond this, whoever copies this sacred text without permission from the editor will be damned.

I'm not terribly superstitious, nor am I creeped out by the mortal

---

[3] *Please notice that for these books I have included readability rankings, an informal and unofficial hierarchy based partly on what I've read about the book and partly on the book's physical self. Heavy, dun, pica-set flagstones automatically drop several hundred places in the rankings. (The higher the number, the less readable the book).*

consequences that a reckless attitude toward such paranormal warning systems threatens to foment, but somehow I felt that the estimable Joseph H. Peterson, translator of and final authority on the *Liber Juratus*, was not fucking around. So I wrote to him, explained about the library, and requested permission to write out one copy without suffering damnation. Mr. Peterson, who was polite and enthusiastic, assented. JB, however, has so far not granted permission, as it would take me an awfully long time on the clock to transcribe and bind the three-hundred-odd pages of the *Liber Juratus*. As of this writing, it is one of the few books whose acquisition remains in abeyance and in question.

Most of the books were easy to get. Just search, place in basket, order, and wait. Between three and eighty days later, the book would arrive, usually via USPS. Bryan, our mailman, suffered. At the height of his labors, during July and August, when the temperatures would reach 109°F—not a dry heat—he would sometimes be thirty parcels burthen per day. But he stuck with it without complaint or vengeance, whereas Joan's mailman, a passive-aggressive cretin given to daily repine, quit midway through the project.

Delivery time was the best part of the workday, though the books delivered sometimes brought woe. Most arrived as described, but occasionally a book marketed as, say, "Very Good," usually by some kitchen-table used-book start-up whose only profits come from shipping overcharges, would arrive looking and smelling like a pan-seared cod. I have noticed that a seller's veracity with regard to a book's condition is proportionate to the flexibility of the seller's return policy. Books that have been, say, pan-scared, cannot usually be returned; there's nothing to do but send the seller a snide note and let the cod lay where Jesus flang it.

The list is hopelessly incomplete, profoundly flawed, shot with errors: amateurism at its most arrogant. It is especially weak in drama, non-English nonfiction, Chinese, Japanese, and Southeast Asian literature of every sort, children's books, history, sociology, and oral tradition. If JB keeps me on the payroll, hopefully I'll be able to feed some of these genres. But at this point, almost all the books that can be bought have been bought. All that remains is one last major schlep—Joan and I have between us some 150 recently received volumes that must still be brought to JB's and shelved. The project will then be over. JB and his library will await the moment of his retirement, Joan will move on to her next film, and I will return to the expensive tedium of muttonthumping.[4] Officially, that is. Unofficially, I will continue to work on the list. It's become a habit, an irresistible one, though not nearly so wretched as, say, heroin or Sudoku. During the period it's taken me to write this essay, I've found five more books that simply must be included in the library: Tacitus's *De origine et situ Germanorum*, Wharton's *Age of Innocence* (how many gimmes like that have I overlooked?), Shannon's *The Mathematical Theory of Communication*, the anonymous *Utenzi: Utendi Wa Tambuka, Utenzi Wa Shufaka*, and *Herculine Barbin: Being the Recently Discovered Memoirs of a Nineteenth-Century French Hermaphrodite*. And to make room for these worthies, five others must be fetched away.

Nominated by The Believer

[4] *Nineteenth-century slang for "bookbinding."*

SELF-PORTRAIT
AS SUPERMAN
(ALTERNATIVE TAKE)

by JAKE ADAM YORK

from NEW ENGLAND REVIEW

At twenty-four frames per second, sixty seconds is two
hundred
      feet of film you'll never see: Christopher Reeve
ready to become mild-mannered Clark Kent—sharp

          trilby and blue chalk-pinstripe suit—
once they call *Action*, the Who-me smile fading
      to bit-lip circumspection, cover story and secret,

hand on the button-down's placket, ready to pull
          the buttons from their eyes, peel
the rough-hewn cotton from the ancient crest, the S

      that curves like a river between the mountains,
a snake curled inside a chest, invulnerable aorta
          of Kal-El's dense alien body, gone spectacular

in the air of his new home planet, to run, almost,
      out of his clothes and into the air, faster than
a speeding track star alone in the Kansas wheat,

faster than Lois Lane's shriek
from the helicopter dangling from the *Daily Planet*'s roof
faster than a B-movie pimp's comic relief:

Say, Jack—woo!—that's a bad outfit! When he swings,
     centrifugal, the hotel's revolving door,
when he leaves his suit, his glasses, his *Aw shucks*

   for the prop girls to gather, he just rises,
just lifts off Broadway in his Funkadelic boots,
     like he landed from the swing set, but

in reverse. Here, there's no thought of a ladder,
    no pause at the top of the McDonald's-colored
slide, no turn where the cape unfurls

     common as a hotel towel clasped
with an outsized safety pin around the neck,
    no miraculous misremembered pause

in midair when the grass darkened in the shape
     of a four-year-old boy who could
heat-vision ants with a grandma's magnifying glass

   before Tara Skinner looked out her window
and gravity, in on the game, pulled him down,
     trying not to give anything away.

He will not stand, his stained knees stomach-
    ache green. He will not limp to the back
door or hide what the doctor says must have been

     excruciating pain for weeks. He won't
have lain in bed, believing so plainly
   in the helium of Odd, the fracture

just the splintering of polar ice he could feel
     half a globe away, seismic as the twist
of the spine a physical therapist will describe.

He'll smile again as he always does, boyish
and pure, the curl's wag ready to swing free,
                    waiting for the call that lets him arc

across the sky, high over the heads of any tragic
            chorus, arms open to catch the screaming woman
who, it seems, is hardly ever there. He'll ease

                    again, two hundred feet of acetate,
to the ground, where they'll curl in their questions—
            Who are you? What was that?—in a darkness

where he can unbutton his shirt and graze
                    cramped fingers over skin
burned like a meteor in the rays of our yellow sun.

Nominated by New England Review, Dan Albergotti, David Wojahn

SPECIAL MENTION

(The editors also wish to mention the following important works published by small presses last year. Listings are in no particular order.)

POETRY

Coronagraphy — Samiya Bashir (Poet Lore)
I Find God On Facebook — Barbara Price (Silk Road)
Unsleeping — Timothy Liu (New South)
The Lives of Cells — Kathryn Winograd (Chautauqua)
In The Ear of Our Lord — Brendan Constantine (Beloit Poetry Journal)
A Boy In A CNN Transcript Shoots Marbles — Mia Leonin (New Letters)
Literacy — XJ Kennedy (Evansville Review)
If Mamie Till Was The Mother of God — Joseph Ross (Little Patuxent)
Disappearing Town — J. Scott Brownlee (Birdfeast)
In The Lion's Cage — David Starkey (Georgia Review)
Dear Andy C — Jim Daniels (Hotel Amerika)
The Sweet Drive of History — Al Maginnes (New Madrid)
The Mother — Stephanie Lenox — (*Congress of Strange People* (Airlie Press)
Between Chinese and English — Ouyang Jianghe (Zephyr Press)
I Am Happy Living Simply — Marina Tsvetaeva (*Dark Elderberry Branch* (Alice James)
Ludwig Josef Johan — Arkady Dragomoshchenko (Little Star)

After Grass and Long Knives — Olena Kalytiak Davis (Ploughshares)

Libraries & Museums — Kathleen Ossip (A Public Space)

Delirium — Endi Bogue Hartigan (Verse)

Bats — Brian Barker (Cincinnati Review)

Lessons In Woodworking — D.A. Powell (Normal School)

God's Gym — Lisa Russ Spaar (*Vanitas, Rough: Poems*, Persea Books)

To The Field of Scotch Broom That Will Be Buried by The Wing of the
Mall — Lucia Perillo (*On The Spectrum of Possible Death*, Copper
Canyon)

Coffee Lips — David Ferry (Poetry)

An Absence — David Bottoms (Georgia Review)

What Stays Here — Colleen McElroy (*Here I Throw Down My Heart*,
University of Pittsburgh Press)

We're Small on The Rim — Julie Suk (Georgia Review)

The Invisible Hand — Bruce Bond (Raritan)

FICTION

Séamus-Luigi Makes Three — Jenny Smick (Crab Creek Review)

Driving In Snow — Stephen Taylor (Kenyon Review)

Life Lessons — Edith Pearlman (Cincinnati Review)

Upper Middle Class Houses — Claire Burgess (Third Coast)

The Dancing Bear — Maxim Loskutoff (Minnesota Review)

The Baghdadi — Joan Leegant (Normal School)

San Sebastian — Jacob White (Salt Hill Journal)

Arya — Dina Nayeri (Alaska Quarterly Review)

The World To Come — Jim Shepard (One Story)

Building Walls — Dustin M. Hoffman (Puerto del Sol)

Lessons — Laura Van Den Berg (American Short Fiction)

The Kontrabida — Mia Alvar (One Story)

Hello Everybody — A.M. Homes (Recommended Reading)

Drouth (1944) — Wendell Berry (Threepenny Review)

Grimace In the Burnt Black Hills — Thomas Atkinson (The Sun)

Snake River Gorge — Alexander Maksik (Tin House)

Souvenirs — Tate Higgins (American Short Fiction)

from Adam In Eden — Carlos Fuentes (Dalkey Archive)

A Cruel Gap-Toothed Boy — Matthew Baker (Missouri Review)

Farewell, My Brother — David Means (Zoetrope)

Analogue — Jay Hosking (Little Fiction)

One For The Road — Holly Goddard Jones (Epoch)

Eulogy for Rosa Garsevanian — Naira Kuzmich (Blackbird)

The Muskeg — Jay Irwin (Gettysburg Review)

Dinosaur Bones — Evan Morgan Williams (Water-Stone)

Boundaries — Thomas Wolf (North Carolina Literary Review)

The Conversations — Tim Horvath (The Collagist)

Wretch Like Me — R.T. Smith (Austin State University Press)

Charade — Nancy Huddlestone Packer (*Old Ladies*, John Daniel & Co.)

Long Bright World — Jacob Newberry (Southwest Review)

The Scientist — Dena Afrasiabi (Enizagam)

The Geometry of Starting Over — Caroline Patterson (Southwest Review)

Angry Blood — Estella Gonzalez (Kweli)

NONFICTION

A Translator's Confession — Jonathan Galassi (Yale Review)

Bear Country — Philip Gerard (*The Patron Saint of Dreams*, Hub City Press)

Devil's Slide Utah and The Three Forks Portland Cement Company — William Lychack (American Athenaeum)

For Allah — Krista Bremer (The Sun)

Not A Butler to the Soul — G.C. Waldrep (*A God In The House*, Tupelo Press)

A Frog In Every Pot — Derrick Jensen (Orion)

And So It Is Again: Michigan Central Station and The History of Ruin Porn — Christopher Kempf (The Pinch)

Varieties of Quiet — Christian Wiman (Image)

Bridges and Tunnels — Suzanne Farrell Smith (Kenyon Review)

The Girls of Apache Bryn Mawr — Abby Geni (Camera Obscura)

The Lion of Gripsholm Castle — Caitlin Horrocks (Five Chapters)

Damn Cold In February — Joni Tevis (Diagram)

Fall of the Winter Palace — Melora Wolff (Brick)

What Should be the Function of Criticism Today? — Anis Shivani (Subtropics)

On The Varieties of Obsession — Steve Almond (Mt. Hope)

Detroit Wrecks, 1982 — Peter Stine (Antioch Review)

Fifty Shades of Beige — Kerry Howley (Bookforum)

The Fracking of Rachel Carson — Sandra Steingraber (Orion)

The Mercy Kill — Joe Oestreich (Normal School)

The Ledger — Lawrence Jackson (n+1)

City of the Dead — J. Malcolm Garcia (New Letters)

Bruised — Joe Wilkins (The Sun)

Osama Pecha Kucha — Natalie Vestin (Chautauqua)

A Gathering Menace — Neil Shea (American Scholar)

In The Hall of German Memory — Robert Zaller (Boulevard)

Some Reflections on Tragedy — C.K. Williams (Yale Review)

On Hair — Brenda Miller (Sweet)

Removing My Curse — Robin Hemley (Lapham's Quarterly)

Sometimes A Romantic Notion — Richard Schmitt (Gettysburg Review)

Mouseskull — Ann Pancake (Georgia Review)

Found In Translation — Mark Jarman (Hudson Review)

The Princes: A Reconstruction — John Jeremiah Sullivan (Paris Review)

The Guinea Pig Lady — Jen Percy (Ninth Letter)

Falling Overboard — Robin Beth Schaer (Paris Review)

On Modesty — Anna Vodicka (Shenandoah)

Meat — Brian Doyle (The Sun)

Liminal Scorpions — Carole Firstman (Colorado Review)

Silly Lilies — Amy Leach (*Things That Are*, Milkweed)

With Nathanael West in Hollywood — Peter LaSalle (Memoir)

In A Room With Rothko — Anthony Wallace (The Arts Fuse)

After The Massacre — Lee Hancock (Dart Society)

Attention — Jennifer Bowen Hicks (North American Review)

Ostrander At the Door — Aaron Gwyn (Missouri Review)

Uncommon Sense — Rachel Riederer (Tin House)

Elizabeth Bishop At Summer Camp — William Logan (Virginia Quarterly)

Occupying the Real West — Judy Blunt (New Letters)

O'Connor Plus Bishop Plus Closely Plus Distance — Marianne Boruch (Georgia Review)

Suffering — Robert Clark (Image)

Observations from the Jewel Rooms — Beth Ann Fennelly (Ecotone)

River Camp — Thomas McGuane (McSweeny's)

A Drunkard's Walk — Gerald Shapiro (Michigan Quarterly)

American Despair In An Age of Hope — Peter S. Fosl (Salmagundi)
Ruth Stone's Funeral — Toi Derricotte (Water-Stone)
Hair Piece: Derrida In the Wilderness — Andy Martin (Raritan)
My Job Search — Emilie Shumway (The Point)
Believe — Nick Ripatrazone (Los Angeles Review)
The Girls In My Town — Angela Morales (Southwest Review)
A Little Bit of Fun Before He Died — Dagoberto Gilb (ZYZZYVA)

PRESSES FEATURED IN THE PUSHCART PRIZE EDITIONS SINCE 1976

A-Minor
Acts
Agni
Ahsahta Press
Ailanthus Press
Alaska Quarterly Review
Alcheringa/Ethnopoetics
Alice James Books
Ambergris
Amelia
American Circus
American Letters and Commentary
American Literature
American PEN
American Poetry Review
American Scholar
American Short Fiction
The American Voice
Amicus Journal
Amnesty International
Anaesthesia Review
Anhinga Press
Another Chicago Magazine
Antaeus
Antietam Review
Antioch Review
Apalachee Quarterly

Aphra
Aralia Press
The Ark
Art and Understanding
Arts and Letters
Artword Quarterly
Ascensius Press
Ascent
Aspen Leaves
Aspen Poetry Anthology
Assaracus
Assembling
Atlanta Review
Autonomedia
Avocet Press
The Baffler
Bakunin
Bamboo Ridge
Barlenmir House
Barnwood Press
Barrow Street
Bellevue Literary Review
The Bellingham Review
Bellowing Ark
Beloit Poetry Journal
Bennington Review
Bilingual Review

Black American Literature Forum
Blackbird
Black Renaissance Noire
Black Rooster
Black Scholar
Black Sparrow
Black Warrior Review
Blackwells Press
The Believer
Bloom
Bloomsbury Review
Blue Cloud Quarterly
Blueline
Blue Unicorn
Blue Wind Press
Bluefish
BOA Editions
Bomb
Bookslinger Editions
Boston Review
Boulevard
Boxspring
Briar Cliff Review
Bridge
Bridges
Brown Journal of Arts
Burning Deck Press
Cafe Review
Caliban
California Quarterly
Callaloo
Calliope
Calliopea Press
Calyx
The Canary
Canto
Capra Press
Carcanet Editions
Caribbean Writer
Carolina Quarterly
Cedar Rock
Center
Chariton Review

Charnel House
Chattahoochee Review
Chautauqua Literary Journal
Chelsea
Chicago Review
Chouteau Review
Chowder Review
Cimarron Review
Cincinnati Review
Cincinnati Poetry Review
City Lights Books
Cleveland State Univ. Poetry Ctr.
Clown War
CoEvolution Quarterly
Cold Mountain Press
The Collagist
Colorado Review
Columbia: A Magazine of Poetry and
    Prose
Confluence Press
Confrontation
Conjunctions
Connecticut Review
Copper Canyon Press
Cosmic Information Agency
Countermeasures
Counterpoint
Court Green
Crawl Out Your Window
Crazyhorse
Creative Nonfiction
Crescent Review
Cross Cultural Communications
Cross Currents
Crosstown Books
Crowd
Cue
Cumberland Poetry Review
Curbstone Press
Cutbank
Cypher Books
Dacotah Territory
Daedalus

Dalkey Archive Press

Decatur House

December

Denver Quarterly

Desperation Press

Dogwood

Domestic Crude

Doubletake

Dragon Gate Inc.

Dreamworks

Dryad Press

Duck Down Press

Dunes Review

Durak

East River Anthology

Eastern Washington University Press

Ecotone

El Malpensante

Eleven Eleven

Ellis Press

Empty Bowl

Epiphany

Epoch

Ergo!

Evansville Review

Exquisite Corpse

Faultline

Fence

Fiction

Fiction Collective

Fiction International

Field

Fifth Wednesday Journal

Fine Madness

Firebrand Books

Firelands Art Review

First Intensity

Five A.M.

Five Fingers Review

Five Points Press

Five Trees Press

Florida Review

Forklift

The Formalist

Fourth Genre

Frontiers: A Journal of Women Studies

Fugue

Gallimaufry

Genre

The Georgia Review

Gettysburg Review

Ghost Dance

Gibbs-Smith

Glimmer Train

Goddard Journal

David Godine, Publisher

Graham House Press

Grand Street

Granta

Graywolf Press

Great River Review

Green Mountains Review

Greenfield Review

Greensboro Review

Guardian Press

Gulf Coast

Hanging Loose

Harbour Publishing

Hard Pressed

Harvard Review

Hayden's Ferry Review

Hermitage Press

Heyday

Hills

Hollyridge Press

Holmgangers Press

Holy Cow!

Home Planet News

Hudson Review

Hunger Mountain

Hungry Mind Review

Ibbetson Street Press

Icarus

Icon

Idaho Review

Iguana Press

Image
In Character
Indiana Review
Indiana Writes
Intermedia
Intro
Invisible City
Inwood Press
Iowa Review
Ironwood
Jam To-day
J Journal
The Journal
Jubilat
The Kanchenjunga Press
Kansas Quarterly
Kayak
Kelsey Street Press
Kenyon Review
Kestrel
Lake Effect
Latitudes Press
Laughing Waters Press
Laurel Poetry Collective
Laurel Review
L'Epervier Press
Liberation
Linquis
Literal Latté
Literary Imagination
The Literary Review
The Little Magazine
Little Patuxent Review
Little Star
Living Hand Press
Living Poets Press
Logbridge-Rhodes
Louisville Review
Lowlands Review
Lucille
Lynx House Press
Lyric

The MacGuffin
Magic Circle Press
Malahat Review
Manoa
Manroot
Many Mountains Moving
Marlboro Review
Massachusetts Review
McSweeney's
Meridian
Mho & Mho Works
Micah Publications
Michigan Quarterly
Mid-American Review
Milkweed Editions
Milkweed Quarterly
The Minnesota Review
Mississippi Review
Mississippi Valley Review
Missouri Review
Montana Gothic
Montana Review
Montemora
Moon Pony Press
Mount Voices
Mr. Cogito Press
MSS
Mudfish
Mulch Press
Muzzle Magazine
N + 1
Nada Press
Narrative
National Poetry Review
Nebraska Poets Calendar
Nebraska Review
New America
New American Review
New American Writing
The New Criterion
New Delta Review
New Directions

New England Review

New England Review and Bread Loaf
    Quarterly

New Issues

New Letters

New Ohio Review

New Orleans Review

New South Books

New Verse News

New Virginia Review

New York Quarterly

New York University Press

Nimrod

9X9 Industries

Ninth Letter

Noon

North American Review

North Atlantic Books

North Dakota Quarterly

North Point Press

Northeastern University Press

Northern Lights

Northwest Review

Notre Dame Review

O. ARS

O. Bl k

Obsidian

Obsidian II

Ocho

Oconee Review

October

Ohio Review

Old Crow Review

Ontario Review

Open City

Open Places

Orca Press

Orchises Press

Oregon Humanities

Orion

Other Voices

Oxford American

Oxford Press

Oyez Press

Oyster Boy Review

Painted Bride Quarterly

Painted Hills Review

Palo Alto Review

Paris Press

Paris Review

Parkett

Parnassus: Poetry in Review

Partisan Review

Passages North

Paterson Literary Review

Pebble Lake Review

Penca Books

Pentagram

Penumbra Press

Pequod

Persea: An International Review

Perugia Press

Per Contra

Pilot Light

The Pinch

Pipedream Press

Pitcairn Press

Pitt Magazine

Pleasure Boat Studio

Pleiades

Ploughshares

Poems & Plays

Poet and Critic

Poet Lore

Poetry

Poetry Atlanta Press

Poetry East

Poetry International

Poetry Ireland Review

Poetry Northwest

Poetry Now

The Point

Post Road

Prairie Schooner

Prescott Street Press
Press
Promise of Learnings
Provincetown Arts
A Public Space
Puerto Del Sol
Quaderni Di Yip
Quarry West
The Quarterly
Quarterly West
Quiddity
Rainbow Press
Raritan: A Quarterly Review
Rattle
Red Cedar Review
Red Clay Books
Red Dust Press
Red Earth Press
Red Hen Press
Release Press
Republic of Letters
Review of Contemporary Fiction
Revista Chicano-Riqueña
Rhetoric Review
Rivendell
River Styx
River Teeth
Rowan Tree Press
Ruminate
Runes
Russian *Samizdat*
Salamander
Salmagundi
San Marcos Press
Sarabande Books
Sea Pen Press and Paper Mill
Seal Press
Seamark Press
Seattle Review
Second Coming Press
Semiotext(e)
Seneca Review
Seven Days

The Seventies Press
Sewanee Review
Shankpainter
Shantih
Shearsman
Sheep Meadow Press
Shenandoah
A Shout In the Street
Sibyl-Child Press
Side Show
Sixth Finch
Small Moon
Smartish Pace
The Smith
Snake Nation Review
Solo
Solo 2
Some
The Sonora Review
Southern Indiana Review
Southern Poetry Review
Southern Review
Southwest Review
Speakeasy
Spectrum
Spillway
Spork
The Spirit That Moves Us
St. Andrews Press
Story
Story Quarterly
Streetfare Journal
Stuart Wright, Publisher
Subtropics
Sugar House Review
Sulfur
The Sun
Sun & Moon Press
Sun Press
Sunstone
Sweet
Sycamore Review
Tamagwa

Tar River Poetry

Teal Press

Telephone Books

Telescope

Temblor

The Temple

Tendril

Texas Slough

Think

Third Coast

13th Moon

THIS

Thorp Springs Press

Three Rivers Press

Threepenny Review

Thunder City Press

Thunder's Mouth Press

Tia Chucha Press

Tikkun

Tin House

Tombouctou Books

Toothpaste Press

Transatlantic Review

Treelight

Triplopia

TriQuarterly

Truck Press

Tupelo Press

Turnrow

Tusculum Review

Undine

Unicorn Press

University of Chicago Press

University of Georgia Press

University of Illinois Press

University of Iowa Press

University of Massachusetts Press

University of North Texas Press

University of Pittsburgh Press

University of Wisconsin Press

University Press of New England

Unmuzzled Ox

Unspeakable Visions of the Individual

Vagabond

Vallum

Verse

Verse Wisconsin

Vignette

Virginia Quarterly Review

Volt

Wampeter Press

Washington Writers Workshop

Water-Stone

Water Table

Wave Books

West Branch

Western Humanities Review

Westigan Review

White Pine Press

Wickwire Press

Wig Leaf

Willow Springs

Wilmore City

Witness

Word Beat Press

Word-Smith

World Literature Today

Wormwood Review

Writers Forum

Xanadu

Yale Review

Yardbird Reader

Yarrow

Y-Bird

Yes Yes Books

Zeitgeist Press

Zoetrope: All-Story

Zone 3

ZYZZYVA

THE PUSHCART PRIZE FELLOWSHIPS

The Pushcart Prize Fellowships Inc., a 501 (c) (3) nonprofit corporation, is the endowment for The Pushcart Prize. "Members" donated up to $249 each. "Sponsors" gave between $250 and $999. "Benefactors" donated from $1000 to $4,999. "Patrons" donated $5,000 and more. We are very grateful for these donations. Gifts of any amount are welcome. For information write to the Fellowships at PO Box 380, Wainscott, NY 11975.

Siv Cedering
Dan Chaon
James Charlton
Andrei Codrescu
Tracy Crow
Dana Literary Society
Carol de Gramont
Karl Elder
Donald Finkel
Ben and Sharon Fountain
Alan and Karen Furst
John Gill
Robert Giron
Doris Grumbach & Sybil Pike
Gwen Head
The Healing Muse
Robin Hemley
Bob Hicok
Jane Hirshfield
Helen & Frank Houghton

Joseph Hurka
Diane Johnson
Janklow & Nesbit Asso.
Edmund Keeley
Thomas E. Kennedy
Sydney Lea
Gerald Locklin
Thomas Lux
Markowitz, Fenelon and Bank
Elizabeth McKenzie
McSweeney's
Joan Murray
Barbara and Warren Phillips
Hilda Raz
Mary Carlton Swope
Julia Wendell
Philip White
Eleanor Wilner
David Wittman
Richard Wyatt & Irene Eilers

MEMBERS

Anonymous (3)
Betty Adcock
Agni
Carolyn Alessio
Dick Allen
Russell Allen
Henry H. Allen
Lisa Alvarez
Jan Lee Ande
Ralph Angel
Antietam Review
Ruth Appelhof
Philip and Marjorie Appleman
Linda Aschbrenner
Renee Ashley
Ausable Press
David Baker
Catherine Barnett
Dorothy Barresi
Barlow Street Press
Jill Bart
Ellen Bass
Judith Baumel
Ann Beattie
Madison Smartt Bell
Beloit Poetry Journal
Pinckney Benedict
Karen Bender
Andre Bernard
Christopher Bernard
Wendell Berry
Linda Bierds

Stacy Bierlein
Bitter Oleander Press
Mark Blaeuer
Blue Lights Press
Carol Bly
BOA Editions
Deborah Bogen
Susan Bono
Anthony Brandt
James Breeden
Rosellen Brown
Jane Brox
Andrea Hollander Budy
E. S. Bumas
Richard Burgin
Skylar H. Burris
David Caliguiuri
Kathy Callaway
Janine Canan
Henry Carlile
Fran Castan
Chelsea Associates
Marianne Cherry
Phillis M. Choyke
Suzanne Cleary
Martha Collins
Ted Conklin
Joan Connor
John Copenhaven
Dan Corrie
Tricia Currans-Sheehan
Jim Daniels

571

Thadious Davis
Maija Devine
Sharon Dilworth
Edward J. DiMaio
Kent Dixon
John Duncklee
Elaine Edelman
Renee Edison & Don Kaplan
Nancy Edwards
M.D. Elevitch
Failbetter.com
Irvin Faust
Tom Filer
Susan Firer
Nick Flynn
Stakey Flythe Jr.
Peter Fogo
Linda N. Foster
Fugue
Alice Fulton
Eugene K. Garber
Frank X. Gaspar
A Gathering of the Tribes
Reginald Gibbons
Emily Fox Gordon
Philip Graham
Eamon Grennan
Lee Meitzen Grue
Habit of Rainy Nights
Rachel Hadas
Susan Hahn
Meredith Hall
Harp Strings
Jeffrey Harrison
Lois Marie Harrod
Healing Muse
Alex Henderson
Lily Henderson
Daniel Henry
Neva Herington
Lou Hertz
William Heyen
Bob Hicok
R. C. Hildebrandt
Kathleen Hill
Jane Hirshfield
Edward Hoagland
Daniel Hoffman
Doug Holder
Richard Holinger
Rochelle L. Holt
Richard M. Huber
Brigid Hughes
Lynne Hugo
Illya's Honey
Susan Indigo

Mark Irwin
Beverly A. Jackson
Richard Jackson
Christian Jara
David Jauss
Marilyn Johnston
Alice Jones
Journal of New Jersey Poets
Robert Kalich
Julia Kasdorf
Miriam Poli Katsikis
Meg Kearney
Celine Keating
Brigit Kelly
John Kistner
Judith Kitchen
Stephen Kopel
Peter Krass
David Kresh
Maxine Kumin
Valerie Laken
Babs Lakey
Linda Lancione
Maxine Landis
Lane Larson
Dorianne Laux & Joseph Millar
Sydney Lea
Donald Lev
Dana Levin
Gerald Locklin
Linda Lacione
Rachel Loden
Radomir Luza, Jr.
William Lychack
Annette Lynch
Elzabeth MacKierman
Elizabeth Macklin
Leah Maines
Mark Manalang
Norma Marder
Jack Marshall
Michael Martone
Tara L. Masih
Dan Masterson
Peter Matthiessen
Alice Mattison
Tracy Mayor
Robert McBrearty
Jane McCafferty
Rebecca McClanahan
Bob McCrane
Jo McDougall
Sandy McIntosh
James McKean
Roberta Mendel
Didi Menendez

Barbara Milton
Alexander Mindt
Mississippi Review
Martin Mitchell
Roger Mitchell
Jewell Mogan
Patricia Monaghan
Jim Moore
James Morse
William Mulvihill
Nami Mun
Carol Muske-Dukes
Edward Mycue
Deirdre Neilen
W. Dale Nelson
Jean Nordhaus
Ontario Review Foundation
Daniel Orozco
Other Voices
Pamela Painter
Paris Review
Alan Michael Parker
Ellen Parker
Veronica Patterson
David Pearce, M.D.
Robert Phillips
Donald Platt
Valerie Polichar
Pool
Horatio Potter
Jeffrey & Priscilla Potter
Marcia Preston
Eric Puchner
Tony Quagliano
Barbara Quinn
Belle Randall
Martha Rhodes
Nancy Richard
Stacey Richter
James Reiss
Katrina Roberts
Judith R. Robinson
Jessica Roeder
Martin Rosner
Kay Ryan
Sy Safransky
Brian Salchert
James Salter
Sherod Santos
R.A. Sasaki
Valerie Sayers
Maxine Scates
Alice Schell
Dennis & Loretta Schmitz
Helen Schulman

Philip Schultz
Shenandoah
Peggy Shinner
Vivian Shipley
Joan Silver
Skyline
John E. Smelcer
Raymond J. Smith
Philip St. Clair
Lorraine Standish
Maureen Stanton
Michael Steinberg
Sybil Steinberg
Jody Stewart
Barbara Stone
Storyteller Magazine
Bill & Pat Strachan
Julie Suk
Sun Publishing
Sweet Annie Press
Katherine Taylor
Pamela Taylor
Elaine Jerranova
Susan Terris
Marcelle Thiébaux
Robert Thomas
Andrew Tonkovich
Pauls Toutonghi
Juanita Torrence-Thompson
William Trowbridge
Martin Tucker
Jeannette Valentine
Victoria Valentine
Hans Van de Bovenkamp
Tino Villanueva
William & Jeanne Wagner
BJ Ward
Susan O. Warner
Rosanna Warren
Margareta Waterman
Michael Waters
Sandi Weinberg
Andrew Weinstein
Jason Wesco
West Meadow Press
Susan Wheeler
Dara Wier
Ellen Wilbur
Galen Williams
Marie Sheppard Williams
Eleanor Wilner
Irene K. Wilson
Steven Wingate
Sandra Wisenberg
Wings Press

Robert W. Witt
Margo Wizansky
Matt Yurdana

Christina Zawadiwsky
Sander Zulauf
ZYZZYVA

SUSTAINING MEMBERS

Agni
Betty Adcock
Anonymous (2)
Dick & L.N. Allen
Russell Allen
Carolyn Alessio
Jacob M. Appel
Philip Appleman
Linda Aschbrenner
Renee Ashley
Jean Auel
Jim Barnes
Catherine Barnett
Ann Beattie
Joe David Bellamy
Madison Smartt Bell
Beloit Poetry Journal
Linda Bierds
Bridge Works
Rosellen Brown
Fran Castan
David S. Caldwell
Dan Chaon
Chelsea Associates
Suzanne Cleary
Martha Collins
Ted Conklin
Bernard Connors
Daniel L. Dolgin & Loraine F. Gardner
Elaine Edelman
Dallas Ernst
Ben & Sharon Fountain
Eagene Garber
Robert L. Giron
Emily Fox Gordon
Susan Hahn
The Healing Muse
Alexander C. Henderson
Bob Hicok
Kathleen Hill
Helen & Frank Houghton
Mark Irwin
Diane Johnson
Christian Jara
Don & René Kaplan
Edmund Keeley
Judith Kitchen

Peter Krass
Maxine Kumin
Wally Lamb
Linda Lancione
Sydney Lea
Thomas Lux
William Lychack
Norma Marder
Michael Martone
Peter Matthiessen
Alice Mattison
Robert McBrearty
Jane McCafferty
Deirdre Neilen
Neltje
Daniel Orozco
Pamela Painter
Horatio Potter
Jeffrey Potter
David B. Pearce, M.D.
Barbara & Warren Phillips
Kay Ryan
Elizabeth R. Rea
James Reiss
Stacey Richter
Sy Safransky
Maxine Scates
Alice Schell
Dennis Schmitz
Peggy Shinner
Maureen Stanton
Sybil Steinborg
Jody Stewart
The Sun
Elaine Terranova
Susan Terris
Robert Thomas
Pauls Toutonghi
William Trowbridge
Hans Van de Bovenkamp
BJ Ward
Rosanna Warren
Galen Williams
Eleanor Wilner
David Wittman
Susan Wheeler
Ellen M. Violett

CONTRIBUTING SMALL PRESSES FOR PUSHCART PRIZE XXXVIII

A

A-Minor Magazine, 7C, 42 & 42A Hollywood Rd., Hong Kong
aaduna, 144 Genesee St., Ste. 102-259, Auburn, NY 13021
Able Muse Review, 467 Saratoga Ave., #602, San Jose, CA 95129
ABZ Press, PO Box 2746, Huntington, WV 25757-2746
Accents Publishing, P.O. Box 910456, Lexington, KY 40591-0456
The Adirondack Review, 107 1st Ave., New York, NY 10003
The Adroit Journal, 1223 Westover Rd., Stamford, CT 06902
Agni Magazine, Boston University, 236 Bay State Rd., Boston, MA
    02215
Airlie Press, P.O. Box 434, Monmouth, OR 97361
Airways, P.O. Box 1109, Sandpoint, ID 83864
Akashic Books, P.O. Box 46232, West Hollywood, CA 90046
Alabaster & Mercury, 5050 Del Monte Ave., #6, San Diego, CA 92107
Alabaster Leaves Publishing, 1840 West 220th St., Ste. 300, Torrance,
    CA 90501
Alaska Quarterly Review, 3211 Providence Dr., Anchorage, AK 99508-
    4614
Aleph Book Company, 161 B/4, Ground Floor, Gulmohar House, Yusuf
    Sarai Community Centre, New Delhi, 110049, India
Alice Blue, 4019 NE 39th Ave., Vancouver, WA 98661
Alice James Books, 238 Main St., Farmington, ME 04938
Alligator Juniper, Prescott College, 220 Grove Ave., Prescott, AZ 86301

Alligator Press, 1953 S. 1100 E Unit 526368, Salt Lake City, UT 84152-5015

American Athenaeum, P.O. Box 2107, Lusby, MD 20657

American Arts Quarterly, c/o Bergmann, 400 East 77th St., NY, NY 10075

American Circus, 330 E. 6th St., NY, NY 10003

The American Poetry Journal, P.O. Box 2080, Aptos, CA 95001-2080

The American Poetry Review, 1700 Sansom St., Ste. 800, Philadelphia, PA 19103

The American Scholar, 1606 New Hampshire Ave. NW, Washington, DC 20009

American Short Fiction, P.O. Box 4152, Austin, TX 78765

Amoskeag, 2500 No. River Rd., Manchester, NH 03106-1045

Ampersand Books, 5040 10th Ave. S., Gulfport, FL 33707

Ampersand Communications, 2901 Santa Cruz SE, Albuquerque, NY 87106

Anaphora, 163 Lucas Rd., Apt. I-2, Cochran, GA 31014

Anatomy & Etymology, 1915 Maple Ave., Apt. 809-A, Evanston, IL 60201

Ancient Paths, P.O. Box 7505, Fairfax Station, VA 22039

anderbo.com, 270 Lafayette St., Ste 705, New York, NY 10012

Annalemma Magazine, 112 Second Ave., Ste. 30, Brooklyn, NY 11215

Another Chicago Magazine, MC 162, 602 So. Morgan St., Chicago, IL 60607-7120

Anti-, 4237 Beethoven Ave., St. Louis, MO 63116-2503

The Antioch Review, PO Box 148, Yellow Springs, OH 45387-0148

Antrim House Books, 21 Goodrich Rd., Simsbury, CT 06070

Anvil Press, 278 East First St., Vancouver, BC V5T 1A6. Canada

Any Puppets Press, 6065 Chabot Rd., Oakland, CA 94618

Apercus, 8321 Via Rocosa Rd., Joshua Tree, CA 92252

Apple Valley Review, 88 South 3rd St., #336, San Jose, CA 95113

Apt, 70 Commercial St., #1R, Boston, MA 02110

Aqueous Books, P.O. Box 12784, Pensacola, FL 32591

Arcadia Magazine, 9616 Nichols Rd., Oklahoma City, OK 73120

The Archstone, 250 W. 50th St., 15L, New York, NY 10019

Arctos Press, P.O. Box 401, Sausalito, CA 94966-0401

Arizona Authors, 6145 West Echo Lane, Glendale, AZ 85302

Arkansas Review, P.O. Box 1890, State University, AR 72467-1890

ArmChair/Shotgun, 377 Flatbush Ave., No. 3, Brooklyn, NY 11238

Arroyo Literary Review, C.S.U. 25800 Carlos Bee Blvd., Hayward, CA 94542

Arsenic Lobster, 1830 W. 18th St., Chicago, IL 60608

Arte Publico Press, 452 Cullen Performance Hall, Houston, TX 77204-2004

Artichoke Haircut, P.O. Box 22541, Baltimore, MD 21203

Artifact, 1139 N. Harrison St., Stockton, CA 95203

The Arts Fuse, Boston University Writing Program, 100 Bay State Rd., 3rd Flr., Boston, MA 02215

Asheville Poetry Review, P.O. Box 7086, Asheville, NC 28802

Ashland Creek Press, P.O. Box 1379, Ashland, OR 97520

The Asian American Literary Review, P.O. Box 34495, Washington, DC 20043

Askew, P.O. Box 559, Ventura, CA 93002

Asymptote, 31 Locust St., #36, Brooklyn, NY 11206

At Length, 716 W. Cornwallis Rd., Durham, NC 27707

At the Bijou, 71 Bank St., Derby, CT 06418

Atelier 26, 4156 S.E. Bybee Blvd., Portland, OR 97202

Atlanta Review, PO Box 8248, Atlanta, GA 31106

Atticus Books, 26525 Clarksburg Rd., Damascus, MD 20872

Augusta Heritage Press, 123-C North Orlando, Los Angeles, CA 90048

Autumn House Press, 87 1/2 Westwood St., Pittsburgh, PA 15211

The Awakenings Review, P.O. Box 177, Wheaton, IL 60187-0177

The Awl, 875 Avenue of the Americas, 2nd Floor, New York, NY 10001

B

Bacopa, P.O. Box 358396, Gainesville, FL 32635-8396

The Bad Version, 2035 W. Rice St., Chicago, IL 60622

The Baffler, 200 Hampshire Street, No. 3, Cambridge, Mass 02139

The Bakery, A. Abonado, 12 Strathallan Pk., #2, Rochester, NY 14607

Ballard Street Poetry Journal, P. O. Box 7171, Worcester, MA 01605

The Baltimore Review, 6514 Maplewood Rd., Baltimore, MD 21212

Bamboo Ridge Press, PO Box 61781, Honolulu, HI 96839-1781

Barbaric Yawp, 3700 County Route 24, Russell, NY 13684

Barely South Review, Old Dominion University, Norfolk, VA 23529-0091

Barge Press, 3729 Beechwood Blvd., Pittsburgh, PA 15217

Barn Owl Review, 275 Melbourne Ave., Akron, OH 44313

Barrelhouse, 793 Westerly Pkwy., State College, PA 16801

Barrow Street, PO Box 1831, New York, NY 10156

Bartleby Snopes, 917 Kylemore Dr., Ballwin, MO 63021-7935

basalt, Eastern Oregon Univ., One University Blvd., La Grande, OR 97850-2807

Baseball Bard, Box 90923, San Diego, CA 92169

Baskerville Publishers, 9112 Camp Bowie Blvd., West #214, Fort Worth, TX 76116

Bat City Review, 1 University Station B5000, Austin, TX 78712

Bayou Magazine, 2000 Lake Shore Dr., New Orleans, LA 70148

Bear Star Press, 185 Hollow Oak Dr., Cohasset, CA 95973

The Believer, 849 Valencia St., San Francisco, CA 94110

Bellevue Literary Review, NYU School of Medicine, 550 First Ave, OBV-A612, New York, NY 10016

Bellingham Review, MS-9053, WWU, Bellingham, WA 98225

Beloit Fiction Journal, 700 College St., Box 11, Beloit, WI 53511

Beloit Poetry Journal, PO Box 151, Farmington, ME 04938

Berkeley Fiction Review, 10 B Eshleman Hall, UCB, Berkeley, CA 94720-4500

Bernheim Press, 5809 Scrivener, Long Beach, CA 90808

The Bicycle Review, 1727 10th St., Oakland, CA 94607

Big Fiction, 7907 8th Avenue NW, Seattle, WA 98117

Big Lucks, 3201 Guilford Ave., #3, Baltimore, MD 21218

The Binnacle, 4 Kimball Hall, 116 O'Brien Ave., Machias, ME 04654

Birch Brook Press, P.O. Box 81, Delhi, NY 13753

Birdfeast, 1302 Grant Blvd., #11, Syracuse, NY 13208

Birds, LLC, 207 Bertie Drive, Raleigh, NC 27610

Birkensnake, 559 30th St., Oakland, CA 94609-3201

Birmingham Poetry Review, HB 215, 1530 3rd Ave. S., Birmingham, AL 35294-1260

Bizarro Press, 20 Noble Ct., Ste. 200, Heath, TX 75032

BkMk Press, UMKC, 5100 Rockhill Rd., Kansas City, MO 64110-2446

Black Clock, CalArts, 24700 McBean Parkway, Valencia, CA 91355

Black Lantern Publishing, P.O. Box 1451, Jacksonville, NC 28541-1451

Black Lawrence Press, 41 Varick St., #208, Brooklyn, NY 11237

Black Warrior Review, P.O. Box 870170., Tuscaloosa, AL 35487-0170

Blackbird, PO Box 843082, Richmond, VA 23284-3082

Blank Slate Press, 2528 Remington Lane, St. Louis, MO 63144

Blink-Ink, P.O. Box 5, North Branford, CT 06471

Blip Magazine, 2158 26th Ave., San Francisco, CA 94110

Blood Lotus, 307 Granger Circle, Dayton, OH 45433

Blood Orange Review, 1495 Evergreen Ave. NE, Salem, OR 97301

Bloodroot, P.O. Box 322, Thetford Center, VT 05075

Blue Fifth Review, 267 Lark Meadow Circle, Bluff City, TN 37618

Blue Lycra Review, 275 W. Main St., Forsyth, GA 31029

Blue Mesa Review, UNM, Humanities #217, Albuquerque, NM 87131-1106

Blue Print Review, 1103 NW 11th Ave., Gainesville, FL 32601

Blue Unicorn, 22 Avon Rd., Kensington, CA 94707

Bluestem, Eastern Illinois Univ., English Dept, 600 Lincoln Ave., Charleston, IL 61920-3011

BOA Editions, 250 North Goodman St., Ste 306, Rochester, NY 14607

Bold Strokes Books, P.O. Box 249, Valley Falls NY 12185

Bona Fide Books, P.O. Box 550278, Tahoe Paradise, CA 96155

Bone Bouquet, 317 Madison Ave., #520, New York, NY 10017

Book Thug, 260 Ryding Ave., Toronto ON M6N 1H5, Canada

Booktrope Editions, 1019 Esplanada Circle, El Paso, TX 79932

Boone's Dock Press, 235 Ocean Ave., Amityville, NY 11701

Booth, English Dept., Butler Univ., 4600 Sunset Ave., Indianapolis, IN 46208

Border Crossing, Lake Superior State Univ., 650 W. Easterday Ave., Sault Ste. Marie, MI 49783

Borderline, 1915 Maple Ave., Apt 809-A, Evanston, IL 60201

Bordighera Press, 25 West 43rd St., 17th Floor, New York, NY 10036

bosque, 163 Sol del Oro, Corrales, New Mexico 87048

Boston Literary Magazine, 383 Langley Rd., #2, Newton Centre, MA 02459

Botticelli Magazine, 5982 Goode Rd., Powell, OH 43065

Bottom Dog Press, P.O. Box 425, Huron, OH 44839

Boulevard, 7507 Byron Place, 1st Floor, St. Louis, MO 63105

Bound Off, P.O. Box 821, Cedar Rapids, IA 52406-0821

Box Turtle Press, 184 Franklin St., New York, NY 10013

Boxcar Poetry Review, 630 S. Kenmore Ave., #206, Los Angeles, CA 90005

Brain, Child, 341 Newtown Turnpike, Wilton, CT 06897

Brevity, English Dept., Ohio University, Athens, OH 45701

The Briar Cliff Review, 3303 Rebecca St., Sioux City, IA 51104-2100

Brick, P.O. Box 609, Stn. P, Toronto, Ontario, M5S 2Y4, Canada

Brick Cave Media, P.O. Box 4411, Mesa, AZ 85211-4411

Brigantine Media, 211 North Ave., St. Johnsbury, VT 05819

Brilliant Corners, Lycoming College, 700 College Place, Williamsport, PA 17701

Brink Media, P.O. Box 209034, New Haven, CT 06520-9034

Broadkill Review, 104 Federal St., Milton, DE 19968

The Broadsider, P.O. Box 236, Millbrae, CA 94030

Brooklyn Arts Press, 154 N. 9th St., #1, Brooklyn, MY 11249

The Brooklyn Rail, 99 Commercial St., #15, Brooklyn, NY 11222

The Brooklyn Review, English Dept., Brooklyn College, 2900 Bedford Ave., Brooklyn, NY 11210

Brothel Books, 116 Ave. C, #17, New York, NY 10009

Bull, 343 Parkovash Ave., South Bend, IN 46617

Bull Spec, P.O. Box 13146, Durham, NC 27709

Burnt Bridge, 6721 Washington Ave., 2H, Ocean Springs, MS 39564

Burntdistrict, 2016 S. 185th St., Omaha, NE 68130

C

C&R Press, 812 Westwood Ave., Chattanooga, TN 37405

C4, 17 Cameron Ave., Cambridge, MA 02140

Café Review, c/o Yes Books, 589 Congress St., Portland, ME 04101

Cairn: The St. Andrews Review, 1700 Dogwood Mile, Laurinburg, NC 28352

Caketrain Journal, PO Box 82588, Pittsburgh, PA 15218-0588

Caitlin Press, 8100 Alderwood Rd., Halfmoon Bay, VON 1Y1, BC

California Quarterly, 23 Edgecroft Rd., Kensington, CA 94707

Callaloo, 4212 TAMU, Texas A&M Univ., College Station, TX 77843-4212

Calliope, 2506 SE Bitterbrush Dr., Madras, OR 97741-9452

Calyx Inc., Box B, Corvallis, OR 97339-0539

The Camel Saloon, 11190 Abbotts Station Dr., Johns Creek, GA 30097

Camera Obscura, P.O. Box 2356, Addison, TX 75069

The Carolina Quarterly, Box 3520, UNC, Chapel Hill, NC 27599-3520

Carve, P.O. Box 701510, Dallas, TX 75370

Casperian Books, P.O. Box 161026, Sacramento, CA 95816-1026

Catfish Creek, Box 36, Loras College, 1450 Alta Vista St., Dubuque, IA 52001

Cave Moon Press, 7704 Mieras Rd., Yakima, Washington 98901

Cave Region Review, North Arkansas College, 1515 Pioneer Dr., Harrison, AR 72601

Cave Wall Press, PO Box 29546, Greensboro, NC 27429-9546

Central Recovery Press, 3321 N. Buffalo Dr., Ste. 200, Las Vegas, NV 89129

Cerise Press, 2904 E. Eleana Lane, Gilbert, AZ 85298-5776

Certain Circuits, 1315 Walnut St., Ste. 309, Philadelphia, PA 19107

Cervena Barva Press, PO Box 440357, W. Somerville, MA 02144-3222

Cha: An Asian Literary Journal, Flat 3615, Shui Kwok House, Tin Shui Estate, Tin Shin Wai, Yuen Long, Hong Kong

The Chaffey Review, 5885 Haven Ave., Rancho Cucamonga, CA 91737-3002

The Chattahoochee Review, 555 North Indian Creek Dr., Clarkston, GA 3002

Chatter House Press, 7915 S. Emerson Ave., Ste. B303, Indianapolis, IN 46237

Chautauqua, UNC Wilmington, 601 South College Rd., Wilmington, NC 28403

Chelsea Station Editions, 362 West 36th St., #2R, New York, NY 10018

Cherokee McGhee, 124 Peyton Rd., Williamsburg, VA 23185

Chicago Poetry, 2626 W. Iowa, 2F, Chicago, IL 60622

Chicago Quarterly Review, 251 Peyton St., Santa Cruz, CA 95060

Chicago Review, Taft House, 935 60th Ave., Chicago, IL 60637

ChiZine Publications, 67 Alameda Ave., Toronto, ON M6C 3W4, Canada

The Chrysalis Reader, 1745 Gravel Hill Rd., Dillwyn, VA 23936

Cider Press Review, P.O. Box 33384, San Diego, CA 92163

Cimarron Review, Oklahoma State Univ., Stillwater, OK 74078

Cincinnati Review, Univ. of Cincinnati, PO Box 210069, Cincinnati, OH 45221-0069

Cinco Puntos Press, 701 Tenth St., El Paso, TX 79901

Citron Review, 933 Pineview Ridge Ct., Ballwin, MO 63201

The Claudius APP, 220 20th St., Apt. 2, Brooklyn, NY 11232

The Cleveland Review, 1305 Andrews Ave., Lakewood, OH 44107

Clock, 1203 Plantation Drive, Simpsonville, SC 29681

Clover, A Literary Rag, 203 West Holly, Ste. 306, Bellingham, WA 98225

Coal City Review, English Dept., University of Kansas, Lawrence, KS 66045

Codex Journal, English Dept., Eastern Illinois University, 600 Lincoln Ave., Charleston, IL 61920

Codhill Press, One Arden Lane, New Paltz, NY 12561

Codorus Press, 34-43 Crescent St., Ste. 1S, Astoria, NY 11106

The Coffin Factory, 14 Lincoln Place, Ste. 2R, Brooklyn, NY 11217

Cold Mountain Review, ASU – English Dept., Boone, NC 28608

Cold River Press, 11402 Francis Dr., Grass Valley, CA 95949

The Collagist, 318 Ridge St., Marquette, MI 49855

Colorado Review, Colorado State Univ., Fort Collins, CO 80523-9105

Columbia Poetry Review, 600 South Michigan Ave., Chicago, IL 60605-1996

The Common, Frost Library, Amherst College, Amherst, MA 01002-5000

Common Ground Review, 40 Prospect St., #C-1, Westfield, MA 01085-1559

Conclave, 2410 W. Memorial Rd., Ste., C-238, Oklahoma City, OK 73734

Concrete Wolf, PO Box 1808, Kingston, WA 98346-1808

Confrontation, English Dept., LIU/Post, Brookville, NY 11548

Conium Press, 120 NW Trinity Place, #103, Portland, OR 97209

Conjunctions, Bard College, Annandale-on-Hudson, NY 12504-5000

Connecticut Review, 39 Woodland St., Hartford, CT 06105-2337

Connotation Press, 714 Venture Drive, #164, Morgantown, WV 26508

Consequence Magazine, P.O. Box 323, Cohasset, MA 02025-0323

Constellations, 127 Lake View Ave., Cambridge, MA 02138

Conte, AAB 321 32000 Campus Dr., Salisbury, MD 21804

Copper Canyon Press, PO Box 271, Port Townsend, WA 98368

Copper Nickel, Campus Box 175, P.O. Box 173364, Denver, CO 80217

Corium, P.O. Box 2322, Richmond, CA 94802

Counterpoint Press, 1919 Fifth St., Berkeley, CA 94710

The Country Dog Review, P.O. Box 1476, Oxford, MS 38655

Court Green, 600 South Michigan Ave., Chicago, IL 60605-1996

Crab Creek Review, PO Box 1524, Kingston, WA 98346

Crab Orchard Review, SIUC, 1000 Faner Drive, MC 4503, Carbondale, IL 62901

Crack the Spine Literary Journal, 2016 Main St., #1907, Houston, TX 77002

Crazyhorse, College of Charleston, 66 George St., Charleston, SC 29424

Creative Nonfiction, 5501 Walnut St., Ste. 202, Pittsburgh, PA 15232

Cross-Cultural Communications, 239 Wynsum Ave., Merrick, NY 11566-4725

Crosstimbers, 1727 W. Alabama, Chickasha, OK 73018-5322

Curbside Splendor, 2816 N. Kedzie, Chicago, IL 60618

Curbstone Press, 321 Jackson St., Willimantic, CT 06226-1738

CutBank, University of Montana, MST410, Missoula, MT 59812

Cutthroat, A Journal of the Arts, PO Box 2414, Durango, CO 81302

The Cyberpunk Apocalypse, 5431 Carnegie St., Pittsburgh, PA 15201

Cyberwit.net, HIG 45, Kaushambi Kunj, Kalindipuram, Allahabad – 211011 (U.P.) India

D

Dahse Magazine, 80 Leonard St., #2C, New York, NY 10013

Daniel & Daniel Publishers, P.O. Box 2790, McKinleyville, CA 95519-2790

Dappled Things Magazine, 600 Giltin Drive, Arlington, TX 76006

Dark Valentine Press, 4717 Ben Avenue, Valley Village, CA 91607

Dart Society, 1601 Barnum Rd., Kaycee, WY 82639

The Darwin Press, P.O. Box 2202, Princeton, NJ 08543

Deadly Chaps, 86 Stanton St., #14, New York, NY 10002

decomP, 726 Carriage Hill Dr., Athens, OH 45701

Deep Kiss Press, 101 Stafford St., Staunton, VA 24401

Deep South, 203 Iris Lane, Lafayette, LA 70506

Deerbrook Editions, P.O. Box 542, Cumberland, ME 04021-0542

Defunct, 1028 Earlville Rd., Earlville, NY 13332

The Delmarva Review, PO Box 544, St Michaels, MD 21663

DemmeHouse, P.O. Box 2572, Brentwood, TN 37024

Denver Quarterly, University of Denver, 2000 E Asbury, Denver, CO 80208

The Destroyer, 3166 Barbara Court, L.A., CA 90068

Devil's Lake, UWM, 600 North Park St., Madison, WI 53706-1474

Devilfish Review, 200 Willard St., #201, Mankato, MN 56001

Diagram, New Michigan Press, 8058 E. 7th St., Tucson, AZ 85710

DIG, P.O. Box 608, Wainscott, NY 11975

Diode, 421 S. Pine St., Richmond, VA 23220

The DMQ Review, 16393 Bonnie Lane, Los Gatos, CA 95032

The Doctor T. J. Eckleburg Review, 1717 Massachusetts Ave., NW, #104, Washington, DC 20036

Dos Gatos Press, 1310 Crestwood Rd., Austin, TX 78722

Drash, 2632 NE 80th St., Seattle, WA 98115-4622

Dreams & Nightmares, 1300 Kicker Rd., Tuscaloosa, AL 35404

Drunken Boat, CCSU, 1615 Stanley St., New Britain, CT 06050-4010

Drunken Monkeys, 5016 Bakman, #110, No. Hollywood, CA 91601

Dunes Review, P.O. Box 1505, Traverse City, MI 49685

Dzanc Books, 1334 Woodbourne St., Westland, MI 48186

E

Echo Ink Review, 9800 W. 83rd Terrace, Overland Park, KS 6621

ecotone, UNCW, 601 S. College Rd., Wilmington, NC 28403-5938

Edgar & Lenore's Publishing, 13547 Ventura Blvd., Sherman Oaks, CA 91423

Edge, PO Box 101, Wellington, NV 89444

Educe Literary Review, 712 ½ W. Franklin, Boise, ID 83702

Eiso Publishing, 3450 Wayne Ave., #12P, Bronx, NY 10462

Ekphrasis, PO Box 161236, Sacramento, CA 95816-1236

Electric Literature, 147 Prince St., Brooklyn, NY 11201

Elephant Rock Books, P.O. Box 119, Ashford, CT 06278

Eleven Eleven Journal, 1111 Eighth St., S.F., CA 94107

Emerge Literary Journal, 9 Waterford Circle, Washingtonville, NY 10092

Emerson Review, Emerson College, 120 Boylston St., Boston, MA 02116

Emprise Review, 2100 N. Leverett Ave., #28, Fayetteville, AR 72703-2233

Encircle Publications, P.O. Box 187, Farmington, ME 04938

Engine Books, P.O. Box 44167, Indianapolis, IN 46244

The Enigmatist, 104 Bronco Dr., Georgetown, TX 78633

Enizagam, Oakland School for the Arts, 530 18th St., Oakland, CA 94612

Epiphany, 71 Bedford St., New York, NY 10014

Epoch, 251 Goldwin Smith Hall, Cornell University, Ithaca NY 14853-3201

Equus Press, 22 rue Claude Lorrain, 75016, Paris, France

Erie Times News, 205 West 12th St., Erie, PA 16534-0001

Escape Into Life, 108 Gladys Drive, Normal, IL 61761

The Evansville Review, 1800 Lincoln Ave, Evansville, IN 47722

Event, PO Box 2503, New Westminster, BC, V3L 5B2, Canada

Every Day Publishing, 1692 Windermere Pl., Port Coquitlam BC V3B 2K2, Canada

Exit 7, 4810 Alben Barkley Dr., Paducah, KY 42001

Exit 13, P.O. Box 423, Fanwood, NJ 07023

Expressions, MiraCosta Community College, 1 Barnard Dr., Oceanside, CA 92056

Exter Press, 116 Greene St., Cumberland, MD 21502

Extract(s), 464 Rockland, Manchester, NH 03102

Eye to the Telescope, Science Fiction Poetry, 1300 Kicker Rd., Tuscaloosa, AL 35404

F

F Magazine, 3800 DeBarr Rd., Anchorage, AK 99508

FM Publishing, P.O. Box 4211, Atlanta, GA 30302

failbetter, 2022 Grove Ave., Richmond, VA 23220

Fantastique Unfettered, 21 Indian Trail, Hickory Creek, TX 73065

The Farallon Review, 1017 L St., #348, Sacramento, CA 95814

Faultline, English Dept., UC Irvine, Irvine, CA 92697

Feile-Festa, 15 Colonial Gardens, Brooklyn, NY 11209

Fender Stitch, 9301 Fairmead Dr., Charlotte, NC 28269

Fiction Advocate, Oxford Univ. Press, 198 Madison Ave., New York, NY 10016

Fiction Fix, 370 Thornycroft Ave., Staten Island, NY 10312

Fiction International, SDSU, San Diego, CA 92182-6020

Field, 50 North Professor St., Oberlin, OH 44074-1091

Fifth Wednesday Books, Inc, P.O. Box 4033, Lisle, IL 60532-9033

Finishing Line Press, P.O. Box 1626, Georgetown, KY 40324

The First Line, PO Box 250382, Piano, TX 75025-0382

First Step Press, P.O. Box 902, Norristown, PA 19404-0902

Fithian Press, P.O. Box 2790, McKinleyville, CA 95519

5 AM, Box 205, Spring Church, PA 15686

Five Chapters, 387 Third Ave., Brooklyn, NY 11215

Five Points, PO Box 3999, Atlanta, GA 30302-3999

Fjords, 2932 B Langhorne Rd., Lynchburg, VA 24501-1734

Flame Flower, 3322 King St., Apt. B, Berkeley, CA 94703

Flash Fiction, University of Missouri, 107 Tate Hall, Columbia, MO 65211

Flash Frontier, P.O. Box 910, Kerikeri 0245, New Zealand

Flashquake, 804 Northcrest Dr., Birmingham, AL 35235

Fledgling Rag, 1716 Swarr Run Rd., J-108, Lancaster, PA 17601

Fleeting, 125 Lower Green Rd., Tunbridge Wells, TN4 8TT, UK

Flint Hills Review, Campus Box 4019, 1200 Commercial St., Emporia, KS 66801

The Florida Review, P.O. Box 161346, Orlando, FL 32816-1346

Flycatcher, 5595 Lake Island Dr., Atlanta, GA 30327

Flying House, 3721 N. Greenview Ave., #2, Chicago, IL 60613

Flyway, English Dept., 206 Russ Hall, Iowa State Univ., Ames, IA 50011

Folded Word, 5209 Des Vista Way, Rocklin, CA 95765

Fomite, 58 Peru St., Burlington, VT 05401-8606

Foothill, Jagels Bldg., 165 East Tenth St., Claremont, CA 91711-6186

Fordham University Press, 2546 Belmont Ave., University Box L, Bronx, NY 10458

Forge, 1610 S. 22nd, Apt. 1, Lincoln, NE 68502

Fort Hemlock Press, P.O. Box 11, Brooksville, ME 04617

Fortunate Childe, P.O. Box 130085, Birmingham, AL 35213

Four and Twenty Poetry, P.O. Box 61782, Vancouver, WA 98666

4 Stops Press, 225 S. Olive, #101, L.A. CA 90012

Four Way Books, P.O. Box 535, Village Station, New York, NY 10014

Fourteen Hills, S.F.S.U. 1400 Holloway Ave., Humanities 372, S.F., CA 94132

Fourth Genre, 235 Bessey Hall, East Lansing, MI 48824-1033

The Fourth River, Chatham University, Woodland Rd., Pittsburgh, PA 15232

Freedom Fiction Journal, Nirli Villa, 7, Village Rd., Bhandup west, Mumbai – 400078, India

Freight Stories, Ball State University, Muncie, IN 47306-0460

Freshwater, Asnuntuck Community College, 170 Elm St., Enfield, CT 06082

Fringe Magazine, 93 Fox Rd., Apt. 5A, Edison, NJ 08817

Fugue, University of Idaho, P.O. Box 441102, Moscow, ID 83844-1102

Full of Crow, P.O. Box 7, Freeport, PA 16229

Future Cycle Press, 313 Pan Will Rd., Mineral Bluff, GA 30559

Fwriction, 519 E. 78th St., Apt. 3G, New York, NY 10075

G

Gallaudet University Press, 800 Florida Ave. NE, Washington, DC 20002-3695

Garden Oak Press, P.O. Box 1606, Fallbrook, CA 92088

Gargoyle Magazine, 3819 North 13th St., Arlington, VA 22201-4922

Gemini Magazine, PO Box 1485, Onset, MA 02558

The Georgia Review, University of Georgia, Athens, GA 30602-9009

Gertrude Press, P.O. Box 83948, Portland, OR 97283

The Gettysburg Review, Gettysburg College, Gettysburg, PA 17325-1491

Ghost Ocean Magazine, 3650 N. Fremont St., Apt. 1, Chicago, IL 60613

Ghost Town Literary Review, CSU SB, 5500 University Pkwy, San Bernardino, CA 92407

Gigantic, 496 Broadway, 3rd floor, Brooklyn, NY 11211

Gigantic Sequins, 1 19th Ave., SF, CA 94121

Gival Press, PO Box 3812, Arlington, VA 22203

GlenHill Publications, P.O. Box 62, Soulsbyville, CA 95372

Glimmer Train Press, P.O. Box 80430, Portland, OR 97280-1430

Globe Light Press, 8411 Cienega Rd, Mentone, CA 92359

Gold Gable Press, 1405 Michaux Rd., Chapel Hill, NC 27514

Gold Man Review, P.O. Box 8202, Salem, OR 97303

Gold Wake Press, 5108 Avalon Dr., Randolph, MA 02368

Good Men Project, 83 Beech St., #3, Belmont, MA 02478

Grain, Box 67, Saskatoon, SK, S7K 3K1, Canada

Granta, Grove Atlantic, 841 Broadway, 4th Floor, New York, NY 10003

Gray Dog Press, 2727 S. Mt. Vernon #4, Spokane, WA 99223

Graywolf Press, 250 Third Avenue No., Ste. 600, Minneapolis, MN 55401

Great Lakes Review, 2050 Kingsborough Dr., Painesville, OH 44077

Great River Review, PO Box 406, Red Wing, MN 55066

Great Weather for Media, 515 Broadway, #2B, New York, NY 10012

Green Lantern Press, 1511 N. Milwaukee Ave., 2nd Floor, Chicago, IL 60622

Green Mountains Review, 337 College Hill, Johnson, VT 05672

Green Poet Press, P.O. Box 6927, Santa Barbara, CA 93160

The Greensboro Review, UNC Greensboro, Greensboro, NC 27402-6170

The Greensilk Journal, 1459 Redland Rd., Cross Junction, VA 22625

Greenwoman Magazine, 1823 W. Pikes Peak Ave., Colorado Springs, CO 80904

Greta Fox Publishing, P.O. Box 571, Coarsegold, CA 93614

Grey Sparrow Press, P.O. Box 211664, St. Paul, MN 55121

Grist, 301 McClung Tower, Univ. of Tennessee, Knoxville, TN 37996

Groundwaters, PO Box 50, Lorane, OR 97451

The Grove Review, 1631 NE Broadway, PMB #137, Portland, OR 97232

Gulf Coast, University of Houston, Houston, TX 77204-3013

Gypsy Shadow Publishing, 222 Llano St., Lockhart, Tx 78644

H

H.H.B. Publishing, 9550 S. Eastern Ave., Ste. 253, Henderson, NV 89123

H.O.W. Journal, 12 Desbrosses St., New York, NY 10013

The Habit of Rainy Nights Press, 900 NE 81st Ave., #209, Portland, OR 97213

Hackwriters, 58 March Court, Warwick Drive, Putney, London SW15 6LE, UK

The Hairpin, 111 River St., Hoboken, NJ 07030

Hamilton Arts & Letters, 92 Stanley Ave., Hamilton ON, L8P 2L3, Canada

Hampden-Sydney Poetry Review, Box 66, Hampden-Sydney, VA 23943

Hand Type Press, P.O. Box 3941, Minneapolis, MN 55403-0941

Harbour Publishing Co., P.O. Box 219, Madeira Park, BC V0N 2H0 Canada

Harpur Palate, PO Box 6000, Binghamton University, Binghamton, NY 13902

Harvard Review, Lamont Library, Harvard University, Cambridge, MA 02138

Harvard Square Editions, 851 E. Belmont Ave., Salt Lake City, UT 84105

Haunted Waters Press, 1886 T-Bird Drive, Front Royal, VA 22630-9038

Hawaii Pacific Review, 1060 Bishop St., Ste. 7C, Honolulu, HI 96813-4210

Hawthorne Books, 2201 NE 23rd Ave., 3rd Floor, Portland, OR 97212

Hayden's Ferry Review, A.S.U., P.O. Box 870302, Tempe, AZ 85287-0302

The Healing Muse, 618 Irving Ave., Syracuse, NY 13210

The Hedgehog Review, UVA, PO Box 400816, Charlottesville, VA 22904-4816

Hedgerow Books, 71 South Pleasant St., Amherst, MA 01002

Hennen's Observer, 9660 Falls of Neuse Rd., Ste. 138, Raleigh, NC 27615

High Coup, P.O. Box 1004, Stockbridge, MA 01262

High Desert Journal, P.O. Box 7647, Bend, OR 97708

High Hill Press, 2731 Cumberland Landing, St. Charles, MO 63303

Hippocampus Magazine, P.O. Box 411, Elizabethtown, PA 17022

Hither & Yahn, P.O. Box 233, San Luis Rey, CA 92068

Hobart, PO Box 1658, Ann Arbor, MI 48106

Hobble Creek Review, PO Box 3511, West Wendover, NV 89883

Hobblebush Books, 17A Old Milford Rd., Brookline, NH 03033

The Hollins Critic, P.O. Box 9538, Roanoke, VA 24020-1538

Home Planet News, PO Box 455, High Falls, NY 12440

Homebound, P.O. Box 1442, Pawcatuck, CT 06379-1968

Honest Publishing, 21 Valley Mews, Cross Deep, Twickenham TW1 4QT, UK

Hoot, 1413 Academy Lane, Elkins Park, PA 19027

The Hoot and Hare Review, 16631 CR 178, Tyler, TX 75703

The Hopkins Review, John Hopkins Univ., 081 Gilman Hall, 3400 N. Charles St., Baltimore, MD 21218-2685

Hotel Amerika, English Dept., 600 S. Michigan Ave., Chicago, IL 60605

Hub City Press, 186 West Main St., Spartanburg, SC 29306

The Hudson Review, 684 Park Ave., New York, NY 10065

Hulltown 360, 7806 Sunday Silence Lane, Midlothian, VA 23112

Hunger Mountain, 36 College St., Montpelier, VT 05602

I

I-70 Review, 5021 S. Tierney Dr., Independence, MO 64055

Ibbetson Street Press, 25 School Street, Somerville, MA 02143

The Idaho Review, Boise State Univ., 1910 University Dr., Boise, ID 83725

The Idiom Magazine, 2739 Woodbridge Ave., Edison, NJ 08817

Ideomancer Speculative Fiction, 141 Howland Ave., Toronto, Ontario, M5R 3B4, Canada

Illuminations, College of Charleston, 66 George St., Charleston, SC 29424

Illya's Honey, PO Box 700865, Dallas, TX 75370

Image, 3307 Third Avenue West, Seattle, WA 98119

In Other Words: Merida, Calle 58, #301A, X25A Y27, Colonia Itzimna, Merida, Yucatan 97100, Mexico

In Posse Review, 11 Jordan Ave., San Francisco, CA 94118

Indian Literature, Sahitya Akademi, Rabindra Bhawan, Ferozeshah Rd., New Delhi, 110001, India

Indiana Review, 1020 E. Kirkwood Ave., Bloomington, IN 47405-7103

InDigest, c/o Nelson, 2815 34th St., 3A, Astoria, NY 11103

Inkwell, Manhattanville College, 2900 Purchase St., Purchase, NY 10577

International Poetry Review, UNCG, P.O. Box 26170, Greensboro, NC 27402-6170

iO: A Journal of New American Poetry, 1402 N. Valley Pkwy, #404, Lewisville, TX 75077

Ion Drive Publishing, 6251 Drexel Ave., Los Angeles, CA 90048

The Iowa Review, 308 EPB, University of Iowa, Iowa City, IA 52242

Iron Horse, English Dept., Texas Tech Univ., Lubbock, TX 79409-3091

IsoLibris, 4927 6th Pl., Meridian, MS 39305

J

J Journal, 524 West 59th St., 7th fl, NY, NY 10019

Jabberwock Review, Mississippi State Univ., Drawer E, Mississippi State, MS 39762

Jacar Press, 6617 Deerview Trail, Durham, NC 27712

Jaded Ibis Press, P.O. Box 61122, Seattle, WA 98141

Jersey Devil Press, 30 Galway Dr., Hazlet, NJ 07730

Jet Fuel Review, Lewis University, #1092, Romeoville, IL 60446-2200

jmww, 2105 E. Lamley St., Baltimore, MD 21231

John Gosslee Books, 2932 B Langhorne Rd., Lynchburg, VA 24501

The Journal, 17 High St., Maryport, Cumbria CA15 6BQ, UK

The Journal, Ohio State Univ., 164 West 17th Ave., Columbus, OH 43210

The Journal of Experimental Fiction, 12 Simpson Ave., Geneva, IL 60134

Journal of New Jersey Poets, 214 Center Grove Rd., Randolph, NJ 07869-2086

Jovialities Entertainment Co., 521 Park Ave., Elyria, OH 44035

Juked, 17149 Flanders St., Los Angeles, CA 91344

Junk, 16233 SE 10th St., Bellevue, WA 98008

K

Kartika Review, API Cultural Center, 934 Brannan St., San Francisco, CA 94103

Kattywompus Press, 2696 W. Saint James Pkwy., Cleveland Heights, OH 44106

Kelly's Cove Press, 2733 Prince St., Berkeley, CA 94705

Kelsey Review, Mercer County Community College, 1200 Old Trenton Rd.,, West Windsor, NJ 08550-3407

Kenyon Review, Finn Cottage, 102 W. Wiggin St., Gambier, OH 43022

Kerf, 883 W. Washington Blvd., Crescent City, CA 95531-8361

Kestrel, 264000, Fairmont State Univ., 1201 Locust Ave., Fairmont, WV 26554

Kitsune Books, P.O. Box 1154, Crawfordville, FL 32326-1154

Kiwi Publishing, P.O. Box 3852, Woodbridge, CT 06525

Kore Press, P.O. Box 42315, Tucson, AZ 85733-2315

Korean Expatriate Literature, 11533 Promenade Drive, Santa Fe Springs, CA 90670

Kweli Journal, P.O. Box 693, New York, NY 10021

L

La Muse Press, 1 East University Pkwy, Unit 801, Baltimore, MD 21218

The Labletter, 3712 N. Broadway, #241, Chicago, IL 60613

Lake Effect, 4951 College Drive, Erie, PA 16563-1501

Lalitamba, 110 West 86th St., #5D, New York, NY 10024

Lamberson Corona Press, P.O. Box 1116, West Babylon, NY 11704

Lapham's Quarterly, 33 Irving Place, New York, NY 10003

Lavender Review, P.O. Box 275, Eagle Rock, MO 65641-0275

Leaf, Box 416, Lantzville, B.C., V0R 2H0 Canada

Levellers Press, 71 S. Pleasant St., Amherst, MA 01002

Levins Publishing, 2300 Kennedy St., NE. #160, Minneapolis, MN 55413

The Lindenwood Review, 209 S. Kingshighway, St. Charles, MO 63301-1695

Lines + Stars, 1801 Clydesdale Place NW #323, Washington, DC 20009

Lips, 7002 Blvd. East, #2-26G, Guttenberg, NJ 07093

The Literarian, 17 East 47th St., New York, NY 10017

The Literary Bohemian, Po Vode 381 01 Cesky Krumlov, Czech Republic
Literary Juice, 511 Travers Circle, Apt. C, Mishawaka, IN 46545
The Literary Lunch Room, 209 Riggs Ave., Severna Park, MD 21146
Literary Orphans, 440 Lake St., Crystal Lake, IL 60014
The Literary Review, 285 Madison Ave./M-GH2-01, Madison, NJ 07940
Little Balkans Review, 315 South Hugh St., Frontenae, KS 66763
Little Fiction, 728 Willard Ave., Toronto, ON M6S 3S5, Canada
Little Patuxent Review, 5008 Brampton Pkwy., Ellicott City, MD 21043
Little Red Tree Publishing, 635 Ocean Ave., New London, CT 06320
Little Star, 107 Bank St., New York, NY 10014
The Lives You Touch, P.O. Box 276, Gwynedd Valley, PA 19437-0276
Livingston Press, Station 22, Univ. of West Alabama, Livingston, AL 35470
Lookout Books, 601 South College Rd., Wilmington, NC 28403
Lorimer Press, PO Box 1013, Davidson, NC 28036
The Los Angeles Review, P.O. Box 2458, Redmond, WA 98073
The Los Angeles Review of Books, 4470 Sunset Blvd., #115, Los Angeles, CA 90027
Los Angeles Poets' Press, 24721 Newhall Ave., Santa Clarita, CA 91321
The Los Angeles Review of Los Angeles, 1316 Lemoyne St., #22, L.A., CA 90026
Lost Horse Press, 105 Lost Horse Lane, Sandpoint, ID 83864
The Louisiana State University Press, 3990 Lakeshore Dr., Baton Rouge, LA 70803
The Louisville Review, Spalding Univ., 851 South Fourth St., Louisville, KY 40203
Loving Healing Press Inc., 5145 Pontiac Trail, Ann Arbor, MI 48105-9279
Lowestoft Chronicle, 1925 Massachusetts Ave., Cambridge, MA 02140
Loyal Stone Press, 13549 36th Ave. NE, Seattle, WA 98125
Luminis Books, 13245 Blacktern Way, Carmel, IN 46033
Lunch Ticket, Antioch University, 400 Corporate Pointe, Culver City, CA 90230

M

The MacGuffin, 18600 Haggerty Rd., Livonia, MI 48152
Magnapoets, 13300 Tecumseh Rd. E., #226, Tecumseh, Ontario N8N 4R8, Canada

Main Street Rag, P.O. Box 690100, Charlotte, NC 28227

MAKE, 2229 W. Iowa St., #3, Chicago, IL 60622

make/shift, PO Box 27506, Los Angeles, CA 90027

The Malahat Review, PO Box 1700 STN CSC, Victoria BC V8W 2Y2 Canada

The Manhattan Review, 440 Riverside Dr., #38, New York, NY 10027

Manoa, English Dept., University of Hawai'i, Honolulu, HI 96822

Many Mountains Moving, 1705 Lombard St., Philadelphia, PA 19146-1518

Marco Polo, 153 Cleveland Ave., Athens, GA 30601

Marin Poetry Center, P.O. Box 9091, San Rafael, CA 94912

Marriage Publishing House, 800 SE 10th Ave., Portland, OR 97214

Martha's Vineyard Arts & Ideas, P.O. Box 1130, West Tisbury, MA 02575

The Massachusetts Review, South College 126047, Amherst, MA 01003-7140

The Masters Review, 1824 NW Couch St., Portland, OR 97209

Matchbook, 31 Berkley Place #2, Buffalo, NY 14209

Matter Press, P.O. Box 704, Wynnewood, PA 19096

Mayapple Press, 362 Chestnut Hill Rd., Woodstock, NY 12498

McSweeney's Publishing, 849 Valencia, San Francisco, CA 94110

Measure, University of Evansville, 1800 Lincoln Ave., Evansville, IN 47722

The Medulla Review, 612 Everett Rd., Knox, TN 37934

Memoir Journal, 1316 67th St., #8, Emeryville, CA 94608

Memorious, 409 N. Main St., 2A, Hattiesburg, MS 39402

Menacing Hedge, 5501 31st Ave. NE, Seattle, WA 98105

Menu, 87-16, #501, Daejo-dong, Eunpyong-Ku, Seoul, South Korea 122-030

Metazen, Ulrich-von-Huttenstr. 8, 81739 Munich, Germany

Michigan Quarterly Review, 915 E. Washington St., Ann Arbor, MI 48109-1070

Michigan State University Press, 1405 S. Harrison Rd., East Lansing, MI 48823-5245

Mid-American Review, Bowling Green State Univ., Bowling Green, OH 43403

Midway Journal, 8 Durham St., #3, Somerville, MA 02143

Midwestern Gothic, 957 E. Grant, Des Plaines, IL 60016

The Mighty Rogue Press, P.O. Box 19553, Boulder, CO 80308-2553

Milkweed Editions, 1011 Washington Ave. So., Ste. 300, Minneapolis, MN 55415

The Millions, 107 Birch Rd., Highland Lakes, NJ 07422

Milspeak Books, 3305 Lightning Rd., Borrego Springs, CA 92004

the minnesota review, Virginia Tech, ASPECT, Blacksburg, VA 24061

Minnetonka Review, P.O. Box 386, Spring Park, MN 55384

MiPOesias, 604 Vale St., Bloomington, IL 61701

Misfits' Miscellany, 28 Edward Rd., Hont Bay, Cape Town, 7806, South Africa

Mississippi Review, 118 College Dr. #5144, Hattiesburg, MS 39406-0001

The Missouri Review, 357 McReynolds Hall, Univ. of Missouri, Columbia, MO 65211

Mixed Fruit, 925 Troy Rd., Edwardsville, IL 62025

Mixer.com, 3013 Woodridge Ave., South Bend, IN 46615-3811

MMIP Books, 416 101st Ave., SE, #308, Bellevue, WA 98004

Mobius, the Journal of Social Change, 505 Christianson St., Madison, WI 53714

Mobius, the Poetry Magazine, 14453 77th Ave., Flushing, NY 11367

Modern Haiku, PO Box 33077, Santa Fe, NM 87594-9998

Mojo!, 38 Exeter St., Arlington, MA 02474

The Monarch Review, 5033 Brooklyn Ave., NE, Apt. B, Seattle, WA 98105

Monkeybicycle, 206 Bellevue Ave., Floor 2, Montclair, NJ 07043

Moon Maiden Productions, P.O. Box 70, La Pryor, TX 78872

Moon Pie Press, 16 Walton St., Westbrook, ME 04092

MoonPath Press, P.O. Box 1808, Kingston, WA 98346

Moonrise Press, 8644 Le Berthon St., Sunland, CA 91040

Moonshot Magazine, 416 Broadway, 3rd Floor, Brooklyn, NY 11211

Mootney Artists, 213-B Main St., Woodbury, TN 37190

The Morning News, 6206 Wynona Ave., Austin, TX 78757

MotesBooks, 89 W. Chestnut St., Williamsburg, KY 40769

Mount Hope, Roger Williams Univ., Global Heritage Hall 201, Bristol, RI 02809

Mountain Gazette, P.O. Box 7548, Boulder, CO 80306

Mouse Tales Press, 19558 Green Mountain Dr., Newhall, CA 91321

MousePrints, 43200 Yale Ct., Lancaster, CA 93536

Mouthfeel Press, 15307 Mineral, Horizon City, TX 79928

Mozark Press, P.O. Box 1746, Sedalia, MO 65302

Muddy River Poetry Review, 15 Eliot St., Chestnut Hill, MA 02467

Mud Luscious Press, 2115 Sandstone Dr., Fort Collins, CO 80524

MungBeing Magazine, 1319 Maywood Ave., Upland, CA 91786

Murder Slim Press, 29 Alpha Rd., Gorleston, Norfolk, NR31 0LQ, UK

Muse-Pie Press, 73 Pennington Ave., Passaic, NJ 07055

Muzzle Magazine, 312 N. Geneva St., #5, Ithaca, NY 14850

Mythopoetry Scholar, 16211 East Keymar Dr., Fountain Hills, AZ 85268

N

N + 1 Magazine, 68 Jay St., #405, Brooklyn, NY 11201

NaDa Publishing, 1415 Fourth St. SW, Albuquerque, NM 87102

NANO Fiction, 738 Minor Ave., Kalamazoo, MI 49008

NAP, 5824 Timber Lake Blvd., Indianapolis, IN 46237

Narrative, 2130 Fillmore St., #233, San Francisco, CA 94115

The National Poetry Review, P.O. Box 2080, Aptos, CA 95001-2080

Natural Bridge, English Department, One University Blvd., St. Louis, MO 63121

Naugatuck River Review, PO Box 368, Westfield, MA 01085

Nazar Look Journal, Luntrasului 16, 900338 Constanta, Romania

Neon, 8 Village Close, Wilberforce Rd., Norwich, Norfolk NR5 8NA, UK

NeoPoiesis Press, P.O. Box 38037, Houston, TX 77238-8037

New American Writing, S.F.S.U., 1600 Holloway Ave., SF, CA 94132

The New Criterion, 900 Broadway, Ste. 602, New York, NY 10003

New Delta Review, English Dept., 15 Allen Hall, L.S.U., Baton Rouge, LA 70803

New England Review, Middlebury College, Middlebury, VT 05753

The New Guard, P.O. Box 10612, Portland, ME 04104

The New Inquiry, 747 Baker St., San Francisco, CA 94119

New Issues, 1903 W. Michigan Ave., Kalamazoo, MI 49008-5463

New Letters, UMKC, 5100 Rockhill Rd., Kansas City, MO 64110-2499

New Madrid, Murray State University, 7C Faculty Hall, Murray, KY 42071

New Mirage Journal, 3066 Zelda Rd., #384, Montgomery, AL 36106

New Ohio Review, Ohio University, 360 Ellis Hall, Athens, OH 45701

New Orleans Review, Box 50, Loyola University, New Orleans, CA 70118

The New Orphic Review, 706 Mill St., Nelson, B.C. V1L 4S5 Canada

New Plains Press, P.O. Box 1946, Auburn, AL 36831-1946

New Rivers Press, MSUM, 1104 Seventh Avenue S., Moorhead, MN 56563

new south, Campus Box 1894, Georgia State Univ., Atlanta, GA 30303-3083

New Southerner Magazine, 375 Wood Valley Lane, Louisville, KY 40299

New Urban Review, Box 195, Loyola University, New Orleans, LA 70118

New York Tyrant, 676 A Ninth Ave., #153, New York, NY 10036

New Verse News, Les Belles Maisons H-11, Jl. Serpong Raya, Serpong Utara, Tangerang-Baten 15310, Indonesia

Newfound Journal, 1576 Portland Ave., #10, St. Paul, MN 55104

News Ink Books, 22848 State Route 28, Delhi, NY 13753

NewSouth Books, P.O. Box 1588, Montgomery, AL 36102

Newtown Literary, 91-31 Lamont Ave., #2D, Elmhurst, NY 11373

Night Ballet Press, 123 Glendale Court, Elyria, OH 44035

Nightblade, 11323 126th St., Edmonton, AB T5M 0R5 Canada

Nightwood Editions, Box 1779, Gibsons, BC, VON 1VO, Canada

Nimrod, 800 South Tucker Dr., Tulsa, OK 74104

918studio, 918 N. Cody Rd., Le Claire, IA 52753

Ninth Letter, 608 S. Wright St., Urbana, IL 61801

Noon, 1324 Lexington Ave., PMB 298, New York, NY 10128

The Normal School, 5245 N. Backer Ave., M/S PB 98, Fresno, CA 93740-8001

North American Review, Univ. of No. Iowa, 1222 West 27th St., Cedar Falls, IA 50614-0516

North Carolina Literary Review, ECU Mailstop 555, Greenville, NC 27858-4353

North Dakota Quarterly, 276 Centennial Drive, Grand Forks, ND 58202-7209

North Star Press of St. Cloud, Inc., P.O. Box 451, St. Cloud, MN 56302

Northwest Review, 5243 University of Oregon, Eugene, OR 97403-5243

Northwind, 4201 Wilson Blvd., #110-321, Arlington, VA 22203

Not One of Us, 12 Curtis Rd., Natick, MA 01760

Notre Dame Review, 840 Flanner Hall, Notre Dame, IN 46556-5639

Now Culture, 90 Kennedy Rd., Andover, NJ 07821

O

Oberlin's Law, P.O. Box 27, New Hampton, NH 03256

Obsidian, African Amer. Cultural Cntr, 2810 Cates Ave., Raleigh, NC 27695-7318

OCHO, 604 Vale St., Bloomington, IL 61701

Off the Coast, PO Box 14, Robbinston, ME 04671

The Offending Adam, 1319 11th St., #5, Santa Monica, CA 90401

Ohio University Press, 19 Circle Dr., The Ridges, Athens, OH 45701

Old Mountain Press, 85 John Allman Lane, Sylva, NC 28779

Old Red Kimono, 3175 Cedartown Hwy. SE, Rome, GA 30161

Omnium Gatherum, 9600 Tujunga Canyon Blvd., L.A. CA 91042

One Co., P.O. Box 517, Oneco, CT 06373

One Eye Two Crows Press, 4335 SE Hawthorne Blvd., Portland, OR 97215

1110, (One Photograph, One Story, Ten Poems), 54 Lower Rd., Beeston, Nottingham, NG9 2GT, UK

One Story, 232 3rd St., #E106, Brooklyn, NY 11215

One Teen Story, 232 3rd St., #E106, Brooklyn, NY 11215

Orange Quarterly, 3862 Hidden Creek Dr., Traverse City, MI 49684

Orchises Press, George Mason Univ., English Dept., Fairfax, VA 22030

Oregon Humanities, 813 SW Alder St., #702, Portland, OR 97205

Origami Poems Project, P.O. Box 1623, E. Greenwich, RI 02818

Orion Magazine, 187 Main St., Great Harrington, MA 01230

Orphiflamme Press, P.O. Box 4366, Boulder, CO 80306

Osiris, PO Box 297, Deerfield, MA 01342

Other Voices Books, 2235 W. Waveland Ave., Apt. 1, Chicago, IL 60618

Out of Our, 1288 Columbus Ave., #216, San Francisco, CA 94133-1302

Outpost, 301 Coleridge, SF., CA 94141

Overtime, PO Box 250382, Piano, TX 75025-0382

OVS Magazine, 32 Linsey Lane, Warren, NH 03279

Oxford American, 201 Donaghey Ave., Main 107, Conway, AR 72035-5001

Oyez Review, Roosevelt Univ., Literature & Languages, Chicago, IL 60605-1394

P

P.R.A. Publishing, PO Box 211701, Martinez, GA 30917

PAC Books, 72 Tehama St., San Francisco, CA 94105

The Packinghouse Review, 1030 Howard St., Kingsburg, CA 93631

Palabra, P.O. Box 86146, Los Angeles, CA 90086-0146

Palettes & Quills, 330 Knickerbocker Ave., Rochester, NY 146155

Palm Beach ArtsPaper, P.O. Box 7625, Delray Beach, FL 33484

Palo Alto Review, 1400 W. Villaret Blvd., San Antonio, TX 78224

Palooka, P.O. Bo 5341, Coralville, IA 52241

PANK Magazine, Dept. of Humanities, 1400 Townsend Dr., Hancock, MI 49931

Papaveria Press, 145 Hollin Lane, Wakefield, West Yorkshire, WF4 3EG, UK

Paper Nautilus, I-4 Bradley Circle, Enfield, CT 06082

Paperbag, 255A 19th St., Top Floor, Brooklyn, NY 11215

Parallel Press, 728 State St., Madison, WI 53706

Parcel, 6 E. 7th St., Lawrence, KS 66044

The Paris-American, 4 Center St., Apt. 97, Sussex, NJ 07461

The Paris Review, 62 White St., New York, NY 10013

Parody, P.O. Box 404, East Rochester, NY 14445

Parthenon West Review, 1516 Myra St., Redlands, CA 92373

Passages North, English Dept, 1401 Presque Isle Ave., Marquette, MI 49855-5363

Paterson Literary Review, 1 College Blvd., Paterson, NJ 07505-1179

Pear Noir, P.O. Box 178, Murrysville, PA 15668

Pearl, 3030 E. Second St., Long Beach, CA 90803

PEN America, PEN American Center, 588 Broadway, Ste. 303, New York, NY 10012

Pen & Anvil, Boston Poetry Union, 30 Newbury St., Boston, MA 02216

Penmanship Books Poetry, 593 Vanderbilt Ave., #265, Brooklyn, NY 11238

Pennduline Press, 14674 SW Mulberry Dr., Tigard, OR 97224

Perceptions, Mt. Hood Community College, 26000 SE Stark St., Gresham, OR 97080

Permafrost, Univ. of Alaska Fairbanks, P.O. Box 75570, Fairbanks, AK 99775

Perugia Press, PO Box 60364, Florence, MA 01062

The Petigru Review, 4840 Forest Dr., Ste. 6B, PMB 189, Columbia, SC 29206

Petrichor Review, 2 Short St., New Market, NH 03857

Phantom Drift, P.O. Box 3235, La Grande, OR 97850

Philadelphia Stories, 93 Old York Rd., Ste. 1/#1-753, Jenkintown, PA 19046

Phoenicia Publishing, 1397 rue Rachel E., #102, Montreal H2J 2K2 Quebec, Canada

Phoenix in the Jacuzzi, 19 Maple Dell, Saratoga Springs, NY 12866

Phrygian Press, 58-09 205th St., Bayside, NY 11364

PigeonBike, 611 Wonderland Rd. N. Ste. 379, London, Ontario N6H 5N7, Canada

Pilot Light Journal, 3809 Cliffside Dr., #4, La Crosse, WI 54601

The Pinch, English Dept., 467 Patterson Hall, Memphis, TN 38152-3510

Ping-Pong, Henry Miller Memorial Library, 48603 Highway 1, Big Sur, CA 93920

Pink Narcissus Press, P.O. Box 303, Auburn, MA 01501

Pink Petticoat Press, P.O. Box 130085, Birmingham, AL 35213

Pirene's Fountain, 3616 Glenlake Dr., Glenview, IL 60026

Pixelhouse, P.O. Box 1476, San Mateo, CA 94401

Plan B Press, P.O. Box 4067, Alexandria, VA 22303

Pleiades, Univ. of Central Missouri, English Dept., Warrensburg, MO 64093-5046

Ploughshares, Emerson College, 120 Boylston St., Boston, MA 02116-4624

Plume, 740 17th Ave. N, St. Petersburg, FL 33704

Poecology, 1749 Kappa Ave., San Leandro, CA 94579

Poems and Plays, MTSU, P. O. Box 70, Murfreesboro, TN 37132

Poet Lore, 4508 Walsh St., Bethesda, MD 20815

Poetry Center, CSU, 2121 Euclid Ave., RT 1841, Cleveland, OH 44115-2214

Poetry for the Masses, 1654 S. Voulstia, Wichita, KS 67211

Poetry In the Arts Press, 5110 Avenue H, Austin, TX 78751-2026

Poetry Kanto, 3-22-1 Kamariya-Minami, Kanazawa-Ku, Yokohama, 236-8502, Japan

Poetry Magazine, 61 West Superior St., Chicago, IL 60654

Poetry Northwest, Everett Community College, 2000 Tower St., Everett, WA 98201

Poetry South, MVSU 7242, 14000 Hwy 82 West, Itta Bena, MS 38941-1400

The Poet's Billow, 245 N. Collingwood, Syracuse, NY 13206

The Poet's Haven, P.O. Box 1501, Massillon, OH 44648

Poets and Artists, 604 Vale St., Bloomington, IL 61701

Poets Wear Prada, 533 Bloomfield St., Apt. 2, Hoboken, NJ 07030

The Point, 732 S. Financial Place, #704, Chicago, IL 60605

Pool, 11500 San Vicente Blvd., #224, L.A. CA 90049

Pomeleon, 5755 Durango Rd., Riverside, CA 92506

Post Mortem Press, 601 West Galbraith Rd., Cincinnati, OH 45215

Post Road, Boston College, 140 Commonwealth Ave., Chestnut Hill, MA 02467

Potomac Review, 51 Mannakee St., MT/212, Rockville, MD 20850

Prairie Journal Trust, 28 Crowfoot Terrace NW, P.O. Box 68073, Calgary, AB, T3G 3N8, Canada

Prairie Schooner, UNL, 201 Andrews Hall, PO Box 880334, Lincoln, NE 68588-0334

Precipitate, 1576 Portland Ave., Apt. 10, Saint Paul, MN 55105

Presa Press, PO Box 792, Rockford, MI 49341

Press 53, PO Box 30314, Winston-Salem, NC 27130

Primal Urge Magazine, P.O. Box 2416, Grass Valley, CA 95945

Prime Mincer, 401 N. Poplar, Carbondale, IL 62901

Prime Number Magazine, 1853 Old Greenville Rd., Staunton, VA 24401

Printed Matter, 910 T St., Vancouver, WA 98661

Printer's Devil Review, 74 Park St., Apt. 2, Somerville, MA 02143

The Prose-Poem Project, Equinox Publishing, P.O. Box 424, Shelburne, VT 05482

Proverse Hong Kong, P.O. Box 259, Tung Chung Post Office, Lantau Island, New Territories, Hong Kong, SAR

Provincetown Arts, 650 Commercial St., Provincetown, MA 02657

A Public Space, 323 Dean St., Brooklyn, NY 11217

Publication Studio, 717 SW Ankeny St., Portland, OR 97205

Pudding Magazine, 5717 Bromley Ave., Worthington, OH 43085

Puerto Del Sol, N.M.S.U, P.O. Box 30001, MSC 3E, Las Cruces, NM 88001

Q

Qarrtsiluni, P.O. Box 8, Tyrone, PA 16686

Queen's Ferry Press, 8240 Preston Rd., Ste. 125-151, Plano, TX 75024

Quiddity, Benedictine University, 1500 N. Fifth St., Springfield, IL 62702

Quiet Lightning, c/o F. Karp, 734 Balboa St., SF, CA 94118

Quiet Mountain Essays, Box 261, Scotland, SD 57059

Quill and Parchment Press, 2357 Merrywood Dr., Los Angeles, CA 90046

The Quotable, 520 W 21st St., #230, Norfolk, VA 23517

R

R.KV.R.Y Quarterly, 72 Woodbury Dr., Lockport, NY 14094

R. L. Crow Publications, PO Box 262, Penn Valley, CA 95946

Radius, 65 Paine St., #2, Worcester, MA 01605

Ragazine, Box 8586, Endwell, NY 13762

Raintown Review, 5390 Fallriver Row Ct, Columbia, MD 21044

Raleigh Review, Box 6725, Raleigh, NC 27628-6725

Raritan: A Quarterly Review, Rutgers, 31 Mine St., New Brunswick, NJ 08901

Rattle, 12411 Ventura Blvd., Studio City, CA 91604

The Rattling Wall, 269 S Beverly, #1163, Beverly Hills, CA 90212

The Raven Chronicles, 12346 Sand Point Way, N.E., Seattle, WA 98125

Ray's Road Review, P.O. Box 2001, Hixson, TN 37343

REAL, P.O. Box 13007-SFA Stn, S. F. Austin State Univ., Nacogdoches, TX 75962

Rebel Satori Press, P.O. Box 363, Hulls Cove, ME 04644-0363

Red Alice Books, P.O. Box 262, Penn Valley, CA 95946

Red Fez, 304 W. 15th St., Georgetown, IL 61846

Red Hen Press, PO Box 40820, Pasadena, CA 91114

Red Lightbulbs, 4213 S. Union Ave., Floor 2, Chicago, IL 60609

Red Luna Press, 2616 West Verdugo Ave., Burbank, CA 91505

Red River Review, 4669 Mountain Oak St., Fort Worth, TX 76244-4397

Redactions, 604 N. 31st Ave., Apt. D-2, Hattiesburg, MS 39401

Redivider, Emerson College, 120 Boylston St., Boston, MA 02116

Reed Magazine, SJSU, English Dept., 1 Washington Sq., San Jose, CA 95192-0090

Referential Magazine, 8324 Highlander Court, Charlotte, NC 28269

Regent Press, 2747 Regent St., Berkeley, CA 94705

The Republic of Letters, Apartado 29, Cahuita, 7032, Costa Rica

Requiem Press, 4501 42nd Ave. S.. Seattle, WA 98118

Rescue Press, 1220 E. Locust, #209, Milwaukee, WI 53212

Resource Center for Women & Ministry, 1202 Watts St., Durham, NC 27701

Revolution House, 516 N. 6th St., #3, Lafayette, IN 47901

Rhino, P.O. Box 591, Evanston, IL 60204

River Otter Press, 812 Hilltop Rd., Mendota Heights, MN 55118

River Styx, 3547 Olive St., Ste. 107, St. Louis, MO 63103-1024

River Teeth, Ashland University, 401 College Ave., Ashland, OH 44805

Roanoke Review, 221 College Lane, Salem, VA 24153

Rock & Sling, Whitworth Univ., 300 W. Hawthorne Rd., Spokane, WA 99251

Rose House Publishing, P.O. Box 3339, Grand Rapids, MI 49501

Rose Red Review, 13026 Staton Drive, Austin, TX 78727

Rougarou, PO Box 44691, Lafayette, LA 70504-4691

Ruminate, 140 N. Roosevelt Ave., Ft. Collins, CO 80521

S

S.F.A. Press, P.O. Box 13007, SFA Station, Nacogdoches, TX 75962-3007

2nd Wind Publishing, 931-B S. Main St., Box 145, Kernersville, NC 27284

Sacramento News & Review, 1124 Del Paso Blvd., Sacramento, CA 95815-3607

Saint Paul Almanac, 275 East Fourth St., Ste. 735, Saint Paul, MN 55101

Salamander, 41 Temple St., Boston, MA 02114-4280

Salmagundi, Skidmore College, Saratoga Springs, NY 12866-1632

The Salon, 294 N. Winooski Ave., Burlington, VT 05401

Salt Hill, 123 Strong Ave., Syracuse, NY 13210

San Diego City Works Press, 1313 Park Blvd., San Diego, CA 92101

San Pedro River Review, P.O. Box 7000-148, Redondo Beach, CA 90277

Sand Hill Review, 1076 Oaktree Dr., San Jose, CA 95129

Santa Monica Review, 29051 Hilltop Dr., Silverado, CA 92676

Saranac Review, SUNY, 101 Broad St., Plattsburgh, NY 12901-2681

Scapegoat Press, P.O. Box 410962, Kansas City, MO 64141-0962

Scarlet Literary Magazine, 1209 S. 6th St., Louisville, KY 40203

Scarlet Tanager Books, 1057 Walker Ave., Oakland, CA 94610

Scarletta Press, 10 South 5th Street, #1105, Minneapolis, MN 55402

Schuylkill Valley Journal, 240 Golf Hills Rd., Havertown, PA 19083

Scribendi, MSC06-3890, 1 University of New Mexico, Albuquerque, NM 87131

Sea Storm Press, P.O. Box 186, Sebastopol, CA 95473

Seal Press, 1700 Fourth St., Berkeley, CA 94710

The Seattle Review, Univ. of Washington, Box 354330, Seattle, WA 98195-4330

Seems, Lakeland College, PO Box 359, Sheboygan, WI 53082-0359

Serving House, 29641 Desert Terrace Dr., Menifee, CA 92584-7800

Seven Hills Review, 2910 Kerry Forsest Parkway, D-4-357, Tallahassee, FL 32309

Seventh Quarry, Dan-y-bryn, 74 Cwm Level Rd., Brynhyfrd, Swansea SA5 9DY, Wales, UK

Sewanee Review, University of the South, 735 University Ave., Sewanee, TN 37383

SFA State University Press, 1036 North St., Nacogdoches, TX 75962-3007

Shabda Press, 3343 East Del Mar Blvd., Pasadena, CA 91107

Shadow Mountain Press, 14900 W. 31st Ave., Golden, CO 80401

Shenandoah, Mattingly House, 2 Lee Avenue, Lexington, VA 24450-2116

The Shit Creek Review, 90 Kennedy Rd., Andover, NJ 07821

Shock Totem, 107 Hovendon Ave., Brockton, MA 02302

Shoppe Foreman Co., 3507 Homesteaders Lane, Guthrie, OK 73044

Short Story America, 2121 Boundary St., Ste. 204, Beaufort, SC 29907

Sibling Rivalry Press, 13913 Magnolia Glen, Alexander, AR 72002

Signal 8 Press, P.O. Box 47094 Morrison Hill Post Office, Hong Kong

Silk Road Review, 2043 College Way, Forest Grove, OR 97116-1797

Silver Birch Press, 13260 Moorpark St., #3, Sherman Oaks, CA 91423

The Single Hound, P.O. Box 1142, Mount Sterling, KY 40353

Sinister Wisdom, P.O. Box 3252, Berkeley, CA 94703

Sink Review, 95 Graham Ave., 2nd Floor, Brooklyn, NY 11206

Sixth Finch, 95 Carolina Ave., #2, Jamaica Plain, MA 02130

Slake Media, 3191 Casitas Ave., Ste. 110, Los Angeles, CA 90039

Slapering Hol Press, 300 Riverside Dr., Sleepy Hollow, NY 10591

Sleet Magazine, 1846 Bohland Ave., St. Paul, MN 55116

Slice, P.O. Box 659, Village Station, New York, NY 10014

Slipstream, Box 2071, Niagara Falls, NY 14301

Slope Editions, 34 Juckett Hill Dr., Belchertown, M 01007

Slough Press, Texas A&M University, College Station, TX 77843-4227

Small Doggies Omnimedia, 4432 SE Main St., Portland, OR 97215

Smartish Pace, PO Box 22161, Baltimore, MD 21203

SmokeLong Quarterly, 5708 Lakeside Oak Lane, Burke, VA 22015

So to Speak, George Mason University., 4400 University Dr., MSN 2C5, Fairfax, VA 22030-4444

Solas House, 853 Alma St., Palo Alto, CA 94301

Solo Press, 5146 Foothill Rd., Carpinteria, CA 93013

Solstice, 38 Oakland Ave., Needham, MA 02492

The Southampton Review, 239 Montauk Hwy., Southampton, NY 11968

The Summerset Review, 25 Summerset Dr., Smithtown, NY 11787

Song of the San Joaquin, PO Box 1161, Modesto, CA 95353-1161

South Dakota Review, USD, 414 East Clark St., Vermillion, SD 57069

South Loop Review, Columbia College, 600 S. Michigan, Chicago, IL 60605

Southeast Missouri State University Press, 1 University Plaza, MS 2650, Cape Girardeau, MO 63701

The Southeast Review, English Dept., Florida State Univ., Tallahassee, FL 32306

Southern Humanities Review, 9088 Haley Center, Auburn, AL 36849-5202

Southern Indiana Review, USI, 8600 University Blvd., Evansville, IN 47712

Southern Poetry Review, 11935 Abercorn St., Savannah, GA 31419-1997

The Southern Review, L.S.U., Old President's House, Baton Rouge, LA 70803

Sou'wester Magazine, Southern Illinois Univ., Edwardsville, IL 62026-1438

Southwest Review, PO Box 750374, Dallas, TX 75275-0374

Sow's Ear Poetry Review, P.O. Box 127, Millwood, VA 22646-0127

sPARKLE & bLINK, 215 Precita Ave., San Francisco, CA 94110

Specter, One Market St., Apt 417, Camden, NJ 08102

The Speculative Edge, 149 W. Trottier Rd., S. Royalton, VT 05068

Spillway, 11 Jordan Ave., San Francisco, CA 94118

Spirituality & Health, 444 Hana Highway, Ste. D, Kahului, HI 96732

Spoon River, Illinois State Univ., Campus Box 4240, Normal, IL 61790-4240

Spork Press, 216 N. 3rd Avenue, Tucson, AZ 85705

Spudnik Press Coop, 1821 W. Hubbard St., Ste. 302, Chicago, IL 60622

St. Andrews College Press, St. Andrews University, 1700 Dogwood Mile, Laurinburg, NC 28352

St. Petersburg Review, Box 2888, Concord, NH 03302

Star Cloud Press, 6137 East Mescal St., Scottsdale, AZ 85254-5418

Star*Line, W5679 State Road 60, Poynette, WI 53955-8564

Steel Toe Review, 1521 16th Avenue So, #J, Birmingham, AL 35205

StepAway, 2, Bowburn Close, Wardley, Gateshead, Tyne & Wear, NE10 8UG, UK

Still, P.O. Box 1121, Berea, KY 40403

Still Crazy, P.O. Box 777, Worthington, OH 43085

Stirring, 114 Newridge Rd., Oak Ridge, TN 37830

Stone Canoe, 700 University Ave., Ste. 326, Syracuse, NY 13244-2530

Stone Highway Review, 1606 South 27th St., St. Joseph, MO 64507

The Stone Hobo, 16 Holley St., Danbury, CT 06810

Stone Telling Magazine, 200 Nebraska, Lawrence, KS 66046

Stoneboat, Lakeland College, P.O. Box 359, Sheboygan, WI 53082-0359

Stonewood Press, 97 Benefield Rd., Oundle, PE8 4EU, UK

Storm Cellar, 2387 Deer Pass Way, Decatur, GA 33035

Storysouth, 3302 MHRA Bldg., UNC Greensboro, Greensboro, NC 27402-6170

The Storyteller, 2441 Washington Rd., Maynard, AR 72444

String Poet, 10 Tappen Drive, Melville, NY 11747

Structo, 2 Mordaunts Court, Woolstone, Milton Keynes, MK15 0BT, UK

Stymie, 1965 Briarfield Dr. Ste. 303, Lake St. Louis, MO 63367

subTerrain, P.O. Box 3008 MPO, Vancouver, BC V6B 3X5, Canada

Subtropics, PO Box 112075, University of Florida, Gainesville, FL 32611-2075

Sugar House Review, PO Box 17091, Salt Lake City, UT 84117

The Summerset Review, 25 Summerset Dr., Smithtown, NY 11787

The Sun, 107 North Roberson St., Chapel Hill, NC 27516

sunnyoutside, PO Box 911, Buffalo, NY 14207

Sun's Skeleton, 274 Bay Rd., #1, Newmarket, NH 03857

Super Arrow, 121 N. Normal, #3, Ypsilanti, MI 48197

Supermachine, 388 Myrtle Ave., #3, Brooklyn, NY 11205

Superstition Review, 3931 E. Equestrian Tr., Phoenix, AZ 85044-3010

Sweet, 110 Holly Tree Lane, Brandon, FL 33511

Swink, 1661 10th Ave., Brooklyn, NY 11215

Switchback, MFA Program, USF, 2130 Fulton St., S.F., CA 94117

Sycamore Review, Purdue Univ., 500 Oval Dr., West Lafayette, IN 47907

T

Tawani Foundation, 104 S. Michigan, Ste. 525, Chicago, IL 60603

Telling Our Stories Press, 185 AJK Blvd., #246, Lewisburg, PA 17837

Ten Thousand Tons of Black Ink, 716 Columbian Ave., Oak Park, IL 60302

10 X 3 Plus, 1077 Windsor Ave., Morgantown, WV 26505

Terrain.org, 10367 East Sixto Molina Lane, Tucson, AZ 85747

Texas Review Press, Box 2146, Sam Houston State Univ., Huntsville, TX 77341-2146

THE2NDHAND, 1430 Roberts Ave., Nashville, TN 37206

Third Coast, Western Michigan University, Kalamazoo, MI 49008-5331

Third Flatiron, 4101 S. Hampton Circle, Boulder, CO 80301-6016

Third Wednesday, 174 Greenside Up, Ypsilanti, MI 48197

32 Poems Magazine, Valparaiso University, 1320 Chapel Drive South, Valparaiso, IN 46383

THIS Literary Magazine, 315 W. 15th St., #12, Minneapolis, MN 55403

Thought Publishing, 73 Alvarado Rd., Berkeley, CA 94705

Three Coyotes, 10645 N.Oracle Rd., Ste. 121-163, Tucson, AZ 85737

Three Mile Harbor Press, Box 1951, East Hampton, NY 11937

Three Rooms Press, 51 MacDougal St., Ste. 290, New York, NY 10012

Threepenny Review, PO Box 9131, Berkeley, CA 94709

Thrush Press, 889 Lower Mountain Dr., Effort, PA 18330

Thunderclap!, 1055 Thomas St., Hillside, NJ 07205

ThunderDome. 6655 Esplanade #3, Playa del Rey, CA 90293

Tidal Basin Review, P.O. Box 1703, Washington, DC 20013

Tiger Bark Press, 202 Mildorf St., Rochester, NY 14609

Tiger's Eye Press, P.O. Box 9723, Denver, CO 80209

Tightrope Books, 167 Browning Trail, Barrie, Ontario, L4N 5E7, Canada

Tikkun Magazine, 2342 Shattuck Ave., Ste. 1200, Berkeley, CA 94704

Tin House, PMB 280, 320 7th Ave., Brooklyn, NY 11215

Tipton Poetry Journal, PO Box 804, Zionsville, IN 46077

Toasted Cheese, 44 East 13th Ave., #402, Vancouver BC V5T 4K7, Canada

Toadlily Press, PO Box 2, Chappaqua, NY 10514

The Toucan Literary Magazine, 6156 W. Nelson St., Chicago, IL 60634-4043

Trachodon, P.O. Box 1468, St. Helens, OR 97051

Transition, 104 Mt. Auburn St., 3R, Cambridge, MA 02138

Transom Journal, 185 Vernon Ave., Apt. 4, Louisville, KY 40206

Traprock Books, 1330 E. 25th Ave., Eugene, OR 97403

Travelers' Tales, Solas House, 2320 Bowdoin St., Palo Alto, CA 94306

Tree Killer Ink, 33 Sioux Rd., PO Box 80002 Woodbridge, Sherwood

Park, Alberta, Canada T8A 5T4

Tree Light Books, 3650 N. Fremont St., #1, Chicago, IL 60613

Treehouse Magazine, 113 S. Front St., Wilmington, NC 28401

Treehouse Press, P.O. Box 65016, London N5 9BD, UK

Trinacria, 220 Ninth St., Brooklyn, NY 11215-3902

TriQuarterly, Northwestern Univ., 339 E. Chicago Ave., Evanston, IL 60611-3008

Truman State University Press, 100 E. Normal Ave., Kirksville, MO 63501

Tuesday, PO Box 1074, East Arlington, MA 02474

Tule Review, Sacramento Poetry Center, 1719 25th St., Sacramento, CA 95816

Tupelo Press, PO 1767, North Adams, MA 01247

Turbulence, 29 Finchley Close, Hull, East Yorkshire, HU8 0NU, UK

20 Something Magazine, 4429 Ebenezer Rd., Perry Hall, MD 21236

A Twist of Noir, 2309 West Seventh St., Duluth, MN 55806-1536

2 Bridges Review, NY City College of Technology, 300 Jay St., Brooklyn, NY 11201

Two Hawks Quarterly, Antioch Univ., 400 Corporate Pointe, Culver City, CA 90230

Two Serious Ladies, 31 Maxwell Rd., Chapel Hill, NC 27517

Typhoon Media, P.O. Box 47094, Morrison Hill Post Office, Hong Kong

Tyrant Books, 676A Ninth St., #153, New York, NY10036

U

URJ Books, 633 Third Ave., New York, NY 10017-6778

U.S. 1 Poets' Cooperative, PO Box 127, Kingston, NJ 08528-0127

U.S. 1 Worksheets, P.O. Box 127, Kingston, NJ 08528

Umbrella, 5620 Netherland Ave., #2E, Bronx, NY 10471-1880

Umbrella Factory Magazine, 1720 SW 4th Ave., #617, Portland, OR 97201

unboundCONTENT, 160 Summit St., Englewood, NJ 07631

Under the Sun, Tennessee Tech U., English Dept., Box 5053, Cookeville, TN 38506

Underground Voices, 4020 Cumberland Ave., Los Angeles, CA 90027

University of Arizona Press, 1510 E. University Blvd., Tucson, AZ 85721-0055

University of Chicago Press, 11030 South Langley Ave., Chicago, IL 60628

The University of Georgia Press, 330 Research Dr., Athens, GA 30602-4901

University of Louisiana Press, P.O. Box 40831, Lafayette, LA 70504-0831

University of Massachusetts Press, P.O. Box 429, Amherst, MA 01004

University of Nebraska Press, 1111 Lincoln Mall, Lincoln, NE 68588-0630

University of Nevada Press, MS 0166, Reno, NV 89557-0166

University of North Texas Press, 1155 Union Circle #311336, Denton, TX 76203-5017

UNO Press, University of New Orleans Publishing, New Orleans, LA 70148

Unshod Quills, 39391 SE Lusted Rd., Sandy, OR 97055

Unsplendid, 265-B S. Peter St., Athens, GA 30601

Unstuck, 4505 Duval St., #204, Austin, TX 78751

Unthank Books, P.O. Box 3506, Norwich, NR7 7PQ, United Kingdom

Unthology, P.O. Box 3506, Norwich, NR7 7PQ, UK

Uphook Press, 515 Broadway, #2B, New York, NY 10012

Uptown Mosaic, F. Swan Creek Rd., Ft. Washington, MD 20744-5200

V

Vagabondage Press, P.O. Box 3563, Apollo Beach, FL 33572

Vallum, P.O. Box 598 Victoria Stn., Montreal, QC H3Z 2Y6, Canada

Valparaiso Poetry Review, English Dept., Valparaiso Univ., Valparaiso, IN 46383

Vandal, 526 Cathedral of Learning, 4200 Fifth Ave., Pittsburgh, PA 15260

VAO Publishing, 4717 N. FM 493, Donna, TX 78537

Vector Press, 5612 Beacon St., #1, Pittsburgh, PA 15217

Vered Publishing, 1352 W. 25th Ave., Anchorage, AK 99503

Versal, Postbus 3865,1001 AR Amsterdam, The Netherlands

Verse Wisconsin, P.O. Box 620216, Middleton, WI, 53562-0216

Vestal Review, 2609 Dartmouth Dr., Vestal, NY 13850

Victorian Violet Press, 1840 W 220th St., Ste. 300, Torrance, CA 90501

Vinyl Poetry, 814 Hutcheson Dr., Blacksburg, VA 24060

The Virginia Quarterly Review, 5 Boar's Head Lane, P.O. Box 400223, Charlottesville, VA 22904

Virgogray Press, 2103 Nogales Trail, Austin, TX 78744

VoiceCatcher, P.O. Box 6064, Portland, OR 97228-6064

Voices, PO Box 9076, Fayetteville, AR 72703-0018

The Volta, 1423 E. University Blvd., Modern Languages Bldg. 472, Tucson, AZ 85716

vox poetica, 160 Summit St., Englewood, NJ 07631

W

Waccamaw, PO Box 261954, Conway, SC 29528-6054

Wag's Revue, 710 E. Davenport St., Iowa City, IA 52245

Wake: Great Lake Thoughts & Culture, 1 Campus Dr., Allendale, MI 49401-9403

Walkabout Publishing, P.O. Box 151, Kansasville, WI 53139

The Wapshott Press, P.O. Box 31513, Los Angeles, CA 90031-0513

Washington Square Review, 58 W. 10th St., NY, NY 10011

Water-Stone Review, MS A1730,1536 Hewitt Ave., St. Paul, MN 55104-1284

Water Street Press, 108 Fifth St., Ste. 2, Healdsburg, CA 95448

The Waterhouse Review, 105 E Barnton St., Stirling, FK8 1HJ, UK

Wave Books, 1938 Fairview Ave. East, Ste. 201, Seattle, WA 98102

Wayne State University Press, 4809 Woodward Ave., Detroit, MI 48201-1309

Weave Magazine, 7 Germania St., San Francisco, CA 94117

Weighed Words, 1326 Sleepy Hollow Rd., Glenview, IL 60025

Wesleyan University Press, 215 Long Lane, Middletown, CT 06459

West Branch, Stadler Center for Poetry, Bucknell Univ., Lewisburg, PA 17837

West End Press, P.O. Box 27334, Albuquerque, NM 87106

West Marin Review, P.O. Box 984, Point Reyes Station, CA 94956

The Westchester Review, Box 246H, Scarsdale, NY 10583

Western Humanities Review, Univ. of Utah, Salt Lake City, UT 84112-0494

Westland Park Press, P.O. Box 9594, Canton, OH 44711

Whispering Prairie Press, P.O. Box 8342, Prairie Village, KS 66208-0342

White Dot Press, 707 Carl Drive, Chapel Hill, NC 27516

White Pelican Review, P.O. Box 7833, Lakeland, FL 33813

White Pine Press, P.O. Box 236, Buffalo, NY 14201

White Whale Press, 2121 Cleveland Pl. 1-N, St Louis, MO 63110

Wicked East Press, P.O. Box 1042, Beaufort, SC 29901

Wigleaf, English Dept., Univ. of Missouri, 107 Tate Hall, Columbia Mo 66211

Wild Goose Poetry Review, 838 4th Avenue Dr. NW, Hickory, NC 28601

Wilderness House Press, 145 Foster St., Littleton, MA 01460

Willow Springs, 501 N. Riverpoint Blvd., Ste 425, Spokane, WA 99202

Willows Wept Review, 17313 Second St., Montverde, FL 34756

Wilson Quarterly, 1300 Pennsylvania Ave., NW, Washington, DC, 20004-3027

Wind Publications, 600 Overbrook Drive, Nicholasville, KY 40356

Wings Press, 627 E. Guenther, San Antonio, TX 78210

The Winter Anthology, 414A Altamont St., Charlottesville, VA 22902

Winter Goose Publishing, 2701 Del Paso Rd., 130-92, Sacramento, CA 95835

Wising Up Press, P.O. Box 2122, Decatur, GA 30031-2122

Witness, Box 455085, Las Vegas, NV 89154-5085

WomenArts Quarterly, UMSL, One University Blvd., St Louis, MO 63121-4991

Woodley Memorial Press, 2518 W.View Drive, Emporia, KS 66801

The Worcester Review, 1 Ekman St., Worcester, MA 01607

Word Palace Press, P.O. Box 583, San Luis Obispo, CA 93406

Word Riot Press P.O. Box 414, Middletown, NJ 07748

Wordcraft of Oregon, P.O. Box 3235, La Grande, OR 97850

Wordgathering, 7507 Park Ave., Pennsauken, NJ 08109

Wordrunner eChapbooks, 333 N. McDowell Blvd., #A231, Petaluma, CA 94954

Words without Borders, 3800 N. Lawndale Ave., Chicago, IL 60618

Work Literary Magazine, 8752 N. Calvert, Portland, OR 97217

Workers Write!, P.O. Box 250382, Piano, TX 75025-0382

World Literature Today, 630 Parrington Oval, Ste. 110, Norman, OK 73019-4033

Writecorner Press, PO Box 140310, Gainesville, FL 32614-0310

Writers Ink Press, 1104 Jacaranda Ave., Daytona Beach, FL 32118

The Writing Disorder, P.O. Box 93613, L.A., CA 90093

Writing Knights Press, 7406 Kingston Ct., Mentor, OH 44060

Writing on the Edge, Writing Program, UC Davis, Davis, CA 95616

Wyatt-MacKenzie Publishing, 15115 Highway 36, Deadwood, OR 97430

Y

The Yale Review, Yale University, PO Box 208243, New Haven, CT 06520

Yarn, 26 Hawthorne Lane, Weston, MA 02493

YB, 401 Zanzibar, Billings, MT 59105

YU News Service, P.O. Box 236, Millbrae, CA 94030

Yellow Medicine Review, J. Wilson, English Dept., SMSU, 1501 State St., Marshall, MN 56258

Yemassee, USC, Columbia, SC 29208

Yes Yes Books, 1232 NE Prescott St., Portland, OR 97211-4662

Z

Zephyr Press, 50 Kenwood St., Brookline, MA 02446

Zoetrope: All Story, 916 Kearny St., San Francisco, CA 94133

Zone 3, APSU, P.O. Box 4565, Clarksville, TN 37044

ZYZZYVA, 466 Geary St., Ste. 401, San Francisco, CA 94102-1262

CONTRIBUTORS' NOTES

STEVE ADAMS won *Glimmer Train*'s New Writer Award. He lives in Austin, Texas.

CHARLES BAXTER teaches at the University of Minnesota. He is the author of ten books of fiction and recently won The Rea Award for the Short Story.

SCOTT BEAL serves as writer-in-the-schools for Dzanc Books. He teaches at the University of Michigan. His most recent books are published by Red Beard Press.

MEI-MEI BERSSENBRUGGE lives in New York City and New Mexico. A book of poems, *Hello, The Roses*, is forthcoming from New Directions.

TINA LOUISE BLEVINS died last year in an accident. This is one of her first published stories.

AYSE PAPATYA BUCAK teaches at Florida Atlantic University. Her work has appeared in *The Kenyon Review*, *The Normal School* and *Witness*.

ROBERT COOVER is the author of three story collections and ten novels. A new novel, The *Brunist Day of Wrath*, is just out from Dzanc, as part of a boxed set.

EDUARDO C. CORRAL's *Slow Lightning* was selected as the 2011 winner of the Yale Series of Younger Poets. He lives in New York.

BILL COTTER's second novel, The *Parallel Apartments*, is soon out from McSweeney's. He lives in Austin, Texas.

HAL CROWTHER is an essayist, critic and former newsmagazine editor, screenwriter and syndicated columnist. He is the author of four essay collections and was a finalist for the National Book Critics Circle prize for criticism.

KWAME DAWES is the author of many poetry collections, two novels and several plays. He has won two Pushcart Prizes, a Guggenheim Fellowship and an Emmy.

NATALIE DIAZ was born and raised in Needles, California. She is Mojave and Pima. She played professional basketball in Europe and Asia. Her *When My Brother Was An Aztec* is recently published by Copper Canyon.

MATTHEW DICKMAN is poetry editor of Tin House Magazine. He is the author of volumes from Copper Canyon Press and W. W. Norton & Co. His poems have appeared in *The New Yorker*, *McSweeney's*, *Ploughshares* and elsewhere.

W. S. DI PIERO won the 2012 Ruth Lilly Poetry Prize. His *Tombo* is due soon from McSweeney's.

STEPHEN DIXON is the author of thirty books of fiction. His most recent book is the collection *What Is All This?*

ANDRE DUBUS III is the author of *Bluesman*, *House of Sand and Fog* and The *Garden of Last Days*. His *Dirty Love* is just published by W. W. Norton & Co.

ELIZABETH ELLEN is the author of the story collection *Fast Machine* and edits the journal *Hobart*. She lives in Ann Arbor, Michigan.

TIMOTHY DONNELLY was awarded The 2012 Kingsley Tufts Poetry Award. He is poetry editor of *Boston Review*.

ERIC FAIR lives in Bethlehem, Pennsylvania.

ROBERT LONG FOREMAN lives in Wheeling, West Virginia. His work has appeared in *Michigan Quarterly Review*, *Pleiades*, *The Massachusetts Review* and elsewhere.

SARAH FRISCH teaches at Stanford University. She recently completed a Wallace Stegner Fellowship.

BECKIAN FRITZ GOLDBERG lives and teaches in Arizona. She is the author of seven volumes of poetry.

LOUISE GLÜCK lives in Cambridge, Mass. Her collected poems were published in 2012.

JEFFREY HARRISON is a previous winner of Pushcart Prizes for his poetry and nonfiction.

SABINE HEINLEIN is the author of *Among Murderers: Life After Prison* (University of California Press, 2013). She has received numerous awards and been published in The *Brooklyn Rail*, *Art in America* and *Die Zeit*.

AMY HEMPEL is the author of four short story collections. She won the PEN/Malamud Award for the short story and other citations.

DAVID HERNANDEZ's *Hoodwinked*, won the Kathryn A. Morton poetry prize. He lives in Long Beach, California.

DAVID HORNIBROOK is a student at the University of Michigan. His poems have appeared in *Columbia Review*, *Flyway* and *Dunes Review*.

PAM HOUSTON's five books include *Contents May Have Shifted*, *Cowboys Are My Weakness* and *Waltzing the Cat*. She lives in Colorado.

SAEED JONES' chapbook is *When The Only Light Is Fire*.

PHILIP KELLY has worked as a housepainter and craftsman for over thirty years. He considers Hawaii his home.

PAUL KINGSNORTH is a poet, novelist and author of two non-fiction books. He is co-founder and director of the Dark Mountain Project (www.paulkingsnorth.net.)

YUSEF KOMUNYAKAA's most recent book is *The Chameleon Couch*. He teaches at New York University.

SARAH LINDSAY's *Twigs And Knucklebones* is available from Copper Canyon Press. She received a Lannan Foundation Fellowship.

JACK LIVINGS' collection of short stories will soon be published by Farrar, Straus & Giroux. He lives in New York.

JILL MCDONOUGH's books of poems include *Habeas Corpus* and *Where You Live*, both from Salt Press. She received an NEA, Cullman Center, and Stegner Fellowships. She directs the MFA in Creative Writing of U. Mass-Boston and the Fine Arts Work Center Online.

LORRIE MOORE is the winner of the 2004 Rea Award for The Short Story. Her books include *Birds of America*, *Who Will Run The Frog Hospital* and *A Gate At The Stairs*.

HOWARD NORMAN is the author of seven novels, including *The Bird Artist* and *The Museum Award*. He lives in Washington D.C.

SIGRID NUNEZ's most recent book is *Sempre Susan: A Memoir of Susan Sontag*. She lives in New York City.

JUDE NUTTER's third collection, *I Wish I Had a Heart Like Yours*, *Walt Whitman* (University of Notre Dame Press) was award the 2010 Minnesota Book Award and voted Poetry Book of the Year by *ForeWord*. She lives in Minneapolis/St. Paul.

MOLLY PATTERSON's debut story collection, *Just Because You Can*, is due out from Five Chapters Books. She teaches at the University of Wisconsin.

CARL PHILLIP's most recent poetry book is *Silverchest* (Farrar, Straus & Giroux, 2013). He teaches at Washington University, St. Louis.

CLAUDIA RANKINE is the author of four poetry collections. Her *That Were Once Beautiful Children* is coming soon from Graywolf Press.

MATT RASMUSSEN is co-editor of Birds, LLC and teacher at Gustavus Adolphus College. His first book of poems, *Black Aperture* (LSU Press, 2013) won the Walt Whitman Award.

ROGER REEVES lives in Chicago. He can be reached at poexeries@yahoo.com.

PAISLEY REKDAL is the author of four poetry books including *Animal Eye*, a finalist for the 2013 Kingsley Tufts Prize, plus an essay collection, *The Night My Mother Met Bruce Lee*.

SUZANNE RIVECCA is the author of "Death Is Not An Option", a finalist for the PEN/Hemingway Award. She lives in San Francisco.

RACHEL ROSE lives in Vancouver, BC. She has authored three books of poetry, most recently *Song & Spectacle*, which won The Audre Lorde Award for Lesbian Poetry and was a finalist for The Pat Lowther Award.

DAVY ROTHBART is the creator of *Found* magazine. His essay collection, *My Heart Is An Idiot*, was published in 2012.

MARY RUEFLE's books are published by Wave Books. She lives in Bennington, Vermont.

JOANNA RUOCCO co-edits *Birkensnake*, a fiction journal. She is the author of books from Ellipsis Press, Tarpaulin Sky Press, Noemi Press and FCZ.

DAVID ST. JOHN is the co-editor of *American Hybrid: A Norton Anthology of New Poetry*. He has authored ten poetry collections and lives in Venice Beach, California.

SUSAN SLAVIERO's poems have appeared in *Rhino, Fourteen Hills, Flyway, Jet Fuel Review*, and *Ghost Ocean*. Her book *Cyborgia* is out from Mayapple Press.

SUSAN B. A. SOMERS–WILLETT poetry books are *Quiver* (University of Georgia Press, 2009) and *Roam* (Crab Orchard, 2006). Her collaboration documentary poetry series "Women of Troy" aired on PRI and BBC radio.

TESS TAYOR's books of poems, *The Forage House*, is published by Red Hen Press. She reviews poetry for NPR's "All Things Considered."

NATASHA TRETHEWEY is Poet Laureate of the United States and a Pulitzer Prize winner. She teaches at Emory University.

DEB OLIN UNFERTH is the author of the memoir, *Revolution*, a finalist for The National Book Critics Award. She lives in Ann Arbor, Michigan.

MADHURI VIJAY is from Bangalore, India. She was an Iowa Arts Fellow at The Iowa Writer's Workshop.

FRANCOIS VILLON (1431-1464) French poet, is best known for his *Le Testament* and his poem *Ballade des Pendus*.

OCEAN VUONG was born in 1988 in Saigon, Vietnam. His chapbooks are *No* (YesYes Books, 2013) and *Burnings* (Sibling Rivalry Press, 2010). He received a Kunitz Memorial Prize and an Academy of American Poets Prize.

AFAA MICHAEL WEAVER teaches at Simmons College in Boston. His poetry collection, *The Government of Nature*, is published by The University of Pittsburgh Press.

MARCUS WICKER is the author of *Maybe The Saddest Thing* (Harper Perennial) selected by D. A. Powell for The National Poetry Series. His work has appeared in *Poetry*, *Third Coast*, *Ninth Letter* and *American Poetry Review*.

JESSICA WILBANKS is at work on a memoir about Pentecostal Christianity. She attended Hampshire College and received an MFA from The University of Houston, where she was an editor for *Gulf Coast*.

RICHARD WILBUR, translator, was the second Poet Laureate to the Library of Congress in 1987. He is a two-time winner of Pulitzer Prize in Poetry.

JAKE ADAM YORK (1972-2012) taught at the University of Colorado and was co-editor of *Copper Nickel*. He was the author of three books of poetry including *Persons Unknown* (Crab Orchard).

TAYMIYA R. ZAMAN teaches at The University of San Francisco. She holds degrees from Smith College and the University of Michigan.

PAUL ZIMMER is happily retired on a Wisconsin farm after a long career in publishing.

ANDREW ZOLOT was born in South Florida and now lives in Brooklyn.

INDEX

The following is a listing in alphabetical order by author's last name of works reprinted in the *Pushcart Prize* editions since 1976.

618

620

622

627

631

634

639

643

648

650

651